Duncan Falconer grew u... the first ten years of his ... He became a Special Forces operative at the age of nineteen (it is unlikely there will ever be one as young again). He is now a director to two companies operating in hostile environments.

DUNCAN FALCONER
OMNIBUS

The Protector

Undersea Prison

SPHERE

This omnibus edition first published in Great Britain in 2010 by Sphere

Copyright © Duncan Falconer 2010

Previously published separately:
The Protector first published in Great Britain in 2007 by Sphere
Paperback edition published in 2007 by Sphere
Reprinted 2007, 2008, 2009 (twice)
Copyright © Duncan Falconer 2007
Undersea Prison first published in Great Britain in 2008 by Sphere
Paperback edition published in 2008 by Sphere
Copyright © Duncan Falconer 2008

The moral right of the author has been asserted.

*All characters and events in this publication, other than those
clearly in the public domain, are fictitious and any resemblance
to real persons, living or dead, is purely coincidental.*

A CIP catalogue record for this book
is available from the British Library.

ISBN 978-0-7515-4416-9

Printed and bound in Great Britain by
Clays Ltd, St Ives plc

Sphere
An imprint of
Little, Brown Book Group
100 Victoria Embankment
London EC4Y 0DY

An Hachette UK Company
www.hachette.co.uk

www.littlebrown.co.uk

THE PROTECTOR

To Ricky

1

Mallory's Treasure

The Royal Navy Search and Rescue Sea King helicopter flew low and fast over the flat grubby desert, all eyes in the cockpit focused on a thin trail of black smoke half a mile ahead. Beyond it was a blurred collection of dilapidated dwellings on the other side of a road that marked the northern edge of the town of Fallujah that was a short flight west of Baghdad. Visibility was poor in every direction, a fine dust filling the air like smog and with more trails of carbon smoke dotting the hazy landscape like plumes from the stacks of distant steamships, columns of dark vapour bending gently on a south-easterly breeze. The pilot was tracking a signal that had its focus point a little to the left of the closer, finer plume. It was on an emergency bandwidth emitted by a radio in the hands of a British Tornado pilot whose aircraft had been shot down in the last twenty minutes.

Royal Marine Corporal Bernard Mallory stood beside his Royal Navy partner, Petty Officer Mac Davids, in the narrow doorway that connected the cabin to the cockpit. At thirty, Mac was a couple of years older than Mallory, a head taller and not as strongly built but a hundred yards faster in a mile race. Mallory pushed the inside of his helmet against his ear as he strained to listen to the weak, intermittent radio message from the Tornado pilot who was answering the co-pilot's request for his situation report.

'All I want to know, for Christ's sake, is if the area is hot or not,' the pilot said, a little tense, more to himself than to anyone else. His eyes darted back and forth across the range of his vision, looking for any sign of a threat that he knew was out there somewhere. It would not have been this crew's normal responsibility to carry out the rescue of a downed pilot in hostile territory. That task usually went to Special Forces flights and the rescue crews were normally made up of SAS and SBS operatives. But when the distress call came in none were immediately available and Samuels, the Sea King pilot, a gung-ho type who had missed the first Gulf War by only a couple of months, elected to at least check the level of hostility. The duty watch officer running the operations desk had allowed him to give it a go but only if there was zero enemy ground activity.

Mac and Mallory had exchanged glances when they'd first heard their boss's request to do a recce, knowing his hankering for a bit of the excitement whose lack he had been complaining of. His appetite was more urgent now that the war was fast coming to an end.

The tension in the helicopter increased perceptibly as Samuels took some lift out of the rotors and dropped the heavy beast to a couple of hundred feet above the ground. They were now exposed not only to anti-aircraft guns and rockets but also to small-arms fire.

In the back of everyone's mind was the questionable logic of risking the lives of four men to save just one but that was a danger they had accepted before joining the search-and-rescue service. This was the wrong time to dwell on it anyway but the arithmetical reasoning was more acute at this stage of an operation.

Mallory stepped back from the cockpit doorway, pulled his black-tinted sunshade visor down, gripped the heavy handle of the large side door and yanked it across on its runners until it engaged the catch that locked it open. The wind charged in aggressively, ravaging every inch of the cabin and tossing around anything that could not hold firm against it. He held on to the winch above to lean out and get a better look to starboard while Mac went to a port-side window.

Mallory looked down at the arid ground a hundred feet below as it shot past: dirty gold sand with a sprinkling of black giving way to sparsely cultivated patches of bracken-like vegetation, a track with a battered pick-up trundling along it, a line of parched, dust-coated eucalyptus trees, a herd of scattering goats with the shepherd boy twisting in their midst to look up at him. What sounded like far-off explosions were barely discernible above the noise of the engines and rotors chopping the air and except for the handful of distant smoke columns he could see little evidence of the heavy air assault taking place in the southern part of the town.

The Sea King had originally been on its way to an American base – confidently named 'Camp Victory' – at Baghdad International Airport on the west side of the city when they'd picked up the downed pilot's distress call. Soon after diverting from their course and picking up the location of the emergency beacon they heard the Tornado pilot's voice confirming that he was alive. The level of Iraqi resistance in the area was unknown since there were no coalition troops close enough to make that assessment. But it was believed to be light since the main ground-fighting in the sector was concentrated further south on the Baghdad side of Fallujah. The Iraqi military had for the most part disintegrated. Isolated groups of Republican Guard were putting up a token resistance in places but the back of the enemy had been broken and the majority of the army had abandoned their weapons and uniforms. However, a lone helicopter close to the ground was an irresistible target to any Iraqi who still had a gun. One lucky shot could turn the rescue mission into a fight for survival. That danger would only increase when the moment came to hover close to the ground and pick up the downed pilot.

A loud *thwack*, like the noise of a stone striking the helicopter's thin metal fuselage, made everyone start. The pilot banked the lumbering whale of a craft as sharply as it could go, the rotors complaining loudly as he put excessive torque on the engines.

'What was that?!' he shouted.

Mallory instinctively ducked back into the cabin, suspecting that it had been a bullet. Then, gritting his teeth, he leaned back outside to inspect the helicopter's body and saw a small hole only a couple of feet from him, towards the tail. 'Got a strike low on the cabin skin below the numbers,' he shouted into his mike against the wind. He looked inside for the corresponding hole but could not see anything: wrinkled padding and a row of folded hammock seats obscured the inside wall. 'From what I can see we're fine,' he said, guessing while looking at the other side of the cabin for an exit hole. He didn't find one. Mac scanned the roof for any sign of damage, then went back to the port-side window.

The immediate question on everyone's mind was if the attack constituted a high enough level of danger to abort the mission. They all knew that as far as operational procedures were concerned the answer was affirmative — but the important issue was whether Samuels agreed.

Any indecision the Sea King pilot might have had evaporated when the Tornado pilot's voice broke through to say that he could hear them. Samuels reacted by pulling the chopper's nose back around and on track towards the emergency beacon.

Mallory spotted several puffs of smoke above a low wall, giving away the firing position of a machine gun that he could not hear above the helicopter's engine noise. 'Contact starboard! Four o'clock! Four hundred!' he shouted. Samuels responded with another violent turn as a bright-orange tracer flew across the front of his windshield, heading skyward.

Mallory checked the outside of the craft again as best he could, hanging on tightly against the torque, then looked inside for signs of damage before stepping back and going to the cockpit door to see how his crew were doing. 'Everything looks OK,' he said, seeing that they were fine. But Samuels ignored him as he gripped his steerage and power controls while the co-pilot's hands whipped from one instrument button to the next, flicking switches and turning dials.

'Systems functional,' the co-pilot said as he turned off an engine alarm that had been triggered by the violent manoeuvring and tapped a gauge that had gone into the red: he did not seem overly concerned about it. He threw Samuels a couple of anxious glances in between his checks, wondering if his boss still intended to press on. But with no response from the pilot other than a fixed expression of concentration the answer for the moment appeared to remain affirmative.

Mallory was confident in his crew, having been with them for more than three months, and he went back to the external cabin door to maintain his surveillance. He had no say over their actions anyway and he had his own responsibilities. Being the only soldier on board, and a Royal Marine no less, he felt an inherent duty to be the cool-headed bulwark of the team. That was not to say that the others weren't up to the task. But as a Marine he was expected to be a stalwart. There was no doubt in Mallory's heart that he would uphold the pride of the Corps as well as his own if called upon. But this was the first time he had been under direct enemy fire and as the adrenalin coursed through his veins anxiety accompanied it. He was on his guard as he ventured into this level of fear for the first time, not truly knowing how he would react. Crouched in the open doorway of such a large, lumbering and attractive target he felt vulnerable as well as helpless to defend himself. His SA–80 assault rifle was secured in a bracket on the bulkhead behind him but grabbing it to engage an enemy he could not accurately see was pointless. More importantly, his crew would not appreciate him turning the rescue craft into a gunship unless there were clearly no other options.

Mallory had been a bootneck for six years and since graduating from Lympstone Commando Training Centre had spent most of that time in a fighting company of 42 Commando based in Plymouth. But six months after a long-awaited transfer to Recce Troop (42 Commando's reconnaissance team), the most expert fighting group in a commando unit, he tore a ligament in his knee playing rugby. To add to his disappointment he was transferred to the Regimental Sergeant Major's staff in the Company Headquarters to keep him employed during his rehabilitation, not an uncommon post for the walking – or hobbling – wounded. Then, at the outbreak of war, shortly before he was declared fit for duty, his boss read out an e-mail to the office from Naval Command requesting search-and-rescue volunteers. Mallory knew that he would not be able to slip back into his Recce Troop slot within the immediate future. His position had been filled and all he could hope for was to get back on the standby list. Therefore, when he heard the request for search-and-rescue volunteers, a somewhat specialised position, he asked immediately to be considered for the post. Mallory had never previously had aspirations of that nature. Being a part of a helicopter crew had not entered his head before that day. But his decision to volunteer was encouraged by rumours that few if any members of 42 Commando, including the Recce Troop, would join the war, at least the planned early stages of it. Having missed out on the fight in Afghanistan he desperately wanted the opportunity to see action.

The RSM agreed to put Mallory's name forward and within a week he received his acceptance notice. But by the time he had finished the training he had come to doubt the course he had chosen. Rumours abounded that the navy search-and-rescue squadron he was being attached to had little chance of seeing action since only Special Forces rescue teams would be permitted to operate in hostile areas. And for the early stages of the war that had been how it had panned out.

But now that Mallory was heading into the thick of it, having taken a bullet strike already, the old adage 'Be careful what you wish for' sprang to mind.

The Sea King pilot swung the heavy craft in a wide arc away from the source of the gunfire. But once again, as the downed Tornado pilot's voice came over the speakers sounding increasingly desperate as he claimed to have the helicopter in sight, Samuels brought the nose back around.

'I'm showing green smoke,' the downed pilot said, the quality of the communication suddenly better than it had been.

It was now obvious to all that short of a seriously

damaging strike against the Sea King they would not abandon the desperate stranger. The man had fully committed himself by igniting a smoke grenade and would stay close to it, well aware that it could also attract the enemy.

Mallory strained to look through the haze and saw the puff of dark green that was quickly billowing into a substantial cloud in front of a collection of huts several hundred metres from the black smoke that marked the Tornado pilot's crash site. It indicated that the pilot was at least able to move.

Before Mallory could report the sighting he heard Samuels confirm to the downed pilot that he had the smoke visual. They were going in.

Mac joined Mallory in the doorway and both men checked that they had their 9mm pistols in holsters at their sides. The pair contemplated their next move. They glanced at each other, looking for signs of weakness, any talk unnecessary. Mallory forced a grin from which Mac appeared to take little reassurance.

Mac pushed his mike aside and moved his mouth closer to Mallory's ear. 'You ever read "Rendezvous with Death"?' he shouted above the noise.

'What?' Mallory shouted, having heard Mac's question but then unsure if he had done so correctly.

'"Rendezvous with Death." You ever read it?'

'No, but I think I saw the film,' Mallory replied.

Mac rolled his eyes. 'It's a poem.'

'I must've missed that one,' Mallory replied sarcastically. He had never read a poem in his life and suddenly felt a tinge of inferiority. It was not an uncommon feeling for him. Mallory envied servicemen who'd had a good education. It made him want to improve himself in that regard but he had never made the effort. His excuse was the company he kept: fellow bootnecks. A commando unit was not the ideal environment in which to cultivate culture. 'Sounds a bit dramatic,' Mallory shouted, regretting his initial sarcasm.

'First World War,' Mac shouted. 'You should read it.'

Mallory didn't dwell on the matter and concentrated on catching a glimpse of the Tornado pilot.

'Stand by,' Samuels warned over the radio as they drew closer and dropped lower towards the green smoke that was moving along the ground in the breeze before rising and spreading out. Mallory eyeballed the medical pack strapped to the bulkhead near the door as he adjusted his bulletproof jacket. The plates that covered his chest and back were heavy but he had worn them for so long now that they felt like a part of him. He went over the procedure and his responsibilities that they had rehearsed endlessly back in the UK as well as when they'd arrived in Iraq. This was the second live rescue he had taken part in but the other one had not taken place under fire. Although Samuels was bringing the helicopter in as fast as he could it felt as if they were moving through the air like a barrage balloon.

The Sea King suddenly shuddered heavily as Samuels increased the pitch and brought the nose up sharply to slow the massive aircraft. Mallory and Mac reacted by crouching in the doorway, their hands firmly gripping the sides of the opening as they leaned out, hoping that the Tornado pilot would reveal himself.

The ground was close enough for Mallory to pick out fine details such as a goat lying near a bush. The animal must have been dead because the others had scattered. Mallory disconnected the communication cord from his helmet as he got ready to exit the craft.

The down draught of the helicopter's rotor blades hit the ground with tremendous force and just as Mallory caught sight of a man in a grey one-piece flight suit scurrying from behind one of the buildings the dust rose up to mix with the green smoke and obscured his view. Mallory studied the ground as it drew closer, calculating the best moment to jump. It was an exhilarating feeling, getting ready to abandon the safety of the craft to leap into the unknown.

The Sea King jolted as it turned through ninety degrees, its tail majestically sweeping around, its rotors blowing all before them, before dipping a little as it came to a wavering halt. Samuels was positioning his cabin door to face the Tornado pilot, a sign that he too had seen the man and was giving his boys the shortest route and ensuring that they would not have to run around the 'copter's nose or tail.

Mallory estimated that he was a body's length from the ground and jumped out of the doorway, hitting the packed sand hard. He dropped to one knee, his outstretched hands only just stopping him from falling on his face. He cursed himself for not allowing for the added weight of his body armour and equipment. As Mac landed beside him he pushed himself up and, though all he could see ahead was swirling dust and

11

green smoke, he ran on into it, knowing that the downed Tornado pilot was somewhere beyond.

As Mallory emerged a few paces ahead of Mac, his mouth and the back of his throat coated in dust, he saw the pilot on his knees the length of a tennis court ahead and wondered why he was not running towards them. As Mallory closed the distance the pilot wobbled as he got to his feet, one of his legs unable to support him – it was clear the man had an injury.

Mallory glanced left and right for any sign of the enemy as he covered the last few metres. He threw an arm around the pilot's back as Mac grabbed him from the other side.

'You OK?' Mallory shouted.

'Did something to my bloody leg on landing,' the pilot said in a refined English accent, his breathing laboured. 'Just get me going and I'll be fine,' he added, displaying a strength of character as he clung on to both men's shoulders.

Mac and Mallory part-carried, part-dragged him back towards the dust storm as he tried to put his weight on his good leg when he could.

A shot rang out close by, followed by another. The three men kept up their pace as Mallory looked in the direction of the firing, an action made difficult due to the pilot's arm wrapped tightly around his neck. More bullets ripped into the sand in front of them and as the men responded by increasing their speed Mallory was struck by what felt like a hammer blow to his right foot. It was followed by a searing, burning

12

pain. His leg gave way as if the nerves had been severed and he dropped, unable to stop himself.

The pilot released him and Mac slowed to look back for his partner. 'Mallory!' he cried.

'I'm OK,' Mallory shouted as he got to his feet. 'Keep going! Keep going!'

Mac saw him stand and obeyed, taking the pilot's weight onto his hip and pushing on into the swirling dust and smoke.

Mallory took a step but his leg gave way and he dropped to the ground again. The limb seemed to be losing its strength near his hip, as if a major nerve had been severed, even though the wound appeared to be in his foot. He pulled himself up, forcing his wounded leg ahead of him in an effort to kick-start it back into action. But a painful spasm short-circuited the muscles and it buckled again. He looked up from the ground to see Mac and the pilot disappear into the dust storm and with a growling shout intended to inspire a supreme effort he pushed himself up once again. It appeared to have the desired effect but as he moved forward the ground immediately in front of him exploded in a series of bullet strikes from a machine gun close by and a round slammed into the side of his helmet, throwing him over like a rag doll. It was as if he had been kicked in the head by a bull and his vision blurred.

Mallory's animal will to survive took charge and he staggered to his feet once more. But as he lurched towards the helicopter another swarm of bullets spat around him. His subconscious screamed at him to take cover and he dived towards a low wall, misjudging the distance and hitting the top of it. As another volley struck the wall beside him he slipped over the top to fall hard on to his back. The voice in his head continued to cry out for him to move and he crawled as fast as he could, scurrying on his belly like an alligator, every limb pushing and clawing at the dirt, keeping his head and backside low. He reached a small gap in the wall and caught a glimpse of the helicopter inside its shroud of dust – the green smoke had dissipated now that the dispenser was exhausted. The seconds were ticking away and Mallory knew that the Sea King would lift off as soon as Mac and the pilot were on board. They had to. The extraction had turned hot and the chopper pilot had a responsibility to the others.

Mallory braced himself to get up and run towards the craft but as he raised his body and brought his good leg beneath him the Sea King's screaming engines powered up to the max and the rotor-driven sand-storm intensified. The hub of the 'copter's blades then emerged from the top of the dust cloud. The craft followed its nose in a tight turn before straightening up as it continued to rise, gaining speed with every second. The nose dipped as the helicopter moved away from Mallory, the aircraft banking to one side and then the other like a fish trying to avoid a shark snapping at its tail. Mallory was compelled to stare at it, partly in disbelief and partly hoping that it would turn in an arc to come back for him. But deep down he knew that it had gone for ever and a voice inside his head urged him to run . . .

Mallory could hear his own heavy breathing as the sound of the chopper's engines faded. He scanned around, assessing his options, and saw his only way out: the collection of buildings where the Tornado pilot had originally hidden. He dropped to the ground and scrambled as far as he could on his stomach away from the wall, keeping it between him and the original source of the gunfire. But Mallory was moving far too slowly and, unable to bear it, he leaped to his feet, gritted his teeth against the pain in his leg and ran for all he was worth. The nerves in his hip seemed to have rediscovered their connections and he got into his stride. But he had covered barely a dozen metres when he was struck by a fierce blow to his back that punched him forward with the force of a flying sledge-hammer and he sprawled in the sand. Mallory did not pause to speculate about what had happened nor about his condition. If he was alive he would keep going and if he was seriously wounded he would not be able to. He pushed himself up and onward and another round whistled past him. He dived over a waist-high wall as several bullets struck it and he rolled ungracefully onto his knees. Then, pushing off like a sprinter starting a race, he propelled himself forward, straightening up as he gained speed, and ran as if the very hounds of hell were snapping at his heels.

Mallory arrived at the first building and skidded around the corner where a dirt street separated two blocks of shacks opposite. Not a soul was about: the only movement that caught his eye was a goat wandering along the street. He sped across the gap,

15

the pain shooting up his leg which he fought to control.

As he ran down the line of dilapidated buildings he reached for his holster, finding the pistol and wrapping his hand around the grip, his thumb pushing aside the Velcro tab that held it in place. He pulled the gun free. His feet lost traction on some slimy garbage as he made a sharp change in direction into an alleyway but hitting the far corner wall helped him to regain his balance. He jumped over a mound of trash and charged on through a long puddle of rancid water, close to slipping several times. But his momentum kept him going. Unable to look back as he ran in case he lost his footing, a strangely euphoric feeling spread through him. Perhaps it was the release of endorphins into his bloodstream, or the buzz of fear itself. Whatever the cause he suddenly felt he had the wings of Mercury on his heels. But the high was not enough to kill the pain in his leg or lighten the reality of his position. Although the shooting appeared to have stopped he had to believe that the bullets could fly his way again at any second.

A woman carrying a bundle suddenly stepped from a doorway and, unable to change direction, Mallory slammed into her with such force she hit the wall of her house and bounced off it to fall flat on her back in the dirt. Mallory hardly felt the impact: his weight, more than twice hers with his body armour, and the kinetic force of his speed must have been like having a horse hit her. Mallory kept on going without a backward glance, every sense concentrated ahead.

The end of the dead-straight alleyway was still some distance away and Mallory's fear of being shot from behind became more intense. Unable to bear it any longer he slammed on the brakes and swerved into the opening of a hut, bouncing off the wall as he fell in and slipping onto his side on the dirt floor. He got to his feet right away, hunched in a stoop because of the low ceiling, and spun in a circle, gun held tight in a two-handed grip, ready to shoot, gulping in air as perspiration flowed, his eyes straining to see into the darkened corners. The room looked like someone's home: rugs, cushions and cooking implements were laid out as if the occupants had recently departed in a hurry. An opening in the opposite wall, looking as if it had been fashioned with a sledgehammer, led to an adjoining room and Mallory moved to look inside. It was another living quarters, with blankets and pillows on the floor, its walls bare but for a jagged hole high up that served as a window.

Mallory was breathing heavily and he removed his helmet, feeling stifled by it. He wiped away the sweat that was flowing into his eyes as he moved into the smaller room where he jumped up and held onto the edges of the opening to take a look outside. It was another narrow alleyway like the one he had just run down but the point was that it was a different one. He tossed his helmet out, pulled himself up, wriggled through like a maggot and dropped hands first without dignity onto the mucky ground outside. As he got to his feet and picked up his helmet the pain shot through his leg again and he part-jogged, part-limped along the cramped passageway. He checked behind him every few paces, anxious to increase the distance from his landing place but at the same time mindful of the risks of remaining out in the open. Moving increased the chance of running into other dangers and the wisest option was to find somewhere to hide. That would also give him time to formulate a plan, sort himself out and, most importantly, open up communications with his people.

A wrecked car blocked the end of the alleyway, as if someone had once tried to drive it through, got stuck between the buildings, given up and left it to rot. Tatty flat-roofed mud huts lined either side of the alley and just before Mallory reached the car a gap appeared on his right as if one of the buildings had collapsed. He slowed as he reached it, his gun held in front of him, and turned the corner into what looked like a small yard surrounded by buildings on three sides. Each had an opening although only one had a door, fragile and battered, which Mallory opted for since it offered concealment. He approached it stealthily with his pistol leading the way and eased it open, helmet in his other hand, and looked inside. It was dark with no windows and he quickly moved into the room, stepping away from the doorway and out of sight in case someone passed. The air was musty, smelling like rotten rags, and the room did not look as if it had been recently used, although there were some signs of a previous occupation: cooking pots, wooden boxes containing what appeared to be rusty electrical fittings, a stripped engine block and an

18

assortment of other junk. A rug covered a large portion of the dirt floor but like everything else in the place it was decomposing and caked in dust.

Mallory closed the door and, feeling overheated, took a moment to get some air. He would have liked to undo his bulletproof jacket to let the air circulate around his sweating body but he knew better than to relax. His injured foot was throbbing and he allowed himself the luxury of squatting on a log for a moment to stretch out his legs and ease the pain. He moved the injured foot into a shaft of sunlight coming in through a crack in the door and inspected it. There was a hole through the instep of the sand-coloured suede boot with a corresponding one on the other side, a dark bloodstain around both. But there was no sign of blood leaking from the wound at that moment. A bullet had passed through the fleshy part of the sole of his foot but it had missed the bone or at worst had only grazed it. An inch higher and the outcome of his escape might have been different, not that it was by any means a done deal at the moment.

The foot grew more painful as blood was allowed to circulate more freely through it and Mallory contemplated removing the boot to put a dressing on it. He had a small medical pack on his belt but the risk was too great. And the boot might be difficult to get back on if his foot swelled. If it had been bleeding he might have taken the chance but no one ever died from pain, he mused, and decided to forget about it. The worst that could happen to it now was infection and that would take days before it showed.

He picked up his helmet which gave no ballistic protection and inspected the entry and exit holes in the top of it. He felt the top of his head in case it had been nicked by the bullet and though it was soaked a check of his fingers revealed only sweat – no blood. He had been lucky there, too – an inch lower and it would have been curtains. He reached around his back to search for the third bullet strike in his body armour, his finger finding the hole in the shock-absorbent powdery material that had done its job. Mallory had used up a lot of luck so far but he was going to need more if he wanted to make it home in one piece. The thought of what he needed to do to get out of this mess was depressing and he considered his options for escape.

The first thing he had to do was set up communications to let his people know he was alive and where he was. He removed his standard-issue SARBE emergency search-and-rescue radio and beacon from its pouch on his belt. It was a waterproof and robust device no bigger than a cigarette pack, and he checked it for damage. He turned it to the radio function long enough for a light to flicker – indicating sufficient power – before turning it off and putting it back in its pouch. This was not the place to send his emergency signal. Mallory needed to be in a secure open area for any rescue craft to land.

He checked his watch. The ideal location for a pick-up was outside the town and that meant waiting until dark. The Tornado pilot had initiated his beacon immediately because he was in dire straits but Mallory had

20

a responsibility to ensure the rescue team's safety as well as his own. That meant he had to find a safe landing site.

Mallory was parched, his mouth dry as a bone, but he had no water. Adding a bottle to his belt kit was something he had considered but decided against, limiting the amount of equipment he carried to enhance his mobility.

Mallory's eyes gradually became accustomed to the dim light and he noticed a dirty sheet that was hanging on a couple of nails on the opposite wall and that appeared to cover a hole. He got to his feet, ignoring a stab of pain from his stiff foot, limped over to the sheet and moved it aside. The roughly hammered hole was an entrance to a smaller, darker room that seemed to be filled with more junk. He removed a small pencil light from a pouch and switched it on. The light revealed a weapons store, an Aladdin's Cave of armaments: dozens of AK47 assault rifles, RPG7 hand-held rocket launchers and an assortment of metal ammunition boxes. Mallory's first thought was to get out of there, imagining that the owners of such an important storage facility might not be far away. But on the other hand a high-velocity rifle would be more useful in a fight than his pistol.

He stepped inside, allowing the sheet to drop back across the opening, and took a closer look at the cache. There were hundreds of AK47 magazines, many of them filled with bullets, and inside an open ammunition box were several pistols. On closer inspection much of the ordnance turned out to be old and rusty, while the wooden stocks and butts on some of the AK47 rifles were badly damaged. Mallory holstered his pistol to inspect an AK47 that looked in better condition than the others and carefully drew back the working parts to check the breech and ejection mechanisms. It didn't look too bad – a touch of oil would do it the world of good. The AK47 was a cheaply manufactured weapon but that was also its advantage. Its low-tolerance moving parts could function even when poorly maintained, one reason why it was the most popular weapon with poorly trained ragtag armies.

Mallory sorted through the ready-filled magazines, all of which were in bad condition. A couple of empty ones were in reasonable shape but he needed some loose ammunition to fill them with. The next ammunition box he inspected contained pistol rounds and the one beneath that was empty. Another ammunition box was filled with spare parts for an 82mm mortar: a rusty tube and base-plate lay on the floor beside it.

A clean, relatively new-looking metal ammunition box sitting alone in a corner under a stack of empty sandbags caught his eye. Mallory squatted on a bundle of dirty Iraqi army uniforms in front of it to take the weight off his throbbing leg. He removed the sandbags and pulled on one of the box's catches but it was tight. He put the end of the flashlight in his mouth, allowing him to use both of his hands, and after a struggle the catch sprang open. He gripped the sides of the lid and raised it. The light bathed the inside of the box and Mallory almost dropped the small torch from his mouth when he saw what was inside.

He pushed the lid back fully and removed the pencil light from his mouth – which stayed open in disbelief. The box was filled with neatly packed rectangular bundles of green-grey printed paper, each sheet of which had the image of Benjamin Franklin in its centre and the figures '100' in each corner.

Mallory took out one of the bundles to examine it more closely, turning it on its side and flicking through the crisp notes with his thumb to find every one identical apart from its serial number. He took out a couple more bundles to reveal that the ones beneath were also all made up of United States of America hundred-dollar bills. Suddenly worried that the owners might appear at any moment he went back to the opening to peer through it.

He stepped into the outer room and crossed to the front door to listen. The only sound was a distant rumble but the urge to get out of the building consumed him.

Mallory hurried back into the small room, grabbed an empty sandbag, shoved several AK47 magazines – loaded and unloaded – into it, picked up the assault rifle he'd selected and his helmet and looked down at the box of money. It suggested to him more than anything else in the room that the owners could return any time. Nobody would leave that amount of money unattended for long, certainly not these people to whom it was worth ten times its western value. At the same time he found it impossible to simply walk away from that amount of cash.

He had at least to satisfy a nagging curiosity. He

put down his hardware booty, sat back down in front of the box, picked up a bundle of notes and riffled swiftly through it. A rough calculation put the bundle at ten thousand dollars and there were ten bundles per stack and eleven stacks. Mallory whistled softly to himself as he realised he was staring at over a million US dollars – worth well over five hundred thousand pounds, more than he could earn in the Marines if he stayed in for the next twenty years.

Mallory got to his feet, his stare fixed on the treasure, and wondered how a person could have the worst and best luck in his life all in one day. That was so typical for him, though, he thought. In this case each sort of cancelled the other out, leaving him with a fat zero and the rest of the day still to go. Even if he were to take the money, and assuming that all went well with the rescue, the first thing he would be asked about would be the contents of the box. And once declared, there was no doubt about how much he would be allowed to take home with him: none of it, since it was war loot and hence illegal.

But on the other hand he *could* take a little if he hid it on his person. So he stuffed one bundle into a thigh pocket, another into a breast pocket which was only barely big enough – and then he stopped himself. Greed simply increased the chance of discovery. After his rescue Mallory would be escorted to the hospital where he would have to discard his clothing. He could probably secure one bundle but more would be pushing it. It all depended on so many things: being left alone for even a few seconds before he was examined; his clothes being taken away once he was in hospital garb; finding somewhere in the examination room to hide the bundle so that he could retrieve it later. He knew he was probably being too paranoid but it worried him nevertheless.

A noise outside startled him and he drew his pistol, grabbed up the bag, AK47 and helmet, carefully pushed the concealing sheet aside and moved stealthily across the room to the door. There was no follow-up to the sound, the source of which was unclear, but it was yet another warning to get out of there as soon as possible.

As Mallory placed a hand on the door to open it he paused and looked back towards the storeroom. There was one possible low-risk solution to keeping the money that was admittedly a long shot but better than simply walking away and eternally regretting that he had not given it a go. He was already succumbing to peer pressure, imagining some of the names he would be called by the lads back home if he told them how he had found a cool million and then just walked away from it.

Mallory reached into a pouch, pulled out his GPS and turned it on. A message window declared it was searching for satellites and he turned it off, satisfied that it was working. He weighed the pros and cons of his hastily thought-out plan and the pros came out on top, no doubt enhanced by thoughts of a fancy new house with a pool, a new car, et cetera. Enough, he told himself. He could daydream later, which was another positive aspect of the plan since it gave him something more to look forward to, not that the prospect of survival wasn't encouraging enough.

He pocketed the GPS, placed his helmet, AK47 and bag on the floor by the door and went back into the storeroom.

He took the bundle poking out of his breast pocket, tossed it back into the box, leaving the one in his thigh pocket, closed the lid and picked it up to test its weight. It was heavy but manageable. The problem was that he would need his hands free to hold his gun. He scanned around the room, found a length of old nylon rope that appeared to have the strength for the job and threaded it through the handles at either end of the box, tying it off to form a loop. He bent forward, placed the line over his head, stood up, moved the box around so that it hung low across his back and tested it. It was not perfect and would annoy the hell out of him but it was worth a try.

The urge to get out of the building was now over-powering. Mallory went back to the front door, took up his Kalashnikov and bag, elected not to wear his helmet at that moment since it impeded his hearing, clipped it around the nylon line by the chin strap, took his pistol from its holster and opened the door.

He crossed the yard and checked inside the opposite building. There was a partially open door at the far side and he crossed the dirt floor towards it.

The door led onto a street and Mallory carefully looked out and checked in both directions. A man was on the road in the distance but far enough away not to be an immediate threat. Otherwise it looked clear.

Mallory focused on the entrance to an alleyway directly opposite and, holding the box in place with the same hand that was holding the bag and AK, his pistol in the other, he moved off.

Mallory wasn't far along the alleyway when the difficulties he had expected to have carrying his load became a reality. He paused long enough to undo the helmet, drop it to the ground, and kick some rubble over it. Then he moved on.

Halfway along the alley he ducked through a gap between the houses, stepping around what looked like an old generator to arrive at a corner where he stopped. In front of him was a large expanse of open ground, marked with the rudimentary boundaries and goal-posts of a football pitch, whose perimeter was lined by brick buildings, many of them two-storey. A few metres away in a corner of the waste ground was a flimsy wooden shed that looked as if it had been built to keep animals. He needed somewhere to wait until dark; he didn't fancy backtracking and since he couldn't risk moving in the open any more it was the only option he felt he had.

Mallory moved towards it at the crouch, eyes checking in every direction while the box swung awkwardly behind him. He ducked inside the rickety construction.

The dirt floor was covered in old palm leaves and the ceiling was not high enough for him to stand upright. He dropped to his knees, quickly removed the line from around his neck and moved to the back of the hut to watch the direction he had come from in case he had been followed. The smell and the absence of any man-made implements suggested that animals had probably been the hut's last occupants. Mallory remained still for several minutes, listening intently to the local sounds, until his breathing returned to normal.

A glance at his wristwatch told him he had at least another hour before the sun began to set and probably an hour more until it was really dark. He couldn't remember if there was a moon or not that night but it didn't matter. He was moving out whatever happened.

Mallory quickly set about his next task and emptied the contents of the sandbag onto the floor. He quietly unloaded two old AK47 magazines and one by one pushed the bullets into the ones that were in better condition. Once they were loaded he firmly pressed a magazine into its housing on the weapon until it clicked home. Then, pulling the working parts to the rear, he controlled the return spring, letting the breech-block slide forward to push a bullet out of the magazine and into the breech. He could not allow the return spring to fly forward as normal because of the noise it would make and so the breech had not seated properly and he spent a couple of minutes working it into place. Once he had the AK47 properly loaded he left the safety catch off and rested the gun across his lap – not normal safe practice as he was taught but this wasn't a normal situation, alone and unsupported.

His ears gradually tuned to the noises that surrounded him, far and near, and he leaned back against the wall that moved a little under his weight but held firm. He stretched out his legs. The pain in his foot had eased and Mallory's thoughts drifted home to Plymouth and to the apartment he had shared with Jenny, his girlfriend, until she'd dumped him for a policeman two days before Mallory left for Iraq. Her reason for leaving after two and a half years together was that she did not want to live with someone who was not home every night. He knew the real reason was that she didn't fancy him any more. If she had loved him she wouldn't have left. But then, the truth was that *he* didn't love *her*. He couldn't have or it would have been more painful than it had been. It made him wonder why he had lived with Jenny in the first place. But there had been some good times – in fact, it had all been quite good for him. Clearly not for her, though. But at that moment she would have been nice to come home to.

Mallory exhaled heavily as he checked his watch, calculating that it was three p.m. back in England. It was also Sunday and the lads would be watching football down the pub. What he wouldn't give to be with them at that moment, having a pint and a fish-and-chip lunch covered in tomato sauce and salt and vinegar. His mouth was dry as paper and thoughts like that only made it worse. He forced himself to think of something else.

A sudden noise took care of that. He pointed the Kalashnikov at the hut opening and his ears focused on the sound. It came again, like a tapping noise but not in any kind of rhythm. It seemed to be coming from the direction he had arrived from and was getting closer.

Mallory placed the butt of the weapon against his shoulder as the noise stopped. When it started again Mallory leaned forward onto one knee, both of his eyes open and looking down the length of the rifle, the pad of his index finger resting lightly on the trigger.

Something came into view below the end of the barrel and he dropped the front sight enough to see the shadowy outline of a goat. The animal continued out of the alley, oblivious to Mallory's presence, and ambled towards the hut where it stopped in the entrance.

Mallory and the goat stared at each other as if each of them was waiting to see who would make the first move. Mallory exhaled slowly in relief and as he lowered the rifle the goat turned on its hooves and trotted away, flustered that its planned rest in the cover of the shed had been thwarted.

Mallory felt suddenly exhausted by yet another shot of adrenalin and he realised that his hands were shaking. The fear of being stuck in a place where anyone who saw him would kill him or alert others who could was getting to him. The million dollars and the comforts it could buy gave him no pleasure at that moment and he wished the damned Tornado pilot had not been shot down.

He leaned back as Mac's last words in the chopper popped into his head – something about a rendezvous with death – and wondered why the man had brought it up at such a moment.

Mallory closed his eyes, let his ears monitor the outside and waited in silence as darkness fell. Eventually he could hardly see the spot where the goat had first appeared.

He crept outside quietly, carrying the box, leaving the empty magazines and the sandbag behind. There were no street lights and only a handful of the houses had lights inside, faint orangey-yellow glows from kerosene lamps. The southern sky was a dull orange, silhouetting the rooftops as if a large fire was burning, but it could also have been the lights of the US military base around Baghdad airport. Mallory considered walking in that direction. It was not more than thirty kilometres away and he could cover the ground by the morning. But that would mean heading through the middle of Fallujah – or going around its perimeter, since he was near the northern edge of the town. Either way, it was not a good idea. He could end up a victim of either side.

Mallory looped the line attached to the box over his head, got to his feet and headed across the waste ground, keeping his distance from the dark, silent, dried-mud dwellings.

His foot throbbed but Mallory ignored it. This was the final phase of his operation, with luck, and he hoped sincerely that the next time he fell asleep would be in the safety of his camp. His basic plan was to make his way out of the town and find a deserted patch of ground large enough for a helicopter to land on and where he could establish communications and activate his beacon. From what he could remember of the terrain, a mile or so should see him well north of the town and in farmland. The moon had not yet shown itself and there was a slight breeze. The temperature had dropped, making conditions as good as he could expect, for which he was thankful. If he needed to run he would have to dump the money but that was part of the deal he had made with himself.

Ten minutes later, moving carefully and then only after frequent pauses to look and listen, Mallory came to a low wall and went to ground as much to rest as to check the route ahead. An inspection over the wall revealed that he was at the boundary of a cemetery. It was difficult to tell how large it was: the awkward, tilted headstones and ragged flags moving gently on poles filled the view.

Mallory lifted the box over the wall and crouched on the other side. The box was a complete pain, not just its weight and awkwardness but the metallic noise it made every time it touched something solid, a sound that carried a long way on the night air.

The cemetery seemed an ideal place to cross as the odds on meeting anyone there at such a late hour were slim. However, there was a risk of being silhouetted due to the lack of background and tall structures: the majority of the graves were bordered by low concrete rectangular frames, and he would have to keep low.

Mallory set off among the graves at a crouch but after several metres he lost his footing and the box scraped loudly against a gravestone. He lay flat and took a moment to listen, worried not only that he had been heard but also that the accident had every chance of being repeated. The graves were close together and it was so dark that stumbling as he walked in such an awkward way was unavoidable.

Then Mallory had a thought. The cemetery could be the ideal location to hide his booty. He had originally planned to bury the box somewhere near his pick-up point simply because if it was quiet enough to serve that purpose it would also be an ideal spot to dig a hole. But the bigger problem at the moment was getting to that location undetected.

He put down the box and sat on the edge of a grave to give the matter some serious thought. Burying the money inside a grave might work – but then, there was a chance that it could be visited in the near future and the freshly turned earth would attract suspicion. Mallory looked down at the narrow path he had been following between the graves and it struck him as actually a highly unlikely place to dig a new grave. Therefore it just might be the perfect place to bury something so that it would not be discovered.

Mallory pushed a finger into the earth. It wasn't too firm. He placed the ammunition box on a grave, set his rifle against it, removed his penknife from its pouch, opened it and shoved the blade into the soil. It sank in easily. He carved out a rectangle slightly larger than the box and began to scrape away the topsoil, placing it in a pile to one side.

Mallory was soon frustrated with the small amount of earth he was shifting and he searched around for a better digging implement. A can with a couple of plastic flowers in it was resting on a nearby headstone. He put the flowers to one side and used the tin as a shovel. Several minutes later he'd dug a substantial hole. He compared its depth with the height of the box. Ideally the top needed to be at least a foot below the surface. After a pause to look around and listen he pressed on.

A minute later Mallory had dug a considerably deeper hole, although now stones began to obstruct his efforts. He discarded the can and pulled the stones out by hand, decided he'd gone deep enough, picked up the box and lowered it inside. It lay at a slant, its highest point nine inches from the top, which Mallory reckoned was good enough. He dragged the loose soil back into the hole with his hands. When he had created a slight mound he got to his feet and, stamping as hard as he dared, used his weight to level it off. Then he spread the remaining soil around, depositing the stones further away.

As a final touch he shuffled up and down the path, trying to obscure any traces of his efforts on the surface for several metres in both directions. It was difficult to tell in the darkness how successful this operation had been and he would never know until the day he came back to retrieve the box. And God only knew when – or if – that day would come.

Mallory put the plastic flowers back in the can, placed it back on the headstone, wiped his hands on his thighs and removed his GPS from its pouch on his belt. As he turned it on he covered the small glowing screen and scanned around while he waited for the device to acquire the local satellites. A screen message eventually indicated this had been achieved and was followed by a display showing his position in latitude and longitude. He hit the 'man overboard' button and went through the menu to select the 'save' option. It asked him to provide a name and he paused to consider the request. He wanted something memorable but not obvious to anyone who might come across it and as he considered several possible names the word *rendezvous* popped into his head. He counted the letters on his fingers, ten being the maximum number of characters he could use, and since the word fitted perfectly he punched them in and saved it to the memory chip before turning off the instrument. He placed it back in its pouch, picked up his weapon and, after a final check around, headed between the graves towards the northern boundary wall, feeling relieved at having rid himself of his main burden.

Mallory saw a tarmac road on the other side of some waste ground beyond the low wall that marked the northern edge of the cemetery and took a moment to watch and listen. The only sounds were distant *booms* from the direction of Baghdad accompanied by flashes of light but ahead was total blackness. He climbed over the wall and moved down a slight incline and onto the waste ground, looking left and right as he dodged across the narrow road before picking up speed on reaching the other side. He carried on without slowing down and covered several hundred metres before he stopped and lay down near what appeared to be a motorway running across his way ahead. He remembered a major artery north of the town, a road that ran from Baghdad to the Jordanian border, and then the sound of a distant vehicle reached his ears and he looked east to see a pair of flickering headlights in the distance.

Mallory's first thought was that it could be a coalition vehicle – but that was not necessarily good news. This was a war zone, at night, and alert and often nervous fingers were constantly poised on triggers, their owners ready to shoot at anything remotely suspicious. A lone figure in the darkness might invite an attack before any recognition was attempted. On the other hand, it would be unusual for a military vehicle to travel alone in a hostile environment and Mallory elected to remain where he was, hugging the ground until it passed.

The dark shape behind the bright headlights gradually took on a form that was distinctly civilian and Mallory watched it as it drove on by and out of sight.

The motorway had two lanes either side of a meridian flanked by crash barriers and it would take Mallory a few seconds to cross. A thought struck him that the road might be watched. Still, the car had driven along unmolested. The other side of the road was in complete darkness and this was, he hoped, the final obstacle. Luck had remained with him so far and he needed it to stick around a little longer.

Mallory got to his feet, moved forward at a crouch and raised his injured foot over the first of the knee-high crash barriers. Pain shot through him as the edge of the tarmac dug into his wound but he did not falter. It then suddenly occurred to him that if troops were watching they would have night-vision aids and the AK47 with its uniquely curved magazine was unlike any weapon carried by coalition forces. They might allow a car to pass but a man with a gun would be an irresistible target. He held the weapon close to his body to remove it from his silhouette, ran to the meridian, climbed the double set of barriers, and hurried across the final stretch of tarmac, over the last barrier and down a sandy bank. Mallory did not slow and ran across a stretch of open ground, still feeling exposed and vulnerable, towards what looked like an earthwork that in the darkness appeared to be further away than it actually was. He was soon upon it, scrambling up a short incline where he dropped over the other side and found himself in a dry ditch. He moved along the earthwork for several metres before crawling back up and looking in the direction he had come from to see if he had been pursued: anyone following would be silhouetted by the glowing horizon beyond Fallujah. But there was no sign of movement and he slid down to the bottom of the ditch, scrambled up the other side and ran on across another flat open space.

A black scar appeared in front of him that did not quite look like a road and as he drew closer it became a railway line that he had forgotten about. Mallory crossed the rails and pressed on into the darkness, his breathing becoming laboured, his dry mouth aching, his foot throbbing wildly. But the promise of freedom pushed him on, with every step making the prospect more of a reality.

Mallory passed through a line of bushes and found himself on the edge of what appeared to be an open area. He dropped to his knees beside a bush, utterly exhausted, and gulped in air through his sandpaper mouth. He could not remember ever being as exhausted: his only truly comparable experience had been during his commando course when he had run with a thirty-foot telegraph pole from Woodbury Common to the Lympstone camp, a six-mile race, sixty men, six poles, ten men on each. With two miles to go and despite his pole being down to just four men they were in the lead by a couple of hundred metres. But then, with under a mile to go, the man beside him dropped out, unable to keep up the pace and Mallory was left with the end of the pole to carry on his own. He began to see stars, almost collapsing under the physical stress and might have done so had he not seen the tops of the rugby posts that were the finishing line beyond some hedgerows a few hundred metres ahead. Those days seemed as far away as his early childhood at that moment.

Mallory decided the location would do and he pulled his SARBE from its pouch, took hold of a bright-orange cord on its side and pulled it, releasing a pin that activated the device. There was no sound and the only indication that the beacon was transmitting was a small flashing LED light. The transmitted signal would include his GPS position as well as his pre-programmed identity. He laid the Kalashnikov on the ground beside him and waited for the voice of the rescue crew informing him that his signal had been received and that they were on their way.

Mallory was supremely confident that he would be picked up some time that night. If there was one thing he had experience of it was the Air Sea Rescue teams. As long as his SARBE was working, and they rarely failed, he was as good as home. Most passing aircraft, or an AWACS if one was in the area, which was likely, would be able to pick up the signal. The information would be passed on to the relevant operations room and the rescue mission would be set in motion.

An hour passed before the voice of a pilot brought Mallory's SARBE to life. He almost jumped when he heard it. He pressed the 'send' button and was horrified when he could not talk. His mouth, without a trace of saliva, could not form an intelligible word. It took what seemed an age before the pilot finally understood and informed him that they would be with him in approximately ten minutes.

Mallory got to his feet and several minutes later heard the distant drone of an aircraft engine. A minute after that he thought he could see a black speck in the sky to the west and although he could not be sure his eyes weren't playing tricks on him his ears were in no doubt. As the sound grew louder the suspicious speck became larger and formed into two separate objects which shortly after became silhouettes that he recognised: Blackhawks.

They flew towards him, one close behind the other and then they suddenly split up, one chopper dropping height while the other moved into a circling pattern above. Mallory knew that the higher craft would have a heavy machine gun mounted in its doorway to provide covering fire if the pick-up point came under attack.

The incoming craft covered the remaining distance in seconds and when the dust kicked up as it came into the hover Mallory ran towards it. Several figures jumped out of its side when it was a couple of feet off the ground and while two knelt in firing positions the others ran forward, took hold of Mallory and unceremoniously guided him back to the craft.

Seconds later they were all aboard and the helicopter lifted off and accelerated away.

'You OK?' one of Mallory's rescuers asked in an American accent.

'Fine, thanks,' Mallory replied in his parched voice. They were US Special Forces – Delta, he suspected – though the Yanks also had guys who trained specifically for hostile extractions. One of them handed Mallory a bottle of water which he practically drained on his first hit. When he sat back, clutching the empty plastic bottle, his hand drifted to his thigh map-pocket and felt the bundle of money inside.

Thirty minutes later they had landed somewhere near Baghdad airport and Mallory was on his way to his accommodation. Worried about the bundle of money he had concealed in his pocket he had not mentioned his injury and expressed a desire to go to his basher where – he said – he badly needed the toilet and to change his clothes before his debrief, hinting that he'd had an accident in his trousers that needed to be taken care of. As soon as he'd secreted the money in his backpack by cutting into the padding and placing the cash inside to be stitched up later he had a shower, got changed and then made his way to the sickbay to have his wound seen to. After a hearty meal Mallory attended a debrief after which he was exonerated of any blame for having been left behind and, since no one had suffered any serious injuries and his crew's Sea King had returned with only minor damage, the affair was quickly forgotten. The war was coming to a speedy end and the powers that be were preoccupied with preparations for the occupation.

Within five days Mallory was on an RAF flight back to the UK and his unit, where he was immediately sent on leave after being congratulated by his RSM for his war efforts.

Mallory arrived at his apartment to discover that most of his furniture, including his television and stereo, had been cleaned out — not by burglars but by his former girlfriend. Under normal circumstances Mallory would have been annoyed enough to go and look for her and demand an explanation since it was his money that had bought everything. But he decided to forget about it as he placed the bundle of dollars on the kitchen table, made a cup of tea, sat down and stared at his money. Chasing after Jenny would have been a hassle anyway and he preferred to focus his efforts on more important matters.

Mallory had checked the exchange rate at the first opportunity and calculated that his dollars were worth just over six thousand pounds sterling. Another calculation revealed that it was more than the Royal Marines had paid him after deductions for the period he had been at war. All he had to do now was find a way of changing it to pounds without drawing any attention to himself and then spend it. The best idea he could come up with, and quite an attractive one at that, was to go on holiday to the United States – Orlando, for instance – have a good time, buy some new technical stuff from the duty-free shop, change the rest to sterling on his way home and then buy a TV and some furniture. There wouldn't be much left after all that and Mallory wished he had stuffed another couple of bundles into his pockets.

Mallory thought about the ammunition box filled with money that he'd buried in the cemetery in Fallujah: a million dollars just waiting for him to dig up and bring home. But the only way he was going to be able to do that was to get over there – and that would require some planning.

The first step would be to find out which commando unit was going next to Iraq, specifically Baghdad, and then explore the chances of it making a trip to Fallujah, something which would probably be difficult if not impossible to find out in advance. He would then need to apply to join that unit, which of course he might not be permitted to do. And there was another even bigger problem. The Yanks were in the centre and north of Iraq and the Brits were in the south, and it didn't take a genius to figure out that those positions were unlikely to change. Even if by some remote chance Mallory could get to Fallujah he would still have to slip away from the rest of his troop without them knowing, dig up the box without being seen, conceal its contents and keep it secure until he was finally moved back to the UK. Each phase was fraught with impossible difficulties and if he was caught at any stage he could end up in jail for his troubles or at best lose the cash.

Mallory gave a long sigh as the possibilities of ever getting his hands on the money shrank – at least while he remained in the Marines.

As soon as the implication of that thought sank home it struck him that the only way he was ever going to get hold of the money was as a civilian. He needed freedom to go where he wanted, when he wanted, to go to Fallujah on his own terms, take as long as he wanted and decide how he was going to get out of the country with the money. The burning question he needed to answer was whether he really wanted to leave the Royal Marines and end a career that he had set his heart on since he was a boy.

Mallory got up and looked out of the window onto the field below where several youngsters were playing football. The thought of quitting the Marines didn't sit comfortably with him. He had planned on doing his full twenty-two years of service up to retirement before seeing what else the world had to offer. But now, out of the blue, here he was contemplating his resignation with only a quarter of his time done. It was a gamble on so many levels, not just on whether the money would still be in Fallujah when he got there but on whether that was more important than quitting his chosen career. But a million dollars was a lot of money, to be sure, enough to buy a damned nice house as well as a damned nice car.

Mallory decided to explore all the pros and cons and only when he was satisfied that he had covered everything would he make a decision. It had to feel right and at that moment the notion of leaving the Marines did not. Perhaps it was just fear of the unknown.

But the period of indecision was not easy for Mallory. He tried at first to forget about the money – which turned out to be impossible – and then took to concentrating on the negative aspects of leaving a fine career in the Royal Marines simply to pursue a pile of cash. But the thought of the box in the grave-yard would not let him go and tormented him endlessly. He didn't take the holiday to Orlando in the end. In the back of his mind he knew that if he did decide to leave the Marines he would need to finance his Fallujah operation.

When Mallory returned to work he was told to report to Recce Troop, the position he had originally longed for. But the satisfaction was no longer there. Finally, a month after his return from Iraq, he made the decision to resign. The money or the adventure of retrieving it dominated his thoughts and he knew that he would remain restless until he did something about it. It was only after he committed himself, when he walked into HQ Company, met with the duty clerk and asked for the necessary papers, that the thought of the cash in the graveyard stopped pestering him and he set about planning his expedition in earnest.

But he was soon to acquire a whole new collection of concerns.

Mallory's initial research had already revealed that his mission was going to be more complicated than simply arriving in Iraq, digging up the box and leaving with it. The struggle between the various religious and political factions in the country as well as the general resistance to the coalition occupation had begun. There was an increase in crime and banditry due to the absence of law and order. Further research revealed that westerners were not permitted visas to enter the country unless they were employed by a certified Iraqi reconstruction contractor. But the Marines were not going to let Mallory go for another ten months anyway, by which time he hoped Iraq would be back to normal. With luck, he could then go there on holiday, hire a car, buy a shovel, dig the money up at his leisure, take a tour of the country, go out by road through Turkey or Jordan and start spending his cash on a relaxing drive back through Europe.

Mallory saw it all as a great adventure and began to feel more relaxed about the whole thing. He started enjoying his work once again and appreciated the company of his colleagues more than ever, knowing that it was all soon to come to an end. And, of course, he spent many hours contemplating the delightful problem of how he was going to spend the money. What finally made everything much more worthwhile was the realisation that whatever happened, even after he'd got the money, he could always rejoin the Marines and pretty much take up where he'd left off. There'd even be an amusing exploit to tell his grandchildren. Mallory would be a winner whatever happened: he looked forward with relish to revisiting Fallujah and concluding the greatest adventure of his life.

2

Abdul's Dilemma

Abdul Rahman stood beside his hand-painted white and blue Iraqi police Toyota pick-up parked near a busy road junction outside one of the north-west entrances to the Green Zone that were heavily guarded by the US military. The elaborate check-point, protected by layers of interconnecting sections of concrete blast-walls, was overlooked by the majestic historical monument known as the Assassins' Gate. It was also one of the locations where a year previously jubilant Iraqis had unceremoniously pulled from its plinth a statue of Saddam Hussein in celebration of his defeat by the US-led invasion forces.

The afternoon was a normally busy one despite the thousand-pound vehicle bomb that had gone off the day before directly outside the checkpoint. The death toll eventually totalled more than twenty people after the most severely wounded had failed to survive the night. One man had been killed almost a kilometre away while shopping in an open market after a piece of the artillery shell that had made up part of the bomb landed on his head. Seven of the dead were at the time inside the van which was ferrying workers who lived in the city into the Green Zone. The only person in the vehicle aware of the explosives packed under the seats and in boxes in the back was the driver. As instructed by his religious guide, he had picked up his passengers after explaining to them how the normal taxi had broken down and, since the replacement van belonged to him, he would be taking the driver's place until the other one was fixed. As they arrived at the checkpoint and waited in line to pass through a security inspection he flicked the two arming switches, cried, '*Allah akbar*' – and pushed the final firing button.

The large crater over a foot deep and surrounded by a wide black scorch mark was a few metres in front of Abdul near the centre of the junction. Like most of the other bomb holes in the city it would not be repaired in the foreseeable future, thus adding to the increasing deterioration of road conditions.

Abdul was holding the butt of an old AK47 against his hip, resting the tip of the barrel on the ground. The tattered, knotted shoulder strap attached at either end of the weapon had broken twice since he had been issued with the gun and it was too heavy to carry all day. He wore black trousers and the sky-blue long-sleeved shirt of the Iraqi Police with the letters 'IP' stencilled on a white band tied over his left shoulder. Abdul had been a police officer for three months after completing a six-week training course in Amman, the capital of Jordan, followed by another week at the Stadium School, the former international football arena, near the centre of Baghdad. The training fell short of the Academy's pre-war standards but the necessity to produce high numbers of officers and get them onto the streets as quickly as possible was paramount. But lack of proper skills and discipline among the police was only one of the problems causing Abdul anxiety in his newly chosen profession – which, it had to be said, had never exactly been a vocational ambition for him. In his younger days Abdul's main feature had been his bright, cheerful smile and although he was a quiet-spoken, introverted young man who tended to daydream when he should have been listening, the little he had to say suggested an above-average level of intelligence. But the smile had rarely been seen since the war and probably not at all since he had joined the police.

The main reason for Abdul's glum feelings while at work was the poor quality of some of the other police officers: there had been a marked lack of vetting procedures when they'd been selected. This was no more evident than in the squad of which he was a member. Abdul's immediate colleagues on the force were, to a man, all Ali Babas, crooks and villains, and one or two of them were possibly far worse than that.

Abdul had been brought up as a good Muslim – the word itself meant 'one who submits', a concept which he fully embraced – and by his late teens he was by far the most religious member of his family, the only one who prayed five times a day. But since the war his faith had slipped, at least as far as his regular acts of worship were concerned. This dilution of his belief was also at the core of his distress since, much as he wanted to re-establish a full commitment to

Allah, possibly even in a more active way than before, he felt unable to. For Abdul believed that he was no longer worthy of Allah's attention. He had allowed an obstacle to come between him and God and was too weak to do anything about it. This obstruction on the divine path was a result of allowing himself to be drawn into a perk of the job, for want of a better term, that had seemed innocent enough at first but had developed into something that in his heart he wholly disapproved of, a disapproval shared by the person he admired most in his life, his sister.

Abdul was a dichotomy. He had never been very strong, physically or mentally, but there were occasions when he was painfully contrary and displayed such levels of determination as to cause suspicion among members of his family, his father in particular, that, as a baby, the boy had been exchanged for an impostor. These moments of defiance were seen as uncharacteristic by everyone else but it was his beloved sister, Tasneen, who was always supportive and read them as evidence of Abdul's great potential. He always showed promise when it came to family duties and honour, motivated as he was by his heritage: tribal, ancestral and, of course, religious. He was unaffected by politics. But it was the ordinary pressure of everyday life that revealed Abdul's character flaws and lack of forcefulness and independence of thought. Those were the qualities of Tasneen, the only other surviving member of his immediate family. Abdul cherished her deeply. She was not just his older, wiser sister. After the loss of their parents she took on many of their functions.

But Abdul often resented her for those very reasons. The strengths she possessed only highlighted his own weaknesses, revealing them not only to others but to himself. Still, he loved her and remained guided by her but only until, he assured himself, he broke through to true manhood.

Abdul had been born on 23 September 1980, the day after Iraq invaded Iran, in Baghdad's Yarmuk Hospital, and was brought up in Al Mansour, one of the city's more affluent districts on the west side of the Tigris river. He was a Sunni Muslim, the same religion as that of his country's leader, Saddam Hussein, a factor that gave Abdul's father undeniable advantages in his business dealings at home and abroad. Abdul's full name, a legacy from twelve successive heads of family, was Abdul-Rahman Marwan Ahmed Mussa Akmed Dawood Sulaiman Abdullah Abdul-Kader Abdul-Latef Abdullah Maath Dulaimy Al Aws.'Dulaimy' was the official tribal name since 'Al Aws' was the name of one of the two main tribes that the Arabs had divided into around the time of Mohamed, the other main tribe being the Al Kharaj. The Dulaimy tribe originated in Saudi Arabia and during Abdul-Latef's reign in the last quarter of the nineteenth century they emigrated to a village called Ana in the open desert region of Al Anbar some four hundred kilometres due west of Baghdad on the Jordan road. Two generations later, Abdul's several-times-great-grandfather Sulaiman fought against the Turks during the great Arab revolt under the leadership of Prince Feisal with the aid of the famed British soldier, Lawrence of Arabia.

The Sunnis were a minority in modern Iraq at around thirty-five per cent of the population. Take away the Sunni Kurds in the north who constituted some twenty per cent and that left the former ruling class in Iraq now holding a considerably smaller percentage.

Abdul had enjoyed a comfortable upbringing and it was not until his early teens that he began to worry about reaching his eighteenth year, when he would be eligible for military conscription. The very thought filled him with dread. Having a well-connected Sunni father might have held some advantages for him when it came to avoiding the draft but unfortunately for Abdul his father believed military service to be an obligation of every young Iraqi. The Sunni – or, to be more precise, Saddam Hussein's family and friends – occupied practically every important position in the government and military. Thinking that it might bolster the rather tenuous advantages of the Dulaimy tribe's somewhat remote connection – Hussein's tribe were the Tekritis from north of Baghdad – Abdul's father also regarded his son's term in the army as a wise and necessary insurance for the boy's future. But Abdul had nightmares about becoming a soldier and the closer that day came the greater grew his desperation to find a way of avoiding it, without attracting scorn from his father. In fact, Abdul was unlikely to be able to avoid his sire's disdain. But he still preferred parental abuse to three years under arms.

His first and most simple plan to delay conscription was to enrol in a university and embark on a long and difficult degree course. He chose computer technology, normally a four-year programme. But, even so, after it he would still have to join the army. His second delaying tactic was to drag out the degree course for as long as he could by failing examinations. There was a limit to how long Abdul could use this technique and by year six his father began to suspect his son's plot. He warned Abdul that if his next results were not a satisfactory pass he would take him out of university and enrol him in the army himself. Abdul did not take his father seriously enough, perhaps, because to do so would have been unthinkable and maybe he hoped that his father would eventually realise how important his studies were to his son. When Abdul failed to make the grade yet again his father was furious and delivered his ultimatum: join the army or leave the house for ever. His father also made it clear that if Abdul chose the latter course he risked losing all claim to his inheritance.

The threat, particularly its disinheritance component, proved to be more painful to Abdul than his hatred for the military and he finally accepted the inevitable. The day he left the university he registered himself as eligible for conscription and within a week he had received his marching orders. He was sent to a training outpost in the western desert not far from his tribal home of Al Anbar, which was not a coincidence. He arrived at the camp along with four hundred other recruits at six a.m. Within a couple of hours they had received an induction speech, followed by a severe haircut, and were then lined up outside the barracks where their training team introduced them-selves. The recruits were invited to lie down on their stomachs, whereupon the instructors went around kicking and hitting them with a level of enthusiasm that went far beyond even Abdul's expectations. The beatings were immediately followed by a gruelling run without water in the midday sun where they continued to receive kicks and blows for no apparent reason. After a brief rest and a paltry meal the abuse was resumed. By four p.m. the recruits were ordered to return to their barracks and, expecting more of the same the following day, two dozen of Abdul's fellow conscripts conspired to desert. Abdul needed little encouragement to take part in the mutiny and as soon as darkness fell he joined the others at a hole in the perimeter wall through which they filed. Then they dispersed.

Abdul arrived home late that evening, walked into the house and went directly to his father who was horrified to see him. Abdul attempted to relate his terrible experiences but before he could begin his story his father demanded that he return to the camp immediately. Abdul found the strength to refuse abjectly to obey, pleading to be heard and swearing that no matter what punishment his father inflicted he would not go back. His father responded promptly by ordering him out of the house, never to return. Abdul continued to make his pleas but his father shouted violently for him to leave, even picking up a cane at one point to beat him. In a storm of shouts and screams Abdul ran out of the room, bundled some of his things into a bag and left the house.

But Tasneen was waiting for him in the street, having already made a plan to help her little brother. She led him to a friend's house nearby and arranged for him to stay in a small room there. She personally ensured that he was well fed while she embarked on a subtle crusade to change their father's mind. Abdul's world had turned utterly on its head and he believed that Tasneen's task was an impossible one. He was convinced this was the end of the family for him and so he concentrated on how he was going to manage life on the run from the army while making a living. But he could not come up with anything: he slipped into a deep depression and became absorbed in self-pity.

Four days later Tasneen woke him up with the announcement that she had come to take him home. Abdul could not believe it at first, then quickly wanted to know how and why their father had changed his mind. Tasneen gave her brother no explanation, appearing neither pleased nor disturbed by whatever had happened, and simply told him to come back home with her.

When they walked into the house she stayed by the front door and told him to go into the living room alone. Abdul became nervous, not knowing what to expect. The only encouragement Tasneen gave him was an assurance that it would be all right. Abdul believed her but as he approached the living-room doors his doubts grew and he reached for the door-knob with a shaking hand.

When he entered the room his father was standing at the window, looking through it with the kind of empty gaze that suggested he was not so much looking outside as inside at his own thoughts. To Abdul's surprise, when his father turned to face him there was not a trace of anger in his expression. Instead, there was a deep concern and, unless Abdul was mistaken, a trace of fear.

Abdul's father gave a strange kind of slight smile that unnerved Abdul further, although it disappeared as soon as the man sat down and bid his son to sit in the chair opposite. Abdul did not say a word, unable even to begin to guess what his father was about to say to him.

'Abdul, my son,' his father finally said. He was looking down at his hands at first but then he looked up into his son's eyes. 'Do you still refuse to go back to the military?'

Abdul could feel the heaviness of his father's heart. But despite his inability to find a solution for his own plight during his past few days' seclusion one thing he remained certain of was his future regarding the military. 'I will not go back, Father. I cannot. They are animals. I—'

Abdul's father put up a hand to stop his son from saying anything more. They sat in silence for a moment longer as the older man considered a deeper, much more troubling question. 'It will only be a matter of time before they come to look for you. You know that, don't you?'

'Then I will leave . . . ' Abdul began to say. But his father interrupted him once again, this time with a hint of anger in his eyes.

'Let me talk,' Abdul's father said firmly. 'It is not the army who will come here looking for you. It will be the secret police . . . And if they cannot find you they will take *me* away.' There was no shortage of horror stories about the secret police and what they did to people in their custody, no matter how trivial the reason for their arrest, and Abdul knew the tales as well as anyone.

'But . . . ' Abdul began, and again his father stopped him.

'You are a man now, not a boy. The world is a different place for men than it is for boys. There are different rules – rules of survival. It may seem to you, in the protection of this house, with me and your mother here, that there are more choices out there for men, that we have greater freedom than you. But in reality we have much less. There are far more rules for men and the punishments for breaking them are harsh. But I believe these rules to be important. Without them we cannot maintain our values and we will end up living by someone else's rules.'

Abdul listened quietly as his father continued in some detail about the advantages and disadvantages of the decisions, many of them unavoidable, that we all have to make in life and then the consequences of making the wrong decisions, especially in the times in which they lived. It was all so very complicated, intimidating as well, and Abdul could only wish that he had convinced his father not to send him to the army in the first place. There were ways of avoiding conscription but it had to be taken care of well in advance of the call-up date. One solution was to pay a fee, around two thousand dollars, to a certain someone a friend knew in the military who would have annulled Abdul's obligation. But his father would never have done that, partly because the man believed that Abdul would have enjoyed it once he had settled in but mostly because of what he was talking about now: the rules and the penalties for breaking them.

As Abdul watched his father wring his hands while he talked it became apparent that it was his duty, Abdul's, to resolve this most serious dilemma that he had created for his father and the rest of his family. When the older man finally grew silent Abdul stood up, put his hand on his father's shoulder, and with an uncommon resolve in his voice promised, as Allah was his witness, that he would find a solution, and if he failed he would let Allah decide his fate. But Abdul's father took little satisfaction from the declaration and did not look at his son who had always been much more of a talker than a doer. Abdul was aware of that, having been accused of it many times. This time he vowed to be different.

Abdul immediately set about making use of the many friends he had made at university and seeking out those he had heard rumours about in the past, men who had managed to somehow avoid the draft. Within a few days he learned of an army officer who held an influential position in the administrative office that dealt with army deserters and who – for a fee, of course – could have a name removed from the dreaded list. Abdul made contact with the officer through a man who had apparently benefited from his services. At a rendezvous in a coffee shop by the river near the Ishtar Sheraton Hotel the officer confirmed, after the customary ritual exchanges, that he could indeed help Abdul, at a cost of fifteen hundred dollars. Abdul did not want to go to his father for the money, part of his deal with himself and with Allah, and went directly to his mentor and only ally, Tasneen. Together they emptied their own bank accounts and raised the balance from various sources, mostly in the form of loans from other family members. But on the day they were to meet the officer and hand over the cash he called to explain that he was very sorry but Abdul's paperwork had been forwarded to 'other' authorities. Abdul was horrified and immediately asked if it was possible to bribe the new recipient of the paperwork. The officer explained how that would be impossible since the new recipients included the police, the army, the National Guard, the border guards and, of course, the secret police. Abdul's details would remain on file indefinitely or until he turned himself in or was captured.

Abdul had to sit down before his knees gave way. He had failed his father, dishonoured the family, but – far worse – he would be on the run for the rest of his life. The officer had suggested that Abdul's best course of action was to return to the army camp. He could expect imprisonment for a year or so, which would be unpleasant to say the least. There was, of course, a chance that Abdul could be hanged as an example to others, something that Saddam encouraged. But if

Abdul's father made a personal plea it could help his case. If Abdul was captured while on the run his chances of being executed were difficult to judge.

When Abdul's father learned of the news he slipped into a depression as he recounted a recent story of an old friend whose son was wanted for something by the secret police. After failing to find the boy they took the father instead. The son eventually turned up and the police hanged him in front of his father.

Abdul was faced with a serious quandary. If he ran his father might pay the price but it would still mean that Abdul would remain a fugitive. If he gave himself up he could be hanged or at least spend a horrifying time in an Iraqi jail, a period that he did not think he would survive. Abdul told his sister that had he known it would turn out as badly as this he would have done his time as a conscript. But it was too late now.

Abdul's fears were to be short-lived. So too, unfortunately, were his father and mother. A month later the coalition force invaded Iraq and a week after that his parents were killed when their car was crushed by the reckless panic-stricken driver of an Iraqi Army armoured vehicle heading out of the city as the Americans closed in on it.

'Abdul,' a voice growled behind him. He turned to see Hassan, his team sergeant, looking at him, a snarl on his face, an expression that as far as Abdul was concerned seemed to be a permanent fixture. Hassan was a strong, stocky man with a barrel gut that was the result not just of a large appetite but also of a taste for strong drink, a suspicion confirmed most mornings by Hassan's fetid breath. Hassan disapproved of everything about Abdul. But then he disliked everyone, it seemed, except his younger brother Ali. Hassan's animosity towards Abdul was partly due to his resentment of Abdul's more privileged upbringing, something which Hassan often sarcastically referred to. As far as Abdul was concerned the man was a lowlife and rotten to the core. Hassan was one of the thousands of prisoners that Saddam had released from jails all over the country shortly before the war, although he would deny the accusation. But after several men confirmed that they'd known Hassan while in Abu Ghraib prison he took to explaining his incarceration as an administrative error: he'd been inside for nothing more serious than a driving offence. Since most prison records had been lost or destroyed during the war, Hassan's included, it was not possible to disprove his claim. Abdul suspected his team sergeant was lying. To him, Hassan was quite simply a criminal in a police uniform.

The truth was that Hassan had always been a criminal, since childhood, and like his brother and the rest of the squad he had joined the police only to further his unlawful ambitions. They were all Sunni Muslims from the Dora district in southern Baghdad, near the large power station which with its smoking chimneys dominated that part of the city's horizon. It was an area notorious for its criminal element as well as for the insurgents who lurked there. The resistance and the crooks were hard to tell apart: their operational methods overlapped in places, both groups often working hand in hand.

Abdul could not understand why the police hired such men when their backgrounds and motives were so obvious. It seemed bizarre to Abdul and he could not believe his bad luck when, soon after joining the squad, he realised what kind of men the rest of his team were. He had initially assumed that his placement with them had been because he too was Sunni but then he learned that many of the other squads were of mixed faith. A week after joining the team Abdul applied for a transfer to another but his request was not even considered, his bosses having far too many more important things to worry about than a young police recruit's unhappiness with his fellow officers.

Iraqi Sunnis had a reputation for being more aggressive and militant than the Shi'a, and Hassan and his cronies were a perfect example. When it came to murder, for instance, an Iraqi Shi'a was likely to accept a financial payment from the murderer in compensation for the family's loss, as the Koran advised. But a Sunni was more likely to demand blood, an eye for an eye – and immediately, too.

There were two other police officers in the team besides Abdul, Hassan and Hassan's brother Ali. Arras and Karrar were boyhood friends, originally from the Sunni stronghold of Ramadi, west of Fallujah, and they had moved to Dora as teenagers. Ramadi, was notorious for its robbers and highwaymen, skills on which

Arras and Karrar hoped to build in Baghdad. All four officers were strong and determined characters who could see nothing wrong or even un-Islamic in what they did and believed it to be an acceptable way to make a living. The chance to commit crimes while working as legitimate police officers was seen as heaven-sent. It removed practically all the dangers and, better still, their victims had nowhere to turn to complain. They were certainly not the only officers of the law who practised extortion on the general public. Corrupt policemen were an accepted part of daily life in Iraq. Before the war a police officer took his life in his hands if he was corrupt. Saddam once had three officers hanged in public after they were caught demanding the equivalent of three dollars from an errant motorist.

Abdul was the smallest and most frail member of the squad. In fact, he was one of the least substantial men in the entire force. Like the majority of city Iraqis the team all wore their hair short and had well-groomed, closely trimmed facial hair – all except Hassan who wore a beard that he trimmed occasionally when it got too bushy.

'That car,' Hassan barked, indicating a fresh-looking BMW with a well-dressed young man behind the wheel who was waiting to enter the busy junction from the bridge. 'Go!'

Abdul looked at the BMW, knowing what he had to do and hating it. He picked up his Kalashnikov, pushed away from the police vehicle and walked towards the car, reluctant but obedient as always. This was why he loathed being in the police, or at least in Hassan's squad.

Disobeying traffic signals had become a national pastime in Iraq since the end of the war. Not a single electrically operated traffic indicator worked and since many of the major roads were partially or fully blocked off for security reasons drivers drove pretty much any way they wanted to in order to get to their destinations. That included mounting pavements, driving the wrong way down roads – including motorways – and going against the flow on roundabouts. This practice played into the corrupt police officers' hands: they selected their victims like sweets on a tray. When Hassan ordered Abdul to commit his first crime, the extortion of a few thousand dinars, equivalent to a couple of US dollars, from a motorist the peer pressure had been overwhelming and Abdul had not been strong enough to defy it. But since the crime involved little more than a brief conversation with no threat of repercussion, Abdul had slipped into it rather too easily. His excuse was that it was far less hassle to take part in the team's 'extracurricular' activity than to defy it. But if Abdul had examined himself more honestly he would have had to admit that although he did not like doing it he did enjoy the extra spending money it provided. Over a short period of time the battle with his conscience had been lost and at the end of the day all that remained was a general distaste for what he did. But he did it anyway.

Abdul walked to the front of the BMW and held out his hand to stop it. The young driver immediately rolled his eyes as he obeyed and pushed the button that rolled down his window.

'Can I see your registration papers?' Abdul asked.

The young man reached into his inside breast pocket, removed the papers and held them out to Abdul.

Abdul scanned through them quickly with an experienced eye and spotted a discrepancy. 'Where is the court registration?' he asked. The process of registering a new car was not particularly complicated in Iraq but since there was no longer a mail system a new owner had to present himself and the paperwork at the relevant courthouse as well as at his local police station to complete the transaction. It was an inconvenient process for many but a car was technically illegal until the procedure was completed. Although the offence was considered nowhere near serious enough for the car to be confiscated or to have the offender appear in court, technically the vehicle could be temporarily impounded and it therefore left a window of opportunity for corrupt officers to harvest a little bribe.

'Your registration is incomplete,' Abdul said.

'I plan to do it tomorrow,' the driver said, wondering why he was wasting his time debating the subject. But the Arab instinct to haggle was far too strong in him.

'I understand,' Abdul said. 'But do you understand that it is not complete today?'

'Yes, I'm sorry,' the driver said. 'I will take care of it immediately.'

'But you understand,' Abdul said politely, beginning to wonder if indeed the driver *did* understand what he meant without him actually having to say it up front.

The driver sighed as he reached into his pocket and produced several notes.

'I see you do understand,' Abdul acknowledged as he took the money and stepped back from the car to allow it to continue.

Abdul turned away and almost bumped into Hassan who looked down at the cash, took it from Abdul's hand and inspected the amount, maintaining his snarl as he pocketed it. 'Just four thousand? You don't try very hard,' he said.

'I'm not very good at it,' Abdul replied.

'Bullshit,' Hassan said. 'You're weak.'

Hassan walked away, leaving Abdul with the usual bad taste in his mouth. Much as he hated Hassan and the job that he was trapped in, gainful employment was hard to find in Iraq and since Abdul was not the entrepreneurial type it was either the police, the army or the private security sector. The army had been a non-starter since what little experience he'd had of it still haunted him. He did not have the patience and confidence nor the right contacts for a security-guard position, even though a job like that meant better pay if the right employer could be found. Joining the police force was the easiest and most convenient option because it was a simple case of filling in an application form, waiting a few weeks to be vetted cursorily and then completing the brief training course.

At the end of that day's shift, before the team dispersed to their homes or wherever, Hassan divided up the day's takings among the squad. As usual, Abdul received less than the others because, as Hassan put it, he had showed zero initiative and done the least work. But that day's collection meant fifteen dollars to him and, considering his monthly wage was a hundred and fifty dollars, he could get over twice as much in ill-gotten gains for the same period if he maintained that level of take.

Abdul arrived in Al Jeria Street in the Al Kindi block in the southern part of Al Mansour, not far from the old zoo in the centre of Baghdad. He parked his four-year-old Opal in a spot outside the apartment block where he lived and sat for a moment listening to a cassette tape of an Egyptian band, his current favourite. It was a quiet street with little traffic since it was used only by those who lived in the immediate area, although there were more cars than usual this month. They were owned by the men constructing a new house on the corner.

Abdul pulled up the collar of his leather jacket and held the lapels together to ensure that his police uniform was hidden from the gaze of any passer-by. When the track came to an end he ejected the tape and placed it in a plastic bag among a dozen or so others lying in the footwell of the back seat, climbed out of the car, lifted out a couple of shopping bags, checked there was nothing of any value visible inside the car, shut the vehicle's doors and locked them. After making the usual surreptitious glance around for strangers, he crossed the untidily finished concrete side-walk, walked in through the apartment-building entrance and up the stairs that were clean though poorly appointed. He arrived at the third floor, one from the top, a small landing shared by one other apartment, placed his key in the lock and opened the door.

'Tasneen,' he called out as he entered the apartment and closed the door behind him, making sure it was bolted at the top and bottom.

'I'm in my bedroom,' she replied, her voice young and sweet-sounding.

The clean and tidy apartment was simple and inexpensively furnished. There were signs everywhere that the occupants were young and caring: family photographs in ornate frames, a collection of dolls from Tasneen's childhood, a violin that Abdul's father had bought for him when he was a little boy in the vain hope he would one day learn it, a small hi-fi system and a television on a stand in a corner. The couch and matching side chair were made of high-gloss varnished wood with colourful flower-patterned upholstery. Against a window was a polished darkwood dining table with an empty vase in the centre of a delicate white cotton doily. A long varnished wooden shelf fixed high on a wall bore several local ornaments and an ornately bound copy of the Koran. An inexpensive floral-patterned carpet was fitted throughout the flat, except in the bathroom and the small kitchen. The finishing touch was a small, cheap but delicate chandelier that shone brightly in the centre of the ceiling.

Abdul went to the shelf, reached for the Koran,

gave it a kiss, replaced it, walked into the kitchen and put the shopping bags on the counter-top beside the sink. He went back to the door to check if Tasneen had come out of her room yet, heard a tap running in the bathroom and reached for the top of one of the two small wall cabinets. He moved a cooking pot aside and took down a china vase. He quickly stuffed the day's illicit takings inside and as he reached up to replace it he heard Tasneen walk through the living room. He hurriedly slid the cooking pot back in front of the vase and went over to the shopping bags as she walked in.

Tasneen was beautiful. Her classic dark Middle Eastern eyes were large, her olive skin perfect, her dark hair long and slightly curly with a little pink ribbon holding the ends together in the middle of her back. She smiled on seeing Abdul and gave him a kiss on his cheek, her usual greeting for him that never failed to soften his mood.

'How was your day?' she asked as she leaned over the shopping bags to look inside. She was slightly smaller than Abdul but unlike him could not be described as frail.

'Usual,' he said, moving to the window beside the sink.

'How was Hassan today? Your friends still mean to you?'

'That's like asking me if there were traffic jams in the city today,' Abdul replied as he watched Tasneen take items from the bag and place them in their correct places in the cupboards. 'There was a car bomb in Sadoon Street. It went off right across the river from us.'

Tasneen sighed. 'You know I don't like to hear those stories.'

Abdul shrugged. 'You asked how my day went . . . We went to investigate. You know how Hassan likes to drive anywhere that gives him an an excuse to use his siren and flashing lights . . . It wasn't too bad, though. Only three people killed. They think the driver blew himself up by mistake because there wasn't any target that anyone could see . . . As usual, Hassan told anyone who cared to listen that it was an American rocket . . . The man's an idiot as well as everything else.'

Tasneen folded the empty bag, put it into a drawer and started on the second one.

'I was thinking about getting a job as an army interpreter,' Abdul continued.

'You should. Your English is almost good enough,' Tasneen said as she placed a bag of rice on the counter for use later.

'Almost?' he queried.

'Almost, but not quite. But I will help you,' she said as she pulled out a jar of coffee, inspected the label and then turned to face Abdul while holding it up for him to see. 'Turkish Abala?' she asked, a frown spreading across her face.

'Yes,' he said, shrugging. 'So? It's your favourite.'

'It costs seven thousand dinar.'

'I got it because you like it.'

'There are a lot of things I like that we can't afford

70

any more.' Tasneen stared into her brother's eyes, her frown intensifying until he could no longer hold her gaze.

'Why do you always do this?' he said as he walked out of the room.

Tasneen put down the coffee jar and looked into the bag at the rest of the contents. As she picked out a couple of other expensive items her frown was replaced by a look of hopelessness.

She left the kitchen, saw that Abdul was not in the living room and walked across to his bedroom. She stood in the doorway, watching as he removed his jacket.

'You're still taking money, aren't you?' she asked accusingly.

Abdul ignored her as he removed his semi-automatic pistol from its holster and placed it on a dresser. Then he sat down on the bed and started to untie his shoelaces.

'My brother is a thief,' she said resignedly in response to his silence.

'I'm *not* a thief,' he snapped, glaring at her.

'You take money that is not yours under false pretences. That is stealing.'

'They're fines.'

'Fines,' she said, hitting a higher note. 'Fines go to the government. When you put the money in your pocket it's theft.'

'They owe us it, anyway.'

'Who does?'

'The government. You know how little we get paid.'

'Is that what you tell yourself? Or is that what your new friend Hassan tells you to get you to do it?'

Abdul held onto his temper as he removed his boots, got up and walked past her. 'What's for supper?' he asked as he sat on the couch and picked up the remote television control.

'I'm not your wife, Abdul. I work too.'

He sighed heavily, struggling to overcome his anger as he repeatedly clicked the remote, unable to get it to respond correctly. 'There is no government anyhow.'

'You're getting more like them every day. You're not in a police force. You're in a gang.'

The television came on too loudly – an Egyptian soap opera – and Tasneen moved briskly across the room to turn it off. 'Abdul? Listen to me. Don't you realise what you are doing?'

'I'm earning us a living, that's what I'm doing,' he said, raising his voice unconvincingly in his effort to dominate her.

Tasneen might have been delicate in stature but the fire in her bright oval eyes showed greater determination than her brother possessed. 'At what price?' she said, placing her hands on her hips. 'Our mother and father would be horrified if they knew.'

'Father left us nothing. The house was practically destroyed and no one will buy it for years.'

Tasneen exhaled heavily, calming herself in an effort to bring down the temperature. 'We earn a good enough living between us. You don't need to steal.'

'This is not a living. You work for an American contractor in the Green Zone. You have to hide yourself each time you go in and come out, every day wondering if a suicide bomber will blow himself up at the checkpoint, always wondering if someone will follow you home and one day kill you for working for the Americans.'

'And what about you?' she snapped. 'It's the same for you, isn't it? You hide your police uniform when you come home for the same reasons. It's how things are, Abdul. It's how we live. But at least I have my self-respect.'

'I'm not a thief! You know that. But you don't know what it's like working with those people. I can't refuse them.'

'Why not?'

Abdul shook his head in frustration at her complete ignorance. 'What do I say to them? That I'm not going to be a part of the squad any more?'

'Yes,' Tasneen said, hitting her high note again.

'I would have to quit the police.'

'And what's wrong with that? It's better than doing what you do.'

'And then how do we live? You don't earn enough money for the both of us.'

'Get another job.'

'Doing what?'

'As a security guard. You can earn maybe four, five hundred dollars a month doing that.'

The first thought that popped into Abdul's head was that he earned more than that with his supplementary income anyway. But he dared not say that to her. 'Then get me a job,' he said.

Tasneen gritted her teeth in irritation as she watched him fold his arms across his chest and stare at the blank television screen. 'We cannot go on like this, Abdul,' she said. 'You know it as well as I do. It can only get worse.'

He didn't move other than to direct his sullen stare down at the floor.

'I hate this bad feeling I have for you,' she said. 'I hate it when we talk like this to each other . . . You don't even seem to want to try to change the way you are living . . . What happened to you, Abdul? You were always a good boy. You and I were always happy together.'

'*You* were always happy,' he snapped. 'But you're a girl. It's easy for you. I'm a man.'

'Are you?' she said softly.

Abdul glared at his sister and for the first time in his adulthood he wanted to hit her.

'I still only see the little boy in you,' she went on. 'I love you, Abdul, my little brother, but I have never seen the man in you yet.'

He jumped to his feet and took a step towards her, his fists clenched, one of them slightly raised as if he was about to strike. But she did not waver, her eyes staring into his.

Tasneen had not seen this coming and she was shocked. She did not flinch or try to avoid his threatened blow, mainly because Abdul's aggression had taken her completely by surprise – not that she would have moved to avoid it, anyway.

But, after all, Abdul could not hit her and was

immediately filled with remorse at the thought of it. He lowered his hand and went back into his room, closing the door behind him.

Although he had not struck her, Tasneen had felt a sting of a kind. She had not been aware of the level of stress that Abdul was experiencing and instead of remaining horrified she was suddenly filled with pity for her brother. She always listened to his daily stories about his work with interest, except when he talked about death and explosions. But she realised that she was listening without really hearing, especially what he was saying between the lines. Abdul had always been highly strung and talkative about his woes, often painting an exaggerated picture – as far as she could tell, anyway. She knew he was different from her: weaker, or more sensitive, to put it kindly, but she never made allowance for that when she heard how he reacted to events. He always laughed at things that didn't amuse her, trivial things like children's cartoons, for instance. But then he became stressed over things that she hardly took seriously. Money was one example. But then, Abdul was more materialistic than she was.

Tasneen was a strong-willed self-sufficient woman. She was modern by Arab standards – far too modern for Abdul's liking, despite his attraction to western trappings such as cars, digital watches and electronic gadgets. He was technically head of the household and was strongly drawn to the family's ancient tribal doctrines, ethics and religion, things that his sister had little time for even though she was in effect its driving force and the guardian of its principles. She liked equality of the sexes and was interested in other cultures, though she had never been outside Iraq. The idea of one day going to London or New York would set her daydreaming. She could gaze for hours at pictures of the Alps and she loved modern movies, especially those filmed in places like Florence or Paris, and not always only because of the story. It was the views of the lives of others she liked, specifically those of Americans and Europeans. The attraction was the freedom that she felt those countries offered.

As a woman Tasneen was stifled in Iraq and since the end of the war, or more specifically since working in the Green Zone among Americans and Europeans, the kind of people whose company she had never experienced before, she had begun to believe that she might have a chance to live her dream. She hated every aspect of the war but the end of the dictatorship, despite its violent circumstances, had given her a hope that she'd never had before. She had no real plans to travel across Iraq's borders in the immediate future, but one day she hoped to. She was relying on fate to turn her dreams into reality and hoped that it would one day free her to fly away and explore all the places and experiences she had so often imagined.

She faced Abdul's door, wanting to speak to him, to apologise for not understanding him. But she decided to let it go for the time being. He was clearly deeply troubled and the best thing she could do, she felt, was what she always did at times like this: to simply be there for him if he needed her. The fact that she had no real solutions for him either sometimes made her feel like a hypocrite anyway. Perhaps one day fate might be good to him too. She knew he would never have deliberately chosen to be a thief and Tasneen could only hope that he would find a way out of his dilemma.

'I'll make us some supper, Abdul,' she said softly.

He did not answer. She raised a hand to touch the door, changed her mind and walked away into the kitchen.

Abdul lay on his bed, staring up at the ceiling. He had heard his sister but had chosen to stay silent. His anger was already receding. She was right, as always. But then, it didn't take a genius to figure out how wrong his position was. It might take one to figure out what he was going to do with his life, though, for he could see no hope or opportunities on the horizon. He felt as if he was wasting his existence on this earth. So many people he knew were making a fortune out of the war and there were so many stories of success. The truth was that he had no idea what 'success' really meant to him. It wasn't money. Not really. Abdul appreciated it but it was not what drove him. His problem was that he didn't know what did. That was Allah's job, to direct him, guide him, show him what to do. Perhaps Allah was unable to do this while Abdul conducted himself as he did, stealing from drivers. It was an impossible dilemma.

Another thing that was starting to bother Abdul was his marital status. He needed to find a partner and get married, and soon. It was important for a young Arab man and an essential religious as well as social step. But there were two important obstacles he needed to overcome. The first was that he didn't know a girl whom he wanted to marry and the second, which he needed to solve before he could deal with the first, was his income. A police officer's pay was far too low to attract the kind of woman he wanted or, more to the point, impress the *parents* of the kind of woman he would like to wed. Good families expected suitors at least to provide a home for their daughters, preferably one they owned and did not share with other members of the suitor's family. He needed a higher income and therefore a better job. And as for sharing the apartment, the only way around that was for Tasneen to get married to a man who had his own house so that she could move out. But that was not going to be easy either since Tasneen was not a normal girl.

Abdul's sister was eligible, beautiful and intelligent, not that any of those factors mattered except the first while the last one was valued least of all. The biggest problem was Tasneen herself. She didn't seem to like any man, not enough to marry him, anyway. The disadvantage of her having no parents was that there was no one pressuring her into marriage other than Abdul who had about as much influence over her on that subject as the Pope. Tasneen was far too western in her outlook and attitude. She was too free a thinker, too liberated and most un-Islamic. Considering the concern that she endlessly expressed for him Abdul found it irritating how Tasneen could not see that his advancement was directly related to her getting married as soon as possible.

It was all an impossible situation and one over which he seemed to have little or no control. Abdul decided that the best thing he could do was concentrate on the main issue of the moment which was his job with the police or, to use Tasneen's admittedly accurate description, with his gang of thieves. Since he could not get a transfer he would simply have to tell them that he could no longer take part in their corrupt activities. But the thought of actually telling them filled Abdul with dread. Everyone in the team had to be in on the game. Even Abdul could see the reasoning behind that. Hassan would not allow it to be any other way. There was only one other thing Abdul could do and that was to quit. Deep down, he knew that was the only way out.

Abdul's phone began to chirp a cheerful Arab tune that got louder the longer it remained unanswered. He dug it out of his pocket and looked at the screen to read the number. It was Hassan.

Abdul did not answer it right away, wondering what the man could be wanting. Perhaps God had made Hassan call so that Abdul could tell him he was quitting. Abdul immediately erased that thought out of fear of Hassan's reaction.

He took a grip of himself. There was nothing to be afraid of in the long run. Hassan couldn't kill him just for quitting the police. It was possible that Hassan might even find the prospect acceptable since he did not like Abdul in any case.

Abdul hit a button on the phone and put it to his ear. '*Salom alycom*, Hassan,' he said.

'Shut up,' Hassan growled. 'We are meeting at the police academy tonight at ten.'

'But I am not working tonight—'

'Shut up, I said. You *are* working tonight. There is an operation and we are a part of it. We will meet at the rear entrance to the academy on Palestine Street. Don't be late.'

It was pointless to argue with the man. He was the sergeant and an order was an order. It was not unusual to be called at home to take part in an operation even when you'd just come off duty. There was a shortage of police officers and the bosses usually called in as many men as they could if the job was anything to do with capturing insurgents. This was only the second time Abdul had been called out for a night operation and although he had been looking forward to an evening in front of the television and a good night's sleep, duty called. At least he would not have to stop cars and ask for bribes.

'I'll be there,' Abdul said and the phone went dead.

He tossed it onto the bed and massaged his hands. Hassan always made him tense.

Abdul got to his feet and exhaled deeply as he rolled his shoulders in an effort to relax and compose himself. His thoughts went back to his sister as he heard a noise from the kitchen. He would go and be nice to her and even help prepare the meal. She did far more than he did in the home, all the cleaning and laundry as well as making most of the meals. Abdul often washed up the dishes afterwards but he did little more than that. That was OK for ordinary Arab girls but

Tasneen was different and she meant more to him than their sisters did to other Arab boys.

Abdul decided not to tell her about his plan to quit the force. He would break the news to her once he had told Hassan. And for the rest of the evening until he left he would be his old cheerful self.

Abdul opened the door, stepped into the living room and was about to cross it towards the kitchen when he stopped and looked up at the Koran on its shelf. He reached for it, took it down and held it to his heart as he begged Allah to watch over him and help him with his plans. Then he kissed the book, put it back on the shelf and, suddenly feeling a lot better about everything, headed for the kitchen, a broad smile on his face.

3

Abdul's Miscalculation

Abdul drove along Palestine Street, a dual carriageway that ran into the southern corner of the infamous Sada City in the north-east quadrant of Baghdad. He glanced over his left shoulder at the rear entrance of the police academy as he passed it, a narrow opening in a high wall that looked like it led into a long alleyway with a heavy steel security gate at the end. It was a dark, chilly night. There were no street lights and, due to the nightly curfew, traffic was light, one of the few benefits of being a policeman and driving at night in Baghdad.

Abdul caught sight of several vehicles parked off the road against the perimeter wall near the entrance, one of which looked like Hassan's sparkling new red Opal.

A couple of hundred metres further on Abdul reached a wide junction beneath a motorway under-pass where he made a tight U-turn into the oncoming lanes and headed back towards the academy entrance.

He pulled off the road and onto the rubble-strewn ground, stopped behind the group of cars he recog-nised as belonging to Arras, Karrar and Ali, killed the engine and climbed out. There were several groups of men huddled together along the perimeter wall, and Abdul saw his squad standing in front of Hassan's car, all of them smoking. Abdul locked his car doors, pulled his leather jacket tight against the chilly air and walked over to join them.

None of the men greeted Abdul as he stepped in among them. He was used to their coldness towards him and bid them hello despite it, determined to remain positive for his planned conversation with Hassan. The only thing Abdul had not decided on was the ideal moment to broach the subject. But as soon as he saw the faces of the others he suspected that something was not quite right with them, as if they had heard some bad news and were unable to look at him squarely. Another oddity was that he could always expect a rude or insulting comment from at least one of them but tonight they appeared to be too distracted even for that. Perhaps they were unhappy about being dragged out to work at a time when they all would have preferred to be at home.

'What's the job, then?' Abdul asked, deliberately acting perky as proof that he did not mind being out at that time.

Ali took a last draw on his cigarette, dropped it between his feet and ground it into the soil with the toe of his boot. As if it was a signal to the others, Arras and Karrar also tossed their cigarette butts away.

'You have a balaclava?' Hassan asked Abdul.

'No,' Abdul replied. Many officers carried some kind of headwear that they could cover their faces with, often wearing them while on the job. Police officers were perceived by many Iraqis as lackeys of the Americans and there were considerable dangers in being recognised. Depending on where a man lived or where a task took him there was a risk of retribution. A high number of officers had been killed while off duty, although no one knew the exact figure because the authorities did not like to publicise it. Many policemen had simply disappeared, never to be heard from again, while the corpses of others had been found in one of the several popular places to dump bodies. There was a large piece of open ground to the east of Sadar City for Shi'a victims, another east of Dora for Sunni. Or there was always the Tigris river. Mothers, wives and children often turned up at police headquarters looking for their loved ones, having seen or heard nothing of them for days. Abdul never bothered to disguise himself, mainly because none of the others in the squad did. He also lived in a relatively safe neighbourhood and considered the precautions he took to be adequate.

Hassan reached into a pocket, removed a balaclava and tossed it to Abdul. It hit his chest and dropped to the ground. Abdul picked it up and shook the dust off it.

'Button your jacket up to the top,' Hassan growled at Abdul. 'Hide your uniform.'

Abdul obeyed. 'What is the operation?' he asked again, hoping for a reply.

'A raid,' Hassan said.

'A raid?' Abdul asked. 'Where?' No one replied but

Abdul had the feeling they knew more about it. 'Who are we raiding?' Abdul persisted, finding the courage to push them a little.

'You ask too many questions,' Hassan growled. 'We'll take two cars,' he said to the others, disconnecting from Abdul. 'Yours and mine,' he said to his brother.

Several cars appeared in the alley heading out of the police academy towards Palestine Street.

'That's the chief,' Hassan said. 'Let's get in the cars.'

The other police squads dispersed to their vehicles and Abdul followed Hassan. He had been on one previous night raid and had been told nothing about it beforehand either, which was understandable. It was no secret that the police had been infiltrated by supporters of the insurgency and in the past warnings had been communicated to evacuate targeted premises before the police squads arrived. Abdul wondered if Hassan actually knew the location himself but that did not explain the strange atmosphere within the group.

'What are you waiting for?' Hassan shouted at him. 'Get in with Ali.'

Abdul climbed into the back of Ali's BMW while Arras occupied the front passenger seat. The cars started up, their headlights flashed on and Hassan followed the last of the other squad vehicles onto the road with Ali moving in behind.

Abdul thought he could sense a level of tension among the members of his team which was unusual, especially if they didn't know where they were going or what they were doing. Abdul thought he was imagining it until both men lit up cigarettes having only just put one out.

'Do you think this will be a short raid or an all-night one?' Abdul asked. He didn't receive an answer and sighed audibly. 'Why do you people always treat me like an idiot?'

'Because you *are* one,' Arras snapped, looking around at him, his eyes cold.

'There are several raids tonight,' Ali eventually said.

Ali was the most intelligent of the bunch. But it was a sly intelligence, like that of a desert fox. He was the least abrasive towards Abdul but for no other reason than it was his nature to be more controlled. Karrar, driving with Hassan, was generally mute most of the time but that was because he was as thick as a tombstone and incapable of independent thought. Abdul judged Arras to be the most lethal of the bunch. He was utterly ruthless, had a short fuse, and without Hassan to control him Abdul suspected that he could be very dangerous if upset.

'Several raids?' Abdul asked, surprised.

Arras glanced at Ali as if wondering why he had revealed so much. But Ali was as confident as always. 'They are taking place concurrently,' Ali said.

'Why did Hassan not say?' Abdul asked.

'There's no secrecy,' Ali said smoothly. 'It's only security. Why do you need to know? Why do any of us, other than Hassan, need to know, for that matter? He is the only one who needs to know where we are going. When you see the place and are doing the job you will know everything.'

'Why don't you just shut up and relax, eh?' Arras said, glancing back briefly at Abdul.

They passed the old sports stadium, crossed the motorway flyover and headed into the Karada district. Traffic was light but as they turned around the Ali Baba roundabout – where there was a statue of Kahramana filling the fabled forty pots – a combined US Army and Iraqi police checkpoint came into view ahead. The other squad cars were passing through it and Hassan looked as if he was about to follow when he suddenly swerved past the turning and took the next roundabout exit.

Ali followed Hassan and Abdul sat forward in his seat, looking at the road ahead and wondering why they had left the other police vehicles.

'We are going to do our part of the job,' Ali said, as if he had noticed Abdul's concern.

Abdul sat back again and looked out of his window, Ali's suggestion that he would know soon enough echoing in his head. The car's heater was on too high for Abdul and he undid the buttons on his leather jacket to let in some air.

Hassan pulled off the main road and slowed as they entered a quiet residential street. There was no street lighting and no moving traffic. Parked cars were drawn up on both sides of the road. Most of the houses were in darkness, indicating a power cut in the neighbourhood which was normal for this time of night. Those that had lights obviously had their own generators or benzene lamps but with the current fuel shortage only those who could afford the black-market prices enjoyed the luxury of power at night.

Hassan turned his vehicle along another narrow street, pulled over and parked against the kerb. Ali tucked in behind him and both cars fell silent as their engines and lights went off.

Abdul was expecting everyone to climb out right away but they sat still in the darkness without even communicating. This seemed like further evidence of a pre-raid plan to which he was not privy.

After a couple of minutes, Hassan climbed out of his car and, leaving Karrar in the passenger seat, walked down the road looking at the houses on both sides as if searching for a particular one.

Hassan walked out of sight into the darkness and was gone for several minutes before Abdul saw his silhouette walking back on the other side of the street. He crossed back to his car, leaned in through the open window to say something to Karrar, then headed for his brother's car as Karrar climbed out.

Ali opened the door and Hassan looked in at the men. 'Everyone out and follow me,' Hassan said.

Ali and Arras obeyed. Abdul followed, but the sudden palpable rise in tension infected him and he began to feel uneasy.

Hassan walked down the pavement a short distance before stepping sideways into a large doorway and out of what little light there was. The others followed him, Abdul bringing up the rear. He stayed just outside the small recess.

'Get in here,' Hassan hissed.

Abdul moved in closer, aware of a distinct rise in Hassan's anxiety as his stare flicked in all directions.

Hassan removed his balaclava from his jacket pocket, put it on his head and pulled it fully down over his face, adjusting it so that his eyes were centred in the oval slits. The others followed his example.

Abdul took his balaclava out of his pocket and paused before putting it on. 'What is my part in this?' he asked in a low voice.

'Just put on your balaclava,' Hassan growled.

'When will you tell me?' Abdul asked.

Hassan gritted his teeth and clenched his fists as if he was about to thump Abdul.

'Do what you are told, you prick,' Arras snarled.

Abdul stepped back from the men in their black balaclavas, their white eyes glaring at him. They looked like a pack of satanic beasts. There was something unholy about whatever they were up to, Abdul was certain of it. The mistake he had made with this evil partnership was getting involved in the first place. Whatever these men were about to do was worse than taking petty bribes from drivers, he was sure of it. 'I don't want to do this,' Abdul suddenly blurted out.

The others looked between Hassan and Abdul, wondering what the boss was going to do about this untimely and wholly inconvenient outburst.

'I don't want to be in this team any more. I wanted to tell you earlier but you never gave me the chance,' Abdul added quickly. 'You don't like me. You treat me like a leper. Why don't you just let me go?' he demanded.

Hassan was staring at him, weighing his response,

barely controlling a gut instinct to pound Abdul into the ground.

Arras had no doubts about what he wanted to do with Abdul but he would have to wait for Hassan to give the word.

'I've made my mind up,' Abdul said. 'I'm going to go back to the car and wait for you there.'

But as Abdul started to turn away Hassan grabbed his arm with one hand and gave him such a brutal swipe around the side of his face with the other that Abdul would have fallen to the ground had Hassan released his grip. Abdul raised his hands to protect himself against another blow which Hassan was about to deliver when Ali caught his hand.

'Hassan,' Ali said in a loud whisper. 'This is not the place for this.'

Hassan glared like a maniac at his brother for a few seconds before the words filtered through his rage. He lowered his hand and faced Abdul, pulling him close and holding him firmly so that their noses were inches apart.

'Listen to me, you little turd,' Hassan said with intense malice. 'You will do as you are ordered. One more word out of you and I'll break your neck. Do you understand me?'

Abdul had seen Hassan this angry once before. On that occasion the recipient of his ire, an errant driver who had made the mistake of telling Hassan to go screw his mother, apparently did not regain consciousness for several days. Abdul nodded.

'Tell me,' Hassan hissed, tightening his grip around Abdul's neck until his windpipe started to hurt.

'I understand,' Abdul croaked.

'Put on your balaclava,' Hassan said again, releasing Abdul but staying threateningly close.

Abdul took a few seconds to regain his breath before pulling his balaclava onto his head and over his face.

Hassan pulled his weapon out of its holster and moved out of the doorway. 'You,' he said, looking back at Abdul. 'With me.'

Abdul moved alongside Hassan who grabbed his arm and pushed him ahead. 'Take the lead,' Hassan said.

Abdul walked slowly up the pavement for a short distance before looking back to see the others following in a line. Fear and anxiety began to course through his body as he wondered what Hassan was going to do with him – and what was going to happen on this raid that he was now leading.

Abdul walked on a little further and when he slowed to look behind him again Hassan urged him on with a stiff shove.

Halfway down the street Hassan grabbed the back of Abdul's jacket to halt him. When Abdul turned to see why, Hassan was looking at a car parked against the pavement beside him. It was an old dark-blue BMW and Hassan looked back at his brother who nodded in confirmation.

Hassan pushed Abdul forward again. 'Keep going,' he whispered.

They reached a house where a light glowed dimly on the second floor. Hassan moved nimbly past Abdul and went to the front door. He paused to look around before moving closer and pressing his ear against it.

A moment later he beckoned Abdul to join him. Abdul stepped beside Hassan who suddenly grabbed him roughly. 'Keep your ear to the door and listen,' Hassan whispered. 'You hear a sound, you let me know.' Hassan did not wait for a response from Abdul and moved to join his men who had gathered in a tight group in the shadows of the building.

Abdul watched the devilish quartet whispering together and kept his ear to the door as he'd been ordered. He thought he heard a sound from inside and as he focused his attention on it he was suddenly yanked unceremoniously back. Arras moved to take his place, opened his jacket and removed a hefty crowbar as he pressed his ear to the door.

The others stood close by, Abdul a head shorter than any of them and hemmed in tightly, unable to escape even if he had dared to try.

Arras stepped back from the door and worked the crowbar into the frame. As he slowly levered it to one side the wood began to split but the lock held. He wiggled the bar further in and then levered it back once again. There was a loud crack and the door popped open.

Hassan did not waste a second and pushed past Arras and into the house with anxious haste. Ali and Arras followed quickly while Abdul was shoved inside by Karrar who brought up the rear.

Karrar closed the door behind him and the five men stood like black sentinels in the hallway as if waiting for a signal to move. Halfway along the dark narrow hallway a flight of stairs led to the floor above and Hassan moved to the foot, his pistol in his hand. Without looking back he signalled for the others to move and they obeyed stealthily.

Arras and Ali passed Hassan and continued along the hall to the first door, which was partly open. The room was dark inside. The two men went inside and a few seconds later reappeared and moved further down the dark passageway to the next door.

A few seconds later they came out and went further back into the house, disappearing into the darkness.

Abdul hardly moved, watching Hassan who kept his pistol aimed up the stairs. Karrar breathed deeply behind him. Judging by Hassan's air of intensity and his cautious stance, the man was expecting resistance. Abdul hoped it would end soon but then he realised that he would still be left to deal with Hassan and the matter of his resignation. Abdul was no longer confident that the issue was going to be resolved quite as easily as he had hoped.

Ali and Arras returned from the dark hallway and Ali shook his head at his brother.

Hassan directed his full attention to the top of the stairs. As he placed his foot on the first step it creaked. He paused before applying his full weight but the step creaked again as he raised his other foot and placed it on the next one. That creaked too but the third did not and Hassan continued slowly towards the top, the business end of his pistol leading the way.

The others mounted the stairs behind him. Ali and Arras avoided the first two steps. Karrar nudged Abdul forward: he placed his foot on the first step that once again creaked loudly. Arras stopped to look back with a scowl and Karrar jabbed Abdul viciously in his side.

Abdul winced at the blow and placed his other foot higher up. Arras maintained his warning glare for a moment longer before looking back towards the top of the stairs and taking another step up.

Hassan reached the final step where a closed door blocked access to the floor. The others closed in behind him.

Hassan looked back at his pack to ensure that they were ready. Every white eye, encircled by its black woollen slit, was wide and alert – except Abdul's. His eyes flickered with frightened uncertainty. He was jammed tightly between Arras and Karrar, both of them holding their pistols at the ready.

Hassan faced the door which was painted dull brown, leaned forward and pressed his ear to it. His free hand reached for the doorknob and slowly turned it. He gave it a slight push but the door did not move. Hassan exhaled through his nose – the sound was quite loud in the still air – and stepped back until his arm holding the doorknob was at full stretch. The others leaned back to give him room. With a sudden sharp intake of breath, Hassan shoved his full weight forward. His shoulder struck the wooden door, the bolt inside sprang free and it flew open.

Hassan moved forward with his own momentum and his men followed. Abdul was caught up in the press of bodies as Karrar shoved him hard and they spilled into a room that was bathed in a dull golden glow from a benzene lamp.

The room was not very big and was sparsely furnished with a couch and a dining table. A kitchenette took up one corner. Abdul saw two people lying on mattresses, one a man in his fifties, his eyes wide in shock and holding a book next to the lamp. Ali and Arras were upon the two figures like hyenas, Ali grabbing the man by his neck and jamming a gun into his face. The other figure, a woman as old as the man, awoke and sat up as her eyes tried to focus, her mouth opening in fear. Arras threw his weight onto her while shoving his hand over her face, brutally pushing her head back onto the mattress.

Meanwhile, Hassan continued through the room to its only other door. He raised his leg and kicked open this latest obstruction. Karrar shoved Abdul across the room to the doorway where he left him. In the second room a man and woman were in bed under a sheet. Karrar joined Hassan as they sat up. Hassan pulled back the sheet to reveal that they were both naked and, grabbing the woman by her hair, dragged her off the bed as she screamed. Karrar took hold of the man by his throat and shoved his pistol in his face.

Abdul watched in confused horror. These pathetic-looking people were not the hardened desperados he had been expecting.

'Bring him,' Hassan shouted. Karrar obeyed, brusquely turning the frightened man over, twisting his arm halfway up his back and pulling him off the bed. The man yelped at the pain while complying as best he could with Karrar's efforts to get him to his feet, around the bed and to the door.

The slender woman was in her early thirties and Hassan kept a firm hold of her thick long dark hair as he pulled her past Abdul and into the main room. The naked man followed, grimacing while balancing on tiptoe as he struggled to reduce the pressure on his arm. The man's skin was white and his hair was light, neither feature uncommon in the western reaches of Iraq, but his overall look was distinctly Anglo-Saxon.

The naked woman yelped at every tug on her hair while the Anglo-looking man groaned in response to Karrar's brutal grip. Abdul was conscious of the balaclava over his face and felt distinctly weird as he looked through the narrow eyelets at the unfolding scene.

The older couple were forced to their feet by Ali and Arras who shoved them against the wall. Hassan pushed the naked woman beside them and released her. She held her hands over her breasts and genital area as she cried out. 'Please, please don't hurt us,' she kept begging.

'Shut up!' Hassan shouted as he aimed his gun at her face, his eyes intense. She immediately stopped speaking, although she could not control her whimpering. Karrar kept hold of the male westerner as Ali and Arras stepped back, their pistols levelled at the terrified older couple.

Then Hassan seemed to calm down a little as everyone in the room came under his control. He turned his attention to the naked man. Karrar pulled the man's head back by his hair so that he was forced to face the boss.

'What's your name?' Hassan demanded. The man did

not answer as he looked fearfully at Hassan and then at the naked woman. 'Abdul,' Hassan growled. 'Ask him his name.'

Abdul was almost as frightened as the man and did not understand what Hassan had asked him. 'W-what?' he stammered.

'I said ask him his name,' Hassan repeated.

Abdul looked at the frightened man who was only slightly bigger than himself. 'What is your name?' he said.

'In English, you idiot!' Hassan shouted. 'He is not Arab.'

Abdul made an extreme effort to compose himself as his mouth suddenly went dry. 'What your name?' he asked in broken English.

The naked man glanced at Abdul with pleading eyes when he recognised his language, perhaps sensing in the tone of his voice that this Arab might have some sympathy in his heart. 'J-Jeffrey Lamont,' the man stammered, his face a picture of utter fear. 'You will be paid a lot of money if you—'

'Who does he work for?' Hassan snapped.

'What you company work for?' Abdul asked in heavily accented English as he struggled to get his lips and tongue around the language that he had learned in school. He had only spoken it very occasionally with his sister in the last few years.

'Detron Communications,' the man said.

'A communications company,' Abdul relayed to Hassan.

'What kind of communications?' Hassan asked.

'I don't know,' Abdul said.

'Ask him, you idiot!' Hassan shouted, his temper going up and down with his blood pressure.

Abdul took a moment to form the words but he was not quick enough for Hassan. 'You said you could speak English,' Hassan said accusingly.

'It's been a while,' Abdul said nervously.

'Ask him!' Hassan shouted again.

Abdul swallowed hard and made an effort to concentrate. 'What you communications?' he asked.

'I . . . I don't know what you mean,' the man said, desperately wanting to comply but too confused.

'What . . . kind . . . of communication you work for? What communications?' Abdul asked.

'Phones. We put up mobile phone masts. We're bringing communications to your country,' Lamont said, pleading. 'Please don't hurt us.'

Abdul felt desperately sorry for the man but tried not to let it show as he spoke to Hassan. 'He builds mobile phone masts.'

The man's stare dropped to Abdul's jacket that had opened and he caught a glimpse of his chest badge on his blue shirt. 'You're police,' the man said.

Hassan looked at Abdul's open jacket, then at the naked woman and the old couple who were staring at the badge.

'I have a DoD pass,' the man said. 'In my pocket,' he added, suddenly hopeful that this could be resolved. 'In my trousers. In the room,' he went on.

Hassan looked at the man. He knew what a DoD pass was. It was an identification badge that all foreign reconstruction contractors carried. Issued by the US Army, it allowed them into the Green Zone as well as into coalition camps anywhere in the country. As a police officer, often running checkpoints, Hassan had seen hundreds of them. 'Where's his DoD?' he asked Abdul.

'In his trouser pocket in the bedroom,' Abdul answered.

Hassan went into the bedroom.

'And my passport,' Lamont said. 'I'm an American citizen,' he added, clarifying his legitimacy.

Hassan returned with the man's DoD, passport and wallet. He checked the documents and then the wallet: it contained a few hundred dollars which he pocketed. Then he turned his attention to the woman.

She had calmed down a little on realising that the intruders were police but she was still frightened.

'Are you a whore?' Hassan asked her coldly.

'No. I am not a whore,' the woman said in a defiant tone.

'Are you Muslim?' Hassan asked her.

'Yes,' she replied.

'Then why are you sleeping with this infidel?' Hassan asked as he looked down at her naked body, his gaze resting for a moment on her hand cupped protectively over her vagina.

'Because I love him,' she declared.

Hassan removed his balaclava and looked at her, a grimace of disgust on his face. He raised his gun, aimed it at her eyes, and squeezed the trigger. The pistol fired. Blood shot from the back of the woman's head and splashed the wall behind her as she dropped to the floor, the life instantly gone from her.

'NO!' the naked man yelled, struggling in Karrar's grip. The other woman screamed. Hassan gave Ali and Arras a cold look and the men fired their guns into the heads of the older couple who dropped instantly to the floor, their corpses sprawling next to each other.

Arras took a step forward and fired a bullet into each of their heads and another into the naked woman's for good measure.

Lamont howled despondently, his face contorted with grief, his mouth wide open as his eyes filled with tears.

'Take him,' Hassan said as he stepped over the bodies towards the door.

Karrar pulled the westerner towards the door but the man wrenched himself out of his grasp and threw himself at the dead naked woman. 'Fatima!' he shouted, the pain in his voice startling in its intensity.

Arras moved quickly to help Karrar control Lamont who fought strongly to resist them. Arras had a simple solution to the problem and slammed the butt of his pistol down onto the top of the man's head, following it up with a savage punch to his kidney. The man went limp but remained conscious and Karrar lifted him to his feet and steered him to the door.

Hassan let Ali lead the way out of the room, followed by Karrar and the American. He was about to follow when he realised that Abdul had not moved and was staring down at the bodies.

'Abdul!' Hassan called out. 'Move!'

But Abdul could not hear him through the dreadful mist of revulsion that filled his mind.

'Get him,' Hassan growled. Arras responded, grabbing Abdul by his lapel and pulling him to the door. Abdul did not resist, as if he had lost control over all his motor functions other than his breathing and the beating of his heart. He stumbled over the legs of the dead couple and the near-fall brought him back to life: as he reached the doorway he grabbed the door frame to stop himself.

Abdul looked back at the corpses of the old couple and the naked woman. Then he peered at Hassan who was staring at him.

'You want to join them?' Hassan asked.

The words were as sincere as any that Abdul had heard in his life. He shook his head.

'Get going, then,' Hassan said, his voice soft.

Arras pushed Abdul through the doorway and he clambered down the stairs, hanging on to the banister to stop himself from rolling down into the darkness.

Arras followed closely and as Abdul reached the bottom he was shoved along the corridor and out through the front door. Arras did not let up – he took hold of Abdul's lapel again and pulled him along the pavement, following Karrar and Ali as they manhandled the naked Lamont towards the cars. Hassan was in the rear, his gun held by his side, ready in case they should be challenged.

Karrar and Ali speeded up as they reached Hassan's red Opal and bundled the American into the back.

Arras shoved Abdul into the back of Ali's car where he joined him. Ali climbed in behind the wheel.

Both cars came to life and seconds later were turning out of the side street and onto the main road.

Arras and Ali removed their balaclavas and Arras pulled off Abdul's, giving him a hard shove in the process. 'What's your problem?' Arras shouted. 'Why are you so pathetic?'

'Leave him,' Ali said, still on full alert, his stare darting everywhere.

But Arras's blood was up and he could not back down easily. 'Why is he in this team?' he demanded.

'Because he is, that's all,' Ali said.

'But why? Why do we keep him? Why don't we get rid of him?'

'Because we can't,' Ali stated.

'I mean as in get *rid* of him,' Arras said, putting his gun at Abdul's head, itching to pull the trigger.

Ali grinned as he looked in the rear-view mirror at the pair, Arras with murder in his eyes and Abdul with total fear in his. 'We'd have to make a report. We don't want to draw attention to ourselves. Don't you think Hassan would have thrown him into the river ages ago if he'd wanted to? He's been given to us by God and we must look after him.'

'But he's useless,' Arras said, exasperated. 'He's a liability.'

'He won't be. Isn't that right, Abdul? You're a good little boy who does what he's told.'

Abdul had hardly heard a word. His head was filled with the images of those people being shot, replaying the scene over and over.

'He's a hypocrite,' Arras spat. 'He takes money but he disapproves of how we get it. What kind of a person is that?'

'Be fair, Arras. He gives us legitimacy,' Ali said.

'Legitimacy!' Arras exclaimed.

'Of course. Anyone who looks at our squad sees that pathetic individual and thinks, they may be rough-looking guys but they can't be all that bad.' Ali chuckled, amused by his own wit.

Arras took his gun away from Abdul's head and looked out of the opposite window, unconvinced. Then a thought struck him and he looked back at Abdul. 'Give me your gun,' he growled.

Abdul didn't respond and Arras hit him in the chest. 'Give me your *gun*!'

Abdul looked startled as Arras pulled his jacket aside, found the pistol in its holster and snatched it out. 'I don't trust him,' Arras said. He moved his face closer to Abdul's and spoke softly. 'You ever tell a soul about this, about anything, one word to anyone, I don't care who, and I'll kill you – and that sister of yours. You understand me?'

Abdul did not respond outwardly but he felt a rush of fear flooding through his system. He believed the threat wholeheartedly.

Arras dug his elbow viciously into Abdul's ribs, either to get an answer or out of sheer malice. Abdul pulled his jacket closed and moved as far away from Arras as he could, cowering against his door.

'Pathetic little animal,' Arras said, turning away as if he had done with him.

The cars headed south, using backstreets to avoid any checkpoints, and reached the southernmost Tigris river bridge in the city. After crossing it they continued towards Baghdad's largest power station, its slender smoking chimney stacks towering into the night sky. The cars turned off onto a minor road well before they reached the power station and slowed to a crawl as the road surface deteriorated drastically, with numerous water-filled potholes close to each other.

Abdul had been so preoccupied with the night's events that he had not been paying attention to where they were going. Only when the car went over a large bump, jolting him out of his trance, did he realise they had not headed back towards the academy. Then he realised how unlikely it would be if they did: they were carrying a westerner whom they had kidnapped, clearly without the blessing of the authorities. Abdul wondered why on earth they had kidnapped the man anyway. It had obviously been the aim of the operation. He could not imagine why they had killed everyone else in the room – until it suddenly struck him that it was because his police uniform had been exposed. If that was true then *he* was responsible for their deaths. Abdul suddenly felt sick at the thought. He could hear the woman declaring her love for the westerner and then he saw Hassan shoot her in the eye. The horrific images made Abdul feel more nauseous. Hassan and the others were even lower forms of humanity than he had originally thought. And they called themselves Muslims. Hassan had even accused that woman of not being true to Islam and then had executed her as if it was his right to do so. The cold way in which the team had murdered those people was like nothing Abdul could ever have imagined. He was sharing a car with genuine servants of hell – and he was one of them.

Abdul looked out of his side window at the power station. Its proximity meant they were in Dora, a notoriously bad part of the city. The Americans did not venture into it unless they were looking for a fight and the police were just as unwelcome with the locals. The area was home to insurgents and criminals but Hassan was not here on police business.

Abdul watched the back of Hassan's car bathed in the beams of Ali's headlights as it lurched from one side of the road to the other, weaving between the potholes in an effort to avoid the worst of them.

It seemed an age before they finally came to a stop. Abdul looked out the other side of the car to see that they were outside a run-down two-storey house, the glow of benzene lights inside seeping through gaps in tatty curtains.

Ali followed Hassan's lead and turned off his engine and lights. The area around them plunged into blackness, except for the glow from the house.

Everyone sat in silence. As Abdul's eyes gradually grew accustomed to the dark he thought he could make out Hassan's silhouette, his phone to his ear, inside the car.

A few minutes later the door of the house opened, allowing a shaft of orange light to illuminate the cars. Several men stepped outside. They wore *dishdashes*, shirts that reached to the ground, and a variety of *shamag* headdresses. They sported untrimmed beards, several of them long. These men looked very serious. And dangerous.

Hassan got out of his car.

Ali opened his door. 'Stay here,' he said to Arras as he climbed out. He closed the car door and joined his brother who was already greeting the men. Hassan's demeanour towards them was visibly respectful.

Abdul watched the meeting with interest until a movement at the side of the house caught his attention. He looked into the shadows to see several tough-looking men carrying AK47 assault rifles. One of them stepped into the light to take a closer look at the cars and stared at Ali's car as if he was looking directly at Abdul. Then he crossed the muddy track to Hassan's car and looked in through the windows. Moving across to Ali's car, he bent down to peer inside.

Abdul looked at the man's face which bore as demonic a look as he had ever seen on a human being: rugged, gaunt features and unsmiling eyes with pure murder in them. He stared at Abdul like a wild beast contemplating its helpless prey, his black pupils large and empty. He then stood upright to display a full bandolier across his chest and a belt with a Russian pistol tucked into it. Another belt of full AK magazines and a long knife in a sheath completed his personal arsenal. He walked around the rear of the car before crossing the track back to the house.

The group of men with Hassan went to his car and Hassan opened the rear door. The naked American, now wearing a balaclava but backwards so that he could not see, was unceremoniously pulled out. The group continued their discussion while Hassan handed over the man's documentation and the American was then taken across to the house and inside. The door closed and the street went dark once again.

Hassan and Ali waited alone in the street, talking quietly, all the time being watched by the demonic-looking fighter standing at the corner of the house. He looked like a leashed attack beast waiting for its master to snap his fingers before it struck.

Abdul could tell from the brothers' body language that they were uneasy about something. The pigs had kidnapped a westerner for a bunch of insurgents, that much was obvious. And three innocent people had been killed because they'd happened to be in the way. It was diabolical.

The door to the house opened once again and two Arabs stepped out and walked over to the brothers. A small bundle was handed to Hassan who thanked the men profusely while bowing with great servility. The men withdrew from Hassan, their contempt for him clearly apparent, and went back inside the house, closing the door behind them.

Hassan and Ali went back to their cars and climbed in.

Ali looked nervous though he tried to conceal it.

'Everything go OK?' Arras asked anxiously.

Ali reached for his cigarettes on the dash, took one and lit it with a lighter. His hands were shaking slightly. 'For a moment there I thought the pigs were going to kill us . . . Hassan asked about the money and one of them said we should be doing this for Islam, not for cash. It's the first time I have seen my brother lost for words,' Ali said as he took a deep drag and then exhaled noisily. The air was cold but the beads of sweat on Ali's forehead joined to trickle down his face.

'So it went all right?' Arras asked, impatient to know.

Ali nodded. 'Yes,' he confirmed.

Hassan's headlights came on. Ali started his car and switched on his own beams. They pulled away, tyres crunching on the loose soil, and headed down the road. Arras turned to look back through the rear window and saw the evil-featured gunman step into the dim glow coming from the house's windows to watch the cars move away.

When the house was out of sight Arras became visibly relieved. 'What did Hassan say?' he asked.

Ali was concentrating on his rear-view mirror. 'What?' he asked.

'What did Hassan say when they told him he should be doing this for Islam?' Arras asked.

'Hassan asked if they did not reward their followers too. That's when I thought they were going to kill us. They didn't answer and walked back into the house. But then they came back with the money . . . I thought we were for it, I tell you,' Ali added, a nervous smirk appearing on his face as he began to loosen up.

'How much did they pay?' Arras asked.

'We didn't stop to count it,' Ali said. 'We didn't want to push our luck . . . But now they know that if they want to do business with us again they have to pay.

If word got out that they had killed us no other police would do business with them.'

'How much do you think they paid us?' Arras pressed.

'Be patient. You'll find out soon enough,' Ali said.

Abdul was feeling sick to his stomach as he listened to them. All they could talk about was the money and not once did they mention the poor fool whose life they had sold as if he was a piece of meat. Abdul could not believe that he was with such people. It was utter madness. He couldn't even use the excuse that he was an innocent bystander. He had been the group's official translator, and it was his police uniform that had caused the deaths of the others.

Abdul fought to drive the voices from his head. They were threatening to send him mad. Tasneen's face suddenly appeared in his mind's eye and he wondered what she would have done. He wondered what she would say if she knew and in his imagination the horror in her face was immediate. He did not need Arras's threat to stop him from telling her.

The vehicle swerved suddenly and Abdul looked up to see that they were on Palestine Street and approaching their other cars. His nervousness increased: he knew that some kind of closure to the evening was inevitable and would no doubt include more threats. All he wanted to do was to go home without talking to anyone. Tasneen would be asleep, thankfully, and he would remain in bed in the morning until she went to work. That way he could avoid her for the rest of the day. He would need the time to compose himself so that he would be as calm as possible by the time she returned. But his sister would still suspect something was wrong even then. He couldn't hide such an emotional trauma from her. The trick would be to replace the truth with a lie. But any untruth he told would have to be about something serious, otherwise she would not believe him and would keep on digging. Quitting the squad would be a positive element to throw in the mix and would help to throw her off the scent. He could say that Hassan had threatened to kill him, which was why he was frightened. It was the truth, anyway. He could not remain with the team now. Not after tonight. He hoped never to see any of them ever again. But if they did threaten him he might have to run away and and take Tasneen with him. They would have to leave the apartment, perhaps even Baghdad. If that happened Tasneen would want to confront the chief of police. Abdul's head began to spin with the pressure.

The car came to a stop and Ali and Arras climbed out.

Abdul remained where he was as Hassan and Karrar walked over to the others. They gathered in a tight group to have a discussion. Hassan took a bundle from his pocket, the one the terrorists had given him, opened it up and handed portions of it to the others. He looked over towards Ali's car and the others followed his gaze.

Abdul went numb and stared back at them, feeling pathetic.

Hassan said something to Arras who left the group,

came around to Abdul's door and opened it. 'Get out,' Arras said.

Abdul wanted to stay in the safety of the car but that was ridiculous. Arras stood back as Abdul climbed out and then he pushed him towards the group.

Abdul stopped a few feet away. Hassan looked at him with displeasure.

'Here,' Hassan said, holding out a bundle of US dollars. 'Two thousand is your cut . . . I should give you nothing, because of the way you acted. But, whether I like it or not, you are part of the squad . . . Take it,' Hassan said, thrusting it at him.

Abdul shook his head.

'Take it,' Hassan growled.

'I don't want it,' Abdul said quietly.

'What?' Hassan asked.

'I don't want it,' Abdul repeated, louder this time.

The others looked from Hassan to Abdul, aware of the serious implications of such a refusal. They were waiting for Hassan's response.

'I don't want to be with this squad any more,' Abdul continued. 'I quit.'

Another nail had just slammed into Abdul's coffin. But still he could not see the real significance of it, even though it was written on the faces of everyone who was looking at him.

Arras leaned close to Hassan and whispered something in his ear that Hassan appeared neither to agree with nor disapprove of. But as Arras looked back at Abdul the young Arab saw something in the man's eyes that he recognised. He saw a similar look in the eyes of the others and suddenly felt like a wounded animal facing a pack of salivating hyenas. He wanted to run. But trying to escape would not help. He wouldn't get far – Arras and Karrar would run him down in seconds. And even if he did manage to escape it would only be temporary. They would come after him and would probably go straight to his apartment.

The group was suddenly bathed in the headlights of several cars as they turned off the main road into the entrance to the academy. The lead car stopped and the rear passenger window opened. It was their police captain.

'Where have you lot been?' the captain asked, none too politely. He did not like Hassan or his squad and knew exactly the kind of people they were. But like everyone else he had to accept that scum like Hassan were a part of the system until things improved and they could be replaced. 'You were not in your position tonight. What happened to you?'

Hassan and the others had hidden their money as soon as the other cars had turned off the road. 'We got split up from the others and ended up in the wrong location, chief,' Hassan said, smiling. 'Maybe it was my fault or maybe not. We came back here, hoping someone would come and tell us where to go but no one turned up. How did it go?' Hassan asked with feigned interest.

The captain looked at Hassan and his men with contempt.

Abdul wanted to say something, anything that might extricate him from the mess he was in. But the end result would be the same, he realised. He and Tasneen would remain in danger. Perhaps the captain's timely appearance and Abdul's silence might have a calming effect on Hassan.

'Get to your homes,' the captain said.

'We're on our way, captain,' Hassan said. 'Good night to you.'

As the captain's car lurched forward between the heavy blast walls and drove away Abdul felt as if a safety net had been removed. The other cars followed and seconds later the group was once more on its own in near-darkness, with all eyes again on Abdul.

Arras whispered again to Hassan and after some thought this time the squad leader nodded in agreement. 'Go home,' Hassan finally said, breaking the silence.

Abdul did not move. Fear and suspicion kept him fixed to the spot.

'Karrar. Put him in his car,' Hassan said.

Karrar took Abdul by the arm and pulled him towards his car.

Abdul glanced over his shoulder to see Arras following them. His fear escalated but he had to believe that they were really letting him go.

'Your keys,' Karrar said as they stopped outside Abdul's car.

Abdul nervously reached into his trouser pocket and pulled out his keys.

'Open the door,' Karrar said.

Abdul fumbled the car-door key into the lock with a shaking hand. When the key finally slipped in and he turned it to release the central locking Karrar grabbed Abdul around the neck in a vice-like choke hold that almost crushed his windpipe. Arras joined them in a second to open the rear door and help restrain Abdul. Abdul tried to cry out but was barely able to breathe. Karrar moved backwards onto the rear seat, dragging Abdul in with him while Abdul fought to prise the man's arm from around his throat. Karrar manoeuvred himself out from beneath Abdul until he was on top and applied his full weight, his arm releasing its hold around Abdul's neck but his hand clamping down on to his face.

The other door opened and Arras leaned in to lend his weight until Abdul was pinned down as solidly as if he'd been set in concrete.

Hassan's head loomed over Abdul as the squad sergeant glared down at him. 'Arras wants to kill you but Ali is right. The captain has seen you tonight and if you disappeared it would look bad for us. Besides, I don't think we need to go that far, do you?'

Abdul could only stare up at Hassan's evil eyes while he did his best to draw a breath.

'So you want to get out of the police?' Hassan continued. 'I agree. If you can't be in our squad you should leave the police completely. We can't have you joining another squad now, can we? You might become chief of police one day and then where would that leave us?' He smiled. 'Of course, there's only one way to ensure that you really do leave,' Hassan said. He looked at Arras and nodded.

Arras grabbed Abdul's right arm, straightened it so

that it was sticking out of the car and knelt on it with his full weight.

'The police don't allow invalids on the force. Did you know that?' Hassan asked.

Arras took a length of cloth from his pocket and wound it tightly around Abdul's wrist. With each turn it got tighter and tighter until the pain became excruciating. Abdul's scream was muffled by Karrar's fingers clamped across his mouth.

Arras tied off the line and Abdul could feel his hand swelling as the blood built up in his arm. Arras produced a large hunting knife from a sheath in his jacket. Abdul struggled with intense desperation, making a Herculean effort to throw his captors off, but he might as well have tried to lift the car itself. Arras lowered the blade to his wrist.

Abdul went rigid as he felt a burning sensation which his senses could not fully explain although logic told him what was happening. The burning intensified as Arras sawed at Abdul's wrist with some effort, cutting through the sinews and arteries, working the blade into the joint to sever the tendons. There was not a great deal of blood due to the tourniquet and as Arras cut through the last strip of flesh Abdul fainted and went limp.

Arras held up Abdul's severed hand for the others to see, grinning as he pushed himself out of the car. 'The dogs can have that,' he said as he tossed the blood-dripping thing away, wiped the blade on Abdul's jacket and replaced the knife in its sheath.

Hassan looked down on Abdul who remained

unconscious as Karrar removed his weight from him and climbed out of the car.

'Drive him to his apartment,' Hassan said to Karrar. 'You follow and take Karrar home,' he ordered Arras. 'Leave Abdul in the car when you get there.'

Karrar climbed off the unconscious body, pushed Abdul's legs inside and closed the doors. He took the car keys, climbed into the driver's seat, started the engine, manoeuvred the car onto the road and waited until Arras was behind him in his own car before driving off down the road.

'I'm wondering if we should have just killed him, after all,' Ali said.

'He'll keep his mouth shut,' Hassan replied. 'He's not stupid . . . I need a drink,' he grunted as he headed for his car.

As Abdul opened his eyes a bright light pierced them. He squeezed them shut and rolled onto his side. He took a moment before he reopened his eyes to discover the morning sun shining in through the front window of his car. A fierce pain shot up his arm and he looked for the source of the stinging sensation. As he focused on the bloody stump the memories of the night before came flooding back – it was like a dam bursting inside his head. In his delirious half-asleep state he thought it had all been an awful nightmare. But it was now horribly clear that it had not been.

Abdul struggled to sit up and raised his stump in front of his face. As he focused on the bloody end, seeing the torn flesh, ripped tendons and scabby holes where the arteries had dried and shrunk, he burst into tears.

Abdul sat there for some time, crying deeply at first and then whimpering like a child, except when a spasm of intense pain burned up through his arm. Then he would let out a loud moan as he rocked forward and backwards.

He felt incredibly thirsty and it was the desperate need for water that eventually forced him to slide over to the car door, carefully protecting his highly sensitive stump in case it should brush against anything. He looked around outside, recognising the road he lived in. The urge to get upstairs to Tasneen was overwhelming. The tourniquet had saved him from bleeding to death but he had to get to a doctor as soon as he could. The sight of the wound made him grimace, the ugly finality of it, and soon he could not bear to look at it any more. Suddenly he began to retch uncontrollably but all he brought up was bile that hung from his mouth in sticky strings. Abdul began to cry again as self-pity welled up in him and he held the stump close to him.

He had to get out of there and do something about it. Gritting his teeth, he made a supreme effort to bring himself under control. The task was simple enough. All he had to do was get out of the car and walk upstairs.

He reached for the door latch and pulled it open, his hand going straight back to the stump to protect it. He barged open the door, shuffled to the edge of the seat and let his feet find the road. He took a moment to gather himself before leaning forward and as he stood up his knees almost gave way. He had to release his stump to grab hold of the door and steady himself.

Abdul straightened up and took a quick look around, worried that someone might see him. The street was empty and he shut the door, leaned back against the car to take another breather, then set off on the last stage of his painful journey home.

He stumbled as he mounted the pavement but kept on his feet and headed towards the entrance of his apartment building, leaning forward like a hunchback unable to stand fully upright. A sudden dizziness came over him and he staggered forward, lurching uncontrollably from side to side as he focused on the entrance. His knees gave way and he instinctively put his hands out to stop himself. The end of the stump slammed into the ground and the pain was so intense that he almost lost consciousness.

Abdul gave a long, deep moan as he rolled onto his back, his entire body shaking. But he fought to regain control and continue with his mission, pushing himself up with his good hand until he could move forward into the sanctuary of the apartment-block entranceway.

Abdul leaned against a wall to support himself while he fought to control the pain. This was almost too much. All he wanted to do was drop to the floor and curl up into a tight ball.

Abdul forced himself away from the wall towards the stairs and began the long march upwards. He got himself into a rhythm, bent over like an old man, raising one leg after the other and moving as if he was not so much climbing as falling up the steps.

He turned the last corner to his landing, clasping his stump, shoulder against the wall, his mouth drooling like a child's. When he reached his front door he leaned heavily against it. It was the final obstacle and he reached with his stump for his right-hand pocket where he always put his keys, momentarily forgetting that he had no hand to retrieve them. He gritted his teeth against the pain as he moved his good hand around to the pocket. But there was nothing inside it. Where were his keys? he asked himself. Then, in a surprisingly lucid moment, he wondered if they were still in the car. If so, who had driven him home?

Nothing could make him go back down and look for them, not even the threat of death, and he slid down the door and slumped on the floor. The need to cry welled up in him once again but this time he fought to control it. He banged his head lightly on the door and then repeated the action again and again, not so hard that it hurt but enough to distract him from the agony of his throbbing stump.

It was early but Tasneen was in the kitchen, making some tea. She had been unable to sleep properly, worrying about Abdul being out so late as she usually did the rare times when he worked nights. She had checked his room several times in case he had sneaked in during one of her fitful sleeping spells. When the sun had come up and he was not home she got dressed to wait for him.

When Tanseen first heard the thumping against the door she was afraid, unable to think what it might be.

As she got to the door the thumping stopped. But it started again as she reached for the lock.

'Hello?' she called out. 'Who's there?'

Another sound came from beyond the door. It sounded like a moan. Then she thought she heard her name and knew immediately that it was her brother outside the apartment.

Tasneen unbolted the door as quickly as she could. When she opened it she froze in horror for a second at the sight of Abdul looking up at her, his face white, his eyes red and with a horrendously painful expression in them. Only then did she realise that he was gripping his truncated wrist. She stifled a scream and dropped to her knees to take hold of him, unsure what to do. She wrapped her hands around his head and Abdul buried his head between her breasts. He burst into tears, sobbing uncontrollably.

'Help me,' he whimpered.

'I'm here,' Tasneen said. Then the tears streamed down her cheeks.

4

Stanza's Dilemma

Jake Stanza walked down the steps of the Royal Jordanian F28 passenger jet and onto the tarmac of Baghdad International Airport. He slung his laptop bag's strap over his shoulder and, along with sixty other passengers, headed towards the modern terminal building. The air was not as hot and sticky as he had expected. He had read that temperatures in Iraq could be blistering, especially in August, but by then he hoped to be long gone. The reputation of the place was bad enough but the excessive heat would only add to the discomfort.

He studied the enormous terminal building that stretched for several hundred yards in front of him, expecting to see evidence of the war that had ended less than a year before. But it appeared to be unscathed. He had taken little notice of news reports about Iraq from day one. It wasn't a war or a place that interested him greatly and besides, he'd never expected ever to come to the country in a professional capacity, not the way his career was going. But on receiving the assignment he'd researched as much as he could in the little time he'd had before leaving home. He'd read more than one report of mortar attacks against the airport and was expecting to see evidence of the brutal fighting as soon as he got off the plane. But the facility looked quite normal apart from a couple of uniformed Nepalese-looking security guards nearby who were carrying rifles. There'd been the unusual approach and landing, of course. Instead of the aircraft gradually descending on a long approach path as one might expect, it remained at fifteen thousand feet until it was directly above the airfield before spiralling down in tight turns and pulling up at the last moment to touch down – a defensive procedure against terrorist anti-aircraft missiles, he was told.

After conducting his initial research, Stanza had originally planned to drive into the country. There were three main land routes into Baghdad: from Turkey in the north, from Kuwait in the south, and from Amman, the capital of Jordan, in the west. According to reports each route had its security-related pros and cons and acting on advice from a so-called experienced source Stanza chose the Amman road. It was the longest route: four hours from Amman to the Iraqi border, an hour or so's wait at immigration and then another four and a half hours to Baghdad itself. It wasn't until Stanza arrived in Amman and hired a local driver that he learned from a security expert at the bar in the hotel how utterly out of date his advice was and that to attempt that way into Iraq was now considered suicide. From the Jordanian border to Baghdad was considered one of the most dangerous stretches of motorway for banditry in the country, especially the section that passed north of the towns Ramadi and Fallujah. It was possible, at considerable cost, to hitch a ride with a PSD (Private Security Detail) convoy that offered armed protection. But even then safety from attack was not guaranteed and there were those who reckoned that the openly aggressive teams only attracted trouble. When Stanza heard of four Japanese journalists who had travelled that route the week before and were now awaiting their fate at the hands of insurgents who had taken them hostage there was no longer any question in his mind of how he was going to arrive in Iraq.

In the early days of the conflict journalists had enjoyed, for the most part, their customary status as impartial observers. But a year into the conflict they were simply seen as westerners – and as spies by many – as much a commodity for economic or political kidnappers as any other foreigner.

Stanza entered the terminal that was a few degrees cooler than the tarmac and joined the line of people waiting to be processed by Iraqi immigration officers. When his turn came he presented his passport, visa and press card and after a brief scrutiny by an officer he was allowed through into the cavernous baggage-reclaim hall.

Twenty minutes later, after his bags had been searched by a Customs officer, he walked through a pair of automatic glass doors into the arrivals lounge and looked around for the security officer employed by his office who was supposed to be waiting to meet him. Stanza had not been given any details of who he was meant to meet, where they were staying in Baghdad or what to do if the rendezvous failed to take place. Like most journalists he arrived with a prima donna attitude, expecting all his needs to be taken care of. Pretty much anywhere else in the world Stanza would have made his own way to a hotel but he suspected this was not the case in Baghdad and that he was going to have to wait. He did wonder briefly about what he might do if his security officer failed to turn up but since he did not have a clue he put the question aside.

Iraq had changed a great deal in the year since the end of the war, with violence increasing tenfold after the initial post-war celebrations. Insurgents were infil-trating every area of civilian life and kidnappings and suicide bombings were commonplace. In the early days after the overthrow of Saddam Hussein journalists were able to tour the country relatively freely in search of stories, from Basra in the south to the Turkish border in the north, from Iran in the east to Syria and Jordan in the west. There were few serious threats, the greatest danger being on the bad roads where horrendous Iraqi driving skills made perilous situa-tions actually lethal. Stanza had been warned in Amman not to expect much freedom of movement these days and that he would probably spend most of his time confined to Baghdad unless he chose to embed with a military unit. More paranoid advice that he received was to stay in his hotel and limit his trips to the convention centre in the Green Zone for press confer-ences and meetings with political and military figures.

The picture was very different from the one painted by Patterson, his foreign editor, who in fact had never been to Iraq. Stanza wondered if the man had deliberately lied to him about the dangers in order to get him to go – there was no one else at the paper who would even consider it any more. Even before Stanza left Amman he had developed an uneasy feeling about the trip.

But no one knew better than Stanza, except for his foreign editor and the other senior mandarins at the paper, that he had little choice if he wanted to hang on to his job as a journalist, or even actually to remain in the media business in any capacity. Ironically, there had once been a time when Stanza would have leaped at the chance to report from a war zone to further his career. Then, after a long period when he was not allowed to go anywhere, he suddenly found himself on a dangerous assignment to save what was left of it. But that was because no one else would do it and to cap it all ultimately there were no guarantees that he would have a job afterwards. If anything, Stanza believed this could well be his swansong – and he was only forty-two years old.

Stanza was a fallen star on the verge of plummeting right out of sight due to a serious incident a year earlier. With sixteen years in the news business behind him he had long since come to accept that he had seen the best of his job opportunities and there was no way a two-month assignment in Iraq, regardless of all that was going on in the country, was going to revitalise his career or even prevent its premature end.

This was the main reason why Stanza could muster little enthusiasm for the trip. It wasn't as if he had been a particularly great journalist – he would admit to that. Nor, if he was honest with himself, had he reached a particularly dizzy height from which to fall, although he had made something of a name for himself in certain circles. Journalism was not Stanza's true vocation in life and if he had ever had one he'd never found out what it was.

Stanza's interest in journalism began some time during high school, probably towards the end of that phase of his education. Several of his friends had decided on careers in the news media and it was more than likely that he'd caught his ambition from them. Whatever its genesis, on leaving high school he made his mind up and firmly set his sights on a career in the news business. But his first significant effort in that direction was shot down in flames, something that was to become a frequent feature of his working life.

Stanza was the only son of an Italian–American middle-class family and had been brought up in a strongly Irish working-class neighbourhood in the Bridgeport section of Chicago. He was described as a generally quiet boy with a pleasant temperament, unnoticed either on the sports field or in the classroom for the same reasons – he was not outstanding but neither was he an embarrassment. He was more attracted to the idea of academic pursuits and never once appeared on the principal's punishment list, avoiding relationships with any thuggish, rebellious or ostentatiously cool fellow students. From an early age he was attracted to all things classy and sophisticated but unfortunately class and sophistication were not attracted to him. Even though many of his so-called best friends during high school came from wealthy families it was an exclusive club whose doors he could not pass through. Had he been noticeably talented he might have broken down more of those barriers than he did. When the time came for him and his friends to leave high school and apply for admission to the Medill School of Journalism at Northwestern University in Chicago, one of the finest schools for journalism in the country, he was denied entry because he had neither the grades, a letter of recommendation nor the money to buy his way in. One journalistic virtue that Stanza did have, though, was tenacity and, determined to pursue his chosen career, he enrolled in community college. Two years later, after leaving the college with an associate of arts diploma, he applied for entry into Northwestern but was again denied. He was, however, accepted into the University of Illinois, Chicago and its college of journalism, and after flunking a couple of semesters he eventually graduated at the age of twenty-six with a Bachelor's degree.

Undeterred by his non-Ivy League education, and still displaying more naivety than courage, Stanza set about applying for internships with such newspapers as the *Chicago Tribune* and the *Washington Post*. After being rejected by all of them, something he was learning to deal with, he pressed on with other notable papers such as the *Sun-Times* and the *Reader*. After months of disappointment and on reaching the bottom of his wish list without a single bite he compiled another list of lesser newspapers, and then another of even lesser journals to apply to. Four months after leaving university Stanza was finally offered a position at the *Champagne Regatta* in southern Illinois, a rag that was second from the bottom of his final list.

Stanza spent four years with the *Regatta* before moving to Gary, Indiana and joining the *Gary Gazette*, a move that was not entirely in defiance of gravity. Gary was a depressing steel town where he was tasked with covering mostly public works and social drama. Undiscouraged, Stanza applied himself to the work and was rewarded four years later with a position at the *Herald* in Milwaukee, which was without doubt several steps up the ladder. The editor had been impressed with Stanza's sensitivity when it came to writing about certain social problems and gave him a post at the metro desk covering urban conflict: crime, mayhem, riots and all things grim and disturbing. In Stanza's case it turned out to be the inspiration he needed.

On his thirty-sixth birthday he received a reward for his hard work in the form of a significant pay rise, along with a hint that he was to be considered for a post on the foreign desk. Stanza had discovered within himself an affinity for the dark side of news gathering – homicides, domestic atrocities and disasters – and so he focused his reporting talent on human conflict of the more brutal variety. Stanza's breakthrough came during a period of violent race riots that seemed to be spreading across the country. At this time he could most often be found in the forefront of the worst clashes between demonstrators and police. His first experience was in New Jersey in 2000, the scene of a clash between blacks and Latinos where he learned some serious lessons in self-preservation that included the proper clothing to wear, defence against various uses of pepper spray and CS gas, and where or – more to the point – where *not* to position oneself in a riot. In February 2001 he covered the violent Mardi Gras disturbances in Seattle and a couple of months later he was in Cincinnati for another round of more of the same until a little too much complacency was almost his undoing. Wearing a balaclava and gloves to disguise his skin colour Stanza found himself in a cauldron of rock- and Molotov cocktail-throwing, where he was first battered by the police and then barely escaped serious injury when a black rioter discovered that he was white and, believing he was a police spy, kicked him almost senseless. Ironically, Stanza was rescued by police who also thought he was an undercover cop.

When asked by his editor one day why he took such risks Stanza couldn't think of a satisfactory answer. He didn't bother to examine this apparent lack of purpose too closely, suspecting that it might turn out to be nothing more than a desperation to succeed. But not wishing to look a gift horse in the mouth, Stanza looked ahead and enjoyed his reputation for daring reporting, finally confident that he could make something of a name for himself. When an editor at the *Chicago Tribune* hinted to him at a cocktail party one evening that there was possibly a position for him at the renowned newspaper Stanza knew he was finally on his way. Then, shortly afterwards, he made the most catastrophic mistake of his career.

Around the time when Stanza was joining the *Herald* in Milwaukee the newspaper industry was suffering numerous blows to its reputation because of the exposure of various hoaxes, gross exaggerations and entirely untrue stories that had appeared in various prestigious journals, many of them written by well-known reporters. On one occasion a Pulitzer Prize had to be returned. Heads, some of them very senior, rolled within the various organisations responsible. Safety measures were introduced across the industry in an attempt to ensure that such scandals could never occur again. However, to vet for authenticity every quote and observation produced by a journalist was impossible. In many cases the problem lay as much with the editors and publishers as it did with the reporters themselves. Competition for readers was fierce and the pressure placed on hacks of all kinds to produce popular stories was intense.

Stanza needed a series of notable stories to propel him into the limelight where the biggest publishers in the country would notice him. His crime, when he eventually committed it, was nowhere near as heinous as those committed by many others – at least, not to those outside the business. But for those within the industry it was precisely the kind of corrupt reporting practice that needed to be stamped out.

Stanza had been searching for an attractive heading

for a political piece about the state's governance that he was developing. He found exactly what he was looking for in an enticing quote made by a local politician that he read on the wires. But the quote came from an interview that the politician had given to another journalist and Stanza needed it to sound as if it had been given to him. So he came up with what he thought was a simple way of making it appear as if that was what had happened.

Stanza telephoned the politician and requested a brief phone interview since he did not have the time to meet him personally. When the man came on the line Stanza asked him if he had indeed given the quote concerned. The politician acknowledged that he had. Stanza thanked him, ended the conversation and finished off his piece in a way that clearly conveyed to the reader that the quote had been made directly to him.

Two days after the piece was printed the *Herald*'s managing editor called Stanza into his office. Also at the meeting were the managing editor's boss, the executive editor, and *his* boss, the publisher himself. Stanza was dragged over the coals for his 'lie' and the only reason he left the office with his job intact was because the publisher wanted to bury any scandal and preserve the paper's reputation. But Stanza took with him a warning – delivered in no uncertain terms – that he did not have a future with the *Herald*, nor with any other paper for that matter. The management strategy was to keep Stanza at the *Herald* until the incident became ancient history and then dump him.

A year later Stanza was called into the office of Patterson, the paper's foreign editor. Due to the notably unimproved attitude of his bosses towards him, Stanza suspected that the time had come for him to be handed his cards. But to his surprise he was offered an assignment to Iraq. Patterson did not hesitate to tell Stanza that he had in fact been due to be 'let go' that week. But as matters stood the paper had a problem and Stanza was the only solution. Patterson's dilemma was that no one else at the newspaper wanted to take the risk of going to a war zone that had already claimed the lives of more journalists than any other in history. Patterson hinted that if Stanza did an outstanding job – and it would need to be exactly that – the paper *might* not be in such a rush to get rid of him. The way Stanza saw it was that if he did an outstanding job he could make Iraq his reporting home. He thanked Patterson before leaving the office but when he closed the door behind him he wondered why he'd bothered.

Stanza carried his two heavy bags and a laptop across the arrivals lounge towards a large set of double doors beyond which bright daylight shone. He stepped through them onto a covered concourse where a dozen or so hardened and grizzly-looking Caucasian men were standing around. They looked like mercenaries or ex-Foreign Legionnaires, unshaven, their hair cropped, obviously waiting for people to exit the terminal. Many had pistols strapped to their thighs and wore bulging khaki waist jackets containing radios, spare magazines and God only knew what other military-style gadgetry in the multitude of pockets and pouches. As Stanza passed between them he noticed that the English some of them spoke came in various accents while others appeared to speak a range of Eastern European languages.

Stanza emerged from this collection of ruffians and dropped his bags at the side of a road that ran along the front of the vast terminal building. A handful of vehicles were parked against the kerb and directly across the road was an immense three-storey concrete car park, the lower floor filled with vehicles.

'Jake?' a voice called out from behind him.

Stanza turned to see a fit-looking younger man heading towards him. The fellow had short neat hair and a closely cropped beard and was wearing a short-sleeved check shirt. He could have mingled easily with the other mercenary types, although his look was not as menacing. He wasn't sporting a combat-ready waist-coat, for one thing, and he carried no visible weapons. However, there was an air of controlled, efficient tough-ness about him and Stanza suddenly felt like a tourist who had arrived in the wrong country.

'Jake Stanza?' the man asked again, with a friendly smile.

'That's me,' Stanza said dryly, doing his best to appear self-assured and cool about being in the most dangerous place in the world.

'Bernie Mallory,' the man said as he held out his hand.

Stanza shook it, suspecting that the man was English

– although he would have to hear him talk a little more before he could be certain.

'I'm your security adviser,' Mallory said.

'I guessed that much,' Stanza said light-heartedly. 'How was the flight?'

'Great,' Stanza replied, looking around and wondering where the transport was. Several people in suits walked out of the arrivals lounge and were ushered into a couple of heavy-duty 4x4 vehicles by some of the armed thuggish-looking types.

'Our transport is in the car park,' Mallory said, pointing across the road. 'Those are VIPs,' he added, suspecting that Stanza was wondering why he had to walk to the car whereas the suits had been met at the terminal. 'Let's try and beat the rush,' Mallory said, stepping past Stanza onto the road. 'We don't want to be hitting the BIAP road with the rest of these targets,' he said, ignoring Stanza's bags.

Stanza picked up his bags and followed. 'What do you mean?' he asked Mallory who was a few feet ahead of him and heading towards a footpath into the car park.

'We're all targets,' Mallory said, half-turning his head. 'Westerners. The BIAP road is the most dangerous in the world. Averages a couple of kills a day . . . They know when the flights come in from Amman, the bad guys, and it doesn't take much savvy to figure out that half an hour to an hour later the passengers will be coming out. They'll be looking for a target.'

It got darker and cooler as they entered the vast concrete car park. Stanza followed Mallory between dozens of civilian cars, many with armed thugs hanging around them.

Stanza's laptop slipped off his shoulder and he shuffled on, trying to ignore the added discomfort and wondering why his security guard had not offered to help with his bags. But the BIAP road was a more important subject at that moment as he thought about the dangers they were to face almost immediately after landing. 'Isn't there another road out of here?' he asked.

'Yep,' Mallory replied. 'It's quieter but if you do get hit you're more isolated. At least on the BIAP road there's a chance that a US convoy might come by if you've had a contact. Then it's down to luck if they get involved. They don't always bother when it's a fight involving civilians.'

Stanza wondered if the man was being serious or just trying to get the new journalist in town all wound up. He decided not to ask any more questions for the time being – he'd try to assess things for himself as they developed. When Stanza had first heard that he was to have a personal security officer in Baghdad he'd been hostile to the idea – not that he'd had any choice in the matter. But that had been back in Wisconsin and despite his uncertainty about this Brit he was beginning to suspect that there might be some sense to it. Apparently the security adviser was just part of the life-insurance package anyway, which was expensive enough for a journalist in Iraq. A personal security guard significantly reduced the premium. Patterson would not have hired one for any other reason. Certainly not out of any altruistic concern for Stanza's well-being.

They carried on into a darker, dustier section of the robust concrete structure. The only light came in through narrow openings on either side, which left the centre area quite dark. Trash was everywhere and there were strong smells of sewage, rotting garbage and urine.

Stanza and Mallory walked past the seemingly endless rows of concrete pillars that supported the vast low ceiling. Most of the vehicles they passed were SUV types, four-wheel drive and solidly built. More armed men were positioned among them, looking like modern gladiators, all adorned with weaponry of various types. One group they passed was guarding four heavy trucks modified with what looked like steel plates that were all painted matt black. *Mad Max* came to Stanza's mind as he studied them. The last vehicle had a large board tied to its rear with the words 'GET BACK OR I'LL KILL YOU' written on it in large letters and an Arabic translation beneath.

Mallory led Stanza around the corner of a broad ramp that came down from the floor above. Ahead, Stanza saw two very ordinary-looking cars parked away from the others. Two smartly dressed Arab men in their thirties were leaning back against one of the cars, chatting and smoking. They stood up and put out their cigarettes as Mallory approached.

On seeing Stanza struggling with his bags, one of the Arabs hurried forward to help him. The other Arab took Stanza's laptop from him.

'Easy with my computer,' Stanza called out, his voice echoing in the concrete cavern as the men opened the boot of one of the cars and loaded the luggage inside.

'These two are Farris and Kareem,' Mallory said, introducing the Iraqis who paused to beam and nod hello. 'They're our drivers.'

'Hi,' Stanza said, forcing a smile.

The men went to hold out their hands, unsure if Stanza was the polite type or not. Iraqis were quite formal when it came to greetings. When meeting one of their own kind they usually broke into a pantomime of traditional gestures and phrases.

Stanza took their hands in turn and shook them somewhat limply in what he reckoned was an adequate effort to bond with the natives.

'D'you have body armour?' Mallory asked.

'No,' Stanza said, apparently unaware that he needed any.

From the back of his car Mallory dragged out a heavy flak jacket covered in a durable blue cotton material and with a stiff high collar. He held it out to Stanza. 'Try that,' he said.

'Do I put it on now?' Stanza asked, looking at it in Mallory's hands.

'I would advise it,' Mallory answered dryly.

Stanza took hold of it. As Mallory released it, it fell to the ground, its weight almost wrenching Stanza's arms from their sockets. He hadn't been prepared for that and after taking a firm grip on it he heaved it up and plonked it on the bonnet of the car.

Mallory opened one of the car's front doors, took off his short-sleeved shirt to reveal a thin nylon T-shirt covering a taut muscular torso and lifted a light pair of armoured plates off the passenger seat. They were connected by a series of Velcro straps and Mallory placed them over his head and fixed them tightly on his shoulders and around his back and chest.

Stanza removed his jacket and after a brief study of the flak jacket's configuration he put an arm through an opening and heaved it on as if it were a saddle.

'I thought these things were lighter nowadays,' Stanza said.

'They are but the *Herald* can't afford 'em,' Mallory replied as he put his shirt back on and buttoned it up. 'That one must be ten years old.'

Stanza zipped up the front of his armoured vest and, clearly unable to get his jacket back on over the top, stood and waited for Mallory's next command. It was all so very foreign to him. 'As long as it works,' he said, trying to sound relaxed.

He watched Mallory pull out of a bag a rifle that he guessed was a Kalashnikov, load a magazine, cock the gun loudly, apply the safety catch and put the weapon on the floor beside the front passenger seat. Beside it was a large pouch with several spare magazines protruding from it. The sound of two more weapons being cocked startled Stanza – the noise was accentuated in the cavernous place – and he looked around to see the drivers casually placing semi-automatic pistols into their hip holsters, which they then covered with their jackets.

Stanza's discomfort became more palpable.

'You set?' Mallory asked Stanza, a serious tone to his voice. 'A quick brief, then.'

The drivers came over to Mallory, the confidence of those familiar with their responsibilities evident in their relaxed yet alert body language. Stanza remembered his wallet in his jacket pocket and decided to put it in his trousers.

Mallory looked at him. 'This is mostly for you,' he said, sounding like a schoolteacher.

'Oh, right,' Stanza said.

'You'll travel in the back of my vehicle,' Mallory said to Stanza. 'I'll be in the front. Kareem will be in that car following behind. His job is to tail us at a distance without looking as if he's with us. If anything goes wrong, if we get hit and our car fails – flat tyre, whatever, anything that stops us – Kareem will pull in front of us and we'll debus into his car. If we run into a contact, a firefight or an IED – improvised explosive device – we'll try and push through if we can. You get your head down but be ready to act if I tell you. Just do whatever I say, OK? If we have to debus you stay close to me. D'you understand all that?'

Stanza nodded since it was all he could do. He didn't feel as if he had any time to think. He had questions but didn't want to appear nervous or overly concerned. He knew they were driving to the hotel but he was not prepared for these warlike precautions. He felt as if he was taking part in a military operation.

'What route do you want to take?' Mallory asked Farris.

Farris shrugged to indicate his indifference as he glanced at Kareem for his thoughts. 'Blue four, seven, then railway red two,' he said, more in the tone of a suggestion than a statement.

Kareem also shrugged. 'That's good,' he agreed. 'My brother he called, said IED one hour past at black nine flyover. There may be 'nother so we not go there.'

'Sounds good to me,' Mallory said. Then, to Stanza, 'You done a hostile environment course of any kind?'

'A what?' Stanza asked, looking confused.

'Your paper not send you on a course to prepare you for here?'

Stanza shook his head. He'd heard of courses for journalists that taught them about weapons effects, military and insurgent tactics and how to be a hostage but they were not cheap, whereas Patterson was.

'How about a medic course?' Mallory said.

'No. Nothing like that,' Stanza said, adding a feeling of inadequacy to his growing nervousness.

'The medic bag's on the back seat. If we have to get out under fire or for any reason, if you can remember, bring it with you. OK?'

Stanza nodded as he looked inside the back of the car at the black bag with a small red cross on it on the floor behind the driver's seat.

'I don't s'pose you know how to use a weapon, either?' Mallory asked.

Stanza shook his head and was about to say he didn't approve of them anyway, which he did not. But at that moment it felt like a pretty lame thing to say.

'I'm not saying you should carry one,' Mallory said.

'But if I was lying next to a gun and a crazed insurgent was coming at me to slit my throat I'd want to know how to use one. You have a financial value to some of them but not to everyone.'

Stanza began to imagine such a scenario but it was all too heavy for him to hold a train of thought. He was beginning to feel as if he had arrived on another planet.

'OK. Let's saddle up,' Mallory said as he unzipped a butt pouch hanging below his navel, took out a pistol and cocked it.

Stanza climbed into the back of the vehicle, an awkward manoeuvre thanks to his bulky vest – which had him wondering just how far he could run in the damned thing anyway. There was some comfort, however, in the knowledge that his torso was protected against bullets.

Mallory sat in front of Stanza, closed his door and tucked his pistol under his thigh for ease of access. Farris climbed in behind the wheel, started the engine and drove slowly out of the narrow parking bay between a pair of heavy pillars. He turned a tight corner towards the exit.

Kareem allowed them to get some distance ahead before driving out of his space and following some way behind.

'Kareem, this is Bernie, check,' Mallory said into his hand-held radio which he kept low on his lap so that no one outside could see it. There was no reply. 'Kareem. *Diswamy?*'

'I hear,' came Kareem's tinny voice.

'That's good to me too,' Mallory said before tucking the radio out of sight.

'Is this car armoured?' Stanza asked.

'Your door would weigh quarter of a ton if it was,' Mallory replied. 'And the glass would be more than an inch thick . . . The *Herald* can't afford armoureds,' he added.

Stanza should have known better than to ask. He looked around the vehicle, wondering what protection they *did* have. 'So there's nothing to protect us?' he asked, hoping Mallory had some good news.

'Just your flak jacket,' Mallory replied.

'And this can stop all weapons?' Stanza asked.

'No. Yours is level-three armour. The *Herald* won't buy level-four,' he added in a tone that emphasised his contempt for how cheap their employers were. 'It'll stop AK rounds maybe, and low-velocity stuff such as pistol ammo. But I wouldn't worry about it. A lot of the shooters out here use AP – armour-piercing. They'll go through the car and you and me like they would through butter. Anyway, IEDs are our biggest threat and one of those'll disintegrate this crate in a second if we're close enough. That, or turn it into a fireball. Your body armour's about all they'll find of you in the wreckage,' he added dryly.

Stanza wondered if this was another wind-up attempt, although it sounded all too realistic. Either way, he wished he hadn't bothered enquiring. 'Any good news?' he asked, forcing a smile, deciding to try and sound a little more cavalier about it all.

'I haven't finished with the bad news yet,' Mallory

said. 'Didn't think you'd want to hear it all in one go.' Then, deciding to be a little lighter-hearted, he went on: 'There's always a bit of good news. Chelsea beat Liverpool last night.'

Stanza didn't find that amusing and looked out of the window as they left the car park. They burst into the sunlight and rolled through a small checkpoint, Mallory waving at the Fijian guard without stopping, and picked up speed as they joined the broad three-lane airport perimeter road still within the heavily guarded confines of the airfield. Stanza suspected that Mallory's bad news, as he put it, was an example of sick Brit humour. He realised that his palms were sweating and he rubbed them on his trousers, tried to get comfortable in his armour and his seat and exhaled deeply in a futile effort to relax.

Mallory adjusted a second passenger rear-view mirror that he had stuck to the windshield for his own use and took a look at Stanza. He couldn't help thinking that he'd just got rid of one wanker, Stanza's prede-cessor, and suspected he now had another.

Mallory moved the mirror again, this time to look at the road behind. Apart from Kareem it was empty as they followed the tall perimeter wall that shielded any view of traffic from beyond the airport grounds.

Mallory thought about telling Stanza that he was not going to get a handover brief from the journalist he was relieving as he might be expecting. But he decided to leave it until they got to the hotel. Mallory reckoned Stanza would have enough on his mind, especially if he was a first-timer – which Mallory assumed he was. The previous journalist, a twit named Jed from California, was supposed to have waited at the hotel for Stanza to arrive so that he could give him a situation brief prior to leaving the following day. But the man had left a couple of days early after his nerves had finally snapped, coming up with some bullshit story about urgent family matters that he had to get home and attend to right away.

In his defence, it had to be said that Jed had fallen into the deep end from the get-go although that had been his own stupid fault. He'd never listened to anything that Mallory had said about security since he was one of those types who thought they knew it all. A week after Jed arrived in Baghdad, one bright sunny morning he decided to take a walk around the hotel complex to familiarise himself with the neighbourhood – something that Mallory had previously said was inadvisable. It was not a particularly dangerous neighbourhood but unfortunately Jed ran into a bunch of locals just returning from the funeral of a relative who had been shot by US troops. They decided to take it out on Jed by giving him a good kicking. If it hadn't been for a local shopkeeper and his sons who didn't agree that violence against a lone individual was the right way to express their objections Jed might have been seriously hurt, or worse.

He didn't step out of his room for a week after that and even a ride to the convention centre a mile away had him sweating. A few weeks later, when Mallory thought that Jed was at last settling in, the journalist took Mallory aside to tell him that he suspected the drivers were planning to set him up to be kidnapped. He asked Mallory to get rid of them. Mallory explained that they needed drivers who knew the city well and if they didn't use Farris or Kareem they would only have to employ two other Iraqis. Jed's response was to say that in that case they should leave their guns at home when they were working with him. Mallory tried to convince him that the drivers needed their guns for their own protection since they were risking their lives by associating with westerners. He added, probably unwisely, that the drivers wouldn't need guns if they wanted to do Jed harm anyway. They'd just drive him to a bunch of insurgents who would take care of him from there. This only served to increase Jed's paranoia. Mallory could only imagine what crap he was writing for his newspaper. Jed had been Mallory's first experience of a journalist and now this replacement wasn't looking too bright either.

'How long will it take us?' Stanza piped up.

'To get to the hotel?' Mallory asked.

'That's where we're going, right?'

'Depends on traffic, roadblocks, checkpoints. If there are no big delays then half an hour should see us home. Traffic's getting worse every day, it seems.'

Stanza nodded as he studied a group of US vehicles parked alongside the road on the other side of the meridian where a dozen soldiers were milling about as if one of the vehicles had a flat tyre. 'How's the hotel?' he asked.

'Delightful,' Mallory replied.

Stanza recognised the sarcastic tone.

Mallory wondered how much longer he would have to spend in this shit-hole of a country. He'd been in Baghdad for two months now and it didn't look as if he was any closer to getting to Fallujah than he'd been on the day he'd arrived. The clock was ticking and the pressure to get on with his plan was increasing. The London-based company he worked for was already asking him to provide them with his return date so that they could organise the rotation of his replacement security adviser.

Mallory's initial plans to catch a flight into Baghdad or drive over the border had been stymied by heavily enforced coalition regulations that refused foreigners entry into the country unless they were employed by a licensed Iraq-reconstruction contractor. There *were* ways to get across the border but the risks were great and the chances of Mallory surviving on his own inside Iraq were slim. The conflict was getting more violent by the week and movement within the country for a single westerner was highly dangerous and tantamount to suicide. The obvious change he had to make to his plan was to examine ways of gaining legal access, which basically meant getting a job. There were, however, obvious advantages to that, especially if he could get employment in Fallujah.

Having decided that a bona fide job was the way ahead, Mallory spent the final weeks before his departure from the Marines compiling a list of security companies that operated in Iraq. Considering his background and his limited experience in other 'reconstruction'-related skills, he reckoned that employment as a security adviser was the best way to proceed. He needed a job in which he would have some freedom to move around on his own. But all the companies he found either provided security for large convoys that ferried clients or equipment between locations across the country, or supplied static guards at installations or compounds. The convoys were usually manned by trigger-happy teams of security personnel who hardly got out of their vehicles between their home base and the delivery point. That was not going to work for Mallory and he widened the scope of his search. Using contacts he'd acquired through former Marines already working in Iraq he eventually found a small 'boutique' company in London that provided security advisers to businesses and media organisations operating in hostile environments. At the time it seemed like a perfect solution, especially if he could work the media angle: he knew that reporters sometimes travelled all over the country.

As soon as Mallory left 42 Commando's barracks for the last time he mailed a slightly exaggerated CV to the London-based security company, along with a letter in which he said how well he knew Iraq, specifically Fallujah and the dreaded Sunni triangle, since he'd served there during the war.

A few days later he received an invitation from the company to travel to London for an interview. In his account of his military experience Mallory had included a stint with 42 Recce Troop, omitting to reveal how little time he'd actually spent with the more elite group. But the detail proved to be helpful to his cause when the company's operations officer came to assess his ability to work independently. To Mallory's surprise he was offered a job on the spot as a security consultant to a media organisation and was asked when he could leave for Iraq. He replied that he could go at any time, with a few days' notice – something else that the operations officer wanted to hear.

Mallory later found out that one of the reasons he had been offered a position so quickly was that the company had a shortage of personnel – quality security companies were having problems finding adequately qualified people despite the number of applications pouring in. People with no military experience whatsoever – or those with only short stints in the Territorial Army, for instance – were applying for work, lured by the relatively high pay and pretending to have the know-how required.

Mallory was contacted a few days later and received his instructions and flight details the following week. Unfortunately for him that was the week when violence in Iraq increased significantly and Baghdad became a much more difficult place in which to operate, especially for the media. The insurgents had embarked on an enthusiastic campaign to kidnap any westerner they could get their hands on, either to cut off their heads or ransom them for financial gain. It was not immediately clear to Mallory how this was going to affect his plans to get to Fallujah but he found out within a few days of arriving in Baghdad. He was basically locked down and unable to move except to safe meetings within the Green Zone, the ministries and one or two other secure locations. But, worse than that, there was big trouble brewing in Fallujah, which had become a fortress town for Sunni rebels led by the new leader of the Iraqi resistance, Abu Musab al-Zarqawi. Several PSD teams had been shot up and blown to pieces while driving through the town, their charred and dismembered bodies hung from lamp-posts and bridges as a warning to all westerners. To make the prospects for Mallory's little scheme even worse, it also looked as if the Americans were soon to mount a serious full-scale military operation against Fallujah to flatten the place.

Mallory had successfully convinced his company in London that since it was his first visit for them three months would be a good spell for him to get his teeth into the job. But that deadline was now only three weeks away.

Mallory considered the option of going home soon and having a go at reaching Fallujah on his next trip. Things might even have calmed down a little by then. But in Iraq it was impossible to predict even the next day's events, never mind months into the future. There was a saying in the country that if you thought you were having a bad day, just wait until tomorrow.

But one positive communication that arrived via the office e-mail system that morning was a letter to all media representatives from a military media-liaison officer attached to the US Marine Corps unit based in Fallujah. The threatened assault on the town was no secret and the Marines were taking applications from reporters who wanted to join the news pool for the campaign if and when it kicked off. There were, of course, pros and cons with that option. A news pool meant a mixed bag of media personnel all being carted around within the security structure of a military unit – which meant no freedom to go where they wanted. The military were strict about that rule, describing it as a safety feature although most journalists saw it as a way of restricting what they witnessed. Another problem for Mallory was that he might not be able to go along anyway since he was technically not a media person. But there were ways around that, such as pretending to be a cameraman or producer. That would depend on how well he got on with this Stanza guy. The man might turn out to be another chicken-shit operator like Jed and refuse to go to Fallujah anyway. For Mallory's retrieval scheme to work he would have to be with the unit that actually passed through the area of the graveyard and then have the time and privacy to carry out the excavation. Frustration was building in Mallory as the situation looked like becoming impossibly complicated. Fallujah was little more than half an hour's drive up the motorway but it might as well have been on another world.

The two cars passed through the last airport checkpoint and out onto the wide three lane BIAP highway heading east towards the centre of the city. The checkpoint also signified the last point of refuge en route before reaching the hotel. There were no other cars on their side of the carriageway that was separated from the westbound route by a stretch of rugged open ground a hundred metres wide.

Mallory began to experience that familiar feeling of loneliness on this particular stretch of road as they gathered speed. Farris changed lanes to avoid a large scoop in the tarmac, an old blast hole from a vehicle bomb. On either side of the eastbound and westbound routes were even wider stretches of wasteland, with dilapidated houses in the distance. The ground was dotted with tree stumps, the foliage having been removed by the US military to reduce ambush cover for the enemy as well as to allow military convoys a clearer field of fire. At intervals there were the shattered skeletons of vehicles destroyed by fire or explosions, victims of the post-war rebellion.

'We call this the lonely mile,' Mallory said.

Stanza looked out of one side of the car, then the other. There was no sign of life in either of the stretches of waste ground but beyond them he could see vehicles cruising the roads in front of the houses. 'Is this where most of the hits take place?' he asked.

'A lot of 'em,' Mallory said. 'Any vehicle on this stretch between the airport checkpoint and the next on ramp is either coming from or going to the airport. That tells anyone targeting this stretch that any vehicle on it probably has something to do with the military or the reconstruction – which isn't true, of course, but the insurgents don't mind getting it wrong. They usually do. They kill more innocent Iraqis than anyone else.'

Heavy traffic appeared up ahead with a stream of vehicles joining the motorway from the first on ramp. Farris slowed the car as they closed on it and moved to the inside lane where the traffic was a little faster.

'PSD coming up,' Kareem's voice suddenly rasped over the radio.

Stanza felt the tension move a notch higher as Farris immediately looked into his rear-view mirror and Mallory turned in his seat to get a better look.

'Shit,' Mallory muttered as he looked to either side of their car, hemmed in by the building traffic. 'We need to get over to the right.'

'Can't' Farris said, his gaze flicking between his mirror and the road ahead.

Stanza looked in all directions, unable to see what they were concerned about. 'What is it?' he asked.

'PSD,' Mallory said.

Stanza knew what it meant but not why it was such a worry.

'Four,' Kareem's voice came over the radio. 'Fast your side.'

'I have eyes-on,' Mallory said into his radio as he saw the four matt-black-painted *Mad Max*-type vehicles that he had seen inside the airport car park. 'I was hoping to be clear by the time those bastards left,' Mallory said, more to himself than to Stanza.

PSDs were civilians but when they drove around in SUVs and in a convoy formation they acted as if they had the right to do whatever they wanted, as if they were genuine military. Since they were mercenaries they were, in fact, often more unruly than regular forces were. Iraq was practically lawless, its police largely ineffectual, and under the rule of the occupying forces there was nothing that anyone could do to stop them. The military did not want to get involved because the

PSDs were effectively aiding in the reconstruction by protecting contractors who were travelling to and from locations such as the airport. Indeed, the military often even hired PSDs to carry out protection duties for US government interests due to the shortage of official military personnel who were trained in such techniques. The PSDs tended to be more aggressive than military convoys in their response to attack by insurgents because they were more vulnerable, lacking the heavier firepower that a military unit might possess. They were also high-profile, drove at breakneck speed, and could not call in fire support such as helicopters or other ground patrols if they were hit. Because of their hair-trigger belligerence the Iraqi public hated them and loved to see them killed.

Dozens of PSD convoys had been hit, especially along the BIAP road. It was a long bottleneck and an ideal location for insurgents to ambush such targets. The local terrorists were pretty adept at mobilising quickly from the nearby housing areas along the BIAP road and could hit the convoys with an array of weaponry that included RPG rockets and armour-piercing machine-gun fire. Another reason why the PSDs didn't like hanging around in traffic and why they drove so aggressively and at such speed was the threat of vehicle-borne suicide bombers. The only tactic the convoys had developed against this form of attack was to bully their way through traffic to the point of physically bashing other cars out of their way. Many of the PSD vehicles had rear gunners whose job it was to ensure that no civilian vehicle tried to follow them or get too close. Most locals had a story of their own or of someone they knew about being run off the road, having their car damaged or being shot at by a western PSD team. Dozens of Iraqis had been killed and hundreds seriously wounded in these acts of violence.

But not all PSD teams behaved like this. Many chose to move around using clandestine or low-profile methods such as driving ordinary-looking vehicles that blended in with local traffic. Some did so out of choice, others because they could not afford to finance the larger convoys. The success of the covert method depended on the skill of those involved at staying un-noticed. Tinted windows, for instance, were an unwise choice because the bad guys often used them to disguise themselves when approaching targets. Not the type of person you'd want to be mistaken for. The biggest problem with the clandestine method was how it left its practitioners vulnerable if they did find themselves in a dangerous situation.

'They're coming up on our side,' Mallory said to Farris.

'I see them,' Farris replied anxiously, his stare flicking from his rear-view mirror to the traffic ahead as they merged with it at speed.

The car was hemmed in on three sides by others, with the waste ground of the wide meridian on their left.

'You have to get over,' Mallory said. PSD convoys favoured the left-hand fast lane.

'Trying,' Farris said, attempting to force the car to

his right into the car beyond by threatening to hit it. But the driver was stubborn and refused to budge, honking his horn at Farris.

'Bastards are coming right at us!' Mallory said in a raised voice. 'Over! Pull over!'

Farris's nerves began to show as his efforts to get out of the fast lane stayed unsuccessful. In a panic move he decided to pull over to the far left, his two left wheels leaving the tarmac and running onto the bumpy waste ground.

'No!' Mallory shouted. 'The other way!'

But as Farris moved back onto the road the lead PSD truck, which was now practically touching their rear bumper, swerved to take them on the inside. Farris quickly adjusted again to let him through, but the PSD vehicle turned with him, unable to guess Farris's intentions: the driver seemed to have the impression that Farris was trying to block him. The PSD driver lost what little patience he had and accelerated into the back of the car. Stanza grabbed the back of Mallory's seat as he realised that things were not exactly under control.

'Let him pass!' Mallory shouted.

'I'm trying!' Farris replied, taking his foot off the gas to make the car slow down.

'No, don't slow down!' Mallory shouted. 'Move right, move right!'

The PSD truck accelerated again, this time swerving to the outside of Mallory's car, its far-side wheels leaving the road surface and kicking up dirt from the meridian. As the truck came alongside, the aggressive driver slammed into the flank of Mallory's vehicle and the barrels of two assault rifles poked out of the rear window.

Mallory showed them his empty hands as he looked up at the white faces snarling at him, hoping they would see that he was a westerner. The truck accelerated hard and pushed past Mallory's car as the next in line followed closely, hardly a gap between them. Again, all the guns inside were poking out at Mallory's car as it passed. The third vehicle sped by, inches behind the other, and then the fourth and final matt-black truck covered in welded steel sheeting thundered past, throwing up clouds of dust. As it moved ahead of Mallory's car the rear gunner, crouching behind a belt-fed M60 that was fixed to a post bolted to the floor of the vehicle, gestured to Mallory to move away.

'Move over,' Mallory said loudly to Farris.

'I try,' Farris said, panic in his voice.

Mallory showed his empty hands again but the gunner continued to wave him over, this time more vigorously.

'What does he want?' Farris asked. 'I can't move over.'

'Slow down,' Mallory said, keeping his hands up. As Farris complied, the car behind hooted in protest.

Farris reacted by moving back towards the verge and behind the tail PSD vehicle.

'No!' Mallory shouted, but it was too late.

The PSD gunner either got nervous or was itching for an excuse to use his weapon. He fired a short burst at the car.

The first round went into the grille, the second smashed into the bonnet and two more punched through the windscreen between Mallory and Farris.

Stanza let out a piercing scream. Mallory spun to see the man clutching the side of his thigh, blood oozing between his fingers.

Farris slammed on the brakes as he swerved the car onto the meridian, his eyes wide in horror.

Stanza moaned loudly as he leaned over onto his side, his face contorted in agony. The engine began to judder and make a rattling sound.

Mallory's brain was flooded by a deluge of alarming thoughts, the worst of which were that Stanza was possibly mortally wounded and that they would break down on the BIAP road that was patrolled by bad guys. The prospects were not good.

Mallory scrambled over the seat and heaved Stanza onto his back as Farris tried to manoeuvre the car back onto the road. It was slowing by the second.

Stanza groaned loudly as Mallory pulled his shaking, bloody hands away from the wound to take a look at it. Blood was seeping steadily through a gash in his trousers but it did not appear to be spurting. Mallory vigorously ripped open the cloth to expose the wound. Blood was oozing from a hole in the flesh: Mallory's concern was that the bullet had gone through the leg into the pelvis or had severed an artery. If the pelvis had been shattered any interior bleeding could be fatal if it wasn't taken care of quickly. Mallory took a few seconds to check and see if Stanza had been hit anywhere else but there were no obvious signs. He knew that he should pull away the rest of Stanza's clothing to check more thoroughly but the hole in the thigh was, as far as he could tell, the only serious wound that the journalist had sustained.

The car came to an abrupt stop and Farris clambered out, leaving his door open.

Mallory ripped open the medic bag, found a trauma dressing, tore open the packet, unravelled the bandage to open up the large square pad and pressed it hard against the wound. Stanza cried out, his head banging against the door as he jerked in agony.

'It looks OK,' Mallory said, trying to reassure Stanza. One of the rear doors opened and Mallory looked up to see that it was Kareem.

'Your car all right?' Mallory asked.

'Yes.' Kareem nodded quickly.

Farris leaned in through the driver's door, out of breath and clearly frightened. 'The car no good,' he announced, scanning the traffic behind him.

The build-up of cars was heavy, with all three lanes filled. Mallory's group was attracting close attention.

Mallory had to act quickly. 'Kareem, we're taking your car,' he said as he bound Stanza's wound tightly. 'Get everything out of this one and into yours. Hurry!' Mallory shouted as he pressed down on Stanza's wound again, making him cry out once more.

Mallory clambered out of the car and hurried around to the other side. As he opened the door Stanza almost fell out. Mallory grabbed him. 'We're changing cars,' he said. 'You have to help me.'

But Stanza appeared to be lost in a world of pain

and confusion and did not respond. Mallory didn't wait on ceremony: he grabbed Stanza under the armpits and hauled him out of the car. When Stanza's feet hit the road he let out another yell and started to struggle with Mallory. Farris hurried across to help, grabbing Stanza's legs none too gently, and together they lifted him off the ground, an action accompanied by more howling. They half-carried, half-dragged the journalist to the other car where Kareem was waiting by the open rear door, practically threw Stanza onto the back seat and shut the door.

'Inside,' Mallory shouted as he hurried around to the other rear door. Kareem was already climbing in behind the wheel and as Farris jumped into the front passenger seat Mallory slammed his door. Kareem let out the clutch and the car screeched away.

Farris looked back at his car. It slumped at an angle on the scruffy verge, steam issuing from its radiator grille. Farris said something to Kareem who shrugged as he gave what appeared to be a philosophical reply. But Kareem had other things on his mind. The team was not yet out of danger. Kareem was a naturally aggressive driver and Mallory had been nagging him from day one not to draw attention to the car by driving recklessly. Kareem's excuse was that that was the way everyone in Iraq drove, which was not far off the mark. Still, Mallory had kept him on a tight rein. On this occasion Kareem was in his element and with a combination of skill and attack he worked his way down the side of the line of traffic, passing cars by a hair's breadth. There was a chance that someone had seen them and telephoned their descriptions ahead. Since there was only one direction they could go, an ambush could be waiting for them at the next over-pass – a favourite tactic of the local insurgents.

Kareem, Farris and Mallory stared up at the over-pass as they approached. Traffic was moving across it: a vehicle could stop at any time and let the enemy debus into firing positions. As it turned out, they passed safely beneath it and Mallory looked back through the rear window as they sped away.

'Where to?' Kareem asked as he emerged from a cluster of cars to find the road clear ahead.

'Gate twelve,' Mallory said.

Kareem responded by swerving hard over to the outside lane and clocked over a hundred mph as he drove towards a broad Y-junction, taking the left fork up a ramp that led away from the motorway. There were hardly any vehicles on this stretch of road because it led directly to the Green Zone and a major checkpoint, with only one other turn-off – into a residential area – beforehand.

'Slow down,' Mallory warned as they sped along the broad empty road. 'Let's not scare anyone else into shooting at us.'

The checkpoint appeared up ahead and Kareem reduced speed swiftly so as not to unnerve the soldiers manning it.

Stanza was no longer moaning and yelling but his expression remained a picture of agony.

'Stanza?' Mallory said.

Stanza did not react. Mallory wondered if the man

160

had lost consciousness and took hold of his ear lobe and pinched it hard. 'Stanza?' he repeated.

Stanza winced and opened his eyes, blinking hard as he tried to focus on Mallory.

'Stay with us,' Mallory urged. 'Don't go to sleep. We're almost at a hospital.'

Some kind of response that Mallory read as positive flickered in Stanza's eyes. He thought about giving the man some painkillers but decided against it. There were other priorities at that moment. Mallory was confident that Stanza was going to be OK. The bleeding appeared to have stopped and the journalist would have been in a lot more obvious pain if his pelvis had been shattered. Mallory gripped Stanza's thumb and pressed the nail before releasing it.

It remained white for a second before returning to a normal pink colour as the blood flowed back – a good sign that Stanza's blood pressure was in fair shape.

Mallory turned his attention to the next obstacle, the Green Zone checkpoint, and pulled his DoD identification pass from his pocket. It was an illegal ID since he was not working for an Iraq reconstruction contractor. But there was a healthy black market operating among those western security companies who were permitted to issue the highly prized certificates without which no civilian could enter the Green Zone. Mallory had paid seven hundred and fifty dollars for his but it had been worth it. The Green Zone was the only place he could shop in an American PX store or take a break from the bad hotel food and have a burger or pizza, all in relative safety and sometimes in the

161

company of colleagues, former bootnecks who were also working as security advisers.

Kareem slowed the car to a crawl as they approached the first set of low concrete blast walls arranged in a tight chicane. He halted in front of a ramp where a stop sign in English and Arabic ordered all vehicles to obey or be fired upon. Half a dozen American troops beyond the next concrete chicane eyed the car with caution. It wouldn't be the first time a suicide bomber driving a car filled with explosives had tried to see how far he could get before detonating his load. An Abrams tank was parked behind the soldiers, its barrel pointed directly at the car. A high-explosive artillery shell would be in the breech: one word from the checkpoint commander and the tank gunner would – literally – blow away Mallory and the others.

Mallory held his DoD pass out of the car window while a soldier inspected it from a distance, using a pair of binoculars. The other soldiers relaxed a little as he told them that the card was in the hands of a white man: so far there had been no white suicide bombers. One of the soldiers waved Mallory forward, stepping closer to a blast wall and gripping his assault rifle while concentrating on the car and its occupants.

Kareem halted the car alongside the soldier who leaned down far enough to study the occupants, scrutinising the two Iraqis in front before looking in the back at Mallory and at Stanza who was lying awkwardly in the corner.

'We had a contact on Route Irish,' Mallory said, using the military designation for the BIAP road.

The soldier, a fresh-faced lad who seemed little more than twenty years old, was unfazed by the bloody trauma dressing and Stanza's wound. He took a closer look at Mallory's badge, comparing the picture to the man holding it. 'These guys with you?' he asked in a Southern drawl, indicating the two Iraqis.

'They're my drivers,' Mallory said. 'We left a car back on the BIAP. I'd like to get this guy to the CASH if I can.' He pointed to Stanza. Mallory was overly polite and respectful, in his experience the best way to communicate with soldiers. The youngster would let them through if and when he wanted to, no matter what condition Stanza was in, and being rude or trying to apply any kind of pressure was usually counter-productive.

'He got any ID?' the soldier asked, referring to Stanza.

'He just arrived in country,' Mallory replied. 'He's a US citizen. He has a passport somewhere. You want me to dig it out?'

Stanza managed a timely moan as the soldier took another look at him and his bloody thigh. 'Welcome to Baghdad,' the soldier said, a thin smile on his lips. 'You can go ahead,' he said before stepping back and waving to his commander who was standing between them and the tank.

'Thanks,' Mallory said as he tapped Kareem on the shoulder. 'Go,' he told him and Kareem pulled slowly away.

They drove through the last chicane, over a speed

ramp and passed the massive sand-coloured tank, speeding up as they drove onto a wide empty road.

The Green Zone was an area that had been traditionally blocked off to locals even during Saddam's time. It was several miles square and contained palaces and important government buildings, including Saddam's equivalent of the Pentagon with an elaborate bunker system. The Zone was traversed by broad roads that had been designed with military parades in mind and had more than its fair share of ornate arches, sculptures and heroic statues. Much of it was still intact although its former splendour was scarred by thousands of towering interconnecting concrete blast walls lining roads, fronting buildings and forming protective entrances to numerous checkpoints.

Ten minutes after entering the Zone Kareem steered the car in through the emergency entrance of the large US military hospital and stopped outside the main building. Mallory jumped out and had a quick word with a guard who called for an orderly. A few minutes later a couple of relaxed, experienced medical staff were easing Stanza onto a gurney and wheeling him into the hospital.

Mallory watched Stanza until he disappeared inside. With some relief he turned to face Kareem who was standing by the car. Farris was still in the front passenger seat.

'Farris needs to get back to his car, right?' Mallory asked.

'Farris would like this,' Kareem agreed.

'Stanza's baggage is in the back,' Mallory reminded him.

'*Inshalla.*' Kareem shrugged.

God willing indeed, Mallory mused. The luggage would still be there only if the car had not yet been ransacked.

'I'm gonna hang around here. Go sort the car out before the army blow it up as an IED,' he added, if they hadn't done so already. Farris would be compensated by the newspaper if his car had been trashed. He would even make money on the deal, something that he and Kareem would discuss on the way back to it, no doubt.

'How you get back hotel?' Kareem asked.

Mallory took a moment to think about the logistics of that minor problem. The hotel wasn't far away but it was in the Red Zone, a designation for anywhere in the country that was not inside a coalition-protected compound. 'You won't be able to get back into the Green Zone without a pass,' Mallory said, thinking out loud. 'I'll figure something out,' he said finally. 'Go get Farris's car.'

Kareem nodded and was about to walk away when Mallory stopped him and jutted his chin towards Farris. 'How is he?' he asked, his voice low so as not to be overheard.

Kareem glanced at his colleague and gave a shrug. 'He was frighten. Me too,' he said, a grin forming on his face.

'You weren't the only ones,' Mallory said. 'You did well today. It was good to have you there.'

Kareem nodded, trying to disguise his glee at having his bravery recognised.

'I'll catch you later,' Mallory said.

Kareem climbed into the car, started it up and drove away.

Mallory faced the hospital entrance, pausing to consider Kareem's question about how he was going to get back to the hotel. There were a number of people he could ask for a ride home. But that would have to wait until he was finished at the hospital and there was no telling how long that would take. His job was to look after Stanza. The first call he would have to make would be to the *Herald* in Milwaukee to let them know what had happened. He would put all the blame on the PSD convoy although in truth the contact could have been avoided if Farris had pushed his way to the inside lane when Mallory had told him to. The good news was that they were all alive. Mallory's next call would be to his boss in London: he'd give him the same story.

He sighed as he dug his phone out of a pocket, hit the memory key, scrolled to the *Herald*'s Milwaukee number and pushed the 'send' button. Seconds later the recorded voice of a young Iraqi girl declared first in Arabic and then in English that the number he was dialling was incorrect. Mallory cancelled the call, frowning. The girl's voice was the most hated in Iraq. The Iraqna mobile system was useless, to put it mildly, the service often shutting down for days at a time. At its best, calls were sometimes unavailable for hours and one of the system's most irritating features was the girl's voice informing the caller that the number they were dialling was wrong when it was clearly correct.

Mallory put the phone back in his pocket, mounted the steps and entered the hospital. He'd survived another day in Iraq.

5

Tasneen's Dreams

After a brief discussion with the hospital receptionist who was too disorganised to be much use to him, Mallory was sent to another desk where a clerk told him to wait in the lobby until someone came to see him. Twenty minutes later a man who might have been an orderly or even a doctor – he didn't introduce himself – informed Mallory that Stanza was not in any serious danger. The journalist was being X-rayed at that moment and would head into surgery at the first opportunity. The man could not say how long it would be before an operating theatre became available and since Stanza did not have a priority wound he was low on a list that could fill up at any time without notice. Mallory understood and was directed to a waiting area where someone would eventually tell him when Stanza was ready to leave.

Mallory found the waiting room but only after exploring two long corridors that met at an L-shaped junction. Countless doorways led off to a variety of rooms and offices and eventually he ended up not far from his starting point. The waiting room was small, narrow, empty, uninviting and it was easy to see why he had overlooked it in the first place. There were two rows of uncomfortable wooden chairs facing each other, a dozen in all, and only when Mallory sat down did he notice a small television bolted to the wall high up in a corner above the entrance. Its volume was muted.

He sat on a chair near the door and looked up at the screen that was displaying a US Army-sponsored broadcast of a sports update. Mallory looked around for the remote but if it was in the room its whereabouts were not obvious. Uninterested in getting up to search for it he rested the back of his head against the wall and stretched his feet out under the chair opposite. As he watched the muted screen where the picture had changed to a jolly army chaplain playing a harpsichord he considered getting up and fiddling with the controls on the front of the set to find another channel. But that would have required him to stand on a chair, an action that struck him as not worth the effort.

Mallory pulled his phone out of his pocket to try the newspaper's foreign desk again and pushed the redial button. After a long silence he concentrated on trying to make out what a faint voice that sounded as if it was at the other end of a tunnel was saying.

'Excuse me,' a girl's voice said.

Mallory looked up, unaware that someone had entered the room. He instantly pulled back his legs and sat upright to let an extremely pretty girl pass by. 'Sorry,' Mallory said as he watched her.

Tasneen smiled politely as she sat down on the furthest seat on the row opposite to Mallory.

Mallory stared at her, unable to avert his eyes. She glanced at him, smiled embarrassedly and looked away.

Mallory looked back down at his phone, conscious of his rudeness, but he had been unable to control his reaction to her. She was the most beautiful girl he had ever seen — or, at least, that was what it felt like — and he could not resist taking another glance at her. When he looked back at the screen of his phone he saw that he had accidentally dialled a wrong number. He cancelled it, found the *Herald*'s number again and hit 'send', stealing just one more sideways glance at the girl as he waited for the call to go through.

It was not so much how pretty she was as that a girl so beautiful could be alone with him in a room in Iraq. It was simply the complete unpredictability of it. Her lustrous black hair had a slight curl to it as it fell over her shoulders, her face was an utter pleasure to gaze upon and her large dark eyes were captivating. She was petite, wore tight trousers that accentuated her shapely bottom and legs and, although the colourful blouse she wore beneath a tailored jacket was modest, it did not completely hide the fullness of her breasts. The only women that Mallory had seen up close in Iraq so far had been the hotel chambermaids but they were all middle-aged and wore frumpy clothing. This girl was in a completely different league of attractiveness and poise.

She looked Arab but if Mallory had been told she was Italian or Brazilian he could have believed it. But despite appearing more liberated in her style of dress than most girls he had seen in Baghdad she still possessed that certain timidity or measured aloofness characteristic of well-brought-up Arab girls. Wherever she came from – and Mallory had not ruled out heaven itself at that point – just being in the small room with her was a complete treat as far as he was concerned.

He realised that a girl's voice was jabbering away in his ear and he fought to shift his concentration to the phone as the recorded Arabic response changed to English to inform him that he had dialled the number incorrectly. He ended the call, put the phone in his lap and stared at it as he contemplated what other ways he could contact the newspaper in Milwaukee. But the angel a few feet from him was spoiling his concentration.

Mallory was not what anyone who knew him would describe as a lady's man. He was by no means a complete failure in that department but chatting up girls had never been easy for him. He'd been a late starter in the pursuit of the fairer sex and by his mid-twenties he had decided that his chat was so bad that he had more chance of success by shutting up and hoping that a girl he fancied would talk to *him*. When he reflected on the girls he had successfully dated they had all been either friends of friends or he had met them in situations where they had grown to know each other over a period of time.

Mallory had never considered a relationship with an Arab girl before and certainly not while he'd been in Iraq. But finding himself close to such a beauty, the fact that when all was said and done he was a man and she was a woman could not be overlooked. As there was a distinct possibility that they might share the room for some time, Mallory didn't think that it had to be in silence. With no realistic ambitions beyond a conversation he shouldn't have felt intimidated. But as he drummed up the courage to say something he experienced a familiar apprehension.

He stared at his phone, wondering if he should just scrub round the whole idea, when, as if another part of him had suddenly taken charge of his personality, he announced emphatically, 'The voice.'

Tasneen glanced at him with a blank expression on her face before looking back down at her hands.

Mallory felt awkward at the outburst but decided to continue now that he had started. 'The voice on the phone,' he said, holding it up. 'The girl. It's a great voice but it's gotta be the most irritating one I've ever heard.'

Her only response was a brief, polite smile.

'I'm talking about the girl on the mobile phone,' Mallory persisted. 'The one who tells you that you can't get through because you've dialled the wrong number when you know you haven't.'

'Yes,' Tasneen said politely.

Mallory put the phone back in his pocket as the bullying presence in his head that had propelled him this far urged him to keep going. 'Would you like me to put the television volume on?' he asked, indicating the TV high in the corner.

Tasneen glanced up at the screen.

'I'm sorry,' Mallory said. 'There I go, assuming you can speak English.' He felt silly and decided to shut up.

'You can turn it up if you want,' she said, her accent as sweet and soft as her voice.

Mallory looked at her, pleased that she had responded and even more pleased she could speak English – although the impression remained that she did not particularly want to. 'I just wondered if *you* did,' he said. 'Sorry. I didn't mean to disturb you.'

The girl's gaze dropped to his hands and he followed her stare to the several large bloodstains on his trousers and the similar blotches on his hands and the sleeves of his shirt. He'd forgotten all about cleaning up and suddenly felt like a scruffy clod.

'Excuse me,' Mallory said as he got to his feet and walked out of the room.

Tasneen was glad that he had left. Normally she wouldn't have minded a conversation, especially with a westerner: they could sometimes be interesting, depending on what they did and where they were from. But on this occasion she was distracted by so many things, all of them to do with her brother and none of them remotely comforting.

Abdul was out of any danger from the wound itself. There had been an infection but the antibiotics had taken care of it. He had been lucky, or at least that was the view she was taking. After several days of silence Abdul had eventually told Tasneen how the squad had argued over some money that they had found and that one of them had gone insane and hacked off his hand with a single blow from a machete, something that the man had apparently not meant to do. She suspected there was far more to it than that

173

but was thankful that the blow had not been to Abdul's head. She could not understand why they had threatened to kill Abdul if he told the chief but it was conceivable they were afraid of losing their jobs at a time when work was hard to come by. But with all the time she'd had to reflect on the event, hours spent in the same waiting room while Abdul lay in his hospital bed, she was certain that she had seen something behind his eyes that had warned her he had not been truthful and that the danger was far from over.

Abdul had given the police chief a completely different story, telling him that he had been jumped by masked men on his way home and had had his hand cut off as punishment for being a police officer. But the chief wasn't buying that story either and was pressuring Abdul for the truth.

Tasneen's concern was that if Hassan and his men knew about the police chief's interest, and they probably did, they might think that Abdul would eventually change his mind and report them. She had never met Hassan but after all the stories Abdul had told her about him in the past she believed he was capable of anything. It was a fear that had caused her many sleepless nights and the stress was beginning to wear her down.

The obvious solution was to leave their home but where they could go was the question for which she had no answer. Iraq wasn't like other countries where a person could leave their home and just move elsewhere. Apart from a cousin in Fallujah, Tasneen and Abdul had no close enough relations outside Baghdad to make a safe move and the problems posed by religious and tribal differences were, as far as she could see, insurmountable. Lack of money was a major difficulty as well. Then there was Abdul himself and all his personal issues and since they were together his problems were hers too. He was an invalid now, a young man with only one hand, and the psychological strains of that alone were only just sinking in – for both of them. When the time came for him to step back into normal life among his friends it would only get worse.

Abdul was already showing signs of becoming a recluse, spending most of his time shut up in his room. Even when he was in Tasneen's company he hardly talked, staring into space as if he was in a dream state. She hoped that would change in time. But there was something else about Abdul that worried her. It was as if he had suffered more than the loss of his arm. She wasn't sure, it was just a feeling, but it was as if he had been wounded far more deeply that night in a place that was not as visible. Tasneen's suspicions that he was psychologically disturbed beyond what she would have expected were aroused not just by his brooding silence but by several odd things that he had said. They were mostly in the form of incomplete sentences and references that did not quite fit his story, phrases such as 'It was my fault' and 'I should have done something.' But when she asked him to clarify these comments he would shut down. Whatever was going on inside his head it was obviously deeply painful to him and therefore distressing to her.

Mallory stepped back into the room. Tasneen raised

175

her head and slipped out of her bleak thoughts as he took his seat again. A quick glance revealed that his trousers and shirtsleeves were wet and that he had made some effort to clean himself. It was obvious that he was at the hospital because someone he knew had been injured but she had no interest in knowing about it. Two weeks had passed since the morning when she'd brought her brother in with the help of the Americans for whom she worked in the Green Zone. She had spent practically every hour of that first couple of days in the hospital, a place filled with bad news and horror stories. Every day she had seen mutilated bodies wheeled in or evidence of the presence of such: bloody trails up the front steps and in through the main doors. And from the waiting room she had heard the screams of victims and their relatives and the shouts of medical staff reacting to the arrival of the latest casualties of the terrorist campaign that was being waged in her country.

In a strange way, before her brother's accident, Tasneen had felt separated from it all, as if she was not really involved and it was happening to everyone else but her. That was until the morning she opened the door to find Abdul lying on the floor and clasping his bloody stump against himself. She would never forget that sight for as long as she lived. In one awful, bloody second she became as much a part of this gross conflict as everyone else and from that moment all thoughts of escaping it had disappeared from her mind. Her little brother needed her and she could not desert him even if someone handed her an air ticket, money and a passport with visas for anywhere in the world.

If Tasneen was to be brutally honest with herself, that loss of the hope of eventual freedom was the true root of her depression. A deeper analysis of her feelings would have revealed a certain resentment towards Abdul, as if he was to blame for holding her back. It was not a new feeling. She had hoped that by this stage in Abdul's life he would have found a wife. That would have released her from her self-imposed obligation towards him, one she had adopted even before their parents had died. But the dream that he would one day become self-sufficient and allow her to finally stretch her wings and fly away had withered in the past couple of weeks. It was as if she too had become an invalid, her wings clipped before they had even been used.

Mallory exhaled deeply as he stretched out his legs and rested his head back against the wall. He tried not to look at Tasneen, having decided to leave her alone, and glanced up at the TV that was now showing a large black US Army sergeant making clay pottery. He wondered if the programmers actually believed that legions of US soldiers were crowded around TV sets all over Iraq, watching this act of creativity in stunned silence. The desire to feast his eyes on the girl once more was too great and he turned his head slightly to have another look.

She was staring at the wall, looking lost and unhappy. Sitting in this room in a building filled with foreigners inside an American fortress town called the Green

Zone she was a foreigner in her own country. Mallory wondered why she was in the hospital or who she was waiting for. As a US military establishment it was not usually available to locals. Technically, it wasn't even available to Stanza and was only intended for coalition military personnel and civilians involved in the reconstruction programme. Perhaps the girl was married to an American or maybe she was American herself – although that would have surprised him if it turned out to be so. Her clothes were western but something about her told him she was Iraqi.

Mallory felt sadness oozing from her and had a sudden urge to help. He chose to make one last attempt to communicate with her. As he studied her, trying to decide how he was going to start the conversation, he was struck once again by her beauty. 'You're . . . ' he began, just about to tell her how pretty she was before crushing that rebel voice inside his head. She looked at him, her expression blank. 'You have someone in the hospital?' he asked.

She looked back down at her hands. 'Yes,' she said, her voice a little croaky. 'Yes,' she repeated after clearing her throat.

Mallory nodded. 'Family?' he ventured.

Tasneen was about to tell him that she did not want to talk, even at the risk of offending him, but there was something about him that made her change her mind. He did not look pushy or insincere – quite the opposite, in fact. He had a calm about him, as if he didn't have a care in the world, which was obviously a façade – or a mistaken perception on her part – since it was impossible to be in Iraq and remain worry-free. His manner did not offend her and his eyes did not display the lasciviousness so common in the looks she usually got from western men. She had never approved of the way Arab men kept their women down but had nonetheless taken the general respect they expressed in their routine etiquette for granted – until westerners came in significant numbers to Iraq. Working among them – mostly Americans – had been a stark lesson in the cultural differences between Iraq and the West. She had quickly learned not to trust their motives and she found their forwardness offensive. It was difficult to know for sure but most of them seemed to be generally insincere and duplicitous.

It was strange how in some ways westerners had more respect for women than Arab men did but in other ways were worse. Tasneen's boss was a nice man whose desk was covered in family photographs and gifts from his children but many of the other men in the office were vulgar and she did not feel comfortable in their presence. She had never been abused in any way nor had anyone been directly rude to her or even propositioned her. But the open eyeing up and down of her body without even an attempt to hide the lust behind the looks often angered her. Then she rationalised that the kind of men who joined the military or came to work in war zones were not typical of all westerners, certainly not of the characters who most attracted her in western books and on television.

This man seemed different, though. He looked about

her age, maybe a few years older, appealing because of his apologetic demeanour – and his looks were not unattractive. He appeared to be making an effort to be respectful and unobtrusive, which she appreciated. She decided that feeling down was no excuse for being rude.

'My brother,' Tasneen said.

Mallory looked up at her in surprise. She had replied when he had given up the hope that she would. 'Nothing serious, I hope.'

'He has lost his hand,' she said.

'I'm sorry,' Mallory replied. 'Was it an accident?' he asked.

Tasneen did not want to discuss the incident itself but she did not feel uncomfortable talking about her brother. 'He's a policeman,' she said. Or he was, she almost added.

'It happened while he was working?' Mallory asked.

'Yes.' Tasneen nodded.

'Today?'

'No . . . a couple of weeks ago. But he has to keep coming back for surgery.'

Mallory nodded, looking down at his own hands and thinking how horrible it would be to lose one of them. 'A bomb, was it?'

She looked away. 'A horrible thing to happen,' she said, avoiding the question. 'Especially to a young man.'

'How old is he?'

'Not very old . . . He's my younger brother.'

That's even worse, Mallory thought, being so young. She looked about twenty-five, though it was hard to tell. Her face was youthful but at the same time she had a mature air about her. 'How long will he be in here?' he asked.

'I don't know. No one ever seems to know anything, or they don't want to tell me. I don't know which.'

'There's nothing unusual about that,' Mallory said, thinking how nice she seemed and wondering what her own story was. 'I would bet it's because they don't know. Then, out of the blue, someone will make a decision.'

Tasneen nodded. 'Why are you here?' she asked.

Mallory was surprised that she had actually asked him a question. 'We were attacked on Route Irish, the road to the airport.'

'I know Route Irish,' she said. 'Nothing very bad, I hope?' she said looking genuinely concerned.

'No. One of my people got a bad graze, or at least I hope that's all he got . . . You work here, in the Green Zone?' he asked.

'Yes. The Adnan Palace,' Tasneen said.

Mallory had suspected that she worked for the Americans, which would explain why her brother was here – that, and him being a policeman. Her English was also very good and she was at ease talking to foreigners. The Adnan Palace was where much of the American and Iraqi bureaucracy was based.

'What kind of treatment is he getting?' he asked.

'What?' she responded.

The way she looked at him, her face so open and beautiful, Mallory wanted to reach out and touch it as one would a piece of fine art. But he looked away

181

in case she could see his feelings in his eyes. 'Your brother. How are they treating his wound?'

'They're doing the skin – er . . . ' Tasneen paused to find the word.

'Skin graft,' Mallory offered.

'That's right,' she said. 'Sorry. My English is not very good.'

'You're joking,' he said, grinning. 'It's better than how a lot of English people I know speak.'

Tasneen grinned back at him.

They sat in silence for a moment but Mallory was determined to keep the conversation going. 'Is he staying in the hospital long?' he asked.

'I hope not,' she said. 'They don't like keeping people in if they can help it.'

'Have *you* been waiting long?' he asked. 'I mean, did you arrive just now, when you came in here?'

'No. I got here early this morning. I had to go back to the office for a bit.'

Mallory nodded, suddenly thought of something and checked his watch. It was gone four p.m. 'Have you eaten since you got here?' he asked.

'No, but I'm not hungry,' Tasneen said.

'What about a drink?'

'I'm OK.'

'Have you had a drink of anything since you got here?'

'I'm fine,' she insisted.

'You don't have to be so polite.'

'I'm not being polite.'

'Let me get you something,' Mallory urged, getting to his feet.

'I'm OK,' she said again.

'I'm getting something for myself anyway. I don't even know you but I feel it is my duty to at least make sure you have a drink.'

Tasneen was about to refuse once again but Mallory held up his hand like a policeman stopping traffic. 'Please. What can I get you? Water? A Coke? Coffee? What would you like?'

She relented, sitting back in her chair. 'OK,' she said, giving in. 'I'll have a Coke. I don't think they know how to make coffee here.'

'Being American they don't know how to make a cup of tea either, which was why I didn't ask.'

'I thought you were English,' Tasneen said, giving a cheery smile that she forced off her face almost as soon as it had appeared. By now she felt very relaxed with this man.

'You don't have a problem with that, do you?' he asked, immediately wondering why he'd asked such a boneheaded question.

'Of course not.'

She said it with complete sincerity. 'One Coke coming up,' Mallory said as he walked out the door.

As soon as he was gone Tasneen felt guilty about her brief flight of frivolity at a time when she should have been dour and miserable. But it was exactly the kind of distraction she would have advised a friend to seek in a similar situation. Nevertheless, the guilt remained.

She stood up, walked out of the room and headed along the corridor in the opposite direction to that taken by Mallory.

Tasneen arrived in the reception area and stood in the centre of the hall, looking around for anyone who looked as if they might be able to tell her about Abdul. The receptionist was behind her desk as always but Tasneen knew by now that the woman was hopeless and always offered the same suggestion: to stay in the waiting room until someone came to see her. All Tasneen wanted to know was if her brother was to be kept in for the night. If so she would see him after his operation, then go home and return the following morning.

A man who looked as if he was employed by the hospital walked hurriedly out of a door but before Tasneen could intercept him he disappeared through another. Tasneen's frustration was rising despite her experience of endless waiting in the hospital but she brought it under control and decided to stay in the reception hall until someone in authority appeared.

Mallory arrived, saw her standing with her back to him and was about to walk up to her when he stopped. It was suddenly obvious to him that she wanted to be alone, otherwise she would not have left the waiting room. As he stepped back to walk away she turned and saw him. He made a pathetic effort to wave, self-conscious that she had seen him.

'Hello,' Tasneen said, suddenly flushed with embarrassment. She wished that she had continued on out of the building, avoiding him altogether. Now that he had seen her she felt foolish. 'I came to see if anyone knew anything about my brother,' she said as she approached him.

'Would you like me to have a go?' Mallory asked, holding the door open, wanting to be of help though still feeling he was a pain to her. 'I might have more luck than you . . . I mean, I can probably shout louder than you can.'

'It's not their fault,' Tasneen said. 'They're busy. But I'm just worried – it's an old habit of mine, worrying about him. I should just go back to that room and wait.'

Mallory shrugged. 'OK . . . well. Er – I didn't have much luck with the drink. They have a canteen but you can't take drinks out . . . I came to let you know in case you wanted to have something to eat . . . I don't suppose you'd like to do that – go to the canteen?'

She hesitated and he took it as confirmation that she wanted to be alone. 'That's OK,' he said. 'I'll see if I can sneak you something out.'

Mallory started to head off as a voice in Tasneen's head urged her to go with him. At least it would kill some time and he was not exactly a horrible person. 'Where is it?' she asked.

'Around the corner and halfway along the corridor on the right,' he said, looking back at her but hardly stopping. He walked on without a glance back, hoping his message was clear that he was giving her space to do what she wanted.

She set off at his pace, several yards behind.

Mallory could hear footsteps behind him on the tiled floor but resisted the urge to look back. He passed the waiting room and turned the corner into the longer, busier corridor where hospital staff seemed to be constantly walking out of one door and in through another. He continued a little further before turning right under an arch into a narrower passageway. He could no longer hear Tasneen's footsteps and wondered if she'd taken the opportunity to slip away. As he reached a junction he felt certain he was alone and looked back as he took a right turn. He was surprised to see her entering the short passage. He paused and stepped aside to let her pass. She stopped alongside him, wondering which way to go.

'That way,' he said, pointing along the passage.

She went ahead, leaving a gentle waft of perfume in the air for him to walk through. The entrance to the canteen was around the next corner and at the end of a short corridor lined with glass-fronted refrigerators packed with every kind of drink.

A narrow doorway opened into a large room and Mallory followed her inside. There were half a dozen tables and about the same number of people spread among them. Close by was a worktop jammed with plastic trays, plates, cutlery, napkins and assorted condiments in small sachets. Beyond that was a serving counter with a dozen different food items spread out on it in silver serving trays. A young Iraqi man wearing an apron and a white paper hat and armed with several serving implements stood behind it.

The food looked bleached and overcooked but Tasneen suddenly felt hungry as she realised it had been many hours since her light breakfast. She looked around at Mallory standing behind her. 'Shall I . . . er?'

'Take a tray and a plate,' Mallory said, seeing her

discomfort but also noticing the way she had looked at the food. 'It's OK. They don't expect you to starve to death while you're waiting.'

She picked up a tray, separated one of the plastic plates from the pile with a manicured fingernail, moved to the food counter and indicated some meat and vegetables to the server who promptly piled a generous mound onto her plate. She looked up at Mallory, surprised at the amount of food. He shrugged. It was enough to satisfy a rugby forward. Mallory gave Tasneen a set of plastic cutlery and collected some food for himself while she hung about looking lost. Then he led the way to an empty table in a corner.

'What would you like to drink?' Mallory asked as she sat down.

'Oh . . . hmmm . . . That's what I came in for,' she said with an embarrassed grin as she looked at the mountain of food in front of her. 'Coke, please,' she said.

Mallory went to one of the large fridges and returned with a couple of chilled Cokes. He sat opposite Tasneen and unwrapped his cutlery. She followed his lead, then waited for him to start eating before dipping a fork into her vegetables and tasting a piece of carrot.

'Edible?' Mallory asked.

'It tastes as good as it looks,' she said, grinning. He smiled back.

He stuck his plastic fork into a large slab of meat and began to saw at it with the knife. Before he was halfway through, the fork snapped. A piece of it went flying into the air and Tasneen broke into a giggle.

'Excuse me,' Mallory said, deadpan as he got to his feet. He went over to the stack of plastic cutlery, collected several packets and sat back down, placing them beside his plate. 'I think I'm going to need spares,' he said as he undid one of the packets. 'Maybe I should double up,' he added, opening another, placing two forks together and poking them into the meat. The experiment was a success and after sawing off a piece he put it in his mouth and pantomimed chewing it with difficulty, all much to Tasneen's amusement. She placed her hand over her mouth to hide her broad grin.

'You know,' Mallory said, pausing to make an exaggerated effort to swallow, 'they deliberately make the food bad in hospitals to take your mind off why you're here.'

'It works,' she said. Her smile faded as she remembered why she was in fact there.

'Life has to go on, though, doesn't it?' he said, trying to make light of the philosophy.

'You're right,' she said as she tried a potato chip. 'I don't know your name.'

'Sorry. Bernie,' he said, wiping his hand on a napkin and holding it out to her.

She put her knife down, looked around at the others to see if they were looking, and shook hands. 'Tasneen,' she said.

Mallory shook her hand lightly, enjoying the contact. 'That's a lovely name. I've never heard it before.'

She smiled a thank-you and went back to her meal. 'It was my mother's name, and her mother's too.'

'I take it you're Iraqi?' he asked.

'Yes . . . I'm from Baghdad.'

'Where did you learn English?'

'At school. My father spoke it very well. He used to go to England when he was a young man.'

'You speak it too well to have just spoken it in school.'

'My father wanted us to learn English. My brother and I . . . the three of us, we would have conversations only in English sometimes. We watch a lot of English-language programmes and films on TV.'

'What does your father do?'

Tasneen's expression warned him of the bad news coming. 'Both my parents died during the war.'

'This last one?'

'Yes.'

'I'm sorry,' Mallory said, putting his cutlery down, feeling it was impolite to eat at that moment.

'What do *you* do?' Tasneen asked lightly as she picked at her food, not wanting to talk about herself any more.

Mallory's instinct was to be cautious about his identity and personal details but then he reminded himself that she would not have been given a job at the Palace without being heavily vetted. 'I'm a security adviser to media,' he said, revealing more than he would to most but still remaining sufficiently vague.

'Television?'

'An American newspaper,' he said, picking up his cutlery again and resuming his meal.

'Is it one of your friends who has been injured?'

'A journalist. I only just picked him up at the airport this afternoon.'

'No, seriously?' Tasneen asked, looking shocked.

Mallory studied her, curious about something. 'I wasn't sure at first but now I think your English sounds American at times.'

'Well . . . I work with a lot of Americans. I'm a bit of a sponge for accents. By the time you and I finish speaking I'll probably be talking with an English accent . . . So where do you stay? Here in the Green Zone?'

'The Sheraton,' he answered.

'Isn't it dangerous there?'

'Where is it safe?'

'I suppose you're right,' she mused. 'But that place is a big target, isn't it?'

'There's a lot of media and westerners there, plus a US Army detachment. I suppose it gets more than its fair share of attention . . . rockets and mortars.' He shrugged. 'We've been hit four times in the last couple of months.'

'You've been in Iraq two months?'

'Something like that.'

'When are you going home?'

'I don't know. I'll be here a while yet, I should think.'

'Then you'll go home?' she asked.

It had always been a foregone conclusion with Mallory that as soon as he got his hands on the money he would be out of Iraq, never to return. But a primal force had suddenly come into play, one of the most basic known to man, over which he had little control. 'It's good to take a break, let someone else have a job. Then I'll come back, no doubt. The work's interesting,' he said. It wasn't a lie, at least. If he didn't get the money this trip he would certainly be back.

They spoke for over an hour at the table, mostly about trivial things, hardly ever referring to the conflict. Tasneen was very interested in where Mallory lived in England and what everyday life was like for him, comparing it where she could with life in Iraq before the war. They were eventually interrupted by the server telling them that the canteen was closing and, realising they were the only customers left, they headed back to the waiting room where they continued their conversation.

This time, Mallory sat opposite Tasneen, their knees almost touching, both of them sitting forward more often than back. Mallory talked about his childhood and school and the events that had led to his decision to join the military while Tasneen described her childhood and life in Baghdad under Saddam. Mallory was charmed by how positive she was about everything, how she emphasised the good times while glossing over the threat under which she and her family had lived constantly. Both of them managed to avoid politics for the most part, mainly because neither had any great interest in the subject but also because it was too depressing a topic and would spoil the mood they both wanted to be in.

Mallory was fascinated with Tasneen's knowledge of

the culture and history of the West. He was amused by how that knowledge bore all the marks of having been derived from television and magazines, lacking the detail one might get from a first-hand visit. But it sparked an interest in him as he listened to her describe the topics with such enthusiasm. She knew more about historical and modern London than he did, for instance, specifically the sights and tourist traps. He was embarrassed by his own lack of knowledge about things that were available to him without hardly an effort. She was not interested in nightclubs, a sentiment he shared, and even though she did not drink she expressed a desire to have her first glass of wine in Athens, the cradle of European civilisation. So many things she talked about left Mallory wishing that he had studied history as well as geography and he made a promise to himself to do something about that at the first opportunity.

Neither of them had noticed the time fly by until a doctor appeared in the doorway, looking for Mallory.

'You here with Jake Stanza?' the doctor asked tiredly, looking as if he'd had a long day.

'Yes,' Mallory said, getting to his feet.

'We're gonna leave him where he is for the night,'

'He OK?' Mallory asked, suddenly realising that he had forgotten all about his client during the past couple of hours.

'He's fine,' the doctor said. 'He had a mild reaction to the anaesthetic so we're gonna leave him on the monitor for the time being. You can come pick him up in the morning . . . You're Miss Rahman, right?' he said, turning his attention to Tasneen.

'Yes,' she said, standing and looking a little pensive.

The doctor's experienced eye recognised her concern. He smiled gently to help put her at ease. 'Abdul's fine. It was a pretty long procedure for the both of us but it went well. He's bushed so we'll let him rest here for the night.'

'Can I see him?' she asked.

'Yeah, we can arrange a five-minute visit, I guess. Why don't you come with me now?' he said, stepping back out into the hallway. 'I'll show you where he is and then I'm gonna get outta here myself.'

Tasneen followed the doctor into the corridor.

Mallory watched her as she headed out of the room, frustrated at the abruptness of her departure. But Tasneen stopped to look back at him in the doorway. Their sudden parting was curiously unpleasant for her too and she stared into the eyes of the man whose polite and interesting company had taken some of the edge off her problems for the past few hours.

She moved towards him, holding out her hand. 'It was very nice to meet you,' she said.

'You too,' Mallory said, taking her hand, enjoying the touch even more than before.

She broke the contact as she turned away and hurried to catch up with the doctor.

As Mallory watched Tasneen head towards the reception hall she turned quickly to look back at him, smiled, waved and continued on her way.

Mallory swallowed his disappointment and walked down to the corner and into the longer corridor that was practically empty now. He continued to a set of glass-panelled doors at the far end.

As he approached the exit he could see that it was dark outside, something he should have considered. He stepped out into the slightly chilly air, through the US Army pedestrian checkpoint manned by a male and female soldier who were dressed in full combat gear and onto the main road.

A couple of Hummvees cruised by with their head-lights on, a soldier standing in each roof embrasure behind a belt-fed .50-calibre machine gun. Mallory looked up and down the road that was empty of other vehicles and pedestrians and as the patrol drove out of sight everything fell silent. It was not a good idea to hang around and, sighing philosophically, he closed the door on the romantic episode, turned his back on the hospital and walked on up the street.

Mallory took his mobile phone from his pocket and considered who he could call to ask for a ride back to the Sheraton. The hotel was only on the other side of the river, no more than a ten-minute drive using the nearest bridge, but the problem was the time of day. The dark hours brought out the criminal and insurgent population of the city in even greater numbers. But they were not the only dangers. The curfew was only an hour away, and the military and police patrols, though fewer at night, were more trigger-happy. Some PSD teams ventured out at night but the wiser ones did so only if it could not be avoided. Mallory himself had been out on several occasions after curfew, mostly to the convention centre on work-related trips, but these excursions had been undertaken only with great reluctance. The US military hierarchy was in the habit of holding press conferences in the evenings, the convention centre being situated inside the Green Zone, and they obviously had scant regard for the dangers faced by media crews who lived outside the zone.

Mallory scrolled through the phone numbers of a couple of PSD friends living in the Green Zone but after selecting one was reluctant to make the call. The odds were small that anyone was going out but that was not the only reason for his reluctance. The PSD guys would ask him how he'd ended up getting stuck in the Green Zone without a ride and frankly he would look like an amateur no matter what explanation he gave short of a pack of lies. He could ask to sleep over until morning but that would still leave his competency suspect. Reputation was everything in the security-adviser world and – something he had not overlooked – if he failed in his mission to retrieve the money from Fallujah he might find himself stuck in this business. The last option was to call one of his Iraqi fixers and ask them to meet him at the Assassins' Gate less than a mile's walk from the hospital. But Mallory would be asking him to take the risk of driving from his home to the hotel and back home again.

There was only one choice left short of walking back to the Sheraton, which would be a stupid and unprofessional risk, and that was to find somewhere in the Green Zone to lie down and wait the night out. But although the worst of Iraq's winter months had passed the nights could still get bitterly cold. Neither was the Zone as secure as people assumed, despite the heavy military presence. Iraqis occupied several large residential areas within the Zone and there had been reports of lone westerners being attacked. Only recently Mallory had read an intelligence report of an American contractor assaulted by three Iraqis while out jogging in broad daylight. They had tried to get him into the boot of a car in an attempt to kidnap him but he had managed to fight them off and make a run for it. Every western company compound in the Zone was heavily guarded – and for good reason.

Mallory paused in the street with his hands on his hips and broke into a grin as he shook his head. 'What a wanker,' he said out loud. One cute babe and all his soldiering skills flew out the window.

A car's headlights blinked on in the distance as it pulled away from the sidewalk and as it approached the other side of the road it began to slow. Mallory could not see the driver and his hand went to his butt pouch where his pistol was. The car was a small white Japanese job and as it came to a stop the driver's window wound down. It was Tasneen. Mallory beamed as he crossed towards her.

'Hi,' she said as he rested his hands on the roof of the car and leaned down.

'Hi,' he echoed, unable to conceal his pleasure.

'I'm glad I saw you,' she said. 'I felt bad about not being able to say goodbye.'

'Yeah . . . I . . . I really enjoyed talking with you.'

She smiled broadly but at the same time felt embarrassed by her forwardness.

A vehicle appeared, heading towards them. It was another Hummvee and Mallory hugged the side of the car as it passed closely by, the driver no doubt making the point that Mallory was standing in a stupid position on the road.

'How was your brother?' Mallory asked, resuming his stance.

'I didn't get to speak to him. He was asleep. But he looked fine. Peaceful. That's the only time he does, when he's asleep. The rest of the time he's either grumpy or in a trance.'

'Can't be easy, losing a hand.'

Another Hummvee approached and Mallory hugged the car again to let it pass.

He leaned back down and looked at Tasneen, unsure how to say what he wanted to. 'I feel like I could talk to you all night . . . I mean . . . you know . . . '

Her embarrassment increased.

'Which way are you going?' Mallory asked.

'I live outside the Green Zone.'

'Yes, you said. Which gate do you leave through?'

'The convention centre.'

'Oh,' Mallory said, looking disappointed and releasing the car. 'OK.'

'Where do you need to get to?'

'I'm heading for the Assassins' Gate,' he said.

'That's not a problem. I can drop you.'

'You sure?'

'Of course. It's not a big detour.'

Mallory hurried around to the passenger side, opened the door and climbed in. 'You're very kind,' he said as he closed the door.

Tasneen set off and they drove in silence, both feeling awkward travelling together, something neither of them had expected to be doing.

'It's cold,' Mallory said, in the absence of anything more interesting to say.

'Yes. But not as cold right now as where you come from.'

'That's the truth. Still, the desert can be so hot in the day and so cold at night. I couldn't believe it when I first got here. I didn't think of bringing a pully. Then I was stuck outside one evening and I was so cold that I was shivering.'

'You should go up north,' she said. 'We get snow in the mountains this time of year.'

'You ever been skiing?' Mallory asked.

'I would *love* to go skiing,' Tasneen replied with childish enthusiasm. 'I love to watch it on TV. Not racing but just skiing for fun.'

'Well, your luck's in. I happen to be an ace skiing instructor.'

'Ace?'

'The best. OK, perhaps not the best, but I'm good. Well, I can handle a novice like you, at any rate. I'll teach you for free, how's that?'

Tasneen slowed at a junction, made a right turn, and accelerated on. Mallory felt an idiot, making such a pointless offer, and her silence was proof of it.

'You would probably be shocked if I called you one

day and asked for my lesson,' Tasneen said. She wasn't sure why she had opted to continue the fantasy but sharing it with another person was excitingly different.

Mallory glanced at her, pleased that she had carried on the game. 'Shocked? I'd be stunned.'

'Why?' she asked.

'Because I haven't even given you my phone number.'

Tasneen broke into a delightful laugh.

'Where's your car?' she asked as she slowed. The Assassins' Gate checkpoint was still some distance away but the first set of barriers was already visible in the beams of her headlights and it was dangerous to stop a car close to them, even more so at night.

'Drop me here. I can walk,' said Mallory.

Tasneen could not see any vehicles on the approach road to the checkpoint. 'Where's your car?' she asked.

'At the Sheraton.'

'The Sheraton Hotel?'

'That's where I live.'

'Yes, but you can't walk there from here.'

'I'm not going to. I'm going to jog,' Mallory said. It wasn't so bad. The foot of the bridge was practically outside the Assassins' Gate. It was a long bridge, exposed, but once on the other side he could drop down onto the tree-covered embankment.

'Run?' Tasneen said, her voice a tone higher. 'But what if someone tries to attack you? You are a westerner. You look like one, even in the dark.'

'I'll jump into the river,' he said. It was meant to sound flippant even though it wasn't.

She carried on driving. 'You are mad,' she said as she closed on the first unmanned concrete-barrier chicane.

'You'd better stop,' he said.

'Not now. They might shoot at us.'

'Then drop me on the street.'

They carried on, obeying a sign that demanded they reduce speed to five mph.

'You're crazy,' Tasneen said, turning off her headlights as they approached some soldiers behind a low blast wall.

She was right, of course. Mallory had put himself in an awkward situation and none of his solutions were particularly smart. What a man will do to spend even a few minutes with a beautiful woman . . .

They passed through the Assassins' Gate, an ornate affair but smaller than Marble Arch. It was damaged in places where a shell had struck it during the war: tiles had buckled or fallen away to expose the wire framework beneath.

They cruised between several high blast walls and over a line of road claws towards several more soldiers standing beside a bunker. Tasneen was waved through and the car left the safety of the Zone.

'Anywhere here will do,' Mallory said.

But Tasneen did not slow down. Instead, she speeded up the gentle incline that was the start of the broad four-lane bridge.

'What are you doing?' he asked, realising her intentions.

'You're *not* walking at this time of night,' she said in the domineering tone she used with her brother.

'But now it's dangerous for *you*.'

'No more dangerous than when I go home every night.'

'But you don't go this way.'

'I think I know Baghdad better than you.'

'I'm not sure that I agree with you.'

'You know it from your work point of view. I know it as an Iraqi who lives here. It's different for me.'

'But I'm a westerner in your car,' Mallory said as they reached the crest of the bridge, the buildings on the other side now looming large. The tallest of them was abandoned and in darkness, shell holes that had been punched into it during the war visible even at night. An American soldier had told Mallory that it had been a YMCA and had not been an intended target. But during the battle for the city Iraqi snipers had made use of it to cover the bridge and so American tanks had come forward and taken care of them.

Tasneen reached behind her seat, pulled out a head-scarf and dropped it onto his lap. 'Put that on,' she ordered.

Mallory inspected the purple and yellow scarf, put it over his head and, making light of it, wrapped it around his face in a gesture of feminine flair.

Tasneen was unable to hide her grin.

'This is still unnecessarily dangerous for you,' he said.

'It's done now. You'll be home in a few minutes.'

They headed down the other side of the bridge towards a large roundabout.

'Don't take Sadoon Street,' Mallory said. 'Continue around the roundabout and go under the bridge.'

'Why? Sadoon Street goes straight to your hotel.'

'Don't argue,' he said, firmly but gently. 'I know this area better than you.' The roundabout was a block away from a street known for its criminals, particularly drug dealers. Car-jacking was common in the city and the roundabout had a reputation as a stake-out point for such activity.

Tasneen passed the Sadoon Street exit and continued around the circle. A couple of cars were on the roundabout and Mallory scrutinised them.

Tasneen decided that Mallory could be quite domineering – but then, he was being protective at that moment. Pressure revealed a person's true self and in these new circumstances he remained as polite and calm as he had been in the hospital.

But Tasneen would be the first to admit that she had little experience of men, having really only known two in her life – her father and her brother. Her father had liked to appear tough but beneath the stern looks and the occasional raised voice he had not been. Abdul was a pussy cat whose temper flared at times, although now she would have to say she no longer knew him. Mallory did not appear to be like either of them. She had conversed more with him in a single period than with any other man in her life, including her brother and father. That was very odd, made even more bizarre because he was a foreigner and she had only just met him. In her culture, if a man from outside her family spent that amount of time with her it would be practically a marriage proposal, one reason why Tasneen had avoided such situations all her adult life. Mallory was safe from that standpoint. But if that was why she had begun talking with him it did not explain why she had stopped her car when she'd seen him in the street. Tasneen now had to question how well she knew herself.

'Go straight,' Mallory said as he twisted in his seat to see the other cars continue around without following Tasneen's vehicle.

Tasneen followed his instructions and turned along a quiet shadowy street, the buildings on both sides seemingly abandoned.

'Left,' Mallory said as they reached a T-junction.

A sign in English on one of the dilapidated buildings declared it to be the headquarters of the Iraqi Communist party. The windows and main entrance were draped in barbed wire with wind-blown trash stuck to its barbs. They passed beneath the bridge they had just crossed through a dank and rubbish-strewn cavern, and when they emerged on the other side the river glistened on their right. Battered three-storey buildings were packed tightly together on the left. The road was separated from the river by a parched green area dotted with trees, the remnants of a public park.

Mallory kept watch to their rear until he was satisfied that they had not been followed. Then he switched his attention to the poorly lit empty road ahead. When they had gone half a mile from the bridge he told Tasneen to pull over.

'The hotel is still a long way,' she said. She did not slow down.

'Pull over, please,' Mallory said insistently. Tasneen was evidently on the stubborn side, he decided, even if her obstinacy was well intentioned. 'The Baghdad Hotel is coming up and they're a little trigger-happy around the checkpoint,' he explained. The Baghdad Hotel was rumoured to be the operational HQ of the CIA outside the Green Zone and if it wasn't it certainly housed a lot of heavily armed Americans with local guards supplemented by PSDs running the checkpoint.

Tasneen obeyed and brought the car to a stop against the kerb. A floodlight came on a few hundred yards ahead, illuminating a barrier surrounded by blast walls. A figure stepped onto the street and into the light to make himself visible.

'Turn your headlights off,' Mallory said.

Tasneen turned them off but left the engine running.

'I'll get out here,' he said as he removed the scarf from around his head and turned to look at her. 'Thanks.'

'Not a problem,' she replied, taking the scarf from his hand.

'Which way will you go home?' he asked.

'Back the way we came. You know where the zoo is?'

'Yes.'

'I live near there.'

Mallory could picture the route to the park were the zoo was. It wasn't very far and didn't pass through any bad areas but he wished he didn't have to let her drive home alone. There was nothing he could do about it and he sighed as he opened the door. 'I need to know that you get home safely,' he said firmly. 'Can I have your mobile phone number?'

Tasneen considered the request for a moment, then reached behind the seat for her handbag.

'I have a notebook and pen,' he said, reaching into his breast pocket.

She gave up trying to lift her large handbag around the seat and held out her hand. He placed the pen and notebook on her palm and she turned on the interior light, scribbled down the number and handed the notebook back to him.

'Would you rather call me?' Mallory asked, wondering if he had been too forward.

'You can call. It's OK.'

Tasneen's eyes were illuminated by the dim bulb in the ceiling and her beauty struck him again. He wanted to kiss her soft lips but he knew that if he tried she would take off like a startled dove. He turned off the light, plunging them into darkness.

'Drive safely,' he said.

'Yes, daddy,' she replied.

'I really appreciate the lift. And . . . can I say, this has been my most enjoyable day in Iraq. In fact, the nicest day I can remember in a long time.'

Tasneen looked away but she nodded. 'I enjoyed myself, too.'

'Do a U-turn and head back the way you came to the roundabout.'

'I know how to get home,' she said. 'But thank you for your concern.'

Mallory wanted some kind of physical contact with her before she left and he offered her his hand. She took it and he held onto her fingers for longer than was polite. But she did not pull her hand away.

Mallory released her, climbed out of the car, closed the door and stepped away as the car moved off. It pulled a tight turn in the road, its headlights came on and Tasneen waved as she sped off up the road.

Mallory watched the car until its red tail lights had dipped under the bridge and the vehicle had turned the corner beyond and was out of sight. He glanced around the dark rubbish-strewn lifeless street as the wind picked up for a few seconds to blow an empty plastic bag and a sheet of newspaper into the air. He walked towards the floodlit checkpoint.

Mallory kept to the centre of the road to remain visible to the guards, took out his identification pouch and hung it around his neck.

As he approached the first of the chicane barriers a couple of young Iraqi guards in scruffy civilian clothes and armed with AK47s stepped into the light to watch him. He showed them his empty hands as he closed in and put on a warm smile as he entered the lit area.

'*Salom alycom*,' he called out.

'*Alycom salom*,' one of the men replied dryly.

Mallory raised his badge. The man inspected it briefly before offering him entry.

'*Shukran*,' Mallory said in thanks and headed past half a dozen more guards who were smoking and talking around a glowing brazier.

Mallory nodded, some responded, and he walked

on down the road, lined by towering blast walls, that ran past the back of the Baghdad Hotel. He reached the end of the block, passed through another barrier and walked towards the first checkpoint, manned by Iraqis, for the Palestine and Sheraton Hotel complex.

He repeated the safety procedures, was ushered through and headed for the main checkpoint to the complex manned by US soldiers. 'How's it going, guys?' he said, recognising one of the Americans.

'How you doin'?' the soldier replied. 'You havin' fun tonight?'

'Yeah. Checking out the local nightclubs,' Mallory quipped.

'Guess you can afford it,' the soldier smirked.

Mallory maintained an ongoing banter with a couple of the soldiers about relative wages: western private-security guards could earn ten times as much as a soldier. Another source of envy was the freedom that PSDs seemed to enjoy moving around as civilians. Mallory had been approached by several soldiers asking how to get a job as a PSD if they left the army but Mallory couldn't in all conscience recommend most of the tasks the PSDs were employed to perform. Much of what they had to do was running convoys through bandit country where many had met their end, caught up in explosive ambushes and fierce gun battles. The media heard about few of these incidents – the US Army didn't publicise their discoveries when they came across the remnants of western PSD convoys that had been wiped out and the companies that hired the men didn't advertise their losses because it was bad for business. Many of these companies were in any case not of a high standard: they sent their teams out in lightly armed soft-skin vehicles without sound intelligence or back-up into places where coalition soldiers would not even venture without heavy air support.

'You take it easy, guys,' Mallory said as he headed towards his hotel. 'I've gotta go call my stockbroker, make some investments.'

'Yeah, you do that, pal,' one of the soldiers called. 'You probably earned my day's wages the time it takes you to walk to your room!' another shouted. The comment was followed by some laughter.

Mallory waved without looking back as he followed a line of ten-foot-high blast walls that shielded the road from the river. He passed a large statue of a couple of Arab youths on a flying carpet. An Abrams tank was parked beside it under a canopy, a soldier standing in the turret. Its gun barrel pointed back towards the checkpoint in case a suicide bomber tried to ram his way through. Mallory headed down a broad avenue towards the entrance of the Sheraton and a minute later was stepping into the cavernous lobby and past a central waterfall towards glass elevators from which guests could look onto the lobby as they ascended. As usual, only one of the four lifts was operating at that time: one of them had been permanently disabled after its cables had been severed by a rocket strike earlier in the year. The lobby was five floors high and then the elevators passed through a transparent roof and continued up the outside of the building for another fifteen floors.

Mallory's lift stopped on the fifth floor and he

stepped out onto a landing that ran around the inside of the building. He walked to his room on the east side of the square, unlocked his door and closed it behind him. He took his notebook from his pocket, found Tasneen's number and keyed it into his phone.

Mallory went to the balcony window and pulled the sliding glass door aside to improve the signal reception. He looked down onto the large blue dome of the Firdous Mosque or Mosque of Paradise on the other side of Firdous Square. An explosion went off in the distance somewhere, followed by the rattle of heavy machine-gun fire, normal sounds for Baghdad by day and by night. As Mallory held the phone to his ear, expecting to hear the irritating recording of the girl telling him that he had dialled the number incorrectly, it actually rang.

'Hello,' said the unusually clear sweet voice.

'It's me, Bernie,' Mallory said.

'I'm just closing the door to my car and walking to my apartment.'

'That's all I wanted to hear.'

'And you got home OK too?' she asked.

'I'm in my room.'

'Good. Then we're both nice and safe.'

Mallory wondered if Tasneen was being facetious.

'Thank you,' she added then, sounding sincere. 'It's nice of you to care.'

There was a pause as both of them seemed to wonder what to say next.

'Would I be out of line if I called you again?' Mallory asked.

There was another pause. 'That would be nice,' Tasneen said finally as she reached her front door and put the key into the lock.

'What time will you be at the hospital tomorrow?' he asked, remembering that he still had to collect Stanza and that her brother was there too.

'I'll get there early,' she said. 'I have to work tomorrow.'

'Maybe I'll see you.'

'That would be nice.'

'OK . . . well, good night, then,' he said.

'Good night.'

Mallory ended the call and remained on the balcony, looking out over the city as he contemplated forming a relationship with a local girl. It was without a doubt pointless. But desire knew no boundaries and he would pursue her until either the obstacles became insurmountable or she refused his advances. There was, of course, his own mission in Iraq to worry about, too – it appeared to have slipped his mind for the moment. He yearned for Tasneen's company, though, and would meet her at the hospital even if it was only for a minute. Life in Iraq had to be taken one day at a time.

Mallory suddenly realised that he had not yet called the newspaper or the boss of his company. He scrolled through his phone numbers and then paused as he thought of two greater priorities at that moment. He needed to call Farris to determine the state of the car that they'd left on the BIAP and he had to organise a ride to the hospital in the morning. When that was sorted Mallory would devote the rest of the evening to reporting the incident to Milwaukee and London: both calls would take time – there would be a lot of explaining to do. Then he would organise himself some supper.

Tasneen closed the front door behind her, throwing across the new deadbolt she'd had installed, as well as the others, and double-checking that they were firmly in place. She walked through the living room, dropped her handbag on the couch and went into the kitchen. She filled a glass with water and took a sip. Mallory was a nice man but it would be impossible to see him again. If she ever managed to get out of Iraq it would be good to have someone she knew in the West but Mallory would probably not be right for what she had in mind. He would want to provide more than just help. It was pointless even to fantasise about it. A relationship with any man at that moment would be impossible and to have a friendship with a foreigner would be ludicrous. Mallory surely knew that for himself and if he didn't then she would have to doubt his common sense. But when she had told him that she would see him in the morning she had to admit that it hadn't been just to get him off the phone. She had enjoyed his company, more than she should have. It had been nice but this was the wrong time and very much the wrong place.

Tasneen looked at the fridge, wondering what to have for supper. But the thought of preparing anything now faded away. The sadness that had engulfed her like a fog for the past few weeks was back. For a little while Mallory had made her feel like a normal girl. More normal than she had ever felt before, probably. It had been a taste of forbidden fruit. But that was what she had devoted a life of daydreaming to. She'd had a glimpse of the real thing and ultimately it had frightened her. What she could not decide was whether she had the courage to either explore her dreams or abandon them.

6

Mismatched Pairs

Mallory stood in the hotel car park, checking his watch as Kareem's car emerged from the outer checkpoint in the distance and headed for the US-manned barrier. He walked through a gap in the blast wall, nodded at the American soldiers there and made his way up the road to meet Kareem.

On seeing his boss, Kareem made a three-point turn. As he completed it Mallory opened the car door and climbed in beside him.

'Hospital?' Kareem asked.

'Yep,' Mallory replied. 'You're half an hour late.'

Kareem shrugged in classic Arab fashion, opening his hands to the sky. 'IED in Karada,' he said matter-of-factly.

Mallory never knew when to believe his Iraqi drivers. They were basically good guys but their philosophy seemed to be that if the truth was not of great importance then there was no need to be scrupulous about it. There may well have been an IED in Karada but Mallory doubted that was why Kareem was late. He had caught both him and Farris lying in the past, always about something too trivial to challenge for fear of denting their delicate pride. Arabs tended to rate themselves highly in all manner of things. Both drivers were former Iraqi military and regarded themselves as experts with small arms but in reality their technique was abysmal. Their drills were dangerous and their accuracy terrible. But to tell them as much would have offended them and could have affected their relationship with Mallory. In Arab culture a man who does not share the high opinion one has of oneself is not a friend, and someone who is not a friend is a potential enemy. It was important to maintain mutual respect because Kareem and Farris were not simply employees. Mallory put his life in their hands every day and so let them get away with the small things and dealt with the more serious matters with great diplomacy. They were well paid, their families would be looked after if something happened to them and their laziness and incompetence were often overlooked. Trustworthy staff were hard to find and, as locals went, Kareem and Farris were OK.

Mallory's anxiety today was entirely about Tasneen, anyway. He had woken up that morning thinking of the girl and after some brutal self-examination and self-directed accusations of mere lustfulness nothing had changed. He could not get her out of his mind and the urge to see her had to be satisfied.

'How's Farris?' Mallory asked.

Kareem exhaled dramatically, a familiar sign usually telegraphing a problem. 'No happy,' Kareem said. 'He very upset.'

'How upset?'

'I no know,' Kareem said, using facial expressions and hand gestures to punctuate his comments. 'Maybe he want time to off.'

That was only to be expected and was not a bad idea. The team was going nowhere for a while in any case. 'You too?'

Kareem shrugged, playing his hand. 'If you like. I no care.'

They drove over the Jumhuriyah, the bridge that Mallory had crossed with Tasneen the night before, and pulled over to join a line of vehicles waiting to enter the Assassins' Gate checkpoint. Passing through any of the Green Zone checkpoints was an exercise in tension because of the number of times that they had been bombed. Police vehicles usually hung around the busy junction but their presence only added to its attractiveness as a target. It took ten minutes for Mallory and Kareem to get through into the relatively safe Green Zone and to the hospital. Mallory jumped out on the main street outside the hospital, leaving Kareem to park the car, and hurried to the entrance where he was searched before entering the building.

Mallory turned the corner at the end of the long corridor and paused to look in the waiting room. It was empty and he carried on to reception where, after the usual pointless discussion, he was directed back to the waiting room. After fifteen minutes the wait became intolerable and he began to wonder if Tasneen had already been and gone.

He looked out the door along the corridor that had become busy and saw Stanza standing in the reception hall with a member of the hospital staff. As Mallory reached the reception doors he could see Stanza supporting himself with a pair of alloy crutches and holding what looked like a paper bag of medication. This was apparently the subject of his conversation with the orderly or doctor who left Stanza as Mallory pushed in through the doors.

'Hi,' Mallory said.

Stanza turned to face him, a move that evidently caused him some pain. 'Hi,' he said.

'So you survived, then,' Mallory said.

'I guess so,' Stanza said, markedly less cocky than he'd been the day before.

'How is it?' Mallory asked, looking at Stanza's heavily bandaged thigh.

'Not too bad at all. They dug a bullet out of the muscle but there was no major damage done. Hurts like a son of a bitch, though. Gonna be living off painkillers the next week or so. But the good news is that I should be running around in a couple of weeks.'

'Have you decided if you're staying or heading home? I talked with your foreign editor in Milwaukee. Patterson.'

'Let me guess. He hooted with laughter.'

'He sounded concerned.'

'I'll bet.'

'He wants you to call him soon as you can.'

'I plan to stick around,' Stanza said. 'Hopefully I've had all my action for this trip.'

'Well . . . Car's outside,' Mallory said, pointing along

the corridor. Stanza took a step and froze as his face tightened against a bolt of pain.

'Want me to get you a wheelchair?' Mallory asked, displaying a motherly attitude he had developed only since working with civilians.

Stanza fought the pain until it eased, his face relaxing as he breathed deeply in and out while blinking away the wetness in his eyes. 'I'll be fine,' he said. 'Perhaps another painkiller . . . I just need to get the hang of these crutches. They're my first.'

'Let me carry your bag.'

'They gave me a bunch of dressings and stuff. I said you could handle that for me.'

'We'll change your dressing every morning. Not a problem.'

Mallory took the paper bag as Stanza concentrated on keeping the injured leg rigid while he leaned forward, put his weight on the crutches and took a step with his good leg.

Mallory took a single step to stay alongside him and, as he pondered the time it was going to take to reach the main street entrance, he saw Tasneen step out of a ward, a young man beside her whose heavily bandaged right arm was shorter than his left. They headed across the reception hall to the exit doors, Tasneen too concerned with her brother to notice anyone else.

Mallory felt a spasm of excitement at the sight of her. 'I need to see someone,' he said to Stanza.

'Huh?' Stanza grunted without looking up, concentrating on his next step.

'Just head down to the end, then go right. I'll catch you up,' Mallory said as he hurried away.

Stanza turned to look for Mallory but a painful twinge forced him back. He sighed, took a breath and concentrated on making his way along the corridor.

'Hi,' Mallory called out to Tasneen as she held the door open for her brother.

'Hi,' she replied, startled and looking immediately uncomfortable.

Mallory followed her outside where Abdul had stopped to look at the stranger.

'Is this your brother?' Mallory asked. The young man looked ill and exhausted.

'Yes,' Tasneen said, her uneasiness clear to Mallory. 'This is Abdul.'

'Hi,' Mallory said. '*Salam alycom.*' Mallory suspected that Tasneen had not said anything to her brother about the time at the hospital that she'd spent with an Englishman. 'I'm sorry to bother you,' he went on. 'Your sister was unfortunate enough to get stuck with me yesterday while she was waiting for you.'

Tasneen held her breath for fear that Mallory would mention the drive. She could not look at him.

'Anyway,' Mallory continued, 'I'm sorry to have stopped you but I just wanted to say that if your brother is looking for some light work when he's feeling better we could do with a translator.'

People were moving in and out of the emergency entrance. Mallory was suddenly aware of someone standing behind him and looked over his shoulder to see Kareem.

Mallory ignored him and faced Tasneen who was looking less panic-stricken than she'd been a few seconds before.

'Let me give you my number,' Mallory said, pulling out his notebook and scribbling on a page. 'You don't even have to let me know if you're not interested. It just struck me that your being a former police officer could be useful to us.' Mallory ripped out the page and offered it to Abdul who looked confused.

Tasneen took the paper. 'Thank you,' she said, looking away.

'Goodbye, then,' Mallory said. 'Nice to meet you, Abdul, and I hope you feel better soon.' Mallory felt that he was acting too cheerful but he was stuck in character.

'Goodbye,' Tasneen said, giving him a quick look. 'And thank you.'

'Hope to hear from you,' he said, praying that she understood the personal element in the request.

Tasneen took hold of Abdul's left hand and led him away.

Mallory's gaze lingered on her until he turned to face Kareem who was staring at him in his usual blank manner. 'I park there,' Kareem said, jutting his chin towards the hospital car park.

'I need you out front,' Mallory said.

'Is busy so I come here.'

Mallory thought about explaining why Kareem was not permitted to bring his car into the hospital car park without permission and also reminding him to listen to the instruction that Mallory had given him to wait out at the front of the building. But he chose to ignore the impulse. It was sometimes easier just to move on. 'OK,' Mallory said, trying to sound patient. 'Drive your car back out to the front of the hospital and I'll meet you there. Yes?'

'No problem,' Kareem said. But he stayed where he was.

'Off you go, then,' Mallory said, adopting the paternal tone he used with his locals.

Kareem finally moved away and Mallory took one last look at Tasneen. He smiled inwardly at having achieved his aim of talking to her. Now all he could hope for was that she would call him. The job offer that he'd made to Abdul had been a stroke of brilliance, an idea that had come from nowhere and was clearly a gift from the gods.

He went back inside, through the reception hall and into the corridor. Stanza was not in sight, which meant that he had either made it to the corner at the end or had collapsed and been taken away. The last look Tasneen had given Mallory was replaying itself in an endless wonderful loop and even the thought of being Stanza's nurse for the next week or so was nowhere near enough to put him in a bad mood.

Tasneen guided Abdul towards the car, resisting the urge to look back. It was not that her feelings for Mallory had blossomed in any way. But she was grateful for the offer as well as for the way he had revealed their relationship to her brother. Just the possibility of a job for Abdul was a monumental boost.

'You OK?' Tasneen asked, wondering if her brother had read anything into the chance meeting with the Englishman.

'My head feels like it is full of weeds,' he said.

'It's the medication. The doctor said you would feel better later in the day.'

'Who was that man?' Abdul asked.

There came the question but Tasneen did not think she could read anything untoward in it. 'I was stuck with him in the waiting room yesterday. He was waiting for his friend . . . He was very kind to offer you a job, don't you think?'

Despite feeling mentally sluggish, Abdul's interest had perked up at the mention of employment. Of the many things that had occupied his thoughts during the past few weeks the need to find a job had become the most important. He had many problems to deal with, real and psychological, but Tasneen had been right when she'd said that a job was the most important rehabilitation phase he had to aim for. He had not reacted positively when she'd first made the comment because he'd thought that she was just saying it for the sake of his morale. It had been hard enough getting a job when he'd had both hands.

'He did say translator, didn't he?' Abdul asked.

'Yes.'

That was certainly a job he could do with one hand. 'What does he do?'

'I didn't take a great interest, I'm afraid. I do remember him saying something about a newspaper. Yes, that was it. He works for an American newspaper.'

'I don't speak English as well as you,' Abdul said, looking for the negative aspects of Mallory's offer.

'You speak it well enough,' she said. 'And you can work on it while you're getting better. It will give you something to aim for.'

Tasneen was right, as usual. Abdul was already feeling better.

They arrived at her car and she unlocked the passenger door for him. He eased himself into the seat while she closed the door, walked around to the other side and climbed in beside him.

'Why don't we speak nothing but English for the next few days?' she suggested. 'Like we sometimes used to with Father. Remember? It won't take you long to get good at it again. Father said your accent was always better than mine. I don't know why we didn't think of a job like that for you before. There are so many jobs here for Iraqis who can speak English.'

Abdul leaned his head back and stared at the ceiling, wondering if he should get his hopes up.

Tasneen placed the key in the ignition and started the engine. 'He seemed like a very good person,' she said. 'That's the impression I got. What do you think? He was polite and well mannered. Not offensive as some of them can be. I feel he was sincere. Why else would he walk up to us like that? And he mentioned you being a former policeman. I told him, of course. He seemed very interested in that.'

Abdul looked over at her and Tasneen wondered if she could detect suspicion in his eyes. She was talking too much, especially about Mallory, selling him too hard. But Abdul smiled in a way that she had not seen in a long time. 'OK, my big sister,' he said with an affection she had not heard in his voice since before the war. 'We'll see what happens.'

'That's all we can do,' she said.

'Take me home,' he said tiredly, closing his eyes.

'Only if you say it in English.'

He opened his eyes and stared ahead in thought. 'Home, Jeeves,' he said.

Tasneen grinned. 'Yes, sir,' she said in an exaggerated American accent as she pulled out of the parking spot.

Kareem watched Tasneen and her brother drive away as he climbed in behind the wheel of his car. He was not sure if he should be disturbed or not by the little he had overheard or understood of Mallory's conversation with the couple. Kareem had told Mallory more than once that if ever another job opened up with the newspaper he could provide a good and trustworthy man. He started the engine and drove out of the parking lot. Kareem liked Mallory – a bit. As much as an Arab could like a white man who was his boss in his own country and who probably earned ten times as much money. All westerners were in Iraq to get what they could, to make as much money as possible and ultimately they did not give a damn about the Iraqi people. Kareem knew, or was very sure, that Mallory often held things back from him too, never revealing to him or Farris anything about the day's agenda until just before they were about to leave the hotel. That was because

Mallory didn't trust them. It was not difficult to work that out. Mallory suspected that Kareem or Farris would set him up or something. It never failed to amaze Kareem how stupid the Englishman was. If Kareem wanted to do him harm it would not be difficult. But like all Iraqis who hated the westerners in his country he needed them – for the moment, anyway – to put food on the table to feed his wife and four children. These were bad times but at least he had a job, and a well-paid one at that. What made it so much more difficult was that although he wished the westerners would go he feared for his family's future if they did. These were certainly troubled times.

Mallory opened the door of Stanza's hotel room, two doors away from his own. He stood back to let the man inside. Stanza struggled through the door into a short narrow corridor and examined the place that would be his home for the next two months. The first impression was of somewhere dark, musky and dreary. Immediately by the front door was a small bathroom, a toilet and bidet cubicle next to it. The soiled carpeted corridor led to a poky bedroom, its walls covered in tired grubby wallpaper with seams that either failed to meet or overlapped. It was sparsely furnished with a low double bed, a desk, a chair, and a long dresser with an old television set on it that had a wire coat-hanger for an antenna.

Stanza's bags were on the floor by a glass balcony door that was partly concealed by a drape whose quality matched that of the wallpaper.

Stanza hobbled on his crutches past the bed and pushed the drape aside to look through the balcony door at a view dominated by the Palestine Hotel across the road. Sadoon Street was to the right of it, the Tigris river to the left, the Green Zone beyond the river's far bank and the Jumhuriyah bridge in the distance.

'Tell me this is one of the best rooms in the house,' Stanza said.

'They're all pretty much the same,' Mallory said, shrugging. 'The hotel doesn't have a problem with you doing it up if you want.'

'I'll bet,' Stanza mumbled.

'Room service is limited. The food can sometimes be OK but we have a good supply of Ciproxin, Flagyl and Maxolon in case you get a bug. Chances are you'll need one of 'em before the month is out.'

Stanza looked at Mallory to see if he was serious but as usual there was nothing in his manner to suggest that he was not.

'I'll leave you to it, then,' Mallory said, stepping back to the door. 'I'll pop by later in the day and give you your contact numbers, emergency procedures, intel brief . . . stuff like that.'

'I'll probably be on my bed for the rest of the day after I've cleaned up,' Stanza said.

'That's a good idea. If you need me I'm on the end of my phone. If I'm not in my room I won't be far. Maybe down the gym later this evening . . . Don't forget to phone your editor,' Mallory added, pausing in the doorway to see Stanza staring at his bed. He wondered what the man was thinking. Mallory headed out of the room and was about to close the door when Stanza called after him.

'Bernie?'

Mallory held the door open and looked back in.

'Thanks. For yesterday. I appreciate what you did.'

Mallory shrugged. 'Just doing my job,' he said.

'Yeah, I know,' Stanza said. 'Thanks, anyway.'

Mallory left the room.

Stanza stared back down at the bed, wondering how best to get from the standing position to lying on it in the least painful way. The journey from the hospital bed to the hotel room had been excruciating – at times he'd thought he was going to pass out.

Stanza let the crutches fall onto the bed and leaned forward slowly. The stretching movement caused a bolt of white fire to shoot up his leg and he dropped onto the mattress like a sack of potatoes and remained in the same position until the pain became bearable. Then he rolled carefully on his back, an inch at a time, and eased himself towards the pillow until his ankles reached the edge of the mattress. He suddenly felt utterly drained, raised a hand to look at his watch and, after a quick calculation, decided it would be another four hours before Patterson arrived at the Milwaukee office. He wondered about the conversation he would have with his foreign editor. If Stanza wanted to stay in Iraq, which he had decided he did, he would have to play down the injury. He should have asked Mallory exactly what he'd told the office – but then, it didn't really matter. It was up to Stanza how he felt and what shape he was in. He would describe the incident as more of a shock than anything else and say that the wound was not as serious as they'd first thought, which was all true. He would emphasise that it would not affect his work and he'd claim that he'd be running around in a week as well as any other journalist in the country.

Stanza's mission in coming to Iraq, to claw back something of his career, remained unchanged and a mere bullet was not going to deter him. Looking at it from another perspective, his hell-raising introduction to Baghdad would make a powerful introduction to his first report. It could not have been better, really. As for the content of the rest of the article, that was going to be the hard part. Every journalist in the country was looking for that insightful piece that would get them talked about. The stories were out there. With all that was going on in this crazy place there *had* to be great stories. But they had to be found and he was going to need some luck. The shooting on the BIAP road had been luck of a kind and he didn't mean just because he'd survived it. He had been shot while in the noble pursuit of his duty to inform the ignorant and he would push on regardless, handicapped by pain, in pursuit of the truth.

He sighed. If only he believed that garbage he would be a better journalist. But Stanza's salvation lay not in trying to gain back the ground he had lost but in forgetting the past and forging himself a new reputation. He needed a rebirth. His past had not been forgotten by his bosses because he had not replaced it with anything better. He decided that he didn't need anything more for his first article. His arrival and the shooting on the BIAP road was it. 'I arrived.' A bit Dickens, perhaps, but that was the point entirely.

Stanza closed his eyes and tried to forget the rest of the world for the moment. He needed to heal and sleep was the key. But try as he might he could not break away from his pain or his problems and so he just lay there until exhaustion finally led him into unconsciousness.

Mallory left his room, walked along the landing and before reaching the lifts pushed through a heavy wooden door bearing an illustration of a stick man running from a flame down a flight of stairs. He continued along a short corridor to another door that led into a dank, poorly lit concrete stairwell that stretched out of sight above and below. The air was warm and smelled of cigarette smoke and urine. He jogged down the steps to the floor below and in through an open door. A short corridor led to another door which he pushed through and emerged onto a carpeted, palatial landing identical to the one above. He carried on past the lifts and towards the open door of a suite that had been converted into an office. As Mallory entered what had originally been the suite's bedroom a burst of cheering and clapping went up from the three white men already there, one seated behind a desk, the other two in comfortable low armchairs opposite.

''Ere 'e is!' declared Des, the sinewy large-eyed man

behind the desk who was wearing a broad grin. 'It's Bernie the bolt. Sit yersel' down, cherub. We 'ear yer dented yer new client five minutes after pickin' 'im op at the airport.'

Mallory sat down tiredly in the remaining empty seat and forced a smile while preparing himself to absorb the well-rehearsed abuse that he knew was about to come his way.

'Give 'im a chance, lads. Let's 'ear your version, Bernie,' Des said.

'Nothing much more than that, really,' Mallory sighed. 'Got whacked by PSDs on the BIAP.'

'Bad, is 'e?' asked Dunce, an ape of an ex-paratrooper from Cardiff who sat nearest the balcony window that was slightly open so he could blow cigarette smoke outside.

'He'll live,' Mallory said.

'What 'appened, then, laddy?' Des asked with his habitual interrogative expression, his unusual eyes slightly out of sync with each other. He was a salt-of-the-earth Northerner, mid-forties, very experienced on the private security circuit and former Royal Artillery, which was why he talked loudly all the time. 'Com' on, out wi' it. We 'eard that soon as the shootin' started you dragged the poor booger in front a' ye to save yersel'. That right?'

Every comment from Des was accompanied by grins and chuckles from the other two.

'PSD. Is that right?' Dunce asked.

'Yep,' Mallory said. 'Usual nonsense. Only this time they aimed inside the cab.'

'Foockers, ain't they?' Des said. 'Shoot back, did yer?' he asked, knowing it would have been suicide but he liked to wind anybody up in any way possible. 'Tell me yer put som rounds inter 'em . . . Ey, wait a minute. Yer grenade. You 'ad it out, didn't ye? Tell me yer did, lad, and all's forgiven.' It was one of those conversations that Mallory knew was pointless to take seriously in any way. Des had got the others in their usual giggly mood and was determined to have a laugh at Mallory's expense. Mallory had pretty much expected it on walking into the room but the truth was that he didn't mind it at all. In fact, there was something therapeutic about the way Brits gave each other stick, especially about their misfortunes. It appeared heartless to some, especially to foreigners, but not to Brits, especially those who had served in the military. It was character-testing – and a bloody good laff, of course.

''Ey. Harpic 'ere were shot at yesterday 'n all,' Des shouted. 'Client shat 'isself, din't 'e, Harpic?'

'Fuckin' right,' Harpic croaked in his Luton accent. Harpic was nicknamed after the well-known toilet-bowl-cleaning product because it claimed to 'clean round the bend' – which was how Harpic was often described.

'O' course,' Des went on, 'stupid bastard were drivin' down wrong foockin' lane towards a Yanky checkpoint int' t' GZ. Weren't yer, Harpic, yer daft bastard?'

'Fuckin' soljer waved me in 'at way, din' 'e?' Harpic said defensively, giving a sniff at the end of the sentence. 'Client shat 'imself, all right. 'E 'ad to wipe 'is arse with

230

a trauma dressin' while I went 'n 'ad a go at the wankers who shot at us.'

'I'd advise yer boss to keep a trauma dressin' strapped to 'is arse all the time, the way you drive roun Baghdad, yer mad bastard,' Des said. A hooting laugh came from Dunce.

There was a knock on the door and a rotund Iraqi stepped in, looking most apologetic for intruding on the group.

'Jamel, me ol' codger,' Des boomed. 'What yer want, lad? We're in top-level meetin' 'ere.'

'Hello, hello, hello,' Jamel said, a forced grin on his face. He was a stoutly built Iraqi who looked as if he had not missed many meals in his life. 'Sorry, Des,' he then said sombrely, the smile fading as he bowed his head, his right hand spread over his heart in a sign of deference. 'Please, I want pill,' he said.

'Pill? What's that, the morning-after pill?' Des said, then burst out laughing. 'You been fuckin' aroun' wi' Akmed again?'

Dunce was drawing on his cigarette and snorted so abruptly that mucus shot from his nose. He did his best to catch it as it ran down his chin.

Jamel forced a smile though he didn't have a clue what Des was talking about. 'I need pill, Des.' Jamel held his stomach with both hands while putting on a pained expression.

'For your fat?' Des asked. 'You know why yer fat, don't yer, Jamel? Yer mouth is bigger 'n yer arse' ole, that's why yer fat.'

Dunce snorted once again but this time held his nose.

Jamel grinned, again not knowing what Des was talking about. 'I'm going to toilet too much, Des. Give me pill, please.'

'Oh. Diarrhoea? Yer know why yer've got diarrhoea, don't yer? Same reason. Yer mouth is bigger 'n yer arse' ole. 'Ow long yer been shittin', then? 'Ow long on toilet?' Des said, pausing between each word.

'All today,' Jamel said.

'Well, if yer still shittin' by tonight, come see me and we'll stick a cork op yer arse, OK?'

Jamel maintained his smile, oblivious to Des's meaning, and nodded. 'Thank you, Des,' he said. 'Thank you.'

'Are all the cars filled op wi' benzine?' Des asked.

'Yes, Des. Yes,' Jamel insisted.

'I'm gonna check, you know I will,' Des said with a sudden serious look as if talking to a child. It was impossible to imagine Des with a natural expression.

'All cars full,' Jamel insisted.

'Spare tyres pomped up? You remember what happened on the way back from Basra last month and we 'ad a flat, don't yer? Put the spare on and it were flat too. Eh? Eh?'

'Very sorry, Des,' Jamel said, bowing slightly several times. 'Not happen again.'

'OK. There's a good lad. Shoot off now, then, and don't eat anythin' and we'll see yer later, all right?'

Jamel remained grinning at them, unsure what Des had said. Understanding Des was a common problem among the Iraqi staff, even those who could speak good English. In fact, they did not believe he was English at all and called him The Scottish.

'Jamel,' Des said with emphasis and Jamel gave him his fullest attention. 'Foock off and com back later, me ol' flower, OK?'

Jamel suddenly realised that the meeting was over and that he wasn't going to get his pill. 'Oh. Hello, hello,' he said as he took a step back towards the door. When Des nodded at him to indicate that he was going in the right direction, Jamel put his hand across his heart again and smiled and nodded, saying 'Hello, hello' to everyone as he backed out of the room.

Mallory had not been in Iraq very long before he'd noticed a flagrant misuse of the word 'hello' by most if not all the locals, especially those who could speak hardly any English at all. It was used in its correct form as a greeting but the same person might also use it as a reply to a query about their health and well-being and, most notably, it was often used in place of 'goodbye'. To the uninitiated it could prove highly confusing and irritatingly extend what would normally be a brief encounter.

'Good lad, is our Jamel,' Des said after the Iraqi had gone. 'Now, Bernie, me lad. You all right, are yer? Cuppa tea?'

'I thought you'd never ask,' Mallory said.

'Harpic. Get the lad a cuppa. 'E's 'ad 'ard day.'

'I'm off,' Dunce said, getting to his feet and moving his large frame between the desk and the chairs as he wiped his hands on his backside and followed Harpic. 'See you lads later,' he said as he left the room.

'See you at scoff,' Des yelled after him. Then he leaned back in his chair, grinning one of his classic grins, his eyes like golf balls and looking at Mallory. 'So. 'Ad a bit of a rough day, 'ave yer?' he asked.

'Not really,' Mallory said stretching out his own feet.

'Ow's the client? Aw right, is 'e?'

'He's fine. Took a round in the thigh. The event itself has probably left a deeper scar.'

'I'll bet,' Des said. 'Can't take gettin' shot, these boogers, eh? Make such a song and dance about it.'

Harpic walked in with four mugs of tea on a tray and put them on the desk. 'Where's Dunce?' he asked.

'Hidin' in t' top drawer of desk but 'e don't want to be disturbed,' Des said. 'E followed yer out, yer blind bastard . . . Now,' Des continued, suddenly serious and looking directly into Mallory's eyes. 'What's your plan for Fallujah?'

For a split second Mallory thought that Des meant Mallory's private plans until simple reason reminded him it was not possible for Des to know anything about them.

'Your man's not gonna be fit to get op there, is 'e?' Des said. ''Ave yer got any slots for the embed?'

'Everything's a bit up in the air at the moment,' Mallory said. 'Have you heard anything that might give a clue as to when the Yanks are going in?'

'Bush called me this mornin' but 'e tol' me not to tell anyone. O' course I don't foockin' know when they're goin' in, yer twat, but it's got to be sometime in the next few weeks. They 'aven't put ten thousand men and a couple 'undred tanks around the bloody town to keep wind out.'

Mallory took a sip of his tea while his mind buzzed

about Fallujah. He needed more information. He had decided that embedding with the troops was not the best option for him simply because he would not have the freedom to go anywhere alone. But then, his other choices were probably worse. If Stanza was fit enough in time to go Mallory would be stuck with him as well as with the US Marines.

'I'll be honest, Des, I don't know what we'll do. It depends on how my new guy's health stands at the time.'

'Yeah, I s'pose you're right. Bit soon, really, seein' as he was only shot yesterday.'

'What about yourself?' Mallory asked.

'What, Fallujah? One producer wants to go but 'er correspondent's crappin' 'isself at the thought. 'Ope they both don't want to go or I'll get mesel' in a tangle.'

Des was working as a consultant to a handful of small media outfits who had arrived in Iraq looking for inexpensive security coverage. That meant no full-time security but Des was available as a consultant and also as a body if needed – at extra cost. It was workable most of the time since all the low-rent set-ups usually wanted was advice on how to operate, occasional threat updates and a hand to hold if every-thing went wrong, such as the threatened civil war that had been rumoured for months. But if more than one media company wanted Des to take them out somewhere at the same time he had to do some juggling.

'Let me run somethin' by you,' Des said. 'If your

guy ain't able to make it, would you take one o' mine if needed?'

'How am I gonna do that? If my guy doesn't go I still have to be here for him.'

'I thought you were goin' 'ome soon,' Des said.

'Perhaps.'

'Why don't you let your relief com on in? But instead o' you goin' 'ome, you stay 'ere and 'elp me out. Same money you're gettin' now.'

Mallory was immediately attracted by the idea, its advantages being the let-up in pressure from the London office and an increase in his freedom of movement. Mallory could take Des's client to Fallujah, escort him to the embed rendezvous and then slip away. The client would be with half a dozen other media types as well as the Marines to look after him. It was a very possible plan.

'You know, Des, you might have something there,' Mallory said.

Des grinned.

'Why don't you keep me in the picture, let me know how things are developing and we'll see what we can do. But I like it,' Mallory said.

'I'll let you know soon as I do, me old chum,' Des said.

Mallory's phone rang in his pocket and he pulled it out to check the small screen. When he saw the name he sprang to life, put his mug down as he got to his feet and headed for the door. 'Got to grab this. See you later,' he said as he went out of the door and pressed the 'receive' button.

'Hello?' he said as he walked along the landing to put some distance between himself and the office. The line was bad, the signal jumping from weak to strong and back again. Mallory cursed the Iraqi phone network and called 'Hello' into the phone several times in case he could be heard even though he couldn't hear much himself. Then, as if his prayers had been answered, the line suddenly became clear and he heard the sweet voice that was music to his ears.

'Tasneen. How are you?' he asked.

'I'm fine,' she answered. Her voice sounded like a song of springtime.

'What's going on? To what do I owe the pleasure?' he asked.

'I wanted to tell you how sorry I was for not talking to you very much this morning,' she said.

'You don't need to. I understood perfectly. I'm not a complete idiot, you know.'

Tasneen laughed. 'I know that. You're not an idiot at all. But thank you for making how we met seem so normal to my brother. I know it *was* normal, but you know what I mean. You put it very nicely.'

Mallory was beaming because she sounded so friendly. 'Well . . . I'm sorry too that we didn't have time to talk. I didn't think I was going to see you again . . . You at work right now?'

'Yes. I got in a little while ago . . . I also want to thank you for something else.'

'This is my lucky day. What else did I do that I was not aware of?'

'Well . . . you made Abdul feel so much better. The

offer of a job. I don't know if you meant it or not but just by suggesting it you made him feel, well, useful, I suppose. Ever since you spoke with him he has been in the best mood I have seen him in since his injury. You can imagine that my brother does not feel on top of the world right now. He feels hopeless about his future. You made him feel better, that's all.'

Mallory's job idea had been a top-of-the-head ploy but as a means to see her again it was working like a charm. 'I wasn't joking,' Mallory said. He was the team's security adviser but he did have some influence with the general running of the bureau. The problem was, as always, a question of money but he was confident that he could figure something out.

'Then you were serious?' Tasneen asked, her voice hopeful. In fact, there was such a tone of excitement in her words that Mallory was suddenly struck by a pang of guilt at the possibility that he might not be able to deliver.

'His English is really quite good,' she went on. 'And it will be even better . . . When were you thinking of hiring him?'

Mallory struggled with his conscience. 'Why don't you give me a few days to work it out?' he said. 'I assumed he would need to fully recover first, anyway. Can Abdul read and write English as well as speak it?' Mallory asked.

'Not very well,' Tasneen said regretfully. 'Is that important?'

It would improve his chances, Mallory thought to

himself. And it was a way out if all went pear-shaped. 'I shouldn't think so.'

The line went suddenly bad and Mallory could not hear her. 'Say again,' he said loudly. 'You were cut off.'

'We should get together and talk about it,' she shouted. 'These phones are terrible.'

'How would we do that?' he asked.

'Don't you have a restaurant at the hotel?'

'Yes.'

'I'll come over for lunch.'

'Sounds perfect,' Mallory said. 'When?'

'I'll call you,' Tasneen said, her voice breaking up.

'OK,' Mallory said. But then the line went completely dead, a repetitive beep indicating that the signal had been lost.

Mallory thought about calling her back but decided against it and leaned on the landing rail to contemplate the brief conversation. It appeared that he was developing a social life of sorts, and all because Stanza had been shot. Fate was a strange beast, to be sure. Mallory was confident he could wangle a job for Abdul. The need for an interpreter was obvious since Kareem was not working out as originally hoped. It was the *Herald* being cheap again, trying to double up on jobs. From a security point of view it wasn't smart – but then, when did the media ever put security as a priority? After the event, was Mallory's immediate and damning answer to his own question. It could become problematic if the newspaper wanted to get rid of one of the drivers to make room for Abdul on the payroll, especially when Mallory explained that the young man only had one hand. It looked like it was going to depend on how easily Mallory could manipulate Stanza.

'There 'e goes,' Des said, leaning on the rail a few metres away and looking down into the lobby. 'See that guy there?' he said, pointing at the reception desk. 'The short-arse in t' black suit.'

Mallory made out a short, well-groomed man in a black suit talking with one of the hotel managers.

''Is name's Feisal,' Des said. 'Ali Feisal something or other. One o' the puppet deputies at the Ministry of Interior. You know what 'e does? Takes suitcases o' dollars out of Iraq and deposits 'em in banks in Dubai.'

Mallory took another look at the small man. 'How do you know that?'

'Mate o' mine works at Palace in the GZ, the one at US embassy. They 'ave a big room in t' basement filled wi' US dollars. Guarded by US soldiers. Loads o' money, so they say. Billions is what I've 'eard. The ministries get an allowance or summat like that. The Yanks keepin' 'em 'appy, I s'pose. Money belonged to Saddam anyway, so they say, or it's part o' the Yankee 'andout. Once a month 'e comes in to embassy wi' 'is suitcase which they fill op and 'e takes to airport . . . Good job if you can get it,' Des said.

Mallory watched the little man moving around energetically, pressing the flesh with several suited individuals as if he was of some importance.

'We never did it for money, did we?' Des said.

Mallory glanced at Des, wondering what he meant.

240

Des was a funny chap, unserious most of the time but prone to the occasional bout of philosophy.

'In the mob, I'm talkin' about. When we first joined op. We did it for love of it, di'n' we? An' it were great, wa'nt it? I remember me first wage. Fifty quid the army gave me for ma first two weeks. I di'n't think yer got paid till yer'd finished trainin'. Fifty quid. We were rich then, 'cause we weren't there fer the money . . . Different now, eh? That's all we're 'ere for, i'n't it? Money. We're all 'ere for that. We're no different than 'im.'

Mallory had to agree with Des, the part about his early days in the forces. He'd never thought about the money, not for a second.

'Good news, was it?' Des asked. 'The phone call. Yer looked 'appy.'

'Oh . . . Nah. Just work.'

Des nodded. 'I'll let you know about the Fallujah job, OK?'

'Roger that,' Mallory said as Des walked away and he headed along the corridor towards the emergency stairs. He would go to his room and watch a bit of TV, catch some news if it was worth watching, take some lunch, read a bit of a book and then visit the gym before dinner. He had some interesting prospects to think about: a meeting with the delightful Tasneen and possibly a move to Fallujah in the next week or so. There was some prepping to be done, mental as well as kit-wise. He needed to be able to move decisively and at short notice. All in all things seemed to be on the up and up.

7

A Life Reborn

Abdul popped a couple of painkillers and washed them down with a glass of water. He remained motionless at the sink for a moment until the worst of the throbbing went away.

He stared at his bandaged stump, as he often did, still unable to believe this horrible thing had happened to him. For days following the amputation he had been consumed not only by his own loss but by the horror of the other events of that night. The image of the woman being shot through the eye inches from him, followed by the brutal slaying of the old couple. The mental picture of the westerner being handed over to the insurgents, his pathetic, shivering obedience as he trotted off with them like a dog to the slaughter. Then there was the guilt for the part he himself had played in the kidnapping, intermingled with bouts of self-pity. Abdul would sometimes burst into tears, often without warning. It was worse still when it happened in front of Tasneen – such an unmanly thing to do.

Night-time brought a fresh intensity to the memories of the atrocities and Abdul slept little more than an hour before being awoken, usually by the voice of the woman declaring her love for the American just before the gun went off.

It was at the lowest point of one of those days that Abdul took hold of himself and reasoned that he could either be a victim of the memories or fight to escape the mental prison they threatened to keep him in.

Unsurprisingly, Allah became a great help and Abdul found comfort in the Koran, reading it for hours at a time, especially after being woken in the night by horrible dreams. When he got to the end of the book he started at the beginning again, always, to his joy, discovering something new or a subtly different interpretation in the wise pages. He began to feel his soul reaching out to Allah more and more and believed it would be only a matter of time before he, Abdul, made true spiritual contact with Him.

Abdul began to see Allah's influence in everything around him and decided that the job offer from the Englishman was a hand reaching down to guide him. There were things he needed to set right over the coming weeks and the word that cried out above all others was 'change'. He was going to have to become a different person than he had been so far in his life. The pathetic way he had acted since the amputation sickened him and the need to stand on his own two feet and let go of Tasneen's apron strings became paramount. The only way to achieve that was to leave her. It would be the most positive single event in his quest for development. She had always urged him to think for himself and forge his own way in life but then her very next action would be to treat him like a helpless little boy. And despite resenting her for it he had been content to allow it to continue. With Allah's help he was going to break free of these chains and the curse of the amputation and become the man he should be.

Abdul went into the living room, sat on the couch, reached for the remote control and turned on the television. The day's plan was to watch English-language programmes until Tasneen came home and then he would tell her he was ready to start work for the newspaper as soon as possible. As he flicked through the channels he paused at an Arabic news broadcast, the image on the screen suddenly turning him cold. It was poor-quality video footage of the man's face that he saw every night in his dreams, the face of the American he had helped kidnap. The man was sitting on a floor, wearing a one-piece orange overall, his hands tied in front of him while several hooded men holding guns stood behind and on either side of him. The commentator was explaining how the tape had recently been released on the Internet by a group calling itself the Holy Jihad Brigade and that they were demanding all American troops should withdraw from Fallujah within a week or the hostage would be executed.

Abdul was stunned to his very core. Having decided to look to the future by cleansing himself of the past he found that it was thrown right back in his face. And then, just as immediately, something became very clear to him. This was not a coincidence. He had been meant to see the footage. He did not know precisely what it meant but one thing he strongly suspected was that it was not over between him and the American.

Stanza swam easily to the shallow end of the Sheraton's outdoor swimming pool and took hold of the side, his breathing laboured. This was his fourth consecutive day of self-supervised physiotherapy and he was doing it days earlier than the doctor had recommended. But Stanza was anxious to get his leg back to a semblance of working order as soon as he could. His earlier belief that he could get almost as much work done in his room, relying on the Internet and talking to other people in the hotel, had turned out to be unrealistic. Patterson had shown a surprising degree of patience with the lack of substance in Stanza's reports so far but he would not put up with it for much longer. There was little chance of finding any story of substance while Stanza was immobilised in the hotel. His leg was still painful but not all of the time and was nowhere near as bad as it had been only a few days before.

He brought his legs beneath him into the standing position and gradually lowered himself, bending his legs at the knees. The dull throbbing around the wound was immediate but bearable until a sudden increase in pain forced him to straighten back up. Undeterred, he repeated the exercise several times and was pleased to note that the aching reduced slightly and he could bend a little lower each time. Worried that he might open the wound again if he overdid it Stanza called it a day, pushed himself out of the water and twisted his body so that he ended up seated on the edge of the pool. He winced as a sharp pain stabbed through him and he waited for it to ease, checking the wound that was still ugly and swollen with tiny scabs of blood around the stitches where they entered the skin. There was going to be a nasty scar but at least he had a good war story to go with it. There were not too many 'war correspondents' around who had a bullet wound.

Stanza eased himself onto his back, closed his eyes, gently extended his legs until they were flat on the hot concrete surface and let the sun, which felt immediately strong on his face, bake him dry. He felt tired and could have drifted off to sleep but forced himself to concentrate on a plan of action for the next few days. He was confident of soon being fit enough to make a trip to the convention centre in the Green Zone.

But there were some administrative and logistical problems that had to be taken care of, the first of which was his security adviser. When Stanza had told Mallory that he planned to go to the convention centre within a day or two the man had appeared unenthusiastic. Stanza had argued that all he had to do was walk a few metres from the drop-off point to the first checkpoint inside the Zone where he would be safe but Mallory had explained how he doubted Stanza's ability to move quickly enough in the event of a 'situation' developing on the way to or from the centre. Mallory's point was that if Stanza needed help getting away he would be putting the rest of the team in jeopardy.

Stanza still felt he had a valid case, though, and rested it on the argument that he had come to Iraq to do a job that he could not do from his hotel room and that Mallory was employed to find solutions, not create obstacles. To drive his point home he suggested that if it was Mallory's job to keep Stanza completely safe he should have kept him at the airport on his arrival and held him there for a couple of months. Mallory had no answer to this facetious reasoning and agreed wearily to take Stanza to the convention centre, a decision that heartened the journalist. He had wondered about Mallory's flexibility. Stanza had heard other journalists complain about their security advisers and how they could be complete pains in the backside. Stanza's philosophy was that he was in the risk business and therefore so too were his staff. It appeared that Mallory now understood that.

Another problem – and this was according to Mallory – was the team itself. It was going through something of a shake-up, with Farris the driver having lost his nerve somewhat: under pressure from his family, he was planning to relocate to Jordan. Rumours of civil war were rife and even Mallory, it seemed to Stanza, was not immune to them.

Mallory had come to Stanza's room on the journalist's first morning in the hotel and had presented him with a list of 'operational procedures', as he called them. They were in a typical military format, covering things that Stanza should and should not do, such as never leaving the hotel without informing Mallory and never making an appointment in the city without

247

getting every possible contact detail and location to enable Mallory to conduct a security-risk assessment. There was also a detailed equipment list of things that Stanza should carry with him at all times. This included his passport and sufficient money, a torch or flashlight with spare batteries, a phone with a list of emergency contact numbers and a map that Mallory provided that showed friendly and not so friendly locations, hospitals and notable bad areas. Mallory also provided an emergency evacuation plan several pages long, containing information on escape routes to Jordan, Turkey and Kuwait that Stanza had promised he would read but hadn't. There were also comprehensive health and hygiene tips. Mallory's 'briefing' had gone on for almost an hour, by which time Stanza felt as though he was on some kind of clandestine mission. He did ask, somewhat impudently, at the end of the briefing if Mallory was going to provide him with a Rolex that was really a tracking device. Mallory replied soberly that there were tracking devices on the market if Stanza really wanted one.

It wasn't as though Stanza thought that Mallory's concerns were pointless. On the contrary. But Stanza's view was that Mallory had his job to do, an important part of which was to make Stanza's life easier. Mallory's responsibilities included the general running of the bureau staff, ensuring they were trained in their respective tasks and that they maintained security standards at all times. But, according to Mallory, the team was apparently not as solid as it should have been. If Farris did quit, and that appeared to be his intention, they would need to hire another driver. When Stanza suggested that Mallory should ask Farris to make up his mind Mallory was against it, arguing that they needed to show the men some loyalty. These were trying times for Iraqis and Farris was under enough pressure from his family without any westerners adding to it. Stanza agreed to let Mallory handle it. Another question that Mallory had raised was the need for a translator. He explained that he had been told on arrival the *Herald*'s budget had originally made allowance for the post.

Stanza was interested. Anyone who could help him was welcome. As for the budget, it wasn't Stanza's money and he reckoned that if the allowance was there they should use it.

Stanza was struck by how keen Mallory was: he already had someone in mind for the job. However, Stanza did question Mallory's judgement when the recruit was described as a twenty-five-year old Sunni with limited experience of working with the media, who could not read or write English well despite being able to speak it adequately and, most bizarrely, had only one hand. Mallory defended each criticism as if prepared for it. The man was indeed young but he was a former police officer and therefore had a useful knowledge of the streets and would also be helpful if the police ever stopped them. It would also help if they were in pursuit of a story that required some assistance from that department. As for being a Sunni, the advantages were obvious when a story involved that particular religious persuasion. And as far as his disability was concerned the man was being hired as a translator and in Mallory's opinion one hand less would not affect this function.

Mallory's presentation of his discovery's case was so thorough that Stanza had little choice but to give the man a try. Still, after his security man's sincere thanks he got the distinct impression that he had done Mallory some sort of favour.

Stanza's mobile phone chirped beside him. He picked it up and hit the 'receive' button. 'Jake Stanza.'

'Jake? It's Henry.'

Stanza was instantly fully alert and would have sat bolt upright had it not been for the pain. 'Hi . . . ' Stanza stammered. Patterson had not introduced himself to Stanza as Henry since before the infamous incident. After that dreadful day Patterson had been unrelentingly rude to him, a constant reminder of his terminal dislike for the journalist who had almost ruined his precious paper's reputation.

'What are you doing?' Patterson asked without a hint of a barb in his tone.

Stanza struggled to gather his thoughts. This was his first conversation with Patterson since his injury, all previous communications having been with Patterson's assistant and mostly by e-mail.

'You there?' Patterson asked with a hint of irritation, sounding a bit more like his old self.

'Yes, sorry, I was just . . . '

'You been watching the news?' Patterson interrupted. 'I know you haven't been writing much of it – anything worth reading, that is.'

Stanza rolled his eyes. Whatever the reason for Patterson's initial civility, it had obviously passed. 'I . . . '

'Listen. What do you know about Jeffrey Lamont?'

Stanza felt that he knew the name from somewhere and as his silence became unbearable even to him it flashed into his head. 'Kidnapped a month or so ago. Worked for—'

'Shut up and get off this damned phone. The walls have ears over there. You at your computer?'

'No. I'm . . . '

'Get to your computer. I'll Skype.'

'I'm down in the lobby.'

'Then get your ass back to your room. Three minutes,' Patterson said. The phone went dead.

Stanza lowered the phone, wondering what on earth the man was so fired up about. He wanted to talk through Skype because it had high encryption, making it more secure than other communication systems.

Stanza moved as quickly as he could, gritting his teeth against the pain as he pushed himself to his feet. He pulled on his T-shirt and flip-flops, gathered up his things and shuffled into the hotel.

The pool entrance was on the mezzanine floor but for some reason known only to the hotel management the lifts did not stop there: it was a choice between walking up to the first floor or down to the lobby in order to call one. Stanza chose to employ gravity and, supporting himself heavily on the banister rail, hopped down the broad curving marble stairs to the ground floor as quickly as he could. He hobbled over to the

251

elevator bank and joined a short podgy man who was pushing the call button repeatedly as if his action might speed up the machinery.

'Goddamned elevators,' the man mumbled as he adjusted a thick pair of glasses on his nose to squint up at the floor indicators that sometimes told the truth about the lift's whereabouts.

Stanza checked the indicator on the elevator on the other side of the lobby to see that it was on the top floor, which was not unusual. KBR, a major general contractor, rented the top section of the hotel and it was their habit to jam one of the lifts on their floor so that they did not have to wait for one. It was a constant irritation to the rest of the guests but KBR was the nine-hundred-pound gorilla.

The man kept his finger on the button as he looked over his shoulder. 'Hey, Jack Stanza, right?'

Stanza looked down at the short man whom he did not recognise. 'Jake,' Stanza corrected him.

'Jake, right,' the man said, holding out his other hand. 'Aaron Blant, *Washington Post.*'

Stanza shook the hand, wondering if he had met the man before. There were several papers staying at the Sheraton and the *Post* was below on the fourth floor. 'Have we met?'

'No. I heard about you. The guy who got shot on his first day, right? How's the leg?' Blant asked, leaning around Stanza to take a look at it. 'Ouch,' he said as he saw the ugly scar.

'It's not so bad,' Stanza said.

'Looks pretty painful to me.'

'It's OK now.'

'You were pretty lucky,' Blant said. Something about his tone was beginning to annoy Stanza. 'Couple more inches towards the middle and you wouldn't have been laughing,' he said, grinning. Blant seemed to trivialise the incident in a way that made Stanza feel more like a loser than a hero.

'That's right,' Stanza said, looking up at the floor indicator that was on the move at last.

The lift arrived and Stanza imagined his computer ringing away while Patterson cursed his name. Blant stepped into the elevator and made a meal out of holding the doors open for Stanza as if he was a cripple.

'Which floor?'

'Fifth,' Stanza said, attempting to collect his thoughts, wishing he had some kind of bone to throw to his foreign editor. He'd been working on a couple of pieces, one about the closing of several local schools because of terrorist threats against the teachers and children and another about a suicide bomber whose device failed to detonate and who was now in jail. But frankly they were both crap and frustration welled up in him as he stared at the shattered plastic ceiling in search of divine help.

'Still painful, huh?' Blant said, watching him.

'What?' Stanza asked, wondering why the little jerk was still talking to him.

'You look like you're still in a lotta pain.'

Stanza sighed inwardly and chose to ignore him, hoping that his silence would be hint enough to make the guy shut up.

'What are you still doing in Baghdad?' Blant persisted, oblivious to Stanza's lack of interest. 'I'd have been on the first flight outta here as soon as I left the goddamned hospital.'

'Yeah. Maybe you're right,' Stanza said, wondering about Patterson's interest in Lamont and his need to go to a secure communication link. Stanza had read a couple of lines on the wires about the guy but there were so many kidnapped victims in captivity, a couple dozen of them American, and there was nothing about Lamont's story that made it more significant than the others.

Stanza looked down at Blant, who was wearing a shirt and tie under a sleeveless argyle pullover. 'Know anything about this Lamont guy who was kidnapped?' Stanza asked, suspecting that if there was anything unusual this little swot would probably be aware of it.

'Nothing new as far as I know. Kidnapped from the Karada district three or four weeks ago. You see him on TV? The vid's out already.'

Stanza was more out of touch than he thought. He should've known there was a terrorist video out on Lamont even if he had no interest in the man. It was his damned job to.

'Only a matter of time before he buys it,' Blant went on. 'You're with the *Herald*?'

'Uh huh.'

'I'd have thought you woulda been all over that story.'

'Why's that?' Stanza asked, suddenly afraid that he had missed more than just the video.

'Rumour has it he's a Wisconsin boy. Any truth to that?'

The lift came to an abrupt stop but Stanza might well have jolted with equal force if he'd been standing on firm ground. 'I . . . I don't know if that's true yet.'

'Well, you take it easy,' Blant said as the doors opened and he started to head out.

'You know anything else about him?' Stanza asked, hoping that he didn't appear as desperate as he sounded to himself.

Blant appeared to suspect something but then shrugged. 'Ain't much of a story,' he said. 'Rumour is he was seeing a local chick. She got blown away, maybe because she was a hooker.'

'I . . . I'd heard something about that,' Stanza said, grabbing the doors to keep them open.

'Maybe it was the girl's brother. You know how uptight these people get about one of their own screwing a westerner.' Blant smirked. 'Catch you later,' he said as he walked away.

Stanza let the doors close and the lift continued up to the next floor. He squeezed through the doors before they opened fully and hobbled, wincing, along the corridor towards his door.

As he entered his room he could hear the simulated standard phone tone coming from his computer speakers. He tossed his things onto the bed, sat at his desk and fumbled to pick up his headphones as a window on his computer monitor screen alerted him to the call from the *Herald*'s foreign desk.

He placed the headset over his ears and fumbled with the jack as he spun the mouse pointer around the screen in an effort to click the 'answer' button.

'Hello,' he said, adjusting the microphone in front of his mouth. 'Hello, hello,' he repeated, unable to hear anything.

'Where the hell have you been?' Patterson grumbled, his voice stretching like a rubber band as the Internet fought to convert the signal.

'Sorry, I—'

'I take it you're alone?'

'Yes.'

'OK. Jeffrey Lamont . . . '

'Yeah,' Stanza interrupted in an effort to show that he was up to date. 'Kidnapped in Karada. A Wisconsin boy. Was sleeping with—'

'So what did you do when you heard he was a local boy?' Patterson asked accusingly.

'I . . . I figured since he was sleeping with an Iraqi girl, she was killed because of that relationship and—'

'And you didn't try and find out what he was doing there, check out his *family*?' Patterson emphasised the last word.

Stanza suspected that Patterson would have made a perfect Gestapo officer. 'If Lamont was sleeping with an Iraqi girl in her house he was, well, frankly stupid. I didn't see any attractive angle in portraying a local guy who was so dumb . . . '

'Where are your goddamned instincts, Stanza?'

Stanza rubbed his forehead in frustration, wondering if Patterson hated just him or everyone.

'I was gonna give this story to one of our people here,' Patterson growled. 'But it's gotta come from Baghdad. And since none of my chicken-shit writers wanna go there it looks like it's gonna have to be you. I'll e-mail you what we have so far but I'll read you the meat of it. This is uncut from research. Jeffrey Lamont is a Milwaukee boy born and bred, but his name wasn't always Lamont. He went to St John's North-Western Military Academy in Delafield, Wisconsin, an all-boys boarding school and considered one of the best in the region: at St John's North-Western, young men learn that with discipline comes character. He ran away from the place twice, was caught and re-enrolled. From there he went to Harvard where he majored in film theory, experimented with psychedelic mushrooms, dropped out to piss off his folks and spent a couple of years burning through his trust fund on a beach in Indonesia. Between Harvard and Indonesia he had a row with his father who wanted him to join the family business. Jeffrey wanted nothing to do with it. Sounds like he finally grew up after Indonesia because he started his own communications business. But things didn't go well and he ended up working for an outfit based in San Francisco called Detron Communications. Six months ago, on his father's birthday, eight years after walking out on the family, he made contact with the old man again and it looked like they were going to patch things up . . . His real name is Stanmore . . . Jeffrey Stanmore.'

As Patterson said the name it dropped inside Stanza's head with a crash. 'Stanmore beer,' he said. It was one of the largest breweries in Milwaukee and was still owned and run by the old man – who was also an influential player on the state political scene.

'The man's a genius,' Patterson said sarcastically, referring to Stanza. 'Now. Why do we have this story before anyone else?'

Stanza could have come up with some theories but Patterson was clearly in a pugnacious mood.

'The *Herald*'s owner is a long-time friend of old man Stanmore,' Patterson went on immediately. 'But that's not why Stanmore called us in on this. You're probably already writing this – least, I *hope* you are – but this is no ordinary kidnapping story. We're talking about a son of Milwaukee, an estranged son, alienated from one of the most powerful figures in the state. We're talking about a father who wants his son back and is prepared to pay a lot of money for him. But it's also the mighty versus the merciless. Democracy versus Islam. When this story breaks we're gonna lead it for two reasons. One, because we're the *Herald* and we'd *better* damn well break it first with the advantage we have. And second, when other media get a hold of it there could be some muck-throwing: young Stanmore sleeping with an Iraqi girl, the enemy, a hooker, gone native, living in the danger zone, et cetera, et cetera. But by then we will have already put the story into perspective, something old man Stanmore is very keen on – and is willing to pay for. It's not just a story about the son, it's about the father too. A dynasty is gonna be exposed. The *Herald* is gonna tell the true story, Jake. It's a story about a young man lost in search of a dream of proving his worth to his father, putting his life on the line in a vile and ugly war in search of love, perhaps, love lost. That's what it is, Jake. It's a story about love and sacrifice . . . Do you hear what I'm saying?'

Stanza knew the smell of bullshit well enough. He was beginning to wonder if Patterson hated him not because of the quote he'd stolen but simply because he had been caught. He decided to play his boss a little, give him some more rope. It was a dangerous move, perhaps, but Stanza had home-field advantage. 'To be honest, I'm not sure if I do, exactly.'

But Patterson was nobody's fool and could read the likes of Stanza from a mile away. 'You know why I'm giving you this story, Jake?' Patterson asked rhetorically. 'You know why I don't hire a freelancer or order one of our people to get on a plane right now and fly into Baghdad to take over from you? It's partly because you are a good journalist, Jake. Good enough to get this job done. It's also because you need this if you still want a future in the news business . . . Jeffrey Stanmore was a passionate boy. I believe he loved that Iraqi girl and he was willing to put his life on the line for her . . . Jeffrey was a hero, a son of America . . . And that's only the first part of this story. This story is also going to propel you into the spotlight. It will end up a story as much about you as about Stanmore, and when I say you I mean the *Herald* . . . Jake, you're going to negotiate his release. The *Herald* is going to get young Stanmore back to his father. Jake Stanza, of the *Herald*, is going to reunite father and son. Do you hear me? You do this job right, Jake, and I'll hand your career back to you on a golden platter. Do you hear what I'm saying, Jake?'

Stanza could hear only too well.

'Jake?'

'Yeah,' he said.

'Am I right? Are you the man for this job?'

For one second Stanza had thought he'd had hold of the rod. But he was always the fish on the end of Patterson's line. Still, Patterson had something. He was right. This could be a big story. Huge, if played well, and Patterson and the *Herald* were behind it one hundred per cent. There wasn't a journalist alive who would pass this one up. It was showtime. 'I can do this,' Stanza said, his voice low and thoughtful.

'Does that pass for enthusiasm where you come from?'

'I couldn't be more enthusiastic. I'm already writing.'

'Good . . . We'll talk later, after you've read the file and thought about it.' The phone gave a click and the window on the monitor indicated that the caller had disconnected.

Stanza pushed himself to his feet, too quickly at first – stiffness was followed by a bolt of pain. He manoeuvred himself to his bed, lowered himself onto it, put his head on the pillow and shuffled his legs until he was in a straight line. Then he exhaled deeply.

Without having to think too hard Stanza could see the warning signs for the minefield ahead. Patterson – or, more to the point, Stanmore – knew what he wanted. The big question was how much the facts would support the current storyboard. Overall, the story was going to have to be a combination of perspective, timing and faith, with parallel strands of past and future narrative. The past was old man Stanmore and the Iraqi girl and would be defined by the struggle between love and worth. The future was the hostage negotiation and its final outcome, defined by a contest of life versus death.

Stanza was going to need help, that much was obvious. Mallory came to mind and Stanza wondered how much he should confide in his security adviser. To write this story Stanza was going to have to stretch beyond the boundaries he had expected to in Iraq and Mallory and his obsession with security would be more of a hindrance than a help.

But if Stanza got it right the rewards were beyond anything he could reasonably have hoped for. A smile formed on his lips, the first in a long time, as he closed his eyes and saw the hero's homecoming welcome that he would receive at the office.

8

Forbidden Fruit

Mallory stood at the last checkpoint before the hotel complex, looking with anticipation from his watch to the street beyond the barrier. Tasneen had sounded so happy to meet him for lunch that it had sparked in his imagination all kinds of daydreams about them together. He had even dared to speculate how he could get her out of Iraq and back to England. All this was absurd on many levels, he knew, especially considering how little he really knew her. On top of it all it was highly possible that he was misreading the signs – and the same could be said for her. Ostensibly, the reason for the forthcoming meeting was to discuss the employment of Tasneen's brother but Mallory's motives had little to do with the young man's qualifications for the job.

Abdul's suitability as a translator was worrying Mallory. Farris and Kareem were going to be annoyed, without doubt. They both had family members looking for employment and would see it as a personal insult that they had not been consulted. Then there was the whole Sunni–Shi'a thing, as well as Abdul's youth and his disability. Mallory wondered what the two drivers would think if they knew it was all because he wanted to get closer to Abdul's sister. That would probably freak them out. On the other hand, Mallory wondered why he cared at all since he was effectively quitting his job as soon as he left for Fallujah.

As Mallory looked again, hoping to see Tasneen's car appear, he saw her walking along the river road towards him. He had specifically told her to drive into the hotel complex, which was why he was waiting at the checkpoint, but the mere sight of her obliterated any criticisms. Her suit accentuated her slim, curvaceous body, while her lustrous dark hair bounced on her shoulders with each step and her face was even more beautiful than he remembered.

He ducked under the barrier and strode past the soldiers towards her. She beamed on seeing him. 'Where's your car?' he called out.

'I left it in the street,' Tasneen replied as she stopped in front of him. 'The Iraqi guards would not let me drive it in because I have no pass for this place. I showed them my Green Zone pass but they said this was not the Green Zone.'

Mallory looked in the direction of the outer barrier, considering whether or not to get her car for her.

'It will be all right,' she assured him, reading his thoughts.

Mallory's concerns were, as usual, alien to her. She would have found it bizarre if he'd told her he was worried someone might put a bomb under her vehicle. Security was all about mitigating risk. He decided to walk out with her after lunch and inspect the car before she drove it away. 'It's good to see you,' he said. 'Do you mind if I tell you that you're the most beautiful girl I have ever seen?' It was forward but he didn't care at that moment.

Tasneen looked away, clearly embarrassed, and then to Mallory's surprise she quickly recovered to look back at him and hold his gaze.

'Thanks for coming,' he said.

'Thanks for inviting me.'

They moved off side by side.

'Did you have any trouble getting off work?' he asked.

'They're used to me taking time off for my brother these days. That's what I told them – but in any case I was not lying, was I?'

Mallory guided her to the women's pedestrian entrance where a girl was waiting inside a small cubicle to search her. One of the soldiers gave a low whistle of approval, intended for Mallory to hear, as Tasneen exited the cubicle, closing her handbag. Mallory ignored him.

'It's so different now,' Tasneen said as they passed the Abrams tank under its awning beside the flying-carpet sculpture. 'I haven't been here since I attended a wedding a couple of years ago. You could drive all the way along the river between the bridges at that time.'

'Was it a nice city?'

'It used to be, yes. But I don't know anything else to compare it to. Maybe you would not have liked it.'

Mallory was not sure how to respond. 'You don't

wear a headscarf,' he commented, something he had wanted to ask her about when they'd first met.

'Iraqi Sunni women are generally less conservative than Shi'a women. Although these days most women in Iraq wear headscarves, since the war at least. I work in the Green Zone so I don't get much trouble from Iraqi men. I wear one when I go to the market.'

'Why since the war? I'd have thought you would have felt more liberated – if you'll excuse the word-play.'

Tasneen smiled, but with a polite expression of understanding. 'When there is no law and order the more extreme people have a louder voice,' she said. 'A woman must be more careful not to bring attention to herself.'

They walked up the steps to the Sheraton's entrance past a pair of smartly dressed security personnel who cheerfully bid him welcome. Tasneen avoided their stares as Mallory opened the glass doors and followed her into the foyer.

The restaurant was on the far side of the cavernous lobby beyond the elevators. A waiter greeted them and led them into the dining room. It was a large well-appointed room that gave the illusion of a level of service and cuisine that the current management could not actually provide. Only a handful of the dozen or so tables were occupied, despite the hotel being almost full. Most of the guests, nearly all westerners, opted for some degree of self-catering even if that meant nothing more than sending their staff out to collect food from local restaurants. The hotel food was expensive and monotonous, room service was abysmal and few guests had the time or inclination to eat in the dimly lit formality of the restaurant. But the hotel was still an acceptable place for Tasneen to dine in public with Mallory. Besides, there was nowhere else in the city that was considered safe for a westerner to openly enjoy a meal. The Green Zone was an option – one of the fast-food stalls outside the PX, maybe – but there was a good chance of meeting people either Tasneen or Mallory knew and Mallory wanted to keep their relationship, such as it was, a private affair.

They chose a table in a corner and the waiter left a couple of menus with them before attending to a group of Arab businessmen across the room.

An awkward atmosphere descended on the pair as they sat opposite one another.

'Would you choose for me?' Mallory asked. 'I've eaten here a couple of times but I've not been very adventurous . . . don't know the dishes.'

Tasneen flicked through the menu, studying the offerings. 'How about some lamb?' she asked.

'Sounds great,' he said. Ever since arriving in Iraq he'd eaten lamb kebabs until they were coming out of his ears and he feared the lack of choice was not limited to the hotel. He had not discovered much variety in Iraqi cuisine but he didn't know if that was because there really wasn't any or whether current poor supplies limited the choices.

Tasneen looked for the waiter but he appeared to

have left the room. 'Well,' she said, sighing. 'It's nice to be here. Thank you for inviting me.'

'I'm glad you could come . . . So. Abdul. How is he?'

'He's fine.'

'Good.'

'You still have a job for him?'

'Of course.'

She smiled. 'What is it you want him to do, exactly? He can do anything you need, I'm sure – except drive, of course. Although, knowing him, he will be driving before long.'

'We don't need a driver. We *do* need a translator and someone who knows the city.'

'That's perfect,' Tasneem said. 'He speaks English better today than he did last week and he knows the city very well.'

'Tell me something. It might be a small point – I don't know, and I'm sorry if it's the wrong thing to ask but – you'll forgive an ignorant foreigner, but – well, just to clarify. Abdul being Sunni: how would he feel about working with Shi'a? My two drivers are Shi'a, you see.'

'That's not a problem for Abdul. Westerners make a big thing out of the differences between Sunni and Shi'a. They mostly get along just fine. Like everything, it's the work of a handful of fools that makes life impossible for the rest.'

'I thought as much . . . just wanted to hear your view.'

'There's every religion in Baghdad, you know, even

267

some Jews, though not many of them now, I suppose. Christians live alongside Muslims where I live . . . Have you asked your drivers how they feel?'

'Not yet. I will. I doubt they'll have a problem.' And if they do, Mallory thought, he'd find a way of dealing with it. 'OK. That's the interview over with,' he said, sitting back with a grin.

'That's it?'

'He has the job if he wants it.'

'You didn't mention the pay.'

'Ah. Money. Yes. Would six hundred dollars a month be OK – to start with?'

'Six hundred,' she repeated, holding on to her surprise. 'I think he'd be happy with that.'

'He would be on probation at first. We have to consider the team.'

'Of course. You will be pleased with him, I'm very sure of that.'

The waiter arrived and asked Mallory in Arabic for their order. Mallory referred him to Tasneen who rattled off a reply and the waiter left them.

'I'm very happy, Bernie.' She was beaming. 'When do you want him to start?' This was something to which Mallory had not given much thought, indicating how little he had considered Abdul in this whole affair. 'When will he be fit for work?'

'He would like to start right away. He's well enough.'

Mallory nodded, his expression blank, and Tasneen suspected he was unconvinced. 'The pain has practically gone from his hand. He hardly ever takes a painkiller now. He needs to get out and do something. This job will be perfect for him and he will work very hard to please you. It will help heal his mind as well as his body.'

'OK. I'm sold,' Mallory said. 'Why don't you send him over tomorrow morning and we'll have a talk. He can meet the others and we'll take it from there.'

'That sounds perfect.' She leaned forward, despite no one else being close enough to hear. For one moment Mallory thought she wanted to kiss him and leaned forward himself. 'You are very kind, Bernie.'

'You make it easy for me,' he said, after she stopped what might as well have been a million miles short of kissing him. She did, however, hold his gaze for a few seconds and Mallory began to believe that Tasneen actually reciprocated the feelings he had for her. He had a sudden urge to say something to that effect but stopped himself, worried that it might ruin the moment. But even if he had shouted undying love for her at the top of his voice she would not have heard a word of it. Not at that moment . . .

A massive explosion blew in all the floor-to-ceiling plate-glass windows that made up two sides of the restaurant and the vast hotel building rocked to its very foundations. Walls and ceilings cracked, lights and cornices fell as the stark sounds of crashing and smashing took over from the initial thunderous boom. Mallory was blown off his seat and as he lay on the marble floor his brain fought to grasp what had happened. It felt as if he had been struck by a wall, dust filling his eyes and nostrils as he struggled to get his mind to refocus.

The thought of Tasneen came into Mallory's head like a detonation and he scrambled to his knees. She was not in her chair and he ducked beneath the table to see her pushing herself up onto her hands and knees. He got to his feet, hurried around the table, grabbed her up and pulled her over to one of several robust pillars supporting the ceiling. His first fear was of structural collapse but as the seconds passed and the building stayed up his next concern was another blast. The hotel had been attacked by rockets or mortars three times since his arrival although none of the previous assaults had been as bad as this.

Tasneen was slightly concussed and did not resist Mallory's protective grasp, although even had she wanted to she would have been unable since he was holding her so tightly to him. The waiter was standing in the centre of the room as if catatonic, his face bloody, his mouth agape as he looked up at the ceiling. Mallory followed his gaze to see the elaborate central chandelier swaying dangerously. A couple who had been at a table by the windows were on the floor, both of them covered in blood and glass. Mallory thought the explosion was down to a car bomb in the street or a mortar, or a walking suicide bomber just outside the restaurant. There had been rumours for weeks now that a member of staff had smuggled explosives into the hotel, a small amount at a time. But in a city that experienced dozens of explosions a day and where rumours of all kinds abounded the general feeling that one could get caught out anywhere at any time tended to offset such threats. It was all up to God and westerners used the word 'inshalla' as much as did the Arabs.

There was a sudden loud whooshing sound as if an aircraft had flown past outside and Mallory held Tasneen even tighter against the pillar. A second later there was a loud boom that sounded close but not close enough to do the hotel any more damage. Mallory decided that it had been a rocket since mortars tended to drop silently or with a whistling sound and, just as he said this loud enough for Tasneen to hear, yet another rocket slammed into the hotel with a force equal to that of the first. A shock wave followed, blasting in through the gap where the window had been and spending its great force against the opposite wall in the restaurant. A wooden dresser was tossed aside, its china contents shattering. Tables blew over and something struck Mallory's back but without harming him. He pulled Tasneen's head against his chest and she held on to him tightly as something heavy struck the floor close by. As the shock wave dissipated the sound of automatic gunfire could be heard over the noise of breaking glass and falling debris.

Mallory's eyes widened as he looked up, his ears straining to gather vital information. Another long burst followed by an answering volley of single shots, indicating that a firefight was taking place. When it came to explosions the best thing to do was get to cover and wait it out. But flying bullets required a different reaction. Another circulating rumour concerned the threat of an assault from the Mardi Army, a Shi'a militia occupying Sada City barely a mile west of the hotel complex. It was generally considered suicide to attempt, bearing in mind the amount of western firepower in and around the hotel but on reflection a suicide attack could not be overlooked. There were thirty or forty US troops stationed in the Sheraton and Palestine hotels plus a hundred or so western PSDs. If the Mardi Army attacked with all its estimated eight-hundred-strong force it would find it costly to take even a section of the grounds and would then find it impossible to hold on to for long. But the rebels were not to be under-estimated: they had attacked hotels and coalition camps in the past, beginning the assaults with various explosive devices such as mortars before pressing the attack with infantry. They had failed to penetrate even the perimeters in every case but that had not appeared to deter them.

Mallory pulled his pistol from his pouch as the rattle of gunfire intensified as more weapons joined the fray. He ignored the moaning injured around him and held Tasneen at his side as he headed towards the restaurant entrance. They passed through the small opening into the lobby where gunfire echoed inside the cavernous hall and, their feet crunching on broken glass, kept close to the walls, avoiding the central area that was exposed to debris falling from the domed ceiling. A couple of hotel staff ran across the lobby shouting something and several US soldiers clutching M4 rifles hurried down the curving stairs from the mezzanine above towards the entrance while pulling on their flak jackets and helmets. One of them tripped and sprawled across the marble floor but a colleague quickly dragged him to his feet and they sprinted on outside together. Broken glass was everywhere, lying on the white marble floor like crystals. A fine dust filled the air along with flakes of black and grey ash from a fire somewhere. Most of the massive sheets of plate glass forming the exterior walls of the lobby had shattered. Mallory was heading for an emergency exit that led to the basement, which he had decided was their best choice. Had he been alone he would have looked for a way to join the fight but Tasneen was his greatest concern now.

The main source of the gunfire seemed to be near the Firdous Mosque on the other side of the round-about below his room. A loud burst from a heavy machine gun came from a floor above and Mallory suspected that it was return fire from the US troops who had a firing position on the sixth floor.

Mallory suddenly wondered if the basement was such a good choice after all. If an assault managed to penetrate the lobby he could get cornered down there. On the other hand, if he went above ground level it could prove disastrous if there was a fire. But he was going to have to make a choice.

Des ran in through the main entrance, holding an AK47 and wearing his chest harness of multiple pouches containing spare magazines and a couple of grenades. Only a trusted few knew about the grenades as they were shunned by the US military.

'Des!' Mallory called out.

Des glanced in Mallory's direction and changed course towards him. 'Ee, this is fun, ain't it, lad?' He skidded to

273

a halt beside them. 'You all right, flower?' His eyes were moving faster and bulging even more than usual.

'Any idea what's going on?'

'It's a battle, me lad,' Des said, grinning with his usual flippancy.

'I gathered that. Is it an assault on the hotel?'

Nah. Doubt it. They're not that stupid. Doing a bit of rescuing, are we?' Des eyed Tasneen with a grin. 'Any left?'

A loud burst of gunfire from above startled all of them.

'Des. What's going on?' Mallory asked trying to be patient.

'Rockets, me old sausage. Little bastards drove a truck alongside t' mosque and fired a bonch o' the boogers. One 'it the first floor, the other somewhere near it. Another went into the park just over the blast walls. A palm tree caught fire out front but there might be another burner on t' first floor.'

'So who's firing at who?'

'Don't know. Could be comin' from the block o' flats opposite. US lads on t' sixth-floor roof opened op on the launch platform and it sounds like some was returned. I wouldn't go out there, though. Yanks are shooting at anything that moves. I'm gonna go check on my clients, make sure none 'ave wet 'emsels. See you later. Nice to meet yer,' Des called out to Tasneen, grinning widely, before he hurried away.

Mallory checked Tasneen who was still frightened but was staying in control of her emotions. 'You OK?' he asked, making sure.

She nodded. 'I'm OK. What are we doing?'

Good question, Mallory felt like saying. 'We can't hang about here or go outside. Only one place, really. Come on,' he said, taking her by the hand.

He led her past the lifts, up the broad stairs to the mezzanine and into the emergency stairwell. The main lights had failed but the emergency lighting was just about adequate, although not on every floor. The gunfire outside sounded amplified in the bare, concrete, windowless stairwell as they trotted up. By the time they reached the fifth floor both of them were breathing heavily. Tasneen paused to catch her breath while Mallory went through the first fire door and along the corridor to the next that led onto the landing. The smoke was immediately thicker and he went to the rail to look down into the lobby. Hotel staff members were hurriedly attempting to organise a fire hose, although Mallory could not see where the fire was.

'Come on,' Mallory called. Tasneen responded and they moved off along the landing. He paused outside his room to dig the key out of his pocket and check below once again. The fire team had managed to divide into two groups, one at either end of the hose as they dragged it across the lobby. But on reaching the fountain the groups moved either side of it and an argument began over which one should take the lead. Mallory shook his head as he found the key and opened his door.

Tasneen followed him inside. He closed the door and went directly to the balcony windows, pausing before opening them. 'Stay back,' he warned.

Tasneen stayed in the narrow hallway. 'Should you go out there?' she asked as Mallory slid open the glass door.

'I'll only be a second.' He inched carefully through the gap, keeping low. The firing had stopped and there was shouting from the street below. He leaned forward until the mosque came into view. Men were running, a pick-up truck parked at an awkward angle across the road was on fire, its doors open, and beyond it were two cars that had been hastily abandoned. A body lay on the road between them. American soldiers came into view, moving stealthily across the roundabout towards the mosque. Others were inspecting more bodies further up the street. Smoke was drifting directly across the front of Mallory's balcony and he looked over the rail to see the top of one of the hotel's palm trees on fire and more smoke coming from inside the hotel directly behind it. Mallory assumed it was the impact point of one of the rockets.

He stepped back into the room. 'It's OK. I think it's over.'

Tasneen did not appear relieved by the news.

'I need to check on my people,' Mallory said, heading for the door. 'Stay until I get back and then we'll get you out of here, OK?'

She nodded.

'You sure you're all right?' he asked.

'I will be,' she said, forcing a smile with difficulty.

'There's a fire downstairs. I think it's only a small one. If it gets any worse I'll be straight back.'

Tasneen nodded again.

'See you in a bit, then,' Mallory said as he opened the door.

'Oh, Bernie,' she whispered. 'My handbag.'

'I'll find it,' he said before closing the door behind him.

A few metres along the landing he knocked on a door. 'Stanza?' he called out. 'Stanza!'

A moment later the door was hurriedly unlocked and opened. Stanza stood in the doorway, looking visibly worried.

'You OK?'

'Yes. What's happened? Are we being attacked? Is there a fire?' Stanza didn't wait for a reply and limped back to his open balcony. 'There's a lot of activity outside.'

'I'd be careful about showing yourself. There'll be some itchy trigger fingers out there.'

Stanza ducked back and then decided to vacate the balcony entirely and close the door.

'As far as I can tell it's all over,' Mallory said. 'There might be a fire risk. I'd have your things packed and ready to go, just in case.'

'Right,' Stanza said as he hobbled to his wardrobe and pulled out his holdall.

Mallory decided the man would move quickly enough if necessary and went back to the door. 'Stay here until I get back. You've got food and water for the night?'

'Yes,' Stanza said without looking up at him as he emptied the contents of one shelf into the bag and went to another. 'Let me know as soon as you hear anything.'

'You'll be the first to know.' Mallory closed the door behind him and a quick check over the rails revealed the abandoned fire hose around the base of the fountain. The smoke was still thick and began to irritate the back of Mallory's throat. He decided to see if Des had found out anything more about the attack. It might also be prudent to head over to the Palestine Hotel and book a couple of rooms in case they had to vacate the Sheraton.

An hour later Mallory was back on the fifth floor outside his room with his key in one hand and Tasneen's handbag in the other. He was concerned about a bit of information he had received and how Tasneen might react to it. He had spent fifteen minutes with a US Army captain who had given him the low-down on what had happened and the plans for the hotel's immediate future. It turned out that six or seven insurgents had been involved in the rocket attack. Four of them had been killed as they'd tried to drive away while the rest had escaped on foot through a block of flats on the other side of Sadoon Street. The fires had been put out and although there had been several injuries only one of them had been serious and no one from the hotel complex had died. Des had placed a sign on his office door that read '4–0' with a footnote reminding everyone not to be complacent since we had enjoyed home-field advantage.

Mallory informed Stanza that all was well, after which the man immediately focused on his work – which seemed odd after his previous two weeks of complete inactivity. The journalist launched into a not entirely coherent listing of requirements that he claimed needed taking care of right away. It included the hiring of a fixer or a city guide. Mallory was anxious to get back to Tasneen and agreed with everything Stanza said. He finally extricated himself with a lie that the army was waiting to see him on a security issue. Stanza let him go but not without getting an assurance that they could hit the road first thing the next day.

Mallory put his key in the lock and tapped the door lightly as he pushed it open. Tasneen was looking out at the city through the closed balcony windows and faced Mallory as he came into the room.

'Is everything OK?' she asked.

'Kind of,' he said, holding up her handbag for her to see. 'At least the fire's out . . . There's just one small problem: the Americans have put the hotel complex on full lockdown.'

A look of horror spread across her face. Tasneen knew from working in the Green Zone what full lockdown meant. 'Full?' she asked, hoping he had exaggerated that part of it.

'Nothing in or out of the complex until further notice. They've done it before and, trust me, they mean it.'

'How long for?'

'I'm going to call them every hour but – well, they said at least until dawn.' Mallory screwed his face up a little as he said the last word, aware of the implications, or at least the more obvious ones.

Tasneen sat down heavily on the edge of the bed,

an expression of utter disbelief on her face. 'I can't stay here until night-time, even.' She looked up at him, hope in her eyes.

'I don't know what to say . . . I tried to get you a room but there aren't any.'

She began shaking her head even before he had finished. 'It doesn't make any difference. I can't stay here, Bernie. Not even in the hotel. You don't understand.'

'I do,' he said coming closer and sitting on the bed.

'No, you don't. This is Iraq. I am a Muslim girl.'

'I know, I know, but there isn't anything we can do. If we went down to the checkpoint to try and force them to let you out it would only draw more attention to you when they refuse – which I know they will. Right now no one knows you're in here. If you walk outside you won't be able to come back in because you'll be seen. You can't stay in the lobby. It's a mess and they've already begun clearing it up. It's open air down there and the furniture is all stacked up.'

The gravity of the implications of all this was almost too much for Tasneen to bear.

'Listen to my plan,' Mallory urged. 'As I said, no one knows you're in here. No one. You stay until you can go, in a few hours or even at dawn. You can sneak along the corridor to the emergency stairs and by the time you appear in the lobby no one'll know where you stayed. That's not so bad, is it? Huh?'

Tasneen pondered it all until she came to accept that there were no alternatives. Mallory's plan had made her feel a little better, at least the part about no one knowing where she was. But there was one glaring problem with it.

'Why don't I leave you alone?' Mallory said, getting to his feet. 'I'll come back when it's OK for you to leave.'

'Where are you going?'

'I might be able to use a friend's room.'

'And what will you say if he asks why you can't use your own room?'

'I'll think of something.'

'What if someone comes looking for you?'

'No one's going to come into the room,' Mallory assured her.

'But the hotel staff have the key. They might come in.'

Mallory suddenly wanted to take her in his arms, hold her close and assure her that everything would be all right. 'What is it you are specifically worried about? I understand the reputation thing and all that, especially with a westerner.'

'It's my brother. He will be worried and he'll want to know where I am.'

'You can't tell him?' Mallory said, making it sound like a question although he meant it as a statement.

'Of course not.'

'Then tell him you're staying with a girlfriend.'

Tasneen shook her head. 'He will want to know who and why and . . . Abdul can be very protective.'

'There's a saying that if you want to hide the truth stay as close to it as possible.'

She did not understand.

'Tell him the truth so far, that you were at the hotel seeing the *Herald* about his job. Then the hotel got hit and you had to stay – but in your own room, of course. That would be the only lie.'

'But what if he comes to find me?'

'He can't get in,' Mallory reminded her.

'He can be very persistent.'

'Not as obstinate as the Yanks. Trust me on this. He's not getting through those checkpoints. A lockdown is a lockdown with these guys and there are no exceptions. Plus he's an Iraqi. I'm sorry but you know what I mean. If he tried too hard the Americans would arrest him.'

Tasneen knew he was right.

Mallory could see her relax slightly, although her expression remained pensive.

She pulled her phone from a pocket, selected a number, pressed the call button and pushed it under her hair to her ear.

'Go to the window,' Mallory said quietly. 'Better reception.'

She got off the bed and went to the window. 'Abdul,' she began and then after he answered rattled off in Arabic. The conversation went back and forth for a while before it ended abruptly. Tasneen looked up at Mallory and then smiled slightly. 'I think he's happy with the story. I emphasised the job. I told him he could start tomorrow. Is that OK?'

'I think that's what we agreed just before the restaurant blew up. Which reminds me. You must be starved.'

'I'm not really—' Tasneen began.

'I've been through this with you before. The last time you said you weren't hungry you embarrassed me by getting the server to pile so much food onto your plate that I had to do the same.'

She grinned and her face lit up.

'I know somewhere I can scrounge a meal,' Mallory said, going to the door. 'I'll check on a few things, see if the checkpoint is going to remain closed. Be back in a while.'

When Mallory left the room Tasneen lowered her head as her thoughts remained on her predicament. She did not regret coming to see Mallory, although she could have done without this situation. If it all turned out OK then securing the job for Abdul would have been worth it.

She felt that her feelings of attraction towards Mallory had increased. He had acted well during the bombing and had protected her. He was so easy to be with and he amused her. But there was something else which she was not sure ought to continue. She had taken to daydreaming again, fantasising about being in different places in the world, but now she was not always alone. Bernie was often there and what surprised her was her willingness to become involved with him, something she had never contemplated with anyone else.

The dangers were obvious but at the same time she felt safe with Bernie. He would not pressure her. It could remain just a fantasy. He had implied that he'd be in Iraq for a while, although she understood that he would have to go home occasionally. But Abdul could never know there was anything between them, even though it was only a game. In the Islamic faith only the man could marry outside his religion – a family's religion was dictated by the male, not the female.

Life was a never-ending series of complications. Tasneen sighed and went back to the window to look out over the city. It was a long time since she'd had such a view of Baghdad. Her heart began to ache for its people and she wondered when they would ever see peace again.

Mallory was back within an hour, carrying a trayful of several plates covered in foil. He'd appropriated the food from Des who, it had to be said, was a generous man. Unsurprisingly, Des had a contact in KBR's kitchen upstairs. As Mallory was leaving the office Des had made a joke about wanting to see the video. Mallory ignored it but was concerned that Des even suspected that Tasneen was with him. It might be worth having a word with him just in case he added it to his repertoire.

They began the meal in silence but after Tasneen asked Mallory what countries he had been to they embarked on a lengthy discussion that included politics, food, fashion and music as well as geography. Before long they had forgotten the brutal conflict outside the room except when a distant explosion or rattle of gunfire interrupted them. But they were determined to keep their thoughts elsewhere.

It was the looming prospect of bedtime that eventually stilled the conversation. Mallory took the initiative by tossing a pillow on the floor, lying down on the carpet and announcing that the spot would suit him perfectly. Tasneen removed her shoes and stretched out on top of the bed. They were out of sight of each other but continued talking until Tasneen quite matter-of-factly said that he could join her if he wanted to. He insisted he was fine. When she said he could stay on the floor if he wanted but said again that she did not mind him being on the bed he changed his mind lest the invitation should not be repeated. He placed his pillow on the bed and lay beside her but left a respectable gap between them.

Mallory had no illusions that the invitation was anything more than a friendly gesture but her close proximity set his imagination going and he fought to control it. They talked for a while longer and then Tasneen rolled onto her side. Mallory glanced over to see that she was facing him. He decided to remain on his back. This was not the time or the place to become intimate with her. Taking advantage of her predicament in such a way would be wholly un-scrupulous. If she became frightened she would be trapped and Mallory could not bear the thought of her being in the room with him and not wanting to be. This was far more than he had expected and it was satisfying enough. They eventually drifted off to sleep, although he remained aware of her presence throughout the night. At one point she turned over and brought her knees up to her chest and Mallory looked at her, feasting his gaze on the heart-like shape of her bottom and wondering what it would be like to caress it with his hands and, better still, feel it pressed tightly against him. He eventually rolled away to ease the feelings of desire and it was not long before dawn reached for the balcony windows and Mallory sat up and went to look at the city. It was Baghdad's most beautiful time of day. The minaret of the Firdous Mosque came to life, its speakers crackling before a voice called for morning prayers. Mallory dialled a number on his cellphone. When the call was answered Mallory asked about the state of the lockdown, closed the phone and went back to the bed to look at Tasneen. She did not stir but as he moved a strand of hair from her face she rolled onto her back with a sigh and opened her eyes. She sat up, startled as she focused on the unfamiliar surroundings but relaxed on seeing Mallory, remembering where she was.

'Good morning,' he said. 'Sleep well?'

'Thank you,' she said as she slid off the bed and stood up.

Mallory watched her find her shoes and pull them on.

'They just opened the checkpoint . . . I shouldn't come down with you,' he said as she pulled on her jacket.

'I can find my way out.'

'Take the fire escape down to the mezzanine floor. It's written on the door in the stairwell.'

'I'll find it,' Tasneen said as she picked up her handbag and checked that she had everything.

Mallory followed her to the door, unlocked it and paused before opening it. 'Maybe one day we can look back and be amused by all this . . . I enjoyed you being here.'

When she looked up at him he could not read her expression. 'I think I will say that I enjoyed it too,' she said. He felt relieved and was suddenly bursting to hold her and kiss her lips. If there had been an invitation in her eyes he would have. He wanted to ask when he might see her again but it seemed pointless. He would let fate play the next hand. 'Wait,' he said as he moved around her to open the door enough to look out onto the landing. 'Mind how you go. Drive carefully,' he said.

Tasneen moved past him in the confined space, her breasts touching his chest, her smell filling his head. Seconds later she was gone and only then did Mallory remember that he'd intended to check her car for bombs. He doubted whether anyone would target her but, as he always told himself, that was not the point. He would have to let it slide this time, though.

Mallory took a look in all directions for prying eyes before closing the door. But he was too far from the edge of the landing to see down onto the third-floor walkway where an Iraqi security guard was leaning on the rails, smoking a cigarette. The man could see the top of Mallory's door from his position and since its opening and closing was the only movement at that early hour it caught his attention. Then he saw the moving head of a woman who was walking along the landing and a moment later she passed through the lobby and out of the hotel.

9

The Team Deploys

Mallory climbed out of the shower and towelled himself dry as he went through the list of things he had to do that day. First he had to contact the office in London and tell them to give his relief the go-ahead to move to Baghdad. Next he needed to inform Des that he would be available to accompany his client to Fallujah – although Mallory was still unsure if that was the best way to proceed. But he had extracted all the pleasure he could from daydreaming about Tasneen and the million dollars and it was time to turn some at least of the fantasy into reality.

There was a knock on the door and he checked his watch. It was ten past seven. Too early for the drivers. The knock came again.

'Who is it?' he called out, standing to one side of the door out of habit. No one to his knowledge had been shot through a door but it was the sort of thing that went through his mind on such occasions.

'It's Stanza.'

'One second.' Mallory went back into his room and pulled on a pair of trousers and a T-shirt, wondering if something was up. Stanza had never called on him this early before. When he opened the door Stanza was standing there, dressed as if ready to go out.

'What time are the men coming in?' Stanza asked.

'I told them to be in at nine.'

'Nine,' Stanza repeated, making a calculation.

'I still don't know about Farris.'

'When will you know?'

'If he turns up then I'll know.'

'This is not gonna work out like this, is it?' Stanza said testily.

Mallory sighed inwardly, wondering when Stanza was going to get the message regarding local staff.

'We need to get together to discuss a plan of operation,' Stanza said. 'We have things to do, places to go, people to see and I need reliable drivers and a guide. I'm sorry, Mallory, but that's your job and it's not going very well.'

Mallory decided that Stanza had a flea up his backside about something. Having started the day in such a good mood he would not allow the little knob to wind him up. 'Give it until nine. By then we'll know about the drivers and we should also have a fixer.'

'A fixer? Who?'

'I told you.'

'Oh. The one-armed guy.' Stanza had left a message about finding a fixer with Blant from the *Post* but he had not received a reply yet. His confidence in Mallory's guy had eroded from the moment he'd agreed to meet him. 'I have some feelers out for a fixer myself. I'll also look for a driver. We'll talk at nine, then,' Stanza said, turning on his heel.

Mallory closed his door and took a moment to calm the anger that was threatening to ruin his morning. The twat had managed to wind him up with his final comment about looking for a driver and fixer himself. Stanza was beginning to show his true colours: he was either a real bastard or he was trying to bully Mallory in particular. If Stanza kept on like this Mallory would simply tell him to shove his job. But that would mean letting Tasneen's brother down, which would not help his cause with her.

He took out his mobile phone and scrolled through the numbers. Stanza was right to a certain extent, though. The team had slipped a notch and that was Mallory's responsibility. In truth it wasn't of huge importance to him but he had standards to maintain.

'Kareem. It's Mallory. Are you coming in this morning at nine? Nine o'clock . . . Good. What about Farris? OK. See you here at nine. Be a little earlier if you can. Bye.'

Farris was apparently on his way in but seeing was believing. Mallory's next call was to Tasneen who was very cheery when she answered the phone. She asked him to hold on while she moved to somewhere more private in her apartment. She had made it home without a hitch to find Abdul asleep on the couch and when he woke up he'd been relieved to see her. He had been visibly excited about starting work that morning and she intended to drop him off at the hotel on her way to work. When Mallory asked if she planned to drop him off and pick him up on a regular basis she said no but since this was his first day she would make an exception. In future Abdul would use the taxi service which was reliable enough. Mallory made a mental note to instruct Kareem to drive Abdul into work and back home when practical. Mallory eventually said goodbye to Tasneen after they agreed to discuss Abdul's first day at the end of it.

At a quarter to nine Mallory stepped out of his room and looked down into the lobby. The wind blew unchecked through the hotel but apart from the missing windows everything looked in place. If there was one thing the Iraqis could do efficiently it was clean up immediately after a bomb.

Kareem and Farris stepped out of the emergency stairwell – the lifts were still out of order – and walked towards him, both lighting up cigarettes even though they were out of breath. It was at times like this that the KBR staff suffered through living at the top of the building, particularly their grossly overweight members – of whom there were many. But because of their selfish antics with the lifts no one had any sympathy for them. Des, of course, had been quick to react by posting a sign in the emergency stairwell on his floor that was aimed at KBR staff. It announced: 'Only 16 more floors to go, you fat bastards.'

Farris looked sheepish as he greeted Mallory but said nothing about his future intentions. Mallory chose not to ask. If Farris wanted to leave the country it would be a problem for Mallory's relief. Some media organisations were easier-going and local staff could organise stand-ins to take their place but Mallory did not allow that. Mallory had trained his drivers in security-driving techniques that included actions to take in the event of various different situations, from a traffic accident or flat tyre to an actual enemy contact. He did not want to endanger the client or the team by having a stranger take over, someone who did not know the drills and procedures.

Mallory looked back down into the lobby and saw a young man who resembled Tasneen's brother standing near the fountain, one of his arms wrapped in a colourful cloth. 'We have a new guy starting today,' Mallory said to the drivers. They looked at each other quizzically. The suspicions that Kareem had confided to Farris on the subject had obviously been correct. 'If you need someone I can find you good man,' Kareem said.

Mallory knew that was coming. It irritated him how these people never seemed to grasp the bound-aries of their rank, often making suggestions concerning matters beyond their authority. 'He will be a translator and fixer and will be working directly with Stanza . . . He's a Sunni,' Mallory added, caring less if that last bit of information annoyed them further.

Farris and Kareem glanced at each other again to ensure that they were in agreement. 'No problem,' Kareem said, shrugging, a sentiment clearly opposite to what he truly felt.

'Be back in a minute,' Mallory said, leaving them.

Abdul recognised Mallory as soon as he saw him step onto the lobby floor and put on a smile for him. Mallory reached out with his left hand, Abdul took it and they shook. The vividly coloured silk scarf that wrapped the bandaged stump was no doubt a touch from Tasneen.

'How are you?' Mallory asked.

'I am fine – thank you for asking,' Abdul said, each word carefully enunciated.

'Your sister drop you off?'

'Yes.'

'Have you had breakfast?'

'I had breakfast with home – *at* home, thank you.' Abdul smiled apologetically at the mistake.

'How is the wound? Still painful?'

'Very little now. I do not need the pills any more.'

'That's good.' Mallory was pleased with his first impression of the young man who was polite, dignified and unobtrusive, qualities that Mallory hoped would sustain. 'We live on the fifth floor. Come and meet the rest of the team.'

'Of course,' Abdul said, extending his left hand in a courteous gesture to indicate that Mallory should lead on.

Mallory headed for the stairs. 'The lifts aren't working at the moment but you need to know the emergency stairs anyway.'

Kareem and Farris were leaning on the rail, smoking cigarettes and chatting, as Mallory and Abdul exited the emergency stairwell. Mallory made the introductions and the men exchanged greetings in Arabic. Kareem and Farris glanced at Abdul's stump several times without mentioning it. The meeting between them seemed cordial enough and, not wanting to waste any more time, Mallory knocked on Stanza's door.

When it opened Stanza looked out, saw his assembled team and stepped back to let them in.

'This is Abdul,' Mallory said as the young man passed the journalist. Stanza forced a smile, extended his right hand and before he realised his mistake Abdul took hold of the journalist's offered fingers with his left hand and shook them.

Mallory closed the door after Kareem and Farris and followed them into the room.

'Find a seat,' Stanza said. The drivers sat on the edge of the bed, leaving the two chairs for Mallory and Stanza. Abdul stood politely to one side until Stanza insisted that he should take a chair.

Stanza sat on the edge of his desk. 'I guess we should first of all welcome – Abdul, is it?'

Abdul nodded. 'Abdul, yes,' he said.

'I take it you guys all know each other?' Stanza asked, looking between the drivers.

'They just met,' Mallory said.

'OK. Welcome to the team . . . um . . . let's see how we all get on and . . . well, let's get straight to it . . . We have a story the paper wants to pursue. But before I get into it I need to stress one important thing, which is that everything about this story has to be kept between ourselves. No other media group out there –' he pointed to his door '– has the knowledge we have about the story and they must not find out. In fact, no one outside of this room must know. Understood? Friends, family, whoever. It has to stay with us only. Is that clear?' He acted like a headmaster, looking hard at each individual until he nodded.

Stanza looked at Mallory last. Mallory was miffed at being relegated to the level of the others and decided that he'd been right in his earlier impression of the journalist: Stanza was a twat.

Appearing satisfied, Stanza adjusted his position before delivering the next part of his brief. 'The story,' he announced, 'is Jeffrey Lamont, the American who was kidnapped from a house in Karada last month. A lady and two other people were murdered at the same time.'

Abdul stiffened, then checked to see if any of the others were looking at him. Suddenly he wondered if this was some kind of bizarre set-up. But all eyes were on Stanza who was looking down at the floor while composing his next sentence.

Kareem and Farris did not know who Stanza was referring to but, typically, nodded as if they did.

Mallory didn't know who Stanza was talking about either. There were dozens of kidnap victims. The mention of the murdered girl rang a bell but triggered nothing specific in his memory.

'I'm not gonna say too much right now,' Stanza went on, 'other than that we're a Wisconsin newspaper and Lamont is a Wisconsin boy.'

That was obviously the appeal of the story but Mallory could not see the reason for secrecy. Stanza was clearly taking this too seriously. From Mallory's experience, Kareem and Farris would have understood about five per cent of what Stanza had said: they made little effort to concentrate, even though they nodded constantly. Abdul, on the other hand, appeared locked onto Stanza's every word.

'I'm gonna need your help on a few things,' Stanza went on, addressing the nodding drivers, clearly unaware of their level of competence. 'Research. First thing. The woman Lamont was seeing, the one who was murdered. Very important. I want to know who she was. Where are her family, parents, whatever? We need to talk to someone who knew her. Next. The house where the kidnapping took place. Where is it? This is where you guys earn your dollars. Any ideas how to find answers to these questions?'

Kareem and Farris were looking at each other as if they had been asked to find the Holy Grail.

'Mallory,' Stanza said.

Mallory looked at him. 'Sorry. What?'

'Any ideas?'

Mallory shrugged. Story research was not his part of the ship. 'Finding the house?' he said, blowing through pursed lips. 'Was the address on the wires?' he pondered, throwing out the first thought that came into his head.

'Research back at the office has come up blank. Someone in this town has to know. What about the police?'

Mallory looked at Abdul who was wearing a bemused expression. 'Abdul?'

Abdul snapped out of his trance and looked at him enquiringly.

'Any ideas?' Mallory asked. 'You're an ex cop . . . Do you know anyone who could tell us where the house is?'

Abdul stared at Mallory for an uncomfortably long

time but his eyes were out of focus again and were seeing something else. He was back in the house in its dark, quiet street, seeing again the tattered entrance, the creaking stairs, the room at the top, the people inside and then hearing a gunshot that made him blink.

Mallory wondered if there was something wrong with the man. Tasneen had mentioned something about psychological stress but she'd never said how bad. 'You OK, Abdul?'

Abdul refocused and saw everyone looking at him. 'I know where it is,' he said matter-of-factly.

'The house where Lamont was kidnapped from?' Mallory asked, unsure if Abdul was on the same page as the rest of them.

'Yes,' Abdul said. His mental reaction to thoughts of the house had varied since that night but his present feelings tended towards morbid curiosity. He had passed by the end of the street a couple of times since that night and had strained to see the building in the few seconds it had been in view. There had to be an explanation of why he was going to offer to take these people to visit it. The thought had come from outside his soul and therefore was not his. Perhaps it came from Allah, he mused.

'The house where Jeffrey Lamont the American was kidnapped?' Stanza repeated.

'Yes,' Abdul said. 'Where Lamont was kidnapped.'

'And where the woman was murdered?' Stanza added, still not entirely convinced that the young man knew what he was talking about. It all seemed too easy, too convenient.

'And another man and woman,' Abdul added.

'Were you on duty the night it happened . . . a police officer?' Mallory asked.

'Yes,' Abdul said.

'Were you involved in the case?' Stanza asked anxiously.

'I was out that night and I know where it is.'

'And you can take us there?' Stanza asked, tense.

'Yes,' Abdul said, calming down as the questions kept coming.

'This is fantastic,' Stanza said, standing up and flexing his leg, which had stiffened a little. 'What about the woman?' Stanza asked.

Abdul considered the question. 'I don't know,' he finally said.

'I'll settle for the house for now,' Stanza said. 'I want to go there. Right away.'

Abdul shrugged. 'OK.'

'So let's go.' Stanza made a move towards the door.

'One second,' Mallory said.

Everyone paused.

'Let's remember where we all are, shall we? Kidnappings, bombings, shootings take place outside the hotel, any time, anywhere. So can we all put our security heads back on? I need to give Abdul a security brief: how we do things, go through a few of the drills, OK?'

Stanza sighed heavily. 'Do we have to do that now?' he asked.

'What if something happens on the way?' Mallory argued. 'He needs to know – for his safety as well as ours – how we operate and what to do in an emergency. You can't take short cuts in this place.'

'OK, OK,' Stanza said, holding up his hands. 'Enough with the lecture. I'll see you guys in the car park.'

'Quarter to ten at the cars,' Mallory said. Kareem and Farris acknowledged and followed Stanza out of the room.

Mallory looked at Abdul, curious about his mental balance though not unduly alarmed by any of the signs of distraction that he'd displayed. Abdul looked far too pathetic to be threatening. 'Let's take a slow walk to the car park. I'll tell you what we do in emergency situations – bombs, shootings, flat tyres, accident, car crash, if we're being followed, et cetera. I would normally take a whole day going over these things. Anything you don't understand, ask me. OK?'

Abdul nodded.

'I don't mind repeating myself a hundred times but you have to know what I'm saying. Don't say you understand something if you don't because I will ask you questions and if you can't answer them correctly I'll be angry. Do we understand each other?'

'Yes,' Abdul said, wondering if the Englishman liked him or not. Abdul was instinctively suspicious of this invader. All foreigners were in Iraq to make money out of Iraqis. Abdul did not feel hate for them, nor malice, but he did not like them either. His attraction to western trappings was not as strong as it had once been. The West and democracy were threats to Islam and they had to go, it was as simple as that. But, simple as the solution was, its achievement would not be easy, he knew that much. He believed in patience but above all else he trusted in Allah. Abdul's faith was founded on the teaching that every single object and action was part of a great and universal design that would eventually prove Islam to be the true guiding light of mankind. It was the only religion that secured man's salvation against himself. Allah oversaw every strata of life and was even watching the faithful at this moment, listening to their plans and ambitions and guiding them where necessary.

The pair left the building and as Mallory talked Abdul listened carefully. He did not want to give Mallory any reason to criticise him and he asked several questions, some of which he already knew the answers to. But he wanted to prove that he was being attentive. All the while, however, in the back of his mind was the forthcoming visit to the house of the murders. It was a living nightmare that he had to confront at some time. There was also the threat from Hassan to consider. As long as Abdul did not implicate the other members of his squad in any way there should be no problem. But that was assuming Hassan was a reasonable man, which he was not. Abdul was aware of another change in himself. He was no longer as afraid as he used to be. He still feared the unknown, though: the house, his future. His recent maturity was Allah's doing, he knew that much. He also had a strange feeling that the journey he needed to take had begun.

Half an hour later the Milwaukee *Herald*'s two cars were passing through the hotel's last security checkpoint. Farris's car still had bullet holes in the windshield and bonnet: Mallory had asked him repeatedly to have them repaired because they drew attention. It was this type of insubordination that took Mallory to the brink of losing his temper and in this case threatening to replace Farris's car and therefore the driver if it was not taken care of. He decided that if the vehicle was not repaired by the end of the week he would deliver just such an ultimatum. Farris and Kareem were slacking and needed a kick up their backsides.

The team drove down a narrow pothole-scarred residential backstreet that connected to Sadoon Street. Des had nicknamed it 'Fingers-in-your-ears Street' because of the number of explosive devices that had been planted in it during the past year – it was the only route out of the hotel complex most of the time and was therefore an attractive ambush site.

Abdul was in the lead vehicle with Farris while Mallory and Stanza followed in Kareem's car. At his feet Mallory kept a holdall containing a short-barrelled AK47 with an extra-long forty-round magazine attached, a chest harness holding six AK47 magazines, a smoke grenade and a shrapnel grenade that he had appropriated from a US soldier.

The general M.O. while driving in the city was for both vehicles to act as if one had nothing to do with the other. Mallory had given Abdul as much of a security brief as he could in half an hour and was relying on Farris to guide him if they ran into a problem.

Stanza wiped his brow and adjusted his body armour. 'This jacket is damned hot,' he complained.

'Wait until the summer,' Mallory said dryly.

'How come the drivers don't wear any?' Stanza asked. Kareem glanced at the journalist in the rear-view mirror and gave a smirk.

'Same reason they don't wear seat belts,' Mallory said. 'Allah will decide when it's time for them to die and no safety equipment will help when that moment arrives. That right, Kareem?'

'*Al hamdillilah*,' Kareem nodded.

Abdul had given Farris and Kareem a rough idea of where the house was and on reaching the Ali Baba roundabout they took the first exit into a popular shopping district. The street was lined on both sides with vendors of every description, most of them utilising the wide pavement to display their wares that included newly made furniture, washing machines still in their boxes and stacked several high, satellite dishes, refrigerators and clothing.

'What's this street?' Stanza asked.

'Tariq Al Karada,' Kareem replied.

'Are we actually in Karada?' Stanza asked.

'We not far from the house — if Abdul is telling truth,' Kareem said.

'Do you think he's making it up?' Stanza asked, curious why Kareem should say such a thing.

Kareem shrugged his shoulders and stuck out his bottom lip. 'We shall see,' he said.

The traffic was heavy and Kareem did not allow more than a couple of cars to get between him and Farris. After crossing a major junction they turned along a quiet residential street. A few blocks further on Farris slowed as he approached the entrance to another.

The area was middle-class by Baghdad standards, or appeared to be. The trick was to imagine it without the trash and rubble that was everywhere other than in the truly affluent sections. Farris's car pulled over to the kerb and Kareem came to a stop close behind it. Mallory was first out, looking up and down the street for anything suspicious. A few months back a westerner could have gone shopping in this part of town and could even have grabbed a bite in a restaurant but now even just passing through had its dangers.

'Let's keep it to fifteen minutes,' Mallory said to Stanza. Abdul was staring up at the first-floor window of a house directly in front of them.

'This it?' Stanza asked.

'Yes,' the young Arab said.

'Who do we see about taking a look inside?' Stanza asked.

Abdul walked to the front door and pushed it open.

Mallory made a mental note of Abdul's direct-approach style. 'Kareem, Farris, you stay here. Come up and get me if anyone looks like they're taking an interest, OK?' he said.

The two men nodded.

Abdul led the way into the hall, followed by Mallory and Stanza, and stopped at the foot of the staircase. Mallory looked along the dilapidated hallway where there were two doors, both closed.

'You sure this is the place?' Mallory asked.

'Yes,' Abdul said, staring up the narrow staircase.

Mallory followed his gaze to the darkness at the top of the stairs and when he looked back the young Arab appeared to be in a quandary of some sort.

'Abdul?' Mallory asked quietly. Abdul's response was to raise a foot and place it on the first step. It creaked loudly. He continued up and the next step squeaked too. Mallory and Stanza followed him to the top where they all stopped outside a closed door.

'You've been here before?' Mallory asked.

'Yes.'

'Does anyone still live here?' Stanza asked.

'I don't know,' Abdul said.

Mallory wasn't comfortable with this half-cocked way of operating but Stanza clearly didn't care.

Abdul reached for the doorknob and paused as he touched it.

'Open it, for Christ's sake,' Stanza said impatiently.

Abdul turned the knob and pushed open the door. They looked inside, Stanza craning his neck to see past Mallory's shoulder.

The room was a shambles, as if it had been ransacked, and smelled of rotting trash. A broad shaft of daylight came in through a broken window that was partly covered by a tattered curtain. Clothes and bedding were strewn around the floor and draped over toppled furniture. Everything was covered in a thick layer of fine sand that had blown in through the window.

The floorboards creaked lightly as Mallory eased past Abdul. Stanza followed.

'Doesn't look as if anyone lives here at the moment,' Mallory offered.

Stanza moved carefully around as if he was afraid of leaving a footprint. He crouched to take a look at a bundled-up sheet that was heavily stained. 'This look like blood to you?' he asked.

Mallory moved the sheet away with his foot to reveal the floorboards beneath. They were covered in a dark crusty substance. 'Yeah. Loads of it,' he said, following a trail to an even larger pool of dried blood.

Stanza wiped his hands on his thighs as he got to his feet, even though he had not actually touched anything. 'Something about murder scenes,' he said. 'They've all got the same spooky feel, as if the ghosts of the dead were standing next to you and watching.'

Mallory pushed open the bedroom door to reveal a window covered by a gaily coloured curtain, a bed with its sheets on the floor and a bedside table on its side with a broken lamp beside it.

'This tells a sad story,' Mallory mused. 'I heard some-where that she was a hooker.'

'No,' Stanza said, perhaps too firmly.

'Would spice up the read,' Mallory joked, unaware that it irritated Stanza.

'You don't think Lamont could have found love in Baghdad?' Stanza asked, only remotely interested in Mallory's plebeian view.

Mallory was at the window, standing on tiptoe and trying to look down into the street when Tasneen's image filled his mind's eye. 'Why not? You can find love anywhere, I suppose.'

'My point is, could it happen between an American man and a Muslim woman here and now, I mean?'

Mallory turned his gaze to the greying sky, wondering if there was a sandstorm brewing. Then he realised what story angle Stanza was hoping for. 'You mean, is love stronger than religion? Before I came here I would have said yes. But . . . well, they're a fanatical lot generally, more than I used to think . . . People back in the West might buy it, though . . . How can you find out?'

'Find someone who was close to her,' Stanza said, glancing at Abdul in the hope of some kind of lead. But the young Arab seemed to be back in a daydream.

'Lamont's not dead yet, is he?' Mallory asked.

'Not as far as we know,' Stanza replied.

'Better get the story right, then. He might turn up one day.'

That didn't matter to Stanza. Writing a story correction only provided more bites of the cherry.

'Would Lamont have been the romantic-hero type or a total ass, d'you reckon?' Mallory said.

'I take it that *you* think an American screwing a Muslim chick in a house like this would be a total ass.'

'These days? For sure,' Mallory quipped.

Abdul was reliving the horror of that night once again but the memory was already becoming blurred. The physical pain of his terrible wound had also lessened but the shame of his part in the atrocity had not. If anything, it had become clearer to him. However he looked at it he couldn't escape the feeling that he could have done something. He'd had a gun but he had been a coward. It was as simple as that. 'She was wrong to give herself to the American,' he said.

Stanza and Mallory looked at him.

'But she wasn't a whore,' Abdul added.

'How do you know that?' Stanza asked.

Abdul moved his gaze from the floor where the woman had fallen and stared sullenly at the two foreigners, confidence returning to his expression. He had been growing steadily irritated with their banter, particularly their comments about love between members of different faiths. The woman had been wrong to give herself to the American but Abdul had felt sympathy for her. She was a lost soul, a sinner, but nevertheless brave, more so than he. She must have sensed that Hassan might kill her for sleeping with the American and yet instead of begging for forgiveness she had declared her love for him. Abdul could not allow these people to cheapen her.

'She loved him,' Abdul said.

Stanza believed Abdul and not just because he wanted to.

'There were rumours of a western man seeing an Iraqi woman,' Abdul went on. 'He came here often.' Abdul could only surmise that but something like it had to be the case since Hassan had been confident that he'd find the American in the house. And then there was the woman's declared love for Lamont – that could not have happened in an instant. 'There are not many hookers in Baghdad. We . . . the police know those who are and she was not known. It is a great risk for an Iraqi woman to have a relationship with a westerner and only one force could have kept them together.' Abdul, satisfied with his deduction, turned around and walked down the stairs.

Stanza glanced around the room, half-hoping that a clue would present itself to him. Abdul's analysis had made sense.

Mallory went to the door to look down the stairs. 'We've been here too long,' he said.

He headed down the stairs while Stanza went to the doorway before pausing to look back into the room. The ghosts seemed to touch him this time and he shivered. Then he followed Mallory.

Mallory stepped out of the house and saw Abdul climbing into Farris's car. Stanza walked out behind him and closed the door. 'I want to drive back with Abdul,' Stanza said.

Being detached from his client wasn't the way Mallory liked to operate but he let it go. He could feel Stanza was close to clashing with him on the security-versus-work issue. 'If you have a problem you must get into this car as soon as you can.'

'Sure,' Stanza said as he opened the rear door of Farris's car and climbed in.

'Sure,' Mallory echoed. He got into Kareem's car.

As Farris pulled into the street and accelerated away Stanza stared at the back of Abdul's head, wondering how best to tackle him. Stanza had been impressed with Abdul's assessment of Lamont's relationship with the murdered woman but at the same time he felt it was too insightful. Stanza leaned forward in his seat. 'Abdul?'

Abdul half-looked around.

'That was interesting, what you said. Can you add to it? Or perhaps you know someone who can.'

'I was speaking as a policeman.'

In Stanza's experience there were several reasons why a person would not elaborate on something that they knew to be important. Fear, whether of retribution or of being implicated. Protecting someone. Holding out for personal gain. And then there was the bullshitter. Stanza had dealt with all of them but he could not say which applied to Abdul – probably not the last one. 'Something I said upset you back there . . . Abdul?'

Abdul made a point of looking at Farris. 'Can we talk later?'

Stanza read the glance and sat back. 'Sure.'

Abdul did not trust the drivers because he did not know them. But most of all he welcomed the break from further questioning. As for the house, he was glad he had visited it. But as he contemplated the possible divine purpose behind it a sudden throbbing in his wound took over everything else on his mind. He closed his eyes in an effort to control the pain.

Traffic was heavy and forty minutes later they rolled into the hotel complex. Mallory climbed out with his heavy holdall and watched Stanza and Abdul walk away from Farris's car to have a private conversation.

'I'll give you a call if I need you again today,' Mallory said to Kareem.

'What about . . .' Kareem said, finishing the sentence with a jut of his chin towards Abdul.

'Not today,' Mallory said, wondering if he would

have a moment with Tasneen when she came by to get her brother.

Kareem said something to Farris who gave Mallory a wave. Both men climbed back into their cars and drove out of the car park.

Mallory thought about waiting for Stanza, decided against it and headed for the hotel. Their conversation had nothing to do with him, anyway. It was hot and he fancied a cold shower and a cup of tea.

Stanza was standing close to Abdul and talking in a quiet yet determined manner. 'If we're going to be a team we have to help each other. If there is something about this story that is a problem for you let's talk about it. One of my most important responsibilities is to protect my sources and certainly members of my team. I wouldn't do anything to put anyone in jeopardy. Do you trust me as far as that goes? We plan to stay here for a long time . . . Abdul?'

'I understand,' Abdul said. 'It's just that . . . lives are under threat, in danger. Not just me. I'm afraid, not for me but for others.'

'I understand that,' Stanza said, looking around to ensure they were still alone, pausing as he spotted a couple of Iraqi guards some distance away, standing around smoking and chatting. 'Walk with me,' he said and they followed the towering blast wall towards the other end of the car park that was deserted. As they left the shade of the eucalyptus trees the sun touched them and the temperature increased notably.

'What I'm about to tell you I've told no one,' Stanza said, pulling the top of his shirt open to let some air in. 'I'm telling you because I believe I can trust you. The other reason I'm telling you is that I want *you* to trust *me* . . . We're not just doing a story on Lamont,' Stanza went on, deciding to keep the American's real name to himself for the moment. 'We're going to negotiate his release, or at least try to.' Stanza had deliberated for some time before deciding to confide this much in Abdul. He needed help from a local and his instincts told him that Abdul was the man. Even if Abdul was connected to the insurgents in some way, that was precisely who Stanza was trying to get in touch with. 'Does that shock you?' Stanza asked.

Abdul's mind was beginning to spin at the consequences of such an undertaking. 'It . . . it is a shock, as you say. But also dangerous.'

It was indeed, and stimulating too, Stanza suddenly thought. 'What do you think about finding the people who kidnapped Lamont and asking for a meeting to discuss a ransom?'

The image of Hassan and the others appeared. But it was not Hassan to whom Abdul would need to talk. He would know the identities of those who'd ordered – and paid for – the American's kidnapping.

'How would we go about that?' Stanza asked. 'In theory, at least. Is it possible?'

'I don't know.'

'We couldn't involve anyone else. No one official.' The US government's policy of non-negotiation with hostage-takers, hijackers and the like was well documented. But it was not against the law for a private individual to do it. 'If we could at least try and make a start. I don't expect it to be easy but . . . What do you think?'

Abdul was thinking about Hassan. The idea of approaching his erstwhile boss filled him with dread. It seemed that he had not become fearless after all. Abdul might now be enjoying the comfort of Allah but Hassan was still a tool of the devil. Hassan could contact those who had bought Lamont, it was his business to. But why would he want to? 'It would be very dangerous,' Abdul repeated, more to himself than to Stanza.

'But would it be possible? Can't we take it in small steps? A feasibility study? What would your first step be?' Stanza was pushing the matter because he was not meeting the resistance he had expected. Whether Abdul could manage such a thing was something to worry about later.

Abdul took hold of his stump that had started to throb again. Stanza was right. Abdul could take a small step. Test the ground. Money was the key to Hassan, though. 'Would you pay for the information?'

'Pay? Pay who?' Stanza was unprepared for talk of money.

'Palms will need to be oiled. You are asking people to put themselves at risk. People who owe you nothing.'

Stanza understood. But journalists like him rarely paid for information. In any case, his budget was small and he only had enough dollars to pay the local staff's wages, plus the hotel bills and expenses. 'How much?' he asked.

'Not for me,' Abdul said. 'But if I found a person

with information he will want money. How much I do not know. I am not experienced in these matters.'

Neither was Stanza but the point was he didn't have any money anyway. He could rustle up a few thousand dollars, more if he withheld the wages until he got a resupply from the *Herald*. He would have to get permission from Patterson, of course, who would in turn have to get it from old man Stanmore. They had not even discussed the size of the ransom yet. The paper wasn't ready. Stanza would be moving ahead unsupported. An immediate conversation with Patterson was required. 'Can you find out how much we might be talking about? For information and such?'

'Maybe.'

'OK. We'll take it a step at a time. See what we need to do to make contact with the kidnappers. Let's not put ourselves at risk. Call me the minute you have anything,' Stanza said before walking away.

If one's fate was always in Allah's hands, then Abdul could not imagine what was in store for him further along the path. But, thinking positively, it would be wonderful if he could achieve something with this Lamont business. Here was a chance to redeem himself, partly at least. Perhaps the idea was not as wild as it first appeared. Meeting Hassan – the only way into the maze that he could think of – was a terrible prospect, of course. But if there was money involved that would interest Hassan more than anything.

This was the most ambitious undertaking of Abdul's

life. But, most important, it was very much an adult mission.

As Abdul stepped off towards the checkpoint he straightened his back and pushed out his chin. This was indeed the start of a remarkable journey.

10

The Lion's Den

Tasneen stepped into her apartment, closed the door behind her and bolted it. As she pulled off her jacket a sound came from the kitchen. 'Is that you, Abdul?' she called out, her breath catching as she became suddenly nervous.

Abdul popped his head around the kitchen doorway. 'Hi,' he said. His smile was unusually broad.

Tasneen's unease was immediately replaced by a different concern. He was supposed to have called her when he was ready to be picked up. She put down her jacket, dropped her keys into her handbag and placed it on the small table by the door. 'How was it?'

When Abdul did not answer she walked to the kitchen doorway. He was cutting a sandwich, using his handless forearm to keep it in place while he sliced through the bread with his good hand. Her instant reaction was to take over but as she reached out he shifted his body to block her and continued sawing. 'I can do it,' he said, a hint of annoyance in his tone.

Tasneen folded her arms and leaned against the door frame, glad to see him showing some independence. 'Well? Are you going to answer me?'

He cut through the sandwich and brushed the crumbs from his stump. 'I was concentrating on not cutting any more of my arm off.'

She grinned. 'You had a good day, then.'

'I have never had a day quite like it,' Abdul said, taking a large bite out of the sandwich as he offered her the other half.

Tasneen shook her head. 'Sounds exciting . . . What did you do?'

He walked past her into the living room while trying to keep the pieces of lamb and tomato from falling out from between the slices of bread. 'We did journalist things,' he said as he sat on the couch, his mouth full of food.

'Tell me. I want to know.'

Abdul swallowed the mouthful before he had chewed it completely. 'We investigated a story.'

'So . . . what's your job?'

'I don't think I have a title. I do things the white guys can't do. I talk to Iraqis, find locations, stuff like that.'

'Sounds like fun,' she said.

'Not exactly how I would describe it.'

'You said you hadn't had a day like it.'

'It was different.'

'So tell me what you *didn't* like about it, then.'

He sighed. 'OK, OK . . . You and your cross-reference analysing . . . It's just, well, not what I expected.'

She studied him patiently. His moods were so difficult to understand these days. It was as if she didn't really know him at all any more.

He appeared about to reveal something deep, then winked at her.

Tasneen gave up, rolling her eyes. 'If you don't want to tell me, fine. You like the job, kind of. At least you don't hate it. And since it was the first day it could get better, or worse . . . What about the others? The Iraqis? Can you tell me how they were?'

'They don't like me. They're suspicious. They're not very bright, either . . . The journalist is strange. I have mixed feelings about him.'

'In what way?'

Abdul shrugged. 'I don't think I trust him. He's hard to understand. I don't think he is very experienced. He knows nothing about Arabs, that's for sure.'

'What about Bernie?'

'He doesn't like me or trust me.'

'I don't believe that,' she said.

'He's hard to read, too. He seems impatient, as if he has other things more important to do. That – or he has no interest in being here.'

'He wouldn't have hired you if he did not like you.'

'It doesn't matter what he thinks, anyway. Stanza is the boss and Mallory will be gone soon.'

Tasneen did not allow her expression to change. 'Oh? When?'

'I don't know. I heard the drivers talking. He's been here longer than he should have, apparently.'

Mallory had told her that he would have to leave but also that he would be back. 'Are you going to stay working with them?' she asked as she picked up her jacket and handbag and carried them into her bedroom.

'Sure . . . Why not?' Abdul said as he sank into the couch, finished off his sandwich, wiped his hand on his lap and looked at his stump. The first thing he did every morning when he woke up was to check his hand to see if it had all been a dream. It was why every day began at a low point for him.

Abdul lowered his arm as he pondered his next step, dark images returning to his thoughts. Since leaving the hotel he had considered the best way to approach Hassan. The telephone was pointless since details could not be discussed over it and Hassan would not meet him unless he was told the purpose of the rendezvous. There was only one solution, not a particularly attractive one. But then, no part of the undertaking was particularly appealing.

'Tasneen?' he called out.

'Yes?' she answered from inside her room.

'Can I use your car for a couple of hours?'

She appeared in her doorway. 'My car? Why?'

'Mine has a problem. I think it's the fuel pump.'

'I meant, why do you want a car?'

'It's not so difficult to drive with one hand. I used to do it all the time when I was using my phone.'

'Where are you going?' Tasneen asked, trying to sound matter-of-fact. But she was concerned for several reasons.

'I have to work.'

'Work?'

'That's why I was home early. My day is not yet over.'

'What work?' she asked, growing suspicious.

'It's confidential.'

'Is that right?'

Abdul sighed. 'I work for a newspaper. The stories are often confidential. Scoops.' He could see the doubt in his sister's eyes. 'If you don't want me to work for them then why did you get me the job?'

'Don't twist this around, Abdul. Why can't I drive you to wherever it is you want to go?'

'Because then you'd know what the job was.'

'What about your drivers?'

'The boss doesn't want them to know, either. He hasn't even told Mallory.'

Tasneen wondered if that was true.

'Why do they all call him Mallory but you call him Bernie?'

Tasneen decided there was something dark about Abdul today. 'How long will you be? Are you allowed to reveal that much?'

'Why? Are you going out somewhere?' he asked cheekily.

'You don't have the keys to the car yet,' she parried.

Abdul conceded the point. 'A couple of hours. No more . . . All I'm doing is going to see someone who might have some information for the journalist about a story he wants to do . . . Look, I'll tell you a little but if you tell anyone else I could get fired . . . The news story is about an American hostage. He comes from the same town as the newspaper and so the journalist is very interested in him. OK? Now you have it.'

Tasneen didn't know what to make of it. It sounded

odd to her. But if her brother was lying he had suddenly become very good at it.

'The problem is that I don't know what time this person will get home so I will have to wait for him.'

'So you could be late.'

'I'm not a child!' Abdul snapped, startling her. Immediately he regretted losing his temper, although he was not sorry for the sentiment behind the outburst.

Tasneen walked back into her room and a moment later emerged from it and tossed the car keys at him.

Abdul sighed again as he leaned back and looked up at the ceiling in silent prayer.

He got to his feet, went into his bedroom, opened up his wardrobe, reached in, took out a shoebox and put it on the bed. As an afterthought he pushed the door until it was almost shut, sat on the bed beside the box and opened it to reveal his pistol and spare magazine. Tasneen had found it on the floor of his car days after the incident. It still belonged to the police and Abdul was supposed to bring it in with him when he went to collect his final pay cheque. He pondered the wisdom of taking it with him. It had no part in his plan but it might be useful if things went wrong. He dithered over the pros and cons before finally allowing his male vanity to decide for him. He shoved the loaded magazine into the weapon, placed the gun in his jacket pocket, closed the box and put it back in the wardrobe. He checked his watch and then the window. It would be dark soon but it was still too early to go. However, the thought of hanging around the apartment with Tasneen made him uncomfortable so he pulled on his jacket and opened the door. 'I'll see you in a while,' he called out as he walked to the front door. 'I'll call you if I'm going to be late.'

He closed the door behind him and a moment later was walking out of the apartment block to Tasneen's car.

Abdul took his time getting the feel of the vehicle and practising his one-handed technique before starting the engine and slowly manoeuvring the car out of the parking space and around the block. The most difficult operation was turning the wheel quickly enough to steer around the tighter corners without crossing to the other side of the road. Once on the wider main streets his confidence increased and he joined the busy late-afternoon traffic.

He took his time, ignoring the usual fierce competition for gaps and lanes, allowing anyone who wanted to push in front of him, and headed due south towards Dora once he arrived at the roundabout beside the Baghdad radio tower. The control building at its base had been destroyed by a guided missile during the war. He crossed the BIAP highway near the great mosque and headed for the towering smokestacks on the edge of the infamous neighbourhood.

Abdul had been to Hassan's house a couple of times although he'd never been inside it. The street was easy to find because of a prominent blue ceramic-tiled mosque at one end and a small produce shop almost directly across the road from the house itself.

The first phase of Abdul's simple plan was to see if Hassan's car was outside his house. It wouldn't necessarily mean that Hassan was home if it was but he would knock on the door anyway. If the car was not there Abdul would wait. But that was the potentially tiresome part. When Hassan wasn't working as a cop he was conducting his nefarious business dealings around the city and he could be out at all hours.

It was dark by the time Abdul arrived in Hassan's neighbourhood. The area looked as bad as its reputation. Several streets around Abdul's neighbourhood had a street light or two that worked most nights but Dora was in darkness except for the glow of benzene lamps from some of the houses.

The mosque loomed ahead, its colourful dome illuminated by a couple of light bulbs powered by a small generator. A cruise along Hassan's street revealed only a couple of vehicles, neither of them his. Abdul carried on to the end of the street, circled around the block, pulled to a stop beside the kerb, from where he could see the house and turned off the car's engine and headlights. He sat in the dark silence for a moment. He felt uncomfortable and, in case he was being watched from one of the unlit houses, he climbed out and walked down the street to the small store across from Hassan's house.

The shop was a hovel of dust-covered tins, sweets and cigarettes. Abdul bought a packet of Marlboro Lights and headed back the way he had come. He considered walking past the car and continuing around the block but decided against it in case he was challenged. He climbed back in behind the wheel. If anyone came up and asked him what he was doing he would tell them the truth. Hassan was well known and respected – or feared – in the neighbourhood and Abdul might attract a measure of the same esteem if it was understood that he was an associate.

Abdul placed the packet of cigarettes on the dashboard, eased down into the seat and rested his head in a position that allowed him to watch the street.

He checked his watch, deciding to give Hassan until nine o'clock. But then, if the man did not arrive by then Abdul would have to come back another night if he was to pursue his plan. He would give the man until ten, or perhaps later. It didn't really matter if he gave him until midnight. His final decision was to leave it to fate, to Allah. If it was His will that Abdul should make this connection then it would take place. But that was the big problem with fate, Abdul decided. In this case, for instance, it was up to him to choose the time until which he would wait. If Hassan arrived in that time it would be Allah's will. But if Abdul decided to then extend the time limit was that then also extending it beyond the divine will? Everything was of course Allah's will, but the outcome might be different if Abdul kept changing his mind.

Abdul decided that the best way had to be to stick to his guns. If he declared to fate well in advance that he was leaving at nine o'clock then that would be the time he should leave.

At a quarter to nine a car drove into the far end of the street and Abdul watched its headlights move slowly towards him. Before reaching the small shop the headlights pulled into the kerb, came to a stop and went out.

Abdul leaned forward in his seat, unable to make out if the car had stopped in front of Hassan's house. Its interior light flickered on as a door opened and a figure climbed out. Abdul suddenly wondered what to do if there were other thugs – such as his dreaded team mates – with Hassan but as he peered into the darkness it did appear that the figure was alone. It disappeared into a house.

Abdul's heart rate had increased, his nerves were tingling and a ripple of fear passed through him as he contemplated the next phase of his plan. A voice inside his head was suddenly arguing that the whole thing was pointless.

But he knew it was the voice of fear and not of reason that was nagging at him. He took several deep breaths, crushed the internal debate and went through a mental rehearsal of what he was going to say to Hassan. Abdul remembered the gun in his pocket. He thought about leaving it in the car in case Hassan decided to search him. The weapon would only make the man suspicious and perhaps even alarmed. But if Hassan did lose control Abdul would be defenceless. He took the pistol out of his pocket, cocked it as quietly as he could by gripping the top-slide between his knees and put it back.

He climbed out of the car and closed the door, making hardly a sound. He crossed the street towards Hassan's house, his nerves tightening even more as he took several deep breaths in an effort to calm himself.

As Abdul arrived outside Hassan's house he looked in every direction, at the same time straining to listen. A light was burning inside on the ground floor. The car that had pulled up was Hassan's red Opal. Abdul stepped into the shadows of the doorway and faced the shabby door that had not been painted in years. His feeling of apprehension grew even stronger and he prayed it would not get any worse – Hassan would sense it and feed off it. He breathed deeply several more times, reached his hand out and struck the door with his knuckles. The knock was pathetic and he cursed himself for his feebleness as he repeated it with more vigour.

An orange glow appeared through several cracks in the door and a noise came from inside the house. Abdul's heart beat faster at the sound of the key turning in the lock. The door opened.

Hassan was holding a pistol. The pale orange light filled the end of the hallway behind him. He stared at Abdul with an ominous expression on his face. Hassan's shirt was unbuttoned to reveal a stained T-shirt beneath and the top of his trousers had been unfastened to ease the strain on his fat stomach. He looked as oily and sleazy as ever.

Hassan's stare shifted to Abdul's stump and his podgy unshaven face broke into a smirk. 'What do *you* want?' he asked, losing the smile and spitting out something.

Abdul swallowed, opened his mouth but was unable to speak. It felt as if he had suddenly been choked by a tightening pressure around his chest.

'Say something or get lost,' Hassan growled.

'I . . . I have to talk to you,' Abdul finally managed to stutter.

'About what?'

Abdul glanced behind him nervously. He cleared his throat but found that he had become tongue-tied with tension again.

'Are you going to say something or are you going to just piss your pants?' Hassan asked.

'I have . . . I have business to discuss with you,' Abdul stammered at last.

'Business?' Hassan said with contempt. 'What kind of business would *you* have with me?'

'I need information.'

Hassan suddenly grew suspicious and looked past Abdul.

'I'm . . . ' Abdul began. But he found himself struggling to remember the verbal strategy that he had rehearsed.

Hassan raised his pistol and levelled it at Abdul's forehead. 'You've got five seconds. If you don't tell me what you are doing here by then I'll shoot you where you stand.'

'The man w-we kidnapped. I have people who want to know where he is.'

'I'll leave your body in the street right here,' Hassan growled. 'No one will care around these parts. I could butcher you with a cleaver into a dozen pieces and no one would bother me . . . Who wants this information?'

'An American. Civilian, not military,' Abdul quickly added.

'I think I *will* shoot you,' Hassan said, turning the weapon to check the safety catch was off before pointing the muzzle back at Abdul's head.

'Please. They will pay for the information,' Abdul pleaded. 'I'm frightened. That's why I can't speak. Give me one minute. Please, Hassan.'

Hassan studied the younger man as if he was a piece of dirt. 'You said the one word that could save your life, you little shit. Pay.' Hassan lowered his gun. 'In,' he said, stepping aside.

Abdul stepped into the house's narrow hallway, past Hassan who smelled of sweat and alcohol, and waited as the man checked outside before closing the door.

Hassan brushed past him, walked to a room partway down the hallway and stopped in the doorway. 'Here,' he grunted.

Abdul shuffled past him and into a squalid room. The only furnishings were a tattered couch, several worn and grubby rugs overlapping each other to cover the floor and a side table.

Hassan went to the side table that was covered in dust-covered junk as well as several bottles of Scotch, one of them half-empty and with its cap off. He put the gun down, picked up a filthy glass containing a fair measure of the amber liquid and took a large swig. He winced as the liquid passed down his throat and then he glared sullenly at Abdul. 'You want a drink?'

Abdul shook his head. 'No.'

Hassan dropped his gaze to Abdul's stump. 'How's the hand?'

'What hand?'

Hassan broke into a guttural laugh. '"What hand?" That's good. I never knew you had a sense of humour.'

Abdul had intended it simply as a stoic statement.

'I hope what you want is not some kind of joke, though,' Hassan said, ominously serious once again.

'I am here to do business.'

'About the American *we* kidnapped,' Hassan said, chortling. '"We." I like that. I hope you don't expect to get paid now that it's *we*.' He took another swig from the glass. 'Who are these Americans?'

'A newspaper.' Abdul felt less tense now that he had engaged Hassan in conversation. 'They want to do a story.'

'What's the deal?'

'They want to know where the man is.'

Hassan drained the glass and refilled it from the bottle. 'Where he is? That's another joke, of course.'

'They want to make contact with the people who have him,' Abdul corrected.

'And how much will they pay for this information?'

'I don't know.'

Hassan looked at him suspiciously.

'This is why I am here, Hassan. You know that I don't know much about these matters.'

'Who are they?'

'I'm not supposed to say.'

'I asked who they are?' Hassan said darkly.

'I . . . I cannot say,' Abdul said, sensing danger but pushing his luck.

Hassan took another swig, put the glass down and picked up the pistol. 'I could fire bullets into you all night and no one would come to investigate. You come into my house and dictate to me! "I cannot say".' He mimicked the words with a fair approximation of Abdul's pathetic tone. He looked at Abdul coldly. 'Who are they?'

'A newspaper . . . called the *Herald*,' Abdul blurted.

'Why do they want to speak to the kidnappers?' asked Hassan.

Abdul was about to reply but Hassan interrupted.

'They want either to interview them, interview him, or they want to pay a ransom. Right?'

'You are right.'

Hassan nodded. 'The ransom will be in the millions.'

'I don't know anything about the money. Not right now,' Abdul said.

'They sent you out looking for the American without money? You are either crazy or stupid . . . I hope you don't think I am either.'

'They also do not know the cost of doing this kind of business. That's why I am here.'

Hassan studied Abdul, weighing him up. 'I'm supposed to give you a price for my information and then you tell those you work for, and then they give me the money – is that how this is supposed to work?'

'Does that not suit you, Hassan? If not, please guide us.'

'Tell me something, you little shit. How did you get into this line of business? I cut your hand off and now you're working in a business that deals in millions. It was good fortune for you. I should take a piece of your money.'

'Can you at least tell me if you can get in touch with the men who have the American?' Abdul asked, desperate to get Hassan on track.

'I think you are trying to make a fool of me, little man.' Hassan swayed a little as the drink soaked into his brain.

Abdul warned himself to be more careful. He had never seen Hassan drunk before but suspected that it made the man even more dangerous. 'Please, Hassan. I am only the messenger. They would not trust me with more than I have discussed with you.'

'I believe that,' Hassan slurred, putting down his pistol and lurching around as he took another swig of Scotch. 'It's a dangerous errand they've sent you on.'

'Perhaps I should come back another time.'

'Is that what you would ask the lion as you stood in his cave?'

Abdul's concern went up a notch as he gauged the distance to the front door, wondering if he could make it outside at the run before Hassan picked up his gun and shot him. Abdul reckoned he might reach the door but he feared it would be as far as he got before Hassan's bullets cut him down. 'Then how must this work, Hassan? Please tell me.'

'You want information and I want money for it,' Hassan said, draining the glass again. 'It is a marriage of the two,' he continued, reaching for a packet of cigarettes. 'You have asked for the information but you do not have money. So how can it now proceed? This is the question.'

Abdul watched Hassan as he laboriously set about lighting a cigarette. 'Why don't you give me a price for your information? Then I will tell those I work for.'

'Idiot,' Hassan scoffed as he picked up the gun and somehow managed to hold on to it while he poured yet another drink.

Abdul felt his own pistol inside his jacket pocket. His advantage lay in Hassan's drunkenness but he would be foolish to underestimate the man's experience with violence of all kinds. Hassan was unpredictable even when he was sober. He could lose his temper at any second and put a bullet into Abdul just because he was there.

Hassan looked over the rim of the glass, fixing Abdul with his heavy-lidded stare. 'One hundred thousand dollars,' he declared.

The price was unimportant now. Abdul had not imagined Hassan being this difficult to deal with and his every thought was focused on getting out of the house. 'I'll tell them,' Abdul said as he took a step towards the door.

'Where are you going?' Hassan said as he put down the glass and swung his gun towards Abdul, holding it level for a moment before lowering it as if it had suddenly become too heavy.

'To tell my people your demands.'

'You think I'm so stupid? Eh? You don't think I know you want revenge for your arm . . . You leave and then the next people through my door are American soldiers who will torture me for the information.'

Abdul was not prepared for such a response. 'If that was true I would not have needed to come here,' he said, thinking swiftly. 'The American government does not negotiate. That is why they do not know. The newspaper is dealing with this. They would not tell the military.'

It took a while but Hassan began to see the sense in Abdul's reasoning. 'I have an idea,' he said. 'I will have my own hostage to make sure that you don't cross me.'

Abdul had no idea what the man meant. He watched as Hassan tucked the pistol into his belt and reached for his jacket. 'I don't understand,' Abdul said.

Hassan burped loudly as he looked at Abdul, a knowing smirk forming on his face. 'I need a hostage to ensure I get my money . . . We'll go to your apartment and I'll stay with your sweet little sister until your newspaper comes up with the money.'

Abdul was horrified. 'You cannot do that,' he gasped, unable to hide the alarm in his voice.

'I do what I want. And if you don't come back with the money . . . well, then you have a problem. And don't be long. I don't know how long I can spend in a room with your pretty little sister without showing her some affection,' Hassan said, a grin forming on his sweaty face.

The blood pounded through Abdul's veins and throbbed in his temples at the thought of Hassan even entering his apartment. The image of the man grabbing Tasneen grew frighteningly clear. There was no way he'd let the pig leave this house with that objective in mind. Abdul took the gun from his pocket and pointed it at Hassan.

Hassan's brain was addled with alcohol and he'd already taken a step towards Abdul before the sight of the pistol stopped him. He swayed as he looked into Abdul's eyes. 'So I was right. This is what you came to do. Murder me.'

'No,' Abdul said. 'But now it seems like a good idea.'

'You don't have the guts.'

'Maybe I didn't before the night you cut off my hand.' Abdul's voice quivered slightly. 'It doesn't take courage to murder a man like this. Look at you. You're not brave. It only takes great cruelty or hate and I have plenty enough of one of those.'

'So. The boy thinks he is a man now. Perhaps you are ready to join us at last.'

'Go to hell,' Abdul said, the pistol shaking slightly in his hand as he tightened his jaw. The boom as the gun fired was the loudest sound Abdul had ever heard, or so it seemed in the small dingy airless room where even the clatter of a cockroach's legs as it scurried up the cracked walls was amplified.

Hassan shrieked, grabbed his thigh and dropped heavily to the floor, falling onto his backside. There was no blood: the round had punctured the skin neatly and the meaty flesh closed around the entry hole. The intense pain that Hassan was feeling came from the red-hot bullet lodging inside the thick muscle and the shattered femur as his weight collapsed the limb that could no longer support him.

Abdul kept the gun aimed at Hassan. The man had not made another sound after his initial scream but his face was screwed tightly against the pain.

Hassan opened his tear-filled eyes and blinked furiously in an effort to focus on Abdul. 'You shot me!'

Abdul was surprised by how easy it had been to fire a bullet into a man – or into this particular man, at any rate. There was something else about the experience that he had not expected. It had felt very good indeed. This chunk of metal in his hand was more than just a tool that fired a projectile. Weapons like it had made kings and brought down nations and now it had in a second reversed his vile relationship of servitude and torment with Hassan to turn Abdul into the undisputed master. But if it was to stay that way Abdul would have to finish the job. So he fired again.

This time Abdul was prepared for the explosion and he watched something red fly off Hassan's shoulder as the bullet struck it. Hassan screamed as he brought a hand up to clutch at the new wound that, unlike the first, immediately bled heavily. The masterful feeling only increased as Abdul took a step forward, adjusting his aim to point the muzzle at Hassan's head. Abdul was about to pull the trigger a third time when he suddenly remembered why he was there in the first place. 'Where is he?' Abdul asked, his voice now cold and decisive.

Hassan looked at him through drooping eyelids, his mouth open while his head and torso moved with every heavy gasp. 'The . . . Islamic . . . secret . . . army have him,' he said, the effort obviously causing him more pain. 'Black Banners.'

'I know that. They were on the television. I want to know who I can contact.'

'And . . . and then . . . you will . . . kill me.'

'You are not in a position to barter.'

'My money. You will . . . keep it for yourself . . . I have taught you well.'

'There is no money, Hassan. Your life is at an end. You are bartering for nothing. Tell me and I will send you on your way. If you do not, then I will leave you here for the rats to finish off. Think about it.'

Hassan understood and quickly came to terms with his drastically shortened future. Death did not horrify him, not as much as it would have appalled a person who had something however small to live for. Hassan had been an unhappy boy who had grown into an unhappy man. To him, no human life had any value beyond what it would fetch in ransom money, not even his own. He had never feared dying and this stoicism had nothing to do with religion. He did not really care what Abdul did to him. Perhaps the alcohol that he'd drunk made this acceptance easier but Hassan would not admit that. He knew this moment was his last and he grinned at the irony. 'My . . . my father told me . . . my . . . my weakness would one day kill me.'

Abdul was not interested but allowed the man to ramble on in the hope that he would eventually tell him what he wanted.

'The others . . . they wanted . . . to kill you . . . I said no. That was . . . my weakness. The old fool . . . he was right after all.'

Abdul realised that Hassan had accepted his fate: it was time to go. Despite his earlier threat to leave the man alive for the rats to gnaw he could not risk abandoning him like this in case he stayed conscious long enough for his brother Ali or the others to find him.

Abdul was about to deliver the *coup de grâce* when Hassan struggled to say more. 'Fallujah,' he said. 'I'll see you in hell.' Hassan looked for his gun beside him, reached for it and wrapped his bloody fingers around the grip.

Abdul squeezed the trigger. The gun jumped in his hand, the noise making him flinch even though he had braced himself against it. Hassan's head jerked back as blood gushed from his eye socket, his mouth gaping open. He moved no more.

Abdul walked out of the room and down the hall, opened the door without any difficulty, stepped outside and headed for his car. He tossed his pistol onto the passenger seat, dug the car key from his pocket, started the engine and accelerated down the road, tyres screeching. He passed Hassan's house, turned the corner at the end of the road too wide, almost hitting a parked car on the other side, switched on his headlights and sped away up the road.

Twenty minutes later he came to a stop outside his apartment block, turned off the lights and engine and sat in silence while he absorbed the implications of the evening's activities. He had achieved much more

337

than he had ever hoped for or would have believed possible. There was no doubt that he had broken down many barriers since losing his hand but Abdul was shocked at the type and speed of the progress he had made. Then it dawned on him how he could have discovered these qualities in himself long ago had he put his mind to it. All those years of weakness could have been avoided. This night had proven how lethally competent he was when left to his own devices.

Abdul took a deep breath, pocketed his gun and made ready to head upstairs, no doubt to an interrogation by Tasneen. He would not tell her anything, of course. She would never be able to imagine how her little brother had killed a man that night.

Abdul climbed out of the car and took a moment to consider his likely fate from now on. The suspicion that he was on a great journey was even stronger now and that he was developing the skills to complete it. Fate had removed one of his hands but he was now more powerful than when he'd had them both.

Abdul looked to the sky as if he was staring into the face of Allah. '*Allah akbar*,' he said softly. Then he walked to the entrance of his apartment.

11

Plans Within Plans

Stanza removed his headset, got up from in front of the computer, poured himself a cup of coffee and looked through the closed balcony windows over the city. He took a sip of the hot black liquid, enjoying just about the only reminder of home in this God-awful place while pondering the hour-long conversation he'd just had with Patterson. It was early in the morning in Milwaukee and the foreign editor had not appreciated being woken up by his bedside phone to hear Stanza on the other end of the line telling him to get to his computer for an important conversation.

When Patterson came online, though, he was in a better mood and immediately pressured Stanza for the story so far. When Stanza began by describing the immediate problems that faced them it was as if Patterson had not heard him. The man launched into a plethora of thematic suggestions of his own, based on the premise of a young heir to a fortune who fled a stifling future in the family business in search of love and adventure. Stanza asked if old man Stanmore would appreciate the monstrous-father inference but Patterson brushed the question aside. He said that every good plot and subplot had a protagonist and antagonist and that this piece was not simply news. It was an epic.

Patterson went on to impress upon Stanza the need to be prepared for several possible scenarios, at which Stanza rolled his eyes. The first and most ideal was young Stanmore's imminent release into Stanza's hands after the payment of a ransom. This would read like a hero's triumphant return to his family after escaping death at the hands of vile Islamic insurgents. The *Herald* would, of course, enjoy the acclaim for their pivotal role in securing the young man's release. Then there was the tragic scenario: young Stanmore getting his head cut off. *That* would read like a eulogy for a young life prematurely extinguished while in pursuit of love and adventure. Patterson suggested it should be written in the first person: 'I did this' and 'I did that', 'I went here to speak to these people', 'I was approached', 'I investigated further.' Stanza had no objections to this idea. Neither did he think Patterson had gone too far when he expressed a belief that the piece would have the potential for a Pulitzer Prize nomination.

Stanza eventually steered the conversation back to his main concerns: the need to find the people who were holding young Stanmore and open up a line of communication with them. To Stanza's utter amazement Patterson said that he thought Stanza was already involved in that stage. Stanza's frustration grew with every revelation of Patterson's ignorance of the realities of Iraq. Finally, unable to contain himself, he burst out exclaiming that it was not a case of simply picking up the phone, calling directory enquiries and asking for insurgency headquarters and the offices of the Black Banner Brigade. Patterson did not appreciate the sarcasm.

When Stanza introduced the subject of money Patterson was not so responsive and simply made excuses about why there was no progress to report in that area. Stanza's mood turned ice-cold at this point and he warned Patterson in no uncertain terms that the success of the story depended on hard cash. Stanza did not allow Patterson to interrupt and went into detail based on Abdul's suggestions. The summing-up was simple: no money, no story. It was the first time that he had experienced Patterson unable to deliver a tirade in defence of an indefensible position. When Patterson finally asked how much money he needed Stanza held on to the first figure that came into his head, doubled it and then doubled it again. 'One hundred thousand,' he said.

Patterson went quiet for several seconds but then calmly said he would get as much of it as he could to Baghdad as soon as he found a quick way of doing it.

'And the ransom amount?' Stanza asked.

'It's being discussed.'

'I need a ballpark figure at least.'

'We don't have one yet.'

Stanza felt it was safe to assume that no one at head office had been willing to start such a discussion. 'Fine,' Stanza said. 'My advice is to be prepared to part with five to ten million.'

Patterson was stunned.

'Those are the figures the French and Italians are rumoured to have paid,' Stanza said. 'I'm afraid they've set a tough precedent for high-profile kidnapping payments.'

Patterson had little more to say after that and assured Stanza that he would get back to him as soon as he had talked with the publisher and old man Stanmore.

Stanza was satisfied by the way the conversation had gone and felt that his stock with the *Herald*'s management had greatly improved. It was now up to him to produce the goods. The only scenario Stanza wanted to see unfold was one where he made contact with the kidnappers and eventually negotiated young Stanmore's release. But for the moment the chances of that appeared to be hanging on the abilities of one young disabled fixer and somewhere between the previous afternoon and that morning Stanza had for some reason lost confidence in Abdul. He began to doubt that he would ever hear from the man again: he'd sent him on an errand that was clearly out of his league. The question was who he could contact next. Mallory was his only source at present but having come up with that one-handed Arab youngster in the first place it reflected badly on him.

A knock on the door snapped him out of his thoughts. He put down his coffee and went to answer it. 'Who's there?'

'Abdul.'

Stanza was surprised. Suddenly he hoped he was wrong about the young Arab. He would learn soon enough, he reckoned, and opened the door to see Abdul standing back politely. 'Come in,' Stanza said.

Abdul entered, closing the door behind him.

'Want a coffee?'

'No, thank you.' It was less than twenty-four hours since his introduction to the team when he'd been so nervous but his self-confidence had soared since the previous night's experience.

'What have you got for me, then?' Stanza asked.

'I managed to track down someone involved with the kidnapping.'

'You did?' Stanza asked, his amazement followed immediately by suspicion. 'How did you manage that, if you don't mind me asking?'

'I was in the police, remember.'

'And you tracked down the insurgents who kidnapped Lamont?'

'No,' Abdul said, shaking his head and wondering if Stanza was being facetious or just plain stupid. 'Most kidnappings are not carried out by insurgents. They are done by criminals who then sell those they've kidnapped to insurgents. Many of these criminals are known to the police.'

Stanza nodded. That made sense. He wanted to ask why the police had not done anything if they knew who the kidnappers were but he chose not to go there, for the moment at least. 'And this person can help us?'

'No . . . But he pointed to where we can look.' Abdul paused to align his thoughts. 'If you want to make contact with those who now have Lamont we will have to go to Fallujah.'

'Why?' Stanza asked. 'I take it you have a reason to believe that Lamont's there.'

Abdul had thought about it long and hard and it was an obvious choice in the end. It had been obvious to Hassan and had been the man's last thought before he died. Fallujah had become a popular location with kidnap gangs over the past year. The bodies of several beheaded western kidnap victims had been dumped outside the town. The place was also the headquarters for the Sunni rebellion. Many of the rebels were also criminals and, being a Sunni himself, Hassan would know them or at least know how to make contact. Abdul had no doubt that Lamont was there. 'It is the Black Banner Brigade that has Lamont,' Abdul said. 'And they are based in Fallujah.'

'But we only need to make contact with those who have him. Surely they have a representative in Baghdad?'

'I agree. But I don't know who to ask.'

'This man you met. He actually told you that Lamont was in Fallujah?'

'He made that suggestion.'

'Did you ask him if he knew a Brigade contact in Baghdad?'

'No.'

'Then go back to him and ask.'

'That is not possible. He has gone and will never return.'

Stanza wished he had been at the meeting and had taken control of it. 'What about others? This guy didn't kidnap Lamont alone.'

Abdul shook his head. 'It is very dangerous, even

with money . . . Fallujah is the best chance you have. The Brigade controls Fallujah. The military and the police will not be able to find Lamont easily. The Brigade will do business. They paid money to get Lamont and they will sell him for a good profit. They are businessmen.'

Stanza sipped his coffee as he contemplated the prospect of going into the infamous town. 'How would we get hold of someone from the Brigade if we went there?'

'I have a cousin who lives in Fallujah. He would find someone who knows. That will not be a big problem . . . You are offering money, yes?'

Stanza nodded. 'How much would we need?'

'My cousin will want some. Not much. A thousand or two. But the insurgents? I don't know. A lot. This will be discussed at the first meeting.'

'And what about our safety – or should I say mine. I'm the wrong colour, not to mention the wrong nationality.'

'My skin or my religion will not save me from them either. We will have the rights of negotiators. This is something they will respect as businessmen,' Abdul said, reflecting on Hassan's comments on the business sense of the insurgents. 'Before you are introduced, I or my cousin would get assurance that they will accept you as a negotiator.'

Stanza could see a distinct change in the young man since the day before. He was far more relaxed and self-assured. 'So you would go to Fallujah and prepare the ground for me to go there at a later date?'

'That is possible.' Abdul contemplated the idea. 'But if I set up a meeting for you soon after getting there I would have to come back for you. Perhaps they will have questions I cannot answer. They might not trust me or believe me. They will believe you because you are a white man. And moving in and out of Fallujah is not easy right now. I think it is best that we go there, do our first piece of business and leave.'

Stanza could see the argument but that didn't make it any easier to accept. Stanza might be white enough to initiate negotiations but at some stage the deal's bona fides would have to be confirmed even further. Verification would be required that the transaction was ultimately being conducted by Stanmore's family. Stanza would like to see some evidence of that for himself.

He decided to play along for the moment, as if he were planning on going to Fallujah with Abdul, and in the meantime see how it panned out. 'How would we get into Fallujah? The Americans have the town surrounded.'

'I will call my cousin. He will know how to get past the Americans.'

'That doesn't sound reassuring. I mean, I'm sure your cousin is a capable guy but there's an entire army out there.'

'It is impossible to cover every inch of ground, even for the Americans. There will be ways in.'

'You're sure about that?' Stanza could not control the constant doubts he had about Abdul.

'You have read of many insurgents from all over,

called by their masters to move into Fallujah for the great battle against the Americans. They arrive every day and bring many weapons with them and the Americans cannot stop them. I have also heard that many of the car bombs that are used in Baghdad still come from Fallujah.'

Stanza had read stories about that on the wires too. He had also heard it from official American military sources. The insurgents' defences were being strengthened and weapons were arriving from Iran and Syria almost daily. 'OK . . . So we find a way in. Then what?'

'Then we will find the Black Banner Brigade and begin negotiations.' Abdul shrugged as if nothing could be simpler.

Stanza felt that he was in danger of becoming infected with Abdul's optimism and had to bring himself down to earth for a reality check. Nothing went that easily, especially in Iraq. 'We would drive, I guess?'

'Yes. But you cannot use your existing drivers. They are Shi'a.'

Stanza suspected that Kareem and Farris would refuse to go anyway. But as far as he was concerned the fewer people the better – which raised the question of Mallory. Judging by the way the guy treated a simple drive to the Green Zone convention centre a jaunt to Fallujah would be way out of the question. But that would mean going without him. Still, a single security guard wouldn't be much help against an army of insurgents anyway and another white man could only increase the danger. Mallory probably wouldn't go anyway. The best thing was simply not to tell him. 'You've not discussed any of this with anyone else? The drivers? Mallory?'

'Of course not. You said I was not to.' Abdul hoped that Mallory would not be brought into it anyway. 'What would you like?'

'What do you mean?'

'What would you like me to do now?' Abdul watched Stanza, gauging him. The man looked doubtful about the operation and Abdul suddenly felt that he would choose not to go. The thought disappointed him and for the first time he found himself anxious for Stanza to act bravely. Abdul wanted very much to reverse the fortunes of Lamont but he had not realised until that moment that his heart was so very much in it.

Stanza went to the window in the hope of inspiration but all he could see was danger. 'I'll think about it. See what else you can find out about the route into the town, checkpoints, that sort of thing.' Stanza needed more time to decide. His journalist side was shouting at him to get on with it. But it was the self-preserving side of Stanza that was holding everything up. He was now fully confident that Abdul would arrange things if he was given the go-ahead but the thought of climbing into a car and driving to Fallujah filled Stanza with dread. His hand reached for his gunshot wound that had begun to itch.

'I will call my cousin. Perhaps he can make contact with someone in the Brigade today.'

Abdul's words only increased Stanza's anxiety. 'That would be great.'

'I'll call you later,' Abdul said as he went to the door. Stanza continued staring out of the window without acknowledging Abdul's parting words.

Abdul left the room, headed for the lifts and pushed the call button. He had not been entirely straight with Stanza and wondered if the journalist had suspected his minor manipulations. It might well have been possible to find someone who knew how to make contact with a member of the Black Banner Brigade in Baghdad but Abdul had no desire to try. Neither was he sure of Stanza's safety. Arabs did indeed respect the inviolability of a negotiations parley. But Abdul could not be certain whether that applied to the fanatical Takfiri who were the backbone of the Fallujah insurgency. Takfiri were the most dangerous individuals on the planet. Zarqawi and Bin Laden were Takfiri, an extreme faction of the Wahabi who were themselves extremists and, like the Taliban, believed that Muslims should live by the strictest rules of Islam. Abdul could only pray that those who were holding Lamont were more fiscally liberated. His focus now was truly on Fallujah. He believed the town was part of the path he had to take and that Allah was his guide. It was not difficult to understand why. Lamont was his salvation and everything that had happened since that night pushed him closer to it. His sister meeting Mallory at the hospital, Stanza, the destruction of Hassan were all signs. Stanza was the perfect means to establish Abdul's contact with the Brigade and he suddenly had no doubt that the journalist would decide to make the journey.

The sound of a door shutting caused Abdul to look up and he saw Mallory heading from his room along the corridor. Abdul stepped out of view and when Mallory did not arrive at the lift he assumed that the man had taken the emergency stairs. Something about Mallory bothered Abdul but he could not put his finger on it. Perhaps it was nothing more than the mistrust Abdul believed they had for each other. The lift arrived, a porter walked out pushing a baggage trolley, and Abdul stepped inside and touched the ground-floor button. A moment later he stepped out into the lobby and marched briskly across it to the main entrance. If Mallory should call after him he would act as if he could not hear him.

Abdul walked out of the hotel entrance onto the road and maintained a brisk pace to the US checkpoint as he ran through his plans. His first task was to get hold of Muhammad, his cousin, if the man was still in Fallujah, which he prayed he was, and get him to remain there. Muhammad was a greedy man and would do anything for money. All Abdul would have to do would be to hint at the possible financial rewards of helping to release an American hostage and Muhammad would cheerfully take his chances with any American assault on his town. Abdul was sure of that.

Mallory walked out of the fourth-floor emergency stairwell door onto the landing and headed for Des's office. He'd had a restless night thinking about his plans for Fallujah and had got out of bed at one point to pore over a map of the town and make notes. At dawn he telephoned his boss in London and arranged for his relief to come out to Baghdad as soon as possible. His boss called back shortly after to let him know that a guy called Johnson would be arriving in Amman in two days and would get into Baghdad the following afternoon to take over from Mallory. Mallory was committed one way or the other – Fallujah or home.

Mallory glanced over the rail and paused as he saw Abdul leaving the hotel. He wondered why Abdul had not contacted him and looked up at Stanza's door. Then again, Abdul was Stanza's fixer and it was really nothing to do with Mallory unless they wanted to go somewhere.

Mallory walked on, knocked on Des's door and on hearing a muffled 'Come in' pushed it open.

Des was at his desk concentrating on his computer monitor and looked up for a second as Mallory entered the room. ''Ello, me ol' cock, 'ow are yer?'

'Not so bad,' Mallory said, falling tiredly into the armchair.

Des concentrated on hitting a couple of keys and when he was satisfied they'd had the desired effect he pulled off his glasses to rub his eyes. 'Cuppa?'

'I'm fine, thanks. How's everything?' Mallory asked, getting on with the formalities.

'Can't complain.' Des sat back in his chair and exhaled heavily. 'We ain't lost anyone this week so it's nay s' bad.'

'Anything more on Fallujah?'

'What, about the Yanks goin' in?'

'Anything, really. Your man still embedding, is he?'

'Not sure now.' Then Des lowered his voice like a real gossip. 'I think 'e's 'ad a touch of the old cold feet about it. 'E's from a small radio network in Oklahoma and I think he's only finally got around to asking 'imself why 'e's riskin' 'is arse to send news over there when 'e can sit back 'ere in t' 'otel and pull it off wires.'

That was not what Mallory wanted to hear. His plan had been designed around the embed.

'Can't blame 'im, really,' Des went on. 'So many bloody rumours goin' around about what the Yanks are plannin' on doin' to the town and when they're goin' in and the resistance an' all. Yer don't know what to believe.'

'Have you still secured his embed?'

'Aye. 'E's still got a spot if 'e wants it. But I'm pretty certain 'e ain't goin'.'

'When is it for?'

'We're on standby. Some journalists 'ave already gone in, some of the big networks, a couple from each. If there's too many o' the boogers runnin' aroun' they'll be gettin' in the way of the Marines. Sounds a bit of a gang-fock media circus but there yer go. Are yer all right?' Des asked, his classic bulging-eyed grin appearing as if by a switch. 'Look a bit tired, lad. Not sleeping well?'

'I'm fine.'

'Tell me,' Des said, leaning forward, his voice lowering once again in a conspiratorial manner. 'Who were that lovely little thing you 'ad 'ere t' other day? Eh?'

'When was that?' Mallory asked, feigning ignorance.

'When was that, 'e says,' Des echoed with a chuckle. 'During rocket attack. In lobby. Little beauty, she were.'

'Oh,' Mallory said. 'She's the sister of one of our locals. She'd popped in to see him and I just happened to be on my way out when the boom-boom hit.'

'Know her well, do yer?'

'Nah. Just enough to say hello.'

'Just enough to say hello? You don't say too much when she stays over, then. I like that. All action.'

'What do you mean?' Mallory asked, looking Des in the eye.

Des winked at him. 'Can't get one past Des, me ol' cock. Jedel, our night watchman, saw 'er leave your room in the wee hours. 'Ay. Me 'at's off to yer. If yer can gerrit, go for it. Just watch yersel', though, laddy. They'll slit yer throat aroun' 'ere if yer dip yer wick in the wrong crease. Know what I mean?'

'Don't read too much into it, Des, me old cock. There was a lockdown, remember. She had to stay somewhere.'

'Well, just watch yersel', that's all, like I said. If Jedel knows then every bastard does.'

It was a concern to Mallory but he had other problems at that moment. 'Des . . . Let me ask you something. Getting back to the embed. If your man doesn't take that spot would you mind if I did?'

'Lookin' for a slot for your bloke then, are yer?'

'It's for me,' Mallory said.

Des raised his eyebrows. '*You?* As in yersel'?'

'Yes.'

''Ave I missed summat?'

'My relief arrives in a couple days and . . . well . . . I'd like to see the fight.'

'You want to go to Fallujah on yer time off?' Des asked with continuing incredulity.

'If you don't fill the slot.'

'You've been 'ere too long, me old cock. You need to get 'ome, 'ave a few ales and a bit o' tatty. When yer've got the taste back then call me and tell me yer'd rather be in that shit-'ole op road.'

Mallory stared at him blankly in reply.

'You serious?' Des asked.

'Yep.'

'Why, fer God's sake?'

'Like I said. I'd like to see the fight.'

Des shrugged and shook his head. 'OK. If yer that focken' mad I'll put yer name down and I'll give yer a shout when the call comes in. You got a press pass? They won't let you on chopper unless yer press.'

'I've got a pass.'

'OK. It's a thirty-minute standby.'

'I'm ready to go,' Mallory said. 'Oh. One other thing. You got a spare room? I hand mine over to my relief when he gets in.'

'Anything else I can do fer yer?' Des said sarcastically.

'Just in case I'm still on standby.'

Des sighed. 'Dougal is heading up to Arbil tomorrow for a couple of weeks. You can use 'is room.'

'Thanks, Des. Much appreciate it,' Mallory said, getting to his feet. 'I'll catch you later, then.'

'Yer not trying to be a reporter, are yer?' Des asked.

Mallory wondered if that might not be such a bad cover story. Des would tell just about everyone and it was better than being thought of as simply a mad bastard. 'Well, truth is I'm going to take a camera. Might be able to sell some pics.'

'Mad sod,' Des said as he put his glasses back on. 'Don't become one of that lot. You know what they say about media, don't yer? Responsible for 'alf the world's problems and all of its ignorance.'

'Photos tell the truth,' Mallory said, defending his cover although he would agree with Des at any other time.

'Do they fock,' Des said. 'It's not what the media tell or show anyway, it's what they don't tell and show that's the problem.'

'Well, it's more for the crack than anything else,' Mallory said, heading for the door. 'Catch you later.'

Des watched Mallory until he was out of sight before focusing on his computer monitor. 'Mad bastard,' he said, his mouth twisting in concentration as he stabbed at one of the keys, none too confident of its effect.

Mallory leaned on the rail and looked down into the lobby as he gathered his thoughts. All he could do now was wait and hope that the embed happened. It would see him to the outskirts of Fallujah in a US helicopter and then with the usual chaos of battle he would slip away from the media gang and head for the cemetery. It had been a long time getting to this stage and, as expected, a tingling of apprehension had arrived with it.

Tasneen entered his thoughts, followed by Des's comments about her being in his room. He would rather no one knew but it was not a major drama. Their conversation the evening before had set him thinking of her until he'd fallen asleep. It had begun with Abdul, of course, but once Mallory had reported how well her brother had done on his first day they had moved on to other matters. They'd ended up not only talking about cycling holidays but practically agreeing to plan a tour of France together one day. It had been bizarre in many ways and Mallory wondered if they were truly hitting it off or just living some kind of fantasy. He had an urge to call her but decided to put it off for the moment. His retrieval mission was, with luck, about to begin and his concerns for its success as well as for his own survival were gnawing at him.

The plan's biggest flaw was that it depended heavily on factors over which he had no control. There were essentially three main phases to his mission: the move to Fallujah; the move to the cache; the extraction back to Baghdad. The embed with the US Marines would cover phase one but the problem there was where precisely that would put him on the map. The Marines had many options for taking the town and Mallory needed to be in the right place on the outskirts before his move in. The Marines might decide to form up on one side of the town and push through on a broad front, herding the enemy back into ambush positions. Or they might drive a wedge through the centre of the town and then continue to subdivide it into pockets to prevent the enemy from regrouping and coordinating their defences. Another option would be to press in from all sides, bulldozing the enemy into a central point while artillery and air power concentrated fire into an ever-shrinking area. Then again, they might just bomb the town flat for several days before walking in to see what was left. Whatever the method, Mallory needed to be in a position to get to the cemetery as soon as it was overrun.

Mallory headed back to his room to pack. Des could call him to move at any time and he needed to be able to just snatch up his gear and go. It was entirely possible that within a few days he could be heading back to the UK with a bag full of cash. It was a nice thought and one that Mallory tried to keep in the forefront of his mind. But it kept on getting overtaken by a feeling that something was going to go terribly wrong.

12

The Betrayal

Abdul cleared the last hotel checkpoint and headed towards Sadoon Street where he hoped to find a taxi. A horn beeped and he looked across the road to see Kareem's car pull over and stop. The window opened and Kareem leaned out. 'Abdul! Come here!' he shouted.

Abdul would have liked to avoid the man but he was too close to walk away and ignore him for no reason.

'Are you going home?' Kareem asked as Abdul approached.

'Yes, but I can get a taxi.'

'Get in. I will take you.'

'No, truly. That's OK,' Abdul said.

'Please. It is my job and I insist.'

'You are very kind but I can get a taxi.'

'Please, it is no problem for me. I would rather drive you than have you wait for a taxi.'

Abdul was sincere and was not indulging in the Arab propensity for extreme politeness. But Kareem clearly took his resistance as simply good manners and, determined to give Abdul a ride, was not backing down.

'Are you sure?' Abdul finally asked, giving up after deciding there was no harm in it. He wanted to be alone but would have to wait until Kareem dropped him off.

'I insist. It would be my pleasure,' Kareem said, smiling thinly.

Abdul walked around to the passenger side and climbed in. 'You are very kind,' he said.

Kareem carried out a multi-point turn in traffic to head back the way he had come. 'Al Mansour?' he asked.

'Thank you.' Abdul nodded.

They drove in silence until they reached the Jumhuriyah bridge, Kareem glancing at Abdul every now and then as if trying to think of something to say. 'How are you enjoying the job?' he finally asked.

'It seems very nice.'

'You have been very useful. Finding the house. Jake was very pleased.'

'Yes. That was lucky.'

'You knew Mallory from before, of course?' Kareem glanced at Abdul for a reaction.

'No.'

'Oh?' Kareem sounded surprised. 'But I thought he hired you because you were friends.'

'I did not know him before I arrived.'

'You mean before the hospital.'

Abdul did not understand. 'Hospital?'

'I first saw you at the hospital talking to Mallory.'

Abdul did not remember seeing Kareem that day. 'That was the first time I met him.'

'Ah . . . Then the woman you were with . . . she knew Mallory.'

'She is my sister.'

'Then that explains it.'

Abdul wondered what it explained but not enough to ask.

'You live with your sister?'

'That's right,' Abdul said, becoming irritated with the cross-examination.

'So she has known Mallory for a long time, then,' Kareem persisted.

Abdul glanced at him, wondering what was up with the man. 'No,' he said.

Kareem looked surprised. 'Are you sure?'

'Why are you asking me? I know my own sister.'

Kareem sighed as if something was weighing heavily on his mind. 'I am confused, then. That is all. So you were at the Sheraton when she was with Mallory?'

'What are you talking about?'

'The day of the rocket attack. Your sister was at the hotel.'

'I know. She was with a friend. A girlfriend,' Abdul said, annoyed with this fat Shi'a sticking his nose into his affairs.

'I am sorry, but the woman I saw you with at the hospital was at the hotel with Mallory and not another girl.'

Abdul stared at Kareem, his eyes narrowing.

'I saw her go into the restaurant with Mallory,' Kareem went on. 'Then the rockets hit. I would have asked you how she was after the attack, but later I heard she was fine.' Kareem glanced at Abdul long enough to see the other man's stare burning into him.

'What are you trying to say?' Abdul asked coldly.

'This is very difficult, you understand,' Kareem said.

'Tell me.'

Kareem was having doubts about taking the subject any further. His purpose for revealing what he knew was straightforwardly malicious. He enjoyed gossip and even though the implications of his information were dire only now did he appreciate the full gravity of it. 'I am only saying this because I am more your brother than I am Mallory's. You are Sunni but you are also Muslim and Arab. That is important to me.'

'I asked you what you are trying to say,' Abdul said softly but firmly.

The horn of the car behind honked and Kareem moved over to let the driver pass. 'A woman left Mallory's apartment early the next morning, after the rocket attack. She was seen by Jedel, a security guard at the hotel.'

'My sister?' Abdul asked.

Kareem shrugged nervously.

'And how can you be certain it was her? Did you see her?'

'No. The description was the same, though.' Kareem suddenly feared he had underestimated the other man who had more of an aura of power about him than he had first suspected. 'You are right. People should not jump to conclusions. This is a serious accusation . . . You would have known if your sister had not come home that night, of course,' Kareem said, glancing at Abdul who was looking ahead. 'I am sorry. Forget all that I have said.'

They did not speak for the rest of the journey and when Kareem stopped the car outside Abdul's apartment block the one-handed young man climbed out and walked away without saying another word.

Abdul walked up the stairs, opened his front door, stepped inside, closed the door behind him and remained rooted to the spot, horrified. The news had rocked him. It was possible the hotel security guard had lied or Kareem had made it up but Abdul knew in his heart that it was true. His sister had lied to him. Tasneen had spent the night with Mallory, a white man, an infidel.

Abdul sat on the couch as his stump began to throb slightly. But this was too serious an issue for him to be distracted even by this reminder of his mutilation. His sister, the most important person in his life, had betrayed him, the family, their name, their heritage, and Allah. She had defiled herself. Not only had she been with a man out of wedlock but it had been Mallory, a man he did not trust. Abdul realised that what he sensed about Mallory's attitude to him, what he took for suspicion, was something far worse. Mallory had been laughing at him.

Abdul rested his head on his hand and closed his eyes tightly as the torment swirled like a storm around him. He had thought that he knew Tasneen better than anyone but now it seemed he did not know her at all. She was everything to him: she was perfection. Now he could barely comprehend how in one short space of time she had destroyed their entire past together. She had lied from the beginning about Mallory and therefore every second, from the moment of their meeting on, had been a lie. Voices in his head began to chant, a single cry at first. Then others joined in, voices of his family but not just those of his father and mother. It was a collective cry from generations of his line. He was head of the family: his was the last remaining name on earth to represent them and they were calling to him from a thousand graves and over a thousand years, gathered in chorus, baying for justice, punishment. Tasneen must pay, they cried. She must pay. They both must pay!

Abdul got to his feet, went into the bathroom, turned on the tap and vigorously splashed his face with cold water. But the voices did not relent. Retribution, they clamoured. Revenge was the cry, and then he heard faint music, an Arabic song that he recognised. It was his cellular phone ringing in his pocket.

He pulled it out and looked at the display. Stanza. Abdul did not want to talk to anyone at that moment and he let it ring on. When it went quiet he walked back into the living room and considered what to do. The phone came to life once again and he checked the screen. It was Stanza again. Abdul knew the man well enough already to know he would call until Abdul answered. He pushed the receive button and put the phone to his ear. 'Yes?'

'Abdul?'

'Yes.'

'I've decided to go – to Fallujah.'

Abdul should have told him that he could not discuss it at the moment but the draw of the town suddenly grew in his mind to equal the overriding obsession of his sibling problem.

'Did you hear me, Abdul?'

'Yes.'

'I've just heard from a reliable source that the Americans may be attacking in under a week. I want to be out of Fallujah before the offensive begins.'

'I have not yet talked with my cousin,' Abdul said.

'Well, do it now, and let me know.'

'OK . . . I will.'

'Is everything all right?' Stanza asked, sensing an oddness about Abdul.

'All is fine.'

'I'll wait for your call, then,' Stanza said and ended the conversation.

Abdul lowered the phone and stared at the flower-pattern carpet as if in a trance. Going out of town would give him time to think, which he needed to do. Grave decisions had to be made. It would be best if he was not in the apartment when Tasneen returned. Masking his feelings would be difficult if he had to face her so soon.

Abdul scrolled through the numbers on his phone and hit the call button. A moment later it picked up. 'Muhammad. It's Abdul, your cousin. Tasneen's brother,' he added.

Muhammad was besotted with Tasneen which was another reason he would be eager to help. He sounded

pleased to hear from Abdul and after the initial pleas-
antries asked about his sister. Tasneen detested the man
but Abdul lied that she had asked after Muhammad's
health and sent her regards. Muhammad expressed his
strong feelings for her, as usual, and at the first opportunity Abdul declared he was coming to visit. The
announcement, as expected, gave Muhammad pause
and Abdul went on to explain how he needed his
cousin's help – and that it involved money. Muhammad
was now all ears. Abdul explained about the American
hostage and the newspaper journalist, emphasising the
funds available to pay those who assisted in the
endeavour. As Abdul had expected, Muhammad was
entirely at his service.

The first thing Abdul asked for was an accurate and
reliable route into Fallujah. Muhammad offered several.
Abdul chose the one closest to the route he knew –
he'd been to Fallujah only once since the war. The
town was forty minutes west of Baghdad by motorway
in normal traffic and the back roads would more than
double the time, depending on any obstacles encountered. Muhammad warned of an American checkpoint
on the motorway that could be avoided by heading
north a mile before it at Abu Ghraib. The route would
then take them along country lanes and eventually
lead into the town from the north. The Americans had
Fallujah pretty much surrounded but there were gaps
in the encirclement with which Muhammad was
familiar. Muhammad warned Abdul, however, that their
problem was not so much the Americans as the insurgents and sympathetic villagers who had set up their

own checkpoints inside and outside the American cordon. These checkpoints were not coordinated – they were run by local thugs monitoring their own patches. Most of the hard-line insurgents were in the town itself, preparing defences for the battle. Abdul should be prepared to bribe his way through these checkpoints but Muhammad was uncertain about the wisdom of attempting the journey with a white man. Still, a western reporter might be allowed in. Some insurgents would want the battle to be recorded from a point of view other than the American military's but others might kidnap the journalist simply because he was a westerner. Abdul told his cousin that he would call if he needed more advice and after Muhammad wished him luck he disconnected the call.

Abdul hit a couple more buttons on his phone and a few seconds later Stanza picked up. 'We go tonight,' Abdul said.

'Tonight!' Stanza echoed, surprised by Abdul's speed.

'Going at night will be best.'

Stanza pulled himself together and silently reassured himself that he could cancel at any moment. 'OK. How will we get there?'

'My car.'

'You want me to drive?' Stanza asked, his voice rising.

'I can drive. Or you can if you prefer.'

There was another long pause before Stanza spoke. 'What time were you thinking of leaving?'

'We should leave soon after dark.'

'OK. Come to my room. I don't want to be hanging

around outside.' A beep indicated that Stanza had cut the call and Abdul checked the phone to make sure.

Abdul took a moment to think what he might need to take with him and pared it down to just a pistol and money. He needed to get fuel for the car – he could quickly get the small mechanical problem it had fixed – but other than that his cousin would take care of all their needs in Fallujah. The rest was up to Abdul and his wits. It was Allah's mission but He used mortal tools to achieve His aims and if they were not up to it then He would allow them to fall.

Abdul went into his room, opened his wardrobe and removed the box that contained his pistol. He pocketed the gun and went back into the living room where he opened a drawer in the side of the coffee table and took out a notepad and pen. He needed to let Tasneen know that he would not be home for several days, otherwise she would be worried and look for him. He would also have to tell her he was going out of the city or she would wonder why he could not come home.

He considered telephoning her and then dismissed the idea in favour of the note. If he spoke to her he would have to deal with a myriad of questions but worse than that his anger might reveal itself and Abdul did not want to deal with the problem of her relationship with Mallory until his return. The ramifications of that issue crowded his mind and the pain of accepting that his relationship with his beloved sister was at an end was like a burning knife in his heart.

But Abdul warned himself not to linger on the past.

His religion, tradition and a thousand ghosts would not allow it: Tasneen and Abdul's lives were inconsequential when compared with the greater scheme of things. He could not begin to fathom why she had done such a thing – but then, there could never be an explanation that would satisfy him. There was no acceptable explanation why she had gone alone to a man's private room. Staying the night put it beyond all reason. Death was a more acceptable option than dishonouring herself and her family. She was a Muslim, an Arab, an Iraqi. What made it even more horrendous, if that was possible, was who she had done this foul deed with. Had he been an Arab and a Muslim Abdul would still have wanted revenge. But to defile herself with an infidel – with Mallory, an Englishman – was beyond comprehension.

Abdul suddenly felt painfully alone, more than ever before, beyond the loneliness that had engulfed him when his father had kicked him out of the house for deserting the army. And it was going to get much worse between him and Tasneen before he could put it in the past. He thought about seeking advice – from a mullah, perhaps. But that would mean airing his family's shame in public and he could not do that. It was bad enough that the likes of Kareem knew. And how many others by now? The shame of it all intensified at the thought of the gossip that was being spread around at that very moment. The stain on his line would be there for ever. It was more than an obligation to exact revenge. It was Abdul's duty.

Mallory should be the first to suffer because Tasneen

would have to know that he had been punished before her own sentence could be carried out. She would have to recognise the enormity of her sin and be aware that her partner in this crime had paid the ultimate price. Abdul would give her time to ask Allah for forgiveness before he sent her to Him.

The horror of what Abdul had to do was vivid in his mind but he believed in its necessity wholeheartedly. He had a great deal to do during these coming days. So much that it began to seem impossible to achieve. But it was not impossible. He had dealt with Hassan, a test of fire that he would have believed beyond him had he consciously made it his mission when he'd set out that night. He would find the American hostage, he would kill Mallory and then Tasneen: when it was over he would have truly reached manhood and would be free of the chains of his youth, his soul cleansed of sins, and free to pursue a purified life.

Abdul took a deep breath and scribbled a few lines on the page. He decided to reveal that he would be staying with Muhammad in Fallujah while he, Abdul, was with his reporter boss. Muhammad would use Abdul's visit as an excuse to call her anyway. It was of no consequence if she knew where he was. He no longer needed to deceive her about anything. Before her execution he would tell her the truth about his hand and inform her that he had killed Hassan in revenge. She would depart this world knowing she was leaving behind not a little brother but a man.

Abdul put the pen down, leaving the page on the

table, and got to his feet, feeling in his pockets for his car keys, gun and identification card. Satisfied that he had everything he needed he went to the front door. Then he paused to look up at the Koran on the shelf. He took it down, held it most reverently, closed his eyes while he asked Allah for the strength that he would need, kissed it and returned it to the shelf.

He closed the door behind him.

Stanza drew the cord tight on his backpack and wondered if there was anything else that he needed to take. He had his satellite and mobile phones, tape recorder, camera, plenty of pens and notebooks, his toothbrush and toothpaste, a flashlight and all of the bureau's money — six and a half thousand dollars — except for a thousand left behind as a reserve. He checked his watch and looked outside to see that the light was fading. The tingling fear had not left him since Abdul had called to say they were going into Fallujah that night. Sometimes it got so bad that he had to sit down and go through his mission to reassure himself. He knew it was madness, that he was taking a great personal risk. But then, great things were never achieved without those elements being present. He told himself he had to keep that in mind. It was the madness of his adventure that would later be interpreted as dedication to his work and set Stanza apart from all the others. He was going into the gorgon's lair for sure, but what he would retrieve would be the envy of everyone in his profession. There wouldn't be a journalist or media organisation in the entire world who would not know his name.

It was the moment of truth. Stanza could grab the chance for fame and glory or let it pass. Few people ever got such opportunities and if Stanza turned away from it his life would effectively be over. At the end of the day the choice was between possible death or certain oblivion for if he ignored this opportunity he would fall into the void. In the end, actual death was better than that.

A knock startled him into standing up. He walked to the door, opened it and Abdul marched straight in. Stanza's stare was fixed on the young Arab as he followed him into the room. 'Is everything OK?' he asked.

When Abdul looked at him his lips formed a thin, reassuring smile. 'Are you ready?'

'I am,' Stanza said, nodding slowly and deliberately.

Abdul could see that Stanza had wrestled with the decision and that his courage had emerged victorious. But he wondered how long it would last. 'Good.'

'How long do you think it will take? I know we can't know for sure – but an estimate?'

'I am hoping that one day will see our first contact made,' Abdul said. 'After that . . . it depends on the result of the meeting. If we are lucky we can return tomorrow.'

'Good.' Stanza nodded. It was precisely what he wanted to hear. 'You have a route?'

'Yes. We head up the motorway and before the main

checkpoint we turn off and head east, then north. I have directions.'

'Why do we need to avoid the American checkpoints?' Stanza asked. 'Surely they would be points of safety for us.'

'The answer is simple. They will not let us through. We do not live there so we cannot pass.'

'And the insurgents' checkpoints? How do we deal with them if we meet them?'

'But that's who we are looking for,' Abdul said. 'We have to meet them sometime and begin our negotiations.'

Stanza had come to the same conclusion but wanted to hear it from Abdul. His confidence in the young man had increased but the fear would not leave him.

'I am in as much danger as you,' Abdul said, reading Stanza's concerns.

Stanza looked at the young Arab. 'Why *are* you doing this?'

Abdul was not sure how to answer. He did not care to reveal his reasons to the American but he still felt an explanation was needed. 'Guilt,' Abdul said. 'Anger.'

'I don't understand.'

'I have no purpose. Up until now I have only been a victim.' Abdul felt his stump. 'I want to become involved . . . This is a beginning perhaps.'

Stanza was still not clear about Abdul's reasons but the young man appeared sincere enough.

'Are you ready?' Abdul asked.

'Let's do it,' Stanza said, removing his jacket from the back of the chair, pulling it on and picking up his backpack. As the two men stepped towards the door there was a distant boom, followed by a low rumble that gently rocked the balcony windows. Stanza paused for only a second before walking out of the room. He locked the door and followed Abdul along the landing.

Tasneen closed the apartment door and tiredly pulled off her jacket as she headed for the kitchen to make herself a much-needed cup of tea. She saw the sheet of notepaper on the coffee table and at first ignored it. But as she turned on the electric kettle she had second thoughts and went back into the living room. On reading the few lines she was instantly filled with dread. Fallujah had been on everyone's lips that day at the Palace: the general consensus among the Americans seemed to be that not only was the battle imminent but the town with its estimated thousand insurgents was going to be levelled.

Tasneen scrambled for her phone and dialled Abdul's number. It rang for a moment until the irritating female voice broke in to inform her that the phone she was trying to call was either switched off or out of the coverage area.

She paced the room, wringing her hands, and then scrolled through the phone list until she came to her code name for Mallory. She waited impatiently for it to ring.

'Mallory here,' he said almost immediately.

'Bernie. It's Tasneen.'

'Tasneen,' he said, delighted.

'Bernie, where's Abdul?'

'Abdul? I don't know.'

'What's he doing? I must talk to him.'

'I haven't spoken to him since yesterday.'

'You must know where he is?'

'What's wrong, Tasneen?'

'Don't you know he's in Fallujah? I just got home and found a note from him.'

'Fallujah?' Mallory said, obviously astonished.

'Why is he going there?'

'I have no idea. Are you sure?'

'I must find him. If he's not going with you, what is he doing?'

'Look. No one's going to Fallujah. Certainly not Abdul. Stanza's said nothing to me.' But as soon as the words left his lips Mallory knew he was wrong. Stanza had been acting weird all day. Then there'd been the sighting of Abdul that morning. Mallory had known that something was up but frankly hadn't cared enough to find out what.

'Abdul would not make it up, Bernie. Not something like this.'

'Can I get back to you?' Mallory said, heading for the door. 'I'll find out what's going on and call you back.'

'Please, Bernie,' Tasneen said pitifully.

'I will. Soon as I know. I'm going now. Bye.' Mallory ended the call as he walked out of his room towards Stanza's. Perhaps Stanza had sent Abdul to Fallujah for something. The man was stupid enough to do that.

He knocked on Stanza's door and when there was no immediate answer he knocked again more loudly. 'Stanza,' he called out. 'It's me. Mallory.'

Mallory dug out his phone, brought up Stanza's number and hit the send button. The line rang and then suddenly stopped as if the phone had been turned off. Mallory dialled Abdul's number and, according to the young lady's recorded voice, it was either switched off or beyond signal range.

Mallory's feelings of concern deepened. Something was going on that he was not privy to and he felt that he was being tugged in several different directions. On the one hand he shouldn't have cared because he had his own mission to complete. But on the other, Abdul's life could be at risk and Mallory had responsibilities on that score, his own as well as those he had to Tasneen. The other issue was of course Stanza's security but Mallory wasn't particularly bothered about that – beyond a niggling sense that it was one of his professional duties. The first thing to do was find out where the pair were. He scrolled to another number and called it.

'Kareem? It's Mallory. I'm looking for Abdul.'

Kareem explained how he had dropped him off at Abdul's apartment and when Mallory asked him if he knew anything about a trip to Fallujah Kareem said that he knew nothing. Kareem had not talked to Stanza all day but he did have one bit of bad news: Farris was leaving with his family for Jordan in the next couple of days. Mallory had no interest in Farris at that moment so he ended the conversation and went to the rail to look down into the lobby. Stanza's absence from his room was bothering him since there was nowhere to go in the hotel, unless the journalist had made some friends. Stanza didn't go to the gym and usually had one of the drivers bring him food from outside at around this time. Kareem hadn't heard from him and Farris was out of the loop now, it seemed. As for his work, Stanza was not booked on an embed – Mallory would have known about that – and he could not have taken an Arab with him anyway.

The little creep of a reporter was up to something but worse, he was avoiding Mallory and Mallory resented that hugely.

Mallory's phone chirped and he snatched it up to look at the screen before answering, expecting it to be Abdul or Stanza. In fact, it was Des. This was not a good time. He hit the receive button and put it to his ear. 'Mallory.'

'Where've you been?' Des asked. 'I've been calling you for ages.'

'You know how the phones are.'

'You still want the embed, yer need to get to helipad in twenty minutes. Go like mad 'n' you could make it.'

Mallory suddenly didn't know what to do. 'Have you seen my journalist?'

'What?'

'Stanza. The one who got shot.'

'No, mate. Do yer want this embed or what?'

Mallory squeezed his forehead with his fingers as he fought to make a decision. Then something else dawned on him. 'Shit, I don't have a driver.'

'Right. One o' mine is just leaving the hotel. I'll

give 'im a call and tell 'im to meet yer outside the far checkpoint. If yer run yer might make it.'

'OK . . . OK. Bye.' Mallory killed the call and stood tensely, trying to decide what to do. This was what he had been waiting months for. It might be his last chance. God only knew what would happen to Fallujah after the Americans went in. The cemetery could get blown to bits. The town could get shut down for months or even longer. He could search for Abdul and Stanza all night and not find them. Or if he did and they were doing nothing more than having dinner in the Palestine Mallory would be furious. And – worst-case scenario – if indeed they had gone to Fallujah, which Mallory still could not believe, it was out of his hands anyway.

'Bollocks,' he said as he hurried back into his room, snatched up his backpack, and broke into a run towards the emergency stairs.

Abdul's car was parked away from any others in the hotel-complex car park, beneath a couple of parched eucalyptus trees, and Stanza paused in front of it.

'You sure you're OK to drive?'

'It's an automatic,' Abdul said as he put the key in the door.

Stanza did not look any more convinced.

'If we get stopped I will have to do the talking,' Abdul said. 'I also know the way.'

Stanza's expression did not change – Abdul could easily mediate and navigate from the passenger seat.

'Then you drive,' Abdul said, shrugging with indifference.

'What the hell. Go ahead,' Stanza said as he moved to the passenger door. 'If I get crazy with your driving we can always stop and swap over.'

As both men opened their doors a dark muscular-looking Mercedes sedan cruised into the car park, the wheels that supported the four tons of armoured glass and bodywork crunching over the gravel. It stopped a short distance in front of Abdul's car, bathing the two men in its powerful headlights.

Abdul and Stanza squinted at the vehicle as the engine died, leaving the headlights burning. Both rear passenger doors opened and two men climbed out. One stayed beside his open door while the other walked to the front of the Mercedes. He gave a discreet hand signal and the headlights died.

'Jake,' the man said.

Stanza strained to see who it was but could only make out that the man was Caucasian and was wearing a tailored jacket with a crisp white open-neck shirt beneath. 'Who am I talking to, please?' he asked, somewhat pathetically. The man standing by the open rear door moved away from the car a little and Stanza saw some kind of rifle in his hands.

'Name's Bill Asterman,' the man at the front of the Mercedes said in a distinctly Midwestern American accent. 'I'm from the embassy.'

'The American embassy?' Stanza asked.

'That would be correct,' Asterman said dryly.

Stanza looked around, wondering if other embassy guys were standing in the darkness. It was very sinister. 'What . . . what can I do for you guys?' The man's features became a little more visible. He looked middle-aged with that polished clean-cut bearing one associated with Secret Service types.

'Where are you headed, Jake?' Asterman asked.

'How do you know me? My name?'

'Jake Stanza of the Milwaukee *Herald* . . . That's not a secret, is it, Jake?'

'Well. That . . . that's me.'

'I asked where you were headed?'

'Headed?' Stanza repeated, sounding pathetic even to himself, unable to be more assertive.

'Yeah. As in where are you going?'

'I'm . . . I'm er, heading out, with my translator.'

'Yes. But where is "out"? Where are you going?' Asterman's voice was a patient monotone.

'Do you mind if I ask who wants to know?' Stanza ventured bravely.

'I'm an official of the US government. *Your* government . . . We have responsibilities to you, Jake. But you also have responsibilities to us . . . So why don't you just tell me where you're headed?'

Stanza wasn't sure of his ground. He'd never come across government types like this before. 'The convention centre . . . We're heading over there for a meeting.'

Asterman took a packet of cigarettes from his pocket, toyed with it for a moment then brought both hands up to his face. A second later a flame appeared illuminating his cropped blond hair and when his hands went back down he had a cigarette in his mouth. One of his hands went back into his pocket while the other returned to his mouth to remove the cigarette and allow a long stream of smoke to escape. 'The convention centre? There are no pressers today. Who you meeting?'

The man had all the airs and attitudes of an interrogator and Stanza had the sudden feeling that this stranger actually already knew a whole lot about what Stanza was really doing. 'Why are you so interested?' The journalist tried to lighten his tone by forcing a smile but he could not sustain it.

'That's my job, Jake . . . So, if you don't mind, I'll ask you again. Where are you going?'

'I told you,' Stanza said, clearing his throat nervously.

Asterman took a slow draw on his cigarette and blew the smoke out towards Stanza through pursed lips. 'I'll tell you something, Jake. In my job I rarely ask questions I don't know the answer to.'

Stanza told himself to get a grip: he was perfectly within his rights to go wherever he wanted in Iraq. He was the press, after all. 'OK,' he said, putting a little starch into his backbone. 'You wanna know where I'm going, then you say you know where I'm going. Fine. I don't know why it's any of your business but I'm going to Fallujah.'

'Why are you going to Fallujah?' Asterman asked in the same monotone. It was beginning to irritate Stanza.

'I'm a journalist. Dozens of journalists are going to Fallujah. There's a damned battle about to take place there,' Stanza said. The growing irritation in his voice was a substitute for genuine confidence.

'But are you going to Fallujah just as a journalist?' Asterman asked.

'Why else would I be going there?'

'What's the story, Jake?'

'What the hell is this all about? Huh? I don't have to tell you anything.'

'And you know why that is, Jake?'

Stanza gritted his teeth. 'Because you know everything? You tapping my phones and my e-mails? Is that it?'

'You're aware of our policy about negotiating with kidnappers,' Asterman said.

'I'm aware of your policy. But that's *all* it is: a policy, not a law.'

'Where did you get the idea that you could do whatever you wanted in this country?' Asterman asked.

'So what are you trying to tell me? That I have no right to try and free an American from captivity? You think that's gonna fly? Tell me some more. I'd love to write that story.'

The man took a final draw from his cigarette and tossed the glowing butt to the ground. 'I have a responsibility for your safety, Jake. It's not true that I can't stop you. But I respect your freedom. I'd just like *you* to respect *our* efforts to maintain national security.'

'You've got to be kidding me. How the fuck does this affect national security?'

There was an uneasy silence for a moment until Asterman eventually spoke. 'What if I told you I could block the ransom money?'

'I'd say you were full of shit. If they cut his head off that would put the knife in your hands.'

There was another long silence.

'You gonna stop me or not?' Stanza asked.

'Like I said, Jake. I respect your freedom . . . Gonna be a tough drive, though.' Asterman looked over at Abdul, his gaze falling on the young man's stump. 'Off the record, Jake. One American to another. That's a mean road you're gonna have to take. A lotta tougher folk than you have tried it and failed.'

The sound of footsteps crunching the gravel caused the spooks to turn instantly. The one by the open door raised his M4 assault rifle as another climbed out of the front passenger side, a pistol in his hand.

Mallory walked past the Mercedes, his small backpack over his shoulder. 'Evening,' he said to Asterman as he carried on across to Abdul. 'Keys,' he said, holding out his hand.

Abdul had remained perfectly still throughout the exchange, unable to understand the game being played and concerned that the American official was going to stop them going to Fallujah. Mallory's arrival caused Abdul's heart to race and he lowered his head, unable to look the man in the eyes for fear that his own stare might reveal his hatred. He dropped the car keys into Mallory's outstretched hand.

Asterman looked from Mallory back to Stanza and sighed deeply. 'You know what happened to Pierre Dusard, John Santez, Mike Kominsky, Paul Jerome, Natasha Kemp, all media freelancers who went into Fallujah a week ago?'

Stanza stared coldly back at Asterman, suspecting that he could guess the answer.

'Neither do we. And we know more than most.' Asterman walked back to his open door and climbed in. His men did the same. The Mercedes's engine and headlights came to life again and after the heavy doors had closed it reversed a short distance, pulled a slow, tight turn and cruised out of the car park.

When Stanza looked over at Mallory his security adviser was staring back at him coldly. 'Are you gonna tell me I can't go too?' Stanza asked. 'Because if you do I'll tell you the same thing I told him.'

Mallory had been jogging past the end of the car park heading towards the checkpoint, when he'd seen Stanza in the headlights of the Mercedes some distance away, just before they went out. He'd heard most of the conversation, unable to tear himself away, and when he realised Stanza was going to stick with his plan to go to Fallujah it seemed that the only thing he could do was join the journalist and Abdul. Travelling with them legitimised his trip to Fallujah – he was respon-sible for their security, after all. It was still crazy but now that it was probably too late to catch his embed he was left with the same choice as before but with a different way of achieving it. He chose to go for it.

'Get in the car,' Mallory said to them both.

Abdul climbed in the back as Mallory sat behind the wheel. Stanza remained standing outside. 'Are you getting in or not?' Mallory called out, starting the engine.

Stanza leaned down to look at Mallory. Several

things were playing on the reporter's mind, but eventually he climbed in and closed the door. Mallory put the car in drive and they headed out through the checkpoints.

After the last chicane the car turned along the potholed road that led to Sadoon Street and they crawled along, steering left and right to avoid the worst of the hazards. Before they reached the main road where traffic was passing in both directions Stanza held up his hand. 'Stop the car,' he said.

Mallory glanced at him. 'What, here?'

'I said stop the car.'

'This is not a good place—'

'STOP THE GODDAMNED CAR!' Stanza shouted at the top of his voice.

Mallory was angered by the sheer petulance of the command but the man was clearly upset about something. He brought the car to a halt.

Stanza clenched his jaw. 'What the fuck is GOING ON?' he shouted before turning in his seat to look at Abdul. 'You ever see that guy before?'

Abdul shook his head. 'No.'

'Tell me something. What the fuck are you doing here? Huh? Why are you here?'

'You asked me that already,' Abdul said.

'A sense of fucking purpose? Bullshit! A chicken-shit kid like you wants to go with me to the most dangerous goddamned town in the goddamned world because you're feeling left out of things?'

Mallory stared ahead, knowing that his turn was surely coming.

Abdul remained calm. 'I will not die for you if that's what you think. I believe in what we are doing.'

Stanza stared at the young man for a few seconds, unable to decide if his reply was in any way convincing. Then he turned to Mallory. 'And what the hell is your excuse? Huh? You have more chance of getting whacked than I do. At least I have some value as a journalist if we get caught. They'll label you CIA and slice your goddamned head off in a heartbeat . . . Well?'

'You'll think my reason is stupid.'

'No kidding. Why should you be the only person in this car with an intelligent reason for going to that shit-hole? . . . No, please tell me. I'd like to hear anyway.'

'Well. The truth is . . . I'd like to see the fighting. I missed most of the war and to be honest this might be my last chance to see a full-on battle.'

'You want to go and watch the battle?! Christ, now I really am worried . . . Do you know why I'm going?'

'Lamont . . . I heard most of the conversation between you and the spook and I can figure out the rest.'

'What were you doing in the car park?' Stanza asked, suddenly wondering.

'I saw you both leaving the hotel and I was curious.'

'And you just happened to have your backpack with you.'

'If you were going out I was going too. You two've been sneaking around devising some kind of conspiracy,' Mallory said, starting to raise his voice. 'I'm the one who should be pissed off here. I'm in charge of security and you two planned a trip to Fallujah without even consulting me.'

'And you can't figure out why?'

'Damn right! I would've said no.'

'Then what the hell are we doing now?'

Mallory exhaled as he lost the edge of his feigned anger. 'I decided that what you were doing was . . . well, a pretty good thing. Maybe you should do it or at least try. And I couldn't just sit back in the hotel room and let you go alone.'

Stanza looked ahead quizzically, then glanced between Mallory and Abdul again before facing the front. 'I don't know what to think any more. But something stinks about this whole thing. You. Him.'

Mallory decided to shut up and let Stanza work his way through it. The man was indecisive but now it looked as if the decision to go was all down to him. Mallory could only wonder how he'd got into this position.

Abdul remained quietly in the darkness of the back of the car, unsure of what to make of the pair of them.

Mallory studied the darker shadows around them. The lone car with its engine running and lights on would eventually attract attention, not only from bad guys but from any army or police who happened to be in the area.

'I'm not sure if I have the strength to say that we should go any more,' Stanza finally said. 'If you leave it up to me I think I'll say go back to the hotel.'

Mallory shifted in his seat, wondering how he could manipulate Stanza's uncertainty. 'Why don't we just head out of Baghdad, assessing the situation as we go? We don't need to take stupid risks if we play it right. If it starts to look dodgy we abort and come home.'

Stanza looked at Mallory. 'You want to go that bad?'

'Stanza,' Mallory began, sounding tired of him. 'I don't care if you want to go back to the hotel. It's fine with me. But I bought into your mission to try and save Lamont. I think it's a noble idea and I have not been on a noble mission for quite some time now. So why don't you just run through all the reasons you wanted to go to Fallujah in the first place – quietly in your head, if you don't mind – and if they no longer work for you then let's turn around. But do me a favour. Make your decision fast because I don't want to sit in this street like a fucking target for a moment longer. And if it's a yes, I don't want to hear you whingeing to go home half a mile up the road. I run the road trip until we start the negotiations and then it's all yours.'

They sat in silence for a moment. Stanza shifted uncomfortably. 'I'm sorry. You're right . . . Asterman spooked me,' he said.

'That's what he was trying to do,' Mallory said.

'I'll leave it up to you. You're the security expert. If you think we should go then we'll go.'

'Oh, for fuck's sake,' Mallory said as he put the car in gear. The bat was back in his hands and he had already decided what he would do with it despite the constant doubts. The car crawled out of a water-filled pothole and bumped its way to the end of the road. Mallory paused at the junction for a gap in the traffic and quickly cut across the oncoming lane to join the handful of cars heading north.

13

Into the Breach

Mallory adjusted the rear-view mirror: he watched it as much as he looked ahead – his normal technique whenever he pulled away in a vehicle. This time his concern was more acute than ever. His usual plan in the event that they picked up a tail was to head for the nearest US checkpoint. But on this night they were heading out of Baghdad, away from nearby safe locations, and picking up a couple of bandits would create problems. It was impossible to detect a follower quickly if the driver behind had any level of skill. The trick was to find a distinguishing feature of any suspect vehicle that would be easily recognisable further into the journey.

Stanza picked up on Mallory's vigilance. 'You think he might follow us?'

'Who?'

'That jerk Asterman.'

'I can't think why.'

'Because we might lead him to Stanmore.'

'Who?'

Stanza sighed. 'Lamont's real name . . . It doesn't matter right now.'

Mallory nodded. The details held little more than a mild interest to him. 'Asterman won't follow. If he gets too far from the safety of the Green Zone he'll attract more attention in that armoured Merc than we will in this piece of shit . . . No offence meant, Abdul.'

Abdul ignored the comment and Mallory glanced at him in the mirror as he steered around the Jumhuriyah roundabout and onto the bridge.

'Abdul knows a route into Fallujah,' Stanza offered.

'Abdul?' Mallory said, looking for a response to Stanza's comment.

'You are heading for the ten motorway?' Abdul asked.

'Yes.'

'Take the ten and I will tell you where to turn off.'

Mallory checked the lights in the rear-view mirror again to see that the configuration had changed. He memorised the new image and settled down as they left the bridge and turned right at the Assassins' Gate towards Haifa Street.

'Don't take Haifa,' Abdul said calmly.

'I wasn't going to,' Mallory said. Haifa Street was probably the most dangerous stretch of residential road in Baghdad after the BIAP. US convoys could expect some sort of attack every time they went down it. Mallory took the next turn left at the Al Mansour Hotel, cut across town towards the disused Baghdad Airfield that was now a US military camp and headed east on the main surface streets to the entrance of the ten motorway. Traffic was light and after they mounted the access ramp a glance in the rear-view mirror revealed that they were alone.

The black surface of the motorway stretched ahead of them with only a sprinkling of tiny red and white lights along it. Ten minutes later they passed a sign for Abu Ghraib and Abdul sat forward in his seat as if suddenly taking an interest in the journey. 'That's the prison,' he said and they all looked to the right at the long, brightly lit and ominous wall topped with razor wire and sentry towers. The car passed through an underpass and Mallory noted they were now the only vehicle on the road in either direction.

'Mobile phones don't work beyond here,' Abdul said, referring to the poor signal reception. 'The first American checkpoint is about a mile further on. We must turn off soon.'

'What do we turn off onto?' Mallory asked. 'A road, track, what?'

'A track through a gap in the barriers,' Abdul said, peering into the distance in an effort to find it. 'There!' he suddenly called out, pointing to the near side.

Mallory slammed on the brakes and the car's tyres screeched loudly. Before it came to a stop Mallory slammed it into reverse and the occupants jerked forwards as the vehicle accelerated backwards, snaking from side to side as Mallory avoided the crash barriers. They passed the gap, Mallory applied the brakes – with less of a screech this time – threw the lever into drive, which caused a crunching sound, and the car shunted forward. He turned off the road and down a steep bumpy embankment after which the ground levelled out again. The headlights exposed deep tyre tracks in the sand and Mallory followed them into the blackness.

'How far along this track?' Mallory asked, deciding to get all the information he could from Abdul ahead of time to avoid any more emergency stops.

'You will come to a road soon. We go left.'

The sandy track was awkward to drive along at any great speed with several soft patches that threatened to suck them to a standstill if Mallory got too slow. He maintained the vehicle's momentum to push them through and after half a mile they mounted a solid bank and bounced over an edge onto a narrow tarmac road. Mallory braked hard as he turned the wheel in an effort to keep all four tyres on the road. He had only partial success. But the verge was firm and eventually he managed to steer back onto the tarmac and accelerate away.

'What's next?' Mallory asked, peering ahead along a straight dark road that the headlights failed to illuminate adequately. Open countryside was on either side of them, with clumps of bushes and trees lining the road.

'Stay on this road for a few miles,' Abdul said.

'And then what?' Mallory persisted.

'We pass through some villages and then we come to a river, which we will follow.'

'What about the US military?' Stanza asked.

'What about them?' Abdul asked.

'For Christ's sake. Where are they?' Stanza asked excitedly.

Mallory glanced at the journalist, wondering exactly how strung out he was.

'I do not know where the Americans are,' Abdul said. 'They could be anywhere . . . They are not your only problem, though.'

'Don't you just love the way he says "your problem" and not "ours"?' Stanza mumbled.

Several squat angular shapes appeared up ahead and a moment later a dull orange glow became evident inside some of them. It was a small mud-brick hamlet of dilapidated dwellings, several with benzene lamps but with no other sign of life other than a corral of aimless-looking cows and goats. The car's headlights swept across the animals as it passed through the village.

Mallory was maintaining a pace that would only just allow him time to react safely if something appeared in the headlights. He took a moment to run through in his mind the technicalities of a handbrake turn. He'd done one only once before – for a laugh when he'd been a young Marine out with some of the lads.

A T-junction appeared eventually and Abdul instructed Mallory to take the left turn. The other minor roads they had been on since leaving the motorway had been quite straight but this one snaked tightly. Mallory soon realised they were following the line of a small river mostly hidden behind a lush bank of trees and bushes. They shadowed the waterway for several miles before eventually moving away from it and straightening up again. A fork in the road appeared and Mallory slowed, expecting Abdul to give him directions but none came. He turned to see Abdul looking ahead, a confused expression on his face.

'Well?' Mallory asked.

Abdul's expression did not change.

Stanza looked around at him. 'Which way?'

'We should come to a crossroads after the river,' Abdul said.

'Which way did your cousin say to go at the crossroads?' Mallory asked.

'Across.'

They stared at the junction for a moment.

'What came after the crossroads?' Mallory asked, breaking the silence.

'A fork.'

Mallory sighed in frustration. 'Which way at the fork?'

'Left,' Abdul said, suddenly irritated that Mallory assumed he had got the crossroads and the fork mixed up. 'My cousin told me a crossroads was first.'

Mallory made an executive decision and accelerated into the left-hand road. 'What came after the fork?'

'Another crossroads.'

They drove along the winding road into increasing darkness that the car's headlights struggled to penetrate. All eyes were glued to the beam as a faint glow on the horizon hinted at a town ahead.

Stanza clasped his clammy hands together, his breathing quicker than normal. Since leaving the city he'd more than once had the urge to slam the dashboard and demand that Mallory turn around and head back to the hotel. The fear of running smack-bang into death at any second grew with every bend in the road – he felt as if he was playing some insane game of Russian roulette. But he could not say what kept him from giving in to his fears. It was not embarrassment, nor the dim hope of getting the story of his life, nor the chance of saving Stanmore's life. What kept Stanza from cracking wide open was the connection he had made with his old self. It was not all that long ago that Stanza would look forward in an odd kind of way to dangers such as the race riots he had experienced. This mission to Fallujah was far more dangerous, of course, but the buzz was similar and he needed to find that part of himself again.

This was a new epoch in journalism, the age of the media warrior. More journalists were dying for the cause of getting a story than ever before and Stanza was a part of this brave new era. But simply holding on while the possibility of unknown horrors loomed closer was proving to be the most difficult thing he had ever done in his life.

Mallory realised he was gripping the steering wheel too tightly and forced himself to relax. His stress was intensifying with the feeling that he was possibly driving into hell on earth. He could imagine his reaction if someone had casually asked him in a pub back in Plymouth if he would risk his life for a million dollars. It would have been a resounding 'not likely'. Yet here he was. It was supposed to have been an exercise in planning and logistics but had grown slowly into an obsession. Pride was a killer of men, he remembered someone saying, a British affliction that the Royal Marines were so good at instilling into young men. Mallory was a finisher at heart, something he had learned about himself during commando training. But he also liked to think that he had *some* common sense, at least. This adventure was proving otherwise. Mallory didn't want to become a victim of his own pride, but it might already be too late.

The headlights suddenly illuminated several cans and large stones in a staggered line across the road and Mallory took his foot off the accelerator as his mind raced to decide if he should stop or keep going. As they moved closer a figure moved from the roadside bushes into the light of the beam, a young man in a scruffy *dishdash*, holding something long that was hidden in the folds of cloth at his side. Another man with a shabby *shamag* wrapped around his head and carrying a short pole stepped into view behind the first.

Everyone in the car tensed, Abdul gripping the back of Stanza's seat with his one hand.

Without any conscious thought Mallory hit the accelerator, pushing the pedal to the floor and willing the car to turn into a rocket. But time seemed to slow to a crawl and the car felt as if it had hardly speeded up at all. Two more men appeared from the other side of the road, stepping into the middle of it. The first man held up a hand, signalling the vehicle to stop, but Mallory bore down on him.

One of the front wheels struck an obstacle and the men made a concerted effort to dive out of the way.

But the corner of the car struck the first man's legs, the second faring only slightly better as one of the headlights shattered. The other pair scrambled in their sandals to take evasive action on the loose surface. Mallory swerved in an effort to avoid them but there was a quick succession of thumps and the remaining headlight exploded.

'Down!' Mallory shouted as he continued to swerve the car from left to right, expecting a volley of bullets to follow them. He could barely make out the road ahead by the dim glow from the sidelights and it seemed like an age before the sound of gunfire eventually started behind them. None of the bullets seemed to strike the car. Mallory hit the high verge on the edge of the road and kept going until they were out of direct line of sight. He pulled the car over in an effort to keep it in the centre of the road and they drove on, the weak sidelights struggling to illuminate the road more than a few metres ahead.

Mallory took his foot off the accelerator to slow the vehicle down. 'Everyone all right?' he called out, glancing at Stanza who had his hands pressed tightly against the sides of his head as if he did not want to hear. 'Stanza?'

Stanza flashed Mallory a startled look.

'You OK?'

Stanza nodded. 'We're not going to do that again, are we?' It was more of a request than a question.

'Abdul?' Mallory asked.

'I'm OK,' Abdul said quietly from a corner of the back seat.

'What now?' Stanza asked.

'What do you mean?'

'We can't continue!' Stanza said, an octave higher.

Mallory steered around a curve, his eyes searching ahead in the gloom and then slowed to a stop before turning off the engine and lights. He opened his door and climbed out.

Stanza suddenly felt vulnerable and climbed out on his side. Mallory was looking up the road in the direction they had come. 'What are we doing?' Stanza asked in a low voice. It had gone strangely silent after the ambush incident.

'I'm listening,' Mallory said.

'You think they might come after us?'

'No.'

'Do you think we hurt anyone?'

The back door opened with a creak and Abdul climbed out.

'Mallory?' Stanza was seeking an answer to his question.

'I think they'll think twice next time before they try to stop a speeding car with their bodies.'

Stanza was in no mood for any flippancy. 'What do we do now?' he insisted.

Mallory wished the man had a little more backbone. He'd given Stanza credit for beginning the journey but had suspected that he might crumble at some point. 'We go on . . . The problem's behind us.'

'What if we want to go back? What if we had to?'

'We can't. Not the way we've just come . . . I'd have thought that was obvious.'

'But if we did want to,' Stanza said. 'If we did, how could we?'

'Don't ask me. Ask Abdul.'

'I only know this route from here,' Abdul said.

Stanza looked up the road ahead, into the darkness, accepting that it was the only way to go but not liking it one little bit.

The sound of a very heavy engine starting up not far away got their attention and seconds later another grumbled to life with a throaty roar.

'Tanks,' Mallory said.

'They coming for us?' Stanza asked, alarm in his voice.

'Doubt it. Changing location, perhaps. They could be half a mile away. Difficult to tell at night.'

Mallory went to the front of the car and looked along the road into the darkness. 'We can't stay here and we can't go back,' he said.

'But what if we run into more of the last lot?' Stanza asked.

It was a good question that Mallory had no answer for.

'You should let me drive now,' Abdul said.

Both men looked at him.

'Get into the back, into the trunk. I will drive us through another checkpoint.'

Stanza's expression went from perplexity to astonishment. 'In the trunk?' he squawked.

Mallory's initial reaction was not far off Stanza's. But as he thought through their options, it seemed to him that, unsavoury as it was, Abdul's suggestion was probably the wiser course. The real question was whether or not Abdul could be trusted. There was something odd about the Arab that Mallory had not noticed before. He appeared more confident and self-assured but there was something else, something less definable, about him.

Stanza was looking at Mallory. 'You obviously don't think it's a bad idea,' he said accusingly.

'Maybe it isn't. Compared to our other choices.'

The rumbling engines grew louder and sounded as if they were heading towards the group.

'If the Americans catch us they'll probably hold us before sending us back,' Mallory said. 'Maybe for a day or so. Point is, this little adventure will then be over.'

That didn't sound like such a bad idea to Stanza.

'We can't be far from Fallujah,' Mallory said, looking at Abdul.

'A mile, maybe.'

The engines continued to draw closer and Mallory went to the trunk of the car and opened it. Inside was a box of what looked like spare parts, an empty fuel container and some rags. 'Now or never, Stanza . . . Make your mind up.'

Stanza could not get his feet to move. Why were there so many opportunities to quit? He groaned. It was like being compelled to jump off the roof of a skyscraper onto a blanket only to find oneself on another roof with yet another small blanket far below to jump onto. This time all he had to do was climb into an airless space and continue into hell blindfolded.

The distant engines sounded as if they were moving

behind them. Stanza looked at Abdul to assess him one more time, a man he hardly knew and in whose one hand he was expected to place his life. 'Ah, Jeezus,' he said as he gritted his teeth, walked to the trunk and placed a foot inside.

'Wait a minute,' Mallory said as he removed the fuel container and box and threw them into the bushes. 'In you get.'

Stanza obeyed.

Mallory joined him. When they were lying down Abdul took hold of the top of the lid and studied them for a moment. 'I'll do my best to get you there,' he said before slamming the trunk shut.

'I could have thought of more encouraging things to say under such circumstances,' Stanza said in a low voice, his lips close to the back of Mallory's head. The car lurched a little as Abdul climbed in.

He started the engine and was about to turn on the sidelights when he changed his mind. He put the gear change into drive and headed slowly down the road.

His eyes gradually grew more accustomed to the dark and he increased his speed.

Mallory and Stanza lay spooned together in the blackness, their hands braced against the sides of the trunk to keep from bashing into them. Mallory's concern inevitably increased now that he had relinquished all control to Abdul. He told himself he could trust the guy but that belief depended wholly on the fact that Abdul was Tasneen's brother. There was something oddly amusing about his predicament and had he been

401

with a fellow bootneck he might have joked about it. But Stanza was clearly not the person to share such bizarre humour with.

Abdul wound down his window, wondering if he would still be able to hear the tanks. He couldn't. The crossroads appeared and he passed straight over without slowing. As he reached the top of a gentle rise a yellowy glow lay spread out ahead of him. It was Fallujah — very close.

He turned on the sidelights to provide some illumination and the bushes and scruffy vegetation that had lined the road gave way to a broad expanse of open ground. Pinprick house lights appeared and Abdul remembered his cousin telling him to leave the road at that point and drive across the open hard-packed ground, heading directly for the town.

Shortly after leaving the road a long dark scar appeared ahead of him. Abdul realised it was the motorway that passed north of Fallujah and connected Baghdad with the Jordanian border. It was the same motorway that they had driven out of the city on and it was empty. His directions were to head right alongside an earthwork barrier in front of the motorway until he found a well-used gap through it. The gap in the silhouette was easy to spot, and Abdul drove through. When he reached the edge of the tarmac he stopped the car.

Muhammad had warned him that crossing the motorway at this point might be dangerous. The Marines were known to take pot-shots at vehicles avoiding their checkpoints and he would be in full view for several seconds.

Abdul took a moment to mention to Allah that he understood his life was in His hands and He was free to take it or otherwise. As soon as he had finished his short prayer he felt confident that Allah would not have brought him this far to die so uselessly. He pushed the accelerator pedal to the floor.

The engine roared as the wheels mounted the road, sped across the lanes, through the corresponding gap in the meridian and across to the other side. But as Abdul reached the edge he panicked as he realised that the motorway was far higher than the ground beyond and he was going too fast. The vehicle shot off the side and was practically airborne for a few seconds as the nose dropped to strike the dirt surface on the other side.

Mallory and Stanza were thrown against the roof of the trunk, against the petrol tank as the front wheels hit and when the rear wheels touched down they were hammered back against the floor.

The car immediately stalled and Abdul worked quickly to restart it, conscious that he was still in the open and a sitting duck. The engine came to life at the first try and, thanking Allah out loud, he accelerated ahead, the car fishtailing in the soft soil as he aimed for a gap between a row of squat buildings.

No sooner had Abdul rounded the corner of the end building when two youths, red *shamags* wrapped around their heads and faces, exposing only their eyes, one of them brandishing an AK47, stepped from the shadows and forced him to brake hard. They approached Abdul's side of the car, the boy with the gun holding it at the ready. He looked as though he meant business.

Abdul wound down his window. '*Salam alycom*,' he said to the boy with the assault rifle who had stopped a short distance from the car.

'Where are you going?' the boy asked.

'To visit my cousin, Muhammad Rahman,' Abdul said.

'Why are you here?'

'I have come to join the fight, of course,' Abdul said.

The boy remained suspicious and moved to look through the windows and inspect the back seat. Abdul noted his gaze wandering towards the trunk. 'Does your friend need a weapon?' Abdul asked.

The youngster's attention immediately went back to Abdul who was reaching into his pocket. He retrieved his pistol and held it out for the boy.

'What's in your other hand?' the boy asked suspiciously, bringing the end of the barrel up to meet Abdul.

Abdul held his stump out of the window. 'A gift from the Americans,' Abdul said. 'I have come to return it.'

The boy appeared to accept Abdul immediately and his stare fell back on the weapon.

'Take it,' Abdul said.

'What will you fight with?' the boy asked.

'My cousin has others.'

It was difficult to judge the boy's expression behind his *shamag* but Abdul thought it softened as he took the weapon. His friend stepped forward, anxious to have it. The boy handed the pistol to his colleague who inspected it eagerly.

'Be careful. It is loaded. Kill as many as you can,' Abdul said as he started to pull away. 'Allah be with you,' he added.

The boy stepped forward as if to stop Abdul. But he changed his mind and let him go, joining his friend to look at the pistol.

Mallory and Stanza had frozen the moment they'd heard the voices. They waited tensely for the trunk to open, their faces red in the glow of the brake lights. Neither of them could scarcely breathe, fearing this was the moment of their discovery. When the car shunted forward and accelerated away they were both exhausted by the tension.

'Are we in the town, do you think?' Stanza asked.

Mallory shushed him. Their fates were in Abdul's hands and there was no point in discussing anything until they were out of the trunk.

Abdul drove slowly along a narrow residential street, trying to work out his location according to his cousin's instructions. Only after turning right at a major road did he recognise where he was. A group of men, some with rifles slung over their backs, were up ahead, working by the light from a benzene lamp. They appeared to be moving some heavy items from the back of a pick-up truck into a house and as Abdul passed he saw a stack of large artillery shells. One of the men looked around at him and Abdul immediately faced ahead, prepared to stop if the man so much as lifted a finger. The man went back to directing his workers and Abdul suddenly felt a heightened nervous respect for the spirit of the town. It was as if the very buildings were holding their breath in anticipation of a coming storm.

He turned a corner clumsily, having to use his knees to get the wheel around before his hand could assist. There was activity in this street too with more armed men stacking sandbags to make what looked like a firing position, a collection of RPG rockets and ammunition boxes inside it. It seemed that everywhere there were signs of the great defence that the insurgent leader Zarqawi had threatened.

Mallory and Stanza lay wide-eyed in their uncomfortable confinement, their faces dimly illuminated by the rear lights of the vehicle. Mallory strained to look through a small hole in the tail light but could make out very little other than that they were in a town. The car was moving more slowly than before, swerving from one side to the other as if negotiating obstacles in the road.

Stanza was practically numbed by the entire experience, unable to see anything, and had somehow placed himself in a Zen-like state in order to get through the journey. His eyes finally opened when the vehicle came to a stop and the engine and lights went off. The pair remained frozen once again, all their senses tuned to the goings-on outside their metal shell.

One of the doors opened and the weight shifted as if Abdul had climbed out. This was followed by the sound of footsteps, but they were moving away.

'He's not coming to let us out,' Stanza whispered anxiously. 'What shall we do?'

'We're doing it,' Mallory said, adding a 'Shh.'

Mallory thought he could hear voices, followed by what sounded like a wooden door closing. A moment later the vehicle sank slightly as someone climbed in, the door closed and the engine came to life. They shunted forward slowly, took an immediate turn followed by another and a few seconds later slowed and went over a bump before coming to a stop again. The engine died, the driver climbed out and this time the footsteps came around to the back of the car. There was some shuffling, followed by the sound of wood creaking and then what sounded like a pair of large doors banging together. A moment of silence followed. Then Mallory and Stanza flinched as the trunk lock clunked loudly and was opened.

The two men remained in their dark pit like a couple of helpless animals, blinking up at a naked light bulb dangling on a wire between Abdul and another Arab who were looking down on them.

'This is my cousin Muhammad,' Abdul said.

Muhammad, who was older than Abdul, much fatter and looked nothing like him grinned broadly as he offered a hand to Mallory. Mallory took hold, assuming it had been offered to help him out, but Muhammad shook Mallory's hand weakly and let go.

'*Salam alycom*,' Mallory said as he pushed himself up, grabbed the side of the trunk, and got out. He stretched to relieve the stiffness in his back.

'*Alycom al salam*,' Muhammad said, placing a hand on his chest as he bowed slightly. 'Welcome, welcome.'

Mallory forced a smile and nodded.

'Hello,' Muhammad said, grinning and bobbing his head in a servile manner. He extended an arm towards an open door. 'Hello,' he repeated, indicating they should go that way, using the word with more versatility than Mallory was used to.

As Stanza climbed out of the trunk Mallory took a look around the dingy room that was filled with junk of all descriptions, none of it valuable. Stanza brushed himself down and shook the cousin's offered hand. The man bid him hello and indicated the open door again. Muhammad shuffled towards the door and Abdul indicated that the others should follow.

Muhammad led them along a short corridor to a doorway with a curtain across it. The air here smelled like a strong mixture of mildew and kerosene fumes, an aroma explained by the contents of the room that Muhammad invited them into. He held back the curtain to reveal a dark interior more than amply furnished with cushions of every size and colour, though black and burgundy were the most prevalent. Rugs covered every inch of the floor and a good portion of the walls. The tobacco-stained ceiling was streaked with cracks. Everything was bathed in an orangey glow from a benzene lamp on a large circular copper-tray centrepiece that was suspended a few inches off the ground on a wooden frame. Muhammad was evidently proud of his living quarters and confidently invited his guests to choose a place to recline.

The sound of cutlery tinkling against glass came from behind another curtain suspended across a corner of the room. Mallory and Stanza lowered themselves onto a cushion each and stretched their feet towards the copper tray while Abdul and Muhammad, who were having what appeared to be an intense conversation, sat opposite. The curtain moved aside and a heavily veiled woman in an *abaya* stepped out of a tiny kitchenette, carrying a tray on which were four small glass cups that were half filled with sugar. A little teapot stood beside them. The woman's dark eyes were barely visible through the narrow slit of her headpiece and she avoided eye contact with everyone as she placed the tray on the table and filled the cups with a tan liquid. No sooner had she completed that task than she went behind her curtain and drew it back across.

Muhammad smiled broadly once again as he invited Mallory and Stanza to indulge in the tea. After the two westerners picked up their cups Abdul and Muhammad took up theirs, resuming their conversation. Mallory was certain that he heard the name Tasneen mentioned a couple of times whereupon Abdul glanced at him. The two men eventually faced the westerners.

'My cousin welcomes you to his house,' Abdul said.

Mallory and Stanza nodded politely.

Muhammad's smile disappeared while he sipped his tea and did not return when he replaced the half-empty cup back on the tray. He asked Abdul something and the reply was accompanied with a shrug. Then Abdul indicated Stanza with a jut of his chin whereupon Muhammad's gaze fell on the journalist. Muhammad said something while looking at Stanza and Abdul nodded.

'Muhammad asks if you have any money with you.'

'What does he want money for?' Mallory asked.

The men exchanged glances while Abdul relayed the response. The cousin appeared annoyed as he rambled on, using hand gestures to emphasise certain points. When he stopped he looked between Mallory and Stanza.

'My cousin asks . . . how can you negotiate without money?'

Stanza was the one who now looked irritated. 'We don't need money to begin negotiations. When we finally agree on a price the funds can be transferred.' Stanza looked at Muhammad in a wearily superior manner. 'Why is he asking me about money? Has he made any contact with the kidnappers?'

Abdul talked at some length with his cousin before facing Stanza, his fingers scratching an itch at the end of his stump. 'Muhammad has made contact with someone who can take us to a member of the Black Banner Brigade. He needs to find out which hostage you are interested in.'

'What do you mean, which hostage?'

'I did not tell Muhammad Lamont's name over the phone. But you have also called him by another name.'

'Stanmore, yes. But they will know him only as Lamont, unless Lamont has told them his real name . . . How many hostages do they have, anyway?'

Abdul said something to Muhammad who shrugged as he rattled off a list of nationalities that Mallory and Stanza did not understand for the most part. Abdul repeated them as best he could in English: 'British, French, Italian, German, Portuguese, Armenian, Turkish, Kenyan, Somalian, Nepalese, Chinese, Japanese, Americans and dozens of Iraqis.'

Muhammad said something as he picked up his tea.

'He . . .' Abdul began. Then he took a few seconds to rethink his words. 'He asks how much he is to get. He thinks it should be a percentage of the ransom.' Abdul looked down at his stump as if distancing himself from the question.

Stanza looked at Mallory, then back at Muhammad. 'Can you believe these fuckin' monkeys?' he said.

Abdul looked up at Stanza sharply.

'How can this guy ask for a percentage?' Stanza asked. 'Is he one of the kidnappers?'

'My cousin has nothing to do with kidnapping. But Muhammad believes that if he is to risk his life for the American he should get something for it.'

Muhammad said something which Abdul repeated. 'Are you getting paid for coming here?' he said.

Stanza sighed. 'I will pay him. But not a percentage.'

Abdul spoke to Muhammad who looked away as if he had been insulted.

Stanza threw up his hands. 'OK. What the hell. Sure, why not? Take a piece of the action. It's not my money and I'm sure Stanmore's old man would agree. What percentage does he want?'

Abdul asked his cousin who replied after a moment

411

of thought. 'He thinks ten per cent is fair,' Abdul said.

'*Ten?*' Stanza said, breaking into a laugh. 'These fuckin' people . . . OK. It's a deal. Who the fuck cares? Just do me a favour. Can we put his money to one side for now? Your cousin will get paid, I promise him that. Can we get this ball rolling now? I'm here to get Stanmore, not spend my time haggling with your cousin over his goddamned fee.'

Abdul said something to his cousin who thought about it for a moment before replying. When Abdul responded there was a hint of frustration in his voice. Muhammad eventually nodded in agreement and got to his feet, said 'Hello' to Mallory and Stanza and left the room by another door that appeared to lead to the front of the house.

Stanza and Mallory both looked at Abdul for an explanation.

'He has gone to contact those who have Lamont.'

'Just like that,' Stanza said. 'What they got, some kinda store down the road with a hostage section?'

Mallory dropped his head into his hands, suddenly feeling exhausted. The stress of the evening was catching up with him. He felt it was going to be a long night and he just wanted to lie back and sleep.

A distant explosion rocked the building enough to fill the air with dust from the many cracks in the walls and ceiling. Stanza looked at Mallory, then at Abdul, both of whom appeared to have ignored the blast. A shot was fired close by, then another in the distance, followed by more. Then silence.

Stanza ran a hand through his hair and massaged his neck. 'I'm bushed,' he said to no one in particular. Then he lay back, rested his head on a cushion, stretched out his legs and closed his eyes.

Mallory contemplated doing the same but then felt Abdul's stare on him. When he looked up the young Arab looked away. Again he sensed something odd about the man. He'd caught Abdul looking strangely at him a couple of times now and each time the Arab looked away as if he was hiding something.

Mallory slid down the cushion until his head was resting on it. He closed his eyes and decided to rely on his hearing for security for the moment. He reasoned that snatching a rest was only sensible as there was no way of knowing when their next opportunity might be. But as soon as he began to relax a distant voice warned him to be cautious, a voice clearly recognisable even though he had not heard it for many years. It was that of his first troop sergeant at 42 Commando, Muggers Mugrich – the unsmiling one, as he'd been known.

It was strange how that particular man's image had emerged from the lower reaches of Mallory's memory. He had not seen or thought about Muggers for years. Shortly after Mallory's arrival in the troop, his first draft since passing out of commando training, it had been tasked with taking part in one of the last tours of Northern Ireland, a pointless task to all concerned as the IRA had long since been defeated. Most of the deployment duties consisted of long walks across stretches of the border where little of any great significance had happened for an age. The last incident had been so far back, in fact, that the intelligence officer whose job it was to provide such historical background information during the operational briefing wasn't quite sure what it had been. The military wing of the IRA had seen the last of the wind removed from their sails when their essential funding and support from the USA was brought to an abrupt end after the 9/11 terrorist attack. What little was left of their struggle was diminished as much by the rising tide of Islamic terrorism as by their own internal corruption.

But Muggers treated the operation the same way he did every task, even the most boring exercises, and that was as if the screaming hordes might come over the top at any second. It was considered a certainty that if any member of the patrol fell asleep on sentry duty Muggers would catch them – and when he did, woe betide that individual. Harsh as his punishments often were he was a likeable character who offended few because he was always right and fair and, after more than twenty years in the mob, there wasn't much he didn't know about the business. Mallory had almost nodded off only once in his entire military career. Muggers caught the young Marine as his heavy eyelids were starting to close. 'Fight it, laddy,' Muggers said softly from behind him and Mallory's eyes snapped open. 'Think of something violent that makes you angry. Like someone attacking your mother, or your sister. It'll get your blood up and put a touch of adrenalin into your system and you won't sleep for a while.'

Mallory never forgot the advice and it had served

him well on many an occasion. But despite his memory of it he drifted away on the feelings of nostalgia it brought with it and while mentally reliving those good old days he forgot to think of something that made him angry. Mallory had no idea precisely how long he had been asleep. What woke him up was another soft voice coming to him as if from the end of a long tunnel.

'What?' Mallory said, his eyes opening abruptly to see the dull cracked ceiling with its flickering patterns created by the light of the benzene lamp.

'I asked if you had any family.'

Mallory fought to marshal his senses and remember where on earth he was. 'Family?' he said as he realised that he was in Fallujah and the voice was Stanza's.

'As in wife and kids,' Stanza said.

Mallory looked over at the man who was lying fully stretched out on the rug, staring up at the ceiling. 'No,' he said. Mallory looked around the room to discover that they were the only two in it. He got quickly to his feet.

'Not even a girlfriend?'

Mallory went to the curtain in the corner and pulled it aside to reveal that the tiny kitchen space was empty. He went to the door Muhammad had left by and opened it enough to look into a dark empty hallway with the front door at the end.

'If you're looking for Abdul he's gone,' Stanza said. 'His cousin came back for a couple of minutes. They had a brief talk, kinda secretive, and then they both left.'

Mallory lowered himself into the chair Abdul had been sitting in and felt the shape of his pistol inside his front pouch.

'*Do* you have a girlfriend, then?' Stanza asked.

Mallory wondered why Stanza was intent on pursuing such a trivial subject in the light of their situation. Then again, trivia was probably what they should be discussing at such a time. They had relinquished control of their lives and were at the mercy of so many different forces that it made a mockery of the central concept of Mallory's job, which was risk management. 'No,' Mallory said. An image of Tasneen's pretty face came into his mind's eye. At that moment his pursuit of her seemed as ridiculous an adventure as the one he was currently involved in.

'I suppose it's difficult in your job,' Stanza said.

'Is it any easier in yours?'

'I don't go away as much as I imagine you do.'

'You have a wife and kids?' Mallory wasn't particularly interested, but since they were on the subject he felt he might as well ask.

A smile twisted Stanza's face. 'No. Never been lucky in that department. Almost. Had a wife, that is, but never got far enough to contemplate kids. I don't think I'd make a good father.'

Mallory thought about asking why and then decided not to.

'I'm too selfish,' Stanza said anyway. 'That's also what went wrong with my relationships . . . all of 'em. Too tied up in my own world. The irony was I was never that interested in journalism. Not really. Not passionately like some. But I did want to succeed. So I kept on trying and didn't have time for anyone else . . . Is that a pointless life or what? Eh?' Stanza glanced over at Mallory to see if he had been listening.

Mallory had been only half-attentive – he'd drifted away to reflect on his own life. But he caught Stanza's question and look. 'My philosophy has always been never to regret anything,' Mallory mused. 'You take the right fork and even though it wasn't ideal you might not have survived the left . . . For what it's worth, that's my philosophy.'

'Yeah . . . Basic, but I guess it works,' Stanza said.

'Well, maybe if I reach your age I'll have managed to work out something a little deeper, but that's where I've got to so far.'

A sound came from the front hallway and Mallory got to his feet while Stanza sat up.

The door opened and Muhammad looked alarmed as he eyed the two men. He immediately stepped aside to make way for a fierce-looking Arab dressed in a dark, soiled *dishdash* with a well-worn leather jacket over the top. He was carrying an AK47 and his stare flicked to Mallory's hand as it moved to his pouch.

The man took a couple of steps into the room and looked around quickly. Stanza got to his feet as Abdul, looking as if he had seen a ghost, walked in behind the stranger. Behind him was another Arab who moved like a beast in search of raw meat. He was far more tense and murderous-looking than his colleague and his leathery face was covered with a wiry black beard. The hatred in his narrow dark eyes was unmistakable. He gripped a Russian PK belt-fed machine-gun rifle, heavier than his comrade's AK47, and looked as though he would like nothing better than to cut loose with it.

The first Arab, who was clearly the senior of the two, said something while keeping his gaze fixed on Mallory.

'He asks who is the one he should talk to about the hostage,' Abdul said.

Stanza forced a smile as he stepped forward to offer his hand. 'My name's Jake Stanza,' he said.

The Arab ignored the hand while he studied Stanza from head to foot. He said something else, his voice cold and assertive.

'He asks what you want,' Abdul said.

Stanza cleared his throat. 'I'd like to interview Jeffrey Lamont. Would that be possible?'

Abdul translated and the Arab replied. 'Is that all you want – to talk to him?'

'N-no . . . no,' Stanza stuttered in an effort to correct any misunderstanding. 'I have the authority to negotiate a payment for his release. A ransom.'

Abdul translated and the Arab scrutinised Stanza before replying.

'He will take five million US dollars,' Abdul said.

Stanza nodded. Sweet and to the point. But now that he was finally in the position he had been looking forward to he felt insecure and unsure how to conduct himself. 'Fine . . . Fine. That's a lot of money,' he said. The only concept of negotiating that Stanza had was, ironically, one of the basic Arab rules of bargaining: don't settle for the initial price.

The Arab's expression remained icy as he uttered a few words.

'What do you offer?' Abdul translated.

Stanza rubbed his brow nervously. 'I was thinking in the region of a couple of million. But . . . Well, I'll gladly put that to my people. I'm only the go-between,' he stammered, forcing a smile that quickly became a nervous grimace.

Abdul repeated Stanza's words and the Arab replied. 'He doesn't think you are in a position to negotiate, which is not a healthy position to be in.'

'B-but I am. I am.'

Mallory looked at Stanza, realising that his life was now in the hands of this twat. This was not a factor he had considered before and he decided that he wasn't about to let Stanza take him down with him. 'Ask him for proof that the hostage is still alive,' Mallory interjected.

The Arab looked at Mallory as Abdul interpreted the question.

'Would you like an ear or a finger?' Abdul translated the response.

'That's not proof of life,' Mallory said. 'Stanza – ask him something,' he ordered.

'Ask what?' Stanza was flustered. 'I don't understand.'

'A proof-of-life question.' The irritation in Mallory's voice was clear to all.

'Like what?'

'I don't know, for fuck's sake. The name of his pet fucking goldfish. Something that only his father would know.'

Stanza rubbed his forehead as he struggled to think. 'Ask him what his favourite beer is.'

'For God's sake,' Mallory said, looking up at the ceiling. 'We are fucking dead.'

'His father owns a brewery,' Stanza shouted.

'They could get that off the bloody Internet,' Mallory retorted. 'Something only his old man would know. His mother's pet name or maiden name. You've come here to negotiate for a man's life and you don't know the first bloody thing about it.'

'Shut up,' Stanza yelled as anger fused with his fear. 'I need to talk to him,' Stanza said to Abdul. 'I need to talk to Stanmore . . . Lamont. That's the proof I want that he's alive. Let me talk to him and then I'll get the money.' Stanza's desperation was clear – and distinctly unappealing.

Abdul relayed what Stanza had said. The first Arab replied and left the room before Abdul could translate. The murderous-looking Arab remained a moment longer to stare at the white men with his hollow black eyes, his hand tight around the stock of his machine-gun. A voice called from the hallway and he walked out of the room, leaving a miasma of tension and fear in his wake.

The four men stood in silence as Abdul closed the door.

'Was that a yes or a no?' Stanza asked.

'He said you are fools who have come here to die.'

'Great job, Stanza,' Mallory said.

'That's it?' Stanza asked Abdul. 'What about Stanmore? Do we get to see him? Does that guy want the money? I don't get it. How have we left things?'

Muhammad said something which led to a heated exchange between him and Abdul. Then they calmed down and seemed to agree on something. 'They will talk further with us,' Abdul said.

'What does that mean?' Stanza asked.

'That was the first negotiation,' Abdul said. 'We can talk more later.'

'How the hell do you know that?' Stanza asked, raising his voice. 'You said the man told us we were dead.'

'That is why I know,' Abdul said. 'You are *not* dead. That is his way of saying you can talk more later.'

'Jesus fuckin' Christ. *When* later?' Stanza asked.

'That I do not know,' Abdul said.

'We don't have time for this,' Stanza said.

'You are in a hurry but they are not,' Abdul pointed out. 'They are preparing for a battle.'

'All the more reason to get on with this,' Stanza said.

'I am only the translator,' Abdul reminded him, for the first time revealing some of his own anxiety. Abdul had been racked by fear since meeting the two Arab men, especially the murderous one. Muhammad had taken him to a house a few blocks away where a dozen or so fighters were digging a deep hole in the floor of the living room. Muhammad told Abdul there were many such excavations in the town but he did not know what they were for.

An hour had passed before the leader arrived and when Abdul saw the murderous one with him he was consumed with fear that the beast would recognise him. It was the demon in human form from the house in Dora where Hassan and the others had delivered Lamont the night they'd kidnapped him. Until that moment Abdul had forgotten the face that had peered in through the car window as they'd waited. When the beast looked at Abdul with those distinctive black eyes it was as if he was looking into his very soul and could see everything. Abdul could not hold his gaze and prayed that the man had forgotten him. The slightest suspicion would result in the immediate elimination of Abdul and his cousin. Infiltration and betrayal were the insurgents' greatest fear and they treated suspects with brutal finality. It seemed that every time Abdul glanced at the man he was looking back at him, the cold malevolent expression unvarying as if nothing existed behind those eyes but hate and a desire for violence.

Stanza exhaled loudly as he walked across the room. 'What now?' he asked, pausing to look at Abdul.

Abdul shrugged. 'We wait . . . They are busy preparing defences. Perhaps tomorrow Muhammad and I will go and see them again,' Abdul said, repeating his suggestion to his cousin who shrugged as a reply.

Stanza sighed as he came to terms with his predicament and slumped down onto a cushion.

Silence descended on the group for a while until it was broken by Muhammad. 'He asks if you want food,' Abdul said.

'Why not?' Stanza said, only half interested.

Abdul nodded to Muhammad who replied with a hand gesture.

'He needs money,' Abdul said.

Stanza reached into a pocket and took out a bundle of notes, a mixture of dollars and dinars. Muhammad took the offering, checked it, appeared satisfied and left the room.

Mallory took stock of their situation as he watched Stanza lower his head into his hands. He wondered if it wasn't time to get on with his own mission. But before he could take a single step towards the cemetery there were several obvious matters that needed to be checked out.

Mallory went to the doorway that led to the garage, decided it was the right time, pushed back the curtain and quietly slipped out of the room.

14

Rendezvous with Death

Mallory opened the door to the garage, shone his flashlight around, found the light switch and flicked it up and down a couple of times without luck. He sat on the edge of a table covered in junk, turned off his flashlight and used the darkness as an aid to concentration.

The first and most obvious problem involved in leaving the house would be having to trudge through a town bustling with insurgents who were preparing for a major assault by the US Marine Corps. Mallory's first option was to wait for the attack to begin and then stay under cover until it had rolled over and past him. That might involve surrendering to the Americans at some stage, which would with luck mean that he'd be told to stay put. But they might transfer him outside the town, which would not do at all. Another problem with waiting for the assault was that it might not happen for days yet or possibly weeks. Still, Mallory reckoned that he could let Stanza head back to the city with Abdul. He felt confident he could strike some kind of deal with Muhammad to lie low in his house, although he did not trust the man an inch. If he ever found out about the money Mallory might well have a problem.

His other option was to head for the cemetery as soon as possible. He could do it if he had a local guide, someone who could communicate with anyone they bumped into, a scout who could move ahead and clear the way for him. The only person available who could possibly do that was Abdul.

It made good sense. Abdul was in a weird mood, or so it seemed, but money was a great facilitator and Mallory had no doubt that ten or twenty thousand dollars would bring him alongside nicely.

The second option was the most attractive and Mallory got to his feet walked back down the corridor and into the living room.

Stanza was in the same position, still holding his head in his hands. Abdul was at the sink, staring into space while holding a glass of water to his lips. Mallory's appearance appeared to set Abdul in motion again and he emptied the water down his throat.

Mallory waited for Abdul to look at him again and beckoned him over. Abdul glanced at Stanza who remained staring at the floor. Mallory stepped back through the curtain and Abdul followed along the corridor to the garage.

When Abdul stepped into the garage Mallory closed the door behind him and shone the torch in his face. 'Do you mind talking in the dark – I want to save my batteries?'

'No,' Abdul replied, wondering what this was all about.

Mallory turned off the light and the room went completely dark. 'I need to ask you something – something private.'

Abdul remained silent.

'I have something very valuable hidden not far from here and I need your help to get it.'

Abdul found this most bizarre. He had been expecting something along the lines of questions regarding their mission in Fallujah but this was entirely unexpected. 'Valuable?' he asked, unsure if he'd understood the English correctly.

'Money,' Mallory said, getting to the point.

Abdul blinked in the darkness. 'I don't understand you.'

Mallory took a deep breath. He did indeed have a lot to explain. 'I have a box of money, US dollars, buried in a hole in the ground not far from here. I was here a year ago, during the war. I was a soldier and I found this box. I could not take it with me so I buried it and now I want to get it.'

This made immediate and perfect sense to Abdul. 'How much?' he asked.

'A lot.' Mallory wondered if he should reveal the amount, then quickly decided against it. 'I'll give you a portion of it,' he said. 'How about ten thousand dollars?'

Abdul's thoughts began to shoot in several directions at once and he decided that he needed time and space to sort them out. 'Where is this money?' he asked.

'In a cemetery.'

'Buried?'

'Yes.'

'How do you know it is still there?'

'I don't . . . There is only one way to find out.'

'Why have you asked me to help?'

'I need you to get me through the town. A guide. A simple job for a lot of money,' Mallory said, hoping that would be the case.

Abdul broke into a thin smile that Mallory could not see. Allah did indeed move in mysterious ways. Here was the answer to his prayers. And the cemetery was a delicious irony. He needed to know nothing else. 'When do you want to go?'

'Now.'

Abdul accepted the risks that could come with meeting insurgents but his confidence had improved since he'd been out in the town already. 'I will help you,' he said.

Mallory flicked on his flashlight and aimed it at Abdul for a second. 'We'll need a shovel.'

They followed the beam around the dilapidated room as it illuminated an assortment of junk. Abdul saw something, walked over to the pile and withdrew a spade from it. 'Will this do?'

'Perfect,' Mallory said, taking it from him. 'A bag would also be useful. A strong, fairly large one.'

Abdul wondered how much money there was.

Mallory moved the beam to another pile of odds and ends. Abdul picked up a filthy canvas bag, fine dust filling the air as he opened it up and tested the handles for strength.

'That'll do,' Mallory said.

As Abdul handed the bag to Mallory his gaze caught something in the brief torchlight.

Mallory went to the garage door to open it.

Abdul crouched to feel for the object.

'Let's go,' Mallory said.

'Coming,' Abdul said. 'Fixing my shoe.'

Mallory cracked open the door, checked that the narrow backstreet was empty and slipped outside.

Abdul found what he was looking for and picked it up. It was a cast-iron hammer with a nasty-looking spike on the reverse head. The shaft was bound in string for an improved grip. Abdul swung it down to assess its suitability. If brought down firmly enough a single blow using the spike would penetrate a skull with ease. He tucked it into his belt and headed for the door.

Abdul walked over to Mallory who was looking at an electronic device in his hand. 'What is that?' he asked.

'GPS,' Mallory said as he scrolled through a list of waypoints and stopped on the one marked RENDEZVOUS. He hit the accept button and a moment later an arrow appeared on the screen, along with several information windows. 'Seven hundred and fifty-seven metres as the crow flies . . . in that direction,' he said, pointing. Mallory looked at Abdul. 'Don't suppose you know a cemetery in that direction?'

'I don't know Fallujah that well.'

'Lead on, then. That way. You go forward, check if it's safe, then I'll join you. We'll keep doing that until we reach the cemetery. OK?'

Abdul nodded and headed off. Mallory put an arm through the carrying straps of the bag that had the shovel in it, pulled them over his shoulder and followed Abdul at a distance.

The sky had grown lighter, most of the cloud from earlier having cleared. The two men kept to the right side of the street where the shadows were thicker, hugging the building line as closely as possible. Abdul paused at the end of the first row of houses, all of which appeared to be empty, and Mallory stepped into a doorway out of sight.

Abdul remained still for a time, checking in all directions while Mallory kept him in view. Just as Mallory was beginning to wonder if Abdul had had second thoughts the Arab set off without looking back and turned right and out of sight. Mallory carried on to the corner, peered around it and saw Abdul walking away up the street. Mallory checked behind him, turned the corner and walked briskly along, maintaining his distance from Abdul. They were in another residential street packed with run-down homes.

A pair of headlights appeared up ahead. Abdul ducked out of sight and Mallory skipped over a low wall outside a front door and got down behind it.

The vehicle passed.

When Mallory got to his feet and looked over the wall Abdul was already out of his hiding place and looking back in Mallory's direction as if impatient to get going.

Mallory stepped onto the street as Abdul headed off to the end of the row of houses and stopped at the corner. Mallory checked his GPS and broke into a jog. By the time Abdul looked back Mallory was just behind him.

Ahead was a broad boulevard and the arrow on the GPS indicated they needed to cross it diagonally. The boulevard had three lanes either side of a meridian and several vehicles, their headlights on, were gathered some distance away outside a mosque.

'That way,' Mallory said, indicating across the boulevard and away from the cars.

'Should I run?' Abdul asked.

'Walk casually,' Mallory said. 'We'll go together, OK?'

Mallory walked out from the shadows onto the boulevard with Abdul by his side. They stepped off the pavement onto the road and headed towards the central meridian. As they reached it a shout came from behind them and the hairs stood up on the back of Mallory's neck. There was another yell, followed by a shot and both men broke into a sprint. A burst of automatic gunfire rang out. It seemed abnormally loud. Several bullets ricocheted off the road nearby as they leaped across the last section of road and onto the pavement. But they were still exposed and some distance from the nearest corner. More bullets, one of them a bright-orange tracer round, slammed into the wall beside them and as they reached the corner Mallory grabbed hold of Abdul and pulled him around it as a couple more slugs cut through the air, dangerously close. The two men did not stop and ran for all they were worth.

Mallory was ahead and, spotting an alleyway across

the street, changed direction towards it. 'This way!' he shouted.

Mallory came to a skidding halt inside the alleyway entrance and urged Abdul ahead. As they emerged from the other end into what looked like a square he nudged the young Arab more to the left.

As they reached the entrance to another street Mallory took hold of Abdul's jacket and steered him into a dark doorway.

They panted heavily and Mallory checked back the way they had come before reviewing his GPS display. 'We must be near the cemetery,' he gasped. 'It has to be behind those buildings. Come on.'

They headed up the street to a gap between the buildings on the other side of the road and a few metres further on stopped at a low wall. Beyond were the jagged silhouettes of tilted stones looking like rows of broken teeth, along with black flags on angled sticks. Mallory did not recognise the place but he remembered that he had approached it from a different direction the last time. He sensed Abdul close behind him and without further hesitation he unslung the bag, tucked it under his arm, hopped over the wall and moved in among the tombs at a slight crouch. He paused by a headstone a few metres in and cloaked the glow from the GPS while he checked the direction. After he moved off, a quick look behind him showed Abdul mimicking his caution.

Mallory slowed as the GPS indicated that the cache was only metres away. He searched around for anything that he might recognise. He was about to learn the answer to one of the greatest worries that had been on his mind since leaving England: had the stash been discovered or not? He held his breath in anticipation.

Mallory realised he was standing on the path that was lower than the surrounding ground level, the path in which he had dug the hole. Then his stare practically lasered into the exact spot where the box was buried. It was undisturbed and more natural-looking than when he had left it. That did not mean, though, that someone hadn't dug it up the day after he'd buried it and he double-checked the GPS, which confirmed their arrival at RENDEZVOUS. He turned it off, its job finally done, and pocketed it.

Mallory looked behind at Abdul who was crouching by a headstone. 'It's here,' he said as he removed the shovel from the bag and, without wasting a second more, rested its blade on the spot beneath which he believed the box lay.

Mallory placed his foot on the shoulder of the shovel and was about to push down on it when a familiar sound stopped him. He looked to the night sky as the thud of a helicopter's rotor blades beat the air somewhere above. With its navigation lights off the chopper was virtually invisible.

After a few seconds Mallory went back to his task, pushing the shovel into the ground that yielded easily.

Abdul stood on the grave directly behind Mallory, which made him a head taller, and watched as the Englishman got into a digging rhythm. He slipped his hand inside his jacket, felt for the hammer tucked into his belt, slid it out and held it against his side with his stump while he took a firm hold of the grip with his hand. It felt good, not too long or too heavy, and he rested it against his thigh, pressing it into his flesh to make sure that the spike was facing behind him. Mallory was moving in unpredictable patterns, making it risky to attempt a blow, and Abdul told himself to be patient. The ideal moment would present itself soon enough. The point of the weighty spike was sharp and one good whack would stun Mallory enough for Abdul to deliver another that would penetrate his skull, drive into the fleshy brain and kill him. Allah was such a thoughtful god. He had not only provided the perfect tool for the job, silent and final, but He had also arranged for Mallory to have his back to Abdul, distracted by his greed.

Mallory struck something metal with the spade and he dropped to his knees to feel around in the hole. A grin spread across his face as his fingers touched the box: at that moment he knew his money was there. No one would have reburied the box if they had emptied it. 'We've hit the mother-lode,' he said softly, turning his head to look up at Abdul.

Abdul moved the hammer out of sight behind his leg and smiled thinly at the man he was about to kill.

Mallory faced the hole again, pulled away several handfuls of earth from the side of the box and felt for the handle. He eventually dug it free, took a firm grip of it and put all his effort into pulling up the edge of the box. It resisted at first but a little more effort and the corner moved and then seemed to spring up. Mallory lifted the box onto its side, got to his feet, pulled it out of the hole completely and rested it on the path.

He stood upright and took a breather.

Abdul was about to raise the hammer when Mallory dropped to his knees again.

'Right. Let's see if the worms have left us anything,' he said as he unclipped the lid with some effort, gripped its edges and prised it open. He could not see inside the box well enough to confirm it was the money although it was obviously full. A layer of fine sand covered the paper and Mallory's smile returned as he pulled out a tight bundle of notes. He shook the remaining dust off, flicked through the bills and held them out to Abdul. 'There you go. Ten thousand US dollars.'

Mallory was not looking directly at Abdul who quickly tucked the hammer under his right arm and took Mallory's offering.

'And you can have another for your trouble later,' Mallory said as he dragged the bag alongside the box and began transferring the money into it.

Abdul stared again at the back of Mallory's head as he put his bundle of money into his pocket and gripped the hammer once again. The rest of Abdul's journey suddenly became clear to him and he knew what he had to do.

Abdul strengthened his grip on the haft and brought the hammer out in front of him. Mallory was busy transferring the bundles of banknotes, his head more or less in the same position, and Abdul stepped down onto the path behind him, adopted a wide-legged stance and raised the spike.

Mallory placed the last of the bundles in the bag, ran a hand around the inside of the box to be sure he'd emptied it and closed the bag. 'Can't believe I've actually got this far,' he said.

Abdul held the spike high and focused on the centre of Mallory's head.

'Wait,' Mallory said suddenly as his ears picked up a repetitive distant concussive sound that alarmed him although he could not immediately identify it.

Abdul froze before lowering his weapon, momentarily confused. He could hear nothing: aware that time was running out, he raised the spike again, grimacing with effort as he started to drive it down.

Mallory suddenly remembered what those distant thumps meant: he had heard similar sounds many times during the war. They were heavy cannon being fired from several miles away, one after the other. The shells would take only a few seconds to land.

As Abdul's hammer spike drove through the air towards Mallory's skull the first shell struck the cemetery, the powerful explosion producing a shock wave that lifted both men off their feet and tossed them aside like rag dolls. The ground rocked as a series of the shells struck in quick succession, half a second between each as they landed across the cemetery and through the houses opposite.

Mallory slammed against a headstone and was knocked close to unconsciousness. Abdul landed on a grave with a metal surround, smashing a collection of flowerpots within it. He tried to sit up as his brain fought to understand what was happening but he fell back as another blast shotgunned him with soil, pebbles and fragmented headstone rock. The barrage raged around them, the ground shaking as masses of earth were thrown into the air. The sound was deafening. Mallory came back to near-consciousness and rolled into a ball, his hands tight around his head as soil and debris rained down. A ton of headstone landed feet from him, then toppled over to hit the edge of a grave, thereby miraculously forming a shelter instead of flattening him. He remained unaware for the time being and stayed curled in a tight ball, jolting with each powerful boom and expecting the next to be the one that tore him to shreds. A nearby headstone exploded as a chunk of shrapnel slammed through it. The incoming shells sounded like screaming freight trains, only a thousand times louder, before they struck the ground. It was a symphony of doom: fiery, ear-splitting blasts, white-hot chunks of shrapnel that shrieked like banshees and shock waves powerful enough to rip stone walls apart.

Mallory was unable to move while death tore hungrily through the air, seeking victims inches above him. He could not think, only pray that it would end soon. There was a brief lull and he considered getting out of there, but just as he did the shells returned.

Mallory had no idea how long he lay in his cocoon of dirt and fear. It seemed like an age before the barrage gradually moved away and into the town. But he was alert enough to know that he too had to move – and soon. Artillery barrages were intended to clear a path for an assault that would follow close on its heels and out in the open was no place to be when tanks and infantry were bearing down on their targets.

Mallory raised his head, banged it on the massive headstone, brushed the dirt from his face and eyes and looked up at the grey slab. Had it landed a few feet to either side it would have flattened him. As he started to crawl out from under it he felt a sharp pain on the back of his head and touched it to find a wet spot that was obviously blood. He pressed it gently to feel if the bone was still intact, which it appeared to be, and went on to check the rest of his body. Satisfied that he had no broken bones or missing pieces he crawled out from under the slab and sat up. He saw the money bag a few metres away, covered in dirt. He got to his feet to look for Abdul and saw him lying on a grave several metres away. As he made his way to him across shattered tombs the young Arab began to stir.

'Abdul?' Mallory called out, hardly able to hear his own voice. His ears felt muffled as if they were filled with dirt. He took hold of Abdul's jacket and gave it a tug. 'Abdul?'

Abdul looked completely disorientated, mouth open, eyes blinking and darting in every direction.

'We have to get going.'

Abdul continued to blink rapidly in fear and confusion as he attempted to focus on Mallory.

'You OK?' Mallory asked.

Abdul looked around as if he was trying to decide where he was. He made an attempt to get up but his legs and arms began to shake and Mallory took his weight as he helped him. 'That's it. We have to get going.'

Abdul reached for a headstone to steady himself while Mallory held him under his arms. 'Stay there a moment,' Mallory said as he made his way back to the money bag, quickly checked it for damage, crouched to put the strap over his head and with a great effort got to his feet. The back of his head began to throb but he gritted his teeth, straightened up and stumbled back to Abdul.

The young Arab was still holding on to the head-stone and staring at the ground as if in a daze. Mallory took hold of his arm. 'Come on. We can't stay out in the open.'

Abdul did not appear to hear him but he responded when Mallory yanked him forward. They stumbled through the graveyard, Mallory scanning in all directions to get his bearings. He decided that the motorway was on his left and north of the cemetery which would make an ideal kill-zone for anyone trying to break out of the town. Alternatively, it would be a good location from which to form up and mount an assault. The only thing to do was head into the town, find somewhere to hide and then surrender to the Americans as soon as it was safe to do so.

The rolling barrage was still heavy, heading towards the centre of the town. But just as Mallory thought they were at least safe from that, a series of powerful explosions behind them alarmed him and he feared it might be the start of a follow-up shelling. They had been lucky with the first barrage but might not survive another.

'Come on!' Mallory shouted as he picked up the pace and pulled Abdul along.

Abdul appeared to understand the need to hurry and increased his speed as they moved across the cratered ground. Mallory wondered if the young Arab was experiencing some kind of shell-shock and could only hope that he would keep moving.

Mallory managed to retrace their route despite much of the ground being churned up. He could make out the gap they had come through between the buildings and he steered Abdul towards it.

The thunder of exploding artillery shells intensified and every few seconds a jagged chunk of metal flew past them. The effort to make it to the narrow alleyway became desperate. They scrambled over a low wall, the money bag falling heavily off Mallory's shoulder as he pulled Abdul across. Abdul dropped to his knees as a shell landed inside the cemetery not far away and Mallory fell to the ground beside him.

'We have to keep going,' Mallory shouted as he got up and pulled Abdul to his feet. They broke into a run along the alley.

It felt as if they were surrounded by explosions. A section of a building up ahead gave way and crumbled into the alleyway but the men hurled themselves over the rubble. They were on a roller-coaster ride from hell and could be blown to bits, crushed or riddled by shrapnel at any second. But to stop seemed more dangerous than to keep moving.

As they ran out of the alley and across the open square an explosion ahead caused Mallory to hesitate and consider dropping down somewhere – anywhere – to wait out the assault. But a series of crunching booms behind changed his mind and they kept up the pace. As they turned a corner into a narrow street Mallory wondered if they shouldn't just keep going until they reached Muhammad's house. Stanza was probably hysterical by now. Mallory had considered leaving the journalist to his own devices, a decision that might have been easier to make had the man not been so pathetic. But Stanza was his responsibility, after all, and Mallory might as well wait out the assault with him as anywhere else – if they could make it back in one piece.

The explosions continued but for the most part appeared to be concentrated behind them. The barrage was as much a psychological weapon – a way of softening up the enemy – as it was a means of destroying defences and covering an assault. Mallory had not heard any small-arms fire and wondered if the Marines planned to bomb and shell the place for hours before sending in the first ground troops. Either way, Muhammad's house now seemed as good as any as a place of refuge.

Mallory and Abdul paused, exhausted, at the corner of the street that led onto the broad boulevard that now looked quite different from when they had crossed it earlier. Several fires were burning fiercely in front of the mosque where the vehicles had been gathered and judging by the twisted wreckage strewn around they had received a direct hit. Craters peppered the roadway and every telegraph and electricity pole appeared to have collapsed, their wires criss-crossing everywhere.

Several louder explosions behind them goaded them on. Mallory pulled Abdul onto the boulevard and they crossed over poles and ducked under wires towards the other side, which they could barely see. The air was filled with a dense acrid smoke that burned the back of Mallory's throat and he tried to cover his mouth as he ran. He lost his grip on Abdul as he tripped over something. When he looked back Abdul was close behind him, nearly blinded by ash, and Mallory took hold of him and led him along the side of the buildings until they reached a street which they hurried into.

The air quality improved dramatically but as they reached the next road junction gunfire erupted. It sounded like heavy machine guns, .50-cal or greater: either the defenders were shooting at anything in reaction to the shelling or the ground assault had begun.

Mallory and Abdul hurried along a street and turned a corner to see Muhammad's garage up ahead. The house across from it had received a direct hit and had collapsed, dragging a section of the next-door building down with it. A fire was burning inside. Mallory hurried to the garage door to discover that a chunk of it was missing. He dragged Abdul inside, leaned him against the vehicle, opened the trunk of the car, threw the bag in, slammed the trunk shut and carried on into the house.

He walked into the living room, expecting to see Stanza. But the place was in darkness, the benzene lamp extinguished and the only light coming from the open doorway – open because the door had been blown in – that led to the hallway. Mallory walked across the debris-covered cushions to look into the hallway only to discover that the front door had been blown off its hinges too and was lying on the floor, along with its frame. A figure ran past outside and Mallory stepped out of sight to consider what to do.

A groan came from somewhere near his feet and at the same time the living-room door moved. Mallory pulled the edge of the door up to find Stanza lying beneath. He quickly shoved it aside.

'Stanza? It's Mallory.' He removed pieces of wood and other debris from Stanza's face and torso. 'Can you hear me? Stanza?'

Stanza was breathing in short, sharp bursts. He opened his eyes, blinking rapidly.

'Easy,' Mallory said. 'You're fine but you need to lie still a moment.'

Mallory checked Stanza for signs of any broken bones or bleeding. 'Can you hear me, Stanza?'

Stanza's breathing slowed as Mallory came into focus. He tried to speak but no words came out and he broke into a coughing fit that forced him over onto his side. 'Mallory?' Stanza finally wheezed as he struggled to get his breath.

'You're OK.'

Stanza continued coughing but not as desperately. 'Where . . . where've you been?'

'Do you have any pain anywhere?' Mallory asked. 'Can you see me OK?'

Stanza nodded. 'I'm OK. I'm OK . . . What the hell happened?'

An explosion shook the house and dust seemed to leap from the walls to fill the room.

'The assault's begun,' Mallory said. 'Can you stand?'

The shelling continued in the distance and Stanza looked through the door at the fire across the street. 'Sweet Jesus. I thought the insurgents had attacked the house.' He made a move to get up and Mallory took most of his weight. Stanza wobbled on his feet while Mallory held him.

'We might need to get out of here,' Mallory said.

Stanza felt all over his head as if checking that everything was still in place Then he looked at Mallory's dust-covered face that had a dozen small, dried cuts all over it. 'What happened to you?'

'Same as you.'

Stanza looked around and let go of Mallory to stand on his own two feet. He looked up as a couple of nearby booms shook the ground. 'The assault.'

'We need to decide what to do.'

Stanza shuffled over to the sink, leaned heavily against it, took the remaining glass off the shelf and held it under the tap as he turned it on. A dribble of water came out before it stopped altogether. Another explosion rattled the building to produce more dust and Stanza looked around at Mallory with fear in his eyes. 'What shall we do?'

'I think all we can do is wait it out and surrender when the Marines arrive.'

'Can we survive until then – in here?'

'We won't live any longer out there.'

'Where's Abdul?'

Mallory suddenly realised that the young Arab had not followed him into the room. He went to the back door, moved down the short hallway and entered the garage. 'Abdul?' he called out. There was no sign of him. Mallory hurried to the back of the car and lifted up the trunk lid. The bag seemed to be as he'd left it and he opened it up to find the money untouched. He went to the garage door to look out through the hole. There was no sign of life. Then a nearby explosion splattered the house with shrapnel, forcing him back inside. He went to the car, lifted the bag out of the trunk and made his way back into the living room where Stanza was still standing by the sink.

Mallory put the bag down and went into the hallway to the front door.

He peered outside into the street that was a mess of debris; chunks of bricks and mortar, splintered wood, trailing wires and lots of smoke. A few feet in front of him lay a buckled lifeless body. The jacket looked familiar and Mallory edged out of the doorway to get a closer view of the face. It was disfigured, one of the eyes hanging from its socket and the lower jaw torn away, but he was just about recognisable. Mallory was certain it was Abdul's cousin.

Large pieces of ash floated by on the warm air like grubby snowflakes. The ground shook as a shell landed close by and showers of powdered masonry fell on Mallory. A man in a tattered *dishdash* who was carrying an assault rifle ran quickly down the street, past Mallory and out of sight.

Mallory decided that Abdul had legged it. The man was shell-shocked and couldn't be blamed. He'd taken a hammering at the cemetery and was lucky to be alive. They both were. Mallory could only wish him luck and hope that the Marines wouldn't shoot him before he had a chance to surrender. He thought of Tasneen and wondered what he would tell her. But then, he'd have to get back himself to do that and at present the prospects of that were in the balance.

Mallory went back into the living room to find that Stanza had not moved.

'This house'll collapse if this keeps up,' Stanza said.

'What do you want *me* to fucking well do?' Mallory shouted, the stress and Stanza's bleating finally getting the better of him. 'Why don't you just accept that if we get out of here in one piece we're going to be lucky, OK?'

Stanza blinked at him innocently as if he, Stanza, was being victimised. Another heavy boom shook the house and Stanza gripped the sink behind him as his stare darted to the ceiling where a crack had suddenly widened. 'Perhaps there's a basement,' he said.

'Why don't you go and look for one, then?' Mallory said, wondering if there was indeed a safe place to wait for the Americans to arrive. The garage, perhaps. Better still, inside the car. Short of a direct hit, being inside a metal box would be safer than being out in the open. A fire would, of course, be a problem if they got trapped. But then maybe they could drive out, at least. Mallory's mind was racing. He looked at Stanza who had not moved but was wearing a most odd expression, a combination of shock and fear. He realised that Stanza was looking behind him and he turned around to see the demonic insurgent they'd encountered earlier standing in the doorway. His *dishdash* was soiled, his machine-gun dusty in his grimy hands. A couple of bandoliers of linked ammunition spanned his chest and a short sword in a scabbard hung from a leather belt around his waist. Mallory took a step back as the Arab's crazed stare bored into him. Then the human devil moved out of the doorway and his leader walked in, dressed in a similar fashion as if ready for battle. A series of new explosions shook the building but no one reacted, not even Stanza.

The leader asked something in a calm, authoritative voice. Mallory did not understand a word and simply looked at him. The leader beckoned to someone behind him and Abdul walked into the room, looking calmer than the last time Mallory had seen him.

Abdul held Mallory's gaze with difficulty. His failure to kill him in the graveyard had left him confused. The Englishman had been saved from Abdul's blow by the very hand of Allah. It had all seemed so clear to him up until that point, what his purpose was and how he was to achieve it. He had seen himself as a tool of Allah but that clearly was not the case, not entirely at least. Somewhere along the road he had misread the signs.

But Abdul had come to his senses and seen the way to complete his mission. Mallory had indeed played a part in it but Abdul had not realised what that was until almost too late. Now he knew what he had to do. 'He asks where the money is,' he said.

Mallory's mouth started to drop open in utter disbelief. 'You little arschole,' he muttered.

'It is payment for Lamont,' Abdul said, as if explaining to Mallory what the money had been intended for all along.

Explosions close by followed by a rattle of gunfire lit a fire under the proceedings and the leader raised his voice.

'He does not have time to waste,' Abdul said. 'Don't try his patience,' he added as a warning of his own.

Mallory exhaled in frustration. It was clearly not an issue for debate and he walked over to the bag, picked it up and dropped it on the floor in front of the leader. The leader nodded to his fighter who crouched to open and inspect the contents. He pulled out several bundles of money, did a quick count, looked up at his boss and nodded.

Abdul suddenly remembered the bundle Mallory had given him, took it out of his jacket pocket and held it towards the leader.

The fighter took it, shoved it in the bag and fastened it back up as the leader eyed Abdul.

Stanza looked from the bag of money to the others in blank confusion.

The leader barked a command and left the room.

'He wants you to follow,' Abdul said, stepping aside.

'Me?' Stanza asked. Everyone seemed to know what was going on except him.

'Both of you,' Abdul said.

'Where are we going?' Stanza asked.

An explosion rocked the building and the dark-eyed fighter shouted at them as he hoisted the bag of money onto his shoulder.

'Now,' Abdul insisted. 'He's taking you to see Lamont.'

Stanza opened his mouth to say something. But the fighter interrupted with an outburst that was clearly threatening and Stanza hurried out the door.

Mallory stared at Abdul, feeling a mixture of loss and humility. The money had driven his every move for almost a year, nearly cost him his life and was now gone. But he could not begin to chastise Abdul for what the man had done. Abdul could have run off with the money himself but instead had continued to risk his life to exchange it all for a complete stranger, and an American to boot. That was altruism above and beyond any level Mallory had contemplated. Tasneen had been right about her brother all along. She had said he was good and honourable and would not let him down. In a way, Mallory felt it was he who had let Abdul down.

Mallory walked out of the room and Abdul followed, the demonic fighter close behind.

Several more fighters were waiting in the hallway and in the doorways at either side of the house and they followed as the leader headed down the street. Devastation was everywhere: fires burning in roofless buildings, pieces of furniture and rubble strewn all over the road, the air thick with ash and smoke. Homes had collapsed, telegraph poles were snapped or bent, water was pouring from severed pipes, mangled human remains lay scattered around. Mallory covered his mouth to stop from choking on the smoke-filled air and as he followed a fighter directly in front of him he had to lengthen his stride to avoid stepping on a severed arm and then on a face that had been stripped from its skull.

An explosion sent a chunk of metal whistling overhead and the leader and those close to him ducked as it smashed into the building above. The staccato of heavy machine-gun fire joined the cacophony and was answered, or so it seemed, by a dozen less powerful weapons. A heavy engine roared angrily beyond the row of buildings in the next street, followed by the clunking of metal tracks crunching through masonry. It sounded like a tank to Mallory and as the leader broke into a trot the others responded likewise. The thunder of battle grew in intensity, a chorus of explosions, flying bullets, crackling fires and grinding machinery. Two Apache helicopter gunships roared overhead, nearly clipping the rooftops as they unleashed a torrent of heavy gunfire at some target a few streets away. Mallory prayed that the dense smoke was masking their group enough. As they ran on Mallory had the feeling that they were heading towards the outskirts of the city – which meant towards the front line of the fight and not away from it. He could only hope that the hostage was in a bunker somewhere and that the four of them would be left to fend for themselves.

The leader turned the corner at the end of the street, followed by his men. Mallory saw Stanza make the corner and when it was his turn he saw to his surprise that the line was filing in through the front door of a house. Mallory followed into the living room that was mostly taken up by a huge hole in the centre, its sides shored up by heavy pieces of timber as in the entrance to a mine. Fighters were climbing down into the hole that was lit from below – Mallory assumed this was the bunker he had been expecting.

A fighter came running in from outside, barging past Abdul who was a couple of fighters behind Mallory, shouting some kind of warning. The leader barked words of motivation that were repeated by his lieutenants. Mallory looked at the faces of the fighters packed around him, expecting to see signs of fear or panic. But there were neither. He looked at the demonic fighter carrying the money and watched as he pulled the bag off his shoulder and handed it to a young fighter, at the same time giving him what appeared to be instructions. Mallory watched as the bag was carried out of the house, thus bringing to an end his relationship with it. It was never meant to be, he mused.

The murderous-looking fighter was then handed a heavy cloth bundle which he thrust at Stanza who looked at it quizzically. The fighter displayed little patience with Stanza's lack of understanding and shouted a command as he shoved the bundle brutally against Stanza's chest. The journalist had no choice but to take hold of it, almost dropping it since it was heavier than it looked. Then he was unceremoniously pushed over to the hole and ordered to go down into it.

Mallory and Abdul had just been shoved into the line of fighters waiting to descend into the hole when a massive explosion outside brought down the front of the house, exposing the living room to the street. Several fighters fell under the cascading rubble and were either killed or seriously injured. The sound of falling masonry gave way to human screams and when the initial cloud of dust dissipated Mallory saw a fighter with a spear of window frame sticking through his chest.

The building across the road suddenly collapsed with a roar but this time it was not due to any explosion. A thundering Abrams tank punched through the walls as if it were a sandcastle, its gun barrel like a battering ram, and bore down on the house.

There followed an immediate scramble for the hole as the tank's tracks screeched painfully as it turned. When it stopped the business end of its gun barrel seemed to explode as a shell burst from it.

The shell was aimed along the street but the shock wave from the end of the barrel almost brought down the rest of the house. Everything went dark as dust completely filled the air, making it almost impossible to see or breathe. All Mallory was aware of after that was being shunted forward until the man in front of him dropped. He followed him into the hole, grasping for anything to hang on to.

The walls quickly closed in as the tunnel became narrower and Mallory had to release his handholds as quickly as he found them to avoid his fingers being stepped on by others descending from above. When he hit the bottom it was so abrupt that his knees collapsed under him and as he recovered the man above landed on him. As Mallory pushed himself to his feet, hands grabbed him and he was yanked in another direction. His face slammed into a dirt wall, breaking his nose, but the lower half of his body continued forward into a space and he dropped into a crouch as he entered a low tunnel.

He was given no time to recover as the man behind pushed him on with his boot and Mallory scurried on his hands and knees in the darkness until he bumped into the man in front of him. The dust was intolerable although it had improved a little from the hole entrance when he'd thought he was going to suffocate. The ground was rocky and quickly became unbearably painful, tearing the skin off his knees. Mallory squatted to put his weight on his feet, which meant shuffling along like a chimpanzee. His hands kept contact with the back of the man in front as he fought to keep going, his head occasionally hitting a jagged lump in the roof.

The shouting was constant, the man behind repeatedly pushing Mallory into the one in front who at one point stumbled, causing Mallory to fall onto him. A pile-up threatened and every effort was made to move on. When the man in front finally got going Mallory stepped on something lumpy that gave way in places and it was not until he reached the head that he realised he had been walking on a dead body.

The air suddenly became even thicker and almost too heavy to draw into his lungs. Mallory's mouth and throat were filled with so much dust that his saliva glands had given up and he wondered if he would ever reach the end of the bunker – wherever that was. He had never experienced anything like this before. The nearest thing to it had been the tunnels on the Royal Marine Commando endurance course on Woodbury Common but at Woodbury there was always light visible at either end and the air was at least breathable.

A loud thud above sent a shock wave through the earth that threatened a cave-in and for a moment Mallory's fear rocketed as it appeared that this was how it was going to end for him. He had never experienced claustrophobia before but he could sense the panic beginning to build and he concentrated on putting himself into a kind of trance as he moved on in order to deal with it, searching for a rhythm in the way he was advancing. As he fought to control his increasing anxiety the man in front came to an abrupt stop and Mallory was pressed into him by the combined weight of those behind. When the man moved again Mallory shuffled after him and saw that there was a distinct change in the light. Mallory's hopes rose that the tunnel was coming to an end.

The man in front paused again before shuffling a few feet forward. He did this several times and then abruptly disappeared. Mallory's outstretched hands found an earth wall and he reached higher to find that the ceiling had gone. He pushed himself upright, banging his back on the ceiling of the tunnel behind him and as he stood up hands from above grabbed him. He was pulled out of the hole and tossed aside onto a stone floor.

Mallory blew gobs of dust from his mouth and nostrils and wiped it from his eyes. Men were coughing and spluttering all around him and he blinked incessantly until his vision returned and he could make out where he was. They were surrounded by walls or parts of walls as if they were inside what had once been a building. But most of it, including the roof, was missing. A dozen fighters in varying states of recovery were hurriedly sorting themselves out, loading magazines into weapons after blowing and wiping dust from the working parts. The shouting had turned into heavy whispering as fighters continued to be dragged out of the hole. There was an intense sense of urgency. Mallory recognised the leader who was marshalling his men, ordering them to spread out behind a low wall.

A body suddenly landed beside Mallory like a sack of potatoes and he realised it was Abdul. The young man looked near to death and when Mallory got to his knees to see if he could help he saw Stanza too, lying in a semi-conscious state a few feet away. Abdul coughed and spluttered as he fought to breathe but Mallory was distracted by a sudden feeling that something ominous was about to happen.

The battle continued to rage with explosions, machine-gun fire, tanks crunching past and helicopters roaring overhead. Mallory initially assumed that they had been retreating as the front line of the assault rolled towards them. But if that was correct something was still not right. He shuffled to where he could look over a wall and saw an armoured troop carrier storm past with several US soldiers running behind it.

It was then that the penny dropped. The tunnel had not gone towards the centre of the town but towards the outskirts. It had been designed to pass beneath the enemy line of advance. The fighters were now behind the US Marines. The crafty bastards had timed it so that the assault would roll over them. But this wasn't an escape. Judging by the way the leader was forming up his men he was going to attack the rear of the assaulting line. The Marines had not pressed forward in depth and had chosen to extend themselves to present a broad front. If there was a second wave it was a substantial distance behind the first, something which the insurgents clearly planned to exploit.

As Mallory stretched up to see the backs of a line of Marines following a tank along a rubble-strewn street he was suddenly yanked around to face the insurgent leader. Abdul was standing beside the demonic fighter who looked even fiercer covered in a thick film of dust, his eyes like dark slits in a rock surface. Stanza was dragged over as the leader spoke and all three men were pushed towards a gap in a wall, an opening that had once been a doorway.

'We're free to go,' Abdul said, coughing.

The dark fighter shoved Stanza through the gap so hard that he sprawled on the ground and his bundle was thrown after him. Abdul did not need further convincing and followed as the fighter raised the barrel of his rifle to point it at Mallory's chest. 'Go,' he said, meaning it.

Mallory walked out through the gap, looking back, wondering if the man would pull the trigger.

A cry then went up from the insurgent leader – *'Allah akbar!'* – and all his men leaped over the wall with him and charged, shooting and screaming as they ran. The demonic fighter looked over his shoulder at his colleagues, back at Mallory, appeared to consider shooting him but then turned away and broke into a run, screaming his epithet as he disappeared into the dust and darkness. Seconds later the sound of gunfire and screams reached a crescendo and the muzzle-flash of discharging weapons became almost constant.

Stanza began to retch violently, crouched over and holding his stomach.

'You can throw up later, Stanza. We have to get going,' said Mallory.

Stanza sat back on his heels and looked up at Mallory, bile running down his chin and neck. 'Stanmore,' he said.

'It's over,' Mallory said. 'The money only bought us our freedom.'

'No,' Stanza said lowering his eyes. 'It bought us Stanmore too.'

Mallory followed Stanza's gaze to the bundle that had fallen open. Inside it was the severed head of a white man.

15

War Without Winners

Mallory, Stanza and Abdul stumbled on through rubble that had once been shops and houses on the edge of the town. The air was filled with the smell of cordite although the three were so used to it by now they hardly noticed. The bodies of dead Arabs had grown fewer as they approached the start line of the assault but Mallory remained alert to every sound and shadow. His two colleagues looked disconnected from the reality of what was going on around them as if numbed by it all, walking like automatons, Stanza carrying his bundle and Abdul following him like a blind man. Mallory had seen vehicles and troops moving on their flanks in the darkness but had chosen not to reveal themselves just yet. It was still dangerous out in the open and the Marines were likely to shoot first and investigate later.

The battle raged a good distance behind them now, although the occasional explosion went off nearby and ahead – probably mortars fired by insurgents in the town.

Mallory led them through a deserted building onto a main road and instantly pulled the others to cover when he saw several Hummvees parked a short distance away with a dozen or so troops gathered around. He told Abdul and Stanza to remain out of sight while he made contact. Then he stepped back onto the road, his hands raised in the air. The soldiers were cautious as he approached them but after he spoke, announcing his nationality, they could see he was a westerner and they relaxed, allowing him to join them. After a brief chat he returned with a sergeant and a couple of his men to collect Abdul and Stanza. Mallory had explained they were press who had got separated from their media pool and they showed their IDs as proof. The sergeant bought their story and allowed them to wait with the platoon. A couple of hours later a Hummvee arrived to take them to a checkpoint on the 10 motorway on the Baghdad side of Fallujah. A taxi was hanging around a few hundred metres from the checkpoint and the driver was happy to give them a ride back to the Sheraton Hotel.

Not a word was spoken during the journey and day had dawned by the time the taxi pulled up outside the first checkpoint. Mallory and Stanza climbed out. Abdul remained in the taxi and as Stanza walked away, carrying his bundle, Mallory stopped to look at Abdul who was staring at the floor. 'You going home?'

Abdul nodded.

Mallory wasn't quite sure what to say. 'I'll give you a call later. OK?'

Abdul didn't respond.

Mallory thought he understood and stepped back as the taxi turned around and drove away. He watched it as his thoughts turned to Tasneen and what he was going to say to her. He looked for Stanza, who was already halfway towards the US Army checkpoint, and then down at his grubby hands covered in cuts and abrasions. He felt his broken nose and attempted to clear his nostrils but they were too blocked with either dirt or dried blood.

As Mallory walked on deliberately slowly so as not to catch up with Stanza he contemplated his immediate future. There was nothing else for it but to head home, and as soon as he could. Tasneen was the only reason to hang about and frankly that looked more of a non-starter now than it had before he'd left for Fallujah. He couldn't go on with Tasneen without telling Abdul anyway, which she probably wouldn't want. As for Stanza, Mallory thought it best to avoid him too. The journalist was no doubt confused about one or two things, especially the sudden appearance of a million dollars, and Mallory wasn't sure if he should try and explain it to him. He decided ultimately to leave any decision-making until the following day and to sleep on it. Things might make more sense once he was cleaned up and rested. It had been a long day, to say the least, and at the end of it he was thankful to be alive.

Abdul sat in the taxi, staring into space as it cruised through the streets of his city that was already waking up. Since seeing Stanmore's severed head he had been trying to retrace every thread of the story from the night of the kidnapping to the point where his motivation became a quest to rescue the hostage in order to cleanse his soul. He had obviously drawn several wrong conclusions about his own role as well as those of various others and was still having difficulty interpreting Allah's overall plan. Allah must have disapproved of Hassan killing the American's Iraqi lover but that did not necessarily mean that He approved of Abdul executing Hassan. Abdul had obviously failed to see how he would have been no different from Hassan had he killed Mallory for the same reason. Fortunately for Abdul as well as for Mallory, Allah had intervened in time. And if Mallory was not meant to die then neither was Tasneen, something Abdul was hugely relieved about. He was going to need help sorting it all out and the first and only person who came to mind was Tasneen. She would figure it out with him. He would have to tell her everything, though, from the night Lamont had been kidnapped to the present. He thought it best not to tell her about his plans to kill her. He would have to tell her how he had nearly killed Mallory, but then, if he did that he would have to say why and then she would suspect that he had also planned to kill her. Honour killings for such reasons usually included both parties. Perhaps he could gloss over the attempted execution of Mallory. It might not affect the story all that much. The important part was about Lamont.

Abdul was feeling strangely better. Just the thought of having Tasneen to talk to again was a tonic. She was wonderful – although not entirely so, of course. Abdul would have to tell her that he knew about her and Mallory. That would put her on the spot but she deserved that much of a punishment. That was fair, he thought. She couldn't get off completely free.

Mallory closed his hotel room door, picked up his two backpacks and, looking clean and fresh despite a swollen nose and tiny scabs all over his face, marched down the landing towards the emergency stairs. He had not been to sleep but a long hot shower followed by a swift cold one and a change of clothes was almost as good. The salts in the water had revealed a dozen more cuts and abrasions, some of them requiring plasters, but apart from a few bruised ribs and the nasty bump on the back of his head he'd fared pretty well, considering everything he'd been through.

He noticed Stanza's door was open slightly and carried on past it, praying that the man would not come out at that moment. He suddenly thought of his relief who was going to turn up to find a most bizarre atmosphere indeed.

Stanza sat in his chair, staring at his desk where the bundle wrapped in its soiled cloth rested. He hadn't noticed until he put the bundle down and sat in the chair that fluids had been leaking from it and had dried into crusty scabs all over his hands and lap where it had rested throughout the taxi ride. He had been unable to bring himself to go into the bathroom and clean up. He felt drenched in despair, not only for Stanmore but for himself. The last twenty-four hours symbolised his life of partial achievements. He'd gone

461

to Fallujah to bring back Stanmore and had returned with only a portion of him.

He tried to think of a single moment during the last month when he'd been in control of his destiny or his purpose on this earth and couldn't come up with one. He couldn't blame anyone else, either. When he thought of Mallory or Abdul nothing remotely flattering came to mind but he couldn't honestly reproach them. There were some questions he'd like answers to, though. Parts of his adventure had been so surreal that he wasn't sure if they had actually happened. If Stanmore's head hadn't been sitting there, leaking on his desk, he might have doubted whether that part of it too had been real.

He wondered what to do with it. It obviously had to end up back in Wisconsin but it wasn't really the sort of thing that one boxed up and took on a plane. Bureaucracy needed to be involved. The embassy was the obvious choice. He could look for that prick Asterman and give it to him.

Stanza sighed. This had to be the lowest point of his life.

There was a knock at the door which he thought he had imagined until a voice called out his name. 'Jeff? You in there? It's Aaron . . . Aaron Blant. The *Post*.'

'It's Jake, you prick,' Stanza wanted to say. But he didn't speak or move.

Blant stepped into the corridor, leaning forward until he saw Stanza sitting in his chair. Then he froze, momentarily horrified by Stanza's condition, caked in dirt and scabs. 'You OK, Jeff?'

Stanza raised his red-ringed eyes to look at him.

'I came by last night but you were out . . . I might have a fixer for you . . . You sent an e-mail.'

Stanza looked away without acknowledging the man's presence.

'You OK?' Blant asked again.

Stanza exhaled heavily.

Blant put his hand on Stanza's desk and into a puddle of viscous liquid. He quickly withdrew his fingers, unsure where to wipe them. 'I guess you heard about Lamont,' he said as he realised the offending liquid was leaking from the stained bundle.

Stanza blinked.

'Did you see the video? They released it yesterday. Cut the poor bastard's head off two or three days ago.'

Stanza rolled his eyes and sighed again.

Blant noticed Stanza's scabby hands and lap. 'You sure you're all right? You don't look so good.'

Stanza looked at his palms and thought he should wash them.

'OK, well, I'm gonna go,' Blant said, holding his sticky hand away from his clothes and looking forward to getting to a sink. 'If you need anything let me know.' Blant sniffed the traces of a foul smell in the air and his nose led him back to the bundle. He looked at Stanza, about to say something. Then he changed his mind and left the room.

Stanza got slowly to his feet, opened the balcony doors, walked outside and looked out onto the city. It might still be an interesting story, he thought. He'd clean up, make himself some coffee and start writing.

And he wouldn't tell Patterson until he'd filed it. *That* was a reaction he would look forward to. Stanza felt strangely confident – or, more to the point, fearless. There was nothing anyone could do or say to him now. He had been through a test of fire and had emerged the other side cleansed in a way. But it would remain to be seen what he had become. He was different, though: he knew that much.

Then it stuck him. He wasn't going to write a news story. He'd write a book. That was his future. He'd tell the world the whole story from beginning to end – his story, his beginning – including all the characters and their roles in his life. Screw the *Herald*. He'd stay in Iraq on the *Herald*'s tab, researching all he needed. Then he'd fly to some remote island and write a goddamned book.

He felt better already.

Des pulled the car over to the kerb outside the departure terminal of Baghdad International Airport where several sniffer dogs were playing with their handlers and took the engine out of gear. 'Well, me old cock. 'Ave a good flight.'

'Thanks for the lift.'

'No drama, me lad. You survived the BIAP for another day. Now all I 'ave to do is survive the trip back.'

'When are you home?'

'Another month. Might 'ave a couple more clients by then. Would yer be interested in working for me?'

'Same job?'

'Sure. Lookin' after media twats. Not brain surgery, is it? As long as we don't lose any. Trick is to scare 'em into not going out the 'otel. And when they're feelin' brave give 'em a bit o' food poisonin'. Yer know t'routine, lad.'

Mallory grinned as he held out his hand. Des took it in both of his and gave it a good shake. 'Mind yersel', yer mad bastard,' Des said.

'You too.'

Mallory opened the passenger door and was about to climb out when Des grabbed his arm. 'There 'e is, the bastard. At it again.'

Mallory glanced at Des and then in the direction he was looking. A short Arab in a smart, expensive suit was dragging a suitcase on wheels away from an immaculate black Mercedes sedan towards the departure lounge entrance, followed by two men who looked like bodyguards.

'That's Feisal, from the Ministry of whatever, the bloke in the 'otel I was tellin' yer about. The one who takes money to Dubai every coupla weeks. 'E's off again . . . Not a bad job, eh?'

They watched until the men had entered the terminal and exited from their thoughts. 'So long,' Mallory said.

'Be seein' yer, mate.'

Mallory took his bags off the back seat, closed the car doors and waved as Des drove away. He shouldered his bags and walked over to a couple of security guards and a sniffer dog.

A few minutes later Mallory walked into the

departure lounge, a large hall with a vast polished marble floor and vaulted ceiling. He looked over at the Iraqi security personnel guarding the entrance to the check-in hall, which was not yet open. A line of people had already formed in front of it, though, a mixture of Arabs and westerners. There were only a couple of flights that day: the others had been cancelled due to the battle that was still raging in Fallujah only thirty kilometres away.

Mallory could not be bothered to join the line and found a seat which he plonked himself down into tiredly. There were rumours that the flight might be cancelled anyway and if so he'd sleep in the airport until he could get a later one. There was no heading back into Baghdad for him, not until he had decided what to do with himself. He had two options as far as he could see. He could rejoin the Royal Marines and continue with his military career, or he could stay in Civvy Street and make as much money as he could doing the security-adviser malarkey.

When he considered returning to Baghdad he could not help but think about Tasneen. He'd spoken to her that morning but she'd whispered that she could not talk for long. Abdul had come home in a bit of a state, physically and mentally, and she needed to be with him. Mallory understood and told her he'd call her at work in a day or so. He didn't tell her he was leaving the country and that his next call would be from the UK. Abdul obviously had not yet told her about Fallujah and the money in the ceme-tery. Mallory decided to leave it all up to fate. Whoever was organising that show certainly had a good sense of humour.

The security guards at the gate seemed to be getting ready to open it. Mallory glanced around at the people converging on the line, suspecting there were more bums than available seats. Feisal appeared with his two burly bodyguards and joined the line. Mallory found it amusing that they had only one suitcase between them and the boss was carrying it. Life was unfair if nothing else. Mallory had gone through hell to acquire and then lose a million dollars and this guy simply walked into a vault once a fortnight and helped himself.

Mallory got to his feet and decided to take his chances with the flight. The opening of the security gate did not necessarily mean the flight was on but it was an indication that the airport still believed it was.

As Mallory joined the back of the line, Feisal and one of his bodyguards walked over to the ticket counter to talk with a member of the airline staff while the other minder remained in the line with the suitcase. The entrance doors to the concourse opened and a large group of men marched in with much bustle and fanfare. They were a mixture of Iraqi police officers and suited ministerial officials and they made a direct line for Feisal. As they surrounded him a boisterous row erupted. Feisal's accompanying bodyguard was dragged aside and the bodyguard who had remained in the line immediately went to the aid of his boss.

The shouting attracted the attention of everyone in the concourse, including airport security guards who unslung their weapons from their shoulders, wondering what was going on. Feisal clearly said something to one of the officials that was less than appreciated: the temperature of the fracas went up tenfold as Feisal's jacket lapel was grabbed. This provoked one of Feisal's minders to grab the grabber, which had a domino effect with everyone seemingly trying to grab a piece of Feisal and his minders. A punch was thrown and then a gun appeared, held high in the air in the centre of the mêlée while hands struggled to reach for it. Inevitably, a shot rang out and the hall erupted in screams as passengers dropped to the floor or ran for the doors. Security guards in various parts of the vast terminal converged on the hall and the pandemonium increased when they started aiming their weapons in a threatening manner, shouting warnings at anyone who looked remotely suspicious. A shot went off outside, fired by an overexcited guard, and was immediately followed by a dozen more that were fired by other guards infected by the excitement.

Mallory crouched behind a planter, just in case. His gaze fell on Feisal's suitcase where it stood in the middle of the hall alongside other luggage belonging to passengers who had been in the line.

Mallory was not sure what inspired him to get to his feet, pick up his backpacks and march through the chaos, stepping over prone passengers until he reached the suitcase, pick it up and walk away with it. Perhaps the dangers in the hall were minuscule compared with what he'd been through during the past twenty-four hours or perhaps it was nothing more than a moment of uncontrollable madness. Whatever the reason, Mallory continued on through the hall, fearing that he might be grabbed from behind at any moment. But as the cacophony continued behind him his confidence increased and, fighting the urge to look back, he walked past a food kiosk and into a public toilet.

The large noxious room was empty and Mallory continued on into one of the disgusting cubicles, closed the door and placed the suitcase on the rim of the foul seatless toilet. He realised that his heart was pounding in his chest and that adrenalin had been coursing through his veins: he fought to control his breathing so that he could listen to tell if anyone had entered behind him. There was no evidence he had been followed.

He reached for the latches on the side of the suitcase. Amazingly, they were not locked and he raised the lid to see rows of bundles of US banknotes wrapped in cling film. A random inspection of one bundle revealed it to be all one-hundred-dollar bills and Mallory fought to control himself. He was on the cusp of walking away with a fortune but also of spending a long time in an Iraq jail that he might not survive. The next few minutes would be crucial. He could not help doing a quick calculation and, experienced in such matters, came to the delightful conclusion that he was in possession of significantly more than one million dollars, probably closer to two.

It was time to speed up. Mallory opened his backpacks, emptied his clothes into the top half of the suitcase and placed the bundles of money into the packs. When he had got them all inside he could stuff only a couple of T-shirts back into the packs, which he strapped up. He opened the cubicle door a little, checked that no one had come in, grabbed his spare clothes out of the suitcase which he left on the pedestal, tossed the clothes into a broom cupboard, pulled a backpack onto each shoulder and walked out of the toilet.

A commotion was still going on in the hall, although it had calmed down a little when Feisal and his men were taken away. Mallory walked across to a stairwell that led down to the baggage-claim and arrivals hall. Once again he became uncomfortably nervous about being followed but as he left the bottom of the stairs and walked into the vast hall that was practically deserted everything seemed relatively quiet. His confidence increased as he headed through a set of double doors, strode past a couple of guards to whom he nodded hello and walked out into the bright sunlight. There was no traffic on the terminal road as Mallory crossed it. He entered the vast underground car park that was practically empty.

Mallory did a quick recce of the dark cavernous structure and found an even darker and more secluded corner beneath one of the massive ramps that led to the floor above. He put down his bags and took a series of deep breaths while he came to terms with what he had just accomplished. It was almost too much to believe and he had to open the top of one backpack and inspect one of the bundles to convince himself that it had really happened, pulling open a corner of cling film to feel the crisp new banknotes. The joke of it was that he was where he would have been had he successfully brought the money back from Fallujah. He now had to figure out how he was going to get it out of the country. It was a phase of the operation that he had resisted planning originally in case it jinxed everything but there were some potential pitfalls with this final leg that were obvious.

Flying the money out would be a problem since luggage searches could be quite thorough, not just in Baghdad but also in Amman. Mallory would never be able to explain away that amount of cash and there was every chance that it would be confiscated. Driving it over a border was probably the best option but not right then. It was far too dangerous and he would lose more than his money if he was stopped. It might end up being a case of finding a secure place to hide it and then getting it out when things calmed down. For the moment the best thing to do was head back into Baghdad, get a room at the Palestine or Sheraton Hotel and take his time coming up with a plan. A pleasant prospect that immediately came to mind was getting together with Tasneen again. Perhaps he could talk her into coming to England with him, or France or Italy or Spain, any of the places they had talked about. He could certainly afford the bribes for visas and so forth. A broad smile spread across his face as he thought how fortunes could change so quickly.

Mallory thought about calling Kareem but risking the BIAP with just one driver for security seemed like a pointless gamble. He told himself to start thinking minimum risk again, a basic rule of his profession that

471

he seemed to have discarded somewhere on the road to Fallujah. As he pondered the problem several heavy engines gunned to life a few rows away and he walked out from under the ramp to investigate. The throaty noises were coming from several matt-black-painted muscular-looking vehicles belonging to the same *Mad Max* PSD team that had shot up Stanza. They were getting ready to move out and Mallory grabbed up his bags and headed towards them. He was certain they would give him a ride into Baghdad for a price. A few thousand dollars should buy him a seat.

The adventure was not yet over but Mallory had a good feeling about it. Perhaps Abdul would take part in it now since circumstances had changed. Mallory suddenly wondered what it would be like having him for a brother-in-law. Now *there* was something to think about.

UNDERSEA
PRISON

Many, many thanks to Christine SS
and to Yorky for so much of the wet stuff

Chapter 1

Major Hillsborough, British Army Intelligence Corps, buckled into the rigid nylon seat of the Merlin troop-transport helicopter. A portly crewman sat by the open cabin door, chatting into his headset. The major was the only passenger; the other two dozen seats folded up against the bulkhead gave the cabin the vacant look of an empty biscuit tin. He couldn't hear a word the crewman was saying above the high-pitched whine of the engines and he leaned forward to look through the narrow opening into the cockpit where the co-pilot was talking into his mouthpiece while consulting a checklist and flicking overhead switches.

The view through the open cabin door revealed nothing but rough angular slabs of concrete: tall inter-locking blast-walls that surrounded the helipad and large pebbles covering the ground to reduce the dust. The crewman slid the large door smoothly shut, muffling the higher and more irritating noise frequencies. These only got louder as the engine power increased and the heavy beast made a great effort to pull itself off the ground.

Hillsborough cleared his throat as he stretched around

to look through the large square window behind his seat. The dust swirled under the thundering rotors, working its way out from beneath the pebbles. The old city beyond the camp's precast angular walls came into view. He had been in Afghanistan only a couple of weeks but that was long enough to acquire what was commonly known as the Kabul cough, an irritation caused by the fine grey dust common to the region. Locals described it as so fine that it could work its way through the shell of an egg.

The helicopter rose to reveal a view of the north-eastern outskirts of the city, the squat dilapidated sandy-grey habitats intermingled with shiny new metal warehouses owned by the UN, Red Cross and various Western food and hardware corporations. The craft slowly turned on its axis, giving Hillsborough a view of the rest of Camp Souter, the British Army Head-quarters in Afghanistan, ringed by layers of imposing walls topped with interlocking spools of razor wire. A soldier stood in the doorway of the nearest sentry tower inside a corner of the wall, watching the heli-copter as it climbed above him. The Merlin continued to turn and Hillsborough saw a massive Antonov cargo plane taxi along the runway of Kabul International Airport. A pair of military C130 transport aircraft were parked near a row of hangars, along with several Apache gunships and some Chinooks.

The chopper dipped its nose slightly as it powered ahead and Hillsborough looked beyond the airfield at a parched mountain range. He had to crouch in order to see the highest point of Khwaja Rawash, a craggy hill he had fancied spending a day walking up but had never got around to. He felt a tinge of guilt about the failed expedition and tried to console himself with the rationalisation that it would have been a pointless risk anyway. But this excuse was quickly negated by the initial justification he'd come up with for doing the walk alone in the first place – which was that he had about as much chance of being mugged on the coast-line near Dover where he lived as he had of running into Taliban fighters in that deserted terrain. He knew that better than most since he was the Regiment's senior intelligence officer – or, at least, he had been until that morning. An aide from the Embassy had arrived un-expectedly in the operations room with a high-priority assignment that had to be carried out by someone who held at least the rank of major and Hillsborough was the only one available.

There was no shortage of men who would have jumped at the prospect of a jolly to London but Hillsborough was not one of them. He had climbed out of bed that morning, as he had every day since his arrival, looking forward to getting his teeth into his new appointment. It was his first senior command posting and having completed his handover from the previous IO the day before he was imbued with an invigorating feeling of his own importance. Now, suddenly, he was nothing more than a messenger carrying an important diplomatic package to Bagram Airbase where a plane was waiting to fly him to the UK. He had no idea what was inside the briefcase chained to his wrist and he didn't particularly care. This trip was a bloody nuisance and he already knew that he wouldn't be able to wait to get back to Afghanistan.

Hillsborough checked his watch, a shiny steel Rolex analogue that his wife had given him on his last birthday. Not more than twenty minutes, the pilot had told him. But Hillsborough displayed none of the sense of urgency and importance that the embassy attaché had ascribed to the mission. The man had not even given him a guesstimated return date and the worst-case scenario was that he could be gone for weeks.

The crewman sat with his elbows on his knees, supporting his large helmeted head while he stared at the floor as he did a rough calculation of his own. He had three days left of his tour of duty and his name was on the operations board under just two more scheduled trips. But since this particular excursion had been unexpected he wondered if he might not have to do only one of his planned trips because of it. At the end of the day it didn't matter, though, as long as in seventy-two hours he was on that big beautiful C130 and heading for England. He could already taste that first pint in his local and hear the boisterous laughter of his mates at the bar.

Hillsborough sat back in his seat and concentrated on easing the tension in his neck muscles that had tightened since boarding the Merlin. He wasn't sure where the stress had come from, since he was generally a relaxed individual even on helicopter flights. He put it down to the anxiety of this unexpected and disruptive mission. He raised a hand to scratch an itch on his eyebrow, inadvertently pulling on the short chain attached to the briefcase, yanking it off his lap and forcing him to make a quick grab for it. Having something chained to his wrist was a new experience for him.

The crewman glanced at the major, wondering if he was nervous. 'You OK, sir?' he called out, leaning forward.

'What?' Hillsborough shouted back, unsure what the man had said.

The crewman was about to repeat himself when he changed his mind, reached above his head, removed a headset from a hook, unravelled the cable wrapped around the earpieces and handed it to Hillsborough who put it on.

'Be there in fifteen,' the crewman shouted.

'Yes. Right,' the major said.

The crewman shook his head as he touched his helmet alongside his ear and pointed to a small control box on the cable at Hillsborough's chest.

Hillsborough found the box and pressed a button on it. 'Yes. Thank you.'

The crewman gave him a thumbs-up and Hillsborough looked back out of the window to see the city already in the distance a couple of thousand feet below. A lonely black road directly below grew from the urban sprawl like a vine and passed below the helicopter. He turned in his seat to examine it as it weaved ahead across a vast, open, treeless land known as the Shomali Plain where half a dozen small villages or hamlets were spaced out on either side, some of them miles back from it. At the end of the plain the road snaked tightly up into a range of lumpy hills before disappearing short of the crest. What appeared to be some kind of ancient fortress came into view almost directly below: a hundred or so neatly spaced blocks of houses surrounded by a high rectangular mud wall. It appeared to be abandoned and Hillsborough studied it until it moved out of sight beneath him.

The Merlin banked easily when it neared the craggy hills, the highest crest a thousand feet above them. Instead of climbing the craft remained at the same height and changed direction once again to fly parallel with the range.

'Two vehicles, eleven o'clock,' said a scratchy voice over Hillsborough's headset. The sighting was on the other side of the craft and he looked away from the window at the crewman who was grabbing the handle of the large cabin door. With a well-practised sharp yank he slid it open a couple of feet. The wind rushed in and the crewman leaned out against it to take a better look, staring ahead of the helicopter.

'Seen,' the crewman said. 'Looks like they're static.'

'People climbing out, I think,' came a voice from the cockpit.

Hillsborough had an urge to unbuckle his belt in order to take a look out the door but immediately thought better of it. Helicopter crewmen could get testy about their passengers moving around the cabin without permission. Instead he took in the dramatic view of the hills that he had from his window. He had read many books about the British occupation of Afghanistan that had happened more than a century ago and he tried to imagine what it had been like for soldiers in those days: the oppressive heat and dust of the summers and the bitter cold of the winters. In many ways life for a rural Afghan had not changed a great deal since those times. Hillsborough wondered what the locals truly made of the Westerners and all their mind-boggling technology. Did they envy them or did they truly want to remain as they were? He was inclined to believe the former, suspecting that most so-called Islamic extremists were nothing more than political tools in the hands of men who could not otherwise vie for power.

'EVADE! EVADE! EVADE!' the crewman suddenly screamed. The last word had barely left his lips before the heavy machine jerked upwards, banked heavily over and dropped out of the sky on its side.

Hillsborough grabbed his seat in sudden panic as his stomach leapt into his throat and the briefcase clattered against the floor.

The crewman had had his suspicions the instant he'd heard the co-pilot sight the vehicles. They only increased as he watched several figures moving hastily around them. He had not seen much in the way of action throughout his tour other than the time when his crew had dropped off a Royal Marine fighting troop on a hillside during a battle taking place some distance away. The Yanks had lost two helicopters in those months, brought down by ground-to-air missiles, and it remained in the back of every crewman's mind each time he took to the air. The route from Kabul to Bagram was considered reasonably secure because of the relatively few numbers of attacks along it in the past six months. The wreckage at the head of the Shomali Plain of a US Blackhawk, shot down the year before, was a reminder to all that no helicopter was safe anywhere in this country.

The crewman had held himself back from hitting the panic button when he'd first thought he could make out the men taking something from the back of one of the trucks. He prided himself on his coolness and his caution against overreacting. But there was no mistaking the sudden flash from within the group and the instant cloud of smoke rapidly expanding behind it, the tell-tale signs of a launched missile.

The pilot had seen the threat and had initially increased power to pull the craft upwards, hoping to get above the missile's altitude limit. But after an instant recalculation he took the lift out of the rotors and banked the chopper away in an effort to gain downward speed and move out of the weapon's horizontal range. As he gripped the controls tightly, willing more speed into the lumbering beast, he knew in his heart that they would not make it. If the rocket was a Strela-7, rumoured to be the most common in use in the region, he needed to be over four kilometres away and above two thousand metres to stand a chance of evading it. He was short of both distances. They were in God's hands now.

The crewman could do nothing but squat in the doorway and stare at the head of the trail of smoke that twisted and curved towards them. The helicopter swung dramatically over onto its other side in an effort to shake its pursuer but the missile's computer nimbly adjusted the projectile's tail fins to compensate for the move. The smoke trail corkscrewed several times in a tight curve, cutting through the crisp, clean air as it homed in on the heat signature of the Merlin's red-hot exhausts.

Hillsborough did not know the nature of the threat but it was evident from the crew's reactions that the situation was a serious one. He put a hand to his seat belt to unfasten it in order to have a look for himself but then he remembered the helicopter crash drills he'd been taught, the fundamental rule of which was to stay strapped into the seat. If they landed he would want to get out of the craft as soon as he could and he focused on the open door in front of him, keeping his hand on the buckle in readiness. The crewman suddenly leapt from the doorway, throwing himself to the floor, and for a split second Hillsborough could see, in the bright sunshine outside, the instrument of their deaths as it homed in.

The impact struck above the cabin at the back of the engine compartment and the blast rocked the craft violently. A second later the fuel tanks ignited, exploding down into the Merlin's interior. The engines died instantly and the tail buckled as the chopper descended in a tight spiral, its nose dipping to lead its dive.

Hillsborough covered his face with one hand as flames engulfed him. The other was restrained by the chain, the briefcase having jammed under the seat. Even so, he managed to undo his seat buckle with his tethered hand and as he fell forward he saw that his body was on fire. He felt the scorching heat pour into his throat as he took his final breath.

'Mayday! Mayday!' the pilot screamed as he and the co-pilot pulled at the controls in a futile effort to get the craft's nose up. Then flames burst in from behind to fill the cockpit and as the men struggled blindly to release their seat belts the helicopter slammed into the ground.

Durrani followed the course of the missile with wide, anxious eyes, his heart pounding in his chest in excited expectation. As soon as he saw it strike and the side of the Merlin burst into flames he shouted for his men to get into the two battered pick-up trucks. He was first into the cab of the lead truck. Its engine was still running, and Durrani yelled again for his men to hurry as they scrambled for the back. Impatiently, he floored the accelerator and the wheels spun in the dry soil before they gained traction and shunted the vehicle forward.

Two of the men gave chase. One of them managed to grab hold of the tailgate and hang onto it, his legs racing at a speed they had never achieved before. Durrani only had eyes for his prey as it dropped towards the horizon. The truck picked up speed as he steered it resolutely across the rough terrain, doing his best to avoid the worst of its hazards. The man hanging onto the tailgate lost his hold after a desperate attempt to pull himself into the back and after sprawling briefly on the ground he scrambled to his feet and leapt into the back of the other vehicle.

Durrani watched the helicopter as it fell out of sight. A second later a mushroom of smoke and flame spouted into the air.

He sped towards it, desperate to complete the planned follow-up phase of the attack. His eyes flickered left and right – he was keenly aware that the road across the plain was a regular military route between Kabul and Bagram and that there was every chance that the attack had been seen by the enemy somewhere.

The trail of black smoke twisting into the clear blue sky was a fast-dissolving record of the doomed helicopter's flight path from the point the missile had struck to the Merlin's impact with the ground. Durrani fought to keep the rising black smoke in his sights but the dust blowing in through his open window was getting in his eyes.

Bright orange flames came into view as Durrani closed on the wreckage. He kept the accelerator to the floor as the pick-up bounced up onto a tarmac road and across it. He looked quickly in every direction, including skyward. If anything remotely military-looking came into view he would turn around and head towards the nearest village at the foot of the hills behind him, his only chance of escape.

The helicopter lay on its side like a gutted beast, its ravaged carcass burning, its rotors buckled, its tail broken off. The cabin and cockpit were fiercely ablaze and Durrani drove in a wide arc around it until he was upwind and away from the direct heat and smoke. He slammed on the brakes, slid to a dusty halt, opened the door and stood out on the sill to inspect his handiwork. His first thought was that it did not look possible that anyone could have survived. Prisoners were a bonus but rare in such attacks.

The other vehicle halted behind Durrani's but the men were more concerned for their own safety, anxiously scanning every quadrant of the horizon like meerkats. As far as they were concerned Durrani was putting their lives at risk by remaining in the area.

Durrani took a long and patient look, scanning the wreckage for anything of value. The destruction appeared to be complete and he was about to swing back inside his cab when something caught his eye. Several metres from the wreckage, lying on the scorched earth, was a twisted, broken body, as charred as the surrounding debris and clearly dead. But a small metallic object lying in the midst of the remains and reflecting the strong sunlight was impossible to ignore.

Durrani stepped down onto the ground.

The anxiety among the others increased as they watched their leader walk casually towards the wreckage. One of them called out that they should be going. The others quickly echoed him. Durrani ignored them, his stare fixed on the body. The wind suddenly changed direction and the searing heat from the flames struck him. He was forced to shield his face with his hands and move back several steps. The wind changed again and he saw that the glinting object was a chain attached to what appeared to be a small case.

Durrani moved in at a crouch and picked up the case, the attached limp arm in a charred jacket sleeve rising on the end of the chain. The metal handle burned him and he quickly dropped it. He drew a knife from a sheath on his belt, pulled the arm straight and dug the tip into the wrist joint, slicing through the sinews until the hand fell away. He looked for the end of the other arm lying awkwardly across the body's back and wiped the thin coat of carbon from the face of the watch to reveal the clear, undamaged glass, the second hand rotating beneath it. The watch was cool enough to touch and he pulled it off the corpse's wrist. He picked the chain up by using the point of the knife. The smouldering case dangled beneath it and, after a quick check around for anything else, Durrani headed back to his pick-up.

He climbed in behind the wheel, dropped the brief-case onto the passenger seat, slipped the scorched watch onto his wrist, put the engine in gear and roared away.

Durrani felt exhilarated as he looked around for the enemy, confident that they would not appear. He was wise enough not to celebrate until his escape was complete but seasoned enough to trust his senses. He bounced in the seat as the pick-up roared back over the tarmac road and headed for the safety of the hills and the villages that ran along the foot of it. Any doubts that he would fail to escape vanished. It had been a well-executed plan.

Durrani looked at his new watch, the shiny metal exposed where the carbon had rubbed off. His gaze moved to the case on the seat, the cracks in the charred brittle plastic exposing more metal beneath. He looked ahead again but the briefcase and its as yet unknown contents remained at the front of his thoughts.

Chapter 2

It was dark by the time Durrani entered the city of Kabul in his battered, dusty pick-up. He was wearing a leather jacket whose condition matched the vehicle perfectly. He was alone. On the seat beside him, concealed beneath a Tajik scarf, was a loaded AK47 with a seventy-five-round drum magazine attached. When Durrani had contacted his Taliban mullah to report the success of the attack and describe what he had subsequently found in the wreckage he was told to report to the mosque with his find as soon as the sun had set and to ensure he was protected. That meant he was to travel with bodyguards.

But Durrani did not like the company of others and avoided it even if it meant increasing his personal risk. He endured the presence of other men only when carrying out tasks he could not physically complete alone. In his younger days, during the fight against the Russian occupation, he had chosen to specialise in mines and booby traps because it was a military skill that he could develop alone. And to ensure he would always be employed in that role and to avoid being thrown into a regular combat company he had worked hard to become one of the best. In the process he'd gained a reputation for innovation and thoroughness, qualities that his peers felt could be employed in other roles – such as the shooting down of helicopters.

Durrani's desire for solitude was not a survival tactic in the usual sense although it had its advantages in that regard. He had been alone, except for a handful of acquaintances, since his early childhood. None of those few friends could ever have been described as close to him. He would not allow that. Durrani was living a lie that if discovered could give rise to dangerous accusations and lead to the loss of his head. He feared that if anyone got close to him they might somehow find out. One way of avoiding unwelcome scrutiny was to gain a reputation for being introverted. He had achieved this but it meant that he could never let his guard down. Success as a soldier bred jealousy and the need to remain enigmatic only strengthened as his celebrity increased.

Durrani was a Taliban – or, to be more accurate, he had joined their cause. The ranks of the Taliban were made up mostly of Pashtuns, the most privileged of the Afghan tribes, and he had been accepted as one of that ethnic group since his childhood. His claim to that heritage was not entirely valid. Durrani was actually half Hazara, a race considered by the Pashtuns to be no better than slave material. The Hazara were also Shi'a whereas the Pashtuns were Sunni. The Pashtuns were the largest ethnic group in Afghanistan and at one time had been considered the only true Afghans. The Hazara were not only different socially, tribally and religiously. They also looked very different: their features were distinctly Mongol – flat faces with flat noses.

Durrani's mother was Hazara and had grown up in Kandahar with her father who was a servant of a wealthy Pashtun family. They had lived in a hut at the bottom of the back garden and the Pashtun master's son, who was a year older than Durrani's mother, had spent his adolescence with her. When she had fallen pregnant in her mid-teens it had been obvious who was responsible and before the bump became too visible the girl's father threw her out of the city.

Durrani knew very little more about his mother's early life than that. He didn't know if her master's son had forced himself upon her or if they had been lovers. Durrani did not suspect rape, though. What little his mother did say about his father, when she eventually told Durrani that he was the son of a Pashtun, revealed no sign of malice or dislike and sometimes even displayed a hint of affection.

Durrani had no great interest in finding his father but even if he had wanted to it would have been impossible. He didn't know where the family had lived or even who they were. All his mother had revealed to him about their identity – it was something she was quite proud of – was that they were descended from Ahmed Shah Durrani, an eighteenth-century Pashtun king of Afghanistan. In the years leading up to the Russian invasion every member of that line had been considered a potential threat to the Communist Afghan government of the day. Those who survived assassination either went into hiding or fled the country along with the rest of the royal family and their relatives.

Durrani had been able to hide any visible evidence of his Hazara bloodline because he had not inherited the distinctive physical Mongol characteristics of that ethnic group. Instead, he had acquired his father's angular, long-nosed, lighter-skinned features. His mother had died of some illness when he was eight before he had developed any curiosity about his male parent. By that time they were living in abject poverty in Kabul in a small mud hut on the outskirts of a residential area at the foot of a hill occupied by an old British military fort that had long since been abandoned.

The memories of the day she died were now cloudy but Durrani remembered being very hungry and his mother lying on the blanket that was their bed, calling weakly for God to help her. God had not heard her: she eventually stopped making heavy and laboured breathing noises and her open eyes became still and unfocused. He shook her and asked her to wake up. When blood trickled from her lips and down the side of her mouth he knew she would never talk to him again. He did not look for anyone to help for there was no one. He could not remember ever talking to anyone else but his mother in those days and as far as he knew she had only ever talked to him – unless begging counted as talking to others. He remembered that his days with her included collecting water in a bucket from a tap and walking miles to get wood for the fire on which she cooked their paltry meals. Looking back it was hard to see how they had survived.

Hunger eventually forced Durrani to leave his mother's body in their dark, miserable hut and walk the streets of the city, ragged and unwashed, scavenging for something to eat. He remembered sorting through rotten food in gutters, competing for it with filthy dogs and cats, and sleeping in abandoned dwellings. Then one day – perhaps weeks later, he had no idea how long – he was literally picked up off the street and carried into a house by a man who turned out to be a schoolteacher. After nursing Durrani back to health the teacher placed him in an orphanage where he joined a dozen or so other children.

Durrani said his name was Po-po, his mother's nickname for him, but when asked for his family name he said, quite accurately, that he did not know. He might have told them what little he did know about his family but for reasons he could not fully understand at the time he was afraid to. His mother had never explained the complexities of race discrimination to him but he was aware that he and she had been different from the Pashtun majority and not in any positive way. Weeks later, after much badgering by the orphanage staff and the other kids, he finally muttered the only name he knew that linked him with his family. To his surprise the reaction had been most favourable, which gave him the confidence to stick with it.

One day a little girl with features similar to his mother's arrived at the orphanage. Durrani immediately went to befriend her but he was pulled aside and told by the other children to leave her alone because she was of a low caste. It was Durrani's first lesson in how

Hazaras were considered inferior to the Pashtuns. The Hazara children were often taunted by the others, treated like animals and made to act as if they were slaves. The schoolmasters did not appear to see anything wrong in it and only intervened when they saw the Hazara being severely beaten.

Durrani soon realised how imperative it was that he should never mention his mother's Hazara ethnicity. He became so fearful of the ramifications that his denial turned into a phobia. When walking the streets he would avoid eye contact with any Hazara he passed for fear that they might recognise him. A memorable exception was the day he saw coming towards him a young woman who looked exactly as he remembered his mother. He could not take his eyes off her until she was feet away, at which point he dropped his gaze and turned his back to her in case she really *was* his parent. He was afraid she might talk to him.

When the woman had passed Durrani he ran up the street as fast as he could and didn't stop until he found somewhere to hide. He did not feel shameful about his reaction. On the contrary, he was relieved at avoiding a close call. But he could not shake loose the memory of the girl's face and he gradually became confused about his mother's death, doubting whether she had actually died at all. The frightening implications of that were that if she was still living he could be exposed.

Since the day Durrani had walked out of his hut, leaving his mother's corpse inside, he had never returned to the area where they had lived. But a few days after

19

seeing the Hazara woman in the street he was filled with the urge to learn if his mother really was still alive. The need to know was not based on any sudden longing to be with her again. His fear of being labelled a Hazara was now greater than any affection he had ever had for his mother. To avoid being seen he waited until the sun had dropped behind the mountains before making his way to the top of the hill that overlooked the area. He crept inside the old British fort and climbed the ramparts of the weathered but still imposing walls to search for the hut from afar. He could not find it where he thought it should have been. But after walking from one end of the fortifications to the other and back several times, identifying some vaguely familiar reference points, he came to the conclusion that the dwelling no longer existed.

Durrani remained on the battlements for many hours, gazing down at the huts and houses, the people coming and going and the handful of children playing where he used to, watching in case his mother should turn up. He left when it was completely dark and all he could see was the glow of kerosene lamps inside the houses, never to return to the place again. From time to time throughout his life, whenever he caught a glimpse of the old fort as he passed through the city, his thoughts went back to those days. The most vivid memory was that of his mother lying in the hut with blood trickling from her mouth.

So fearful was Durrani of being exposed as a Hazara that to maintain his security at the orphanage he decided to keep to himself, rarely talking to the other children.

When asked about his family he shrugged and said he knew nothing other than that they were Pashtun.

Durrani was nineteen and working in a barber shop as a floor sweeper when the Russians marched into Kabul by invitation to support the beleaguered Communist government. He might have stayed in the city if it had not been for another orphan, Rog, a Pashtun boy Durrani's age. Rog was the only person in Durrani's life whom he had allowed to get close enough to call a friend. When Rog one day declared that they should leave Kabul and join the mujahideen to fight against the Russian invaders Durrani experienced his first taste of the lure of adventure. It was an enticement that would subsequently tempt him many times. The following night he and Rog left the city together.

After several days of mostly walking, with the occasional ride on a truck, they arrived at a village in the hills outside Kandahar where Rog had a relative. Within a week they had joined a band of mujahideen.

Thus Durrani began a nomadic guerrilla existence that would span practically all of his next two and a half decades and end with his capture and incarceration in the most impregnable prison on the planet.

The pair were initially employed by the mujahideen as general dogsbodies: carrying ammunition, fetching supplies, cooking and washing. But after Rog was killed in a Russian helicopter attack along with a dozen others in the group, Durrani was handed a rifle and from that day became one of the fighters. A year later, while being treated for a wound and recovering at a training ground in the Hindu Kush mountains, he met a fellow soldier who had recently lost an eye, a quiet, tall, muscular man with an intense and unusually charismatic personality. His name was Omar and the next time Durrani saw him, a decade later, the man had become a mullah and also the leader of a powerful new force that would eventually become known to the rest of the world as the Taliban.

After ten years of fighting the Russians were eventually chased from Afghanistan and Durrani found himself pondering his future and how he was going to make a living. It felt strange to be considering a normal life after so many years as a warrior but it did not take him long to come to the realisation that he had no useful peacetime skills other than the ability to drive a vehicle. And so that was precisely what he did. He got a job as a taxi driver in Kabul, hoping eventually to own his own vehicle and go into business for himself. But the peace he expected to descend on Afghanistan with the end of the war against the Russians did not materialise: the battle for control of the country continued. It was not long before he was lured back into the ranks where he joined the rebellion against the Communist government that was still in power.

Durrani's involvement in the struggle was not motivated by any political loyalty. It seemed to him that the endless battles were for the personal gains of others and that Afghans were merely the tools of Pakistan, Saudi Arabia and the Americans. There was little remuneration other than what could be got from looting. But when he was called to join the fight he went because it seemed better than what he was doing at the time. He was a nomadic warrior purely for the sake of it.

Once again Durrani took part in the capture of Kabul, a new government was installed, and he went back to driving a taxi. During the brief period of calm a pretty young Tajik girl who worked in the taxi company's office came into his life. Durrani set his sights on marrying her. He planned to work hard enough to buy a car, set up his own taxi company and prove his worth to her. But Durrani was to have his heart broken only a few months later when the son of the taxi company's owner announced his intentions to marry the girl, who had accepted his offer. For her he was, financially, a far wiser choice than Durrani.

The failure of the new Afghan leadership to bring order led to the country breaking up into zones, each one led by its own warlord. The two most powerful generals were Massoud and Hekmatyer who both vied for ultimate control at the whim of the same old power-brokers: Pakistan and the US. Crime became pandemic and the general unrest led directly to the emergence of a new clan formed by a sect of Pashtun Islamic-fundamentalist students known as the Taliban. Their banner call was to rid the country of corruption, crime and greedy warlords and they quickly became very popular.

A combination of peer pressure, heartbreak, loss of confidence in the future and the subconscious need to find a purpose to his life saw Durrani leaving Kabul to join in this latest effort to bring order to Afghanistan. He also could not ignore an important characteristic

23

of the Taliban. They were essentially a Pashtun organisation that, in the early days at least, were keen to return the old Afghan monarchy back to power. In such uncertain times it was wise to stick with one's own kind and so Durrani enlisted with the Taliban.

A couple of months later he took part in the battle for Kandahar and after a successful campaign found himself marching on Kabul once again. On his thirty-sixth birthday, a date he had chosen arbitrarily as he did not know his real date of birth, the Taliban took the capital and from there embarked on a crusade to liberate the rest of the country. Durrani approved of the harsh politics of his new leaders, having decided they were necessary to bring order to his war-torn country. Neither was he deterred by the level of brutality used by the Taliban in order to enforce its rule. However, the massacre of Yakaolang left him with scars that never fully healed. Yakaolang was a predominantly Hazara town that had shown the potential for resistance to the new rulers. The truth was that the people had not yet taken up arms against the Taliban but were used as an example to any who might be considering it.

Durrani, now sporting a long black beard, arrived at the town one afternoon along with several hundred Taliban and met up with a force of similar numbers made up of foreign fighters from Pakistan and various Arab countries. Their orders were simple enough: to systematically select every male over the age of twelve and execute him. During the next few days a festival of looting and slaughter took place. More than three hundred men and boys were shot or mutilated along with dozens of women and children who simply got in the way.

On the final day of the massacre the gang Durrani was part of burst into a house and on finding a young Hazara boy of the right age started to drag him outside to execute him. But the boy's older sister tried to stop them, directing her pleas at Durrani. He was standing in the doorway, unable to take his eyes off her – her likeness to his mother was astounding. While pleading for mercy she walked towards him, her hands grabbing the front of her clothes as if she was trying to rip them from her body. She stopped in front of him and became suddenly calm, lowering her voice and talking to him as if she knew him, or so it seemed to him.

'Please spare him,' she said. 'He is just a boy. You know that. You must have sympathy.'

In the Pashtu language it sounded to Durrani as if she could see that he was one of them, one of her kind, a Hazara.

The other Taliban were watching the display as they held the struggling boy, looking between Durrani and the girl, something Durrani suddenly became aware of.

'Please,' she cried, stepping even closer to Durrani. 'You are not the same as the others. I can see that. Spare my brother. I beg you.'

She could see compassion in his eyes but had failed to recognise the overriding fear behind them. Durrani squeezed the trigger of his AK47 and shot the girl once through the chest. She fell back to the floor but managed to support herself on her hands defiantly, refusing to fall all the way back. Her brother wailed on seeing the bloodstain grow down the front of her dress. She never took her eyes off Durrani even as they filled with tears. She looked more like his mother than ever as death came to claim her, a trickle of blood on her lips. She raised a hand towards him as if she wanted him to take hold of it. Durrani wanted her to stop and the only way he could do it was to fire again. The second bullet killed her instantly.

Durrani's colleagues approved of the execution and pushed past him, taking the girl's brother outside. A few seconds later more shots rang out.

Durrani remained staring at the girl's body for a long time, a confusion of emotions swirling inside his head. He felt neither approval nor satisfaction. What he did feel was something that up until that moment in his life had been alien to him. It was guilt.

He left the house, walking past the limp body of the girl's brother hanging lifeless over the front-garden gate, and continued down the main street and out of the town. It was not so much because he was disgusted by what was going on but because he was lost inside himself, consumed by his experience in the house, wondering what was happening to him.

The memory of the girl remained with him for the rest of his life – until his very last breath, in fact.

The Taliban plan to control the whole of Afghanistan did not succeed. The fighting continued for years against the Northern Alliance until the attack on the World Trade Center when it was the Americans' turn to invade the country. The Afghan weapons and strategies that had worked so well against the Russians were no match for US might and the Taliban were swept aside.

Durrani took to the hills and eventually escaped into Pakistan where he stayed for several years. He remained in the employ of the Taliban, for his own security as well as to earn his keep. Occasionally he was sent back over the border on sorties, gathering intelligence on US troop movements, sometimes getting into fights with American or Pakistan border patrols. Some of his comrades-in-arms joined the fight in Iraq but Durrani did not want to move that far from his country. Most of his compatriots believed that, as with the fight against the Russians, and against the British many decades before that, a protracted guerrilla campaign against the Americans would eventually see the Afghans victorious. But the Americans had also learned from those past campaigns and the Taliban found it far more difficult to operate in the same way they had under the Russian occupation.

A degree of order descended upon many parts of the country, Kabul in particular, but this time Durrani could not go back to being a taxi driver or live a normal life in any Afghan city. It would not take long before questions about his past were asked and so his only chance of survival was to stay among those like himself.

He often wondered what his life would have been like if he'd married the Tajik girl. It might have kept him from joining the Taliban, for one thing. But such speculation was pointless. The Durrani who had wanted to marry and settle down was very different from the one who always went to war and there was little left of the former one anyway. Durrani was under no illusions as to how it would all end for him. Thousands of men he had known had died, and all he could remember of them were blurred images of their faces over the years. One day he knew he would join them. He could not look forward to paradise either for he was not a devout Muslim. Deep down he did not believe in such myths. It did not make sense to him that a life devoted to death and destruction could be rewarded with everlasting beauty. He could imagine nothing after life, only dark emptiness.

Durrani drove along a dark narrow street with dilapidated single-storey homes on either side, the rooms illuminated by kerosene lamps or lonely bare bulbs. Grey water trickled from waste pipes onto sodden, crumbling concrete pavements strewn with decaying rubbish. His eyes glanced everywhere as he reached the rear entrance of a sturdy mosque in the midst of the squalor, the largest building in the neighbourhood. The side streets he had used for much of the way after entering the city were unlit and quiet but traffic was busy along the main road that passed in front of the holy building.

He pulled to a stop in a wet and muddy gutter, turned off the pick-up's lights and engine and sat still, his window open, waiting for his senses to grow accustomed to the sounds and shadows.

Durrani looked down at his wrist and the Rolex watch, now clean and shining, more to appreciate his treasure than to note the time. He had few possessions, only those he could carry. The watch was the prettiest trinket he had found in years and he hoped he would not have to sell it, for a while at least. He was curious about the engraving on the back. The next time he met an educated man who could read the language of the enemy he might ask what it said.

He lifted the Tajik scarf off the passenger seat to reveal his AK and the charred briefcase with the chain attached. He placed the case on his lap, the weapon on the floor and the scarf back over it. He wound up the window, checked that the passenger door was locked and looked up and down the street to ensure it was empty. He climbed out of the cab, locked the door, crossed the narrow road, stepped carefully between two parked cars to avoid the muddy gutter, crossed the pavement and passed through a small brick archway.

He entered a stone courtyard, immediately turned the corner towards a large wooden door and on reaching it he knocked on it. He turned his back on the door and studied the dark, silent courtyard that was surrounded by shadowy alcoves. A gust of wind blew a collection of leaves in a circle in the middle of the courtyard before scattering them into a corner. A bolt was loudly thrown back behind the door and Durrani turned around as it opened wide enough for a man with a gun in his hand to look through and examine him.

The man's name was Sena and Durrani had seen him before in the service of the mullah. He was tall and gaunt and, despite the gun, looked unthreatening. Durrani suspected the man had never fired a shot in his life and would probably drop the weapon and run if he were to kick the door open. Sena stepped back to allow Durrani inside, secured the door again, and led him along a corridor, holding the gun at his side as if it was a tiresome appendage. Two Taliban fighters lounged on the floor, staring up at Durrani. They were dressed in grubby black and brown robes and wore long black beards. Two AK47 rifles were leaning against the wall between them. Neither man made any attempt to shift his dirty sandalled feet out of the way as the other men stepped over them.

Sena opened a door at the end of the corridor and led the way down a short flight of stairs to the bottom where two more fighters stood smoking strong cigarettes – the small space stank of tobacco. Sena knocked on the only door on the landing and waited patiently. A voice eventually summoned them and Sena pushed the door open and stepped to one side, indicating that Durrani should enter.

Durrani stepped inside a long narrow windowless room illuminated by a lamp on a desk at the far end. The door closed behind him. Sena remained in the corridor outside.

The room was sparsely furnished: a chair behind the desk, two more against a wall and several cushions on a worn rug. A mullah, dressed completely in black, was replacing a book on a shelf behind his desk. He turned to face Durrani as the door was closed and he studied his guest solemnly. A moment later his face cracked into a thin, devilish smile. 'That was a good job you did today,' he said.

'It was my duty,' Durrani replied courteously.

The mullah's gaze dropped to the case in Durrani's hands.

Durrani stepped forward and placed it on the desk.

'You have not opened it?' the mullah asked as he put on a pair of expensive spectacles.

'Of course not.'

The mullah took hold of the chain, raised it to its full length, released it and turned the case around so the locks were facing him. A brief test proved that they were locked as he suspected. 'Sena!' he called out.

The door opened and Sena looked in.

'A hammer and screwdriver,' the mullah ordered.

Sena closed the door.

The mullah took a packet of cheap African Woodbines from a pocket, removed one, placed it in his mouth and offered the pack to Durrani.

'No. Thank you,' Durrani said.

The mullah pocketed the packet, dug a lighter out and lit the cigarette. He blew a thick stream of strong smoke into the room as he turned the case over to check the other side. 'It was British?'

'Yes.'

'How many dead?'

'I don't know. It was burning. One or two, perhaps, plus the crew.'

The mullah stared coldly into Durrani's unwavering eyes. He had known the fighter for many years, having first encountered him during the Taliban's capture of Kandahar. 'You look tired, old friend. Are you well?'

'I am well. You are kind to ask.'

'Would you like some tea?'

'Not right now. But thank you.'

The door opened and Sena returned with the tools.

'Open it,' the mullah ordered briskly, impatient to know the briefcase's contents.

Durrani placed the case on its side with the locks uppermost as Sena stepped beside him to assess the task.

'Hit the lock,' Durrani said. To the mullah, Durrani appeared to be as anxious as himself to see what was in the case. But in truth Durrani was merely irritated by Sena's sluggishness.

Sena was the mullah's clerical assistant and had been a servant of one type or another all his life. He was graceful, thoughtful and in no way technical and as he placed the tip of the screwdriver in the joint between the two locks every shred of self-confidence had drained from his expression.

'The lock,' Durrani said, a hint of irritation in his voice. 'Put it against the lock.'

Sena moved the tip of the screwdriver closer to one of the locks, gritted his teeth and raised the hammer that looked a touch too heavy for him. Before he could bring it down Durrani snatched away the tools. 'Hold the case,' he snapped.

Sena gripped the briefcase, nervous in the presence of his master and this veteran fighter.

Durrani placed the end of the screwdriver on the mounting of the lock, raised the hammer and brought it down, splitting it. The case was not designed as a safe; its real security depended on its human escort. Another blow split the second lock as easily and the case popped, its top springing open slightly. Durrani would not be so forward as to open it completely himself and he turned it to face the mullah.

The mullah took hold of the briefcase and lifted the top fully to reveal the inside filled with a foam-rubber pad tailored to fit. He removed the top layer of foam to reveal a thin manila file and several letters. He moved them aside and studied the rest of the contents: a grey plastic box the size of a cigarette pack neatly placed in its own little cut-out space.

The mullah decided to open the file first. It contained several white pages with typed paragraphs in English, a language which he could not read. He put it to one side and looked at the letters, each with a name on it. He placed them on the file, his interest now focused entirely on the grey plastic box which he removed from its mould.

He rotated it, searching for a way to open it, and dug a dirty thumbnail under a tab. As he prised it up he fumbled, almost dropping the box as it opened. A grey sliver, part plastic, part metal and the size of a small coin, fell out onto the desk. The mullah put down the box to examine the object that appeared to be a tiny technological device. He picked it up and studied it, with a deep frown on his face.

Sena was unable to resist leaning forward to have a look for himself.

The mullah opened a drawer in his desk, pulled out a magnifying glass and held it over the object to examine it more closely. The device had several gold contact surfaces on one side, similar to those on a SIM card.

The mullah had no idea what it was but the security surrounding it was evidence enough that the device was of significant value. He placed it back inside its box and rested it on the desk.

Durrani looked between the box and the mullah, wondering what his leader planned to do with such a find. The potential value was not lost on him either but how to determine that value precisely was beyond him.

'Leave,' the mullah said to Durrani. 'But do not go far.'

Durrani did not hesitate. The mullah was his boss and if he was to profit in any way from this find it would depend entirely on the mullah's generosity. Durrani headed for the door. Sena sprang to life and beat him to it. They headed back up the stairs, along the corridor where they had to step over the lounging guards again, past the entrance and to a room at the opposite end.

Sena opened the door. 'Make yourself comfortable, please,' he said, stepping back. Durrani entered the small stone room that contained a rug, several cushions and a little cooker with everything required to prepare a cup of sweet tea. 'Would you like some food?' Sena asked.

Durrani considered the offer. He had not eaten since that morning, before the helicopter attack, and although he did not eat very much when he did, priding himself on his ability to operate for days without sustenance, it was also a rule of soldiering to take food when the opportunity presented itself. One never knew when the next meal would come. 'Yes,' he said.

Sena bowed slightly and left the room.

Durrani looked around the cramped space. It was no

larger than the one he was given to use by the mullah in a run-down house on the outskirts of the city on the Jalalabad road. He preferred sleeping outside under the stars, except during the rains and when it was exceptionally cold. But when staying in the city he opted for the better security. This room was more comfortable. It had a stone floor whereas his own dwelling's was earthen and always dusty. There were no windows, though; a naked bulb hung from the centre of the ceiling provided the only light.

Durrani crouched by the cooker to light it and make himself a cup of tea. He wondered why the mullah had asked him to wait but did not trouble himself with the question for long. Durrani took life very much day by day, hour by hour, and was as content sitting back and doing nothing as he was taking part in a battle. It seemed that while he was involved in one he looked forward to the other.

Sena soon returned with a metal plate of rice and chunks of succulent lamb placed on a large thin folded sheet of unleavened bread. After Durrani had eaten it he lay back on the rug, his head resting on a cushion, and within minutes had dozed off.

Durrani did not know how long he had been asleep when he heard the door open and saw Sena looking down at him. The servant immediately apologised for disturbing Durrani but explained that the mullah wanted to see him.

As Durrani followed Sena back down the corridor, stepping over the now sleeping guards and heading towards the staircase, he checked his watch to discover that it had stopped. Durrani shook it but the second hand did not move. He was dismayed and the malfunction was all he could think of as he followed Sena down the stairs. He tapped the timepiece several times and, as they reached the door, to his delight the second hand started to move again. He decided he should sell the watch at the first opportunity.

The door to the office was open and Sena stepped to one side to let Durrani in. The mullah was seated at his desk with another man leaning over it. They were talking in low voices as they inspected the device that was back out of its box and resting on a white china plate between them. The stranger, who looked the intelligent, well-educated type, was dressed in clean traditional Afghan garb made of expensive cloth. He was immaculate, his beard neatly cropped, and Durrani could smell his strong perfume even through the tobacco smoke.

As Durrani entered the room the man looked up at him through a pair of delicate wire-rimmed glasses. He said something to the mullah who glanced at Durrani, then back at him.

'I need you to do it here, in this office,' the mullah insisted.

The man's expression remained one of reluctance but he argued no further.

'Durrani,' the mullah barked as he got to his feet, studying his most trusted fighter as if making a final confirmation of a decision he had come to. 'You have been chosen for a special task. A most important task.'

Durrani looked at the stranger who was staring at him as if measuring him.

'This man is a doctor,' the mullah went on. 'He needs to examine you.'

Durrani could not begin to fathom what this was all about. A special and important task preceded by a medical examination was a bizarre combination, unlike any experience he'd ever had previously. 'I don't understand.'

'You will,' the mullah said confidently.

'Remove your robe,' the doctor said.

Durrani looked at him quizzically. He'd never had a medical examination before in his life and removing his clothing in front of a stranger like this was alien to him.

'We don't have time to waste,' the mullah said testily. 'Do as he says. That is a command.'

Durrani had been obeying orders of one kind or another all his life and during the last fifteen years they had been those of mullahs. To act without question was ingrained in him. He pulled off his robe to reveal a grubby sweat-stained wool shirt.

'And your shirt,' the doctor said.

Durrani unbuttoned his shirt, pulled it off his shoulders and held it in his hand as the doctor studied him from where he stood. Durrani was sinewy, without an ounce of fat on him, his taut muscles and large veins well defined beneath his tight yellowy-brown skin. He was also covered in a collection of interesting scars.

The doctor slowly walked around him, pausing to study the marks of some of the old injuries. He had no doubt that each of them had some kind of horrifying story attached to it. He was not wrong.

A series of deep gouges on Durrani's chest was the result of shrapnel from a missile fired from a Russian helicopter in the Jegay Valley in 1983. A round indentation on his right lat with a corresponding one on his back marked the entry and exit holes of a bullet that had struck him during his first assault on Kabul. A scar across the side of his stomach was from a cut given to him by a Pakistani fighter two days after the Yakaolang massacre when the man accused Durrani of cowardice. Durrani cared little for the man's opinions and was content to ignore him but the man took the lack of reaction as proof of his accusation and drew his knife to kill him. Durrani was not easily riled but a threat of death was sufficient to get his blood up. The Pakistani's thrust to Durrani's side was his last attack. Durrani sidestepped, knocked the man's arm away, closed the gap between them in the next instant, wrapped an arm around his assailant's throat and, while others looked on, crushed his windpipe, letting go only when the man had been dead a good half-minute. His back bore the chequered scars of dozens of lashes that he had once received from a Saudi troop commander who had accused Durrani of stealing loot he was not entitled to. During the next battle a week later Durrani bided his time and in the thick of the fighting he pulled the pin from a grenade and stuffed it down the back of the man's chest harness. No one suspected that the explosion and subsequent disintegration of the Saudi was Durrani's way of taking revenge.

'You have survived much,' the doctor muttered.

'He is my best,' the mullah said with some pride.

'Lie on the desk,' the doctor said. 'On your back.'

The mullah cleared the items off the desk and Durrani sat on the edge of it and lay back.

The doctor moved alongside Durrani, concentrating his examination on the fighter's stomach area. He took hold of the top of Durrani's trousers and pulled them down as far as his pubic hairs, prodding around his lower abdomen. 'It should not be a problem,' the doctor finally acknowledged.

'You must do it now,' the mullah said. 'Tonight.'

The doctor nodded and turned to get his bag from the floor in the corner of the room.

The mullah leaned over Durrani to look into his eyes. 'He is going to perform a small operation on you.'

Durrani stared up at him, unsure how to respond. But whatever was going to happen would happen and, as the mullah had said, Durrani would find out the reason behind it soon enough.

The doctor placed his bag on the desk beside Durrani and removed a bottle of lidocaine, a hypodermic needle, a scalpel, some gauze and a pair of rubber gloves which he pulled on over his hands. Durrani stared at the cracked smoke-stained ceiling and concentrated on detaching his consciousness from whatever was happening to him.

The doctor filled the hypodermic needle with the lidocaine and wiped a small area of Durrani's lower abdomen with an antiseptic swab. 'I'm going to anaes-thetise a small area of skin,' he said reassuringly.

Durrani gave no response and did not flinch when the doctor pushed the needle deep into his flesh and squeezed out the contents of the syringe as he slowly withdrew it. The doctor then took a small plastic bag from his medical kit, placed the tiny device inside it, sealed it by winding thread tightly around the opening and dropped it into a bottle of Betadine antiseptic solution.

There was a sudden flash of flame and Durrani's eyes darted to the mullah who was lighting up a cigarette.

The doctor picked up the scalpel and paused, the blade hovering over Durrani's stomach. 'How do you feel?' he asked. 'Are you OK?'

'You will not bother Durrani with a small cut, doctor,' the mullah said confidently.

The doctor looked at the deep scars on Durrani's torso and shrugged in agreement. 'You should not feel much anyway,' the doctor said. 'Perhaps a small burning as I cut into your muscle.'

Durrani exhaled slowly, wishing the man would stop talking and get on with it.

The doctor placed the scalpel against Durrani's flesh. Durrani felt a sting as the blade cut him and the doctor began a slight sawing motion. He could feel his blood trickling down his side and the doctor swabbing him with a piece of gauze. He raised his head to take a look. The doctor pressed a gloved index finger on the cut and pushed it in until it disappeared inside Durrani's body up to the second joint. Durrani decided it was too bizarre and went back to staring at the ceiling.

The doctor withdrew his finger, wiped the blood off it and produced a pair of tweezers from his kit. He removed the small plastic bag with the device inside it from the betadine and, opening the incision, placed the bag in the hole, pushing it all the way in with his finger. He took a fresh piece of gauze, wiped the wound clean, pushed the sides together and nodded to himself.

As he reached for a suture pack the mullah stopped him. 'No,' the mullah said. 'No stitches. It must look like an untended wound.'

'He must lie still for a while, then,' the doctor said.

'Tape it,' the mullah said.

The doctor suspected that the fighter would not have the luxury of resting at all. But it was none of his business anyway so he took a roll of tape from the bag, tore off several strips and placed them across the cut to hold it closed. He covered the wound with a large dressing which he taped firmly into place, returned his instruments to his bag and closed it. 'It's done.'

The mullah nodded. 'You can go.'

The doctor was about to pick up his bag when he had a second thought. He reopened it and removed a packet of tablets in a strip of foil-covered plastic. 'He should take these. Just in case there's an infection.'

The mullah took the pills and fixed his gaze on the doctor who read the clear message in his eyes. He left the room.

'Sit up,' the mullah said to Durrani when they were alone.

Durrani started to sit up, pausing as he felt a sudden pain where the doctor had cut him. He took his weight on his hands and pushed himself up the rest of the way. He examined the dressing – a bloodstain was forming at the centre – and eased himself to his feet.

'Get dressed,' the mullah said. 'It will stop bleeding soon. You've had far worse than that.'

Durrani pulled on his shirt.

'You are to go to Kandahar and then on to Chaman,' the mullah told him.

'Pakistan?' Durrani asked, buttoning up his shirt. Chaman was a well-known pass out of southern Afghanistan.

'You will be met at Spin Buldak and escorted across the border.'

'And then what?' Durrani asked.

'There is no need to trouble yourself with more information. You will be in good hands. What you carry in your belly is of great importance.'

All Durrani understood was that at the end of his journey someone else would cut him open once again, this time to remove what the doctor had placed inside him. The mullah was going to a lot of trouble to hide the device but he had to concede it was a smart way to ensure that it was not lost. If Durrani had a serious accident or was attacked and robbed, unless his body was completely destroyed the device could still be retrieved. 'I leave right away?'

'Sena will give you all you need. Money and food. You will travel with four of my men.'

'Would it not be better if I travelled alone?' Durrani asked, even though he knew the mullah would not agree.

'I know you like to work alone, Durrani. And it is not that I don't trust your abilities. You are the best of my mujahideen. But this time I need to know where you are every second of every hour. The men who travel with you will not know that you carry anything other than an important message inside your head. Not even those who you will meet in Chaman will know your true purpose. You will be taken to Quetta where you will meet great leaders of our cause who are expecting you. *These* men will know your purpose.' The mullah emphasised the gravity of his words with an intense stare. 'Durrani. I believe that whatever this is inside you is of great importance to us and to our cause.'

'It will be delivered,' Durrani assured him. He was flattered, despite his concealed indifference to the so-called cause.

'Sena,' the mullah called out and the door opened.

Durrani pulled on his robe, a streak of pain flashing through his gut as he raised the garment over his shoulders.

'Allah will watch over you,' the mullah assured him.

Durrani nodded. As he turned to walk away the mullah grabbed his arm and held up the packet of pills. 'Use these if you think there is infection,' he said.

Durrani took the packet and left the room.

The mullah went back to his desk, glanced down at the charred briefcase on the floor, pulled out his packet of Woodbines and lit one.

Chapter 3

Sumners walked into the security-conference 'bubble' on the sixth floor of the Secret Intelligence Service's London headquarters by the Thames and placed a file on a slender chrome podium standing to one side of a wide-screen monitor. Bubble was an obvious nickname for the multi-layered mesh-and-plastic module apparently suspended inside an ordinary room. It had insulated contact points with the floor, walls and ceiling and was protected by layers of various technical screens that prevented all forms of transmission, X-ray and vibration from escaping the module. In short, it was an anti-eavesdropping environment for top-security meetings.

While Sumners attached a memory stick to a USB port on the podium a man in a smart pinstripe suit who looked like a First World War general with his snow-white hair and matching handlebar moustache stepped up into the bubble. He paused in the entrance, planted the tip of his cane on the rubber floor and looked around as if unsure where he was.

'Good morning, Sir Charles,' Sumners said in a jaunty tone without pausing from setting up his presentation.

Sir Charles nodded grumpily. 'Am I early?'

'No, no, you're right on time,' Sumners said, producing the smile he reserved for his superiors.

Sir Charles looked at the four comfortable leather armchairs spread around in no particular pattern. 'Anywhere?'

'Oh, yes, anywhere you like.'

Sir Charles plonked himself into one of the chairs, exhaled heavily, rested his cane against the side of the armrest, put on a pair of spectacles and perused a thin file he had brought with him.

A moment later another man walked in, younger than Sir Charles, lanky, highly intelligent- and sophisticated-looking with his cold eyes and very white skin.

'Good morning, sir,' Sumners said, with distinct gravitas and no smile. This time he paused for the newcomer and there was a hint of a servile nod too.

Sir Charles looked up at the man. 'Van der Seiff,' he said casually before going back to his file.

'Sir Charles,' Van der Seiff replied, a surgical precision in his tone as he selected a chair and sat down in it, straightening the razor crease in his trousers and ignoring Sumners altogether. Van der Seiff's nickname within the lower echelons of the SIS was 'The Spectre' but it referred more to the coldly calculating way he talked and moved than to his actual personality. His pale complexion might also have contributed to the phantom-like impression.

Sumners arranged some papers on the podium and checked his watch as another man entered the bubble. This new arrival looked downright scruffy compared

45

with the others. His suit was clearly off the peg, the knot of his tie was too small and his worn shirt lapels were askew. But if a stranger was to form a lowly opinion of the man based on his clothing he would be making a great miscalculation. His eyes alone threw any negative assessment into confusion. At first glance they appeared weasel-like but on closer inspection they more closely resembled those of a shark.

His name was Jervis and he scrutinised the backs of Sir Charles and Van der Seiff before looking coldly at Sumners. 'This gonna take long?' he asked in a distinct South London accent that was nonetheless far more refined than it had been in his younger days.

Sir Charles and Van der Seiff did not look around at the man although it was clear from their reactions that they knew who he was.

'Hard to say, sir,' Sumners said, trying to sound matter-of-fact but unable to disguise his grudging respect for the man.

Jervis's gaze returned to the backs of the other two men. 'Mornin', gentlemen,' he said as if it were a mild taunt.

'Good morning,' Van der Seiff replied without shifting the direction of his stare, which was fixed ahead at nothing in particular.

Sir Charles gave a grunt without looking up from his file.

Jervis sat down in the armchair furthest from the podium. 'Don't suppose you can smoke in 'ere?' he asked.

Sir Charles frowned.

'I'm afraid not,' Sumners said. 'Apparently it can inter-fere with the bubble's instrumentation,' he added by way of an apology for denying his superior a chance to indulge his habit.

Jervis smiled thinly. He was well aware of the rules but liked to take every opportunity to rub the toffs up the wrong way.

Sumners busied himself checking various cable connections in order to distance himself from the tension-tainted atmosphere. The hostility sometimes displayed by certain department heads towards each other never ceased to perturb him. This was a particu-larly bad lot and he put it down to their extremely diverse pedigrees. Sir Charles was ex-army, Hussars, a retired general, very old school, tough as marching boots and a consultant to the Ministry of Defence and certain lords and monarchs. His brand of diplomacy and numerous highly placed contacts in Europe and America made him very useful in certain areas.

Unlike the other two, Van der Seiff had no military experience. On paper he was the classic brilliant Intelligence recruit: an Oxford graduate, fluent in French, Italian and Spanish with masters degrees in both classics and history. The abilities that placed him a notch above those with similar credentials were an extraordin-ary geopolitical vision, outstanding analytical skills and a cold, ruthlessly logical mind unhindered by emotion. Van der Seiff had been in MI for eight years and was currently with the Directorate of International Special Services. He was tipped to go all the way to the top of the intelligence ladder.

Jervis was more like a common urban fox but with some very *un*common qualities. The events of his earliest years were shrouded in rumours, one of which gave him gypsy origins and another a criminal record. Strangely, all documentation of his life before the age of nineteen no longer existed, the result of either catastrophic bureaucratic failure on several levels or the work of a very senior government official. Jervis had found his way into the Secret Service through the army, signing up to the Intelligence Corps, the first documented proof of his existence. After a year training as an analyst in a camp outside Dover he volunteered for and was accepted on a posting in Northern Ireland. This was during the heyday of the campaign against the IRA, in the late 1960s and during the 1970s, and after showing great promise he was trained and eventually operated as a tout maker, one of the most dangerous jobs in the MI field.

It was during this period of Jervis's life that he began to display some extraordinary gifts. For example, he had a photographic memory and was able, after single and often fleeting observations, to quote countless vehicle registration numbers as well as each vehicle's make and colour. But his greatest skill was an ability to piece together seemingly unrelated or only remotely connected pieces of information. The sum of these talents made him a most useful operative. He was posted to London where his skills developed further and were applied to Cold War diplomatic counter-espionage with impressive results. After his success in piecing together a particularly complicated surveillance operation involving

Russian mini-submarines and Eastern European diplomatic staff in Scandinavia he came under the gaze of the head of MI6.

Despite Jervis's rough edges he began to make his way up through the ranks. He was unlikely to see promotion above his current post but as head of 'special operations worldwide' Jervis had reached far higher than he could ever have originally expected. He had earned his position despite his reputation for mischievousness which some of his peers interpreted as disrespect. His high proportion of successes, however, ensured a long career ahead of him despite the misgivings of his many detractors.

The last man to step into the bubble was Gerald Nevins, department head of the South-Eastern European Section and Sumners's immediate boss. After a quick look around to see if everyone was present he closed the triple-skinned door and turned a locking lever until a green light appeared at one side, indicating the room was sealed.

Nevins ignored the remaining armchair and, looking quite solemn, chose to stand at the back of the room. Folding his arms across his chest he gave Sumners a nod.

'Gentlemen,' Sumners began and then took a moment to clear his throat, sipping from a plastic water-bottle he had brought with him. 'Pardon me.'

Sumners was an experienced briefer but had never before addressed a group made up exclusively of such senior personnel. When he'd been walking up the stairs from his office on the floor below he hadn't been able to help thinking how this was not just a briefing but a personal assessment. These sorts of things always were. They placed a person under the microscope, something which could be both a good and a bad thing. Giving a briefing not only put on display a person's eloquence and ability to address their superiors comfortably. It also exposed organisational, analytical and presentation skills as well as conciseness of expression and general bearing. If a person made a hash of it, especially in front of such an eminent audience, it could have detrimental effects the next time their name came up for review. People always remembered bad briefings.

Success at this stage of Sumners's career was more important than ever to him. He did not possess what would be considered by his peers as the best of pedigrees and it was growing late in the game for him to make a significant step up the ladder. He was the son of a British Army colonel who was not from the right regiment and Sumners himself had not gone to the right university. Jervis might well be proof that pedigree was not everything but Sumners did not possess any of that man's extraordinary skills either. However, because of current world instability, specifically the threat from international terrorism, further promotion was not out of the question by any means. Years ago it had been not only a case of pedigree and contacts but also of dead man's shoes. But since 9/11 the service had expanded rapidly in all directions, with government funding increasing every year. There were many more senior positions opening up all around the globe and Sumners was in a good position to grab one of them.

He could only hope that his fate would not depend on the contents of this briefing, a fear that grew as he compiled the latest intelligence on the day's subject. If it did then his career opportunities would probably terminate immediately on completion of the presentation. In his opinion it was a God-awful mess and heads were undoubtedly going to roll because of it. On a positive note, though, that could only open up new positions which he might be able to take advantage of.

'Sorry for the initial alert two days ago and then the long wait followed by the short notice this morning,' Sumners said. 'Intelligence is still coming in but time is a factor and we have enough – er – info to get the ball rolling.' Sumners glanced at Nevins who was giving him one of his 'get on with it' looks.

'Right. If I can quickly bring us all up to speed regarding the various pertinent regional situation reports.' Summers cleared his throat again as he hit a series of computer keys on the podium. The wide-screen monitor came to life, showing a satellite image of Afghanistan. It continued zooming in on Kabul before moving to the open countryside north of the city, finally focusing on a scorched patch of ground with the charred wreckage of a helicopter at its centre.

'We have positively confirmed that the package was recovered from the wreckage by Taliban fighters immediately after it was shot down. All hard-copy files in the mission briefcase have now been declassified. All operations referred to in the documentation have been cancelled. I can also confirm that the memory tablet carried by the intelligence officer contained all one thousand, four hundred and forty-three British- and US-run indigenous agents and informants operating in Afghanistan and the Middle East – including Iraq of course.'

'Does the list include top tier?' Sir Charles asked.

'Yes, sir.'

'Maple, Geronimo, Mulberry?'

'All of them, I'm afraid.'

'Good God,' Sir Charles muttered as his jowls collapsed to put a seriously unhappy expression on his face.

'What level of personal details exactly . . . for the individual agents?' Van der Seiff asked.

'In most cases, pretty much everything: telephone numbers, addresses, emails, secondary contacts. Many of the attached notes include meeting points, dead-letter boxes and personal contact codes. Suffice it to say that if the tablet was decrypted it would provide enough information to identify every one of them.'

'How many can safely be expatriated?' Van der Seiff asked.

'I . . . I don't have those figures, sir,' Sumners said, glancing at Nevins for help and finding none forthcoming.

'I take it expatriations are in process, though,' Sir Charles said.

'No, sir,' Sumners replied.

'What?' Sir Charles asked, half turning to look enquiringly at Nevins without actually making eye contact.

When Sumners looked at Nevins his boss was already contemplating a response. 'Not at present,' Nevins said.

Sir Charles made the effort to sit forward so that he could turn his stiff old neck around enough to look at him. 'I take it you have an explanation.'

'That's one of the reasons we're all here – to decide if such measures will be necessary.'

'But we're talking about a lot of lives here,' Sir Charles thundered. 'Not to mention the exposure of other information if these people are captured and interrogated. It should have been the first thing to be put into motion.'

'First of all, it would be impossible to bring most of them in anyway. Some of them are on official wanted lists. Others would not be able to run without rousing suspicion. Many have families that cannot immediately be moved. Some are so deep we are unable to make direct contact with them – we wait for many of our agents to contact us when they can. Closing them all down would put us back decades. The repercussions of such a strategy are incalculable. We are, of course, preparing measures for such a course of action but we must first examine every other alternative. I have some suggestions. Perhaps you'll have some of your own,' Nevins added. 'Go on, Sumners.'

Sir Charles did not look confident.

'Excuse me,' interrupted Van der Seiff. 'At the risk of ruining the dramatics of this presentation, do we know the current whereabouts of the tablet?'

'Yes, sir,' Sumners said, miffed on the one hand at the sarcasm but relieved on the other that he could answer the question.

Sir Charles cocked an interrogative eyebrow while

Jervis toyed with a packet of cigarettes as if he was only vaguely interested.

Sumners touched several keys on the computer's pad. 'The security case taken from the wreckage was broken open in the Kalaz Alif Mosque in Kabul where it was delivered the same day it was retrieved from the helicopter wreckage.'

The screen image dissolved to a satellite shot of Kabul before zooming in on a mosque surrounded by narrow streets in a densely built-up area.

'The senior mullah of the Kalaz Alif Mosque,' Sumners went on, 'is one Aghafa Ghazan who we believe to be the most senior Taliban resistance leader in Kabul.'

A grainy image of Mullah Ghazan took up a portion of the screen.

'The fact that Mullah Ghazan received the briefcase before anyone else would lend support to our assessment of his seniority. We have an informer in Mullah Ghazan's staff who witnessed the briefcase being opened. He accurately described the contents. The same informant also witnessed the tablet being removed from its case and inspected by Mullah Ghazan. In the early hours of the following day – the security case was brought into the mosque in the evening – a doctor implanted the tablet into a Taliban fighter by the name of Durrani.'

'You did say implanted?' Sir Charles asked.

'Surgically, yes, sir. In his abdomen. We don't have a photograph of Durrani on file although the Americans have a current image that we have requested through Camp Souter's int cell in Kabul. Durrani was then sent by Mullah Ghazan into Pakistan where we understand he was to hand over the tablet to senior Taliban or al-Qaeda personnel. We suspect the tablet was destined for members of ISI, the Pakistan Intelligence services, where it would have eventually been deciphered. However, fortune, in respect of that dilemma at least, was on our side. Before Durrani could make contact, he and his escort were captured by an American Special Forces patrol while attempting to cross the border. There was a brief firefight. Two of Durrani's escorts were killed and Durrani was taken into custody with minor injuries.'

'Do we know if Durrani was a specific US target?' Van der Seiff asked.

'We understand it was a routine border patrol with no specific orders other than to challenge those intent on crossing the border to avoid the frontier checkpoints.'

'I'm sorry for jumping ahead – it's the suspense thing again,' Van der Seiff said, his sarcasm tangible. 'Do the Americans know anything about the tablet?'

'We think not, sir.'

'Why do we think not?' Van der Seiff asked.

'We would've picked up indicators by now,' Nevins intervened, walking to where he could be seen without the others having to turn in their seats. 'Which brings us to the first issue. The minister would like to avoid the Americans finding out about the missing tablet if at all possible.'

'Obviously,' Jervis mumbled.

'You mean, this Taliban chap . . .' Sir Charles stumbled to remember the name.

'Durrani,' Sumners said.

'This Durrani chap is a prisoner of the United States military?' Sir Charles asked.

'That's correct, sir,' Sumners confirmed.

'That's a very dangerous game,' Sir Charles warned, frowning disapprovingly.

Nevins glanced at Jervis and Van der Seiff for any reaction but neither man was giving anything away.

'The minister does not have the right to risk that information falling into the wrong hands,' Sir Charles continued, haughtily. 'I mean, you say the Americans now have it, but if they don't know they have it who's to say they actually do, or that it can't be lost again, for that matter? If no one is controlling it then it could still end up in the wrong hands. The Americans would never forgive us. And I wouldn't blame them for a moment, either. Oh, no.'

'That's all understood, Sir Charles,' Nevins said, suppressing a sigh. 'We believe the tablet is still inside Durrani and, well, he's going nowhere for the time being.'

'Not the point, old man,' Sir Charles said. 'Doesn't the minister realise this could cost him his job, if it hasn't already?'

'Frankly, Sir Charles, the minister's job security is not our concern. What I *am* concerned about is the security summit meeting next week in Washington. A revelation like this will put the minister in a weak position with the Americans at a time when we can ill afford to be . . . In the simplest of terms, we need to get the tablet back or destroy it before the Americans find out about it. The reason we are all sitting here today discussing our options is because we have some. There is a window of opportunity to retrieve or destroy the tablet before we are forced to come clean with the Americans. It's an opportunity we are here to thoroughly explore. At this moment in time, no decisions have been made.'

'Playing with bloody fire even thinking about it, if you ask me,' Sir Charles mumbled.

Nevins wanted to tell Sir Charles that no one was interested in his opinions about the conduct of operations, only in his contributions towards their success. But he also knew that despite Sir Charles's doomsday reaction the old boy would give his all at the crease if his turn to bat came.

'Do we 'ave a plausible reason to ask the Yanks for an interview with Durrani?' Jervis asked, putting an unlit cigarette in his mouth just for the comfort of it.

'None that won't cause some bright spark to become suspicious enough to dig around,' Nevins said. 'The minister hasn't been particularly supportive of the American propensity for shipping prisoners, terrorist suspects or otherwise, out of countries without the express permission of those countries' sovereign governments and detaining them indefinitely for interrogation purposes. The hypocrisy of us suddenly asking to join in would raise eyebrows at every level.'

'Assuming that your bright spark is already digging around, even routinely, what could he find out about Durrani's operation?' Van der Seiff asked.

'Durrani could be linked to the shooting-down of the helicopter and also to his master, Mullah Ghazan,'

Nevins said. 'Let's assume the Americans know there was something of importance found in the helicopter wreckage. They know it was carrying a senior British intelligence officer. Let's even assume they know that what was found was brought to Mullah Ghazan in Kabul. Outside of this room and our intelligence staff in the Kabul embassy only four other men know the contents of the case: Mullah Ghazan, the doctor Emir Kyran, Sena – Mullah Ghazan's servant – and, of course, Durrani himself. Naturally, none of them know the significance of the tablet.'

'I take it that the servant, Sena, is the informer,' Van der Seiff said confidently.

'That's correct. But he works strictly for us. Doesn't like the Americans and would offer nothing to them. If they brought him in for questioning Sena's handler would be able to inform us.'

'Then the danger lies in the Americans questioning Ghazan and the doctor,' Van der Seiff said.

'Up to this moment they have not. We are monitoring the possibility. I believe, at this present time, the Americans do not know that Durrani is carrying anything inside his body. The tablet is non-magnetic and has such minuscule metallic properties that it cannot be detected by a regular scanner.'

'What about if they X-ray him?' Jervis asked.

'It would show up on an X-ray,' Nevins admitted. 'But we know it is not part of their standard procedure to X-ray detainees.'

'This is ridiculous,' Sir Charles scoffed. 'They probably have the damned thing already and aren't telling us.'

'That's why you're here, Sir Charles,' Nevins said, glancing at him with a chill in his eyes which he quickly warmed with a thin smile. 'If there's anyone who can sniff such a change in the wind, you can.'

'And if they have it?' Sir Charles asked, brushing off the ego stroking.

'We've covered that already,' Jervis said, barely hiding his irritation with the old soldier. 'The minister will be buggered.'

'He won't be the only one, either,' Nevins muttered.

Jervis smiled at the squirming that would take place throughout the organisation when this thing broke open.

'What if our American cousins ask us to contribute to Durrani's file?' Van der Seiff asked, staring into space as he often did when having such conversations.

'I don't see the point in addressing that until they do,' Nevins replied.

Those who did not know Van der Seiff might have expected him to take Nevins's response as lacking in courtesy. He did not. 'Are we prepared to add further lies to the original deceit? That is my question.'

'I know,' Nevins replied. 'I was asking for time to consider that one.'

It was unclear if Van der Seiff accepted the answer but the lowering of his gaze suggested he was not entirely pleased with it.

Jervis's apparent lack of serious interest in the topic was due to the fact that his area of expertise was operational planning and not diplomacy. He knew he would eventually have a significant part to play in this meeting otherwise he would not have been invited so he was anxious to be done with all this banter and move on. He gave his assessment: 'So the continued secrecy of this tablet depends on Durrani and those other characters not telling the Americans that he's carrying something inside his belly.'

'In a nutshell,' Nevins responded, eager to move on himself.

'Bloody marvellous,' Sir Charles grumbled. 'Now we're relying on Taliban terrorists to keep our secrets for us.'

Nevins wanted to tell Sir Charles to stop being so melodramatic but he continued to disguise his irritation.

'I take it everything's in place to knock off the doctor and the mullah,' Jervis said matter-of-factly.

'Of course,' Nevins said with equal callousness. 'If it's any consolation, what little information we have on Durrani is that he is regarded as somewhat special among the Taliban, hence him being entrusted with such an important mission. He doesn't seem the sort to give it up easily . . . And the Americans would have to know what they were looking for before they began searching for it.'

Sir Charles made a disagreeable harrumphing sound.

'Gentlemen,' Nevins declared, as if the word might clear the air. 'I would like to move on to the next phase of this meeting. I want us to examine the feasibility of getting close enough to Durrani to neutralise the tablet. Are we all in agreement?'

'Do we know where he is?' Jervis asked, displaying

his characteristic impatience in the face of protocol, a habit at the root of his unpopularity among his peers.

'I'd like us all to move forward together,' Nevins said. There were some basic ground rules in this game that every man in the room knew well enough and Jervis was obviously trying it on. These meetings were recorded and anyone agreeing to proceed to the next decisive phase was also technically agreeing to favourably conclude the preceding one. In this case it meant approving the minister's request for time to consider an alternative means of retrieving the tablet and to delay informing the Americans. The important subtlety, and also the danger, was that the group would have ostensibly formally agreed to deceive their country's closest allies. If the group decided against moving forward to the next phase the request would not be given operational approval and it would be returned to the minister who would have little choice but to follow a course that would ultimately result in revealing the true situation to the Americans.

But there were some obvious as well as hidden dangers in that course of action. The arc of the swinging crushing-ball is predictable but the collateral damage caused by falling debris is not always easy to foresee. Heads would roll as a result of the action. On the face of it, as it had been laid out by Sumners and Nevins, the safest and most prudent course, for the group at least, was to decide against attempting to 'neutralise' the tablet. However, the reputation of the service was also at stake and that was no small matter. The British enjoyed the most enviable position when it came to international espionage on practically every level. For the group to accept the risk and move forward would take them into territory where the dangers were unknown. Still, one could not get a little pregnant in this business.

'I have another meeting I must attend,' Sir Charles said, getting to his feet. 'I'll see you later, Gerald. Van der Seiff . . . Jervis.'

Nevins and Jervis watched Sir Charles leave the room while Van der Seiff stared ahead as if he was unaware it was happening. One decision against might not be enough to close the case – depending on who made it, of course. But two would seal it. Now the only person Nevins could afford to lose had gone and he waited for one of the others to climb out of their chair and end the meeting.

Sumners resealed the bubble entrance and returned to the podium, unsure if he was to press on or not.

As the seconds ticked away neither of the two department heads spoke and Nevins grew confident that they would remain seated. He took a moment to consider his next move. He was not overly concerned about Sir Charles backing out. The old boy was the sort who could be revisited if advice was needed, even with a task that he had declined to approve. Few people knew that about Sir Charles but Nevins had known him for many years, having served under him in MI6 in his earlier days. Van der Seiff and Jervis were the more important, for the time being at least. The operation to get a team close enough to Durrani was going to need Jervis's particular genius. And Van der Seiff would be essential when it came to political plotting, defending against repercussions and manipulating the players in the international arena.

The Americans were going to have to be played very carefully. They were old allies but had a severe sting in their tail if crossed. Britain's enemies within the US corridors of power would call it mistrust while its friends might understand it was all about saving face. Nevertheless, the hammer would fall, and hard. The danger of the tablet ending up in the wrong hands was a serious one and British Military Intelligence as well as the minister would suffer immensely as a result of their decision if it went wrong. Then there was the risk to the identities of the secret contacts on the tablet if they ended up becoming public knowledge. Pragmatic individuals within The Service would argue that its reputation was more important than the lives of a few wogs.

Fortunately for Nevins that was beyond his area of consideration. He'd been given the job of assessing the immediate options. He was not officially committed to going forward either, even if the others decided to proceed. That was the luxury of his position as the meeting director – for the time being, anyway. His final decision would depend on the ideas and suggestions of the two men in front of him. Van der Seiff and Jervis were the ideal pair to devise an operation of the complexity and subtlety required and were clearly curious to hear more. The prospect of an interesting challenge was probably the only reason keeping them in the room. If they could convince Nevins that it was possible to get to Durrani then he would go along with it. But despite his positive leanings, that would not be easy.

'Let's move on then, Sumners,' Nevins said. 'And since your flair for suspense is not appreciated why don't you cut straight to where Durrani is being held?'

'Yes, sir,' Sumners said, pursing his mouth in irritation at being the butt of Van der Seiff's sarcasm and striking a selection of keys.

A schematic diagram appeared on the screen. It looked like a hill containing dozens of engineered tunnels and compartments in various layers with a large portion of the excavation beneath ground level. As the schematic turned on its axis, showing plan as well as side elevations, more detailed illustrations were speedily created. A slender cord grew skyward out of the top of the hill, curving like a snake. When it reached a considerable height a large barge-like construction with several compartments began to take shape. Antennae protruded from it and it moved gently as if on water. A pair of cable cars left a floating platform and moved at a steep angle down to the hill on a system of heavy-duty wires. Machinery appeared in the lower hollows of the hill with conduits and hawsers fanning throughout the complex, some following the tunnels while others created their own ducts leading to dozens of small rooms in neat rows on several levels.

'Styx,' Jervis mumbled.

'That's right, sir,' Sumners said. 'The undersea prison. Destination of America's highest-category prisoners. And since the announced closure of Guantánamo it has also become a terrorist-detention centre.'

Van der Seiff glanced at Jervis who was grinning slightly. Jervis raised his eyebrows at him in a manner that suggested he thought the situation was becoming much more interesting.

'It's immediately obvious why the minister hopes that time may be on our side,' Nevins said.

'Durrani won't be going anywhere for a long time,' Jervis surmised.

Nevins looked at him as if he might not entirely agree with the comment, a sentiment that Van der Seiff appeared to share. Jervis caught the subtle flicker in both their expressions and narrowed his eyes. 'Why would that not be true?'

'There's a rumble in the jungle,' Nevins replied. 'Styx may be in trouble. Something's going on down below but we're not entirely sure what. It may be a combination of things. We initially assumed the problem was to do with rumours about the CIA using unconventional interrogation techniques. But it could be worse than that. Public interest in Styx has grown with the transfer of prisoners from Guantánamo Bay to the underwater facility. Human-rights groups, the media and political opposition groups are unhappy that they can't even get close enough to look through the bars.'

'Excuse me, sir,' Sumners interrupted politely. He had started off the briefing feeling a little nervous but Nevins's increasing encroachments on what he regarded as his patch were now beginning to irritate him. 'I can expand on that subject.'

'Go ahead. Go ahead,' Nevins said.

'Our analysts have prioritised their trawling for

anything related to Styx and they've come up with some interesting threads. On the subject of interrogation, it would seem that the CIA receives a level of cooperation from the facility's civilian management. The deduction is that the interrogations, under the guidance of the Central Intelligence Agency, may involve pressure and therefore require the assistance of the prison's life-support and engineering staff. This ties in with other evidence that suggests there is a deeper and somewhat nefarious relationship between the Agency and the Felix Corporation that owns and runs the corrections facility.'

As Sumners talked he skilfully produced on-screen visual material in support of each topic. The resulting pictures had even Nevins's full attention.

'The Felix Corp is part-owned by the Camphor Group, an R&D subsidiary of Aragorn Oil. We've also picked up a thread of FBI interest in several executives of the Felix Corp. The Bureau has been conducting covert investigations of offshore accounts connected with the company. The circle begins to close with the evidence that there are connections between certain Felix Corp shareholders and Congress. To examine the relationship between these Felix Corp executives and the CIA I'd like to go back a few years. I'll be brief but I think it's useful to understand the genesis of Styx itself.

'The underwater facility was originally a NASA- and US government-funded research programme experimenting in the subsurface engineering of habitat, mining and agricultural environments. The Camphor Group was one of several smaller investors. NASA's main interest was the relationship between deep-sea and deep-space habitability. The Camphor Group provided funds and technology for the mining module. Early surveys revealed evidence of precious minerals. It was hoped a mine might provide a contribution to the overall costs of the research facility. Construction began in 1983 and the first habitats were occupied on a full-time basis four years later. I should add here that the project was given the security classification of "highly confidential" with security provided by the federal government. This kept media interest to a minimum. By 1993 some sixty personnel were living in the facility which was by then fifty per cent self-sufficient in breathable air, potable water and sewage recycling and was providing twenty per cent of its own energy from wind turbines and solar panels. Two babies were born in the facility,' Sumners added, clearing his throat and instantly wishing that he'd left out that particular snippet.

'Five years ago, in what was apparently a surprise move, NASA and the administration pulled their funding. The government agreed to provide the money to maintain the facility for a period of three years in the hope that an investor might be interested in the site. The pumps were kept operating and vital machinery was serviced. Before those three years were up the decision was made to pull the plug – no pun intended. It was then that the newly formed Felix Corporation stepped in with a surprise proposal. This was aimed at the US Department of Corrections and the intention was to provide the ultimate top-security prison. The idea was greeted with a mixed response. The Agency played no small part in seeing that the proposal received some heavyweight support, enough to see it pass in principle through the House of Representatives. It was awarded a probationary development licence. Technically Styx is still in that category but the first prisoners were interned within its underwater walls two years ago. It's unclear what number of inmates Styx was originally licensed for but it would seem the figure has in any case been exceeded since the invasion of Afghanistan and Iraq. One of the Felix Corp's proposals was to reopen the mine. The running cost of the prison is obviously much lower now than it was at the time of NASA's experiment and the small yield of precious minerals apparently provides five per cent of those costs as well as giving employment to selected inmates. It's the mine that appears to be the focus of the FBI's interest. After this briefing I'll provide you with a more detailed report of the corporate structure behind Styx and the relationship between Felix Corp and the Camphor Group with details of the FBI's investigation to date.'

'Interesting,' Van der Seiff said as he folded his arms across his chest and looked down at his feet extended in front of him. 'I was talking with one of our people in DC the other day. Styx has been popping up as a subject of concern in the White House for some months now. The Oval Office appears to be running its own independent inquiry. They must be concerned about the obvious political implications of an undersea Alcatraz as well as the questionable interrogation techniques taking place down there.'

'It's basically a Guantánamo Bay where outsiders can't get at it,' Jervis said. 'They'll weather the criticism. They'll keep that going for years – decades if they want to.'

'If the White House is conducting its own investigation,' Van der Seiff said, continuing his train of thought, 'it's because they don't want any other government agencies involved. That should provide us with some clues. I have noted for some time now how the White House has shown itself willing to act independently of its intelligence and judicial communities in a variety of arenas. It's no secret that the Oval Office has its own special-operations wing in the guise of "select Secret Service agents". It's also interesting that certain White House staff include people whose curricula vitae are more suited to black ops than to the administrative duties indicated on their payslips. I believe that if the White House decides to close down the prison they're willing and able to go against their various national security agencies.'

'The implications for us right now are how it affects Durrani's future,' Nevins said. 'We have to be prepared for the possibility that prisoners could be moved out of the facility any time soon. We may not get a warning.'

'What about the risk of Durrani removing the tablet himself?' Jervis asked.

'I think that's unlikely,' Nevins said. 'He's a tenacious, pragmatic individual, moderately intelligent and with a stubborn single-mindedness forged by more than twenty years of guerrilla warfare. His mission was to hand the tablet over to those he was ordered to and he'll do his best to achieve that goal no matter how long it takes. Unless someone with authority whom he knows and trusts can get to him and convince him to cut it out and hand it over he's going to hang onto it. It's his simplest and most obvious option. While he remains in Styx the chances of that happening are remote. That won't be the case if he returns to a more open prison on the surface . . . Now, do we have the time to get to him?' Nevins asked. 'Probably more to the point, is it possible?'

Jervis did not need to look at Nevins to know that the man was talking to him. He replied: 'Someone has to get into the prison before Durrani gets out . . . Breaking it down, we have two options: official entry and un-official entry. "Official" means going in as an authorised entity. That means officially requesting to interview Durrani for some reason. Which will without doubt invite curiosity and surveillance by the Agency . . . *Un*official entry of course means getting someone inside the prison without the Agency being aware of that person's true purpose. That would be bloody difficult.'

'But possible?' Nevins asked.

'Nothing's *im*possible. It's all a matter of risk.'

'Risk to the person who goes in?'

'No,' Jervis replied, sounding as if he thought Nevins was retarded. 'Risk of compromise. Risk of failure. We won't know the percentages until we come up with a plan. I don't doubt we can get someone in. But the risk has to be worth it.'

'And what about getting out?' Nevins asked. 'The Americans say that's impossible. I'm inclined to accept that.'

Sumners wished he could suddenly be struck by a

moment of brilliance and present an idea. But his initiative box was utterly empty.

'That might not be necessary,' Jervis said, thinking out loud. He looked at the others. 'The tablet only needs to be destroyed. That reduces the scale of the operation by half as far as I can see.'

Nevins nodded, feeling encouraged so far.

'I don't think this can be done without the help of the Americans,' Van der Seiff said.

Nevins looked at him quizzically. 'But isn't the whole point of this to do it *without* their knowledge?'

'I didn't say do it with their *knowledge*. I said with their *help*.'

Jervis smiled as if he had an inkling of where Van der Seiff was heading.

Nevins was none the wiser. But neither did he feel inferior because of it. The two men in front of him were among the finest in the world at this sort of thing but Nevins had his own specialities. 'You'll have to explain,' he said.

'They could help us get into Styx without knowing why we want to get in,' Van der Seiff said. 'We would provide them with a reason that satisfied their curiosities. Frankly, I can't see how we can do it without them . . . Jervis?'

'The loose ends,' Jervis said. 'It's the loose ends that would bugger us. I see where you're going. Yes. That would be quite sexy.'

'Sexy?' Nevins asked, feeling even more in the dark.

'There's a sniff there, and a cheeky one at that,' Jervis said.

Nevins shook his head, suggesting it was still unclear to him.

'You can smell a solution without knowing it,' Jervis offered.

'When can you give me something more tangible?' Nevins asked. A sniff was not quite sufficient reason for him to propose to the minister that they should go forward.

'Cheeky, yes,' Van der Seiff agreed, the slightest suspicion of a smile on his thin lips.

Nevins frowned. 'Sumners?'

Sumners looked wide-eyed at his boss and shook his head. 'I have no idea what they're talking about, sir.'

'I didn't expect you to. Is there anything else?'

'Nothing significant. The file is available for their eyes on the internal.'

'I need to make a few calls,' Van der Seiff said. 'Can we get together later in the day?' he asked Jervis.

'Sure,' Jervis said.

Nevins took a moment to consider the situation. 'OK. End of the day. Then let's see where we are.'

Van der Seiff got to his feet and smoothed out his suit. 'I take it you're going to clean up Kabul,' he asked Nevins sombrely.

'Of course,' Nevins said. 'That'll go in tonight even if we don't go ahead with the Styx op.'

Van der Seiff nodded and left the room. Jervis followed and Nevins indicated for Sumners to close the door again.

'What do you think, sir?' Sumners said.

'That'll depend on what they come up with.'

'And Kabul, sir? You haven't finalised your options.'

'I want pinpoint accuracy. No bombs. People have a terrible habit of surviving bombs. It has to look like a local hit. Local weapons. That's more to convince the Americans than anyone else.'

'And is that all of them, sir?' Sumners asked, innocently.

Nevins took a moment to consider the question. 'Mullah Ghazan and Doctor . . .'

'Emir Kyran, sir.'

'Yes. Not Sena.'

'I'll pass that on right away, sir,' Sumners said, heading for the door and out of the room.

Nevins put his hands on his hips as he walked over to the wide-screen monitor. He flicked a button on the keyboard. A dozen image windows appeared on the screen like a contact sheet. He touched one of them to expand it. The undersea prison filled the screen and he stared at the complicated diagram. It looked like an impossible task to him. But if Jervis and Van der Seiff said they had a sniff, well, that was good enough for him to wait until they got back to him.

He clicked off the screen and headed out of the room.

Chapter 4

Sir Bartholomew Bridstow sat alone in the back of the British Embassy's black armoured Lincoln Town Car perusing a newspaper through a pair of silver-rimmed reading glasses. His sharp old eyes looked above the small lenses as the vehicle stopped at the first security checkpoint on 17th and East Street in north-west Washington DC. The driver powered down the inch-and-a-half-thick window enough to hang out his pass while another security guard looked in the back. Sir Bartholomew smiled politely at him while holding up his own ID. The vehicle was invited to continue. It passed through two more gated checkpoints manned by members of the uniform division of the Secret Service, the last of whom directed the driver into West Executive Drive.

The Lincoln pulled to a stop outside the West Wing of the White House. As Sir Bartholomew climbed out he was met by a member of the Presidential office staff. The aide escorted him through the entrance where they turned immediately left and up a narrow set of stairs to the Vice-President's office.

Sir Bartholomew was escorted straight in.

Vice-President Ogden eased his heavy frame out of his seat and stepped from behind his desk, wearing a broad smile. 'Good to see you, Barty,' he said, extending his hand.

'You too, Frank.' Sir Bartholomew shook the VP's hand that was almost twice the size of his own.

'How's Gillian?' Ogden asked.

'At this very moment she's being dragged around Georgetown Park Mall by Senator Jay's wife.'

'Kicking and screaming, I'll bet.'

'No fear of that, I'm afraid,' Sir Bartholomew said, with a chuckle. 'Gillian could shop for Britain, I promise you.'

'Tea?'

'No, thank you. I'm not going to keep you long. It's very good of you to see me at such short notice.'

'Have a seat. I have a meeting in ten minutes. Is that enough time for you?'

'Ample. Ample.'

Both men sat down in comfortable antique armchairs, with a dainty coffee table between them. The aide arrived carrying a tray, a jug of ice water and two glasses balanced on it. He placed it on the coffee table and headed back towards the door.

'Hold all my calls,' Ogden called out.

'Yes, sir,' the aide replied before closing the door behind him.

'So. What's on your mind?' Ogden asked, sitting back and shifting his bulk to get comfortable.

'The subject is Styx.'

Ogden nodded. 'OK.'

'You have three British subjects incarcerated in it.'

'Now, Barty. You know that's not a subject that right now you and I—'

'No, no, no,' Sir Bartholomew interrupted, smiling and gesturing dismissively. 'Allow me to start again,' he said, adopting a more appropriate expression. His smile disappeared. 'There are problems involving the prison.'

'Show me a prison that doesn't have problems.'

'Styx is not your usual prison and neither are its current problems. I've heard them described by some as merely problematic for your administration, downright serious by others.'

'Barty, we've known each other many years. We have what I think is more than just a solid working relationship. You can be direct with me. But even as an old friend I'm not about to fill in any of the blanks for you.'

'I wouldn't play that game with you, Frank. To be honest, when I read the request from London I was unsure quite how to approach it. Still am, in fact.'

'I'm all ears,' Ogden said, making a point of checking his watch.

'OK. Well, I'll tell you how we see it and you can ignore me entirely if we're way off the mark and I won't be offended . . . The problems associated with Styx are heating up and when they boil over they're going to cause a substantial mess. Your administration succeeded in taking a lot of the heat out of the volatile issue of political prisoners and foreign terrorists imprisoned without charge with the proposed closing down of Guantánamo. Even if you're now in the process of hiding them all under the waters of the Gulf of Mexico instead. But that's all about to erupt like a volcano. I'm talking, of course, about the corruption within the Felix Corp prison management – the funnelling of money to private bank accounts, undeclared revenue from a mine which utilises inmates as slave labour, that sort of thing. Even more damaging are the Agency's questionable interrogation techniques – with the cooperation of the civilian prison staff, no less. It indicates a most unhealthy, possibly criminal relationship between the CIA and the Felix Corp while at the same time implicating certain members of Congress. One can only imagine what a congressional examination of that relationship would reveal. The leaks have already started . . . Now, of course I'm not here to tell you what you already know . . .'

'You're here to help?'

'What else are friends for?' Sir Bartholomew said, his smile back on his face.

Ogden's suspicions increased.

'Shall I continue?' Sir Bartholomew asked, unsure if he might have gone too far too soon. Personally, he would have preferred more time to prepare the field before setting out his troops. But London had insisted that he should make his way to the proposal as soon as possible. That meant by the end of this meeting.

'I've got a few more minutes.'

'You'd like to shut down Styx but you might run into some obstacles. If you try and point accusatory fingers the resultant inevitable mud-slinging could leave you as dirty as anyone else.'

Ogden stared at Sir Bartholomew, remaining poker-faced, waiting for him to get to his point.

'What if we could provide you with a good enough reason to shut the place down?' Sir Bartholomew asked.

The VP's expression did not change. As he saw it, he had two options at that stage. The first was to end the meeting politely there and then. The other was to acknowledge the existence of the problems and hear out the offer. The Brits didn't usually go to these lengths without being sure of their position and the ambassador did appear confident that he had something of value to offer. It would be timely to present the President with a solution, if the Brits indeed had one. Then there was, of course, the reason why the Brits were doing it – the pay-off. All things considered, though, Ogden didn't see a reason not to continue. Barty had not been far off the mark and the administration was prepared to pay a good price to see the back of this particular problem. 'I'm listening,' he said.

Sir Bartholomew smiled to himself. He was over the first hurdle. It would seem that the transcript he had received from London that morning was accurate. 'Time is a factor, of course,' Sir Bartholomew added.

'I'm interested to hear what you could do that we couldn't,' Ogden said.

'If we were to be of reasonable help in this matter, could we expect our three British subjects to be released into our custody?' The ambassador had to ask for a payment of some kind. Any demand could not be too greedy to risk scaring the VP off. But it had to be weighty enough to divert any suspicions.

Ogden knew Sir Bartholomew to be a shrewd old fox: after all, the Brit had been in the business twice as many years as himself. And the old boy was right about one thing. Time was indeed running out. 'Let's hear what you have to say first.'

'The PM would also like to make the opening address at the summit meeting next week.'

Ogden sat back with a smile. 'This had better be good,' he said. Ogden knew the President could not care less who opened the summit. Who spoke first was more important to the Brits than it was to the Americans and was probably just part of a strategy aimed at one of the other summit members. The three Brit prisoners were not such an easy issue. But, even so, Barty's price was paltry compared to the administration's gains if there was any substance to this offer. Ogden remained suspicious, though.

Sir Bartholomew was about to speak when a gentle knock on the door stopped him. The door opened just enough for the aide to stick his head through. 'Your meeting, sir.'

Ogden nodded to the aide who closed the door. His look conveyed to Sir Bartholomew that time was tight but he had the chair.

'We propose an escape,' Sir Bartholomew said.

'What?'

'An escape. Prove the prison is flawed and the President can immediately order a temporary closure to review security – which will, of course, become a permanent closure. Rather like Alcatraz.'

Ogden frowned. 'First of all that place is escape-proof.

I've been through all the scenarios and, trust me, it doesn't get any tighter than Styx. Therefore you would need help from the inside. We won't get any cooperation from the Agency and we sure as hell can't ask the Felix Corporation to leave a door open.'

'Of course not. We understand that entirely.'

'So how the hell are you going to do it?'

'We'll manage.'

'You guys'll *manage*?' Ogden asked, unable to mask his cynicism.

'Hear me out. First, let me stress that if anything should go wrong at any stage of this operation you'll be protected from having any connection with it. I think that's a most important point to bear in mind. Let me give you the opening scenario . . . The White House will commission a private British company to carry out a survey of the prison's security. We will need a little help with aspects of the initial set-up phase but it's very insignificant and in any case it would be an expected detail in setting up the evaluation. Then we get a man inside – and he escapes. If it looks like the game is up at any stage we say it's just a part of the private security appraisal.'

'You're kinda missing one glaring point here, Barty. Styx actually *is* impossible to escape from. I've been down there. It makes Alcatraz look like a paper bag.'

'*We* don't think Styx is impossible to escape from.'

'Houdini's dead, Barty, and "Beam me up, Scotty" – you know, *Star Trek* – is fiction.'

Sir Bartholomew's smile was like that of a father to a naive son. The truth was that he had no idea what the operation entailed and, like Ogden, believed the prison to be as he described. But he was ostensibly a salesman and on a good day he could sell ice to an Eskimo. 'This private company will be getting a little bit of help, of course.'

'You mean your SIS will do the job.'

'One of those organisations, I suppose.'

'You're serious, aren't you?'

'I'm well known for laughing at my own jokes,' the ambassador said, no sign of a smile on his face now.

'So how are you going to do it?'

'The plans have not been finalised but I'm told the operations department is very pleased with what they've come up with.'

'I sure would like to see those plans . . . Look, I'll be honest, Barty. I can maybe buy someone getting in. I never saw a study on that because, well, who would want to? But getting out? No. Not without help.'

'Of course you can see the plans.'

'I would have to approve every phase.'

Sir Bartholomew sighed. 'Planning by committee is a recipe for disaster.'

'That's non-negotiable, Barty.'

'OK, but let these chaps get on with it. They *are* rather good at it, you know . . . And bear in mind that any interference by your chaps is tantamount to culpability. It would only compromise the authenticity of the independent survey.'

A frown wrinkled Ogden's forehead as he searched for pitfalls. 'How long before the plans are ready?'

'I'm told the latter phases are complete. The initial phase requires some input from your chaps.'

Ogden got out of his chair and went to the window.

'As I said, should anything go wrong at any stage . . .' said Sir Bartholomew.

'Yeah, yeah, we'll be covered . . . You guys just love your secret-service missions, don't you?'

'And you don't, I suppose?'

'You really think you can get a man inside that place and then out without assistance from the prison?'

'Me? No.'

Ogden looked back at Sir Bartholomew quizzically.

'I'm with you,' the ambassador said. 'I think it's impossible. But someone clearly thinks it isn't. Point is, you have nothing to lose by letting them have a go and quite a lot to gain if they should succeed – don't you think?'

Ogden looked back out of the window. 'Assuming the plan has some merit, which I doubt, how soon could this "independent survey" be ready to kick off?'

'I'm told within a week – depending on your contribution.'

'Do you at least have something for me to look at?'

Sir Bartholomew got to his feet, walked over to Ogden's desk, took an envelope from his inside breast pocket, opened it and removed several mugshots of a man. 'They want you to find someone in your criminal system who looks like this man. Any level of criminal will do, even a parolee. You have an estimated one point two million white males at various stages of the judicial process in this country. I'm sure you can find someone who resembles this fellow closely enough. I'm told it doesn't have to be a perfect match. Just close.'

The Vice-President took the mugshots. 'Who's this guy?'

'One of our chaps, I assume . . . Well,' Sir Bartholomew said, before placing the empty envelope on the coffee table beside the photographs. 'I'd better be off.' He held out his hand.

Ogden shook it as he looked into the old man's eyes. He smiled thinly as he watched the ambassador leave and then he looked down at the photographs.

The aide stepped into the doorway.

Ogden looked at him thoughtfully. 'Cancel the meeting. Call the President's office. I need to see him.'

Sumners was seated behind the desk in his small sterile office, reading a file on his computer monitor when there was a knock on his door. 'Come in,' he called out without looking up.

The door opened and John Stratton walked in. He was wearing a worn leather jacket and his hands were plunged deep in its cracked pockets. His hair was tousled and his face was covered in a dark stubble. His clear green eyes betrayed a cold contempt for the man in front of him.

Sumners looked up and his expression immediately darkened. The two men held each other's gaze for a moment, Stratton winning the competition easily. 'Would you mind shutting the door, please,' Sumners said, going back to his monitor and hitting several keys.

Stratton casually pushed the door closed and looked

around the room, his gaze resting on the single pleasant aspect of it: a small window with broad horizontal plastic shutters that partially concealed a splendid view of the Thames. The bottom of the window was too high for Sumners to see the river from where he sat. The half-closed shutters pulled down on one side at a careless angle suggested the civil servant was hardly interested.

The only wall decoration was a world map and a picture of the Queen. There were no family photographs on the desk. Stratton knew Sumners had a wife, or at least had had one a year ago. He was the selfish, callous, pompous type who didn't bother with such trivial mementoes.

Sumners completed his typing and did his best to force a smile as he leaned back, determined to remain superior. 'I see you're still using the same tailor.'

Stratton studied the man he had grown to despise over the years, dismissing a curiosity he'd had before entering the room about whether Sumners had changed even remotely for the better since they'd last met. In Stratton's early days as a member of the operations section he'd seen Sumners fairly regularly, as often as one would expect to see one's SIS taskmaster in this business. That was about a dozen times a year in his case, which was more than most. But then, Stratton was used more than most in those days.

The last time he'd seen Sumners had been over a year ago during a mission neither man would ever forget. Sumners had been long overdue for a shot at the next rung up the ladder and his boss, unwisely in Stratton's opinion, had bumped him up to operational commander. But things did not go well, to put it mildly, and within a few days he'd been relieved of his position. The significant rift that immediately developed between the two men was due to the fact that Stratton had played a pivotal role in that demotion. As far as Stratton was concerned Sumners had deserved it. He had been exposed as inadequate when the going got tough.

Only a handful of people outside the secret operation would have known the facts, though – a select few at the very top. Stratton was probably the only one who knew all Sumners's shortcomings. Sumners was aware of that, too. He had been out of his depth and not only a threat to the operation's success but also to Stratton's survival, as well as that of others. Despite the mission's positive conclusion Stratton had not been invited to take part in another SIS task since then. He suspected Sumners had had a lot to do with that.

Sumners had gone back to the job he'd done prior to that operation which involved selecting operatives for tasks. Stratton had not expected to hear from the SIS again. It was why he'd been surprised when he'd answered his phone that morning to hear Sumners dryly telling him to drop by the office. It did not necessarily mean that Stratton had been summoned for a task but he couldn't think of any other reason why he would be invited to the SIS London HQ. If there *was* a task on offer, Stratton strongly suspected that his name had been mentioned by someone else, one of Sumners's superiors. Sumners must have found it painful to make that call.

'What've you been doing the past year?' Sumners asked.

'Usual stuff.'

'I understand you've been confined to the training teams these days.'

The snide implication was that even the SBS had tired of Stratton. He was beginning to think that was true. The routine of the training slot had been gradually eroding his morale. His commanders in the SBS had clearly become unsure quite what to do with him after his last outing in the USA. Stratton had needed to lie low anyway but instead of sending him away on remote operations somewhere they'd stuck him where they'd thought he couldn't do any harm. Initially Stratton had been relieved that he had not been kicked out of the service altogether. But within a few months he had begun to think that might have been the best choice. Ironically, the man who'd lifted his spirits out of the gutter that morning was the man least likely to. Sumners was one of the few people who knew there was nothing else Stratton would rather do than work for the SIS.

'I take it that you're fit?'

Stratton shrugged. 'Usual.'

'What about diving fit? I'm surprised you were medically cleared to dive after your chest wound.'

'I guess they know what they're doing.'

'Are you medically fit? I can check.'

Arsehole, Stratton thought. Sumners looked as if he was waiting for an opportunity to explode and vent some of his pent-up anger. Stratton didn't care. He even pondered on a comment or two he could make that might provide that trigger. He suddenly began to doubt this was a job offer after all. Sumners was looking far too smug. Perhaps the bastard had brought him in just to screw him about. 'If it was essential to the job I don't doubt you would have checked already.'

'Don't be impertinent,' Sumners snapped, his face flushed with anger. 'Remember this is a military structure and I am your superior – far and above, I may add, the rank of sergeant.'

'Colour sergeant,' Stratton corrected him.

Sumners stared at him while making an effort to calm himself. This wasn't like the old days when he'd had more leverage with his young bucks. Things had changed, even in the last year. The mandarins were taking more of an interest in lower-level decisions than they had before. He could not overlook the fact that his own position had been damaged by that damned operation in Jerusalem. He blamed Stratton for much of it but deep down he knew that he, Sumners, had lost control. Still, he had expected more loyalty from the man. That was unforgivable. The trust had been broken. If he had his way Stratton would never work for the SIS again and certainly not under him.

But there was no denying that the man had carved himself a reputation, albeit a chequered one. He had fans in high places despite his many flaws. The only way forward for Sumners was to get himself another posting. New jobs were opening up all over the place. He needed to patch up the past, get a few feathers back in his cap, and then at the right moment apply for another position. This operation didn't help any, though.

It seemed to him to be doomed to failure. His plan was to distance himself from it as much as possible, do the minimum required to see it through and ensure that he made no operational contributions to it. When the investigation into its failure was conducted his name would appear purely in a lowly coordinating role. The good news was that it could end up being the final nail in Stratton's coffin. A failure of such magnitude on the back of his American fiasco could be his ultimate undoing. Taking an even more brutal view, Stratton might not even survive it. That would probably suit everyone.

'You're under consideration for a task,' Sumners said calmly, suddenly feeling more in control. 'I don't think you're the ideal person, for a number of reasons. But we're hellish busy at the moment with most of our people on the ground – our best are certainly unavailable. You're not at the top of the pile any more, Stratton. As far as you're concerned you're lucky to be here at all.'

Sumners got to his feet, opened a drawer, removed a plastic card and held it out to Stratton. 'Your key card. It'll get you from the main entrance to this floor and the secure elevators only. Let's go.'

Stratton took the pass and followed Sumners out of the room and down a corridor to a pair of elevators. Sumners placed a card into a slot, the doors opened and they stepped inside. Sumners pressed his hand against a glass panel. His fingerprints were scanned in a second but the doors remained open. 'Everyone who steps into this elevator has to have their hand scanned. It won't move otherwise. You're logged in for three days.'

Stratton pressed his hand to the glass. A second later the doors closed and the elevator descended. When it came to a halt the doors opened onto a brightly lit empty corridor. Sumners led the way to a door at the end and used his card and a PIN-code to gain entry. They stepped into a small empty space in front of another door that had a tiny red light glowing in its centre. Sumners waited until Stratton was inside and the first door had closed fully before he pressed a button on the wall. An electronic magnet locked the outer door and the red light turned green, accompanied by a soft click.

Sumners pulled the door open and they stepped through into a large gloomy room with a low ceiling that appeared to stretch to infinity in every direction. Stratton followed Sumners across the carpeted floor past untold numbers of cubicle workspaces, some of them like little islands of light. These were occupied while the others were empty and in complete darkness.

They arrived at the far end of the room where the ceiling rose up to accommodate an enormous plasma screen showing a colourful map of the world on whose edges appeared various calibrations and readings: satellite information, time zones, weather, daylight and nighttime areas, and temperatures.

Three men were standing by a large low table, talking under a spotlight. Two of them were young and were dressed scruffily. The other man, older and wearing a dark suit, had his back to Sumners.

'Excuse me, Mr Jervis,' Sumners said, stopping behind him.

Jervis turned to look at Sumners, a file in his hand. His weasel eyes immediately focused on Stratton.

'This is John Stratton,' Sumners said.

'How are you?' Jervis asked dryly.

'Fine, thanks,' Stratton replied, wondering where he had seen the man before – his face was familiar. The two younger men were strangers to him. Both nodded a greeting that oozed deference. Stratton immediately labelled them as technicians of some sort. They did not look at all like operators. Apart from being young they both had a neophyte discomfort about them, as if they were overawed by the company and where they were.

'Paul and Todd,' Jervis said. 'Has Sumners told you anything about the job yet?'

'I just got here,' Stratton replied. Jervis's London accent reminded him where he'd seen the man before. Jervis had headed up a major Scandinavian operation against Russian mini-submarines years before when Stratton had been purely SBS. It had led to the shutting down of a serious hole in Europe's back-door defences through which the Russians had been ferrying spies, Spetsnaz special-forces infiltrators and information. Jervis looked pretty much the same as he had then – a little older, perhaps. It was his foxlike features that made him so memorable, plus his brilliance. He'd been one step ahead of the Russkis all the way.

'They'll be working the early set-up phases with you,' Jervis said.

Stratton's hope that he would eventually be working alone grew.

'I 'ope a year on your backside hasn't made you soft.'

Stratton's only reply was to stare at Jervis.

'You see that, lads?' Jervis said, a hint of a smile in his eyes. 'That's arrogance. I like a bit of that in my boys. Don't you, Sumners?' he added, well aware that it would wind him up no end.

Sumners forced a smile of his own that quickly crumbled and fell apart.

'This is an unusual operation,' Jervis went on. 'Complex and with little time to put it together. It's an operator-driven task. Tell them what that means, Stratton.'

'I'll be figuring it out as I go along.'

'Unfortunately that means the more important parts,' Jervis said, his cheery tone gone. 'That's why you're back, Stratton. They'd thrown your card out of the company Rolodex. I'm the only one who voted for you on this. Just so happens my vote counts more than anyone else's. Don't let me down . . . You can go ahead,' Jervis said to Sumners as he handed him the file. 'Come with me,' he said to the other two men as he walked away.

Stratton was a little overwhelmed by the compliment. Over the past year his confidence in himself had slipped, along with his hope of being selected for an op again. It was a much-needed slap on the back and greatly appreciated. 'He's the ops director now, is he?' Stratton asked.

'Yes,' Sumners said, miffed that his earlier dressing-down of Stratton had been entirely neutralised. He pushed a button on the side of the glass-covered table, illuminating several flat-screen monitors beneath the glass. The two men's faces reflected the various colours shining up at them. Each screen displayed a different image of the undersea prison. 'You heard of Styx?'

Stratton had heard the name but he couldn't place it. 'No.'

'They probably didn't do Greek mythology in that South London state school you went to,' Sumners said.

It was the clue Stratton needed. 'A river?' he asked, unperturbed by Sumners's dig at his education.

'So you *do* read,' Sumners said. 'Yes – a mythological river in Hades, between earth and the underworld. Dead souls were ferried across it. Well, it's no longer mythology. Today's Styx is the most secure prison on the planet.'

'Gulf of Mexico?' Stratton said, remembering reading something about it.

'It's the focus of this operation,' Sumners said, touching the screens to change the schematics. 'You'll have to study every detail of the place.' Sumners pushed the file over to Stratton. 'There's a list of data files. Read every one of them. You can use that cubicle there. The passwords and links are on the face page. Everything we know about Styx is there. It will become apparent to you that there's a lot we don't know . . . Those two young chaps with Jervis? Paul is the boffin and will help clarify any technical stuff. Todd is a communications specialist. Both show a strong aptitude for field-work and although they're not operatives they can be relied upon to be of assistance – in non-hostile situations only. You have a room booked in your name at the Victory. It includes breakfast. Lunch is in the canteen.

You can expense dinner tonight up to twenty pounds as well as taxis to and from the hotel only. The briefing is tomorrow morning at eight. Be in my office by five to. Any questions?'

Stratton shook his head. He would know all he had to by the end of the following day.

'Tomorrow, then,' Sumners said and walked away.

Stratton watched Sumners go, pulled off his jacket, hung it on the back of a chair and opened the file.

Chapter 5

Nathan Charon sat playing cards with several other inmates in the recreation hall of the Cranston minimum-security prison on Rhode Island, New England. He was a handsome man in his thirties, with mousy hair, and was more sociable and unassuming than his rugged looks indicated. He was a bank clerk, or had been until his association with a small-time cheque-forging syndicate had been uncovered. Since he was not one of the organisers of the scam and was only a first-time loser he received a two-year sentence. With only two months still to serve he might well have completed it without undue drama but for one small accident of nature. He bore a striking resemblance to a man in a photograph that the British ambassador to the USA had handed to the American Vice-President, that man being an English Special Forces operative called John Stratton.

'Ah ha!' Charon shouted as he dropped a running flush onto the table, much to the disappointment of the other players who watched as he scooped up the chips.

'Nathan Charon?' a voice called out from across the room.

Charon looked up, the grin still on his face, as he

searched for whoever had called his name. When he saw the duty officer with one of the guards in tow approaching he got to his feet. 'Here, sir,' he said, grinning. 'Just fleecing these gentlemen of their cigarette coupons.'

The duty officer was not smiling as he stopped in front of the inmate and read his file one more time just in case he had got it wrong. But he had not and although it was one of the most bizarre orders he'd been asked to carry out in his career and undoubtedly an horrendous bureaucratic cock-up he reckoned it was a case of his was not to reason why. He had a job to do and he exhaled deeply before carrying on with it. 'You need to come with me, Charon.'

'Whatever you say, sir. Where we goin'?'

The duty officer licked his lips as he stared unblinkingly at Charon. 'You have a transfer.'

'Transfer?' Charon echoed. The odd expression on the officer's face warned him that all was not entirely well. 'I've only got two months left to do, sir. Where they transferring me to? Disneyland?'

The inmates at the table chuckled.

'Styx. Undersea,' the officer said dryly.

The chuckling ceased.

'That's very funny,' Charon said, grinning broadly and looking at his pals. 'You nearly got me goin' for a moment there, I tell yer.'

The officer's expression remained blank. 'You got twenty minutes to pack your sack before we leave.'

Charon's grin hung on in there but it was becoming a struggle. 'You're pushin' this joke pretty far, ain't yer, sir?'

'It's no joke,' the officer said. 'You can either go easy, or we can do it the hard way,' he said. The severe-looking accompanying guard took a step closer, a restraining system in his hands.

Charon's smile dropped off his face as his colleagues got to their feet and stepped back. 'I got two months left to do.'

'I don't make the orders, son. I got a relocation order here for you signed by the governor himself and no matter how weird it is – and I agree with you that it *is* pretty goddamned weird – I'm gonna carry it out. Now let's get going.'

'But I'm white-collar. I processed a coupla bad cheques. There has to be some kinda mistake.'

'I'm sure someone's sortin' it out right now. But until they do you're comin' with me,' the officer said, nodding to the other guard who came forward to join him. Together they manhandled Charon through the room.

'This is crazy!' Charon shouted. 'You can't put me in undersea . . . For God's sake! I wanna speak to a lawyer!'

A small fishing boat puttered over a rolling black ocean in a growing squall at a minute to midnight. The lights of Galveston Island on the east coast of Texas were little more than a faint glow behind it. The top of a wave broke over the bows and struck the front window of the wheelhouse that was only slightly roomier than a phone kiosk and looked as though it had been stuck on the deck as an afterthought. Paul stood inside, bathed in a fluorescent green glow, his hands gripping the wheel tightly, his eyes flicking between the darkness ahead and a radar tube at his side. Several blips blinked on the glowing circular screen with each sweep of the scanner, the nearest of them only a few hundred metres away. For a second he thought he saw an even brighter object on the periphery of the screen, mixed in with the rain and the rolling swell, and he maintained an unblinking stare on the same spot until it appeared again.

Paul leaned out of the open door, keeping a hand on the wheel, and was immediately pelted with rain and spray as he looked aft for Stratton and Todd. Both were wearing glistening yellow sou'westers and were dragging a heavy bundle to the stern. 'We're coming up on the perimeter buoy!' he shouted.

Stratton and Todd paused to squint at him, unsure what he had said.

'Perimeter buoy!' Paul repeated, cupping a hand around his mouth.

Stratton gave him the thumbs-up and crouched to carry out a final check on the contents of the bundle before clipping it shut. It contained a mixed-gas partial re-breather diving system with extra-large gas bottles and a full-face mask, a set of extra-long glide fins, a digital depth gauge with a pre-programmed ascent schedule and depth alarms, a strobe system, a flashlight, an inflation jacket with an expandable bladder that could reach the size of a VW Beetle when filled and a transponder which he turned on. A small, intense blue LED light blinked slowly on and off and Stratton closed the flap of the bag and clipped together a single large buckle, yanking it hard to ensure that it was secure.

'How long will that set give you?' Todd asked, blowing through one of his clenched hands to warm it.

'Ten hours,' Stratton said.

'Is that how long it takes to decompress?'

'There's a couple of hours to play with.'

Todd shook his soaked head inside his yellow hood. 'First you have to swim and find this thing, then open it, turn it on, put the mask on and all that. It sounds impossible.'

'The toggles glow in water – that'll make it easy to find. One tug and the bag opens. The set's already pressured up. All I have to do is put the teat in my mouth and breathe.'

Todd remained unconvinced. 'And you've got to do all that on one breath.'

'The main umbilical's only thirty metres from the ferry dock,' Stratton said, attaching the end of a long nylon line to a strongpoint on the bag. 'I should be able to make that.'

'Without a face mask?'

'I can't miss the umbilical. It's a metre thick. This line'll be looped around the bottom of it. I find the umbilical, I find the line, I find the bag.' Stratton was running through the scenario in order to convince himself as much as Todd that it was possible.

'And what about your decompression stops? You have to hang about at certain depths for hours.'

'I'll be going up the umbilical, attached to it by the line. The depth gauge is pre-set to the dive stops. I simply tie myself off at each depth and wait. It'll be boring but it'll work.'

'You'll either drown or freeze to death.'

'It's a living.'

'You're bloody mad – with all due respect.'

'Truth is, if I have to depend on this lot to get out of there I'm screwed anyway.'

'I can't tell when you're joking or being serious.'

'I lost track years ago.'

'So why're we going to all this trouble?' Todd persisted.

'Every op has to have emergency RVS.'

'What?'

'Rendezvouses to head for if everything goes wrong . . . even if they're tough to get to.'

'Impossible, more like.'

'Don't dramatise. It irritates me.'

Todd looked apologetic. 'Sorry . . . You're right. It's not impossible – just very, very dodgy.'

'As long as it's *theoretically* possible it allows them to blame me if I don't make it.'

Todd looked bemused. 'Who?'

'Them who tell us what to do.'

'Sorry, I'm confused.'

'For us, on the ground, it's all about how we're going to do the job. For the suits who send us out it's all about win or lose, success or failure, blame and responsibility, medals and demotions.'

'But no one expects you to pull this off anyway. The person who ordered it will surely take the fall.'

'He'll take the blame. But then there's the blame and the *real* blame. If I screw up it'll be my fault . . . Check that line can pay out without catching on anything.'

Todd obeyed but remained puzzled. 'Then you're even more insane,' he decided.

'Perimeter buoy port side!' Paul called out from the bridge.

Stratton went to the side of the boat to see the large red metal buoy holding firm in the heavy sea just ahead. Below the flashing beacon was an illuminated sign warning anyone against trespassing beyond it.

'Less than a mile,' Stratton said, tidying up the bag and ensuring that all was ready. He peered into the darkness, the wind whipping at him, his oilskins flapping open noisily to reveal a black wetsuit beneath.

Todd joined him in the search, shielding his eyes from the swiping rain. 'You been doing this work long?' he asked.

'Breaking into prisons?'

'You know what I mean.'

'A bit.'

'Is that why you're so cynical?'

'No. That came early on.'

'I'd like to get the chance to be that cynical ... I mean, working for who we do ... I'm just a tech,' Todd said. 'One day I might get a chance to do a task ... not like this, of course. I'd never do what you do ... So how did you get to do this kind of stuff, anyhow?'

'I got a call one day.'

It was obvious that Stratton did not want to elaborate but Todd could not resist taking advantage of such a rare opportunity, standing beside a real operative who was actually responding somewhat to him. 'You're SF, I suppose.' He immediately felt uncomfortable asking the question. Prying into an operative's background was not advisable but he decided he had started so he was going to finish. 'Paul and I reckon you're SBS . . . only because this is a dive task and we know the SAS don't really do water – nowhere near as serious as this.'

Since the briefing a week before Todd had spent many hours with Stratton, sorting out equipment and going over the plans and countless procedures. The man was not exactly a chatterbox. They talked about nothing outside of the operation. Todd accepted that Stratton was on a different level – way above his – had different friends, and moved in very different circles. Nevertheless he felt comfortable with him despite how little they appeared to have in common. Stratton didn't make him feel inferior in the way so many other superior types in the SIS seemed to enjoy. Stratton made his underlings feel as if they were every bit as essential a part of the team, which of course they were. The point was, he made them *feel* like they were. That was the difference. When they cocked up, as Paul had done by forgetting to pack the bundle's transponder, an essential element to Stratton's own survival, Stratton simply took the quickest and simplest course to correct the error without undue fuss. What was more, he made you feel just sufficiently bad about yourself to ensure that it never happened again. You wanted to work harder for him. It was the quintessence of leadership and Todd wondered if he could ever be like that one day.

'Sorry,' he said, filling the silence after his question. 'I get a bit carried away . . . Good luck, anyway.'

'You'll always need that . . . In fact, we might need

a little right now,' Stratton said, looking towards the wheelhouse. 'Paul!' he shouted, banging on the side of the small cabin.

Todd wondered what had triggered Stratton's sudden concern and he peered into the rain-soaked blackness. He immediately saw the tiny lights breaking through the weather, a green and red one either side of a patch of white signifying it was a vessel of some kind, the red on the right-hand side indicating it was approaching.

Paul quickly stuck his head out of the bridge door to look ahead. 'I had short-range on. It just came on screen. It's big.'

'Is the support barge showing yet?' Stratton shouted.

'Dead ahead — three hundred metres. What do we do?!'

Stratton looked ahead as he thought, gauging the wind and water. 'Push over to port!' he shouted back to Paul. 'Make them follow us. Give it all you've got! They won't be able to turn as close to the barge as we can because of the sub-sea cables. Make a chase of it!'

Paul turned the wheel, the bows coming about sluggishly against the swell.

'Perimeter security?' Todd asked.

'Who else?'

'Do you think they'll shoot — if we don't stop, I mean?'

'We're about to find out,' Stratton said, squinting ahead. 'There's the barge,' he said, gauging the distances between them, the barge and the security boat as its glowing wheelhouse became clearer.

Several lights came into view dead ahead followed

by the outline of an enormous black rectangular box, like a square island, so large and heavy as to be unaffected by the swell. They were crossing the tide which was against the security vessel, thus improving their chances of getting to the barge first.

'We're aiming too close,' Todd said, alarm in his voice. 'We'll be pushed into it!'

Stratton did not appear concerned as he watched the security boat, still gauging the distances. He banged on the wheelhouse. 'The anchor cables!' he shouted.

'I know!' Paul replied. 'I know what depth we have!'

Stratton was more or less confident that Paul knew what he was doing. He was a careful young man, inexperienced but nonetheless someone who paid close attention to detail. Stratton had checked the anchor-cable angles from the corners of the barge and expected Paul to have done the same, especially since he was the driver.

Paul swung the boat out at the last minute and steered a wide berth round the first corner of the barge. A large wave suddenly shoved them within feet of the massive structure but by that time they were past the submerged cable. The good news was that the security boat was now out of sight.

The barge was a welded and riveted rectangular mass of metal the size of a tennis court, an uninhabited automated service vessel for the prison, held in position by a series of cables anchored to the sea bed. It contained fuel, potable water, emergency oxygen supplies and back-up generators. A structure in the middle bristled with various types of communication antennae. Fixed atop a stubby gantry was a giro-stabilised satellite dish fighting to maintain its position. All the various pipes and conduits were channelled into a single umbilical cord over a metre in diameter that snaked down from the centre of the barge to the prison a hundred and fifty feet below.

The small fishing boat bobbed its way along the side of the barge, the top of which was several metres above Stratton's head. As they closed on the next corner Paul pushed the bows out to avoid the mooring cable he knew went down at a steep angle. But a heavy swell reversed the manoeuvre and the boat heaved over towards the barge. Stratton grabbed up a pole and held it at the ready as Paul struggled to turn the vessel away from the barnacled steel wall.

'We're going to hit as we take the corner,' Stratton called out. Todd searched around for anything he could use, found an old oar and hurried to Stratton's side with it.

As the boat reached the corner it was slammed into the side of the barge. The gunwales cracked loudly, several pieces smashing off. Stratton and Todd did what they could to push the boat off but their efforts were hardly effective. The boat scraped along the barge as the nose went past the corner. Everyone's thoughts went to the cable that was just below them. The wind and tide were running along the edge of the barge around the corner. As the midway point of the boat reached the corner of the barge the bows started to make the turn around it. It looked as if the boat was going to break in half but the stern suddenly pushed out to follow the corner around. As the stern approached where the cable was attached a huge swell lifted the boat up and completed its turn. The crunch of the propeller being ripped off by the cable never came and they shot down the side of the barge towards the next corner.

'Was that luck or what?' Todd shouted.

Stratton ignored him. They were going to need a lot more.

Running with the wind and tide did not make the steering any easier to control but Paul managed a wide sweep of the next corner before turning the bows tightly back in. They passed the corner and entered the leeward side of the barge where the wind was only half as strong and the sea was practically calm. Paul played the engines as he manoeuvred the boat to face the barge, holding position in the tide that was coming at them from beneath it.

Stratton was galvanised into action. He dropped the pole, removed his sou'wester and oilskins, looped the harness attached to a small diving tank over his back and quickly pulled on a pair of fins.

'What if the security boat comes before you get back?' Todd asked.

'Get the bundle ready! Now!' was Stratton's response. He pulled on a face mask, picked up a karabiner attached to one end of the coiled nylon line fixed to the dive bag, clipped it to his belt and leapt overboard. Todd looked over the side into the swirling black water but Stratton was already gone, the line unwinding rapidly and zipping over the gunwales after him.

Paul stuck his head out of the wheelhouse door. 'We're not close enough yet!'

'He's already gone. Get into the barge!' Todd shouted as he hurried to the bundle.

Paul yanked himself back into the wheelhouse and powered the boat ahead. A thought struck him that if Stratton couldn't beat the tide he might go under the boat and get chopped up by the prop. The thought no sooner entered his head when it was brushed aside. He had his job to do and Stratton had his own.

Stratton turned on a powerful small light attached to his mask and headed down to the bottom of the barge. As soon as he slipped beneath it the tide hit him like a wall and threatened to push him back. He battled against it, turning onto his back and at the same time jamming his fingers behind any barnacle or limpet to pull himself forward.

Approaching the umbilical from the leeward side was still the best option as far as keeping the fishing boat in one piece was concerned, but only if Stratton could get to it. He could make out the huge vertical pipe ahead and finned for all he was worth, sucking the air from the bottle as he increased to near-sprint mode. He was certain he could make it. The question was could he get back before the security boat challenged the boys. If not this phase would be a failure.

Stratton reached the umbilical – it felt like a fat conduit of rubber – and pulled himself around it, the nylon line following him. Once he'd got around to the other side the tide catapulted him back in the direction he had come.

★

A spotlight swooped across the small fishing boat and Todd looked up to see the top of the security vessel's superstructure above the barge heading towards them.

The nylon line continued to unravel down into the water and Todd wrestled with the heavy bundle to balance it on the edge. 'Come on, Stratton,' he shouted at the water.

The security vessel made a wide berth round the corner and came into full view. If the security boat caught Todd in its light the bundle would be exposed.

The light struck the rear of the fishing boat and made its way along its deck. Todd had to make an extremely serious decision but then quickly determined he had no choice. He heaved the bundle overboard and it dropped beneath the water as the powerful beam illuminated him.

'Cut the engines,' Todd shouted.

Paul wasn't sure that he'd heard Todd correctly and looked out of the wheelhouse as the security boat bore down on them.

'Cut them!' Todd shouted again.

Paul was in a mild panic, unsure what to do. Stratton was gone. Perhaps Todd knew something he didn't. He reached into the wheelhouse and turned off the power. The engines died, the dull droning replaced by the wind and rain whistling across the boat, which quickly began to drift. As it left the calm leeward side of the barge the wind and sea returned to play with it like a toy.

'STOP WHAT YOU ARE DOING AND STAND IN SIGHT WITH YOUR HANDS IN VIEW!' a voice boomed over a loud hailer as the security vessel powered towards them. Its fierce spotlight was blinding.

The security boat was á large cruiser of the type used by the coastguard and behind the bright lights Paul and Todd could make out men on the bridge wings and in the bows. They were carrying rifles. The big ship came alongside the little fishing boat and slowed abruptly, both vessels rapidly drifting away from the barge.

'YOU'RE IN A RESTRICTED AREA!' the voice boomed. 'STAND WHERE YOU CAN BE SEEN!'

Paul stepped from the wheelhouse with his hands in the air. Todd raised his hands too, looking towards the barge that was almost out of sight and wondering where the hell Stratton was.

'WHAT ARE YOU DOING IN THIS RESTRICTED AREA?'

Neither man answered, unsure what to say or do, despondency suddenly threatening to overwhelm them. All they could think of was that their boss was somewhere behind them in the sea and this entire operation was falling apart before it had even begun.

'Tell them we've a man overboard,' Paul said in a voice just loud enough for Todd to hear.

Todd wasn't sure whether to agree or not. He could see where Paul was coming from. It was concern for the man and not the operation. The question was, what would Stratton do, or want them to do? The answer was easy enough. 'No,' Todd said, squinting at the security vessel.

'Good answer,' Stratton said as he stepped from behind

the wheelhouse, wearing his oilskins and yellow sou'wester. He put his hands in the air. 'Talk to them, Paul.'

Todd didn't look back but he was so pleased with himself, let alone with his boss, that he almost smiled.

Paul breathed a sigh of relief. 'We're truly sorry,' he called out in an Irish accent. 'We're a tad misplaced.'

'We've got engine problems!' Stratton shouted in his own version of the Gaelic twang.

One of the crew relayed the men's reply to the bridge.

'YOU WERE MAKING HEADWAY WHEN WE FIRST SAW YOU!' the voice boomed.

'Just runnin' with the wind, sir,' Paul shouted. 'Why'd we want to be in here anyway? Only tear our nets on all these cables, sure we would.'

'Can you throw us a line?' Stratton shouted. 'Tow us out of here?'

There was a long pause before the security boat's captain came to a decision. 'NEGATIVE. YOU'RE GONNA HAVE TO SOLVE YOUR PROBLEM YOURSELVES.'

Stratton and Todd went to the rear of the wheelhouse, opened the engine compartment and pretended to fiddle with the engine while Paul held the wheel.

'Thanks a bunch there, anyways,' Paul shouted.

'IF YOU ENTER THESE RESTRICTED WATERS AGAIN YOU WILL BE ARRESTED AND PROSECUTED!'

Paul made a gesture to signal that he understood and went back into the wheelhouse to give the impression he was working on their problem.

The security boat's engines roared and it pulled back as the fishing boat drifted away from it.

Stratton kept an eye on the cruiser as it held its position. The captain was clearly still suspicious of them.

'What about the bundle?' Todd asked.

'It's on its way,' Stratton assured him.

'You connected the ends? That's brilliant.'

'That was close,' Paul said, checking on them. 'How long shall we keep the engines off?'

'Who's idea was it to kill them?' Stratton asked.

'Mine,' Todd admitted, wondering if he was going to get in trouble.

'Good,' Stratton said.

A bell clanged and they all looked towards a perimeter-warning buoy a few metres away on the starboard side, a light swaying on the end of its short derrick as if it was a giant fishing float signalling a large bite beneath it.

When Stratton looked back towards the security vessel it had turned its flank to them and was still holding its position. 'Start her up.'

Paul entered the wheelhouse and a moment later the fishing boat's engine gunned to life. Stratton stepped inside to get out of the weather and Todd joined them, closing the door.

'Why were we speaking in Irish accents?' Stratton asked.

'Yeah, I was wondering that,' Todd said.

'I don't know,' Paul said, shrugging. 'I can lie better in Irish. Besides, everyone loves the Irish.'

'That was a crap Irish accent,' Todd said. 'You sounded more like a Pakistani.'

'Better than his,' Paul said, indicating Stratton.

'He's right, Stratton,' Todd said. 'Yours was rubbish.'

The two young men glanced at Stratton, wondering if they'd gone too far.

'Accents have never been my thing,' he admitted.

The others laughed. Stratton's face cracked slightly.

'He smiles,' Todd said, never having seen Stratton wear one before.

The two young men gabbled on, their tensions easing, and the sound of laughter rose above the chugging engine as the boat headed towards the glow on the horizon that was Galveston.

The bundle followed the curving umbilical down into the darkness, bubbles escaping from it as the pressure increased around it. A faint orange glow suddenly appeared below, the light coming from dozens of small windows and portholes in neat rows at various levels around a huge mound.

The bundle finally came to rest on a rocky ledge and hung by its line that went up and around the base of the umbilical where it disappeared into a massive concrete block. As the bundle settled it dislodged several rocks that cascaded down the side of the mound. The rocks dropped past one of the lines of glowing portholes, eventually disappearing into what could only be described as a thick layer of white water covering the sea bed around the underwater hill like an impenetrable mist.

A face came to one of the portholes to look through the thick, grimy glass. It belonged to Durrani who was standing in a small cell in which a bed and a toilet bowl were the only furnishings. He was sure he had seen something fall past his window but after craning in every direction he thought he had imagined it.

Durrani stepped away from the window, went to the bed, picked up a copy of the Koran, sat down and began to read it. But, unable to concentrate, he did not get far, as was often the case. He dropped his head into his hands, stared at his feet in his worn sandals on the concrete floor and wondered, for the umpteenth time since arriving in the prison, if he would ever see his homeland or even the sunlight again.

Chapter 6

Congressman Forbes was seated behind a large oak desk in his sumptuous office on the first floor of the Rayburn House Building on Capitol Hill. He was editing a letter when his phone rang.

He picked it up. 'Congressman Forbes.' His pen went still in his hand as he recognised the voice. 'Yes . . . yes, of course. Where? . . . But . . . OK . . . No, I'll be there . . . Yes.'

Forbes replaced the phone, put down the pen and paused to collect his thoughts. He got to his feet, walked to a coat rack by the door, took his jacket off a peg, pulled it on and left the room.

His secretary looked up enquiringly as he passed her desk. 'I've got to go out. Be back in an hour,' he said as he left the office.

The congressman walked briskly along a shiny marble corridor, doors staggered along either side and adorned with ornate brass plaques bearing the names of various committees. He passed through an arched opening into a palatial hall where a staircase descended to a broad lobby. He skipped down the steps with a degree of athleticism, headed across the mosaic floor, returned greetings to colleagues without stopping and walked through the entrance into the bright sunshine.

Forbes stopped at the top of a broad arc of stone steps and scanned the panorama, starting from the Botanic Conservatory on his far left and sweeping across the manicured gardens in front of Capitol Hill. Halfway across he saw a man wearing dark sunglasses and a brown suit standing alone beside a groomed hedgerow and looking directly at him.

Forbes did not hesitate and walked down the steps, this time with a sense of caution. He crossed a foot-path and deliberately headed in the opposite direction along the hedgerow from where the man was standing. When he reached the end he kept going at a casual pace. The man, who had followed Forbes down the other side of the hedge, was soon alongside him.

They continued in silence towards the Library of Congress until Forbes judged that they looked as if they had been together for the entire stroll. 'I'm assuming this is extremely important for you to meet me here of all places and without more than a minute's notice,' Forbes said without looking at the man, an irritation in his voice as if he were the superior of the two of them.

The man in the brown suit didn't reply as he casually looked behind them and to the sides whilst adjusting the glasses on his nose. Satisfied that they were un-observed he broke his silence. 'The feds are sending someone inside,' he said.

Forbes was perplexed enough almost to stop.

'Keep walking,' the man said casually. He was half Forbes's age and infinitely more composed.

'You mean Styx?'

'Where else?' the man replied dryly. Forbes was no superior of his.

Forbes's mind raced to calculate the implications of the statement. 'This isn't official. I mean, I've not heard anything,' Forbes said, unable to see the irritation in the man's expression.

'It's an undercover operation. They're making their move . . . It was only a matter of time.'

'You people said it would be years before anything like this could happen.'

'It *has* been years. Just not as many as we would've liked . . . We haven't been as nice to the feds lately as we should've. They're punishing us.'

'Just you? I mean, they're not investigating *us*, right?'

The man grinned and shook his head slightly, a gesture that Forbes also failed to register. 'You're the key to closing us down. You always were . . . They're investigating your offshore accounts.'

Forbes couldn't help pausing. The man continued and Forbes caught him up. 'Why're they sending in an agent? I mean . . . they . . .'

'To confirm what they already suspect . . . You can help us — the both of us.'

'How?'

'Give us more time.'

'More time?'

'They're sending in an agent — as a prisoner.'

'A prisoner?'

The man glanced at Forbes, irritated again, this time

with the congressman's panic attack. 'He's on the next scheduled intake.'

Forbes stopped, unable to talk sideways for a moment longer. 'That's in a few days.'

The man stopped and faced the congressman. His eyes were invisible behind his dark glasses but the scowl etched into his acne-scarred skin was plain enough. 'That's right.'

'What . . . what are we supposed to do?'

'Stop him.'

'How?'

'How do you think?'

'I don't think I like your tone.'

'I don't give a damn.'

'Don't you talk to me like that, you son of a bitch. I'm not some CIA lackey. I know what we're doing here. Remember it was the CIA who approached me first, asking for my help in pushing forward the prison concept. I got myself on the congressional delegation trip to Guantánamo. I got onto the House Intelligence Committee so that I could push votes for you.'

'Oh, that's all correct. But we came to you only after we learned you owned a piece of the Felix Corporation and what you were planning for the old NASA facility. You already knew about the possible yield of the mine.'

'That's bullshit. The facility was built on legitimate concepts. The mine was a plus.'

'Is that right? The way I heard it was that a Felix engineer kept the potential mine yield from the various committees that oversaw the original NASA project . . .

what, three years before the proposal of the detention centre?'

'It was you who corrupted it by introducing questionable interrogation methods.'

'And very successful methods too. We saved a lot of lives. You came into this deal a crook, Forbes, and we turned you into a patriot.'

'How dare you! No amount of money from that mine would even begin to compensate me for the risks I've taken for the Agency.'

The man didn't want to put Forbes over the top and softened his manner slightly. 'We still have a problem to take care of.'

'I want you to take that comment back.'

'Which one?'

'I am and always have been a patriot.'

'I'm sorry,' the man said, doing his best to sound sincere and almost making it.

Forbes knew it was the best he could expect and calmed down in order to think. 'Are you telling me it's over? The feds are making their move and so we pack our bags and leave.'

'No. We're not ready for that yet. You're going to stop that agent from getting into the prison.'

'I'll need the name. We can reverse him on a medical issue.'

'We don't know who he is.'

'Then how the hell do you expect me to stop him?'

'Use your imagination.'

Forbes stared at him, unsure quite what he meant. 'My imagination's not that good.'

'You've got people who have imaginations. We went to a lot of trouble to put them in the right places to help you in the event of situations just like this.'

'Mandrick.'

'For one.'

'What precisely are you expecting to happen?'

'There's over half a dozen men in the next intake. Since we don't know which of them is the agent we can't afford to let any of them get inside.'

'We can't turn them all away.'

'I know.'

Forbes struggled to think where the agent's line of thought was headed. When it eventually struck him his eyes widened in horror. 'You're insane.'

'It's the only way. There has to be a little accident before they get to the prison . . . The ferry – before it docks.'

'You don't get *little* accidents at those depths. Even the ones that start little end up big.'

The agent's smile was gone.

'That's going too far,' Forbes said, his voice quivering.

'Too far, congressman, is a distant star we haven't been to yet . . . You want to be a patriot. Nothing is too far when it comes to protecting this country, even from itself. You will block this move. There's a lot more road ahead. We like our little partnership. As always, you help us, we'll help you.'

'This is not cooperation. It's blackmail.'

'Blackmail is for civilians. We strategise. If Styx goes down before we're ready you'll go with it. Is that simple enough for you to understand? You hang in there and you'll get your villa on a mile of Caribbean beach with a little cottage at the end of it that your wife won't know about where you'll keep the little chick – Melissa? – currently living in an apartment you rent for her in Alexandria . . . You back out now and you'll sure as shit remain in the jail business, Forbes. Someone else's.'

The man started to walk away.

'If I go down you'll go with me,' Forbes growled.

'You don't even know who I am,' the man said without looking back.

Forbes stared after him with a scowl that quickly melted into an expression of utter anguish.

A prison transport wagon made its way along the San Luis Pass road from Scholes Field Airport, the sun rising out of the tepid waters of the Gulf of Mexico making a splendid view from the driver's window. There was no view for Nathan Charon and the prisoner seated opposite him, or the guard at the other end of the windowless cabin sealed off from the cab by a steel wall.

The prisoners were wearing crisp new white convict suits with light green stripes made up of small forks, the official inmate uniform for Styx penitentiary. On closer inspection the forks turned out actually to be mythological tridents, an attempt at irony by the uniform's designer.

Charon was staring down at his handcuffs, chained to his seat in utter disbelief at his predicament. The prisoner opposite, a bald-headed, grotesquely scarred beast, was half dozing as the van shook gently.

Charon looked at the guard at the other end of the

119

cabin who was leaning forward in his seat reading a magazine. 'Hey? . . . Hey?'

The guard sighed heavily. 'Give it a rest, will ya, for Pete's sake. You're driving me nuts.'

'You're the last person from the outside world who will see me before I go into that place,' Charon whined.

'Yeah, I know, you said – several times now.'

'Don't you care that you're taking part in this enormous travesty?'

'I'll get over it,' the guard said, turning a page.

'Doesn't anyone think it's just a little odd that a minimum-security prisoner with just two months left to do is being transferred to the highest-classified security prison on the goddamned planet?'

'It is kinda weird, ain't it?' the guard said, turning the magazine and holding it at arm's length to appreciate the centrefold.

'Kinda weird?!' Charon echoed, resting his head back against the van's internal wall with a bang. 'That's the final word, folks. That's what happened to good old Nathan Charon. Kinda weird, though. But hey – these things happen.' He dropped his face into his hands.

'It's gettin' old, Charon. One more word outta you an I'm gonna gag yer. Ya hear me?'

'Yeah, shaddap, Charon,' the other prisoner said without opening his eyes.

The vehicle suddenly shuddered violently, swerving slightly before rolling along with a rhythmic judder. The brakes were applied sharply and the dozing prisoner slammed his head painfully against the frame of the next seat.

The guard got to his feet as the vehicle came to a stop. He opened the small hatch into the driver's cab.

The guard sitting beside the driver turned to look at the cabin guard as he reached for the door. 'We gotta flat,' he said.

'Great,' the cabin guard sighed.

There was the sound of doors slamming, a clunking from outside, and a moment later the back of the van opened and the light spilled in, silhouetting the driver's-cab guard who was standing on the road. 'Get your ass out here, Jerry.'

'Technically, I ain't supposed to get out, Chuck,' Jerry said.

'Oh yeah. Well, *technically* you do, 'cause Harry's got a bad back and health-and-safety says I can't change the wheel on my own.'

'In that case we're supposed to call in roadside.'

'You wanna sit here for the next four hours?'

'I don't care.'

'Well, I do. Besides, we gotta have these guys delivered by twelve.'

'Who cares if they're a little late?'

'Don't screw with me, Jerry. I ain't in the mood. Get your ass outta there. I don't wanna hear anything more about it.'

'Who put him in charge?' Jerry mumbled as he lowered his oversize frame out of the back of the transport wagon and onto the road. A car cruised past with no others in sight as he joined his colleagues who were kneeling on the grass verge inspecting the flat.

'I still think we should call someone,' Jerry said,

unwrapping a strip of gum and pushing it into his mouth.

'It's a flat tyre, not a broken axle,' Chuck said. 'You don't wanna get your hands dirty, fine. I'll do it.'

'Come on,' Jerry said. 'I didn't mean anything. I'm gonna help.'

'You don't have to,' Harry said, removing his jacket.

'I *wanna* help. Can we just forget I said anything?'

'We're all gonna help,' Chuck said, removing his jacket. 'I'll get the spare, you do the jack, you untie the wheel nuts. OK?'

Everyone agreed and set about their respective task.

Fifty metres from the side of the highway Stratton, wearing a pair of overalls, sat in among a dense crop of bushes, unscrewing a silencer from the end of a rifle barrel. He placed it in a box designed to house the weapon pieces and started to unscrew the scope. Paul and Todd, both wearing prison-guard uniforms identical to those of the guards in the prison van, sat a few feet from him. The two young men looked pensive in contrast to Stratton as they watched him place the final piece of the rifle in the box, along with an empty brass bullet casing, close the lid and fasten the clips. Stratton opened a small backpack beside him and removed what looked like an ordinary black tube-flashlight except for its unusual bulbous end.

'Speed they're going they should be done in about fifteen minutes,' Paul said in a low voice, rubbing the palms of his hands together, unaware of his nervous gesture.

'You ever used one of them before?' Todd asked Stratton.

'I haven't seen one in about ten years,' Stratton said as he pushed a test button on the bottom of the device that glowed green for a couple of seconds.

'It's that old?'

'Older. Works even better underwater.'

'SBS,' Todd said decisively, nudging Paul.

Stratton removed the bulbous rubber cover to reveal a thick fish-eye lens. 'They went on to develop a riot-control version but scrapped it because it induced fits in epileptics.'

'What if one of these guys is an epileptic?' Todd asked.

'He wouldn't get a job as a prison guard if he was,' Paul said.

'Good point,' Todd conceded.

'They've got the wheel off,' Paul informed them.

Stratton took a moment to ensure that his kit was organised and he had everything he needed. 'Glasses,' he ordered, taking a pair of dark brown goggles from the bag and putting them on.

Paul was wearing his around his neck and he pulled them over his eyes, tightening the elastic straps that held them firmly in place.

Todd took a long look at the device before pulling his goggles on. Stratton could feel the young man's eyes on him. Todd had hinted more than once the past few days about his desire to move up the ladder to hostile-field status. Part-way into an operation might seem hardly the time to do it to some but not to Stratton.

It depended on the operative and he felt confident that Todd was up to it. He held out the device to him.

Todd looked at him in surprise.

'You want to do this?' Stratton asked.

Todd's mouth dropped open, a mixture of soaring excitement and apprehension. 'Seriously?'

'Your first lesson: when you're sure never hesitate unless it's part of the plan.'

Todd practically snatched the device out of Stratton's hand and then held it as if it was something precious.

'No doubts,' Stratton said, more an order than a question.

'None,' Todd said quickly in case Stratton took it back.

'The beam's forty degrees. You need to get within fifteen metres.'

'I know,' Todd replied, getting himself ready to move forward.

'You're not serious?' Paul asked, looking horrified.

'Watch out for cars,' Stratton continued, ignoring Paul. 'Let's not cause any collateral accidents.'

'You're going to let him do this?' Paul insisted.

'How long does it take to work?' Todd asked Stratton.

'Depends on the individual. Disorientation is almost immediate. Full incapacity can take up to ten seconds. Lasts about five minutes. But you can double-dose if need be.'

'This is madness,' Paul said. 'He's a tech.'

'Chill, Paul. I'm not going to kill anyone.'

'This is where it starts, though.'

'Bollocks,' Todd scoffed, getting to his feet but remaining in the crouching position.

'They've got the spare on. Let's go,' Stratton said.

Todd made his way forward, keeping low through the long grass, as Chuck reached under the truck to release the jack and the new tyre took the vehicle's weight.

Todd eased his way down an incline and through the foliage to the base of the slope that led up to the edge of the highway. The three prison guards had their backs to him as he moved into what he considered to be the ideal position, placed a finger on the trigger and aimed the device towards them. He suddenly couldn't remember if the target actually needed to be looking in the direction of the light or not. It seemed logical to him that they should. He decided not to take the chance – he'd wait for the guards to turn around.

Chuck pulled the jack out from under the vehicle, turned his back to the highway and looked directly at Todd who was partly exposed in an effort to get a clear shot. Chuck wondered why someone was in the bushes in the middle of nowhere pointing a flashlight at him.

Todd immediately recognised that his predicament was expecting all three guards to face him at the same time. Realising how unlikely that was, coupled with the fact that one of them had already seen him, he hit the trigger. A penetrating white light flickered from the lens like a powerful strobe.

Chuck immediately started trembling uncontrollably as the intense light penetrated his retinas. It was designed to pulse at the same frequency as brainwaves, upsetting the flow of information between the compartments and causing massive synaptic short-circuits. The other two guards began to feel odd sensations caused by the light bouncing off the side of the truck. They both turned to look at the source. Harry dropped immediately onto his hands and knees, unable to look away, fell onto his chest and remained still, apart from the fluttering of his eyes. Jerry, beginning to shake uncontrollably, had more resistance to the bombardment and reached for his pistol.

Todd kept his finger pressed firmly on the trigger, squeezing it hard as if the added effort might increase the beam's power. But the guard continued to pull his pistol from its holster.

Jerry raised the barrel of the weapon towards Todd although it began to shake violently in his hand. His knees began to buckle, his face twisting into a grimace as he fought to keep control. He could no longer see the man in the bushes as his brain filled with a white light which suddenly went out as he dropped forward onto his face.

Todd kept hold of the device, transfixed by the fear that he'd almost been shot. A hand gripped his wrist while another moved his finger off the trigger.

Stratton took the device, placed it into his backpack along with his glasses and climbed up the slope. He looked both ways along the highway to ensure there were no vehicles coming and crouched by the guards to check that their vital signs were OK.

Paul arrived, carrying the rifle case and looking flustered. 'That was lucky.'

'Be even luckier if you send the signal,' Stratton said. 'Put your caps on. Look like prison guards.'

Paul chastised himself for forgetting and grabbed his cellphone as he put his hat on. Todd joined him, fitting his own cap and looking seriously chuffed about the success of his task.

'This is Paul. Go, go, go,' Paul said into the phone.

Todd hurried towards the back of the wagon.

'Keys,' Stratton called out as he pulled a bunch from Jerry's pocket.

Todd halted and as he turned the keys were sailing towards him. He caught them and hurried around to the back of the wagon.

Charon and the other prisoner were sitting and staring down at him.

'How ya doin'?' Todd asked in an exaggerated American wise-guy accent that he could not help slipping into. He climbed inside the wagon.

A small van with the same prison markings on its sides arrived, pulled up behind the prison truck and two men in the same-style guard uniforms climbed out.

Todd pulled a syringe from a pocket, removed the sterile cap, plunged the needle into the scarred prisoner's leg and emptied the contents into it.

'Ouch! What the fuck's goin' on?' the prisoner cried as he struggled in his shackles.

Todd removed another syringe from the pocket, took off the cap and stuck the needle into Charon's leg. 'What the hell is *this*?' Charon exclaimed as his vision quickly began to blur. Then he lost consciousness.

Stratton climbed into the prison truck as the others unshackled the scarred prisoner and hauled him out, carrying him to the side door of the small van and putting him inside. Stratton pulled off his overalls to reveal his Styx prison uniform and sat beside Charon. One of the newcomers crouched in front of the two lookalikes in order to study them. 'Hold his head up, please,' the man said. Todd grabbed the back of Charon's head and held it upright.

The man opened up a well-stocked make-up artist's box and set about his work with agile precision. He gave Stratton a super-quick haircut to match Charon's. The colour match wasn't perfect enough for him and he sprinkled a little powder onto Stratton's hair and rubbed it in to lighten it. He compared the two men's faces back and forth, adding colour to eyebrows and complexion. The make-up man finally shook his head and frowned. 'His cheekbones aren't as wide here as his are. I can't do anything about it.'

'Is the difference massive?' Todd asked, moving to where he could make his own comparison. 'He's right. It's noticeable. Your cheeks are slightly thinner than his,' he said to Stratton.

'By much?' Stratton asked.

'Enough,' the artist said.

'A tad, but noticeable, like I said,' Todd agreed.

'Mine need to be bigger?' Stratton asked.

'Yes,' Todd said.

'Hit me,' Stratton ordered.

'What?'

'Hit me. On the cheeks. Mess me up a little. We only

have to fool these guards until they drop me off. The picture in the replacement file is me.'

'He's right,' Todd said, standing back. 'Hit him.'

'I'm not going to hit him!' the artist cried.

'You're the bloody make-up artist. You know where it needs swelling.'

'We never did thumping as a technique in make-up class.'

'Hit me, you little prick,' Stratton shouted at Todd. 'Now!'

Todd didn't hesitate a second longer and belted Stratton across his cheek. 'Well?' he asked the artist, nursing his sore knuckles. 'Bloody check it, then,' he shouted.

The artist looked at the blow, comparing it to Charon's cheek. 'I suppose it confuses the issue. Do the other side.'

Todd lamped Stratton on the other cheek and the artist inspected it. 'I suppose that'll do,' he said, and shrugged. 'It'll be better when the bruising sets in.'

'Get this guy into the van,' Stratton said nudging Charon and the men moved with urgency to obey.

Meanwhile, Paul climbed into the prison truck's cab where he found a metal box file. He sorted through the keys, found the one he wanted, opened the box, removed a file, checked that it was Nathan Charon's, replaced it with another identical file from his backpack and relocked the box.

He climbed out of the cab and put the keys back into the guard's pocket. The guard moaned and started to move.

Paul hurried to the back of the truck. 'They're coming round,' he said.

Everyone speeded the final tidying-up.

Stratton sat in Charon's seat and Todd shackled him in while the others piled into the van.

Todd took a last look around. 'Good luck,' he said. 'Get going.'

Todd was about to climb down when he paused. 'Thanks,' he said holding out his hand. 'Please come back in one piece.'

Stratton looked up at the sincerity in Todd's face. He held out his hand as far as the shackles would allow.

Todd shook it, dropped the keys on the floor, jumped down onto the road, hurried to the smaller van and climbed in. It sped away even before he had closed the door.

Harry pushed himself up into a sitting position and felt his head as he wondered what the hell had happened to him. Jerry rolled onto his back, his eyes flicking open, and stared up at the sky, trying to remember where he was. He suddenly sat up and looked towards the road-side foliage while grabbing for his gun.

Chuck sat up too, blinking his eyes rapidly to help bring them back into focus. 'What the hell happened?' he asked as Harry turned over onto his knees.

Jerry looked towards the rear of the truck, staggered to his feet and used the side of the wagon to help him keep his balance as he hurried around to the back. Stratton, unconscious, was slumped forward in his seat, the seat opposite him empty and the shackles lying on the floor. 'Shit!' Jerry exclaimed. 'We got a break!' he shouted as he moved out into the road to look in all directions.

The other two guards came to take a look. Chuck climbed inside to check on Stratton who moaned as he regained consciousness.

'What the hell happened?' Chuck shouted at him. 'Talk to me!'

Stratton took his time, pretending to gather his senses. The plan was to avoid talking to the current guards because they knew Charon's voice. He shook his head and acted dazed.

'What did you see?' Chuck insisted. 'Where'd Rivers go?'

Stratton continued to act stunned and shook his head, his eyelids drooping.

Chuck gave up and jumped back down. 'We gotta call this in,' he said as he headed for the truck's cab.

'Oh, boy,' Jerry sighed. 'Are we in the crapper.'

Chapter 7

Congressman Forbes sat in his office, staring at his phone. He was weighing his options, all of which looked grim. He had survived many a tight situation in his career but if there was a way out of this one he could not see it. The Agency had him well and truly by the throat and was tightening its grip.

Throughout his professional life Forbes had been an advocate of moderation when it came to the division of spoils. 'Always leave enough for others to fatten on' was one of his sayings. Sharing the profits along with the risks provided allies as well as scapegoats. He had never been greedy – not by his definition, at any rate. Styx was a way of making a tidy income, not without legitimate risk. His mistake had been in allowing the Agency to convince him they could mitigate that risk when all they did was to present him with greater ones. He had not seen the trap coming. The adventure had looked too good to pass on. Now, for his sins, he was faced with the grimmest choice he had ever had to make.

There had been life-and-death decisions to be made in the past but all of these had been in the name of national security. But this was purely to save his own skin. He *could*, he guessed, call it quits, suffer the consequences, the humiliation, the likely prison sentence and bring down a handful of colleagues with him. Better still, he could throw himself off a tall building. But that would take a type of courage that Forbes did not have. He loved life far too much and it was that same love affair that would make the final decision for him. The truth was that it had been made the instant he'd been faced with the ultimatum. This wrestling with his conscience was only a private show, a pathetic effort to convince himself that he was confronting a moral dilemma and therefore this was proof that he did in fact possess such things as a conscience and a moral sense. He had them, all right, but they were just not up to this level of testing.

Forbes stared at the ornately framed picture of his wife and two grown-up children in front of him, all smiles and confidence. It was more than enough to bolster his decision and compel him to get on with it.

Forbes picked up the phone, flicked through a notebook on his desk and double-checked the number before dialling it. The line buzzed rhythmically for several seconds before a voice came on. 'Mandrick? . . . Yeah, it's me. We have a problem . . . a big one. We've been offered a deal we can't refuse from our Agency partners . . . They've informed me we're to have an unwanted visitor . . . an undercover fed . . . Today . . . That's the point. We don't know who. That's why there has to be a terrible accident . . . The ferry, I think. Unless you can come up with something better. But it must be a success . . . This puts us into outer space on the risk chart . . . Can you handle it? . . . What do they say? They don't mind at all. They're the ones insisting on it.'

Pieter Mandrick was half American and half South African. Taking a man's life on the orders of a superior was nothing new to him but he had never received such a request from a civilian employer before and never for a hit that was to be carried out within the USA. And how he'd ended up as warden of the most controversial prison in the world was the story of a fascinating and circuitous journey.

His mother was from Brooklyn and had met his father while on a safari holiday in the Kruger Park. His father, ironically, was a senior prison guard who had spent the last ten years of his life as a shift commander on Robben Island, the notorious prison where Nelson Mandela spent most of his twenty-six-year incarceration. Mandrick had never had the slightest intention of following in his father's footsteps and as a young man would have laughed at the very notion of one day working in a prison, let alone running one. He grew up in South Africa, rather than the States, after his mother became attracted to the new lifestyle she encountered in her husband's homeland. She was not a fan of apartheid but neither was she strongly opposed to it. What she did appreciate were the two live-in maids who practically mothered her baby boy; they fed him, changed his nappies and played with him. That was in between doing every bit of housework including gardening, cooking most of the household's meals – and serving sundowners.

Mandrick was a born adventurer and after leaving university in the mid-1970s he was determined to find more action than the prison service could offer. Before his military conscription papers arrived he volunteered to join the South African army, which was only the first step in his plans. As soon as he could he attended the selection course for the 4th Reconnaissance Commando, a Special Forces unit based in Langebaan, and was accepted after passing with distinction. The unit was set up to perform maritime operations, a subject that interested Mandrick, and after joining the R&D submersible wing he piloted one of the unit's first swimmer-delivery vehicles.

Military life was for the most part enjoyable but after three years it had failed to deliver the adventure that Mandrick had joined up for. As luck would have it, as he was waiting in the HQ building to talk to his sergeant major about quitting the armed forces one of the clerks told him that his unit had just been placed on standby to go to Angola. They were to join in the fight against the South-West Africa People's Organisation (SWAPO), a black guerrilla group fighting for Namibia to separate from South Africa. It was going to be a real war, a deadly guerrilla campaign and more of an adventure than Mandrick had ever hoped to experience. He was overjoyed. To make matters even more exciting, his introduction to the conflict was from the air when his section parachuted deep into enemy territory.

By this time Mandrick was a sergeant in charge of

his own troop. Having shown his talents early on in the campaign, he was given a lead role in the raid to destroy the SWAPO headquarters in the heart of one of the most hostile jungles on earth. The opening battle for the HQ was the most brutal he had experienced and it would only get worse. In the latter stages, when his section found itself cut off from the rest of the unit, it came down to hand-to-hand fighting where empty guns gave way to knives and machetes that then gave way to clubs, fists and boots. By the end of it the black greasepaint he had used to disguise himself as a SWAPO guerrilla in order to get close to the compound had been washed away by blood − fortunately only a little of it was his own.

A few months after the war, while attempting to drink a litre of Scotch alone in his barrack room, Mandrick tried to recall how many men he had actually killed in Angola. But his mind was immediately swamped with images of machetes slicing into limbs, boots stomping on throats, fingers gouging eyes: scenes of carnage that assaulted him until he screamed for them to go away. He woke up a day later, lying in his own urine and vomit. The memories were still vivid and it took many years before they eventually grew foggy and their accuracy became uncertain.

In the mid-1990s he quit the military after turning down a full commission and went to America to visit his mother who had by now divorced his father. The trip was intended as a sabbatical that would last long enough for Mandrick to get his head together and figure out a plan for the future. But the weeks turned into months and he still hadn't discovered a firm direction. To help pay the bills he took employment in a local sports bar. He soon settled into a relaxed routine, although he was plagued by a permanent unease that prevented him from making any kind of long-term commitment to work or relationships. He blamed his disquiet on the political events taking place in his home country. Several options concerning his future that he had considered depended on him returning to South Africa but the growing revolt against apartheid and then the death of his father at the hands of a berserk prisoner influenced his decision to close that door and pursue a life in the USA.

Taking advantage of his mother's nationality Mandrick applied for American citizenship and the year it was granted, in the absence of anything more inspirational, and perhaps still motivated by a latent need for action, he decided to join the New York Police Department. He was not unduly surprised when he was turned down; he assumed it had a lot to do with his politically incorrect South African military background. But several weeks later something extraordinary happened that he later suspected was a result of his application – he had shown up on someone's radar. It was a mysterious meeting that would turn his entire life upside down.

Late one evening, as Mandrick left the bar where he worked, he was approached by a man who introduced himself as an employee of the United States government. The man knew everything about Mandrick's past from the day he'd been born: his parents, his military

137

background (including citations for bravery) and the operations he'd taken part in while serving with the South African Special Forces. Mandrick was invited to a meeting a week later which curiosity more than anything else urged him to attend. It took place in an innocuous sterile room in a downtown office block and was, to all intents and purposes, an interview conducted by three suited men who were also 'United States government employees'. He was asked to keep the meeting secret although he was not told what kind of job the interview concerned and was denied any information that would provide a clue about the government department to which the men belonged. It seemed pretty obvious though that they were connected to the intelligence community.

A week later the mysterious man appeared again. This time he extended to Mandrick an invitation to take part in a personal evaluation. Mandrick was again left without a clue as to what it was all about but neither could he resist continuing with the mystery tour. A few days later, as promised, he received expenses money and travel details for a flight to a small airport in Virginia. On arrival he was met by a man who gave him a password that he had been briefed to expect and he was then driven without further conversation to Camp Peary near Williamsburg, otherwise known as 'The Farm'. It was his first solid clue that these mysterious men were employees of the Central Intelligence Agency.

After signing several confidential contracts and undergoing a fitness and medical examination Mandrick embarked on a week of private schooling. He was the only student in the class. Lessons included the part US embassies played in intelligence processing, agent contact and human-pipeline procedures, field-finance accounting, a basic medical course, clandestine photography and how to operate a sophisticated coded communications system that separated into several innocuous components that fitted into a shaving bag. On the last day he attended a briefing about his potential duties and where he was asked if he would like to go back to Africa and work as an intelligence gatherer and processor for his 'new' country.

Mandrick had then become an operative for the Central Intelligence Agency, although he was no ordinary NOC (non-official cover). Older than most new recruits, he had not gone through the usual agent-induction system at The Farm. His level of knowledge of Africa and his military jungle skills could not be learned in any school and his composure in life-threatening situations was, rightly, taken as proven.

He was given a month to set his regular life in order and prepare a cover story for his mother and a handful of friends. His explanation for moving abroad was that he needed a change and had taken a position in an American travel agency that was opening offices all over Africa. On arrival in Nairobi he was given time to acclimatise and to familiarise himself with procedures under the supervision of the US embassy's operations officer.

Two weeks later he was sent out into the region with the false identity of a road-construction engineer for an American contractor. His main theatre of operations was Uganda, Kenya and the Congo and his main task was to monitor the subversive activities of groups like the Allied Domestic Front and the Lord's Resistance Army. It was not as exciting as Mandrick had hoped but he embraced the role with enthusiasm and within a couple of years he had set up a comprehensive network of couriers and informants.

While carrying out one of his tasks, the processing and collating of information, Mandrick detected the presence of a home-grown, powerful, dark and disturbing influence that was acquiring an operational foothold in the area. But his efforts to get his superiors to take his findings seriously were doomed to frustration. The faction was at the time a relatively unknown group of Arab Islamic militants and only when the US embassies in Dar es Salaam in Tanzania and Nairobi in Kenya were blown up by them, killing more than two hundred and twenty people and wounding over four thousand, were his warnings vindicated. By then it was too late. To add to Mandrick's misfortune he himself was caught up in the Nairobi bombing, barely escaping with his life.

Mandrick was repatriated to the USA to recover from his minor wounds. After sitting at home for a month while waiting to be retasked he was informed, without explanation, that his services were no longer required.

A month later he received what at first appeared to be a severance package that would keep him comfortable for a year or so. But the messenger's parting comment suggested that Mandrick had not necessarily been dumped and was being held in reserve. It was a vague communication but enough to ease the feeling of rejection. Mandrick waited for the call that he hoped would come soon.

A year passed without a word and then one day, as if the serious inroads into his severance package had been monitored, he received a formal letter on headed notepaper from a company called the Felix Corporation. It invited him to attend a meeting at their headquarters in Houston. The way the message was worded, in a minimalist and coldly cordial manner, Mandrick assumed it was an NOC task. Without hesitation he packed an overnight bag and headed for the airport.

Mandrick expected to meet yet another party of anonymous faces in a sterile, nameless office that had been rented especially for the occasion. He was surprised to discover that the Felix Corporation was in fact a genuine company, and an affluent one at that. After being taken to a five-star hotel to freshen up he was escorted to the executive offices of the CEO where, among other senior members of the corporation, he was introduced to Congressman Forbes. The meeting began with lunch and the rest of the day was taken up with detailed briefings that included models and computer-generated images of a proposed undersea prison. The mine was not discussed in any great detail and was presented more as a remedial employment scheme providing, with luck, a nominal contribution to the running costs of the facility.

Throughout the day Mandrick wondered why he was there and figured that there would be a twist of some sort at any moment. At no time was he asked about his background or if indeed he had any level of experience in maritime technology or correction-facility management. Finally, back in the CEO's office, in a meeting where Congressman Forbes appeared to be the most influential force, Mandrick was asked if he would consider a position as assistant warden of Styx once it was built. Forbes outlined the basic remuneration package that included a house in Houston, a car, a generous expenses allowance and some handsome incentive bonuses.

Confused as he was, Mandrick was nonetheless nobody's fool. The whole business had the sniff of the Agency about it. How else had Felix Corp known so much about him – enough not to ask him any questions about his past life and achievements and yet to have such confidence in him? He had been recommended for the post by a covert authority highly placed enough for none of these men to question it and it was therefore wise to assume this influence implied a partnership of some kind. On the other hand, it was a legitimate appointment that he was being offered – or it appeared to be, at any rate.

A couple of weeks before the first batch of Afghan insurgents arrived the warden was suddenly relieved of his position. He was a highly experienced prison officer who had done an exceptional job in getting the facility up and running. Mandrick was handed the job as if that had been the plan all along. His role as assistant warden had been purely so that he could learn the ropes and take over as soon as the CIA's interests became a reality. Styx was not only a top-security prison far from prying and curious eyes. It was a CIA interrogation centre. And Mandrick was its guardian.

The most problematic feature of the prison was the apparently innocuous mine. It caused Mandrick more concern than the interrogation cells themselves. The prison itself was a going concern although its profits were not very big. But the mainstream revenue came from the US government and could therefore be accounted for. The mining department, however, had apparently 'discovered' a tidy vein of precious minerals and was turning over a considerable amount of money. The problem was that it was mostly undeclared revenue. This was the *quid pro quo* aspect of the deal. The minerals were a private bonus as long as the Agency got what it wanted. It was also their leverage. The arrangement was a minor one compared with the deals that the CIA made with major global drugs and arms dealers in the pursuit of international terrorists. Unlike the drug and weapons deals where thousands of lives were lost or ruined daily as a result, the mine gave a handful of American businessmen profits for their patriotism. Mandrick and the prison guards were also beneficiaries.

Before the rather desperate phone call from Congressman Forbes, in the great scheme of things it had all seemed justified. Mandrick had no problems sleeping at night. But the project had suddenly become considerably more sinister and dangerous. He was being asked to kill an FBI agent. Warning bells were sounding in his head.

Mandrick was in his own office seated behind his desk, a high-tech steel construction with a glass surface.

A window made of thick, toughened glass behind him offered a view of bright lights attempting to illuminate a grey darkness. A little shrimp-like creature scurried across the glass as a large fish cruised past in the background. The spacious dome-like room was supported by steel girders set at intervals against the walls, arching to a central point in the ceiling. Rows of cabinets were sunk into the rock walls between the girders on one side of the room and across from Mandrick's desk a bank of flat-screen monitors displayed multiple views of the prison. Some of the monitors showed split-screen vistas while others flipped viewpoints between different cameras at intervals.

Mandrick climbed out of his leather chair and walked over to a complex communications console as he pondered the congressman's unusual and disturbing request. But even as he considered what course to take he was reaching for the internal phone system to start doing his masters' bidding. To ignore them would be to turn his back on his own future – perhaps worse. If the powers that be were prepared to kill an FBI agent to protect their interests then Mandrick himself was of little consequence. But it was not fear that kept Mandrick in line. He was made of more complex and sterner stuff. Since his earliest days he had enjoyed being a part of a team and, even though the Agency was a cold and distant master, he did feel like a small yet important cog in a big and powerful machine – and a winning one at that. He did not know precisely why the FBI agent had to be stopped but he was expected to carry out the order without question. It was the first real opportunity he'd had recently to self-examine his moral fibre. Now that he found it was indeed corrupt, what he'd initially believed to be a spasm of guilt when he'd received the order turned out to be merely a pause for thought before he obeyed.

Mandrick picked up a phone, punched in a series of numbers and held the receiver to his ear. 'Get me the manifest for the next in-transfer,' he said, his accent a cross between New York and somewhere else that few could guess at. 'Who's the transport officer for that serial? . . . Anderson? . . . I want Gann on it . . . Yeah, and send him to my office . . . Yeah, right away.'

Mandrick replaced the phone, pushed his fingers through his short tan hair and walked over to a detailed model of the prison facility.

A buzzer sounded and Mandrick glanced at one of the monitors showing two angled images of a large man wearing a lime-green tailored uniform and standing outside a door. The man looked up into one of the camera lenses, his expression blank, his eyes cold.

Mandrick took a hand-held remote from his pocket and pushed one of several coloured buttons on it. The sound of escaping gas lasted a couple of seconds as a thick rubber seal around a steel oval-shaped door shrank and, after a heavy clunking sound, the door moved back into the room like a filing cabinet drawer before pivoting open.

Gann walked into the room, a big heavy-boned man of distant Scandinavian origins. He was almost a head taller than Mandrick and remained standing by the opening like a barely obedient hound, staring at his master with an arrogant indifference that those who did not know him might have mistaken for insolence.

Mandrick pushed a button on his remote and the door closed with another clunk and a further escape of air as the seal puffed back up to fill the space around it. 'You'll be picking up the next in-transfer,' Mandrick said without a trace of drama.

Gann waited for an explanation. He was not particularly interested but was curious nevertheless about why the schedule was being changed.

'Didn't we have a problem with one of the ferries a couple weeks ago?' Mandrick asked, suddenly remembering.

'Number four,' Gann said.

'What was the problem?'

'The number-three relief valve in the main cabin. The seal needs changing. It leaks.' Gann's accent was soft: many thought he was from Chicago or Philly but no one knew for sure.

'Why hasn't it been changed?'

'It has a scheduled service next week. I guess they're waiting till then.'

Mandrick looked at Gann, gauging him as he often did. The man was a gift from Felix Corp, a special assistant. A thug, in other words. He hadn't gone through the normal vetting procedures and his personnel file was clearly a fairy tale. Gann was supposedly a former US Marine sergeant, an ideal pedigree for the prison service in which he had to look after the most desperate individuals in the world. Mandrick knew soldiers and Gann did not even begin to fit the profile. What Gann did for the company required a pedigree far more ominous than any that the Marines could provide. When they'd first met at the corporate offices in Houston, the day Mandrick was promoted to warden, Gann had been introduced as his key security officer. Forbes went even further, seeming to boast of some secret information when he said to Mandrick, *sotto voce*, that Gann would take care of any 'delicate situations'.

At the time Mandrick could not accurately imagine what that might entail but he got a taste within the first few days Gann was on the job when an inmate was caught stealing gems from the mine. The prisoner, an armed robber and escape artist from Leavenworth penitentiary who was serving three life sentences, had a partner in the guard force who was smuggling the 'merchandise' ashore. The inmate suffered a paralysing injury when a piece of machinery fell on his back and in that same week the guard was involved in a fatal alcohol-related traffic accident. When Mandrick had mentioned that the inmate could have died Gann must have thought he'd said '*should* have' because his reply was that a dead man attracted attention whereas one who'd had an accident and was recovering from his injuries did not.

It was a wise theory. Only one inmate had died in Styx since it had opened, an impressive record which helped protect it from outside scrutiny. But it did have an unusually high rate of injuries, the level of whose seriousness was often concealed. But as Gann so accurately pointed out, as in a war, the 'merely' wounded were hardly taken into account, no matter how serious the damage they'd sustained.

Mandrick had never personally ordered Gann to do anything unsavoury, nothing beyond the bounds of what a normal prison guard looking after category one-plus prisoners might be expected to do. That was indication enough that the man received his orders from someone else. Mandrick had no problem with that. They were all steering in the same direction. And this particular request was going to require a team effort. It was not only serious but technically complicated. Gann could not achieve success without Mandrick's assistance.

The order was also proof that Forbes received his orders from someone. It wasn't easy to get a congressman to become a willing party to a murder – and of an FBI agent, at that. Forbes wasn't a tough guy. Mandrick personally found him weak and pathetic. He was typical of the type: born to wealth and influence, carried through school, did his time in the army in an administrative role, thus avoiding Vietnam, and was handed his political career on a plate. Someone must have dangled him by his testicles over a pool of sharks to get him to do this.

'We have a problem,' Mandrick said in his usual calm, controlled manner. 'One of the prisoners on the next intake cannot be allowed to enter the prison.'

The printer on Mandrick's desk came to life and spat out a sheet of paper. Mandrick picked it out of the tray and glanced over it. 'Six prisoners . . . but we don't know which one is our unwanted guest.' Mandrick glanced up at Gann who was staring at him without a shred of emotion in his expression. 'Would the valve be enough, do you think?' Mandrick asked, knowing the answer but wanting Gann to get involved in the conversation.

'Everyone?' Gann asked, impressed. This was by far the biggest deal he had been presented with since taking on the job. Come to think of it, it was the biggest hit numbers-wise that he had ever been asked to carry out.

'It looks that way. We don't have the time to figure out who it is.'

Gann took a moment to absorb the request. 'I guess the valve would do it . . . with some added insurance.'

'Like what?'

'It would have to happen deep . . . close to the dock would be best but not too close. They'd have to be denied access to the escape suits, for one thing.'

Mandrick was satisfied that Gann was on the right track and would come up with a plan. He looked at the six names again, none of whom he had heard of before. Five would be collateral victims. Once again he was surprised at how easy it was for him to ignore the evil of the decision. Perhaps it was because they were all scum anyway. The list did not include their crimes – he would have to look at the files for that – but he didn't need to. No one got a ticket to Styx who wasn't a special-category prisoner. As for the FBI agent, the risk came with the job.

'We can't afford to screw this up,' Mandrick said, sounding like an officer even to himself. He did not particularly care what Gann thought about him. The man was an ape and needed to be reminded as often as possible of his place in the pecking order, even if his strings were usually pulled from somewhere way above Mandrick's own position. 'What about the other guard?' Mandrick asked. A minimum of two guards was required to ferry an intake of prisoners from the surface. Escape was considered impossible but this minimum was a procedural requirement in case there was a medical incident – like a guard becoming incapacitated due to a bad compression or something similar.

The prison's seventy-five guards were divided into three shifts. When the dark side of the system was designed it had been regarded as dangerous if not impossible to try and recruit only corrupt employees. However, applying principles learned from the infiltration of entire police forces by organised-crime syndicates, the compromising of key positions of responsibility could be coordinated. Once the necessary personnel were in place it was easy to recruit and then manipulate the lower ranks by using the basic motivating principle of greed.

The thinnest of smiles came to Gann's lips. 'Use Palanski.'

'Palanski?' Mandrick was unaware of any significant connection between Palanski and Gann. 'Why him?'

'He's a leak,' Gann said. 'He's been talking to a journalist. They've met a coupla times already. We've been wondering what to do with him.'

We? This was another reminder that Gann had sources and controllers that bypassed Mandrick's own authority. It had CIA written all over it. Mandrick showed no hint of surprise or disapproval. Palanski was a fool for going outside the corporation and deserved whatever he got anyway.

'They won't survive,' Gann said reassuringly, as if Mandrick needed convincing.

'That will be unfortunate,' Mandrick said, checking a screen on his computer monitor. 'Ferry four is officially operable.'

Gann knew nothing about Mandrick beyond his role in the prison. He suspected that the man might be weak. Treating him as a boss was an act. Mandrick was the warden but Gann did indeed answer directly to others and looked upon his official prison duties simply as a cover for his real purpose. Mandrick's cold willingness to be complicit in the deaths of so many people did, however, impress Gann. Mandrick obviously had to have some kind of background that qualified him for the position. But what Gann didn't know he didn't particularly care about as long as it did not directly affect him. 'It must be important,' Gann said, wondering if Mandrick knew more about what lay behind the plot.

Mandrick would not tell Gann the precise nature of the problem, that the victim was an FBI agent – it might even have negative implications if he did. This sabotage was a serious act of desperation and had 'endgame' stamped clearly right through it. The writing was on the wall.

Mandrick didn't want anyone prematurely jumping ship, not before him. If the feds were snooping around it was a warning that the party was coming to a close. The death of one of their agents might only accelerate it. But perhaps the end could be delayed, which was clearly what the Agency was hoping for. It suited

Mandrick too. The mine was still generating cash while the CIA was extracting information from Taliban and al-Qaeda insurgents. All affected parties wanted it to go on for as long as possible.

Mandrick made a mental note to start putting together his escape plans in greater detail. 'We can afford to have at least one serious mishap, I suppose,' he said as he touched a button on his desk and another gush of air announced the opening of the door.

Gann smirked, wondering if Mandrick knew anything at all. He walked out of the room.

The door closed behind him with a clunk and yet another hiss of air and Mandrick looked once more at the names of the men who were going to die. He dropped the paper onto his desk, walked over to an antique bureau, opened it up and took out a bottle of fine Scotch. He poured himself a small glass and took a sip.

Chapter 8

The prison truck slowed to a crawl in order to negotiate a fat speed-bump, its chains and metal innards
rattling as it lurched over it. Out of the corner of his
eye Stratton watched the guard pull himself to his feet.

Jerry had scrutinised Stratton when he'd eventually
climbed back inside the van after the police had arrived
at the scene of the escape on the highway. The guard's
expression conveyed his irritation with the prisoner for
not being of any help to the investigators.

While a medic had cleaned Stratton's wounds and
inspected his body for anything more serious a police
officer had questioned him. For the most part Stratton
just shook his head and mumbled how he had seen
nothing. They eventually left him alone, unsure if he
was telling the truth or simply protecting a fellow con.
Stratton felt confident that neither of the guards was
suspicious about his identity. They were preoccupied by
their own problems and were also still suffering some
minor after-effects of the strobe.

Before the police had arrived the guards had huddled
outside the truck, trying to clarify the events leading
up to the escape. They were worried about their

descriptions of the strange hypnotic device and wondered if they would be taken seriously. Harry described a multi-coloured flashing light while Chuck remembered the man in the bushes pointing something at them that was not a gun. Jerry could only remember feeling nauseous, followed by an intense paranoid feeling that he was going to die. It all sounded too much like science fiction.

The first thing the police did on hearing the story was to breathalyse all three of them and then take samples of their blood for testing. The cops eventually provided an escort for the rest of the journey while the investigation continued.

Stratton was pleased with how it had gone. He had successfully passed through the phase that many in the planning department had considered the greatest gamble – mainly because it had been left entirely up to the Americans who had failed to send through a photograph of Nathan Charon to confirm the degree of likeness between him and Stratton. Handing control of such an important segment of the operation over to any other outfit had always been going to be difficult but the Yanks had, Stratton reckoned, just about come through, with a little help from Todd's fists. So far, so good. The rest of the journey into the prison would be relatively straightforward.

The vehicle continued slowly around a tight corner before it came to a stop. The guard walked to the rear doors and waited beside Stratton. The outside latch was pulled aside with a heavy clunk and fluorescent light spilled into the cabin as the doors creaked open.

Jerry climbed out of the back and exchanged

greetings with several men. Another guard climbed in and unshackled Stratton from his wrist and ankle chains. 'Let's go,' he said and Stratton got to his feet. 'Prisoner coming out!' he shouted and Stratton was helped down.

'Stand still,' Stratton was ordered as his feet touched the concrete floor surface inside a large hangar. A robust wire-mesh belt was fastened around his waist and his hand shackles were secured to it, in front of his stomach.

Chuck appeared from the front cab, holding out a box file. 'Here's his files,' he said to the handover guard who took the metal box.

'Hey, you managed to bring half of 'em home,' the handover guard said sarcastically, much to the amusement of the others. 'Walk on,' he said to Stratton as another guard joined them.

Several more prison wagons were parked around the hangar, with clusters of guards standing around them, chatting and smoking. Stratton walked up a short flight of metal stairs onto a concrete platform and stopped in front of a heavy-duty steel door. The handover guard pressed a button on the wall by the door, a buzzer sounded inside and he looked up at a video camera. 'Come on, wake up,' he mumbled impatiently. Seconds later there was an electrical buzz followed by a clunk.

The guard pulled the steel door open and Stratton was led into a white room where a female officer seated inside a steel cubicle watched them from behind a thick glass window. The guard bringing up the rear closed the door behind them and a red light above another steel door on the other side of the room turned green. 'Walk on,' the female officer said over a loudspeaker.

The two guards moved Stratton towards the door, one of them in front, the other behind. The handover guard pushed open the steel door and they entered a sterile concrete corridor with a high ceiling. Halfway along they turned and entered a room with yet another heavy steel door already open.

Stratton was led to a metal bench that was bolted to the wall. When he sat down a chain attached to the bench was threaded through rings on his mesh belt and fastened with a lock. The handover guard left the room while the other stayed by the door, one hand on his holstered baton alongside a Mace dispenser, a zapper and a radio.

'You're gettin' booked in,' the remaining guard said in a Southern drawl. 'Gonna be a while. You need the can?'

Stratton shook his head.

'That's just fine,' the guard said, taking a toothpick from his pocket to service his tobacco-stained teeth.

Stratton remained in silence for almost an hour before the handover guard returned to release him from his seat and lead him out of the room. The trio continued to the end of the corridor, their footsteps echoing, and through another door. They had to wait until the entry door had locked magnetically before the exit door was unlocked by an officer inside a bulletproof cubicle.

Stratton was ushered into another room where four male prisoners wearing the same uniform as him were chained to a long metal bench. Stratton was placed at the end of the row where he was secured beside a surly unshaven individual who ignored him.

An older guard walked in, carrying a clipboard. Judging by his demeanour he was the senior officer.

He stopped in the centre of the room, planted his feet wide and addressed the group. 'Listen up,' he said in a gravelly voice. A couple of the prisoners sat up but the rest ignored him. 'You've arrived at Styx transfer point. Shortly you'll be moved to the dock where you'll board a boat that'll take you to the ferry platform. From there you'll commence the final leg of your journey. Did anyone have a problem understanding what I just said?'

A dirty-brown-skinned Latino inmate with a straggly goatee glanced up at the senior guard, a quizzical expression on his face.

'*Comprende*, Ramos?' the senior guard asked him.

Ramos shrugged to convey his ignorance, a malicious smirk on his face.

'Give Ramos the Spanish card,' the senior guard said.

One of his colleagues responded by walking over to Ramos and holding a plastic card in front of him. It had the requisite information written on it in Spanish.

'I take it you *can* read?' the senior guard muttered.

Ramos glanced over the card, shrugged again and muttered something that amused only himself. The guard returned to his position.

The senior guard walked to a steel door at the end of the room, reached for a small hatch at face level and opened it. He pulled a two-way radio to his mouth as he looked through the opening. 'Transfer room to dock . . . Transfer room to dock.'

'Dock reading you loud and clear,' a voice crackled over the radio.

'This is Perkins, senior watch. Those guys from Styx ready for transfer of five packages to the dock?'

'That's an affirmative. Officer coming up now.'

A look of irritation passed across the senior guard's face as he closed the hatch and turned to look at the prisoners. There was a deafening silence, one that Ramos chose to break with an extended fart.

'You fuckin' stink, Ramos,' said a large, muscular, tattooed neo-Nazi beside him.

'Shut it,' the senior guard said before Ramos could respond. 'You're still mine until you get on that boat and I ain't too pleasant if you get me riled.'

The other guards remained watching silently, their cold expressions reflecting their boss's threat.

A minute later a clunk signalled that the outer door had been unlocked. The senior guard checked through the hatch once more before unlocking the door on his side.

It opened to reveal a Styx prison guard in his tailored one-piece lime-green uniform. 'Hi,' the Styx guard said, a broad smile on his face that was destined to irritate anyone who saw it.

The senior guard retained his grim look as he checked his clipboard. 'You Gann or Palanski?'

'I'm Palanski.'

The senior guard handed Palanski a sheet of paper from the clipboard. 'You taking any of your stores down with you this trip? They're piling up all over my goddamned hangar.'

'Sorry. Not this time. I hear they're gonna be runnin' ferries all day tomorrow, shippin' stores.'

'They better be.'

Palanski smiled again as he finished reading the paper,

took a pen from his breast pocket and signed the bottom of it.

'No matter how often I see that uniform I can't help thinking how cute it is,' the senior guard said mockingly.

His fellow guards grinned. There was a distinct one-sided animosity between the regular land-based prison guards and their Styx equivalents. The land guards resented the sizeable disparity between their perks and remunerations and those of the Styx custodians. The rumour was that with bonuses and special allowances the undersea guards got twice the annual pay of the land ones. It was also well known that, apart from the negative aspects of living under pressure at the bottom of the sea, the Styx amenities such as food and leisure facilities were of a far higher standard.

'It is kinda nice, ain't it?' Palanski replied, not remotely insulted. Indeed, the Styx guards were quite used to being needled by their surface colleagues. 'Designed by Ralph Lauren, tailored to the individual, breathable fabric for added comfort. Oh, and a real large wallet pocket inside the jacket . . . for extra-large wallets.' A wink finished off the rejoinder.

The senior guard's smirk turned into a scowl. 'Let's do it,' he said and stepped outside as one of his men took over his position and closed the door.

Stratton looked down the line of prisoners, a variety of disagreeable-looking individuals. The man beside him finally glanced at him but when Stratton met his gaze he looked away.

A few minutes later the door opened and the senior

guard stepped back into the room while Palanski waited outside. The prisoner closest to the door was unshackled. 'On your feet,' the senior guard said. The prisoner was escorted out of the room and the door was secured once again.

Several minutes later the guards returned to collect the next prisoner and the process was repeated. Ten minutes later Stratton was the last remaining prisoner and the guards returned to unshackle him. 'On your feet.'

As Stratton stepped through the door and walked through a narrow low-ceilinged hangar he could smell the distinctive odour of ripe sea kelp and hear the distant cavernous echo of lapping water. A curtain of mildew-stained overlapping strips of opaque plastic hung from the ceiling across the width of the hangar. The escorting guard pushed through, holding it open for Stratton. The hangar continued for a short distance, the concrete floor meeting a flight of metal steps that led down onto a landing made of heavy steel girders. As Stratton walked along it he could see black lapping water through the chequered metal pattern of the flooring.

Up ahead, moored alongside one of several landing fingers, was a low, slender fibreglass passenger craft, its cabin and cockpit enclosed. Gann stood on the open aft deck, eyeing him coldly.

Stratton was led up a short gangway and onto the deck. Gann took hold of him brusquely and shoved him towards the opening into the cabin. Stratton ducked inside to find the other four prisoners already shackled to a long metal bench. Palanski was standing at the far end of the cabin, his back to a couple of pilots inside the sealed cockpit. Gann followed Stratton inside and after chaining him into his seat he went back outside to complete the exchange formalities with the senior guard. When he returned he shut the door behind him, leaving two guards outside on the aft deck pulling on life jackets.

Gann unhooked a handset from the wall and held it to his mouth. 'Clear to depart,' he said before returning the handset to its clip. His words were echoed over a speaker by the pilot and the engine revved loudly. A large door at the end of the hangar opened, pulled up into the ceiling, and the boat puttered through it.

'Should for any reason the boat develop problems and begin to sink a device at the end of the row might be activated that will release your chains,' Gann said. 'You notice I said "might".' He grinned. 'The mood I'm in right now it ain't gonna happen so do something to cheer me up . . . Under your seats you'll find life jackets. I'm supposed to show you how to put them on like I was an air hostess but you'll figure 'em out for yourselves if you need to. Anyone don't understand what I'm saying, then tough shit,' he said, looking at Ramos whose sudden smirk implied that he understood well enough. Gann smiled back for just a second.

The sun spilled in through the windows as the boat moved out of the hangar and the grey ocean took up the forward panorama. A prisoner said something to the one beside him and Gann walked down the narrow aisle and stopped in front of the offending talker. 'I'm gonna say this just once, fuckwit. No one talks on this

161

boat except me . . . and Mr Palanski. You belong to me now. This ain't like the cushy little numbers you just left,' he said, addressing all of them. 'You have any complaints, you talk to me. Any problems, you talk to me. Just one word of advice, though. I don't like people talking to me. Got that?'

'Whatever you say, boss man,' the prisoner replied, sarcasm clear in his tone.

Gann slammed him brutally across the face with the back of his hand and leaned in even closer as if he wanted to bite the prisoner's face off. 'I said no talking – and no fucking attitude, neither. Now. You got any complaints?'

The man licked his split lip, tasting the blood as he looked at Gann with death in his eyes. But, wisely, he choked back his response.

'Learn fast. It'll keep you healthy in Styx. It's unhealthy enough down there as it is.'

The boat rocked in the swell but Gann did not grab hold of anything to steady himself, spreading his large powerful legs to maintain his balance.

Stratton could not see very much of the ocean outside from where he was sitting but he knew the ferry platform was only a couple of miles away. Gann brushed past him to take up his position by the rear door, his hand on his utility belt beside his baton and zapper, his other hand on his Mace dispenser, his stare fixed on the prisoners as if hoping one of them might give him an excuse to launch himself at them.

The ferry platform eventually loomed into sight as the vessel manoeuvred to enter a docking bay. It was an impressive construction, like the top section of an oil platform. The most prominent feature was a towering derrick with a dozen heavy cables passing over large wheels at the top before they stretched down at an angle into the roof of a building on the edge of the platform.

The cabin cruiser slipped snugly into its tailored dock and gently hit the bumpers at the end. Several platform guards, all wearing life vests over brilliant yellow jackets, secured the vessel into place, its gunwales level with the landing deck.

Gann opened the rear door and faced his passengers. 'I'm gonna unlock your chains and we're all gonna walk together in a line across the platform to the ferry housing. For those of you who think it might be risky on our part to have all prisoners walkin' at once even though you still got your hand chains, that's because there's nowhere to go from this platform – nowhere but down, that is. And you can either do that in the comfort of the ferry where you can breathe, or you can jump or get shoved off the side. Either way you're going to the bottom . . . I know you'll be surprised to hear I don't give a rat's ass which you choose. Anyone screws around I'll personally toss 'em over the side.'

Gann undid a latch at the end of the bench, took hold of a lever and pulled it up with some effort. Every prisoner's hand shackles were released from the bench between their legs although their hands remained chained together at the wrists. 'Stand up,' he called out and the prisoners got to their feet with a clatter of metal. 'Turn towards me.'

Stratton faced Gann's broad chest an arm's length away.

'Forward march,' Gann said as he stepped back through the door. 'Move it.'

Stratton walked outside and onto the short gangway.

'Keep going,' Gann said. 'Follow the guard.'

Stratton stepped off the gangway onto the wooden deck of the jetty, walked across it and up another steep gangway with a hinge at the top that allowed it to rise and fall with the ocean swell. He stepped onto the main platform, the sea visible through a steel-mesh floor, and followed the guard at an easy pace that allowed the others to catch up. The prisoners' ankle and wrist chains clinked behind him as they walked along a covered ramp that led to another platform connected by massive chains that allowed it to move independently of the docking section.

They approached the entrances to two hangars joined together, each with several thick wire cables coming down at steep angles from the derrick wheels and passing through openings in the roofs. A sign above the entrance to the left-hand hangar read *FERRY 1 & 2*, and above the right hangar *FERRY 3 & 4*. Stratton was directed towards an archway into the right-hand hangar.

Inside, the hangar was fully enclosed, the mesh floor limited to a central pathway with open water either side. A squat craft that looked like some kind of submarine occupied the right bay, while the left bay was empty. Thick, greasy cables entered through the hangar roof, one set dropping into the left bay and disappearing beneath the water, the other set crossing over the top of the squat vessel and through a complex series of wheels on a heavy framework rather like that of a cable car. As Stratton looked at the steel vessel, which was painted white with the number four stencilled in black on the top and sides, the blueprints he had studied in detail came to life in his head. There were four ferries in total, the conveyance method much the same as a classic cable system with a car at either end, both moving at the same time to counterbalance the driving mechanism and passing each other at the halfway point.

The ferries were identical, each with a safe operating capacity of fourteen persons. They were divided into two compartments: a larger main passenger cabin and a smaller section designed for emergency escape. Both compartments had escape hatches but only the emergency compartment had an airlock-tube system that allowed one person at a time to escape without flooding the entire compartment. The escape hatch in the passenger cabin was a standard maritime docking system that a rescue submarine could attach itself to prior to opening.

Massive weights were fixed to the base of the ferry to keep it in the correct attitude as well as to provide negative buoyancy. Along its sides were neat rows of high-pressure gas bottles that provided fourteen passengers with breathable air for up to twenty-four hours at a hundred and fifty feet of pressure.

'Stop there,' a guard called out and Stratton came to a halt halfway along the length of the ferry. The other prisoners shuffled to a stop behind him.

'Turn and face the ferry,' Gann called out as he walked down the line, his voice echoing.

The men obeyed, all looking at the vessel, in particular at the single open door that led into the main passenger compartment.

'You are about to take the last stage of your journey to Styx max-security pen,' Gann said. 'This may look like a submarine but it ain't. There are no pilots or crew. It's an underwater cable car controlled from the prison – unless somethin' goes wrong, then it can be controlled from here. There's a toilet on board but it ain't workin' at the moment so if you wanna go, say so now or do it in your pants 'cause once you're in your seat you don't get out of it until we reach the prison. We won't be serving any snacks or drinks, either. The journey'll take about twenty-five minutes. I ain't gonna go into the technicalities but it's as safe as takin' a bus ride. There's only gonna be me and Mr Palanski on board with you so behave yourselves. For safety reasons, if anyone should get outta line we have the legal right to use whatever we have at our disposal as a restraint to prevent putting other lives at risk. I love that legal right. I've got an iron bar inside and my idea of restraint is a crushed skull. So don't piss me off.'

Gann nodded to Palanski who stepped inside the vessel, remaining by the door.

'We're gonna go in one at a time, just like before, and you'll be secured to your seat,' Gann continued. 'Lead off,' he said to Stratton, who stepped towards the vessel's entrance. The man beside him began to follow and was grabbed harshly by Gann around the throat and held before his leading foot had touched the ground. 'One at a time, I said.'

166

The man choked, unable to grab Gann's hands because his own were secured to his waist-belt. Gann gazed into the man's reddening eyes before pushing him back into line.

Stratton was led by Palanski to the end of a back-to-back double row of metal seats fixed to the floor along the centre of the cabin.

'Sit down,' Palanski said. Stratton obeyed. The woven steel seat was cold. His hand chains were removed from his waist-belt and placed over a hook poking up through the metal seat. Palanski pushed the hook down into a slot in the seat until it clicked into place. 'That's a release mechanism,' he said. 'We can release you if there's a problem. But don't worry, there won't be.'

Palanski talked without any threat or cruelty in his tone, the good cop to Gann's monster. Stratton watched him walk back to the door to receive the next prisoner. It was the same dark surly-looking individual that Stratton had sat beside since joining the group and he watched as the securing procedure was repeated. When Palanski walked away the prisoner gave the hook a firm tug. It was immovable. He glanced at Stratton and they held each other's gaze for a few seconds. Stratton was surprised to see no real malice in his eyes, nor any sign of the cold macho aggression that the others naturally exuded. They were intelligent and without the torment that an incarcerated convict of his level usually possessed. Stratton wondered what his crime was. It was obviously a serious one to have got him a trip to Styx.

Stratton went back to studying the vessel, as much of it as he could see from his seat without stretching around too much. It was interesting to identify various components from the blueprints and those added since. The docking hatch was the same, almost directly above him with its interesting dual lock-and-hinge system designed to open either inwards or outwards. The interior of a regular submarine remained pretty much at surface pressure no matter how deep it descended, which meant the forces against the outer skin were always greater than those inside. The Styx ferries, however, were designed so that the internal pressure increased as it descended, constantly equalising with the outside pressure. For the return phase the pressure remained at the prison depth to allow slow decompression even as the ferry ascended. The ferry was therefore built to prevent it blowing open as opposed to the conventional imploding. Decompression could be carried out inside the ferry or, once on the surface, the vessel could be connected to a habitat chamber and the passengers transferred into it to decompress in more comfort.

The prison was kept at the same pressure as its depth which was an average of a hundred and fifty feet. There were a number of reasons for this, both security and structurally related. If the forces inside the structure equalled those outside (or were just fractionally lower, to be more accurate) there would be less chance of structural failure and fewer leaks. As for the security aspect, an escaping prisoner would have to decompress for hours or risk dying of the bends.

Stratton studied the door to the emergency escape room, hoping he might get a chance to look inside at some stage. From this point on he would have to constantly evaluate possible ways to escape from the prison despite the fact that it was not essential to the plan. His orders were to attempt it only once he had disposed of the tablet and ensured that there was no risk to himself or to others. He reflected on how stupid the 'no risk' part of those orders was. He was in the extreme-risk business. An escape would only give closure to the counterfeit aspect of the plan which was the 'independent evaluation' of the escape potential of the prison. It would be nice if Stratton could manage it all but no one was expecting him to get even close to that. But as long as he destroyed the tablet first he could make an escape attempt if he so desired.

Stratton decided that he would have a go for the adventure of it. His other option, the one most popular with the mission's planners, was that once he had successfully destroyed the tablet he was to give himself up. By doing so he would technically have failed as far as the evaluation was concerned but his real mission would have been achieved. The truth was that Stratton himself did not really expect to succeed in escaping. To do so certainly appeared impossible after he'd studied the plans and experienced the system thus far. But he still fancied the opportunity if it should arise even though he was less inclined these days to take the kind of risks he used to have scant regard for. He'd come close to dying too many times and the incidents were more than just vague memories. The emotions he had experienced during the worst of them were deeply etched into his psyche. It was as if he were two people: one eager to volunteer for any operation, the other warning of the consequences. He could have done with a little less of both.

A heavy clang yanked Stratton out of his thoughts and at the same time he felt the pressure change in his ears. He looked at the entrance to see Gann spinning the central wheel on the closed watertight doors. The action pushed out a dozen clips around the seal, squeezing it shut.

'You're soon gonna feel the pressure build in your ears,' Gann said. 'Sorry you can't use your hands to help relieve it if it hurts. If you get any pain wiggle your jaw or try to yawn. If that don't work then just sit it out. Your eardrums'll burst but that's not a problem. There's nothin' in Styx worth hearing other than me and I'll always make sure you know what I'm sayin' . . . Some pearls o' wisdom for you before we set off. From here on in you're gonna be under pressure, and I don't mean just from me. You're gonna be under *sea* pressure. That means the only way you can get outta the prison is by decompressing, which takes hours. Give you an idea how it works. If you somehow got outta the prison and floated up you'd be big as a Buick by the time you reached the surface. Course, long before you got there you'd explode into a thousand pieces. So if you did escape no one would know about it. A little piece of advice to add to that: if you piss me off too much or you're caught stealin' from the mine – you'll get to learn about that – or you're just a pain-in-the-ass troublemaker I'll see to it that you *do* escape. This ain't like no other prison on Earth. There's nowhere to hide, no way to escape, no one to run to if you ain't happy. No visitors, no lawyers, no press.' He glanced at Palanski who thought he saw something in Gann's look. 'We do our own cleanin', our own cookin', our own laundry. We even do some of our own equipment servicin' if we find out any of you are geniuses. And then we've got the mine for you to play in. What's up, Ramos?'

Everyone glanced at Ramos who was looking agitated. 'I don't like small spaces,' he said, his lips quivering.

'Ain't you spent most of your rat life in a cell?' Gann asked.

'Not at the bottom of the fuckin' sea,' Ramos mumbled.

'Don't worry yourself about it,' Gann said, amused. 'You'll soon be in an even smaller, deeper space.' Gann took a handset off the wall and put it to his mouth. 'Control, this is ferry four, come in.'

A speaker crackled for a few seconds before a voice broke from it. 'Ferry four, control hears you. That you, Gann?'

'Yeah. We're ready to push from the platform. That's five packs plus two guards, total seven persons.'

'Copy, you're ready to push, seven up. Stand by, ferry four . . .'

'Oh, I almost forgot the emergency procedures,' Gann said as he hung the handset back onto its hook. 'If in the event of an incident, like a fire or the cables snap and we sink like a stone' – Gann glanced at Ramos and others who were beginning to look uncomfortable, enjoying their unease – 'your chains'll be disconnected from your seats by me or Mr Palanski.

Anyone panics or gets outta control I'll zap you or knock you out,' he said, pulling a zapper from his belt with one hand, a blackjack with the other and holding them up. 'Whichever, chances are you'll get left behind. I got no time for assholes. If we have to bale out you'll be directed to the emergency escape room through that door over there where your cuffs'll be removed and you'll put on escape suits and go to the surface one at a time.'

''Scuse me,' said the large neo-Nazi. 'Can I ask a question . . . please?'

'Since you asked so nicely,' Gann replied.

'I thought you said we'd be the size of a Buick if we go straight up to the surface.'

'That's only if we're down on the bottom of the ocean more'n a few hours. If that's the case we'll stay in here and wait to be rescued by a special sub.'

The prisoners looked at one another, mumbling their concerns and dissent.

'I said I'm the only one who talks,' Gann grumbled.

Everyone shut up, already conditioned to their guard's potential to cause suffering.

The vessel jerked heavily as the cables above began to move and there was a long creaking sound outside like the tearing of sheet metal. Ramos started to tremble violently, his breathing quickening. He pulled on his chain in the hope that it might disconnect from the hook in the seat. Gann walked down the row and stopped in front of him. 'I'm warnin' you, Ramos. You fuck aroun' and I'll zap yer.'

'I . . . I can't take this shit! Let me outta here!' Ramos

shouted. 'I told 'em I couldn't go down to that place but they wouldn't believe me.'

Gann gritted his teeth as he held the zapper in front of Ramos's face. 'I'm warnin' you, wetback. Settle down.'

Ramos ignored him as if his only obstacle to safety was the hook securing his chain to the seat.

Gann pressed the button on the device and a bright blue and white spark connected the tips of the chrome terminals an inch from Ramos's nose.

But Ramos could not be deterred, his claustrophobia more powerful than Gann's paltry threat. 'Lemme outta here! I gotta get outta here!' he screamed. 'LEMME OUT!'

'Prisoner's outta control,' Gann called out, as if formally declaring the way clear for his legal solution. Without further hesitation he rammed the terminals of the zapper into Ramos's throat where it clicked loudly in time with the high-voltage pulses. The two prisoners on either side of Ramos leaned away as he howled and shook violently. A short zap would have sufficed but not for Gann. He held the device firmly against Ramos's neck for an age. Palanski cringed as he watched. Some of the prisoners found it amusing.

Ramos had gone silent by the time Gann removed the zapper, his body shuddering, his head back, eyeballs rolled up, tongue hanging out, foamy saliva dribbling from the sides of his mouth.

Gann leaned over the Mexican to observe him like a crackpot indulging in an experiment. 'He's OK,' Gann declared, none too confidently. 'That's how they usually go.'

The vessel shunted again and this time there was a perceptible feeling of movement that gradually increased as the craft gracefully pulled out of its holding bay. As it left the guide tray it dropped, taking up the slack in the cables. Everyone experienced that lost-stomach feeling, to the point where several of the prisoners groaned.

Gann tapped Ramos on the side of his head, still unsure if he had done any serious damage – not that he cared much. He gave up and shrugged. 'You got the picture, guys,' he said, walking back along the row. 'No fuckin' around or you'll get the same.'

Stratton focused on a map board at the other end of the bench row. The ferry's position was indicated on an angled line marked at regular intervals like a metro map, except the lit beads were depth markers between the surface platform and the prison's arrivals dock. A bright green LED light indicating the surface platform extinguished and a blue one blinked on further down the line.

Gann stopped in front of a bank of valves and gauges that displayed the internal and external ferry pressures, air-storage volume, air quality, and the carbon dioxide, nitrogen and oxygen percentages of the air. He tapped a couple of the gauges, noting with satisfaction that the internal pressure was several pounds per square inch lower than outside. As he turned around to check on the prisoners his eyes drifted to the line of relief valves in the ceiling, three in total. A drop of water fell from one onto a prisoner's head, causing the man to look up curiously.

'Lemme know if that turns into a fire hose,' Gann said, with a wink.

The prisoner wasn't amused and looked up as another drip fell onto his face.

Gann walked to the front of the cabin to Palanski. 'Did you check the escape suits?'

Palanski was looking at Ramos who, although still in a daze, appeared to be recovering. He raised an eyebrow at the request. 'That's the senior man's job.'

'I only asked in case.'

'I can do it if you want.'

'Nah. I'll check 'em.'

Palanski moved aside. Like most of the prison guards, Gann intimidated him.

Gann unlocked the six dog hasps around the emergency escape-room door. Stratton watched as he tugged at the handle, unable to shift it. Both men looked up at a gauge on the wall above the door. 'Fuckin' room ain't equalised,' Gann mumbled as he turned a valve beside the gauge that allowed air into the escape room. Seconds later the door popped slightly towards him and he turned off the valve and pulled the door fully open.

He stepped inside and as he turned to close the door he caught Stratton staring at him. Stratton looked away and Gann watched him a little longer before closing the door. Stratton looked back to see a couple of the dog hasps turn to secure it.

Gann went to a rack containing more than a dozen bright yellow packs with ESCAPE SUIT written on them in large letters. He took one of the packs, pulled open the seal, removed the bright yellow suit and draped it over the side of the rack. He opened a red box on the wall. Inside were a couple of small air cylinders. He removed one, checked that the contents gauge was green and that the full-face mask was secured to the end of its high-pressure tube. He turned the bottle valve, put the mouthpiece in his mouth, took a quick guff to ensure that it was working and placed it on the shelf beside the escape suit.

He faced the emergency escape tube which was basically a large pipe welded vertically to the ceiling and big enough for a man to crawl up inside. The bottom end, covered with a hatch, was just below his waist. He checked a gauge to ensure that the pressure inside the tube was the same as the ferry's and squatted to take hold of the hatch wheel. He turned it a couple of times and the heavy hatch dropped open on its hinge and returned almost all the way back up on a pair of robust springs designed to counter its weight.

Gann got onto his knees, pushed the hatch fully open against its springs and poked his head up inside to take a look at the narrow space that was illuminated by an internal lamp. A hatch covered the other end of the six-foot-long tube, the brass wheel at its centre wet with condensation. A breathing umbilical was secured halfway up and he crawled sufficiently inside to reach up and press the spring valve inside the teat. An instant gush of air revealed that it was working and he inspected the small collection of valves and gauges that operated the flooding system. Satisfied that everything was in working order, Gann manoeuvred his large frame out of the awkward space and got to his feet.

He looked around to make sure there was nothing else he needed to prepare for his murderous plan and took a deep breath to steel himself. This was by far the biggest job he had ever taken on.

He walked back to the door and unclipped the two dog hasps. When he pulled open the door his gaze met Stratton's again.

Gann stepped through the door, left it open a little and crossed over to Stratton. 'You got somethin' you wanna say to me?'

Stratton looked down, playing the passive-submissive card.

'Then stop lookin' at me. You ain't my type.'

Gann brushed past him and Stratton watched as he stopped in front of the route-marker board where a blue light put the ferry a quarter of the way to the arrival dock.

Stratton sat back in his seat, beginning to wonder if this operation had any chance of success. It was always easier to see where the cracks were from the outside. On the other hand, the inside was where the reality was. He had no experience of penitentiaries and, frankly, the level of security so far was significant enough to suggest the job was going to have to rely much more on chance than the briefing had allowed for. There were things about the ferry that had not been reflected in the diagrams he had seen. They were small but significant enough. The control panel was in a different location for one thing, and there were three relief valves in the ceiling when he was sure there had only been one on the blueprints. Stratton's knowledge of the layout of the prison was based entirely on plans that had not been updated in several years.

Then there was the total lack of information about the everyday routine life of the prisoners as well as the guard system. Procedures could change overnight, anyway. There were also the various unquantifiable characters who ran the place – such as Gann. Asinine prison officers were only to be expected but Gann was more like some kind of classic medieval dungeon guard more comfortable running the torture chamber than looking after the everyday welfare of an inmate. He could screw up the operation all on his own.

'Hey, leave that open,' Gann called out.

Stratton looked over to see he was addressing Palanski who was about to lock the door to the emergency escape room.

'But it's supposed—' Palanski began but was cut off.

'I said leave it open.'

Palanski walked over to Gann at the console. 'We're supposed to keep it closed while we're in transit,' he said in a low voice, as if he didn't want the children to see their parents arguing.

Gann couldn't have cared less what the prisoners thought. 'And I want it open, OK,' he said, glaring at his colleague. And then, as if regretting his anger, he calmed down, mimicking Palanski's lowered voice. 'I wanna go back in there and check on somethin', OK? Between you and me I think one of the relief valves is sticky.'

Palanski looked up at the valve. 'This whole friggin' ferry needs a service if you ask me.'

'Go check on Ramos,' Gann said.

Palanski stepped back, glad that Gann had calmed down. He leaned over the Mexican whose eyes were heavily red-rimmed and looked as if he had taken a drug overdose. Palanski had no idea what he could do for the guy and so he made a meal out of checking him over.

Gann went back to the route indicator. The timing of the next phase was crucial. The ferry needed to be close to the prison dock but not too close. The dock was designed on a moon-pool concept. The ferry arrived from beneath, the cables rolling under a series of wheels before heading up inside at an angle. Once the ferry moved below the wheels it followed the cables and emerged as if from a pool inside an air-filled cavern. Gann's plan was to sabotage the ferry and leave the prisoners for dead before it arrived at the dock. But the prison maintained a rescue team on standby whenever a ferry was operating in case there was a serious incident.

Gann estimated he would soon have to commence the operation and as he checked his watch he experienced a touch of nerves such as he had not felt since his earliest days in the business of skulduggery. He glanced up at the leaking relief valve, a pivotal element to his plan, and then at the prisoners sitting in a row, wondering which of them was the reason they all had to die. It was obvious that things were not well with the prison but perhaps his mission would solve the problem. The man was not just a threat to the future of the facility but also to Gann's employment. This was a great gig for him, the best he'd had. It was more money than he had ever earned and he didn't want it to end.

It was typical of Gann that never once did he question if all the men had to die. It made perfect sense. He was used to following orders that would result in the injury or death of people whom he did not know. He was more interested in how he was going to succeed. Gann knew his place in the great scheme of things. He always did. He was not the kind of man who could set up a company or a criminal organisation by himself. But he made a good lieutenant. Working at Styx had given him levels of responsibility he had never before been entrusted with and tasks such as this made it all so much more satisfying. If there was anything he could do to safeguard his job he would.

Gann's introduction to inflicting violence on others as a means of gainful employment came at an early age, shortly after he'd left school in Toronto, the city of his birth. He became an 'enforcer', a glamorous title bestowed upon him by his first boss, a ruthless housing developer who specialised in turning low-class neighbourhoods into upper-middle-class luxury homes. Gann's job was to put pressure on owners who did not want to sell. This he managed in a number of occasionally imaginative and usually violent ways. Once the houses had been bought the tenants were evicted. Normally the sight of Gann stepping in through the door and telling them that they had to get out was enough. If not, creativity was called for.

The turning point in Gann's life came when a particularly tough tenant organised a group of friends to beat him up on the day he arrived to press his demand to vacate the premises. It was a serious case of misjudgement: several days later Gann followed the man to his place of work, approached him in an underground car park as he was getting out of his vehicle and beat him to death with an iron bar. At first Gann was worried, never having gone that far before. But instead of panicking he kept his nerve and rigged the murder to look like a mugging that had gone wrong.

A few months later Gann's boss was slain as the result of a private business disagreement and Gann was hired by a powerful loan shark in whose employ opportunities to improve his particular skills were plentiful. Gann's reputation grew and he became a freelancer on the books of several major collecting agencies, becoming involved in bounty hunting abroad in places like South and Central America. The next honing of his developing skills was his introduction to assassination, a trade he took to effortlessly with his first task: the strangling of an accountant who had embezzled money from a New York crime family.

Gann carried out a number of similar 'jobs' for the same people until one day things took a turn for the worse. He was picked up by the FBI just before a job and, convinced he was looking at several decades in jail, he agreed to turn state's evidence. As luck would have it, Gann managed to avoid imprisonment altogether due to shockingly poor management of the evidence against him. The feds, however, stuck with their witness-protection agreement and, armed with a new identity, Gann was free to start life over again.

Gann's big concern now, however, was how he was going make a living. The feds had been quite clear in their threats about what would happen if he went back to his old ways. But depression and desperation soon set in when he failed to find satisfactory employment and just as he was contemplating his first armed robbery he received a call from a man who knew not just his real identity but every detail about his past. This man had called to offer Gann a job utilising his particular type of skill but this time for a legitimate company. Gann was curious, to say the least, and agreed to take a meeting in Houston at the headquarters of an outfit called the Felix Corporation.

After a brief interview he was hired as a special-duties prison supervisor, a position that, although he had zero experience of such work, filled him with excitement at the thought of its possibilities. His responsibilities were left vague for the time being and he was placed on a handsome retainer for six months. During that time he attended courses on the duties of a corrections officer, followed by training in sub-sea environments. Gann arrived at the prison several months before the first inmate and spent his time familiarising himself with the jail's layout and procedures, its life-support systems and the ferry procedures. At the end of it he received his special-duties brief, which included giving every assistance to Mandrick, the new warden, as well as to the government agents who would be conducting prisoner 'questioning'.

Gann had matured greatly since his early days and, anxious to keep his position in a company that, in his

eyes, showed great potential for his personal enrich-
ment, he made sure he did precisely what he was ordered
to and did it as efficiently as possible. In the exclusive
world of murderous lackeys, Gann was at the top of his
game.

Therefore, when Gann was told it would be convenient if everyone in the ferry that day should die it was
as good as done. He could also expect a handsome
bonus at the end of the month.

Gann went to the communications set, surreptitiously
unplugged the handset and put it in his pocket. He
went to the control panel and pretended to study the
various gauges while taking hold of an adjustable wrench
attached to a chain fixed to the panel. The tool was
used for turning tight valves. A screwdriver was similarly attached and he used it to prise open one of the
wrench's chain links and disconnect it. He reached for
the interior main air valve and turned it until it was
fully closed. The needle of the interior pressure gauge
moved very slightly to indicate a drop in cabin pressure. With the screwdriver he undid the screw that
secured the interior valve handle, removed the handle
completely and, using the wrench, bent the valve stem
enough to ensure that it could not be turned by hand.
He placed the wrench in his pocket.

The gauge indicated that the pressure was dropping
slowly and Gann looked up at the leaking relief valve
in the ceiling to see the flow of the dripping water
increase. He could feel the sudden decrease in cabin
pressure in his ears and as the leak became a steady
stream the other two relief valves began to drip. The

prisoners beneath wondered what this sudden shower was all about.

Stratton also felt the drop in pressure and looked up as Gann walked past him towards the emergency escape-room door. The three relief valves popped and sea water burst into the cabin as if from fire hoses, soaking the prisoners who shouted and struggled in their seats.

Palanski was as confused as he was alarmed. 'Gann!' he shouted over the sound of gushing water as his colleague stepped through the doorway into the emergency compartment. 'What the hell's happening?!'

'Looks like we got a problem,' Gann shouted back.

Stratton sensed something odd about Gann's tone. He looked between the control panel, the rapidly flooding vessel and the empty doorway into the escape room. The relief valves were designed to allow any increase in internal air pressure over a specific setting to bleed out of the vessel and not allow any water into the cabin if the pressures reversed. But all three valves had failed – which suggested they had been tampered with.

The frothy grey sea water had already filled the shallow sump beneath the flooring grille and was lapping around Stratton's feet. He instinctively pulled on his chains – they were fixed solid – while his mind raced to search for a solution to a situation that was clearly catastrophic.

Palanski hurried to the control panel to check the gauges. 'The pressure's still dropping,' he shouted to no one in particular. He reached for the inlet valve, only to discover that the handle was gone. He searched frantically for it, on the panel and on the floor. Unable to find it he reached for the wrench, only to discover nothing on the end of the chain. In desperation he tried to turn the valve stem with his wet fingers but it was impossible.

Stratton watched Palanski give up on the valves and look around in despair.

'Break the pipe!' Stratton shouted.

Palanski focused on him, a confused expression on his face.

'Break the inlet pipe! The one the valve's attached to!' Stratton yelled above the hissing water. The extreme gravity of the situation was horrifyingly stark. Stratton might have little experience with prisons but he knew a hell of a lot about submersibles and the dangers of them flooding under pressure. The situation had 'extremely serious' written all over it.

Palanski realised the prisoner was making perfect sense. If he could puncture the inlet pipe between the valve and the exterior air bottles it would have the same effect as opening the valve. But there was something else Palanski realised he could do in the meantime and his eyes went to a large red button near the door. He reached up and punched it in. An alarm sounded.

He grabbed up the screwdriver and began to force it behind the high-pressure air pipe in order to prise it away from the wall.

Gann appeared in the escape-room doorway wearing the yellow one-piece emergency escape suit, the transparent hood hanging down his back. The suit made him appear twice as big as he was. He waded through the cabin, the water already to his knees, and brutally grabbed Palanski's arm to spin him around. Palanski looked at him wide-eyed, confused by the escape suit.

Gann did not give his colleague a second more to consider the implications and brutally slammed him across the face. But Palanski was no slouch when it came to fighting and, driven by the added desperation of the situation, he surprised Gann by bringing the screwdriver down hard towards the man's face. Gann would have been skewered had the chain attached to the screwdriver not reached its full length and abruptly halted the tool's progress in mid-air, an inch from his eye. Gann did not hesitate and punched Palanski in the gut with a mighty uppercut.

Palanski bent over double but recovered enough to lunge at Gann with a mid-body tackle. Both men bulled down the row of prisoners. Gann only barely managed to stay on his feet, his back slamming into the steel wall of the escape room with Palanski still bent down in front of him. Gann took hold of Palanski's arm, spun the man around and, positioning the limb across the open doorway, slammed the steel door on it, crushing the elbow joint. Palanski howled as he grabbed at his injury and Gann slipped the wrench from his inside pocket and brought it down onto the side of Palanski's head. Blood streamed across Palanski's face as he fell into the water.

Satisfied that Palanski was no longer a threat, Gann stepped through the emergency escape-room door, took a moment to look back and glare at the prisoners, and closed it behind him.

Stratton watched the dog hasps, waiting for them to turn to secure the door, but they did not and the door opened slightly though he could see nothing inside.

The water continued to flood in through the roof. Every man knew this was the end if they could not free themselves. They fought with their chains, their wrists bleeding as the shackles cut into the flesh. They shouted, growled, whimpered as they fought in desperation for a way out of the watery coffin that they were trapped inside.

In marked contrast, Stratton sat almost still as the ice-cold water lapped around his waist. He had been through every possible escape scenario in his mind but any one of them depended on first getting out of the seat chains. He looked down at the only possible chance of survival that was left – Palanski, sitting in the water, his chin just above it, teetering on the edge of consciousness. 'Palanski!' he shouted. But the guard did not respond.

The two duty controllers in the prison OCR (Operations Control Room) sprang to life with the triggering of the shrill ferry alarm, both of them flashing looks at a blinking red light on the master control board. Beneath it were four route-indicator maps, each similar to the one on the ferry: a small blue LED light was flashing on the far-right map indicating that the number four ferry was five hundred metres from the prison dock.

The senior controller reached for a button on the console and pushed it as he leaned towards a slender microphone protruding from it. 'Ferry four, this is Styx control room . . . Ferry four, this is Styx control room. Speak to me. Pick up the handset and speak to me!'

When no reply came the controllers looked at each other, unsure what to make of the lack of response. The operations-control technology was sophisticated when it came to the general running of the prison but there were few sensory or diagnostic transmissions from the ferries, apart from indications of the vessel's depth and its progress along the cables. Since the opening of the prison there had never been a problem with the ferries apart from some minor incidents and the OCR relied on the communications system and standard procedures to monitor the craft.

'Ferry four, this is Styx control,' the senior controller said again, frustrated that it was all he could do at that moment to contact the vessel. 'Do you copy?'

The only sound from the speakers was the gentle hiss of the carrier wave.

'Still moving towards us,' the assistant controller said, an observation that his boss could make for himself. 'Maybe it's an electrical glitch.'

'The alarm sounds and there's no one on the end of the radio?' the senior controller said. 'That's good enough for me something's gone seriously wrong. Alert the standby divers,' he ordered as he strode across the room and reached for a phone on the main console. 'Call the surface dock. Tell 'em to launch the rescue boats and to start looking for escape suits . . . Mr Mandrick,' he said into the phone. 'OCR duty officer. I think we have a situation . . . it could be a serious one.'

★

Gann had intentionally left the emergency escape-room door unbolted because the room needed to flood if his evidence during the inevitable subsequent investigation was going to be believed. It was that post-incident phase of the operation that had caused him his only misgivings about this task. If it was discovered that the ferry had been sabotaged then any investigation would become a murder inquiry. A motive would have to be found, which could lead to a scrutiny of the goings-on in the prison. If the feds learned that Gann was possibly involved his past would come flying out of the closet and he would never see the light of day again. Gann had a lot riding on the prison's future, hence the personal risk he was willing to take to save it. Everything would be fine as long as the incident looked like an accident.

As he zipped up his suit and positioned the hood on top of his head he pondered the risks to his own survival one more time. He looped the strap attached to the small diving bottle over one shoulder and faced the emergency escape tube. Water was streaming in through the gap in the open door to the main cabin and had reached the opening to the tube.

Gann got down onto his knees, felt for the hatch under the water and pushed it open against its counterweight springs. He took a breath, dipped below the surface, reached up into the tube and pulled himself inside. The tube was dry and he could breathe the air. He climbed up into the narrow space like a grub making its way back inside its cocoon, pulled his feet out of the water and stood on the inside rim of the hatch.

The tube was a tight fit for a man Gann's size and he had not forgotten how hard it had been to reach down and close the hatch during his training course. It had become easier once he'd developed a few techniques. He reached down with a foot and kicked the hatch away as hard as he could. When it sprang back up he caught the inside wheel with his foot and held the hatch shut while stretching one arm down. With an effort, he managed to get a couple of fingers to the wheel, his face pressing painfully against the tube's sides, and, aided by his foot, he turned the wheel several times to screw the locking cleats into place. When the wheel would turn no further Gann wiggled himself upright, his head an inch below the wheel of the top hatch and a small built-in light that shone in his face.

He looped the air-bottle harness over his head, making sure that he knew where the mouthpiece and mask were on the other end of the hose and, by the glow from the small light, he found the breathing tube that was plugged into the vessel's air supply. He placed the mouthpiece between his lips, took a couple of breaths to confirm it was working and turned the flood valve in front of him. Water immediately began to gush into the tube and bubble up over his legs.

'Palanski!' Stratton shouted. If the threat of drowning didn't wake the guard no amount of yelling was going to. Stratton felt around with his feet and found one of Palanski's legs. He dragged it closer with his heel and stamped on it repeatedly. 'Palanski! Get back here! Wake up!'

Palanski began to choke as the water lapped over his mouth. He suddenly made a move towards consciousness as his eyes fluttered open and he fought to raise his head out of the water.

'Palanski! Concentrate! You have to get us out of here! The chain-release lever. Palanski!'

Palanski battled to get a hold of himself as blood continued to seep from the wound on his head. He looked around, suddenly conscious of the desperation around him. Men were screaming, pulling at their chains. One was praying loudly, begging God to forgive him for his sins.

Palanski made an abortive move towards Stratton. But when he put his weight onto his broken elbow he cried out as the pain shot through him like a bolt of lightning.

'Fight it, Palanski!' Stratton shouted.

The sudden pain seemed to help Palanski stay conscious and he appeared more focused as he locked stares with Stratton.

'The chain release,' Stratton shouted. 'Get us out of here.'

The guard pushed himself away from the bulkhead with his good hand.

'That's good. Keep coming!'

Palanski reached out and Stratton offered a shoulder for the guard to take hold of. Palanski pulled himself alongside.

'Under my seat. The lever. You know where it is.'

Palanski nodded, his breathing laboured, and shuffled around to face the end of the row.

'Come on, Palanski!' the man beside Stratton shouted past him. 'All you gotta do is pull that fuckin' lever.'

Palanski reached down and felt for the box and the small opening on the face of it. His face dipped into the ever-rising water as he reached inside the opening and then he appeared to give up.

'Palanski. We're going to die if you don't get us out,' Stratton urged.

Palanski looked dazed. 'Gettin' . . . a . . . breath,' he muttered. He winced against the excruciating pain, then gritted his teeth, took a breath and plunged beneath the surface of the water that was now lapping at the prisoners' chests.

Ramos, shorter than the others, was crying out as he struggled to keep his chin above the froth.

Palanski surfaced, choking and coughing. 'Can't . . . can't reach it,' he stammered.

'It's there, Palanski! You know where it is. All you have to do is grab hold and pull it. Forget the pain. You'll have years to remember it.' Stratton was becoming stressed, his mind chasing ahead to what little he could do even if he did get free of his chains. The first problem was going to be everyone else. If Palanski did release them there would be half a dozen men thrashing around in an ever-decreasing space. It didn't look good and Stratton was starting to try and come to terms with the fact that he was not going to survive this one. There was just too much to overcome. The water was now up to his shoulders.

A high-pitched scream made him look over his

shoulder to see Ramos going absolutely frantic, yelling insanely as he forced his mouth up above the rising water as far as it could possibly go. The water began to pour into it and he spat it out as quickly as he could.

Stratton looked back at Palanski in time to see him take a deep breath and disappear below the surface. He watched the swirling space that Palanski had occupied a second earlier, knowing that he himself would soon be beneath the water.

Ramos was spitting and gurgling as the water finally covered his mouth. He stretched to take another breath and his eyes bulged as he held on to the last few precious seconds of his life. He shook violently as he made a final Herculean effort to free his hands and then the water covered his eyes. Bubbles broke the surface around Ramos's head and he went still.

Stratton looked up at the ceiling but what he was seeing in his head was the chain-release mechanism, having studied it and every other device in the ferry and the prison that had anything to do with escape. It was a ring-shaped handle inside a tube in a box, not the most convenient design, low to the deck, intended to prevent easy access by a seated prisoner. Palanski had to get close to the floor and reach inside before he could grip the ring and pull it towards him.

As the water touched Stratton's chin he put his head back a little. He was cold but that was the least of his problems. His mind singled out the smell of the sea, an indication of how tuned his senses had become as adren- alin coursed through his body. The shouting had all but ceased. Stratton wondered how many prisoners were already dead. Those that still lived were, like him, coming to terms with the approaching end.

The water reached Stratton's mouth and as he automatically stretched his neck and head up to hang on for as long as he could he felt his hands move up an inch from the seat, enough for him to forget his imminent death for a moment. He took a breath, dropped his head below the water and felt between his thighs for the hook in the seat. Palanski had not managed to pull the handle all the way and had only partially released the securing cable. Stratton yanked on it with all his remaining strength. It suddenly came up another inch and he unhooked his chains and burst to the surface. A second later the man beside him appeared, spluttering and gulping for air. None of the others, including Palanski, joined them.

All Stratton could think of now was that he'd been given a little more time, only seconds perhaps, and that he had to find a way to survive this. He believed in his theory that there was always a solution, the only limitations being his inability to find it.

The airlock door to the OCR hissed and clunked as it opened inwards and Mandrick entered. 'What's the situation?' he calmly asked the senior controller who was standing at the console looking at a row of monitors. A couple of them showed murky, poorly lit exterior images. A white blob in the distance was the slowly approaching ferry.

'We think it could be flooded,' he said, looking vexed.

'It's rolling heavy,' the assistant controller offered. 'The buoyancy's way off. See how low in the water it is? It's almost in the milk,' he said, referring to the bizarre white phenomenon that covered the sea bed like a mist in that part of the Gulf.

'Anything from the surface?' Mandrick asked.

'Nothing. They say it's pretty calm up there. If anyone makes it to the surface they'll see 'em . . . It's gonna go into the milk,' the senior controller said, stepping closer to the monitor.

Mandrick came alongside him to scrutinise the monitors. 'It's still moving.'

'Slow but coming on.'

'How long before it reaches the dock?' Mandrick asked.

'Four, maybe five minutes.'

Mandrick looked at the other monitors, one of them showing the arrivals dock where two men dressed in thick wetsuits were hurriedly donning tanks, aided by other guards. 'If it *is* full of water it won't be able to surface in the dock. Isn't that right?'

'Yes, sir,' the senior controller acknowledged. 'It'll be too heavy. Soon as it comes beneath the pool we'll stop it. The divers'll open it up right away and get some air in there.'

'What's your guess?' Mandrick asked him.

The controller shrugged as he stared at the monitor. 'I don't want to even begin to.'

Stratton and the surviving prisoner faced each other, illuminated by a dim emergency light, their heads pressed against the ceiling, the water at their chins.

'Any ideas?' the man asked, placing his hand against the relief valve, which was still letting in water, in a vain attempt to stop it.

'Top of my list is the emergency escape tube. Or we can try and get air in here using the console.'

'I don't know anything about the console but I can check out the escape tube.'

'If you can get up inside it there should be a breathing hose.'

'I'll come back and let you know,' the man said as he took a deep breath and disappeared.

Stratton couldn't help thinking how a promise to return was not something he would have expected from a desperate prisoner. He headed along the cabin, the bodies of the dead men in their seats under his feet. He stopped above the console where high-pressure air pipes entered the cabin from the tanks outside and then he ducked below the water to search for anything he could use to break one of them. The escaping air would increase the cabin pressure and stop the leaks. It might even reverse the flooding to some extent. But all he could find was the empty chain that the wrench had been attached to. He broke the surface to find the air gap even smaller and grabbed the air pipe in the hope it was loose. But it was solidly fixed to the bulkhead and with no tools he would die trying to break it with his hands.

The other prisoner resurfaced, choking and gulping for air. He looked for Stratton, saw him at the other end of the cabin and made his way over to him. 'The hatch is shut tight. I tried to turn the wheel but I couldn't even budge it.'

That meant the outer hatch was open. There was a hand-crank mechanism for closing the outer hatch but Stratton was not sure exactly where it was located. If they could close it they would then need to drain the tube before opening the lower hatch. To do that they would need to operate the control valves which were located somewhere on the side of the tube. They simply did not have the time.

'What's next on your list?'

'This is all I have left,' Stratton said, gripping the wheel that operated the hatch of the docking system.

'We take a breath, open it and then what?' the man asked.

'Follow the cables to the dock.'

'That easier than heading for the surface?'

'Depends how close we are to the dock.'

They held their lips to the ceiling as the water lapped at their cheeks.

'The valve's stopped leaking,' the man observed, his lips beside it.

'We've got enough air for another minute. We go or we stay,' Stratton said, gripping the wheel.

The man glanced at him. 'I'm going for the surface,' he said after some thought.

'Take your boots off,' Stratton suggested as he ducked below the surface.

The man followed Stratton's lead and they removed their boots and socks. When they surfaced they both gripped the escape-hatch wheel.

'Which way you going?' the man asked, unsure of his choice.

'The dock.'

The man thought about it some more and for a second he found the funny side of it. 'Decisions, decisions,' he quipped.

'I hope it's not your last,' Stratton said sincerely. 'Good luck.'

'Name's Dan,' the man said.

'John.'

'Good luck to you, John. Hope to see you again.'

They tugged at the wheel and it began to turn. Water seeped in through the seal, the flow increasing with each revolution of the wheel. Stratton took a final deep breath as the air gap disappeared.

Gann filled the narrow escape chamber, his eyes blinking in the murky water, air escaping from the sides of his mouthpiece with every exhalation as he heaved up the outer escape hatch. After the initial effort it opened easily and the remaining air in the tube combined with the bubbles escaping from Gann's mouthpiece and made its way up into the gloom. He looked up to see the ferry cables illuminated by the dim light from inside the tube and felt around his body for the air bottle attached to the nylon harness looped around his neck. He found the valve on the end of the bottle and followed the hose to the attached mask and mouthpiece.

Gann made ready to swap breathing devices. He hoped he had calculated the distance correctly and that he had enough air to get to the dock once he left the safety of the tube. But there was one major thing bothering him, despite the dangers of the moment, and that was Palanski.

When the time came to be questioned about his actions Gann had planned to say that the ferry flooded so quickly that he'd charged into the emergency escape room to organise the suits and escape tube while Palanski was supposed to free the prisoners. By the time Gann got his suit on the ferry was almost completely flooded. When he went back to find Palanski there was no sign of him and the water was already above the heads of the prisoners, who had obviously drowned.

The big problem was how he was going to explain Palanski's injuries. He had never intended to give Palanski a beating. Palanski wasn't supposed to have attacked him. The only way that Gann could resolve this problem was to go back into the ferry to remove Palanski's body entirely. He could open the outer docking hatch and adjust his story to make it appear that Palanski had not unchained the prisoners as ordered and had in fact panicked and opened the escape hatch, killing everyone. There were a few holes but it was better than leaving Palanski's corpse inside the ferry. If he hurried he might be able to get away with it.

Gann took a deep breath, removed the mouthpiece attached to the escape tube and pulled the full-face mask over his head. Holding the top of the mask firmly against his forehead he exhaled through his nose in order to remove the water in the mask by forcing it out of the bottom. He managed to do this after a couple of breaths, having learned the technique in the diving

199

course he had attended as part of his pre-prison officer training.

He pulled himself out of the tube but did not take account of the motion of the ferry moving through the water. As he emerged he was forced against the side of the hatch, which he grabbed in a moment of panic. He had not reckoned on how travelling at even a slow speed underwater could create such a force. He looked ahead to see if the dock was close, discovering in the process that the ferry was almost in the milk. It was like some strange underwater snow scene. He'd seen the strange substance from the prison windows but it looked even more surreal from this close. Above the white blanket in the distance was a collection of hazy lights; the ferry cables led to the largest cluster, which marked the entrance to the dock. He gauged it to be a hundred yards or so.

The force of the water suddenly decreased, indicating that the ferry was as usual reducing its approach speed. Gann then realised the ferry was actually going to sink beneath the surface of the strange milk.

He turned around to face the docking hatch when, to his utter amazement, a stream of bubbles began to escape from around its edges and it slowly opened. Gann's reaction was immediate.

Mandrick stood with the two controllers, staring at the images on the OCR monitors. The screens appeared to be split, the bottom half white, the top black, with a murky white ferry in the middle dropping deeper into the white section. They all saw the blurred images of movement on the top of the ferry just below the cable struts.

'Looks like someone getting out,' the senior controller said.

'It's the emergency escape hatch,' said his assistant.

'We're going to lose them in the milk,' the senior controller said as he grabbed the mike. 'Send in the divers. Now!' he shouted into the handset.

Gann pushed himself towards the figure coming out of the hatch. He had no idea who it was but that did not matter. No one could survive the ferry now, and not just because it was the original plan that every prisoner should perish. A survivor could accuse Gann of the sabotage. With the power of the water at his back he struck the man forcefully, wrapping his arms around him and hauling him from the opening. The momentum and the force of the water carried them along the top of the ferry and off the end.

Stratton was just below the other prisoner when he felt him shoot from the hatch as if snatched by something passing overhead. But there was not a second to spare to consider what had happened. He pushed himself free of the hatch and up towards the cables. The ferry began to slow to a crawl, cancelling any thoughts he'd had about simply hanging on and hoping he could last until it reached the dock.

He hit the cables and grabbed hold of one, immediately dragging himself forward. He could make out a dim light ahead and pulled for all he was worth. He kept telling himself that the dock was within his range

201

and he could make it. But suddenly the light ahead disappeared and everything became murky white. Stratton immediately remembered the 'milk' that was known to surround the prison most of the year round. The cable had dropped into it, dragged down by the weight of the flooded ferry.

Stratton's lungs began to cry out for air. The lights had been a psychological hub, something he could have used to focus on and help blank out the pain. All he could do now was imagine them getting closer with each pull and simply keep going until he rose up into the dock or went unconscious.

He pulled in a rhythmic motion, one arm over the other, his legs trailing behind him. He fought the urge to increase the pace and concentrated on keeping the pulls firm and controlled. The last time Stratton had swum underwater for any distance had been many years before. Fifty metres was the distance he'd been required to swim that day, two lengths of the camp pool as part of a general diving-fitness test. And he'd had to collect a brick off the bottom of the five-metre deep end before finally surfacing. But on that occasion he'd had a chance to practise a couple of times. Even then he had only barely made it. This time he had the additional incentive of avoiding death – which had to be worth a few metres more.

His face began to tighten and the palpable increase in fear made him pick up the pace. He prayed the cable would rise out of the milk, which would mean he was very close. He wanted to see the lights again. They would give him hope for another few seconds. If not, this was it. Stratton was going to perish at the bottom of the Gulf of Mexico after all. For a split second, in desperation, he almost let go of the cable to swim out of the milk. But his cold logic kept hold of him and refused to give his hands the permission. The cable led to air and dragging himself was quicker than swimming. It was that or die.

But the urge to open his mouth and suck in anything to relieve the increasing pain of oxygen debt only grew. His face tightened further and felt as if it was going to explode. His arms pulled faster, all discipline gone now. His fingers tingled, his temples throbbed. He had seconds to arrive in the dock or he was finished. His lungs were on fire, his heart pounding in his chest like a drum. His mouth started to open and his grip on the cable loosened. There was nothing left, no more oxygen, his last drop of will-power. The carbon dioxide saturating his body demanded that he open his mouth, insisting he draw in whatever there was. He entered the state of madness that accompanies a total lack of oxygen and he stopped, released the cable and inhaled.

The spasms began and he fought to hold on to his soul. The white changed to dark and he could see a light ahead. And then suddenly it all went quiet and serene. The pain that had tightened his face and body had gone and he drifted like a spirit in space, as if he had already left the water, all human senses gone. He could see himself, knew he had passed into another place and he did not care. The power that drove his life had ceased. Stratton was dead.

Chapter 9

Mandrick walked out through the hissing airlock of the OCR as it closed behind him and headed along a broad steel walkway suspended inside a black rock cavern. The OCR entrance hissed again seconds later as the senior controller emerged from it at a pace calculated to let him catch up with Mandrick before he reached the top of a broad stairway. The cavern echoed with the clatter of their feet as both men hurried along briskly. The controller, wearing a slender headset over one ear, listened intently as he followed Mandrick closely along a lower platform to another airlock door. A small red glass screen required Mandrick's thumbprint which it analysed before turning green. As with just about every other door in the facility, any minor pressure difference on either side of it needed to be equalised before the air-seal was withdrawn and access permitted.

'The standby diver's brought in a body, sir,' the controller said, pressing the earpiece closer to his ear to help cut out the sound of vents and metallic clunking that filled the everyday air in Styx. 'And one more . . . alive . . . it's Gann, sir.'

The door opened and Mandrick walked through while listening to the operations controller but without making any form of acknowledgement. He needed to act like a warden who had just experienced the worst catastrophe of his career, dealing with the horror of half a dozen souls lost, not all of them inmates, while at the same time maintaining calm and control. But he was having problems acting the horrified-warden part — acting was something he had never been any good at anyway. Mandrick had other things on his mind. Now that the deed was done something else was disturbing him, a premonition he'd had shortly after accepting the order to neutralise the new arrivals. Whatever had been achieved this day was going to give birth to even greater problems. And greater problems usually meant having to formulate proportionately more drastic solutions.

The two men made their way down a short flight of broad steps cut into the stone and reinforced with steel and concrete. Vegetation grew down the walls, large clumps of it in places. At the bottom was a bulky, robust steel door made of layers of riveted plates and covered in a dozen coats of thick red paint that had failed to prevent patches of corrosion. The area had become noticeably more humid, the walls moist and covered in mildew, the rock ceiling dotted with stalactites that dripped onto their opposite numbers on the uneven rocky surface beneath the metal-grid floor.

'The ferry's come to a stop below the dock,' the controller reported as he moved ahead to open the door.

The door was an exterior access point and required

a higher level of clearances as well as a series of preliminary safety and security checks.

'Senior OC requires access to gate four Charlie,' the controller said into his mike as he punched a code into a keypad on the wall. 'Release four Charlie dock primary.'

After a brief pause a heavy clunk came from inside the door. The controller checked the pressure levels on several gauges beside the door as part of a mandatory procedure before punching in another code. 'Pressures are equalised . . . Release four Charlie secondary.'

Another clunk and the controller grabbed a large wheel on the side of the door and, with a little difficulty at first, began to turn it. After a couple of heaves it practically spun around at only a light touch. When the dozen cleats that surrounded the frame were clear of the breaches the massive door moved perceptibly outwards as cold air rushed in through the seams. The controller gave it a shove to help the electric motor on the hinge and the door slowly opened.

Mandrick stepped through into a large cavern hewn out of the rock and reinforced by steel girders and concrete. Every surface seemed to be contaminated by some variety of kelp and mildew, some of the ceiling species several metres long. The two men paused on a steel-and-concrete landing facing a pool the size of a couple of tennis courts, its water gently lapping several inches below the edge. Four separate clusters of taut dirty-brown heavy-duty cables rose out of the water and passed over large wheels suspended from the ceiling before heading back down. A lone ferry was parked at the far end with the number '1' stencilled on its surface in places. The water looked black, reflecting the dark rock, although it was crystal clear. The doomed ferry was visible several metres below a placard on the wall that had the number '4' stencilled on it behind the strings of vertical cables. A diver was making his way around the ferry, a line attached to him, its other end held by a guard on the landing.

Mandrick looked along the landing to where a metal ladder curved from the jetty into the pool. Several men were gathered in a circle, one of them wearing a diving suit, a set of dive-tanks close by. The other men were prison guards, all bent over a body lying prone on the wet concrete. Standing back a little from the group was Gann, pulling off his bright yellow escape suit as he kept an interested eye on the group's activities.

Mandrick glanced back to the number four ferry below the surface and saw the cables wobble as the diver pulled on the side door with some effort. He looked ahead at the group of men and walked towards them.

Gann's gaze met Mandrick's for a second as he closed in. The diver was giving cardiac massage to the man lying on the ground, pushing down on his chest in a quick rhythm. A guard stood aside to let Mandrick enter the circle as the dripping-wet diver halted the compressions long enough to feel for the man's carotid artery. A guard kneeling the other side of the body looked into the diver's face for signs of hope. The diver showed none as he recommenced his pumping action.

'I can spell ya, Zack,' the kneeling guard offered.

'I'm OK,' the diver replied.

A guard arrived and quickly placed a mask over the body's mouth, turned on an oxygen bottle connected to it and squeezed a bag attached to the mask, filling the body's lungs.

The man looked dead to Mandrick. His eyes were slightly open, water was trickling out the side of his mouth and his only movement was caused by the diver's efforts. Mandrick was reminded of the first time he had given a man the same last chance for life. Three times he had gone through the process during his military days and had never won back any of them. All three had bled away beneath him. The diver was obviously a tenacious bugger, or something was inspiring him to hold on.

The man with the air bottle checked his watch. The rule in the prison for cardiac massage was eight minutes. Mandrick had done his three for about a minute each, not much more. He'd known the men were dead before he had started but he had continued anyway. He'd had the time and people were watching. Maybe that was why this guy was still doing it.

'Sir,' the controller said and Mandrick turned around to look at him. 'Diver's inside the ferry and it isn't good. He counts four prisoners and Palanski – all dead.'

Mandrick looked back at Gann to find the man staring at him. He looked as if he was asking him for some kind of acknowledgement. Whatever doubts Mandrick had had about Gann's insanity were gone. The man was deranged, to say the least.

'I think we got something,' the diver called out excitedly.

Gann's expression blackened as his eyes snapped to the man lying at their feet. The diver's fingers were deep into his neck to one side of his throat. 'Yeah – we got a beat,' he said. 'Weak but I'm sure of it. The gurney on its way?' he called out.

'Doc's on his way down,' the controller informed everyone.

'Way to go, Zack,' one of the guards said, patting the diver on the shoulder.

Mandrick glanced at Gann who was staring at the lone survivor. Mandrick's initial thought was what the odds were on him being the fed. Even if it was it would not be smart to kill him now. No matter how much of an accident it looked. It would seem far too suspicious. Mandrick's prime objective was survival and he did not want to do anything that implicated himself in too obvious a manner. He had pushed it way too far as it was. One man was easy enough to keep an eye on. And there was always the possibility that he had suffered serious brain damage.

'Anyone know his name?' the diver asked.

The senior controller flicked through his file of the incoming prisoners, pausing at each picture. 'Charon,' he said. 'Nathan Charon.'

'Come on, Nathan,' the diver said. 'You can make it. Breathe. That's it. All right. He's back.'

Stratton opened his eyes to see a chequered steel mesh with bright lights spaced at uneven intervals set into the ceiling behind it. Fatigue tugged heavily at his eyelids but he fought to keep them open. The feeling of utter exhaustion lay on him like a lead shroud and he wondered how long he had been lying there. He fought to remain conscious, trying to remember what had happened and how he had ended up in what seemed like a small, clean hospital room. He knew who he was and that he had been on a submersible cable-car heading for an undersea prison. But other recent memories appeared to be missing or fractured. He remembered the ferry flooding and his desperation to get out of it. From the point of leaving the ferry he was unable to piece together the snippets of sounds and images he retained into a coherent pattern of events. He could see the face of a man and hear his voice while water lapped around his neck. The face of another prisoner appeared and Stratton remembered opening the hatch with him. After that it was all a confused blur.

He wanted to look around the room to see if there were other occupied beds but his head felt as if it was bolted to the pillow.

Stratton could hear a tapping noise as if it was floating around in his head all alone. He was unsure if it was a memory or if it was really happening. As he fought to collect the jumble of images speeding through his mind the tapping seemed to get louder. He couldn't lie still any longer and, desperate for clarity, fought to activate the muscles in his neck and turn his head. He slowly rolled it to one side but his eyes would not readily refocus and he looked back up at the ceiling. The mesh was clear but when he turned to look at the room again it was as if his eyes were jammed and unable to adjust.

Fear crept through him as he suddenly wondered what other parts of him no longer functioned. He broke into a cold sweat at the thought of being an invalid and concentrated on moving his arms. They rose up off his stomach where they came into focus and he let them back down with a feeling of relief. Next he had to see if he still had his legs. With a supreme effort he raised his head off the pillow until he could see two ridges under the sheet going from his hips to small mounds at the ends of them. They moved from side to side at his will and he dropped his head back with another heavy sigh of relief.

Stratton began to scan the rest of his body with his mind, tensing various muscles and then relaxing them. Suddenly, the ceiling light he had been staring at was replaced by the face of a beautiful dark-haired woman looking down at him. Her complexion was pale, her eyes and lips dark within the shadow of the light behind her. He was sure she was real only because he could suddenly smell her, a fresh soapy aroma. It was odd because his sense of smell had never been particularly acute. Perhaps he had been reborn, or he was in heaven and this was an angel.

'You're back, then,' she said, without a trace of emotion, looking at one of his eyes and then the other in search of something.

Stratton could only blink up at her. The total absence of a smile or any trace of cordiality ruled out paradise.

'What's your name?' she asked. Her voice was soft

but at the same time strong, and her accent was American.

Stratton started to open his mouth but found it difficult, his lips sticking as if they had begun the process of healing together.

The woman moved out of his sight to reach for something and when her face returned she put a straw to his mouth. 'Have some water.'

He took a sip, feeling the cold liquid pass through his mouth and down his throat like the first rains along a parched river bed.

'Do you remember your name?' she asked again.

A dim alarm throbbed inside his head as his training and years of experience warned him never to talk unless he was *compos mentis*. Then he realised he couldn't remember the answer to her question anyway. He knew his real name but he also remembered that he had a cover. The false identity was just beyond his reach. He thought he saw it flit across his mind but he couldn't get hold of it. He found the image of the man sitting in the back of the prison truck. He saw Paul and Todd. And then the name was suddenly there in front of him. Nathan Charon. Then it was as if the effort had triggered the bursting of a bubble of information inside his head as other elements of his assignment fell into place.

Stratton decided to ignore the woman's question until he had gathered more information on who she was and on his own situation. One of the most important questions he needed an answer to was whether or not he still had a mission. Where on Earth he was would be a good start.

He tried to bend his arm to bring it under his shoulder but what should have been a simple effort proved difficult. He felt eighty years old.

'You want to sit up?' she asked.

Stratton nodded. The woman made a poor effort to help him, unsure where to hold him. This suggested she was not accustomed to helping someone sit up in a bed. That seemed to rule out nurse or doctor as her job. She was wearing jeans and a sweatshirt, both clean but not the usual attire of a professional. As she gripped his shoulder he could feel her strength. She was slender but strong and athletic. Nothing about her was adding up yet.

She pulled the bedclothes away to allow him to slide his feet off the mattress and onto the floor. He was wearing a tracksuit that he did not recognise. His body ached all over. The discomfort reminded him of the time when he'd fallen halfway down the side of a snow-covered mountain in Norway after narrowly avoiding a small avalanche.

Stratton looked around, his ability to focus gradually improving. He realised he was actually inside a steel cage in a corner of a room. The bars went from floor to ceiling on two sides and the door was open. The room beyond looked like a cross between an office and a laboratory. There was a desk with a lamp, pens, paper and a computer. A long workbench was against one wall, next to a row of glass cabinets filled with medical paraphernalia. Another counter was bedecked with technical apparatus and on the wall there was a flat-screen monitor that was switched off. The aspect of the situation that struck him most was that his was the only bed.

Behind the desk was a window with a clear view outside. There were skyscrapers, the central one of which was familiar: the Empire State Building. He was looking at the top half from a similar height which meant he was in another Manhattan skyscraper. The mission was over. He had failed. After surviving the ferry he'd been transported to a surface hospital in New York. But then who was this woman and why was he not with his own people? The feeling that he should stay on his guard intensified.

'Where am I?' Stratton asked.

'You were going to tell me your name,' the woman said. The chill in her voice did not alter.

He wondered why she was asking for his name. Surely she knew who he was. If she didn't then who the hell was she? He decided to give her something. Until he was sure that the op was at an end he would continue to play the game. 'Nathan . . . Nathan Charon.'

He caught her expression just before she turned away and he had the feeling that she was disappointed. Or perhaps it was irritation. He looked out of the window as a bird flew close to the ledge before veering away. 'How long have I been here?' he asked.

'Two days,' she said, walking out of the cage without closing the door and leaning against the steel work surface of the counter from where she could study him.

He did the same, noting her sneakers, her strong, shapely legs, her square shoulders. This girl was in shape and was also very pleasing to the eye.

'Do you remember what happened?' she asked.

'I remember the ferry flooding,' he said, looking at a row of bottles containing different-coloured liquids on top of the medical cabinets behind her. It was certainly an odd-looking hospital room.

'Where are you from, Nathan?'

The question highlighted an aspect of this charade that Stratton had been most uncomfortable with. Charon was from Vermont but a cover story of years in the UK was intended to explain Stratton's English accent. The background details had been placed in Charon's file but Stratton's problem was not so much the alleged period during which he'd lived in the UK, it was the rest of his life, supposedly spent in Vermont. He'd read a brief prepared by the analysts but it would never be enough to get him off the hook if he was questioned. If the woman pushed the issue he would go to the emergency plan for that eventuality which was to go on the offensive and demand to see his lawyer if they were going to interrogate him. 'Vermont, originally. But I moved around a lot.'

'England, I suppose.'

'I spent a lot of years there.'

She took her time with her questions as if weighing each answer carefully.

'What happened on the ferry?'

She was cutting right to the chase. 'It began to flood. One of the guards released our chains.'

'Go on.'

The girl was acting more like an investigator or inter-rogator. He wondered about revealing Gann's part in the incident but decided it was in his best interests to appear to remember nothing. Once he became an integral part of the investigation it would detract from his purpose – if he had any purpose left, that was. 'I can remember hardly anything. I don't seem to remember getting on board, even. Certainly nothing after we climbed out of the escape hatch.'

'We?'

'I was with one other prisoner.'

She looked down at her feet. Stratton decided she was not a professional interrogator. She gave too much away with her eyes and body language. Something wasn't right about her. Whatever her job was it was privileged or she would not be here. She had rank. He would have expected the first person to question him to be highly qualified. She looked as if she was in her late twenties or early thirties. Subtract the years spent in college getting the degrees a person in her position would need and she could not have been in her job very long. She was acting professional but it was just that: an act. She had little real experience of what she was doing. That was obvious to someone like him, at least. It made his circumstances even more curious.

'Where is he?' Stratton asked.

'You and one of the guards were the only survivors.'

Stratton saw an image of Dan leaving the hatch just before him. He felt sorry for the man.

The bird returned to the window ledge before veering away again. Stratton realised there were no bars on the window. That didn't make sense. He was in a detention centre of sorts but one without bars on the

216

windows. There would have to be some kind of exit control no matter how high up from the street the room was. The door into the room was made of frosted glass. The bird returned to the window but this time he realised there was something odd about it. The bird was performing exactly the same action every time.

'What am I doing in New York?' he asked.

The girl looked at the window and rolled her eyes, walked behind the desk, reached for the side of the frame and flicked a switch. The image disappeared. 'Doctor Mani thinks it's healthy to at least maintain a sense of natural surroundings down here.'

'I'm in Styx?' Stratton asked.

'Sorry if it confused you,' she said, without sounding sorry at all.

Stratton felt a sudden partial relief. But a residual fear remained. He was still on the mission, as far as he could tell, but it was all going wrong. Six men were dead, the cause of their deaths was sinister and he had only barely survived. The need to proceed with extreme caution was paramount. 'You a doctor?' he asked.

'No. I'm a prison inspector. I work for the Federal Bureau of Prisons, the programme-review division.'

She spoke as if it was a declaration, a statement of fact, defining her position clearly to him. Her attitude towards him was still hard to pin down. She was cold and authoritative, confident and aggressive. But she was not talking down to him.

She looked as if she was struggling with a thought. 'You have a problem,' she decided to reveal.

He couldn't begin even to guess what she meant.

The girl leaned on the desk and tapped the keypad on a laptop. The screen came to life and she turned it to face him. It was a copy of Nathan Charon's prison file.

'You've put me in a difficult position.'

'I don't understand.'

'You're not Nathan Charon.'

Stratton forced a smirk while at the same time trying to deal with this most dangerous development. Everything seemed to be unravelling before he could even get his foot in the bloody door of the place. 'Do I have brain damage?'

It was a pathetic effort which she was not even going to waste a second on. 'Who do you work for?' she insisted.

'I don't know what you mean.'

'Prior to your arrival at Styx your personal file was wired here from the Vermont Department of Corrections. The files of the other inmates were like-wise wired from their respective state corrections depart-ments. You also arrived with hard copies, which were recovered from the ferry. The files from the Vermont Department of Corrections and your hard copies match. The problem is that neither of your files match the one I have. I received mine from the Federal Bureau of Prisons Atlantic regional office. Whoever set you up as Nathan Charon was powerful enough to change your state file but not influential enough to alter your *federal* records – either that or they overlooked them. Your photograph is close, but it's not you. Most damning are your fingerprints. I did a comparison and they don't match. More interesting is that they don't match anyone's records. Not even the FBI's. I checked. Either you never had a US driving licence or you're a foreigner who skipped Immigration on his way into the US. You don't work for the CIA because there are enough of them down here already. But you *do* work for someone in the US government otherwise you couldn't have got in here.'

Stratton could only look at the girl blankly. He was well and truly busted. But there was something curious about the way she was presenting her findings. She seemed to be acting independently, for one thing. Another oddity was that there was no locked door between them, as if the fact that he was not a threat was a given. He thought about revealing his cover story about being an independent security surveyor. But his instincts warned him to keep that to himself for the moment. It was his get-out-of-jail card and he wasn't ready to get out yet. Perhaps there was mileage to be gained from her thinking that he was a US-government-sponsored implant, which technically he was. That put them on the same side, as long as she was who she said she was. 'What now?' he asked.

She went to her laptop, closed it and put it in a small briefcase which she zipped up. 'Do you know why they sabotaged the ferry?'

He did not but neither did he want to admit that he knew it had been sabotaged – not yet, at any rate. She was probably guessing anyway.

The young woman seemed to read his mind. 'You weren't the only undercover prisoner on the ferry. They either knew about you or about him.' She stared at him, waiting for something back. He just looked at her. 'Christ, you're some kind of asshole. I'm sticking my neck out here and you're giving me nothing.'

It did indeed appear that she had gone over the top to help him. By admitting she knew there was a fed on board and the reason for the sabotage she was also coming clean about her true affiliations. It was doubtful that she was one of the bad guys looking for a confession because she wouldn't need any more than she already had on him. 'What do you want from me?' Stratton asked.

'Something that tells me I haven't risked making myself vulnerable for nothing.'

They locked stares. She could sense he was no longer suspicious of her and, although she had initially been concerned over giving away too much about herself, it did calm her fears. She had not wanted to give him anything at first but her conscience would not allow her to ignore the danger he was in. He was clearly a US government employee and had almost died trying to do his job. It was a miracle he had survived. But he was still in serious danger and she could not turn her back on that. On the flip side, she could not do much to help him, either. It was all down to what kind of a man he was.

'Does anyone else know?' Stratton asked.

She shook her head. 'You want my advice, whatever panic button you have that gets you out of here, I'd push it now.'

It was sound advice, but he was not ready to act on

220

it quite yet. 'I appreciate what you've done,' he said sincerely. 'Trust me, I do . . . I'm going to stay.'

His appreciation seemed genuine and that was good enough for her. He had come clean. She had never expected him to tell her which department he worked for or the details of his task although it was obvious enough. Everyone but the CIA wanted the facility closed down. His intention to stay on track with his task, considering what had happened to him and the dangers that remained, revealed a quality that impressed her. She could sense that she was in the company of no ordinary man.

There was a hiss from the next room that alerted them to someone arriving.

The girl quickly closed Stratton's cage door, picked up her bag and walked to the entrance. 'We probably won't meet again,' she said, reaching for the door. 'Good luck.'

'You too,' he said.

She paused for a second before opening the door and Stratton thought he saw her expression soften. She closed the door behind her.

He could hear her talking with a man for a few seconds then there was another loud hiss and a clunk. A moment later the frosted-glass door opened and a portly Indian man wearing the classic uniform of a doctor – a white coat and a stethoscope poking out of his breast pocket – walked in. He looked over his glasses at Stratton. 'Ah. Lazarus rises. And if you're not a Christian I don't mean to offend. How are you feeling?' he said cheerily, his Indian accent only barely perceptible behind some North American overtone whose identity Stratton could not begin to guess.

'Fine,' Stratton replied.

The doctor looked across the room at the false window and made a beeline for it. 'My name's Doctor Mani. I expect you're thirsty,' he said as he toggled the switch on the side of the frame until the New York skyline returned. The bird immediately attempted to land on the ledge. 'There. Can't stand the feeling I'm under the water all the time. I understand they're considering providing something like this for the inmates' cells. Or is it the galley? Yes, I think it's the galley. A bit of atmosphere during mealtimes. They come in practically any landscape. I think they even have one of Mars, though God only knows who would want to feel they were on another planet. As if this place wasn't enough,' he added as he adjusted the brightness and then stood back to admire it. 'Now then, soon as we have a drink I'll run a series of tests, see how you're coming along, and then let's see if we can get you back into the mainstream as soon as possible.'

Stratton remained seated on the edge of the bed, wondering what this man had done to deserve his job.

'Cat got your tongue?'

Stratton looked up at the doctor. He was still feeling unwell and was content to make it appear he was worse than he was.

'Can you hear me? Can you talk?' Dr Mani asked, putting on a professional smile.

'I can hear you OK.'

'Good . . . Now,' the doctor said, reaching for a small

plastic container, 'first thing I need is a urine sample. Can you manage that for me?' he asked, handing the container to Stratton.

Stratton took it and forced a smile.

'I'll leave you alone for a moment,' the doctor said, leaving the room.

Stratton held the container and sighed. He decided now that he was in Styx he had officially begun his mission. He thought if he looked at it that way he could put behind him all the mishaps so far and start afresh. He was not surprised that this perception had not made him feel the slightest bit better.

Christine walked along a broad central corridor, the rock walls and ceiling dripping water onto a suspended shroud, intended to protect pedestrians, and on the outer edges of the metal walkway. A couple of prisoners wearing face masks and canisters on their backs were spraying the mildew and weeds that gathered in the crevices. A guard stood idly by. 'Mornin', ma'am,' he said as she passed, eyeing her bottom. The prisoners paused to do the same.

Christine ignored them and headed along the corridor, the sound of her footsteps mingling with the noises of running water moving along channels beneath her feet and hissing air ducts above. An indistinct voice came over a loudspeaker further down the tunnel, followed by what sounded like a gong. The prison provided a kind of talking clock accompanied by various sounds but as far as she could tell it was grossly inaccurate. Like so many aspects of the prison, the seeds of good intention were visible but the execution was abysmal.

She headed up a spiral staircase inside a vertical rock tunnel that opened into a spacious cavern. It was constructed of a combination of steel girders, concrete and rock. One wall had a line of large round portholes, the six-inch-thick glass yellow with reflections from outside lights that illuminated any creatures that passed by. There was a single large white airlock door in the cavern that was more ornate than the others, suggesting it was an 'exclusive' entrance. She pushed a button on the side of the door and looked at a camera in front of her.

'Give me one minute, would you, please,' a metallic voice asked.

Christine turned her back on the camera. She knew she looked as distracted as she felt and made an effort to calm herself. She crossed her arms and then quickly unfolded them, dangling them at her sides until her laptop case almost fell off her shoulder. It wasn't just the Nathan Charon situation that was unnerving her. The mysterious agent was an issue but was the least of her concerns at that moment. Time was her problem and compounding the pressure on her. It was running out and she had not yet devised a plan to complete her mission.

The door hissed and clunked behind her and she turned to watch it move back into its frame before it rolled out to one side.

Christine walked into Mandrick's office as the door hissed again and closed behind her.

Mandrick was seated at his desk facing her but he

was looking at a computer monitor while he tapped at a keyboard. When he finished he unplugged a mini-computer from a cable attached to the mainframe and got to his feet. She watched as he clipped it onto his belt, averting her eyes as he looked at her.

'Christine,' he said, beaming as he walked from behind his desk, a hand outstretched to greet her. 'You always bring a smile to my heart whenever I see you.' He took her hand and kissed her on the cheek, clearly savouring the contact.

She smiled, struggling to make it look as natural as possible. He held her gaze beyond cordiality before she broke it off, appearing to be a touch embarrassed.

'I can't help being forward with you,' he said. 'I have such little time left to impress you.'

'You impress me, Pieter. No need to worry about that.'

'Oh? How?'

'You run the most dangerous prison in the world for the most powerful country in the world. That's impressive.'

'And that's all that impresses you about me . . . my job?'

'No. But that's all we're going to talk about right now . . . What does a girl have to do to get a cup of coffee around here?'

Mandrick reluctantly broke away from her and walked over to an ornate wooden dresser with a couple of thermos flasks on a tray alongside some cups. 'When do you leave?' he asked as he filled two cups with the black liquid.

'I have a couple more inmates to interview, a guard or two. That's me pretty much finished.'

'Which prisoners would you like to interview?' he asked as he passed her a cup.

'You choose,' she said and shrugged, taking a sip. 'I'm just playing the numbers game.'

'You haven't asked to see any of our political prisoners.' He gave her a sideways glance.

'I told you the day I arrived. This inspection is apolitical. I'm here to review health and living conditions for staff and inmates . . . To tell you the truth, those Taliban guys scare the hell out of me.'

Mandrick stared at Christine for a moment, his smile growing thin. 'I don't believe you,' he said, his expression serious.

'What don't you believe?' she asked, her smile hanging in there.

'I don't believe you scare that easily. I know potency when I see it. Particularly in a woman.'

'I'm sure you're very experienced. But you're wrong this time,' she said. 'I'm a pussycat.'

His eyes flicked to her body, unable to resist looking at it. 'And how is our Mr Charon?' he asked. 'You've spent quite a lot of time with him since he arrived.'

Christine shrugged. 'I was waiting for him to regain consciousness. I'm going to be asked questions about the ferry incident.'

'There'll be an official inquiry.'

'Yes, but I was here when it happened. I'll have to refer to it in my report. I'll probably get roped into the inquiry.'

'Good. So we will see more of you.'

'Not down here, I hope.'

'My sentiments exactly.'

Mandrick was giving her the creeps and she hoped it didn't show.

'What did Charon have to say?'

'Aren't you going to talk to him yourself?'

'Of course. But you hogged his initial reaction.'

Christine made a show of rolling her eyes at the word 'hogged'. The subtle implication that she had a special interest in seeing Charon first was not lost on her. Mandrick often made little digs that suggested she was doing more than merely inspecting the prison. Sometimes she wondered if he really did know what she was doing and was just playing her along because he fancied his chances of getting her into bed. 'He can't remember much about it,' she said. 'All he recalls is the ferry flooding, the guard freeing them and him getting out of the hatch. I think he's just thankful to be alive.'

Mandrick considered her answer as he sipped his coffee, his eyes lowering to admire her body again. When he looked back at her face she forced another smile.

'Let's get down to more important matters,' he said. 'When you've finished your task I'm going to escort you back to Houston and take you to dinner. And until you promise me that you will accompany me I can't guarantee that any of the ferries will be working.'

'How can I refuse such charming blackmail?' she said.

'It wasn't an idle threat.'

227

'I didn't think it was,' she said, looking away.

'Why do I get the feeling that deep down you really don't like me? Or am I being too sensitive?'

'No. You're not . . . I despise you. But you've discovered one of my darkest secrets,' Christine said, putting down her cup and stepping closer to him. 'There's always been something sinister about the men I'm most attracted to. It's a good sign if I start off by loathing you.' Her face was inches from his.

'Not the characteristics of a pussycat,' he said. Mandrick enjoyed the closeness but despite her forwardness he could feel the wall between them as if it was made of granite. He trusted no one at the best of times but Christine was an uninvited and unwanted guest over whom he had limited control. He would be a fool to believe she was a mere inspector. He would doubt her as a matter of course but something about her made that doubt more emphatic. Even so, he would still scheme to bed her even if she turned out to be an undercover Supreme Court judge. Every time he saw her all he could think about was how she would look naked. He wondered if she deliberately wore tight jeans just to taunt him. He would have taken her to his bed while she was in the prison if she had allowed him to. But she was proving difficult to ensnare.

It was all a part of that wall between them. They ate dinner together every evening, along with the doctor and any visiting engineers as was normal when there were guests. But when the others were ready to leave Christine departed with them. He wondered if she would evade their dinner date in Houston. Without a doubt, there was something phoney about her. But her body was real and desirable enough and he wanted her despite his doubts.

The phone on his desk rang. 'Excuse me,' Mandrick said as he walked over and picked it up. He talked in a low voice, the background hum that seemed to permeate every corner of the prison helping to mask his words. He removed his minicomputer, opened the cover, selected one of a dozen micro data-storage cards and inserted it into the side of the device. After pushing several command icons he gave the caller some information.

Christine stared at the device. It had become the holy grail of her mission, the final phase before she could get out of the damned place. She had been sent to reconnoitre the prison and look for information. Her brief was not actually to acquire that information but to pinpoint its location. Any more would have been asking too much of her. Further ops would be devised to obtain it.

But Christine wanted to complete the mission in one go. She promised herself not to take unnecessary risks but the drive to get the computer was strong in her. Technical attacks against the prison and corporation data files had failed to produce anything of value. From the moment she first saw the minicomputer she knew it contained everything Mandrick reckoned was secret. If she could get hold of it, or the memory cards, she would have achieved far more than she had come for. If she left the prison that minute and reported her find her mission would have been a success. But she was impetuous and hungry for success. She knew it was recklessness encouraged by her ego. Still, the closer she got to Mandrick, or the closer she allowed him to get to her, the more she believed she could succeed. If she attempted it while she was in the prison it would be a two-phase operation: first to get her hands on the material, second to get it and herself to the surface. It didn't matter if Mandrick knew she had it once she was clear of Styx.

But that was the difficult part. If he found out before she reached the surface Christine would be in serious danger. The other option was to meet him in Houston and do the whole dinner thing. The risk with that would be if it was his habit to leave such a precious item in the safety of the prison.

Mandrick put down the phone and came back to her. 'Where were we?' he asked. 'Oh, yes. You were telling me how you loathed me enough to have dinner with me in Houston.'

A buzzer interrupted them. Mandrick looked up at the bank of monitors that displayed practically every part of the prison. One of them showed a man in slacks and a jacket standing in the cavern outside his office. 'There's my luck again. I know you were about to give yourself to me. But duty calls.' He produced his remote control and hit a button on it. There was a clunk as the door hissed and opened.

The man strode into the room, his manner author-itative. He was grim-faced and large, like a former lineman, still naturally tough but aged and out of condition. He seemed anxious to say something but held back as soon as he saw Christine.

'Hank. How was your trip?' Mandrick asked.

'Fine,' Hank replied dryly.

'This is Christine Wineker from the Federal Bureau of Prisons.'

'Yeah, I heard.' Hank could not make his reluctance to meet her more obvious.

'Pleased to meet you too,' Christine said. She knew he was CIA, probably one of the senior guys if not *the* senior, and that he suspected her and loathed her.

'Hank's one of our VPs,' Mandrick explained. 'I don't know what the hell he does, though. Just turns up here once in a while to get in the way.'

'We need to talk,' Hank said, ignoring the charade.

'I was on my way out,' Christine said, shouldering her laptop and heading for the door.

'Thanks for stopping by,' Mandrick said.

Christine did not look back. Mandrick closed the door behind her.

'What the fuck is going on?' Hank blurted out as soon as the door had sealed shut.

'You sound in a bad mood,' Mandrick said, walking over to his desk.

'I'm gone three goddamned days and the goddamned wheels start falling off the place. You gonna tell me that ferry disaster was an accident? I could tell it was a goddamned massacre all the way from Florida.'

'Why are you acting so surprised?' Mandrick's question was sincere.

'Are you fuckin' kidding me?!'

'Hank. The order came from your own people.'

'Bullshit!'

'OK. The order came from Forbes. Now, if you suddenly believe he'd make a decision like that on his own then you are crazy.'

Hank was stunned. His voice became quieter. 'You're serious?'

'He told me it was a direct request from your outfit.'

'Why?'

'The feds were trying to slip one of their people inside as an inmate. We had no ID so . . . everyone had to buy it . . . You clearly didn't get the memo?'

'They're out of their friggin' minds.'

'But we know they're not. They thought it through and decided it was a good idea.'

'It could close this place down.'

'They have to prove it wasn't an accident.'

'That's the first really dumb thing I've heard you say. I don't care how you did it – there'll be a clue and someone'll find it.'

'Hank. You've misread me. I couldn't agree more.'

'Then why the hell did you do it?'

'I didn't realise the Agency had given me veto power.'

'You should've called me.'

'Now you're starting to sound pretty dumb yourself.'

Hank had to agree. He just couldn't believe it. 'There were smarter ways of handling this.'

'There's one clue lying in the hospital.'

Hank looked at him. 'Styx hospital?'

Mandrick nodded. 'The lone survivor – from the prisoners, that is. The other one was Gann.'

Hank shut his eyes and squeezed his temples tightly. 'Shit. I should've guessed that moron was involved.'

'You thought I would get my own hands that dirty?'

Hank pondered the situation for a moment. 'How do we know he's not the fed?' he eventually asked.

'We don't.'

Hank went silent again.

'Interesting, isn't it? We don't kill him we could be damned, but if we do and he's the fed . . .'

'It doesn't seem to bother you,' Hank said accusingly.

'I take life as it comes.'

'You can afford to.'

'I'm not in control. I'm just a hired hand.'

'And getting well paid, too. How is that offshore bank account? Don't forget that's the reason this place came about in the first place.'

'This place was built by your people to interrogate political prisoners.'

'Maybe. But the mine's drying up, isn't it? I know that. You people want out now, don't you? And while we're on the subject of money, my bank account hasn't seen any zeros added to it for a couple months now. That looks to me like someone's planning on leaving without paying the rent that's due.'

'Why're you bitching at me? I'm on the same level as you when it comes to distribution.'

'Sure you are. How 'bout we take a look in your safe? I'll give odds there's a bag of gems sitting in there right now.'

Mandrick sighed, tired of the line the conversation was taking. 'When I first met you at the start of this project you gave me a long and patriotic speech about the purpose of this prison. You cited national security, revenge for nine-eleven, protection of fossil fuels and the lifeline of this great country's economy. You never mentioned money. I'm not pointing the finger, Hank. In the end it all comes down to money. And you're due your share.'

Hank looked away as if Mandrick had wounded him – which, in fact, he had. Hank was a patriot who had lost his way.

Mandrick saw the effect of his dig but he knew he could not afford to make an enemy out of Hank. 'You're wrong, anyway. We're not planning on leaving any time soon. I would know . . . No one's ripping you off, either. Pay's been slow the last couple of months because of the market. It's not the first time. It'll pick up . . . You're wrong about the mine, too. It's doing just fine.'

Hank regretted his own outburst. He didn't like to hear himself talking about money. There was a time when he would not have given it a second thought. But he was older now and the disillusionment of the job had been wearing him down over the years. He was still a patriot but he also wanted his share of the spoils since everyone else around him seemed to be getting theirs. There was no end to the stories about people he had either worked with or for who had made fortunes along the way.

He had begun to weaken around the time he started calculating the pension he could look forward to when he retired, realising how paltry it was considering all he had done for his country. Normally he didn't lose control the way he just had but the ferry disaster had set him off. It had been a crazy stunt but Mandrick was right. He needed to examine all the implications and possible Agency motives before he did or said anything else. The first thing he wanted to know was why the hell he hadn't been informed.

'When's that bitch outta here?' Hank asked, wanting to change the subject. 'I came back for a specific interrogation and I don't feel comfortable while she's snooping around.'

'I think she'll be gone tomorrow. I'm doing everything I can to facilitate her.' Mandrick privately enjoyed the double meaning. 'Anything I can do in the meantime?'

Hank walked over to Mandrick's drinks cabinet and poured himself a whisky. 'I need a pre-interrogation.'

Mandrick picked a pen up off his desk. 'Who?'

'Durrani. Four seven four five.'

'Duration?'

'I need him ready by tomorrow midday. You need to start right away.'

'He's not been through pre-int before. That makes it easier.'

Hank finished his drink and put the glass down. 'You tell your boss to make sure I get my money. Unless he gets a cave alongside Bin Laden there's nowhere on this planet he can hide from me.'

Mandrick hit a button and the door hissed as the seal deflated. Hank walked out of the room, leaving Mandrick with his thoughts. He set them aside, picked up the phone and punched in a number while at the same time opening a computer file. The senior operations controller answered the phone.

'I've got a pre-int for Durrani, number four seven four five,' Mandrick said, consulting his monitor. 'Cell number three eight eight . . . and get the right cell this time . . . Yeah, yeah, yeah. Just make sure. It's important.'

He put down the phone and sat back to resume thinking.

Chapter 10

Stratton, handcuffs securing his wrists, a clean laundry bag over one shoulder containing his bedsheets, towel and spare underclothes, walked along a dripping, dingy corridor that had been cut through the rock and smelled of strong disinfectant. The roughly hewn ceiling was arched and no more than a couple of feet above his head at the highest points. Water leaked through cracks and ran down the walls, providing moisture for the slimy kelp-like vegetation that clung to the rock in green and grey sheets. A gum-chewing guard wielding a baton which he spun on the end of its leather strap sauntered alongside Stratton. One of the low-voltage fluorescent lights flickered and dimmed up ahead as if it was about to die. The guard gave it a tap with his baton as they passed but the blow had no effect.

They were on level three which was where all Western prisoners were accommodated. Level one was operations, level two was given over to the kitchen, laundry and galley while level four housed the foreign and Muslim prisoners. The layers below that housed the pumps, storerooms and various pieces of life-support systems machinery and were the main source of the constant humming that filled the prison. Then there were the various split levels and sections that contained the hospital, the ferry dock, Mandrick's office and what was commonly known as the spook wing where the Agency had its various quarters.

Stratton and the guard walked along a row of identical heavy steel doors spaced at regular intervals a few metres apart. All were painted in a dull green and displayed brown streaks that radiated from suppurating rust sores. Each had the same characteristic bulging rubber seal around the edges, indicating that they were pressure doors.

'Here we go,' the guard said, stopping outside one of the doors. 'Two, one, two.' He checked a pressure valve on the wall and pushed a button on the side of a small flat-screen monitor inside a clear protective plastic box. A fish-eye image crackled to life, showing a small room with a bed either side of it and a man in prison uniform seated at a small desk. A curtain drawn across one of the corners partially hid a toilet bowl.

The guard pushed several buttons on a keypad beside the monitor. 'Pete to OCR,' he said into a mike clipped to his jacket lapel. 'Prisoner Charon at cell two one two requires entry.'

'Copy Charon entering two one two,' a voice echoed and a second later there was a loud hiss, followed by a heavy clunk. As the seals shrank the door was free to move inwards.

'Comin' in, Tusker,' the guard called out as he pushed open the door and remained in the opening. The man at the desk was typing on a laptop and acted as if he was not aware of the intrusion. 'I got some bad news for you, Tusker.'

The man continued to ignore the guard who grinned as if he was about to enjoy what he had to say next. 'We got you a room-mate.' He chewed his gum noisily as his grin broadened.

The man stopped typing and slowly looked around at the guard. Then he shifted his gaze to Stratton. Tusker was in his sixties and nothing like what one might expect a special-category prisoner to look like.

'We got no space, for a few days at least,' the guard explained. 'Charlie section's got a serious mildew problem. We had to shut it down for the prison inspector. Soon as the inspector babe's gone we'll open it back up and you'll have your room back to yourself. That sound OK?'

The older man frowned and went back to his typing.

'Step inside,' the guard said to Stratton, who obeyed. 'Turn your back to me. Release the bag.'

Stratton let go of the end of the bag and it hit the floor. The guard unshackled him, pushed him into the cell and stood back as Stratton felt his wrists. 'You two get along, now. And don't be teaching him any of your bad habits, Tusker, ya hear?' He chuckled as he put his mike to his mouth. 'Close down two one two,' he said as he pulled the door shut with a clang. A second later there was a loud hiss as the seals inflated. Stratton felt the pressure-change in his ears. It was severe enough for him to have to hold his nose and blow, equalising his tubes.

Tusker winced as his hands shot to cover his ears. He was clearly in pain. 'Assholes,' he growled. 'Sons of bitches always slam it up – they know my ears can't adjust that quickly.'

Stratton looked around at the windowless damp walls, the beds and the toilet behind the curtain. He picked up his bag and paused, unsure which bed he was to use. Both were made up although one had several items of clothing neatly folded on it.

Tusker read Stratton's quandary, got to his feet, walked over to the bed that was covered in clothing, removed the items and placed them on the edge of the desk.

Stratton put his bundle down on the bed as Tusker went back to his desk. The pasty walls covered in mildew patches had been recently scrubbed and Stratton wondered how people could spend years of their lives in such confinement without going crazy.

He wondered what the older man was in this hole for. It must have been a serious crime for someone his age to wind up in Styx.

'Hi,' Stratton said, deciding to break the ice. 'Name's Nathan.'

'One second,' Tusker said, as if he needed to finish a train of thought.

Stratton sat on the edge of the bed and wondered what these people did to pass the time. There was no TV, no entertainment that he could see other than books and the laptop. Perhaps the old guy was writing a book himself. The ones stacked on the desk appeared to be on the subject of engineering, except the one on the end. That was a copy of Jules Verne's *Twenty Thousand Leagues Under the Sea*. Apt, Stratton thought.

A vent in the ceiling came to life as a blast of air blew into the room. It lasted about ten seconds and ended in a low growling noise.

Tusker appeared to finish what he was doing and sat back for a moment as if it had been somewhat tiring. He closed the top of his computer and turned in his seat to look at Stratton. After studying him for a few seconds he held out a hand. 'Tusker Hamlin,' he said in a cordial if neutral tone.

Stratton knew the name immediately. He was in the presence of America's most infamous domestic terrorist. This guy was into everything from deadly toxins and chemical agents to home-made explosives. It must have been ten years ago that the media had been filled with the news of his capture. Stratton remembered the footage of a solitary dilapidated caravan in the midst of some vast forest miles from anywhere in one of the northern US states. He took Hamlin's hand and they shook. The older man's grip was firm and his palm calloused as if he'd been doing hard labour.

'You're lucky to be alive,' Hamlin said, sitting back in his chair.

Stratton could not disagree.

'Zack said if you hadn't floated out of the milk when you did he wouldn't have seen you.'

'Zack?'

'Diver who pulled you out and got your ticker goin' again.'

Stratton had wondered who he had to thank for saving his life.

'You believe in God?' Hamlin asked.

'More than I did last week.'

'Where you from?'

'Vermont. I spent a long time in the UK if you're wondering about the accent.'

'Never been there,' Hamlin said in a way that suggested he didn't care either. 'What you in for?

Stratton shrugged. 'Can't keep outta jail. I guess they think this place'll change my mind.'

'Let 'em think what they damn well want to,' Hamlin said, his mind suddenly elsewhere.

'Aren't you a bit old to be down here?' Stratton asked, genuinely curious. 'I didn't mean that to sound rude,' he added, intent on being respectful. This was the kind of place where a person needed to make friends, especially when he had enough enemies already.

Hamlin took a packet of tobacco from a pocket and proceeded to make a roll-up. 'They think they've finally found a prison that'll hold me . . . I've escaped from three so far.'

'I remember you. You made a lot of news . . . I guess they think you're still dangerous?'

'Assholes,' Hamlin muttered, licking the paper and completing the roll-up. 'I've always been fascinated by what I could make in my garage that would scare the bejeezus out of anyone. Made my first atomic bomb when I was twenty. That was without the plutonium, of course. Science department got into more trouble'n I did,' he said, lighting up and blowing the smoke at the ceiling. He held the tobacco out to Stratton who shook his head.

'Didn't you make some anthrax?'

'That was the one that shot me to infamy. Easiest thing I ever made,' Hamlin said, amused at the memory. 'All I did was go to the old testing grounds in Oklahoma and pluck me up some samples right out of an open field that wasn't even fenced. I grew the stuff in culture dishes – had enough to fill a biscuit tin within months.'

Stratton was fascinated by home-made devices himself, particularly explosives. Hearing such details first-hand from a grandmaster was entertaining. 'I remember you mostly for your mail bombs. I saw a diagram of one of your circuits. Very innovative.'

'You technical?'

'I'm not in your league.'

'My mistake was in getting too political,' Hamlin sighed, taking a long drag and clearly enjoying it. 'I should say, in going for the wrong political targets . . . Up until then I was just some anti-abortion, animal-rights, pro-environment nut who on occasion plucked a member or two of the general public to make a point. There was just one detective lookin' for me in those days. Then I sent a coupla letter bombs to a selection of high-ranking Republicans and the entire FBI was set loose on my ass.' The reminiscing amused him.

Stratton couldn't decide what to make of Hamlin. He didn't appear to be crazy. Had he not known the man's history he would have guessed him to be a normal harmless old codger. 'How do you rate this place – compared to other prisons you've been in?'

'This place? I'm havin' a great time!' Hamlin said. 'It's gonna be a little harder than the others to get out of, though.' He held the last quarter-inch of the roll–up between tobacco–stained fingertips and took a final drag. 'I'm busier than I've ever been,' he said as the vent kicked in again and the cell was filled with a current of air that did not smell particularly fresh. 'I keep those suckers runnin',' for one,' he said, pointing to the vent.

Stratton looked up at the small air duct, its orifice coated in black dust. 'You help maintain the scrubbers?'

'Help? Since they put me in engineering the engineers don't come down here so much. I kinda made myself a little niche. They love it, I love it. They get to spend more time topside. I get to spend less time in here. I should get a piece o' their pay cheque.'

Stratton suddenly thought about his task. It was as if it had been waiting in his head for some attention, had lost patience and jumped out at him. He didn't have a plan yet but before he could begin to devise one he was going to have to get his hands on some information. It was too early to get frustrated although it already felt as if he'd been on this mission for an age. He needed to see the lie of the land, experience the routine and gather details about his target.

Stratton got to his feet, walked to the end of the little cell and turned around.

'You pacin' the room already?' Hamlin asked. He took one of the books off his desk and held it out to Stratton. 'Here.'

Stratton took it and looked at the front cover. It was a history of deep-sea diving, stretching back to ancient Greece and Aristotle.

'Hey. You never know when it'll come in handy,' Hamlin said, winking.

Stratton saw the funny side, decided to shelve his problems for the moment and sat back on his bed. Exercising some patience was sound advice. He opened the book and read the introduction. It made him think of his emergency diving equipment sitting at the base of the Styx umbilical just beyond the prison walls. Stratton shuddered at the thought of being out there once again with only a lungful of air to fuel a one-way journey to an objective he could not see. But there were the standby diving sets in the dock that he could utilise if he could get to them. The problem with that was getting inside the dock itself. But then, before he could escape he had to get the tablet.

Stratton told himself once more to be patient and to put the mission to one side for the moment.

A klaxon sounded somewhere outside and Stratton looked over at Hamlin who had gone back to his laptop.

'The dinner bell,' the older man said. 'Highlight of the afternoon for most. In the early days they fed us in the cells. That got to be too much work for the guards and so they opened up a mess hall.'

The door hissed loudly and the seal around it shrank.

'You been to the mess hall yet?' Hamlin asked as he got to his feet.

'No.'

'Watch yourself. It's a place where things can go wrong.'

The door moved in on its hinges and Hamlin helped it open. There was no one outside and Stratton leaned out to take a look.

Hamlin put a hand out to stop him. 'Steady, son,' he said in a low voice. 'From here on you don't move without being told. There're some guards ain't as kindly as others – one in particular.'

Stratton could guess who he was referring to.

'STEP OUTSIDE YOUR CELL INTO THE CORRIDOR!' boomed a voice from tinny speakers.

Hamlin obeyed and Stratton followed.

All the other doors along the corridor were open. A prisoner walked out of each one.

'TURN TO YOUR LEFT AND FACE THE RED LIGHT,' the voice demanded.

A red light shone above a door at the end of the corridor. Every prisoner obeyed lethargically. There was a loud hiss and a clunk and the door below the red light opened. Stratton could feel the pressure change and looked up at a CCTV camera that was pointing directly at him.

'KEEP THE SAME DISTANCE FROM THE MAN IN FRONT OF YOU. HE STOPS, YOU STOP. DO NOT BUNCH . . . FORWARD MARCH!'

Stratton trooped off behind Hamlin.

Gann stood in the operations control room looking at the monitors, in particular the one that showed Stratton heading through a door. He switched to another monitor showing Stratton stepping through the other side and followed his progress along a rocky, brightly lit corridor. When Stratton went out of sight Gann ignored the other monitors and concentrated on his thoughts.

Stratton, in a line of prisoners, shuffled forward behind Hamlin towards an open airlock door. Before he reached it he got a once-over from a chemical scanner and a metal detector. None of the prisoners were wearing wrist or ankle shackles, which suggested a high level of confidence among the guards that there would be no disorder. On the other hand, since leaving his cell Stratton had not seen a guard other than behind a heavy glass porthole. The inmates' movements between their cells and the galley were controlled by airlock doors and loudspeakers. Stratton wondered what riot-control methods the facility employed in the event of a serious disturbance.

'NEXT,' a metallic voice boomed and Stratton stepped through the doorway. He glanced back at the faces lining up behind him, estimating the number of inmates at around two dozen. None of them appeared to be Afghan or Middle Eastern. 'MOVE ON,' the voice commanded and he continued along a short corridor to a door that led into the mess hall.

The room was large enough to comfortably seat fifty inmates. It was two storeys high, with a narrow balcony running around the four walls midway up. A handful of guards stood around the balcony at intervals, looking down on the prisoners as they filed inside. At each corner was a narrow airlock door with a thick glass porthole at head height. A dozen tables were arranged around the clean stone galley floor, with plastic chairs tucked underneath them. The line of inmates snaked from the entrance along one of the walls to a long countertop that began with a pile of plastic food trays and cutlery. There were no servers. The pre-heated meals, similar to military rations, were in sealed plastic bags and were arranged in labelled trays. A selection of biscuits and plastic drink cartons were stacked at the end. Stratton chose a couple of food sachets without taking much notice of the contents. He was more interested in his surroundings.

He followed Hamlin to a table where they set their trays down opposite each other. Two thuggish-looking inmates joined them. One of them appeared to have more than a mild interest in Stratton. Stratton ignored him and opened one of his food sachets. It contained a meaty sludge of some kind and he checked the sachet's label that described the contents as beef and vegetables in gravy. He was used to military field-ration packs and expected it to taste better than it looked, which was usually the case. He dipped a flimsy plastic fork into the dark brown pool, scooped up a chunk and put it in his mouth. It was as expected and, suddenly feeling hungry, he opened a packet of hard-tack biscuits to dip into the gravy.

One of the thugs at the end of the table was trying, with difficulty it seemed, to read the contents label on a packet. He emptied the sachet onto his tray and frowned at the sight of peaches in syrup. He opened another packet and poured what appeared to be a risotto of some kind into the indentation beside the peaches. He then emptied the contents of a third, which, like Stratton's main course, was beef and vegetables in gravy, into the space between the others where it trickled into both. Unperturbed, he dipped a fork into the mess and began to eat it. His stare wandered back to Stratton as he chomped noisily. Stratton glanced at him. The cold malice in the man's unintelligent eyes was raw. Stratton looked away, fully expecting to see more of that Neanderthal machismo in a place like this.

An airlock door on the balcony opened and Gann stepped out. He leaned on the rail as he looked down at the tables and found Stratton. His gaze moved to the thugs at the same table. One of them surreptitiously nudged his colleague and indicated Gann with an upward movement of his eyes. The second thug glanced up at Gann, looked over at Stratton and then back down at his food. An airlock door on the other side of the galley floor opened.

Hamlin heard the hiss above the general din and looked in that direction, stopping the movement of a forkful of food heading towards his open mouth. 'Now that ain't usual,' he said, putting the fork down.

Stratton followed Hamlin's gaze across the room. Afghan prisoners, all wearing Muslim skullcaps and sporting untrimmed beards, were filing into the room.

'The Talibuttfucks don't normally eat the same time as us,' Hamlin said, looking around the room for reactions from the other tables. 'This ain't good.'

The sounds of chewing and talking died down as practically every Westerner stopped eating to look at the late arrivals. Angry expressions formed on faces, low, conspiratorial comments were exchanged and the tension in the mess hall rose perceptibly.

'What the fuck are these assholes doin' in here?' the thug across from Stratton said, loud enough for those at the tables around him to hear.

Stratton looked up at the guards around the balcony who were watching with the curiosity of those conducting a potentially entertaining experiment. He saw Gann, who'd been looking at the Afghans, shift his gaze to the thugs at Stratton's table. Stratton watched the one thug exchange glances with Gann and look directly at him. A warning bell went off in his head. Something was about to happen and it would appear that Stratton had a part to play in it.

The Afghans picked up their trays and eating utensils and for the most part kept their dark eyes fixed ahead, though one or two glanced uncomfortably at the Westerners.

Stratton had lost interest in the thugs for the moment as he searched for the focus of his mission. He had studied photographs of Durrani, courtesy of the CIA after the British SIS had requested copies, but he knew from long experience how difficult it was to identify a person from a photograph. The good news in this instance was that the photo was a recent one. Durrani's hair was bushy, his beard uncropped. The problem was that nearly all the Afghans were sporting similar styles.

Stratton scanned each man down the line, stopping at the second-to-last one coming through the door. Stratton was positive that it was Durrani. Because of the prison uniform the man was wearing he could not see any of the listed VDMs (Visual Distinguishing Marks) since they were all on Durrani's torso. The small incision in his lower abdomen would be the ultimate proof. Stratton went back along the line of faces just to make sure and by the time he reached the end he was certain his original man was Durrani.

There was something exciting, even exhilarating about being so close to his quarry. This was the first stage in the target-information-gathering phase. Durrani was alive and well and in the prison.

A packet of food flew from somewhere and landed on the wall above the line of Afghans.

'Shit!' Hamlin cursed. 'I know how *this* is gonna end up.'

'We should move back and stay out of it,' Stratton said, taking hold of the older man's arm.

'There's nowhere you can escape what they're gonna do to us now.'

Stratton had no idea what the old man meant as they got to their feet.

A chair sailed across the room towards the Afghans.

The two thugs at Stratton's table stood up. Both men appeared to be more interested in Stratton than they were in the Afghans.

Stratton and Hamlin headed for a far wall as the shouting and missile-throwing intensified. The Afghans closed ranks and retaliated by launching anything to hand at the front line of aggressors. One of them chucked a tray like a frisbee, striking an inmate in the face and giving him a bloody injury. It was the starting signal

251

that set the Western prisoners going and a group of them hurled themselves at the Afghans. The clash was brutal and fists and feet swung violently.

The two thugs did not join the mêlée, taking advantage of the disturbance to close in on Stratton. He moved away from Hamlin, looking around for a weapon to replace the plastic fork in his hand.

Hamlin moved into a corner and slid down it until he was sitting on his heels. He put his hands over his head as if the building was about to fall on him and waited for what he believed to be inevitable.

The thugs split up to come at Stratton from different angles. Having failed to find a weapon he raised his fists in a boxer's stance, shuffling back. His right hand was cocked close to his chest with the thumb towards his opponents, concealing the end of the plastic fork protruding from the back of his fist. Working on the principle that it was generally a good idea to take out the biggest danger first he manoeuvred himself closer to the larger thug. The other thug then showed signs of wanting to engage first when he picked up a plastic chair.

As the men closed in the thug with the chair launched it. Stratton did not duck low enough and a leg struck the side of his head. The larger thug took advantage of the distraction and made his move.

Stratton was nothing if not decisive when it came time to attack and he did not hesitate. The thug came in quickly and swung at him with a powerful haymaker. Stratton ducked nimbly underneath it, stepped to one side of the big man and released his cocked fist. But instead of punching straight he swung it in a tight arc and plunged the end of the fork into the man's eye – which exploded in a spurt of retinal fluid, followed by a geyser of blood.

The thug let out a scream as his knees buckled. The second thug was already on top of Stratton and grabbed his collar as his other hand followed up with a blow. Stratton threw his arm over the top of the extended arm of the thug who had a hold of him, bringing it down the other side and up again in between them. The action straightened the thug's arm by applying pressure to his elbow. Stratton continued the move, standing on tiptoe, and his momentum snapped the joint. The second thug's howl rose above the general cacophony. At the same time Stratton swung his other hand with the plastic fork in it high and then down onto the corner of the man's neck, driving the prongs of the fork deep into the flesh. The broken elbow had done the job but the follow-up certainly added to the thug's agony. He dropped to the floor, screaming.

Stratton looked up to see the guards on the balcony stepping through the airlock doors that closed behind them. Hamlin was still sitting on the floor with his head in his hands.

The battle was in full swing. Some of the Afghans tried to stay together while others who had been dragged away from their colleagues were receiving a hiding.

The balcony was now void of guards and Stratton had the distinct feeling something ominous was about to happen. But at the same time it was a great opportunity to get closer to his target.

He saw Durrani and another Afghan scurry behind the counter. He headed towards them, pushing his way through the mêlée while fending off blows. He leaped over the counter, dropped to his knees on the other side and found himself facing Durrani an arm's length away. There was not a trace of fear in the man's eyes. Durrani's colleague was busy fighting behind him, clutching at the throat of a man who was doing the same to him. Durrani stared at Stratton, years of battle experience etched into his brain.

He lunged at Stratton who moved deftly aside while at the same time slamming his forearm against the Afghan's throat and forcing him against the side of the counter and down. Durrani was trapped and grabbed Stratton's arm in an effort to release the choke hold. Stratton replaced his arm with his knee, pinning the Afghan even more firmly. He took advantage of the moment, not to strike another blow but to confirm what he most needed to know. He raised Durrani's shirt and pulled down his trousers to expose the scar. It was still pink, the cut itself ugly due to it healing without stitches.

Durrani was momentarily confused.

Stratton looked into his eyes and for a second they weighed each other up. 'Durrani?' he asked.

Durrani was suddenly horrified. This man was not here to beat him. He wanted his treasure. More alarming was that he knew exactly where to look for it. With a combination of rage and desperation Durrani mustered every ounce of strength he possessed and threw Stratton off him. Stratton fell onto his back and the Afghan was on him like a wolf. He grappled for Stratton's throat, driven not just to defend himself but to destroy this man who knew his precious secret.

Stratton was momentarily overpowered by the force of Durrani's attack and struggled to twist out of his grip.

As Durrani fought to cut off Stratton's air he was suddenly overwhelmed by a feeling of giddiness. The face of the man around whose neck his hands were tightening started to blur. Stratton punched up an arm and pushed his fingers into Durrani's larynx but as he did so he too felt horribly dizzy. His eyes went in and out of focus and he struggled to breathe.

They were not the only two experiencing such difficulties. The riot had suddenly ceased with everyone in the room down on the floor and fighting to breathe. A man screamed as another lurched to his feet, staggered across the room as if blind and fell down hard onto his face.

Stratton fought to hold on to consciousness but his brain felt as though it was being squeezed like a sponge. All he could do was lie still and concentrate on breathing. A few seconds later his mind drifted into unconsciousness.

Chapter 11

Mandrick was at his desk going through a list of emails while Hank Palmerston sat on the other side of the room nursing a cup of coffee and scowling to himself. His head jerked up at the sound of a buzzer. Mandrick glanced at the monitor on his desk and pushed a button on his remote. The door to the office hissed and clunked as it swung inwards and Gann stepped into the room.

Hank's eyes narrowed as he stared at the senior guard whom he disliked intensely.

'You wanted to see me,' Gann said, looking confident despite knowing why he had been summoned.

'You're either a total dumb-fuck,' Hank said, putting down his coffee, 'or . . . nah. There ain't any other explanation. You *are* a dumb-fuck.'

Gann's barely visible reaction was a subtle tightening of his jaw. Having always been employed by aggressive hard-ass men physically inferior to him, controlling himself was something he'd had plenty of opportunity to practise. Gann knew his place in the pecking order and calmed his intense desire to attack the man. Maybe one day, when this was all over and if by chance he happened to bump into Hank somewhere, he'd tear him apart. But for the time being he could not. Hank was a senior CIA field operative and that was reason enough to allow the prick to walk all over him.

'Anyone wanna hear my reasonin'?' Gann asked.

Hank's face broke into a smirk of stupefied disbelief. 'It's got reasoning,' he said to Mandrick. 'Go on. Please do go on. I've got to hear why one of my Talibutts is dead with a broken neck, two of 'em are blinded, one has a broken back and may never walk again and three of 'em have been so badly beaten in the head that I might as well send 'em back home for all the good they are to me now. And all while a federal prison inspector is crawling around the goddamn place. Do tell.'

Gann's expression suggested he conceded that the number of casualties was excessive. Otherwise, he remained confident of his actions. 'I think that Charon guy is a federal agent.'

Hank looked at Mandrick for an explanation. Mandrick raised his eyebrows in denial.

'I ain't as stupid as you think I am,' Gann said. 'I figured out there was a fed agent on the ferry myself. Why else would we have to kill everyone? But now I think the only guy to escape the ferry was the only one who shoulda died.'

Hank's jaw clenched. 'You mixed my Talibutts with the regular prisoners knowing it would cause a riot because you think there's a fed in the building? You know something . . .' he said, pausing to control himself, 'you're so fuckin' dumb I'm irritated just by the sight of you.'

Gann wondered just how problematic it really would

be to kill a CIA agent. 'I didn't suspect it so much before the riot.'

Hank's brow furrowed.

'I always suspected there was something strange about the guy,' Gann went on. 'Right from when I first met 'im. Even before the accident. There was somethin' about him, the way he was always lookin' at people and things, but not in a normal way.'

Hank squared up to Gann who was a head taller and much broader. 'I don't give a damn if J. Edgar fuckin' Hoover himself turned up for lunch . . . Federal agent my ass. You must think I'm as stupid as you are. I know why you want to kill Charon. He's the only person who can finger you for the ferry sabotage.'

Gann smirked. Hank was completely right, up until the fight in the galley. 'So I guess you're not interested to know if one of my inmates is interested in one of yours?' Gann looked smug.

Hank squinted at the oversized guard. 'What're you talking about?'

'Like I said. Charon is a motherfuckin' spy. He ain't here to do time. He's here for one of your Talibutts. I got proof, too,' he said, producing a mini-CD from his breast pocket. 'Take a look at it. It's from one of the cameras in the galley.'

Hank took the CD, eyeing Gann suspiciously, placed it in a slot on the panel and hit the play button. Mandrick got up from his seat and walked around the desk to get a closer look.

An image of the galley looking down from above flickered onto one of the monitors.

'This is just before it went off,' Gann said, moving to the monitor to point things out. 'While everyone else is movin' towards the Talibutts, Charon and his cellmate Hamlin move back. They don't want any of the action. Now, my boys move in . . .'

'Your boys?' Hank interrupted.

'My job – orders from your boss, as I understand it – was to take out the people in that ferry and it ain't done until Charon is history.'

Hank's expression tightened. He glanced at Mandrick, wondering if he was in on this. Mandrick remained poker-faced.

'Now look at this. Charon here wastes my guys in just two moves. He didn't learn that in the joint . . . Then he starts to move back to safety. Remember, he don't want any part of this fight. But then he sees somethin' and in a second he's the other side of the room and on top of one of the Talibutts. But take a look at this. He ain't there for the fightin'. He even says somethin' to the guy. Whatever it is, the guy gets mad and then the depressurisation got to 'em.'

Hank was not entirely convinced and replayed the last segment of the recording.

'I don't know what he's doin',' Gann said. 'But I know when something stinks – and that guy stinks.'

Hank freeze-framed on a close-up of the Afghan.

'The Talibutt's name is Durrani,' Gann offered. He could see that he had scored with the video.

Mandrick remembered the name as the one Hank had given to him earlier when he'd asked him to carry out a pre-interrogation softening-up. He stared at the side of Hank's head, wondering what was going on inside it.

Hank knew it was Durrani the moment he saw him on the monitor. The Afghan was the reason for his present visit. He pondered the various permutations of the situation, unable to make anything out of it at that moment. But the observations, if accurate, certainly gave food for thought. Cogwheels of possibility began to turn and click as an intelligence with twenty-two years of experience in the business filed the information in readiness for any future connections.

Hank had spent the last ten years specialising in inter-rogation and information-extrapolation techniques with Asian and Middle Eastern Muslim subjects. He began his Agency career in Pakistan near the end of the Russian occupation of Afghanistan, spending much of those early days operating out of an office in the US embassy in Islamabad. For most of that period he liaised with the Saudi Arabian and Pakistani intelligence services in their combined efforts to finance, supply and train the Afghan mujahideen in order to oust the Russians. Then, when the Communist grip on Russia finally collapsed along with the Berlin Wall, Hank was already taking seriously the new danger shaping up to take its place in the form of Islamic fundamentalism. He was in Langley when Mir Aimal Kasi gunned down five CIA staff as they waited at the checkpoint to drive into the CIA head-quarters. A month later in New York Ramzi Yousef parked a vehicle on level B-2 of the World Trade Center and detonated a bomb that killed six people in a cafe-teria above. The two young men, both of Pakistani origin, neither of whom knew that the other existed, casually left the country on flights to Pakistan hours after their attack.

Hank moved to Afghanistan to begin the overseas hunt for them. He also got involved in several operations intended to kill or kidnap a dangerous upstart called Osama bin Laden. He lived through the formative days of the great jihad against America that eventually led to the successful destruction of the Twin Towers. He remained in Afghanistan to welcome the first American troops and followed them into Kabul to set up the Agency's new offices. Hank played his part in the defeat of the Taliban only to then suffer the indignity of their subsequent reorganisation with the help of many of his 'old friends' in the Saudi Arabian and Pakistani intelligence services who had their own agendas that were far removed from his.

With the rise of the Iraqi insurgency after the US-led invasion of that country Hank was assigned to aid in the setting-up of information-gathering cells around the world. But following the constant media attacks against Guantánamo Bay and the subsequent witch-hunt by many countries against CIA interrogation centres within their borders, he was grateful for a chance to take a key development role in what could only be described as a bizarre and audacious undertaking. Not only did Styx eventually open for business but it ended up yielding high-quality information while attracting the minimum possible outside scrutiny. When it came to security, media curiosity, eavesdropping and covert investigations, a prison beneath the surface of the ocean was like having one on the Moon. It was almost perfect . . . almost, but not quite.

Hank had never been under any illusion that Styx would last for ever. But he thought it would at least survive for a decade or two and, with luck, perhaps even see the Agency through to the end of the jihad. Now, after only two years, organisational cracks were starting to form in the administrative structure of the little oceanic citadel that he'd had such high hopes for. The FBI was trying to investigate the CIA interrogations as well as the so-called mining infractions by the host corporation. The media had become equally keen to report on anything to do with the prison. The White House was afraid of what the FBI and the media might find. And the only thing holding it all together outside the Agency was the greed of a handful of civilians who ran the place. The key, with them at least, was to ensure that their greed was not completely sated. Rumours that the mine was drying up did not help matters at all. Quite the reverse, in fact. He was in danger of losing the only glue holding it all together.

But it wasn't over yet. Not by a long shot. Not if Hank could help it. 'I want you to listen to me carefully,' he said to Gann. 'Nothing else happens to anyone in this prison unless I say so. Is that clear?'

'What about Charon?' Gann asked.

'If he dies after surviving one dubious disaster already it'll only bring a hundred of his buddies crawling all over this place. He isn't going anywhere and he has no one to talk to but us – so relax.'

Mandrick thought about mentioning that Christine

had met with Charon when he first became conscious. But that might upset more than one apple-cart. If Gann knew as much he might just be stupid enough to try and kill her too. Hank would be none too pleased either, especially with this new implication. Mandrick had a lot of plans in various stages of development, all of them based around his own interests. One of them was Christine and if he smeared her with more suspicion than she had already attracted he might as well forget about her. But he didn't want to, not just yet. He would hold on to his information for the time being.

'I want you to hoist in one last thing,' Hank said to Gann. 'One important piece of information that you should never forget . . . You listening?'

Gann nodded, a feeling of superiority stealing over him. He felt he was a little more equal to the agent than when he'd walked into the room minutes earlier.

'You're a moron,' Hank said with utter conviction. 'You've always been a moron and nothing will change that.'

Gann felt his temples throb as he stared into the eyes of the chubby man within a haymaker's reach of him.

'Morons don't think for themselves,' Hank went on. 'You got that?'

Mandrick knew Gann a lot better than Hank did but it would appear that the CIA agent was a far better judge of character. Mandrick was waiting for Gann to slap Hank in the chops, almost tensing in expectation of the blow, and wondering what his reaction should be. He was impressed with both men, and somewhat relieved, when the punch did not come.

Mandrick had to agree with Hank's basic sentiments, though. Gann was not the brightest lamp in the street. But then, neither was he a complete idiot. He had managed to carry out what had to be acknowledged as a complicated sabotage of a Styx ferry that, with a little help from Mandrick, would be difficult to prove had been foul play. Admittedly, there was the Charon factor, of course, but that aside it had been a good effort. And the fact that he had refrained from dropping Hank was a further indication of Gann's basic good sense. However, he doubted that Gann would forget the insult soon – or ever, for that matter. Mandrick might have misjudged Gann's ability to hold back his violent impulses in the short term but he was confident that at that very moment the man was plotting Hank's demise for some day in the future.

'You people are falling apart,' Hank said, redirecting his ire at Mandrick. 'You don't have the balls to hold this place together.'

Mandrick sighed. 'We're tougher than you think. A lot's happened but we can get away with a lot more.'

'You always tell people what they want to hear, don't you, Mandrick? You want me to think you believe we'll come after you when you jump. But the truth is, guys like you never really do believe it until it's too late.' Hank stared into Mandrick's eyes. 'I've been buying and selling truth and lies for a long time and from people far better equipped to play the game than you. You're lying to me, Mandrick. It's clear as a mountain stream to these old eyes. You know what's better than getting even with someone who screws with you?'

Mandrick didn't bother to try and guess. He was busy assessing Hank's sincerity and to his alarm he found him convincing.

'Getting even with him *before* he screws you,' Hank said. 'That's the smart play. Open the door.'

Mandrick did not react to the threat although more than a tingle of discomfort rippled through him. He opened the door and watched Hank walk out of the room.

There was always going to be an endgame to this whole scenario and Mandrick often felt concern at his apparent powerlessness to influence it one way or another. But perhaps that was not the case any more. It would appear that the ticking clock was going faster than he'd thought a few hours earlier. Hank had shone a narrow beam of light onto the pitfalls that faced all the players in this complicated game. The Agency controlled almost everything, but not quite. Every player had a destructive force that they could unleash and in such a game the advantage went to him who struck first. Mandrick and the Felix Corp were in it for the money but receiving it wasn't enough. The real issue was holding on to the freedom to spend it when the top eventually did blow off.

'He thinks he's in charge around here but he ain't,' chirped Gann.

Mandrick glanced at Gann, wondering why Forbes had inflicted such an uncontrollable beast on him.

'Mr Forbes is in charge of this place. And until he tells me to lay off Charon I'll do what I think is best for this place. The CI friggin' A can go screw themselves.'

Gann headed for the door. Mandrick considered trying to convince him not to go against Hank but decided not to bother. The seams were cracking all over the place and Mandrick felt it was now beyond his ability to hold them together. Gann was, understandably, concerned about being accused of sabotaging the ferry and therefore had every right to protect himself. There was no way that Gann was going to let Charon get out of the prison alive and so he might as well get on with it.

Gann left the room and Mandrick went back to his desk and slumped into his chair. He suddenly felt more vulnerable than he had ever been and there was only one solution. He needed more control of his destiny. To get that he needed to act first. In short, he needed to escape. But it wasn't *getting* free of Styx that was a problem. He could leave that afternoon. He was the warden. The problem was *staying* free. Hank had underlined that fact most clearly. The only way Mandrick could keep the CIA off his back was to have a value to them. It was that lack of value that was frustrating him.

The phone on his desk chirped, taking him out of the depths of his thoughts, and he plucked the receiver out of its cradle. 'Mandrick.'

'Hi,' a woman's voice said.

It was Christine and the image of her body immediately acted like a tonic. 'Hi yourself.'

'I'd like to see you.'

He never believed her when she was so forward. If she wanted to see him it was nothing to do with romance. 'See me or interrogate me about the mess hall incident?'

'What mess hall incident?'

'That's very good, Christine. You'll become more memorable with comments like that.'

She laughed. 'I was told one of the guards got his timings mixed up.'

'It's inexcusable. We're taking it very seriously, of course.'

'I wanted to tell you I'm pretty much finished.'

'I'm sorry to hear that. You're the only breath of fresh air in this place. You'll be at dinner tonight?'

'Of course.'

'I'll see you then . . . Perhaps we can talk afterwards.'

'That would be nice . . . Can I book a ferry for later this evening?'

'You want to leave straight after dinner?'

'After our little talk,' she said coquettishly.

'I see,' Mandrick said, the excitement rising in him despite his better judgement. The thought then struck him that he might leave with her. Perhaps they could both depart after dinner and enjoy the following day together in Houston, relaxing at his apartment after the decompression. It was worth considering. 'I'll make the arrangements.'

'See you later.'

'Bye,' he said, replacing the phone.

That was pleasantly unexpected, he thought. Christine was suddenly within his grasp and it made him feel far more excited and attracted to her, a very welcome distraction from everything else. Mandrick's natural suspicion brought up the question of why she had changed from challenging to amenable so suddenly. He decided that perhaps it was not so sudden. He had been working his charm on her from the moment they'd first met. And time was running out for them to get it together which could have helped to encourage her. Or perhaps it was simply one of the mysterious complexities of the female gender.

On the other hand, this was probably a bad time to be leaving the prison. Things could get ugly over the next few days and being topside would lose him any control he might have. Perhaps it was time to put together his endgame plan. It was based on the premise that, when this house of cards toppled, if he could not be of value to the CIA alive he would have to let them think he was dead. Its magnitude was unnerving and challenging, not the most perfect solution but a good one and, more important, the only one he had.

Christine was highly desirable but he couldn't allow the craving for a beautiful woman to cloud his common sense. That would be fatal.

Christine put down the receiver and stared thoughtfully at the colourful eiderdown covering her small bed that took up almost half of the otherwise drab white-painted concrete room. She sat down at a simple dresser, the only other piece of furniture in the room, and brought up an internet mailing page on her laptop screen. The vent in the ceiling clicked on to adjust the air. She paused to clear her ears before typing a short message that explained to the recipient that she was preparing to finalise her plans for departure.

She had set her own clock ticking. She could quit

there and then, throw in the towel, tell Mandrick that she needed to get out of Styx immediately and turn her back on the rest of her plans. But that was not about to happen. Not without reasons better than those she had. She had waited her entire life for this moment, not that she ever knew what it would entail. But it had all the ingredients she had dreamed of as far back as her teens: an operation concerning national security; dangerous and, most significant, operating alone and under cover. She was a woman doing a man's job in a man's world and in the highly competitive arena she had chosen to work in that was no small achievement.

It had been a relatively short and hazard-free journey to the rare, enviable and highly classified position of Secret Service Special Operative to the Oval Office. The post achieved the highest level of secrecy by circumventing the channels used by all other mainstream and military intelligence-agency recruitment procedures. But Christine was nobody's fool and was aware that getting the important job had been due more to luck than to ability. On the other hand, as her grandmother had always told her, 'The harder you work, the luckier you'll be.' The words were true enough. Her appointment had had a lot to do with being in the right place at the right time. But she had certainly worked tirelessly towards the job throughout her life.

Right from childhood Christine had refused to conform to the generally accepted standards of her gender – by refusing to wear dresses, for instance. She would only ever agree to put on traditional female trappings after heavy negotiations with her parents, always bartering an occasional act of conformity for things considered too masculine for a young lady. At ten she wanted boxing lessons, at eleven she accepted bridesmaid duties only if she could join a boys' soccer club since there was no local girls' team. Other demands over the years included baseball, fencing, rock climbing, karate and clay-pigeon shooting, not all of which she persisted with. But her hunger to pursue such energetic pastimes never seemed to diminish.

Christine's parents regarded her macho aspirations as delusional, superficial and immature until the day she returned home for dinner after a game of 'Smear the Queen', a full-contact American football game without pads or helmet. She was clearly in pain as she sat down for the meal but stoically refused any attention. It later transpired that her collarbone had been broken in two places and she had several cracked ribs, a fractured wrist and a broken thumb. What was more, Christine had received the injuries at various points throughout the game but had refused to leave the field until the end.

By the time Christine attended college she had not only grown into a very beautiful girl but her femininity had blossomed along with it. Her interest in boys was growing beyond them as mere objects to compete against physically but although there was never a shortage of admirers she found it impossible to attract one who matched her strength of mind and spirit.

Christine attended the University of Virginia to begin an MBA course but soon after arriving she was invited to take a Juris doctorate. Her parents were keen on her becoming a lawyer and so Christine accepted the challenge but only if she could take up barrel racing. They agreed.

In her final year at university she placed second in the Quarter Horse World Championships and graduated *summa cum laude*, finishing third in her class. The prospect of becoming a lawyer failed to inspire her but she had put the work in, achieved the grades and had to face the simple fact that dreams were dreams and reality was reality. And so it was with a sense of fatalism and little enthusiasm that she prepared to apply for an internship.

But things were never to develop in that direction and fate played its hand. The law school held a job fair the week of her graduation which Christine decided to visit out of curiosity. To her surprise she happened upon a recruiting booth for the Federal Bureau of Investigation. The agent who ran the booth did not make it sound as attractive as she had expected although she reckoned it was still more inspiring than becoming a lawyer. But any desire to sign up was squashed when he explained the qualifications required. Christine would need at least a college degree, an MBA and three years' work experience or be fluent in a foreign language. She had the degree but not enough work experience and no foreign language.

Christine left the booth and as she headed for the exit she was consumed by a feeling of loss and disappointment. She stopped to look back in the direction of the FBI booth, wondering if there was any other way she might be able to join, when she saw a booth inviting applications for the United States Secret Service.

The Secret Service did not interest Christine as much as the FBI did but for reasons she could not explain she felt compelled to talk to the agent. After telling him about her qualifications he offered her a position on the next recruit intake. He was much older and wiser than the FBI agent and, although her academic certificates were more than enough, what impressed him more were her other accomplishments. He noted that her riding showed dedication, her captaincy of the college hockey team and her position as pitcher for the local baseball team displayed leadership and toughness, and her experience as a hockey referee indicated an ability to make quick decisions and to stick with them. A month later she was on her way to the Secret Service Training Center in Beltsville, Maryland.

The course began with a two-week initiation phase designed to assess the candidates' general fitness and their skills with small-arms weaponry. On completion, the recruits travelled to the Federal Law Enforcement Training Center in Glynco, Georgia where they spent ten weeks learning small-arms skills, hand-to-hand combat and basic law concerning arrest, search and seizure. The final phase took place back at the Secret Service School in Maryland, specifically at the famed James J. Rowley Training Center where the remaining students faced gruelling physical tests while at the same time learning personnel-protection procedures and investigation skills. Christine graduated top of her class in all disciplines, including fitness, outdoing all the men. But at the end of it she suddenly doubted that her new career would give her the adventures she had always yearned for.

After graduation the new agents were asked to list their job preferences and, unsure of what she now wanted to do, Christine selected the Presidential Protection Division, a competitive posting with a long waiting list. It was beginning to look as if her destiny was to be little more than a glorified bodyguard. But fate was not yet done with her.

The First Lady wanted a female agent as her personal minder but her son, a keen sportsman in his early teens, baulked at the idea. The President's wife also doubted whether the service had a woman who would be able to keep up with him but she asked to see a list of candidates anyway. When she read Christine's resumé she demanded that the agent should be fast-tracked to the residence immediately.

When Christine learned that she was to be a babysitter it gave her even more pause for thought. But with little choice in the matter she took on the job, albeit with forced enthusiasm. The boy was soon impressed with Christine's knowledge and experience in so many sports disciplines, none of which he could best her in. He was a polite, disciplined and pleasant boy whose company Christine eventually began to enjoy though it did little to erode the lingering doubt that she was wasting her time.

A few months into the job Christine accompanied the First Lady and her son on a short politically motivated holiday to Cape Town. During an early dinner at a popular restaurant three local robbers, one of them armed with a revolver, chose the location to practise their profession. They were unaware that the wife of the President of the United States was dining inside at the time and apparently did not notice the collection of immaculate black-tinted suburbans and limousines outside the front, each with a smartly dressed driver at the wheel.

The robbers, posing as staff, made their way through the kitchen and into the dining room without attracting the attention of the Secret Service agents having dinner at a table in a corner away from the VIPs. Christine was eating with the First Lady, her son and a South African dignitary when the dastardly intruders revealed their purpose with a shout, the one with the revolver coincidentally holding it up near the First Lady's head.

The robbers ordered everyone to lie face down on the floor and contribute their watches, cellphones, jewellery and the contents of their wallets. Every agent had a concealed semi-automatic pistol but the robber with the weapon was behind the First Lady, thus presenting a difficult situation for them. They could never allow any harm to come to their charges which meant they could do nothing to escalate the situation.

Christine's pistol was in her tailor-made bumbag around her waist but she was directly under the gaze of the robber with the gun. The First Lady showed her grit when she looked at Christine with an expression of stone-cold malevolence. The robber was swinging his gun around as he shouted, the barrel sometimes moving to aim at the President's son who was looking extremely nervous, his eyes darting between Christine and the other agents as if he was about to run to them.

Christine gestured to him to stay calm, worried that he might do something to increase the nervousness of the robbers.

The handful of people at the surrounding tables began lowering themselves to the floor when the First Lady got up from her chair and looked contemptuously at the armed robber. 'Why don't you lower your gun? Then perhaps I'll do what you say,' she said.

Christine initially feared that her boss was simply flirting with the danger and then a second later realised she was deliberately trying to distract the man. She was later overheard saying she knew Christine would take the opening.

As Christine lowered herself to the floor she paused in a position not unlike that of a hundred-metre sprinter waiting for the starter pistol.

'Shut up!' the robber shouted, pointing the revolver directly at the President's wife. 'Get down on the floor or I'll shoot you.'

When Christine made the lunge she put all her power behind it. On making contact with the robber, her outstretched hand pushed the barrel of the weapon towards the ceiling and she practically knocked the man out as her shoulder struck him in the side of his ribcage. The blow launched him across the room and over a table where his head hit a wall, finishing off the job.

The other agents did not lose a second in tearing into the other two crooks, throwing them to the floor where, seconds later, they were bound tightly in plastic cuffs, napkins secured over their eyes. Christine quickly ushered the First Lady, her son and the dignitary out of the restaurant and into the limo which sped away, followed by a couple of the heavy suburbans.

The incident hit the media, although the identity of the agent who saved the day was kept secret, except around the Washington corridors of power. The President heard the details first-hand: his son gave him glowing accounts of Christine's lightning reactions and decisiveness.

A couple of weeks later a vacancy for a Special Secret Service Operative to the Oval Office occurred and Christine's name was placed on the list. But despite her recent heroics it was reckoned that she was unlikely to get a position that in the past had always been filled by men. Another argument against her was her lack of experience.

The First Lady, however, was determined to reward Christine for her valour in the Cape, intuitively aware that the young woman would much rather be doing something more adventurous than working as a bodyguard and sports instructor. Despite stiff opposition from several senior staff members the First Lady demonstrated her influence over the President and within a month Christine was swearing her allegiance to the country's leader in a private ceremony before heading off to Fort Bragg to begin a three-month training course. It was the first of five different locations in the USA and two in Europe where she would learn a variety of skills that included the use of sophisticated communications systems, imaging, the handling of explosives and a variety of weapons, unarmed combat, aggression training and, finally, a couple of weeks learning a special operative's general knowledge base of skills and techniques.

When Christine graduated she was provided with an apartment in Alexander and received instructions to no longer associate freely with her former Secret Service colleagues. Those agents also understood that if they were ever to see her outside the confines of the White House they were not to acknowledge her. That included an agent with whom she was having an affair, which was a blessing since he was madly in love with her but she could not reciprocate to the same extent. It was not a major concern to her that she seemed unable to find a man who was even remotely right for her but she was beginning to wonder if the problem lay with her own personality. But this was the wrong time in her life to cultivate any kind of relationship anyway and so it wasn't even worth thinking about. She could only hope she was kept busy enough so that she did not have time to dwell on such issues. She was not to be disappointed.

She got her first assignment a few days after she'd settled into her apartment, although it was no more than a simple courier task to an embassy contact in Warsaw. Her next dozen jobs were similarly low-level adventures and even though she suspected that she was still being assessed she did begin to wonder if there was ever going to be anything more interesting for an Oval Office operative. And had the world remained on the same even keel the chances were that she might not have seen a great deal more excitement. But if history really is 'philosophy by example' the world will always be a roller coaster swooping up and down between war and peace.

Christine had been an operative for only nine months when New York's Twin Towers were brought down by Muslim extremists, after which her life – like those of so many others – was never to be the same again. The tasks she was assigned suddenly became more intense, secretive and dangerous as America's Cold War infrastructure was ripped out by its roots and the machinery to wage a world war against Islamic terrorists was hastily assembled. There was an immediate shortage of experienced operatives and Christine found herself busier than she could ever have imagined. In between jobs she was sent on crash courses to learn Arabic and Farsi where she was taught to converse, read and write in those languages at a basic but workable level.

There is nothing like a war to sort the true men and women from the boys and girls and within two years it was hinted to Christine by a senior member of the White House staff that she was near the top of the most-favoured-operatives list. A year later, when she was called to a briefing and given her task at Styx prison, she knew she had finally arrived at the place she had dreamed of since her youth.

But the more difficult and dangerous a task, the greater the risk of failure: the higher one climbed the further one could fall. As she listened to the details of the mission it became clear that it could be a matter of physical survival, not just of boosting her reputation.

Christine closed her laptop, got to her feet, sat on her bed and lay back on the pillow. It was time once more to go through thoroughly the various steps she needed to take in this final phase, to examine the many things that could go wrong and, as far as possible, to determine what her reactions to them might be.

Chapter 12

Stratton woke up to the sound of his cell door depressurising and the feeling of his ears popping. He struggled to open his eyelids – they'd been sealed shut by the dried eye discharge that everyone in Styx appeared to suffer from while they slept. He felt for a bottle of water on the floor by his bed, dabbed some on his eyes and pulled the lids apart as someone came in.

Hamlin walked unsteadily into the room and the door closed as he sat down heavily on his bed. The drastic depressurisation of the mess hall during the riot had clearly taken its toll on the older man. Stratton had recovered minutes after the pressure levels had returned to normal but several of the inmates, particularly the injured, had required medical attention. Hamlin was one of those who'd been taken away on a gurney. Some people were more susceptible than others to variations in the pressures of the gases that make up air, notably in the oxygen level. Hamlin was one of those who did not fare well under such conditions and judging by his startled reaction immediately before the 'attack' he had obviously experienced something like it before and had known he was about to suffer.

'You OK?' Stratton asked sympathetically.

Hamlin did not acknowledge him and seemed to be focusing all his mental resources on simply keeping breathing. He eventually raised his head and opened his red-rimmed eyes to look at his cellmate. 'I don't have the constitution for this place,' he said, sounding strained. 'I can't survive here much longer.'

Stratton could not help wanting to give Hamlin some kind of psychological support. The man was a jailbird and would remain so for the rest of his natural life but Stratton had seen his 'normal' side and had to admit to liking that aspect of him. Perhaps it went deeper than that. Stratton was, after all, stuck inside a maximum-security prison in a grotty cell surrounded by a host of dangers, most of them unknown. It was only natural under such circumstances to seek out friends and allies, particularly when you had none to start with. 'I don't suppose there's anything I can do?' he asked.

Hamlin looked slightly amused by a thought that came to him. 'After my conviction, the FBI showed me a letter they found in my files that I wrote some years before. It was to the President of the United States, letting him know how I felt about some of his foreign and domestic policies. I suggested he should quit or go the way of JFK. I never sent it but the feds decided it was a serious threat because it came from me. I never meant it as a direct threat. It was just a suggestion, you know? . . . They told me I'd never make parole. The only way I was leaving jail was in a body bag.' His expression changed to one of determination. 'I'm gonna prove those sons of bitches wrong,' he said, glancing at Stratton for any reaction to his comment.

Stratton took it as bravado.

'You're an odd fish, fellah, ain't yer?' Hamlin enquired.

Stratton wasn't sure how he was intended to take this comment.

'Somethin' about you. Can't point to it but . . . I don't know. Somethin'.'

'I don't mean to make you feel uncomfortable.'

'Ain't nothin' like that. More like the opposite . . . Maximum-security cons have one thing in common. They ain't ever goin' anywhere, other than another prison. They don't kid themselves about it, either . . . least, not deep in their souls they don't . . . We're all partly dead because of it. You can see it in the way we move, walk, talk. Part-dead people can't hide it . . . You ain't part-dead.'

Hamlin continued to search Stratton's eyes in case he was wrong. 'Maybe it's because you just don't *know* you're part-dead,' he eventually decided, looking away.

He remembered something else he wanted to say to Stratton and, putting a finger to his lips, reached across to his desk and switched on a tape recording of some classical music. He increased the volume and leaned towards Stratton in a conspiratorial manner. 'You know Gann's got a problem with you, don't yer?' he said in a gruff whisper.

Stratton shrugged, going along with the intrigue. 'Why?'

'There ain't a lotta secrets in a prison. If the guards know somethin' the cons'll soon learn about it . . . I don't know why he wants you, though. That never came down the vine . . . Gann don't need a reason to hate someone, anyhow. He's just a mean son of a bitch.'

'I don't suppose there's much I can do about that.'

'I guess not,' Hamlin agreed.

'Unless I got to him first.'

'Fat chance of that.'

Stratton studied Hamlin, weighing him up, trying to decide if he could use him in a plan he had been hatching. The trick would be to make it of benefit to the older man too. It was something Hamlin had said that had triggered the idea. He had expressed a desire to get out of Styx — not that any such yearning was exactly surprising. But it had been more than a simple wish. Hamlin had implied that he really could escape and Stratton had to take this seriously, no matter how much of a long shot it was. Escaping from Styx would take some brilliant planning and knowledge of the prison if it was to be done without help from the outside. Hamlin had the credentials and, in his role as prison engineer, had perhaps also had the opportunity to come up with something. The more obstacles Stratton could break down the better chance he had of finding a way to Durrani.

Nothing was impossible and Stratton felt confident that if he had the time he could at least devise a plan. Successfully carrying it out would be another matter, of course. The point was that escape wasn't impossible. You just had to be smart enough to work it out. There was a risk in involving Hamlin but since Stratton had nothing else to go on but the few hours he had spent in the man's company he decided to rely on his instincts.

Stratton turned his attention to the heavy steel door with its thick rubber seam surrounding it. 'You know these doors are sensitive to external pressure?' he asked.

Hamlin looked at him oddly. 'I know just about everything there is to know about this place, including these doors. I service the machinery that maintains the pressure tanks, remember?'

Stratton looked at him soberly. 'So I'm right.'

'It don't take a genius to figure that out, considering there ain't any locks. Day one I calculated the difference between the inside and outside pressure and at its lowest there's over eight tons keeping that door closed. It would take you, me and a herd of Percherons to shift it, and only if there was a handle strong enough to tie them to which there ain't.'

'Unless the pressure was equalised.'

Hamlin smirked. 'That's what everyone spends day two trying to figure out. The pressure in every corner of this entire rabbit warren is controlled from the OCR and even the operators couldn't override the system without tripping a whole bunch of safety devices, procedures, airlocks, alarms and what-you-gots.'

Stratton didn't seem perturbed by Hamlin's negativity. 'Way I understand it is there are a pair of sensors that monitor the different pressures either side. Those sensors are inside the actual door.'

Hamlin scrutinised Stratton more closely. 'It took me till near the end of day three to figure that out.'

'If the sensors detect the pressure on one side equalising with that on the inside they'll automatically compensate,' Stratton continued.

'Unless they're overridden by the OCR which is what happens every time the door is opened . . . I know what you're thinking. Same thing everyone else does eventually. How to manipulate the sensors? There's only one problem, though—'

'And that's the reason you've never been able to figure out how to do it,' Stratton interrupted. 'You don't know precisely where the sensors are.'

Hamlin was growing fascinated with Stratton's line of speculation and he moved closer, his gravelly voice low. 'That's right,' he said, staring into Stratton's eyes. 'If you did, and if you had the right tools, you might be able to isolate the "inside" sensor and make the "outside" one think the pressure inside was higher than what it actually is.'

'And if that could be achieved the system would compensate by decreasing the inside pressure.'

'And when it drops below that of the outside, the door'll pop open . . . Nice theory, ain't it? . . . So far that brings you up to date with me.'

'Unless I knew precisely where the sensor was,' Stratton said.

Hamlin leaned back to look at Stratton from a broader perspective, his expression a mixture of surprise and suspicion.

'You got a pen?' Stratton asked. 'Better still, the tip of a small blade?'

Hamlin continued to study Stratton, trying to make up his mind about him. The guy was either full of shit or he had something very interesting to offer. There was only one way to find out.

Hamlin got to his feet, went to his desk, felt the back of one of the legs and opened a compartment that had been cleverly carved into it. He pulled out a thin strip of metal that had been fashioned into a blade the length of a pen, with string wrapped around one end to form a haft. He handed it to Stratton who got to his feet, faced the door and rubbed the pads of his fingers gently along the seal. Hamlin moved to his side, studying the seal as if he might have missed something the hundred or more times he had meticulously examined it in the past.

'You've noticed these small flaps in the seal?' Stratton said, poking the tip of the blade into one of the creases and prising it open. 'They go all the way around.'

'Sure. They're breathers. Otherwise the seals could blow up like balloons if there was a pressure spike. It's where the hiss comes from when the door opens.'

'And you know there's another seal inside this one.'

'The operating seals, one either side. I've seen these doors stripped down.'

'Did you notice that the operating seals don't have any of these breathers?'

'That's because the sensors are inside them. That's obvious. But it wouldn't have to be no bigger than a pinhead. And if you didn't know exactly where it was you'd never be able to isolate it without ripping out the entire seal – by which time it would no longer operate and you'd be stuck until a team of engineers came down to get you out.'

'The engineers know where the sensors are because they have to service them on occasion.'

'Sure. They just never let me in on that secret,' Hamlin said, starting to get irritated.

'What if I said I knew exactly where the inside sensor was?'

'How the hell would you know that?'

'I got friends,' Stratton said, keeping his voice low. 'I used to be into sat diving. When certain old buddies learned I was heading for Styx they made sure I got a few details they happened to have on this place in case I could use them. I don't know how much use it is,' he added, stepping back to look at the door and then at Hamlin. 'What would you do if you could get the other side of this door?' he asked, tossing out a little bait.

Hamlin remained very much unsure of his new cellmate. 'I want nothin' to do with puttin' the hits on Gann.'

'So you're saying that even if we could open this door without anyone knowing, it wouldn't be of interest to you?'

Hamlin sniffed the bait and found his mouth watering a little.

Stratton read Hamlin's silence to suggest he would be very interested.

'The inside or high-pressure sensor is dead centre on the door-hinge side,' Stratton said, rubbing the spot. 'If we could cut the outer seal just here, then cut into the operating seal, isolate the sensor with a cup of some kind, increase the pressure inside the cup . . . bingo!'

Hamlin was with him every step of the way. 'We could do that easily with a small electric pump.'

'You can get a pump?'

'We're at the bottom of the ocean. Pumps we got.' But Hamlin was still very unsure about a lot of other things. He leaned forward to whisper over the music. 'You open this door, you just got more doors. You got cameras too. Anyone in OCR, the warden's office or the guardroom sees you and that's it. They'll seal you off wherever you are and do what they did in the galley.'

'Then I suppose I'd need to know where Gann was when I opened the door.'

As the notion took root Hamlin's thoughts turned to his own purposes rather than Stratton's. He was hooked on the idea but tried not to show it. If he could get through the door he didn't give a damn what Stratton wanted to do. He knew exactly where *he* would head for.

Stratton sighed dramatically as part of his charade. 'I guess the theory is fine but the practical side would be pretty impossible,' he said, backing off and sitting on his bed.

Hamlin sat down opposite, watching his room-mate and still trying to figure him out. 'But if you could? You beat Gann to death and then walk back into your cell? You ain't gettin' any further.'

'Maybe you're not the only one with an escape plan.'

'Who said I had a plan?'

'You did.'

'I said I'd like to prove 'em wrong. That could mean a lotta different things.'

Stratton looked away as if he'd grown tired of Hamlin's games.

'So you've been here five minutes and you've got an escape plan,' Hamlin scoffed.

'Like I said . . .'

'Yeah, you got friends.'

'Let's just forget it.'

Hamlin didn't want to. He enjoyed nothing more than talking through new technical matters. But this one was of much greater personal interest to him. 'Supposin' we could get through that door. I'm into the whole mutual support thing but only so far. I'd wanna do my own thing. I wouldn't want anything to do with your problems – or your plans.'

'I would neither expect nor want you to. No disrespect but you're no spring chicken any more.'

Hamlin rested back against the wall, still eyeing Stratton suspiciously. 'I don't know about you, my friend . . . It's still the missing part–death side of you that bugs me.'

'Maybe you haven't been around a true optimist for a while.'

Hamlin was not sure why, but he was beginning to trust Stratton.

'Tusker?' a voice boomed over a speaker in a grille beside the air duct.

Hamlin got to his feet and turned down the tape player. 'Yes, sir.'

'How you feelin', Tusker?'

'Not too bad. I'm still gonna sue, though.'

'You know I'd be a witness for yer if I could, Tusker.'

'Generous of you to consider it, anyhow.'

'You feel up to doing some work? We got a torn filter on number two scrubber.'

'I warned you about that one a week ago.'

'Yeah, well, now it's torn. You wanna take a look at it?'

'Where's the engineer?'

'He's not feeling too good.'

'And if I don't?' Hamlin said, winking at Stratton. A short silence followed. 'He'd have to get his drunken ass off his mattress, wouldn't he?'

'You gonna do it or not, Tusker?'

'I'll do it for a cup o' one of them fine clarets the warden always has for dinner.'

'I'll try.'

'Come on, Busby. You can do better'n that.'

'OK,' the operations officer agreed. 'I'll send someone down to escort you in five minutes.'

Hamlin looked at Stratton as a thought struck him. 'Hey? Busby? Those scrubbers are a bitch to pull and, well, I ain't feelin' all that good. How 'bout my cellmate here givin' me a hand?'

'Not a problem. Maybe you can teach him a thing or two for when you're too goddamned old to do it any more.'

'That's thoughtful,' Hamlin said, making a lewd gesture. He slumped back tiredly and looked at the door again, studying the frame around it. He got to his feet and felt the area where Stratton indicated the sensor lay beneath the rubber. 'We're gonna get ourselves a pump and open us a door,' he said in a low voice. 'But not this one.' He looked at Stratton. 'I've got me a door that, I admit, suits me very well, but I think you'll find it'll also suit you better'n this one.' Hamlin went back to the door and his own selfish motives. 'Then I'm gonna show those motherfuckers that Tusker Hamlin still has a few tricks up his old sleeve.'

Stratton watched as the man's faced cracked into a strange smile and asked himself who was manipulating who.

Durrani was kneeling on the bare floor of his cell, sitting back on his heels, his palms flat on his thighs, his back to the door while he prayed towards the far left corner of the concrete room. He had been told by fellow Muslims when he'd first arrived that the apex of the angle of the corner pointed in the direction of Mecca. With no way of ascertaining the accuracy of the claim he took it as fact. He was not permitted a prayer mat and his copy of the Koran had been confiscated for reasons unknown to him the day before so he uttered what chants he could remember, praising Allah and leaning forward to kiss the floor at intervals.

Durrani had never been particularly religious but since his incarceration in Styx, with encouragement from his colleagues, he had found the incentive to at least go through the motions of daily prayer. This kind of prison, without sunlight, a view of his beloved land-scape or even the smell of it, was like a living death. He found it ironic that having never seen the sea until the boat ride to the surface ferry platform and coming from a country that was landlocked he now lived deep inside an ocean. Even if he could escape the walls he would be unable to swim.

But despite his past and present circumstances Durrani was not entirely convinced of the rewards that the Koran promised its followers on the other side of the grave. Praying did, however, break up the day: it gave him something to do and if God did turn out to be all he was cracked up to be then at least Durrani was hedging his bets. On completion of each prayer session he mentioned to Allah that he would forgo the promised paradise if he could see his homeland one last time. It was all about maintaining a level of optimism. But deep down Durrani feared his lifelong trend of general misfortune would persist until the end.

One of the difficulties with praying, however, was working out the timings of the five different prayer sessions each day since he was not permitted a timepiece and there was no rising or setting of the sun. Trying to divide the day into five equal portions did, however, confirm his suspicions that the guards were messing with his head beyond what one might expect from the normal rigours of prison life. He received three meals a day, occasionally in the mess hall although most often a tray was brought to his cell. But the periods between meals varied between what seemed to be a couple of hours to five or six or more. The cell lighting worked hand in hand with the feeding. The lighting programme was supposed to simulate sixteen hours of daytime and eight hours of night but Durrani was convinced that some cycles were at least twice as long as they were supposed to be while others were only half the 'official' duration.

There was never a period when he felt completely well, either, although he was not the only one. He was always getting coughs and throat and lung irritations and, like most prisoners in Styx, had developed horrible sores and rashes all over his body. But then, living under constant pressure, far greater than anywhere on the surface of the planet, was not normal and it undoubtedly did strange things to the body as well as to the mind. The temperature also varied greatly but on average it was far too warm and the ambient atmosphere was always humid. Mould and fungus built up quickly in his cell and the guards often failed to provide enough disinfectant to kill the bacteria that thrived in such conditions.

Another source of suffering was the poor air quality. Durrani would sometimes wake from a deep sleep unable to breathe properly, as if there was not enough oxygen in the air. At other times he would feel intoxicated and experience blackouts, unable to remember what he had done only hours before. According to colleagues these were the symptoms of oxygen poisoning and, again, he reckoned it was due to deliberate manipulation by the guards.

The combinations of these physical and mental assaults were gradually wearing him down but the most significant change in his state of mind, and one that probably went unnoticed by his jailers, was his attitude towards his fellow Afghans. Having spent all of his life deliberately avoiding close human contact, with a couple of notable exceptions concerning the fairer sex, he now cherished the rare occasions when he was allowed to mingle with his colleagues. He was still aloof and distant, never discussing his personal history and certainly not his lineage. But he looked forward to the gatherings with anticipation. It was not so much the physical closeness that he sought, nor his compatriots' advice or encouragement. It was simply the direct experience of seeing them there. Durrani sometimes woke up in the darkness with the fear that he was the only prisoner left in Styx.

He suddenly stopped in mid-prayer, his senses, which had become highly tuned, warning him of a sudden drop in pressure. He felt a burning sensation in his lungs and his face reddened as his heart rate increased significantly. This was the third attack since he'd been returned to his cell after the mess-hall incident. He dropped to the floor and lay on his back, complete lack of movement his only defence against the drastic reduction in the amount of oxygen he was able to extract from the air.

The small light bulb on the wall above his bed suddenly went out and his cell was plunged into total darkness. Durrani concentrated on remaining conscious, calculating by estimating the duration of his prayer sessions how long the day had been. He heard the door seals hiss and knew why the air had been thinned and what was coming now. It was barely hours since they'd last come for him. He had hoped they had finished with him. How foolish of him. It would never end.

The door opened with a loud creaking sound and the beam of a sharp blue halogen light searched the room until it rested on his face. 'Stay still!' a voice commanded in heavily accented Farsi as two figures moved inside. He was grabbed around the arms, raised to his feet and held as a sacking hood was placed over his head.

Durrani did not resist as he was manhandled out of the cell in his bare feet and along a slippery damp stone walkway. His guides were not particularly rough with him as long as he remained compliant. Resistance was futile, a lesson he had learned during his first visit to the Styx interrogation room. If he struggled his arms were twisted up his back. If he refused to walk he was released and seconds later a powerful electrode was thrust into his groin, racking his entire body with a pain so intense that it induced vomiting and rectal evacuation. After that he was not interested enough to find out what they would do to him if he resisted further.

Durrani was brought to a halt while a door hissed open in front of him. He was guided through it and up a flight of stairs. This was the usual route he remembered. It led to another corridor at the top of the metal stairs where he was steered left into a room and then into a chair. His hood would then be removed and he would find himself sitting at a table, with a white man sitting on the other side, aiming a microphone at him. A wire leading to a recording device was attached to the mike.

On the whole his interrogations had not been particularly harsh. The first series had been at a camp in Germany, his first stop after being flown out of Afghanistan. It had been run by soldiers and a handful of men in suits and had been all very unsophisticated and procedural. After confirming his identity, place of birth and the school he went to Durrani was asked about the operations he'd taken part in, the names of various commanders and the locations of meeting places, training camps, weapons caches and so on. He answered many of their questions in one of two alternative ways: the ones he felt were inconsequential he answered truthfully, those that he considered more important he lied about. His interrogators did not appear to know anything about him such as the identity of his true father or the fact that he was part Hazara. 'Tell us now for we will always find out in the end and it will be worse for you,' they had threatened. He did not believe them.

As Durrani shuffled along the corridor between his guards their grip on him tightened perceptibly and he was alarmed by the feeling that they had passed the point where they usually turned off into the interrogation room. He wondered if he was confused about the route but when they took a sharp left-hand corner and passed through a narrow rocky corridor only wide enough for one person he knew this was a different place.

Durrani was guided through a narrow doorway and brought to an abrupt halt, turned around and pushed down into an uncomfortable metal chair. His arms were placed on the hand rests where spring-loaded clamps held them in place, something else that was new to him, and his feet were secured in the same manner to the chair legs. The guards had, without doubt, become more aggressive and the rate of Durrani's breathing increased in line with his nervousness as a horrible thought suddenly nagged at him. He recalled a story, told during a previous gathering of the Taliban prisoners in the food hall, about a special room in Styx with a metal chair in the centre of it and how those who visited it were usually not heard from for weeks after. Sometimes never again.

Durrani's hood was pulled off and he struggled to focus his eyes in the dim light. His shirt was pulled open to expose his bare chest, whereupon a man proceeded to stick small pads on the ends of wires to his flesh in various places. Several were taped to his chest in the area of his heart while others were attached to his neck and temples. Rings with wires coming off them were placed over a finger on each hand as well as on both of his big toes. The wires all came together at a box attached to the wall and after a brief check of the connections the man left the room followed by the guards.

The door closed behind them with a hiss and a clunk.

Durrani looked around him. The small concrete room was circular and otherwise empty. A light glowed on the wall directly in front of and slightly above him. Its source was a rectangular piece of glass, behind which a figure could be seen. The glass was foggy and several inches thick making it impossible to determine the person's features. Only when a voice filled the room through tinny speakers, a voice which Durrani presumed belonged to the person behind the glass, did it become plain that the blurred figure was that of a man.

'Why were you crossing the border the day you were

captured by American soldiers?' the man asked in passable Farsi.

Durrani did not answer. In the silence he could hear the echo of dripping water. He looked at the floor, his eyes by now almost fully adjusted to the dim light. It was wet. A drip struck the top of his head and he looked up to see a circle in the vaulted ceiling directly above him. It was a robust metal hatch set within a thick concrete ring. Another drip struck him in the eye, the salt water stinging, made worse because he was unable to reach it with either of his clamped hands.

'Do you refuse to answer my question or are you considering your reply?'

Durrani looked at the ghostly figure and thought now that he could make out another in the background. He expected some form of punishment for not answering. After his earlier interrogations he had wondered to what extent his captors were prepared to torture him and how he would react. When sleep deprivation, loud noises, physical discomfort and shouting appeared to be the full extent of their techniques he had put their restraint down to the usual weakness of Western institutions and their fear of the media, human-rights groups and liberal politicians. But as he stared at the figure behind the glass and took in the character-istics of his confines it struck him that this time he might have made an error of judgement.

'I will ask you once more,' the voice boomed. 'Why were you crossing the border the day you were captured?'

Durrani looked down at the floor, a signal that the

man behind the glass appeared to take as a refusal to answer. There was a loud clunk from somewhere in the room, followed by a whirling sound and the noise of the sucking-in of air. Durrani immediately felt the change in pressure in his ears and his face flushed as his entire body tightened. He shook uncontrollably and struggled to breathe. It was as if he'd been gripped by a giant hand that was squeezing him like a sponge. It lasted only a few seconds before he was released, only to swiftly experience the opposite effect. Now he felt as if he was being blown up like a balloon.

The resulting intense discomfort and confusion were unlike anything he had ever experienced before. Just as it seemed his body was going to blow apart, his rib joints straining to disconnect, another loud clunk signalled a reversal of the pumps and a return to normal pressure. When Durrani unclenched his hands he looked down at them to see the fingers had swollen to twice their normal size.

'You just went for a trip towards the surface,' the voice echoed. 'Another few feet and you would have started to stretch like a balloon . . . You see, there's gas in every inch of your body, dissolved into your flesh, blood, other fluids. Even your bones. Nitrogen mostly, the rest oxygen, carbon dioxide, inert gases . . . You ever open a bottle of fizzy drink? Of course you have. Remember how the bubbles suddenly appeared everywhere in the bottle as if by magic? And if you took the top off too quickly the froth would gush out of the bottle? Remember that? Well, that's exactly what happens to the human body if it's depressurised too quickly. Divers call it the bends . . . That's what I'm doing to you . . . Of course, it's not an exact science. I drop the pressure a little, you get a body full of bubbles – the more I drop the pressure, the bigger the bubbles get. Problem is it only takes one little bubble to block the wrong vein in your brain and that's it. Permanent brain damage. Even death. What I'm aiming to do is keep you alive. I'm getting pretty good at it now. Had a bit of practice . . . Made some mistakes, but that's life. Now, let's go back in time a little, to before you were captured. Only a few days before . . .You were in Kabul, is that right?'

Durrani's breathing remained laboured, the pains in his chest still severe, as if every joint in his ribcage had been pulled apart and then harshly pushed back together.

'You've got to give me something soon,' the interrogator said. 'Even if it's something small. Otherwise this is going to be a long and very painful day for you.'

Durrani stared at the floor ahead, trying to control the shaking that suddenly gripped his body. The heavy clunk came again and he jerked in fearful anticipation as the sound triggered the air pump and the drop in pressure. The pain was immediate and even more intense than it had been previously. Durrani let out a howl as the veins in his neck seemed to swell beyond their physically possible limits. He could feel his eyes bulging in their sockets and heard cracking sounds in his head as if the bone plates that made up his skull were pulling apart. Seconds later another clunk signalled another reverse of pressure and Durrani exhaled massively before breaking into a coughing fit. His nose began to run,

300

but it was blood, not mucus dribbling into his mouth. Durrani could taste it and as the more intense pains subsided he let out a long moan.

'You came from Kabul,' the voice continued as Durrani's shoulders sagged with relief.

Durrani could not see the floor clearly any more – his eyes were out of focus, and he feared for the damage the torture was doing to his body.

'Talk to me, Durrani!'

Durrani looked up at the window, no longer able to see any figure behind it, and nodded as he muttered something inaudible.

'I can't hear you.'

'I . . . I will talk,' Durrani said louder.

'Good . . . you know it makes sense . . . Let's go back a little further, just for a moment. Not too far back. A day or so before you left Kabul for the last time there was an attack on a military helicopter, a British helicopter. It was brought down by a rocket. Everyone on board was killed. You know anything about that helicopter? You know anything about the rocket?'

Durrani's breathing increased in anticipation of the next assault on his body, the very thought of which filled him with horror. He wanted very much to say something, to answer the question, but somehow found the strength not to. When the clunk came he tensed so fiercely that he cut the skin against the clamps holding his arms to the chair. Then suddenly another clunk announced the mechanism moving quickly into reverse.

'You don't ever have to hear that sound again if you don't want to . . . You're going to tell me what I want to know in the end. Everyone who sits where you are right now always does. Why go through all that pain, all that damage to your body? Some people have never walked again after leaving this room . . . I'm told it has something to do with bubbles expanding in their lower spine. If that damage goes higher you may lose the use of your arms as well. Is it worth it? Really? Ask yourself if it's really worth it . . . Do you know about the helicopter that was shot down?'

Durrani lowered his head and nodded slightly.

'I didn't quite get that. Was that a yes?'

Durrani nodded again, this time more emphatically.

'Was it you who shot that helicopter down?'

Durrani nodded.

'And then you went to the wreckage, didn't you?'

Durrani did not move.

'What did you take from the wreckage?'

Durrani clenched his jaw. The interrogator knew something but not everything. If he did he would have already cut his abdomen open and found the little packet. Durrani had arrived at the point he could not go beyond without shaming himself, without failing.

'I know you took something from the wreckage. What was it, Durrani? What did you find that you were taking to Peshawar?'

Durrani breathed deeply and tried to prepare himself for the pain that was about to come. He hoped that it would bring death, for that was his only escape now.

The clunk came, followed by the whirling and sucking of air. The pressure dropped, one of his eardrums burst and his eyes pushed out against his eyelids that were squeezed tightly shut. He let out a high-pitched scream as if the life was being squeezed out of every inch of his body. Then something inside him snapped and what light there was went out.

Hank Palmerston sat behind the interrogator, both men squinting through the thick glass at Durrani slumped in his chair.

'You went too far, you assholes,' Hank muttered.

The technician who had stuck the sensors to Durrani was seated in a corner in front of several life-monitoring devices. 'He's not dead,' he said. 'He's just unconscious.'

'That machine tell you when he's gonna come out of it and in what condition?'

'He has normal brain and sensory nerve activity at all extremities,' the technician confirmed. 'We just took him beyond his pain threshold.'

Hank shook his head as he got to his feet. 'Two fuckin' years you've been doing this and you still can't get it right . . . Now you listen to me,' he said, leaning heavily over the back of the young Ivy League CIA interrogator who remained sitting in his chair and facing the glass. 'We know that helicopter was a British intelligence operation carrying a VIP passenger to Bagram. We know this guy shot it down. We know he found something in the wreckage. We know he took it to his boss in Kabul who then sent him into Pakistan with it . . . What we *don't* know is what he found in the wreckage, if it was the same thing he was carrying, who he was taking it to or why, or where the hell it is now! But maybe he could help us with a few of those questions, that man sat unconscious in the chair, the one who can't talk to us ANY FUCKING MORE!!! . . . And now it would seem that we're not the only people in this place interested in talking to him. When I heard the feds were sending an agent down here I assumed it was to spy on us and the pricks who run this place. If that's true, which I have every reason to believe it is, then who's this guy Charon and what's his interest in Durrani? Is he a fed? If not, who's he working for? Now you're probably asking yourself, why should we care anyway? Well, I'll tell you. This place, and places like it, produce the information that allows our citizens to sleep safely in their beds at night, to go about their normal daily lives, to fill up their gas tanks without worrying if they'll be able to fill them up next time they get low. But the only threat to places like this, information-providing institutions of national importance, comes not from our enemies but from ourselves. We're falling apart from the inside, like the Roman Empire. We're eating our own flesh, coming up with laws and rules we can't possibly live up to. They might be great and righteous rules, but they're a thousand years too early. And so it's up to us to keep this country safe any way we can. And if it means taking on our own people, then so be it. How we do it is to find ways of convincing the doubters to see things our way. Now I'm an intelligence officer. The only weapon I've ever used is information. But it's more powerful than any gun or any bomb. Whatever Durrani knows is worth something, a lot maybe. I want to know what it is – but I can't get information from

UNCONSCIOUS PEOPLE!!! . . . Have I made myself clear?!'

The interrogator remained motionless as Hank's voice echoed in the small stone and concrete room. He was intimidated by Hank, his overbearing boss, but arrogant enough to show no reaction to Hank bawling him out.

Hank left the room. When the door closed the technician looked over at the interrogator like a sixth-former after a scolding from a teacher. 'He'll be OK. His signs are rising.'

'Get him to the hospital,' the interrogator said. 'Then, soon as he's ready, get him back in here.'

The interrogator's voice crackled from a speaker as Mandrick sat listening in his chair behind his desk. He stared thoughtfully up at his vaulted stone ceiling with its damp rusty scars leading from the ends of massive central bolts down to the tops of the walls where they disappeared behind ornate façades erected to hide the unsightly concrete. The CIA were unaware that a listening device had been secreted in their interrogation room. Hank would have been very upset to discover that the tiny transmitter was linked to a receiver in the warden's office. Mandrick was surprised how easy the bug had been to fit: he'd ordered it online from a commercial spyware supplier in Los Angeles and had then taken an installation lesson from a private detective agency in Houston. It had been just as easy to keep it from being discovered since, as warden, he was informed whenever the Agency's electronic eavesdropping detection unit was due to arrive.

Mandrick's reason for planting the device was to help him collect personal insurance against any CIA backlash when the time came for him to pull out of Styx. His eventual departure was always going to be interesting, he realised. He knew far too much about the irregularities of their operation and being a civilian made controlling him complicated. On the other hand, it was the CIA who had originally installed him in the position and that meant they'd also have an exit strategy for him.

There was no doubt in Mandrick's mind that the Agency had a plan in place for whenever he might leave. His fear, reality-based or otherwise, was that any such scheme would not be agreeable to him. He wanted to leave on his own terms, which could prove dangerous. He knew as well as the Agency did that if he happened to vanish one day it would go largely unnoticed. For those few who might wonder about where Mandrick might have gone his disappearance could be simply explained. Rumours of the corruption that went on in Styx could be leaked, specifically stories of tax evasion. Since Mandrick was at the helm of Felix Corp's undersea interests, any mysterious vanishing by him would not be a huge surprise to anyone.

But his most valuable insurance so far against such an event being engineered by the CIA was the evidence he had accumulated showing the Agency's use of decompression as a torture. It was a serious violation of the Geneva Convention, for one thing. Still, the Agency could probably get away with the explanation that it was some localised misconduct by Hank Palmerston done without Langley's knowledge. They would suffer but not long-term. There was a war on and it was not the time to start ripping into the nation's most important anti-terrorist information gatherers. Therefore it was not the quality of insurance Mandrick was looking for. He needed something big enough to barter for a long-lived amnesty, something he could either offer as exchange for his safe departure when the time came, or use as a deterrent that he could threaten to release if anything suspicious should befall him. It was a dangerous game – but then, that was the business he was in.

Mandrick unclipped his minicomputer from his belt and plugged it into the mainframe lead. He inserted a new storage card into the minicomputer's socket and downloaded the recent interrogation conversation onto it. After unplugging the minicomputer and clipping it back onto his belt he saved the original conversation to a file.

A gentle beep sounded and he looked at the control panel to see a small red light blinking. It was the secure landline and, knowing who it was, he picked up the receiver. 'My office is empty,' Mandrick said.

'So's mine,' a voice replied. It was Forbes. 'I don't think our problem has gone away.' Forbes sounded edgy. 'Frankly, I'm concerned . . . Can you hear me OK?'

Mandrick was tired of what he considered to be Forbes's ever-increasing spinelessness. 'I'm here.'

'We may have taken this train as far as it's going to go. I'm getting hints of building pressure within the House. Several Representatives have sent me enquiries.

Felix executives have reported probes into their assets, which has to be the work of the FBI. It doesn't look good. This thing could explode any time. You may have to start making preparations.'

Mandrick sighed to himself. Wasn't the FBI undercover agent clue enough? 'I understand,' he said, allowing Forbes to maintain the illusion that he was in control of everything.

Mandrick found it bizarre how the man did not understand that when jumping from a sinking ship it was a case of every man for himself. Forbes always sounded as if the dissolution of Styx was going to be an orderly evacuation with some kind of convivial reunion afterwards where all the players met for drinks and canapés. He wanted to suggest to the congressman that he should not only be concentrating on his own escape but also how he was going to *stay* escaped. But if the man was unable to see the obvious dangers then no amount of advice Mandrick might offer would be of help. Not that Mandrick gave a damn about his boss anyway.

'Doesn't it bother you?' Forbes asked after Mandrick's long spell of silence. 'You don't sound concerned.'

'We knew it was going to end one day.'

'But not like this. Not now. Of course we considered it. I have my contingency plans. But we never really believed it would happen so soon – at least, I didn't. I don't think you did either, did you?'

'It's always wise to be prepared.'

'Then you're saying you're ready to go ahead?'

'Not entirely. I will be when the time comes.'

'I'm asking you if you're prepared to carry out the doomsday phase, God damn it – as we discussed?'

'Of course.' Mandrick wanted to add that it was a most essential phase of his own plan of escape but he refrained. It was evident the senator could not be trusted and was more than capable of offering Mandrick up to save himself. Come to think of it, that would make good sense on his part.

Mandrick suddenly felt uneasy as the notion took root. It was immediately followed by a tinge of panic as he feared he was falling behind and that Forbes was actually setting him up. He suddenly wondered if he should be making his move sooner than he'd thought.

'Minimum risk to crew and inmates. I think that's essential. It's the ramifications of our actions that will be our undoing.'

'Of course,' Mandrick said. Inwardly he was in complete disagreement, wondering if Forbes was just being smart.

'You must see that if we cover our tracks as best we can then there will be less interest in pursuing us.'

'I understand,' Mandrick said, deciding that if Forbes was not subtly trying to entrap him then the man was sounding like an idiot.

'As long as you do . . . Fine, then. I'll get back to you as soon as I hear anything else. Do nothing without my say-so. Is that understood?'

'Of course.' That was it, Mandrick decided. As far as his suspicions were concerned that last instruction gave Forbes's game plan away. Forbes was trying to control the final stage of the abandonment of Styx, the doomsday phase, which included both their escapes. Mandrick reasoned that if he was wrong and had misjudged Forbes it did not matter. He could not afford to take the risk and had to stay a step ahead of his boss.

'I'll speak to you later,' Forbes said and the phone went dead.

Mandrick replaced the receiver. The feeling of independence he had once enjoyed while in Styx had turned into one of isolation. The lines of control from the shore had stretched to breaking point as his ship headed towards the void. Mandrick had to scuttle it while he still could.

Since it was now unlikely that he would obtain any kind of insurance against the CIA he would have to fall back on his original plan – which was to devise a scenario that provided substantial evidence of his death without his body having to be found. That was not impossible. It would all depend on the execution of his plan.

As Mandrick got to his feet the door buzzer sounded and he looked at the monitor to see Christine standing outside. She appeared relaxed and confident as usual but as he studied her, zooming the camera in on her face, examining her extraordinary natural beauty, he thought he could detect a trace of tension in her body language.

He checked his watch. Dinner wasn't for a couple more hours. She was early. An enigma, he mused. His gut feeling told him that she was as much a prison inspector as the pope was. She'd been the first person to talk to Charon when he came around. Charon was a damned spy for someone. The place was probably crawling with spies. But he could care less now. It was time to pull the plug on the operation – an apt way of putting it, he reckoned.

Mandrick considered sending her away but decided that he couldn't. If she was a spy then the blossoming romance between them was an act on her part. She was planning on leaving that evening but he couldn't go with her now. Their 'affair' would end this night. She was here for something, to give or to take. Perhaps it was to give first and take later. Having his way with her for half an hour or so would not cripple his plan. The thought amused him. He had the weight of the world on his shoulders, desperate to finalise a strategy for his own survival and yet here he was pausing to consider a piece of ass. What a maverick he was. It gave him a feeling of masterfulness, of superiority. He was a true buccaneer, a mercenary to the core, a rebel and adventurer. What could be more heroic than to take a break at such a crucial juncture for a romantic interlude?

He hit the button beside the intercom and as the door hissed, clunked and opened he stepped from behind his desk and into the centre of the room.

Chapter 13

Hamlin, followed by Stratton and a guard, led the way down a narrow, sloping, dimly lit corridor. The mould and fungus common to Styx had taken a particularly firm grip of this section of the prison. Dripping lengths hung from rusting ceiling girders and intertwined between the conduit and cables that followed the contours of the walls. Hamlin slipped on a patch of slimy plankton and Stratton only just managed to grab him before he fell on his backside.

'Thanks,' Hamlin said, taking a moment to recover and catch his breath. 'This road is long overdue for a clean-up, Jed.'

'You know we don't have enough inmates to maintain the whole place,' the guard replied.

'I don't see why we can't use the Buttfucks,' Hamlin said, taking a grimy cloth from his pocket and wiping the sweat from his face and neck.

'I don't make the rules,' the guard said, loosening his jacket. Sweat stains were clearly visible on it around his chest and armpits.

'If you got rid of these damned plants you could reduce the humidity down here,' Hamlin argued.

'And then you guys'd complain about the disinfectant.'

'It ain't disinfectant, Jed, it's industrial-strength weed-killer,' Hamlin sighed, as if he had complained about it a hundred times. 'Like we ain't got enough health hazards down here we gotta soak up that shit.'

'Quit bitchin', Tusker, and get movin'.'

'Just give me a minute, will yer? My old lungs don't process the air as good as they should. I use the term "air" loosely, of course. Smells like raw sewage. We can only guess what we're taking into our lungs.'

The guard rolled his eyes.

A tinny computer-generated voice announced the time over the speakers.

Stratton wiped the sweat from his face with his sleeve as he waited for Hamlin to move on. He pondered on the humming sound that had grown louder with their descent. The sound of water was still the most notice-able noise; a green, frothy liquid ran down a gutter on one side of the concrete path. The wall on the same side was practically hidden by a variety of piping and conduits, some of it hanging loosely where the orig-inal fastenings had corroded or broken off.

Hamlin sighed heavily and moved on, ducking below a large metal brace that secured a cluster of enormous air ducts to the ceiling. The men weaved between clumps of dripping fungus as they headed steadily downhill.

The lights dimmed suddenly as the voltage dropped. The guard produced a flashlight as Hamlin slowed to a more careful pace. The sloping path became long steps as its angle steepened. Stratton reckoned that they were approaching the lowest depths of the prison. A broad tunnel appeared ahead, cutting across their path. As the lights returned to full brightness voices penetrated through the other noises, accompanied by the sound of heavy footsteps. Stratton realised the sound was coming from behind them.

'Step aside,' a voice called out and the three men moved against the pipe-covered wall.

A guard led half a dozen prisoners at a brisk pace down the long steps. The perspiring inmates were all wearing heavy-duty overalls, robust boots, mining helmets and harnesses from which various tools and pouches hung. They shuffled past, their hammers and chisels clanking, each man carrying an emergency breathing tank on his back with a full-face mask hanging from the valves by the head-straps.

'That's you in a couple of days, buddy,' Hamlin said to Stratton.

'They're still mining pretty actively,' Stratton observed. The report on the old mine had made only scant reference to current activity.

'Some prisons do licence plates and street signs. Our extracurricular is workin' the face.'

As the tail-end guard went past them into the larger tunnel he called for a halt. 'Take a breather,' he said, his voice echoing. 'Last smoke before we go in.'

The guard looked at Stratton with sudden recognition and gave him a nod. 'How you feelin'?' he asked.

Stratton thought it was a strange question from a guard but he nodded anyway.

The guard joined Jed and his colleague and they all lit one up.

'You don't remember him, I s'pose,' Hamlin said.

Stratton shook his head. 'Should I?'

'That's Zack. He's the guy who saved your ass from drownin'.'

Stratton looked back at the guard. These were odd circumstances in which to show appreciation to someone for saving your life.

'Don't worry about it,' Hamlin said as if he could read Stratton's thoughts. 'He's just as likely to take it back if you step outta line. He's one of the fair ones . . . It's what this place was before they converted it,' Hamlin said.

Stratton looked at him, wondering what he was talking about.

'This place. It was a mining and agriculture experiment.'

Stratton acted as if he knew nothing about the facility's past. 'What are they mining?'

'Gems. When it was an experiment it cost the taxpayer a fortune to run and the yield didn't even begin to cover the expenses. When it got closed down they kept the water pumps running. Rumour is that an engineer working on the site in those days wasn't straight-up about the mine's true potential. As they were closing down he found a new strike – a big one. Next thing you know a bunch of private investors came up with the plan to reopen the project as a prison. Pretty obvious all they really wanted was access to the mine. Pretty smart to get Uncle Sam to pay for the reopening and running of the facility. Even smarter to have a work force that don't cost anything, ain't goin' anywhere and can't tell anyone what's goin' on down here. Some of the guys have kept a few rocks for themselves but they ain't goin' anywhere with 'em. The guards get a nice fat tax-free bonus each month in a brown envelope to keep 'em sweet. And the CIA turns a blind eye to it all and even plays safety for the corporation because they get what they want.'

'Pretty smart set-up all around,' Stratton agreed.

Hamlin looked at him, the trace of a scowl on his face. 'You think I'm as dumb as you, don't you?'

Stratton looked into his angry eyes and was reminded of how unhinged the man really was. 'We're the ones down here working for them,' Stratton said, pushing it, curious about the old man's mental state. Hamlin was probably a genius which, as the saying went, was often close to madness.

'Not for long, my friend. These pricks'll remember the day they locked Tusker Hamlin up in here. They said it would be the last anyone ever heard from me. Well, they're wrong, Mister Charon. They're wrong.'

Hamlin continued to stare at Stratton, his look turning to one of curiosity. 'Charon,' Hamlin said, this time pronouncing it 'Kar-on', a smirk forming on his lips. 'That's very amusing . . . Now I know who you are.'

Stratton held his gaze. Since the guards were within earshot he was prepared to defend himself against any accusation that Hamlin might make.

'You're the ferryman.'

Stratton had no clue what the man was talking about.

'The Styx ferryman,' Hamlin continued. 'Karon was

sent by the gods to carry the dead souls of evil men down the Styx river and into hell.'

Stratton remembered the mythological story although he did not recall a ferryman. Hamlin had had him worried there for a moment.

'OK, you guys,' the guard called out. 'Let's get going. See yer later,' he said, waving to his colleagues.

Stratton and Hamlin watched the miners trudge into the mine entrance. 'What's it like in there?' Stratton asked.

'Dunno,' Hamlin said. 'Never wanted to find out. Another reason I made myself an indispensable engineer.'

The two men followed their guard further down the low-ceilinged tunnel for a short distance and stopped outside a large airlock door set in a broad reinforced concrete wall. The door had originally been painted blue but most of the coating had fallen off to reveal rusting metal below.

'Jed at the air room,' the guard said into his radio as he looked up at a black semi-sphere fixed to the ceiling above them. A second later there was a loud hiss, followed by a heavy clunk, and the door moved but only a couple of inches. The guard leaned his shoulder against it to help it open. 'Piece o' shit door,' he grunted as he put all his effort behind it. The door opened slowly and he stepped back, out of breath, to let Hamlin and Stratton lead the way inside.

Two things struck Stratton with some force as the door opened. One was the sudden increase in machinery noise, the other was an intense smell like rotten eggs.

'You'll get used to it,' the guard said, pushing him in.

Hamlin stepped through the door as if eager to get on with the job. 'I find it almost refreshing,' he said above the increased noise, sucking in the air as if it was nectar.

'You would, you strange motherfucker,' the guard said.

Hamlin pulled two pairs of ear defenders out of a box by the door and handed one set to Stratton. They afforded some relief from the high-pitched noise.

They were in a cavernous space, the largest single chamber in the facility. A thousand miles of ducts twisted in and out of several machines and up to the ceiling which they practically covered, finally disappearing through the walls in several places. In the spacious centre was a large wooden workbench covered in various machine parts and tools, with power jacks dangling from the ceiling. It was a dishevelled-looking place, untidy, rusty and disorganised, like the bowels of a neglected supertanker. Metal stairways led up to various service gantries and walkways surrounding the bigger machines.

'I'll leave you guys to get on with it,' shouted the guard.

'Don't hurry back,' Hamlin replied caustically.

The guard waved him off and stepped back through the door, which closed behind him and sealed shut.

When Stratton looked back at Hamlin the man was grinning at him. 'Welcome to my office,' Hamlin shouted.

Stratton walked into the cavern, turning around to take it all in. 'How much of the prison's air does this place scrub?' Stratton asked.

'These only run the mine and inmate levels now. You'd need twice the number of scrubbers, all working efficiently, plus a couple thousand litres of oxygen a day to cover the entire place. There's a mother of a surface barge takes care of the living quarters . . . The desalinators over there only provide part of the potable water. Those pumps're pretty essential, though,' he said, indicating four squat machines along one of the far walls, two of them running and responsible for much of the noise. 'They dump a lot of the water. If they fail you're lookin' at shuttin' down the entire lower sections, including the mine.'

'If this place is so important how come they let you down here on your own?'

'They got pretty lax with me over time. I do a good job, I'm twenty-four seven, and I'm free. I guess they think I'm harmless. There's nothin' serious I can do down here – or so they think. But they don't know Tusker Hamlin as well as they think they do.'

Stratton chose not to question the remark and walked over to dozens of large steel gas bottles stacked in frames along a wall. They were an argon-oxygen mix, all connected together through an array of high-pressure pipes.

'OCR emergency gas,' Hamlin said. 'It ain't essential, though. Just a back-up.'

Stratton reckoned that two men could barely lift one of the bottles, never mind carry it very far. He had no specific interest in them and was simply filing away anything that might be of value.

'Shall we get on with it, then?' Hamlin asked, standing behind him.

Stratton had not heard him draw close. He looked around at the man and saw that he was wearing a strange smirk.

'The door,' Hamlin said. 'Let's test your theory.'

'You mean open it?'

'Sure. What else?'

'It's not something you can test and put away for another day. They'll know in OCR as soon as it opens. We'll only get one hit.'

'Time's running out for the both of us, especially for you,' Hamlin said. 'Gann ain't the patient type. He's gonna make his move soon.'

Hamlin was attempting to manipulate him by playing up the Gann threat. But the older man did not know how right he was. Gann was coming after him because he was the only witness to the ferry sabotage. This was no longer just a mission to get the tablet from Durrani. It had also become largely about Stratton's survival.

He suddenly felt overwhelmed, his confidence about completing the mission in tatters. There was no way out for him, either. Even giving himself up and telling the truth about why he was in Styx was not going to save him. It would only make matters worse since his credibility as a witness would be too high. Stratton had bounced into the operation, all cocky and confident, not only about getting hold of the tablet but also making an historic escape. What an arrogant prick he was, he thought.

Stratton could feel his temples tighten as he realised the true level of his desperation. He was well and truly screwed. And now Hamlin wanted to open the door. But into what? Stratton had no idea where to go or what to do. Was everything down to waiting in ambush in some dark corner in the hope that Gann would amble past so that he could jump him? That was the best Stratton could come up with. It was pathetic. He felt like an amateur.

He looked at Hamlin who now represented the last vestige of hope he had to cling on to. His survival depended now on the plans of an old lunatic. Things could not get any worse. 'Where're you going if we get through that door?'

'Let me explain somethin' to you. I've spent two years, ever since the first day I walked into this joint, figuring out how to get out of here. One thing I hadn't been able to figure were the doors and you walked into my life with the answer. That's providence and I'm grabbing it with both hands. But I don't owe you anything.'

'Nothing for showing you how to open the door?'

'You need that as much as I do. Maybe more. At least I have time on my hands. Yours is running out.'

'You don't even know it'll work.'

'It'll work. You gave me the missing piece of the puzzle.'

'Why can't you take me with you to the ferry? That's the only way out.'

'Why don't you just concentrate on your own problems?'

'Getting out that door doesn't get me to Gann.'

'Oh, I dunno. A resourceful guy might stack things in his favour.'

'You're full of shit, Hamlin. You're just a crazy old man. I don't see why I should help you if you can't help me.'

Hamlin started to grin widely, displaying his stained and cracked teeth. 'Maybe I can.'

'I'm beginning to think you're just an old windbag.'

Hamlin was still smiling. 'I don't know why I like you, ferryman. But I do . . . I know this place better'n anyone, even the people who built it, because I know the changes that were made when the corporation moved in. The original experiment needed independence from a surface barge. A life-support system floating on the surface defeated the whole idea. Failure in that department was probably why it got cancelled. The current surface barge was put in for the prison. They depend on it. It's the key to helping the both of us. We need confusion. The barge provides air, water, power. We screw the barge up and we got ourselves a pretty neat diversion, just like a military operation.'

'How can you do that from down here?'

Hamlin gave him a knowing smile once again. 'This room houses all the distribution conduits for the prison since it was intended to be the main life-support factory. When they brought the barge in it made sense to utilise the distribution system that was already in place. That's what I figured, at least. So I searched around. I discovered I was wrong to a certain extent. They rebuilt the water- and air-distribution system, added water pumps to level three, shut down the sterilisers and desalinators, reduced the workload for the air scrubbers. But what they did end up utilising was some eighty per cent of the power-distribution conduits.'

Hamlin walked over to a metal staircase and climbed to the top. 'Come take a look,' he said.

Stratton followed.

Hamlin led him along a gantry, around a corner, behind the line of scrubbers to an ordinary door. He reached for a small rock in the stone wall, removed it, put his hand inside the hole and withdrew a key. 'One of the service engineers always used to leave the key in the door while he was working in here. I made a mould out of putty, took the key out of the lock one day and made an impression. Took me a while to make a copy of the key,' he said as he put the key into the lock. 'It ain't a perfect copy,' he said, concentrating while manipulating it, massaging it back and forth. The key finally raised the tumblers and turned. 'But it works in the end,' he said as he opened the door.

Inside were several large dust-covered electrical cabinets. 'These are just two of the transformers. But they're an important pair – if you wanna screw up the others, that is.'

Hamlin opened the cupboards and Stratton looked at the complex array of high-powered cables, switches and junctions. 'How do you know what feeds what?' he asked.

Hamlin was still wearing that know-it-all grin. He reached behind one of the cabinets and retrieved a long tube of paper, placed it on a table and unrolled it. It was an electrical blueprint, a complex diagram that was practically meaningless to Stratton. 'I took this off one of the engineers about a year ago. I know every damn circuit on here.'

'You can control the prison's circuitry from here?'

'No. Can't do that. But I can sure as hell screw it up. I can trip circuit-breakers all over that damned barge. The barge isn't manned twenty-four seven. Even if there was an engineer on board it'd take him a while to figure it out. And no engineer would reconnect a circuit before they knew why it broke in the first place.'

'You can cut the power to the prison?'

'Some of it.'

'But there's an auxiliary power system.'

'Sure. But it only runs essentials. In this place that's mostly life support. Security always comes second to safety. I'd say you'd have as much as eight hours before the system was back on line. That long enough for you?'

'Internal doors?'

'Level access will become emergency access, not security. They'll all go green.'

'The ferry dock?'

'Uh-uh. External access is safety so they'll stay secure. I don't know about cell doors and internal security such as that one,' Hamlin said, indicating the door to the scrubber room. 'That's why we have to open it manually before we blow the fuses, otherwise we'd have no power to do it after. You see what I'm tellin' you?'

Stratton did. His mind raced at the possibilities. He could get back up to the other levels. But he still wouldn't be able to get to Durrani unless he knew precisely where the Afghan was. His only chance was to get to Gann first. If he could then he might be able to resume his original plan, having neutralised the main threat to his life. It looked like that plan still amounted to nothing more than lying in wait. But if the entire facility was in turmoil there was a good chance Gann would turn up and an equally good chance Stratton could find a dark, unobserved place from which to jump out at him. The overall plan was sketchy at best but it opened up possibilities. Suddenly he reckoned that once he was through the door he didn't need Hamlin after all. That was a relief in itself. 'OK,' he said.

'You go right. I turn left,' Hamlin said, wanting assurance.

Stratton could not imagine why Hamlin would want to head deeper into the complex. Left was essentially down. As far as he could remember there was nothing in that direction but the mine and some more caverns. 'You go where you want. I'm heading up.'

'Good.' Hamlin grinned. 'To make the most of it we should open the door at the same time the circuit-breakers snap. That way, when the alarm triggers in OCR they'll think it's part of the electrical fault. They'll have too much else to worry about than a door opening down at this level anyway.'

Stratton began to prepare himself mentally for the push. Like a runner approaching the starting line, he was thinking ahead to the first curve in the track. Charging up the corridor would be no different from crashing into a house and not knowing where the enemy was.

'Let's do it,' Hamlin said as he left the room and

headed along the gantry and down the steps. 'A drill saw and something to isolate the sensor,' he called out as he hurried down the steps.

Doctor Mani stood over Durrani who was lying on the operating table in a near-unconscious state. As usual, the medic was not expecting to find much in the way of outward signs of injury after an over-zealous pressure interrogation but he did a cursory check as always. Durrani moaned as Mani pushed open his eyelids to inspect his pupils with a light, looking for any sign of brain damage.

The door opened and Gann walked in. 'How is he?' he asked, towering over Mani.

'They might've gone too far with this one. How many times have I warned those idiots?' Mani said, pulling open Durrani's shirt. He plugged the two earpieces of his stethoscope into his ears and moved the other end from one place to another around the Afghan's chest while listening to the man's erratic breathing. 'God knows how many of his bronchial sacs are ruptured.' Mani felt along the sides of Durrani's ribcage. 'I think he's dislocated several ribs.'

'Is he gonna live?' Gann asked, not particularly interested from any humane point of view. He collected knowledge of the human body's endurance to violence like a stunt-car racer took an interest in car wrecks.

'He'll live. Question is how comfortably. Unless he's suffered brain damage in which case it won't matter, I suppose.'

'I heard the tech say they took him equal to almost

halfway to the surface. His lungs must've been tryin' to push outta his backside.' Gann grinned at his description.

'Charming,' Mani said dryly as he wheeled a scanner over to the table and positioned it above Durrani's throat. 'Would you move aside, please?' he said to Gann who was blocking the doctor's view of a monitor on a nearby counter.

Gann obliged just enough, craning to look down at Durrani. 'He's gotta bit of red froth comin' out the side of his mouth.'

'Thank you. Now, please, give me room.' Mani slowly moved the scanner down Durrani's torso, his eyes glued to the monitor that showed the Afghan's chest cavity in a variety of colours indicating bone, air spaces, flesh and fluids. 'This man cannot go back into that chamber – ever. He won't survive another massive decompression.'

'They've got other methods,' Gann said matter-of-factly.

Mani glanced sideways at Gann who was now concentrating on the monitor. He had known the man since arriving at the prison a year and a half ago to relieve the original doctor and had never ceased to be amazed at the depths of human depravity Gann was capable of reaching. Mani had never come across such an animal before. He more or less understood the need for such types in a high-security guard system of this nature and accepted it was a small community and that contact was unavoidable. But he wished he did not have to communicate face to face with him and his kind quite so much as he did. Preferably he wouldn't have had anything at all to do with them. What irritated Mani most was how Gann treated him as some kind of colleague or, worse, accomplice. Mani accepted that he was a part of the Styx corruption but he never saw himself as anywhere near Gann's sordid level.

'You can speak their language, can't you?' Gann asked.

'A little. I'm not fluent.'

'When he comes around I want you to ask him some questions.'

'Fine. Come back next week sometime.'

Gann looked at the side of Mani's head as he suppressed an urge to punch it. He regarded the doctor as a subordinate and was not used to being talked to by him in that way. He wondered if it was perhaps time to remind the man of his position in the prison hierarchy. 'I wanna know what Charon was doing with him in the galley,' he said.

Mani sensed the irritation in Gann's voice and realised his last comment had not gone down very well. 'Sure. I'll ask him . . . Anything else?'

Gann sensed the new patronising tone. 'Maybe I'll just wait until he comes around.'

Mani was always careful not to upset Gann, having experienced his venom on his first day on the job. Styx's original doctor had also been an Asian – a coincidence, although that fellow was a Sikh. He had arrived wearing his turban, which did not go down very well among the guards, particularly with Gann. It was too similar to the traditional black headdress of the Taliban and as far as Gann was concerned the doctor had to be more or less the same as them. Mani never met the man and did not know how he had come to be employed as the prison doctor but when he'd refused to remove his turban he'd had to go.

When Gann found out that Mani was Hindu he confronted him right away, telling him he didn't trust anyone who was religious, especially on this job, and a religious Asian was off the chart. Gann didn't think there was any difference between Hinduism and Islam and therefore Mani was considered to be doubly untrustworthy. It took a long and patient conversation to persuade Gann that Hinduism was not a religion but a way of life, a philosophy. It was far older than Christianity, which in turn was hundreds of years older than Islam. Mani did not worship a god or single out any prophet and he had no set rituals or performances – like praying on a mat, for instance.

Gann only began to accept Mani when the Indian assured him that he had no time for Muslims. Hinduism, he explained, did not get in the way of making money even by dubious means as long as there was a sound philosophy behind it. Mani pitched himself as simply a healer. The philosophy was flawed but not sufficiently so to keep Mani from turning up to work. Besides, there was also the small matter of him being unable to practise his profession anywhere else in America.

Mani had been struck off the medical register after a patient he was treating had died. He was running a detoxification clinic at the time and was accused of serious malpractice after giving a heroin addict an experimental cocktail of opiate antagonists that led to a fatal seizure.

Mani might have avoided the subsequent litigation had it not come to light that he also happened to be a director of a company that was concentrating on commercialising an ultra-rapid detoxification treatment that had not been officially approved. In addition, he recruited heroin addicts as guinea pigs for experiments without informing them of the extreme risks. Mani was lucky not to have been incarcerated when it also transpired that the dead patient was not his first failure. No others had died but many were found to be suffering from a variety of debilitating physical and mental conditions. Fortunately for him the evidence that his treatment had been directly responsible was inconclusive. But the court case cost Mani every penny he had and, unable to practise, he found himself in a desperate situation.

Mani was an Indian immigrant who had moved to America with his parents when he was five years old and, much as he loathed the thought, he considered moving back to Calcutta where he'd been born to continue making a living the only way he knew how. He sold his car, the last remaining possession of value he had, in order to buy the air ticket. But two days before he was due to leave America he was approached by a man who said he represented the Felix Corporation in Houston and that they had a job they would like him to consider.

When Mani started to explain he was no longer able to practise the man said he knew everything about Mani's past and that the Indian had all the right qualifications for the job. By that he meant Mani was not only a doctor but was also corrupt. And there was no need to be concerned about the legalities since the job was not on the American mainland. When Mani learned the whereabouts of his new practice he brought up the obvious point that the prison was still in sovereign waters. It was explained to him that certain legal technicalities allowed him to work offshore as a medical-supplies officer as long as he didn't call himself a doctor.

As a medical-supplies officer Mani was permitted to give demonstrations to the guards of how to use the most basic of equipment, which he was required to do whenever there was an illness or injury. It was one of the reasons why Gann felt free to come and go as he pleased – not that the man needed a reason. Gann enjoyed watching Mani ply his trade, the more serious the medical problem the better.

Mani loosened Durrani's trousers and pulled them down to expose his abdomen. He felt around the area, firmly pressing the flesh in places in search of any muscle tightening that might indicate an internal injury. Finding no obvious signs of damage he realigned the scanner and slowly moved it from Durrani's ribcage onto his abdomen. As it moved down to Durrani's hips a small black object just above his groin area appeared on the monitor.

Mani's brow furrowed as he tuned the scanner's focus. The object became clearer.

'What's that?' Gann asked.

'I have no idea.'

'He swallow something?'

'It's not in the gut,' Mani said as he examined the flesh to find the small pink scar.

'Maybe it's a piece of shrapnel,' Gann suggested. 'These guys've been in all kinds of shit.'

'Maybe,' Mani muttered as he took a closer look at the object on the monitor. 'It doesn't look like a random splinter or a bullet. That bit there.'

Gann drew closer to the monitor, squinting as he examined the dark patch. 'No shit. That ain't no shrapnel.'

Mani went back to Durrani's abdomen and felt around the scar, prodding his fingers into the flesh.

'Cut it out,' Gann suggested enthusiastically.

'You think I should?' Mani was unsure.

'Sure as shit you cut it out.'

'I should call Mandrick.'

'Look, pal. I'm tellin' you to cut that out. He's got somethin' in there. He's smuggled it in. He could come to at any time and . . . I dunno, maybe activate it or somethin'.'

'I don't think it's a bomb,' Mani said sardonically.

'Maybe it's some kinda suicide device. If he wakes up he might kill himself.'

'I didn't think the Taliban were that sophisticated.'

'Maybe he ain't a Talibuttfuck. Maybe he works for the Russians.'

Mani thought that sounded just as ludicrous. 'I think we should go and see Mandrick.'

'OK. I'll stay here. But if he starts comin' to I'll cut it out myself.'

Mani believed Gann would do it too, and probably with his penknife. He ran his fingers through his thick short black hair, frustrated by his indecision. 'OK,' he said finally. 'I'll open him up and take a look.'

'It ain't gonna do him no harm anyhow.'

'I'll do it, OK?' Mani whined, taking a paper bag off a nearby silver trolley and opening it. Inside was a plastic bowl with a collection of surgical instruments each in its own sterile bag, an assortment of absorbent gauzes and a pair of plastic gloves. He took a syringe and a small bottle from a drawer under the counter top, removed the sterile cover from the syringe, pushed the needle through the top of a bottle and drew out some of the liquid.

'He don't need anaesthetic.'

'The pain might wake him up and that would not be a good idea if I've got my hand inside him at the time.'

'I'll take care of him if he wakes up, don't you worry about that.'

Mani shook his head, containing his impatience and anger. He wanted to tell Gann he was the biggest idiot he had ever met but the satisfaction might come at an unacceptable price. 'Would you mind just staying back and allowing me to do my job, please?'

Gann frowned as he took a step back and leaned against the counter.

Mani injected Durrani's skin in several places around the small scar, placed the syringe on the trolley and pulled on the gloves. He inspected the scar closely again, pulling at the skin lightly to test its elasticity. He pulled the sterile wrapping from a scalpel and positioned it over the skin. Gann leaned forward to get a closer look.

Mani cut into the flesh, keeping the incision to the length of the scar. Blood immediately dribbled down the side of Durrani's abdomen. Mani wiped it and dabbed the cut. The bleeding was minimal. Mani stuck a finger into the opening and moved it around. He couldn't feel anything solid and pushed a couple of fingers in up to his knuckles. He shook his head in frustration as he took out his bloody fingers. 'I can't find it. I'll use the scanner – would you mind?' he said, indicating the scanner above Durrani's chest and his bloody hand that he could not use to take a hold of it.

Gann was eager to be of help in this kind of surgical situation and he moved the scanner down Durrani's body, watching the monitor until the black object appeared. Mani took a pair of forceps from its bag and slipped the end into the cut while looking at the monitor. He opened the forceps and soon had the ends placed either side of the object. He carefully closed the ends around the item. He withdrew the forceps, the small device in its little bag sliding out of the bloody hole.

Mani placed it in the bowl and, with Gann literally breathing down his neck, he wiped the bag clean of blood.

'Take it outta the bag. Let's have a look at it.'

Mani took a pair of scissors from the tray and snipped one end of the bag. The small memory card fell out of the bag onto a piece of gauze and both men stared at it.

'What do you make of it?' Mani asked.

'No idea,' Gann said.

Mani used the scissors to turn it on its side. He took a magnifying glass off the counter and examined the object more closely. 'Whatever it is, it's very sophisti-cated.' He held it with the forceps and used the scalpel to gently pick at what looked like a join. The gap widened slightly and he applied a little more pressure. The piece slid fully open to reveal a finely patterned gold strip similar to that on the face of a SIM card. 'It looks like some kind of memory chip.'

Gann took the magnifying glass and had a look for himself. 'Yeah. Like you get in digital cameras,' he muttered. Tumblers started moving inside his head. 'That's why that Charon guy was talking to him. And that's why he pulled his shirt up. He was looking for this. He ain't workin' for our side otherwise he wouldn't need to be sneakin' around as a prisoner. Charon's a friggin' spy.'

Mani wasn't entirely sure what Gann was going on about and didn't particularly care. He took a small zip-lock bag from a drawer, placed the card inside it, sealed it and removed his gloves. 'I'm taking this to Mandrick,' he said.

'Fine,' Gann said, uninterested in the device. 'And I think I'll have that little meetin' with Charon that I was plannin'.'

Mani placed a piece of gauze over Durrani's wound as Gann walked purposefully out of the room. The doctor left shortly after and closed the door behind him.

Durrani's eyelids flickered and slowly opened.

Chapter 14

When Christine walked into Mandrick's office he immediately noticed something about her that he had been unable to see on the monitor. She had groomed herself, only a little, but more than she had in the past. There was also a hint of eyeliner. That was a significant effort for her.

Christine saw the lecherous glint in his eye as she entered the room. Mandrick was standing there with a superior demeanour as if he was all-knowing. Once again she suddenly wondered if he knew who she really was, or at least that she wasn't what she claimed to be. It was not just with Mandrick either. She never completely trusted her cover, always feeling most unlike prison-inspector material. Every time someone looked her directly in the eye she would stare back at them searching for traces of suspicion. There were so many reasons to get the job finished and be out of the damned place.

She forced a smile. 'Have I caught you at a bad time?'

'No. I was about to do my rounds of the prison but I'm happy to put it off.'

'I can come back later if you'd prefer,' Christine said,

stepping closer to him while at the same time wondering if her discomfort at being so close to him was obvious.

Despite being certain of her duplicity Mandrick was struck once again by her attractive qualities. As well as her beauty and intelligence she had an aura about her, an undeniable strength beyond her physical athleticism. She was a superior creature. There were times when he felt strangely inadequate beside her. The feeling was bizarre and on certain levels it irritated him. Which was why he became far more of a predator in her company than he would normally be with women.

He moved towards her. Inwardly she braced herself, expecting him to take hold of her. But he brushed past like a matador.

'Can I get you a drink?' Mandrick asked, going to an antique bureau and a collection of fine crystal decanters and tumblers.

'I shouldn't really.'

'Is that for medical or professional reasons?'

Christine grinned. 'How does it affect you at this depth?'

'You do get more of a buzz for your dollar . . . But don't let me pressure you.'

'Very funny.'

'Bourbon do?'

'Sure.'

Mandrick poured two glasses, opened a small fridge beside the bureau, took out a bowl of ice, plopped a couple of cubes in each glass and brought them over to her.

Christine took the drink and held it to her mouth as she watched him take a sip of his. She let the glass touch her lips and poured a little of the burnt-gold fluid between them. It tasted bitter to her. She didn't like hard liquor but on this occasion it reminded her of younger days in college after a game of touch football or baseball, joining the guys for a drink. They'd been purely bonding moments for her but fun nonetheless. Now those days seemed like ancient history. From college girl to secret undercover agent standing in the warden's office of a damp, humid prison far beneath the Gulf of Mexico.

As she watched Mandrick eyeing her with the confidence of a great cat, she was less sure of her strategy than ever. Her scheme was nothing more complex than to separate him from his minicomputer, remove the memory-storage cards without him knowing and then head for his personal escape pod. There were some glaring flaws in the plan. The first was the difficulty of getting the keypad entry code to gain access to the pod. She didn't know it. The only way around that was to somehow get Mandrick to show her the inside of the pod and then make her move to get inside it and eject. The other flaw was that as she arrived on the surface he could have her picked up by his own people. She would be stuck inside the pod for hours anyway, waiting to decompress. He would also have plenty of time to cancel some of the information on the storage cards; PIN codes and passwords, for instance.

It was not the best of plans by a long stretch but Christine was out of other ideas. She almost scratched the whole notion several times but the only reason she continued to pursue it was that she was not entirely desperate to pull it off. Taking the storage cards was surplus to the mission objective, anyway. It was all about personal ambition. If the ideal opportunity failed to materialise she would cancel it and surface just with her report.

At that moment the scheme was certainly looking doubtful. Mandrick was being more forward with her than he'd been at any other time. He had a hunger in his eyes. She reckoned she had been too overtly sexual in setting him up and he was clearly expecting more than she was prepared to give. 'Why don't you take me on a tour?' she suggested. 'I can come on your rounds with you.'

He put his glass down, moved closer and stopped in front of her, his eyes boring into hers. 'What are you doing here, Christine?' he asked in a cold voice.

'You mean in this room, now?' she replied, holding on to her composure.

'That, yes. But first the prison. What are you doing here?'

'You know what I'm doing here.'

'I know what you *said* you're doing here. But we all know that's a load of crap.'

Christine could never tell Mandrick the truth. Her career would be over. Perhaps even her life. He'd been prepared to kill an FBI agent. Why not an Oval Office agent? There was no real difference at the end of the day. He had no proof that she was not a prison inspector. He couldn't have. He was guessing. She had no choice but to maintain her claim. 'Where has this come from? I don't understand you,' she said.

'OK. So if you won't answer that question, why are you in this room putting on this pathetic display, attempting to seduce me when it's the furthest thing from your thoughts?'

Christine tried to laugh it off. She put her drink down. 'Well. This is interesting. I thought we . . . I'm sorry. I obviously have it all wrong. Perhaps I should go.'

As she moved past Mandrick he grabbed her hand and pulled her close to him.

'Let go of me,' she demanded.

He wrapped his other arm around her before she could pull away. 'How 'bout we make a deal?' he said, holding her tightly, his nose almost touching hers. 'You give me what I want and we'll talk about your side of the deal. I might surprise you.' He moved a hand down her back and over her bottom, sliding it between the cheeks.

A combination of rage and utter disgust engulfed Christine and she slammed her forehead into his nose, breaking it and immediately following through by crashing a heel down onto the top of one of his feet. To his credit he managed to keep hold of her but she punished him further by bringing a knee up into his groin. It was this blow that finally forced him to release her.

She went to the control panel and hit a button. As the door hissed open she made her way past him towards it. But before she could reach it another hiss signalled a reverse of the pneumatic valves and the door remained closed.

Christine turned to face Mandrick. He was straightening himself up, trying to ignore the pain in his groin while dabbing at his bloody nose with the sleeve of his jacket.

'That smart,' he said, blinking away the water in his eyes. 'Never experienced that combination before . . . You make that up or did they teach you that in prison-inspection school?'

'Let me out of here,' she said coldly.

Mandrick exhaled loudly and relaxed his shoulders to help ease the tension. 'Funny how quickly you can go off someone.'

'Open the door,' she said in a deliberate tone.

He held up the remote. 'Why don't you try and take it?'

Christine was experiencing a whole load of feelings, a growing concern predominant among them. But she no longer felt unsure. The job had come down to a physical conflict between the pair of them. She didn't have to pretend to seduce him for a second longer. That was some relief in itself. If she could take him down she might even achieve the result she wanted. But she would have to flatten him, knock him out, tie him up, restrain him for several hours. She knew nothing about Mandrick's past: his dossier was surprisingly slender for a file that was the result of a White House background check. There was a toughness about him which she put down to character rather than physique.

However, he seemed to have dealt with the blows

she'd given him quite quickly. He could take pain. If he did possess some level of fighting skill, which she doubted, she was confident she could take him. She had quite a few tricks designed for the weaker sex up her sleeve, not that she was much weaker than him. They were techniques rather than skills, such as knowing how best to strike at weak points. She was also confident that she was fitter than him.

Had Christine known Mandrick's pedigree, the numerous African battlefields that he had fought on, conflicts she could hardly imagine, she would probably never have entered the room. There was a world of a difference between skills learned in a dojo and those acquired in battle while fighting for one's life. More importantly, Mandrick knew what it was like to kill and, worse still for her, he had never lost the taste for it.

She decided to strike first, which suited Mandrick as he was more adept at countermoves. She lunged at him with a dummy kick intended to bring his hands low so that she could punch him in the throat. But he stepped aside and parried her fist with a calm ease that took her by surprise. She went for a straight kick to his shin. He avoided it and lunged at her but she caught his hand and tried to turn the wrist in. He took her feet away from under her with a side-sweep and she almost fell on her back. But as he came in to take advantage of her lost balance and grab her hand she elbowed him in the face with her other arm. Mandrick went back, reeling a little from the blow and looking at her with malice. Christine was confident that if she could keep this up she just might take him. But Mandrick had home-field advantage.

He lured her forward as he stepped backwards, feigning fear and weakness, dodging attack after attack, blocking where he could as if he was retreating. On the wall behind him was a large air pipe with an opening at chest height that had a mesh grille across it. The warden's office was the only room in the facility apart from the OCR that had a manual air-pressure control. It was an emergency feature, an override that allowed the operator to rapidly increase or decrease the pressure in the room either to open the door or prevent it from being opened.

Mandrick put his back to the pipe so that he knew exactly where he was. As Christine came in for another blow he took a step forward, trapped her arm, pulled her around, slammed her back against the pipe and threw a lever on the side of the vent. There was a sudden rush of air that reached an immediate and painful pitch. Before Christine realised what was happening her back was sucked against the mesh. She twisted violently in an effort to free herself but was stuck like a fly to sticky paper.

Mandrick stepped back, feeling his bruised face and taking his time about it. 'Now it's my turn.'

As Christine struggled to reach behind her back for the valve handle Mandrick punched her on the side of her face as hard as he could. The blow knocked her almost unconscious. Her knees nearly gave way and she could only watch as he drew his fist back for another punch. This time he changed its direction and struck her in the gut. It struck so hard and low that she almost threw up. He followed through with a knee to her groin, then grabbed her by her throat and held her windpipe tightly, squeezing it until she began to choke.

'I'm not interested in who you work for,' Mandrick hissed between clenched teeth. 'That should worry you.' He slammed his elbow into the side of her face and she went limp. Unable to focus properly she fought to stay conscious.

'It would be churlish of me not to take full advantage of the situation, don't you think?' he said, ripping open her shirt to reveal her bra. He squeezed her breasts. 'Very firm . . . Fortunately for you I'm not into necrophilia.'

A buzzer sounded above the hissing of air.

'For Christ's sake,' he muttered.

The buzzer went again soon after and he looked at the monitor to see that it was Doctor Mani. He hit the intercom on his desk. 'What is it?' he asked, still slightly out of breath.

'Mr Mandrick? I have something very important to show you.'

'Can it wait? I have my hands full.'

'I think you would be very angry with me if I said yes. This is most important or I would never dream of insisting.'

Mandrick sighed and straightened his clothes. 'I guess it just wasn't meant to be,' he said, turning the vent lever back into the neutral position. The air stopped hissing, releasing Christine who hit the floor like a sack of vegetables. Mandrick pressed the entry button on the desk and the door opened.

Mani hurried inside.

'What do you want?' Mandrick said, feeling his nose.

Mani paused on seeing Mandrick's somewhat dishevelled appearance but quickly put any disquiet aside and focused on the urgency of his visit. 'Sir,' he began but stopped in his tracks as he saw Christine lying on the floor. 'Dear God,' he exclaimed, hurrying over to her. 'What happened?'

Mandrick was more concerned about his swollen nose and its blocked airways. 'We had a disagreement,' he said nasally.

The doctor looked confusedly between Mandrick and Christine, noticing now that her shirt had been torn open.

'She's a spy – FBI, probably – trying to steal something, I expect. She's one tough bitch, I'll say that for her,' Mandrick added, feeling his cheekbones again.

'What did you do to her?' the doctor asked, his tacit disapproval obvious as he inspected Christine's bruised face and checked to see if she was breathing.

'Christ's sake, Mani, she attacked me. Just because she came off worse doesn't mean I'm the bad guy.'

The doctor shook his head. The girl appeared to be OK apart from a possible concussion. 'I'll have to get her to the hospital.'

'Do what the hell you want with her . . . What was so important?'

The doctor had almost forgotten. Quickly, he got to his feet and reached into a pocket. 'This was inside that

Afghan they brought in,' he said, taking out the plastic bag with the card inside.

Mandrick took the bag and inspected it. 'Durrani?'

'That's right. It was in his abdomen. It had been placed there surgically.'

'Any idea what it is?' Mandrick asked, in case the doctor had an opinion different from his own.

'We thought it was a memory card of some kind.'

'We?'

'Gann was with me when I found it.'

Mandrick took the device out of the bag and examined the embossed gold circuitry, agreeing with the assessment. 'Anyone else know about this? Hank, for instance?'

'I came right here.'

'And Gann?'

'He was going on about that prisoner, Charon – the one who survived the ferry accident. I think he went to talk to him.'

'Talk, eh?' Mandrick muttered to himself. 'Yeah, I bet.' He checked his watch. Things were stacking up rapidly to push him in one direction: a dead FBI agent, a panicking Forbes, a threatening Hank, an unconscious prison inspector, and now this memory card or whatever it was. It was clearly important and unknown to the CIA. Perhaps it was the insurance he was looking for. Hank was interested in Durrani for a reason, and so was Charon who, just to add to matters, was probably about to die at the hands of Gann if for no other reason than that he'd witnessed the ferry sabotage. Mandrick could not risk Hank finding out about the chip, whatever it was, and Gann could not be relied upon to keep his mouth shut. It was time to go.

'I'll be honest with you, Mandrick. I'm beginning to feel very uncomfortable with this whole set-up down here . . . It's beginning to feel like a powder keg about to blow.'

'You're a very perceptive man,' Mandrick said.

'The company would warn us if things were going to go wrong, wouldn't they?'

'I think the signs would be there for all to see.'

'I'll take my lead from you, then.'

'You see me jump, you go right ahead and jump too,' Mandrick said, with a sarcastic smile.

Mani nodded. 'What about that?' he asked, indicating the memory card.

'You think I should take it to the FBI?'

'Why not? Insurance. We need to start thinking about protecting ourselves.'

'Quite right.'

Christine moaned.

'I'd better get her to the hospital,' Mani said, crouching beside her. 'Come on. Up you get. You'll be fine. Help me get you to the hospital.'

Christine appeared to understand enough to help him get her to her feet although everything else was a blur. Mandrick's image kept flashing across her mind, a memory only, disconnected to time and her current location despite her efforts to marshal her thoughts. She heard the doctor's gentle voice that she remembered and trusted urging her to take a step. She obeyed.

Mandrick watched Mani help Christine through the

door. He hit the close button and removed his mini-computer from his belt, opened the leather cover, placed the card inside one of the small pockets and returned it to his belt.

He opened a cupboard beside his desk to reveal a safe with a keypad on its face and punched in several numbers. A beep indicated that it had unlocked. He pulled open the door, removed a CD box on top of a pile of US banknotes, opened it, selected a red CD at the back of the box and carried it over to the main operations panel with a degree of care.

Mandrick hit several commands on a keyboard, following a series of paths offered on the monitor, and pushed the CD into a slot on the panel. A few seconds later an alert flashed on the monitor, warning that the disk was unauthorised and could contain potentially lethal viruses. Permission to continue was authorised for password holders only and Mandrick typed in a code. Seconds later the monitor indicated that the CD had been accepted.

The image changed to a graph of the prison's gas systems, showing the different pressures throughout. As the information reeled off the CD a warning flashed onto the screen that deleting certain files could have disastrous effects.

Mandrick left the program to run as he picked up a waterproof bag, put it on his desk, removed the money from the safe and placed it in the bag along with the other CDs, some paperwork and a pistol. The last item he removed from the safe was a leather pouch whose opening was secured with a drawstring, which he untied.

Inside were a substantial number of gems of various colours and sizes. He refastened the drawstring, placed the pouch inside the waterproof bag and looked around to see if he had forgotten anything. His hand went to his belt and his minicomputer which he unhooked, placed in the bag and pulled an airtight zip tightly across. That was everything.

He went back to the monitor to check on the progress of the virus. The warnings continued as one section after another began to flash red.

Mandrick picked up the phone on his desk and punched in a number. 'Mandrick here. Are the ferries ready for that scheduled stores run? . . . Good. I want you to send them. I want all those stores cleared off the platform and brought down here . . . Yes, do it now. I know there's a ferry booked for the inspector this evening but she's not leaving until tomorrow . . . Just do what I goddamn say, OK?' He put the phone down, checked his watch and went back to the computer monitor that showed how the virus was spreading.

In the OCR a light flickered on the main panel, accompanied by a beep. The controller and his assistant were seated at a table, eating sandwiches and drinking coffee.

The assistant took a large bite out of his sandwich, got to his feet, walked over to the panel and eyed the read-out curiously as he brushed his hands on his chest. 'Pressure spike in C cell,' he said, his mouth full of food.

'The interrogation chamber?' the senior controller asked as he flicked through the pages of a girlie magazine.

'Yep.'

'They've got nothing booked for right now.'

'Nope,' the assistant agreed, checking a calendar on the side of the panel.

'Give 'em a call. Tell 'em we'd appreciate it if they let us know before they start playing their little games.'

'You want me to ask it exactly like that?'

The senior controller frowned without looking at his colleague. 'Just ask 'em what they're doing.'

The assistant picked up a phone and punched in a number.

The CIA interrogation-room technician was in the pressure chamber, checking the wiring to the central chair, when the phone on the wall buzzed. As he stood up to reach for it he felt suddenly flushed and paused to loosen the clothing around his neck.

Two interrogation officers were in the elevated room, going over several files and making notes. 'You getting hot?' one of them asked.

'Yeah,' his colleague replied, loosening his collar as he looked through the thick glass at the tech reaching for the phone.

The tech picked up the receiver. 'C cell.'

'You guys working that room today?' the assistant controller asked.

'Just some routine wiring. No one's touching the pressure.'

'Well, *someone*'s screwing around with it.'

'I can feel it. The air's getting pretty thick in here.'

The assistant controller scrutinised the gauges. 'Holy

cow! You're down more'n a hundred feet below ambient.'

The interrogation room was filled with a loud crunching sound from above. The technician looked up as dust sprinkled down onto him. 'There's something happening with the ceiling,' he said, his expression deepening with concern.

'Harry, we got a problem,' the assistant controller said to his boss as he pushed a couple of switches to check several other read-outs. 'You'd better get outta there,' he said into the phone. 'The pressure's dropping and the oxygen level isn't compensating.'

The technician was overcome by dizziness as his face reddened. Another loud crunching sound and this time a large crack was visible around the ceiling hatch. The technician dropped the phone and headed for the pressure door, which was closed.

The agent in the booth watched the technician stagger to the door and pull on the handle. 'What's up with Marty?' he said, getting to his feet.

The pressure door would not respond to the open button and the technician dropped to his knees as he fought to breathe. A third loud crunch was accompanied by high-pressure water shooting through the cracks. A second later the ceiling collapsed ahead of a wall of water and the technician disappeared under the tremendous force of it all.

The agents in the booth stepped back from the glass as the room beyond it filled with water. The technician's severed head rolled across the glass and both men went for the door. It did not respond to the control

351

lever and they pulled on the handle with all their might. Cracks suddenly streaked across the thick glass and as the two men fought the door the centre of the window gave way and the water burst into the room.

'Hello!' the assistant controller shouted into the phone. All he could hear was static and he looked over at his boss. 'I think we've got a problem.'

Hamlin finished cutting a hole in the thick rubber door seal large enough to poke a couple of fingers into, withdrew the saw bit and inspected his work, using a small flashlight. 'Does that look like it to you?' he said, stepping back so that Stratton could take a look.

Stratton scrutinised inside the hole. 'That's it,' he agreed.

He handed Hamlin a small bottle cap with a heavily greased rim. Hamlin pushed it in through the hole and positioned it over the sensor.

'It's in place,' Hamlin said as he felt around inside the hole, making sure he was right.

Stratton handed him a flat piece of rubber with a sealing-compound coating one side. Hamlin placed it over the hole he had cut, ensuring it made a tight seal. 'Perfect . . . I got a good feelin' about you, ferryman. I think you're lucky.'

Stratton was bemused by Hamlin's upbeat attitude and was burning to know what was fuelling his confidence.

'Let's help things along a ways, why don't we?' Hamlin said as he walked over to the rack of emergency air bottles and, using a wrench, tried to unscrew one of the ends. 'Gimme a hand here,' he asked as he strained.

Stratton joined him and, with their combined strength applied to the nut, it began to loosen. Hamlin repositioned the wrench and they pushed again. As the thread unscrewed, gas began to hiss from the joint until it became almost deafening.

'That should do it,' Hamlin shouted. 'You ready?'

Stratton gave him a thumbs-up.

Hamlin made his way up the steps and into the transformer room. He collected several prepared cables with crocodile clips on the ends and began connecting them to an assortment of cable hubs, leaving the final couple of clips disconnected. He pulled on a pair of rubber gloves and, using a large pair of pliers with rubber tubing over the handles, gripped one of the remaining crocodile clips and connected it to a terminal. A couple of sparks flew and he picked up the last clip with the pliers, leaned out of the doorway and looked down at Stratton. 'How's it lookin'?' he shouted.

Stratton was checking the seals. He looked up at Hamlin and shook his head. 'Can't see a change yet!'

'Give it a minute!' Hamlin remained confident as he stared up at a large square air duct hanging down from the centre of the rock-and-girder ceiling. The fins that ran across its face opened wider, indicating a sudden flow of air coming out of it. 'Here she comes!' Hamlin shouted.

Stratton followed his gaze to see evidence that the pressure compensator had tripped.

The door seals began to flatten slowly and the door

itself moved perceptibly. Stratton gripped the handle and pulled with all his might. The door moved more freely and as it opened he grabbed the inner edge.

When the gap was wide enough he moved his head to look through into the corridor. A large fist slammed into his face and sent him flying back into the room and onto the floor.

Stratton lay on his back, reeling from the punch and with blood trickling from his nose. Through watering eyes he watched Gann step into the room.

Gann picked up a heavy wrench, tested its weight and held it like a baseball bat. 'Not as smart as you think you are, Mister Charon or whoever you are.'

Stratton wriggled backwards, quickly wiping his eyes and searching for anything he could use as a weapon. There was nothing close to hand.

'Just left a friend of yours in the hospital. Your Afghan pal – didn't think I knew about him, did you? And it was me who found you out, not the CIA or the big guys who run this place. And guess what else? We found something inside his gut.'

Stratton was appalled by what Gann was saying but he had more important matters to deal with right at that moment.

Gann moved over him, the wrench held high. 'Your next stop is the morgue.' He grimaced as he made ready to bring the heavy tool back down. At that precise moment Hamlin connected the remaining crocodile clip, causing a massive short circuit that sparked wildly. All the lights immediately went out, plunging the room into total darkness.

Gann brought the wrench down with all his might and the end slammed home.

The emergency lights flickered on as the auxiliary power kicked in, dimmer than before but enough for Gann to see the end of his wrench sitting in a chipped indentation that it had made in the concrete. At first he could see no sign of Stratton. Then he looked up to see him getting to his feet from where he had rolled when the lights had gone out.

Stratton found an iron bar and held it up, ready to do combat. Gann straightened himself as he adjusted the wrench in his hands and smiled thinly. 'This could be more fun than I'd expected,' he growled. He took a step towards Stratton who backed up to the metal stairs between the scrubbers.

Gann came at him, swinging the wrench in a wide arc. Stratton held up his bar to block the blow. Gann smashed it out of his hand and it went clattering across the floor.

As Gann came in for a speedy follow-up Stratton's heels struck the bottom step and he stumbled backwards. Gann brought the wrench down with all his might, Stratton only barely managing to roll aside again as the end of the tool dented the metal step with a thunderous clang. Stratton instantly threw out a kick that connected with Gann's groin. The big man was halted in his tracks and he gave out a moan as the pain shot through his crotch.

Stratton scurried backwards up the stairs, not prepared to tackle Gann man-to-man just yet. The brute had twice his strength and, like a bull in the ring, needed weakening considerably before the power gap between them could be closed.

Gann brought his pain under control, held the wrench ready to resume the conflict and made his way up the steps, his expression a twisted grimace of malicious determination. The only thing in Stratton's reach was a wooden board which he picked up, holding it like a shield in front of himself. Gann reached the gantry and launched a side blow. Stratton brought the shield across to block it but the force knocked him off the gantry and several feet down onto the top of one of the scrubbing machines, which he landed on back first. Gann jumped over the rail and down onto the machine into the cloud of dust that Stratton's impact had kicked up. He loomed above his winded prey, savouring the moment.

Stratton had nowhere to go in the narrow space. There was a long drop either side to the floor. Gann raised the wrench for a deadly blow but a chunk of metal, a machine part of some kind, flew through the air and struck him on the side of his head, knocking him off balance. Stratton took immediate advantage and kicked the side of Gann's knee, causing it to bend, and followed that up with a thrust from his other leg. Gann lost his balance and struggled to grab the gantry rail, missing it and falling off the machine onto an exhaust pipe several feet below before rolling off that and hitting the floor.

Stratton got to his feet and looked down to see Gann lying with his face against the concrete. He was stirring slowly, the wind knocked out of him.

Hamlin hurried along the gantry towards Stratton.

'Get out of here!' Stratton shouted.

Hamlin needed no further encouragement and headed down the stairs. Stratton jumped over the gantry rail and followed hard on his heels.

Hamlin reached the bottom step, lost his footing and fell sprawling on the floor. Stratton hurried to pick him up and as the older man staggered to his feet a dart struck Stratton in the side of his neck. He let out a scream as two hundred kilovolts shot through his body from a Taser in Gann's hand. Stratton dropped to the floor, his limbs shaking as Hamlin ran for the door. Gann dropped the Taser and threw his wrench at Hamlin, catching him around the legs. Hamlin went sprawling once again.

For the moment Gann ignored Stratton who lay on the floor twitching like an epileptic. He went for Hamlin instead. He picked the older man up by his neck, grabbed his head as if he was going to rip it off and jerked it around into an unnatural position to face him. 'Looks like it's time for you to say goodbye too,' Gann snarled as he slammed Hamlin's head into the metal door, spun him around and used him like a punching bag, pounding his hammer fists into the other man's ribs, smashing them one by one. Hamlin went limp and Gann looked around to see Stratton roll onto his knees, the Taser dart out of his neck.

Gann let Hamlin drop to the floor and marched over to Stratton.

Stratton fought to focus his eyes, saw a shackle on the floor within arm's reach and reached for it. Gann grabbed him mercilessly by the back of the neck, picked him up like a rag doll, and spun him round as he raised a fist, his face twisted in effort. But as his knuckles ploughed through the air towards Stratton's head the shackle struck Gann in the jaw, shattering several of his teeth.

Gann staggered back, releasing Stratton who came in quickly for another blow. But Gann was not finished by a long shot and blocked the attack, following it up with a vicious punch to Stratton's sternum that sent him flying back.

Gann stood upright, taking a moment to gather himself and spit out his broken teeth. He felt his jaw as he stared at Stratton, blood trickling from his mouth. The brute was utterly incensed. 'I am going to tear you apart,' he shouted, his voice rising to a crescendo as he lunged forward.

Stratton ducked a haymaker and countered with a blow to Gann's body that seemed to have no effect. Gann swung again as he ploughed on, Stratton managing to dodge blow after blow although it did not look as if he would remain lucky for long. He didn't. A blow connected with the side of his head, sending him reeling back into one of the scrubbers. The machine was running noisily, a powerful electric motor turning a large shaft that was exposed for a metre where it went into the housing, a large knuckle joint in its centre. Gann grabbed Stratton by the neck and hauled him towards the fiercely spinning shaft. Stratton splayed out his hands, grabbing the sides of the machine, desperation taking hold of him as he felt helpless in Gann's powerful grip.

Gann gritted his teeth as he pushed Stratton's head ever closer to the spinning knuckle joint. Blood and sweat poured from Stratton's grimy face as he fought back with every vestige of his remaining strength. But he could not match Gann's power. He blinked at the joint spinning inches from his face, knowing that Gann was intent on seeing his features sheared away. He suddenly saw two large buttons, one red, the other green, just beyond the shaft. He had no idea what they operated but he was out of options. He released his weakening grip on the edge of the machine, twisted his body round, his face passing millimetres from the joint, reached out and hit the red button. The machine immediately slowed to a stop as Stratton fell onto the smooth section of the shaft just beside the joint.

Gann twisted Stratton back over and held him down onto the shaft. 'You wriggle like a worm,' he snarled as he brought his fist down onto the side of Stratton's face.

Stratton was trapped under Gann's weight and strength and one more blow like the last would finish him. Gann raised his fist again, gritting his teeth, his aim clearly to bury it deep into Stratton's bloody face and end the fight. Stratton made a supreme effort and twisted his head to one side just enough to avoid the main impact of the blow that glanced off his cheek. Gann's weight followed him through and his hand slammed down into the knuckle joint. Stratton did not waste a second – he reached out and struck the green button. Before Gann could pull his hand free the shaft turned. He let out a howl that could have been heard throughout the prison as the knuckle joint turned, trapping his hand. As his arm wrapped around the turning joint the bones in the entire limb broke all the way up to his shoulder as they were twisted around it. The machine jammed and Stratton pushed himself out from under Gann's bulk.

Gann screamed like a banshee, sparks flying from the machine as the motor short-circuited. Flames shot from the housing and ignited Gann's uniform as he fought like a wild man to extract his mangled arm. But his efforts were in vain – the arm was jammed fast. The pain was too much for him and he went limp as the fire engulfed his head. His legs gave way beneath him.

Stratton stepped back towards the door, turning to look for Hamlin. But there was no sign of the older man. He hurried outside into the corridor but Hamlin had gone.

Doctor Mani helped Christine through the door into the hospital and sat her down on the edge of the operating table. She was aware of her surroundings and focused all her efforts on pulling herself back together.

'He did you over pretty good,' Mani said, holding a swab and a bottle of antiseptic liquid. 'Let me have a look.' He gently lifted up her chin. The blood had dried around her swollen nose and lips and there was a large bruise on the side of her jaw. She winced as the doctor dabbed a cut. 'Can you clench your jaw?'

Christine clamped her teeth together and moved her jaw from side to side.

'Any loose teeth?' he asked as he felt her cheekbones and nose.

'I'm fine,' she said, moving his hands away.

'What about the rest of you? Any broken bones, you think? I should check.'

'I'm OK,' she insisted as she slid off the edge of the table to stand, a little wobbly at first.

Mani looked down at the table, suddenly remembering that there had been someone on it when he had left earlier.

At the same instant Christine looked past him and froze.

'Where's the Afghan prisoner . . . ?'

'Behind you,' she said softly.

Mani turned to see the Afghan standing on the other side of the room, holding his gut with one hand, a long, slender surgical blade in the other. 'Oh, dear,' Mani muttered.

Durrani took a couple of steps towards them, holding himself erect with some difficulty.

'Why don't you let me fix you up?' Mani said nervously, his gaze flicking between the silver blade in the Afghan's hand and his dark eyes focused on him.

Durrani tottered slightly, fighting to control his limbs. His head throbbed and his lungs ached with every breath. He could barely see — everything was a blur — but he could distinguish the human forms in front of him. He stopped in front of Mani.

'Please put the knife down,' Mani's voice quivered.

Durrani did not understand a word the doctor was saying. He had met him twice since his arrival, both for cursory medical examinations, and knew he could speak some Farsi. Durrani muttered a few words, his voice weak.

Mani was not sure what the Afghan had said at first and then realised he was asking for something to be given back to him.

'I don't have it,' Mani replied in English, suddenly unsure how to say it in Farsi. 'It's not here. I promise you.'

Durrani assumed the man had not understood him. He also knew it was a waste of time and that he would never see the implanted object he had been entrusted with again. It had belonged to the enemy and they now had it back in their hands.

Durrani removed his hand from his wound, exposing it.

Mani glanced down at the open cut, then back to Durrani's eyes that were filled with menace. Beads of sweat formed at the doctor's temples. 'I don't have it, I tell you,' he stammered in Farsi. 'I can stitch up your wound. Shall I do that?' Mani's voice quivered as he gestured towards his instrument trolley.

Durrani held a hand out to stop him. He had come to terms with his failure. He had never had any illusions about escaping but there had always been the possibility of release one day. Now that his secret had been discovered, hoping for anything else was pointless. They would soon take him back into that room and interrogate him further. Durrani would rather die. This was the only opportunity he would ever have to control his destiny and he was going to take it. And like a good soldier he would take as many of the enemy with him as he could.

Durrani shoved the blade deep into Mani's gut just below the sternum. Mani tensed as the cold blade entered him and his eyes widened in horror as he grabbed Durrani's hand. Durrani clenched his jaw with the strain as he pushed the blade to one side. Mani's knees started to give.

Unable to hold Mani's weight, Durrani pulled out the knife and let the doctor drop to the floor. The effort caused a bolt of pain to shoot through his body and he thought he might lose his balance. But he summoned all his will to remain strong and upright, long enough to focus on the next face in front of him and kill whoever it belonged to. The person did not move and Durrani steeled himself to take one step closer to repeat the deadly thrust.

Christine stared at the half-naked man and the bloody blade in his hand. She might be weak and dazed but faced with the threat of death she would muster every ounce of strength to defend herself. She considered making the first move. The man was exhausted and in pain like her. But the knife gave him a serious advantage. Her heart pounded in her chest. Mani was moving at her feet, making gurgling moans, but she put him out of her mind at that moment. Adrenalin coursed through her veins.

'Why are you doing this?' she stammered, trying to distract him. 'I can help you,' she said, even though she suspected he could not understand her. She kept her voice soft and tender, trying to sound compassionate and unafraid. 'Please let me help you.' She stared into his eyes, waiting for the change in them that would signal his thrust. She would try and block it, move aside and counter. Her instincts would take over and unleash all the power she had until he was beaten.

But instead of tensing for the thrust Durrani remained still.

Christine could sense his sudden hesitation and wondered if he had understood her.

Durrani had indeed paused. He had fully intended to close the gap between them and thrust the knife deep into the blurred outline. But the voice stopped him, the voice of a woman, the first he had heard in a long time. He could not understand the words but he could hear the soft, pleading tones. Indelible memories returned. Since his incarceration with nothing to do but think he had experienced countless recollections of his mother, many of them tormenting. He had also been haunted by memories of the girl in the street when he'd been a boy, and in particular of the one he'd shot in Yakaolang while she pleaded for her brother's life. Although they had been separate incidents, over the years those women had become one in his mind. And now she was standing in front of him, talking to him, pleading for him to recognise her.

Christine could only guess at the sudden change that had come over the Afghan. She had not expected her words to alter his murderous intent. But, bizarrely, that was exactly what had apparently happened. 'It's OK,' she went on, maintaining the same soothing tone. 'I know how you feel. I understand . . . I do.'

The room suddenly reverberated with the shriek of klaxons. Durrani snapped out of his trance. His grip on the knife tightened, his jaw clenched, his eyes narrowed. He came out of the fog and back into reality and stepped forward to make his thrust.

The lights went out.

Chapter 15

The auxiliary lights came on in the OCR, triggering a cacophony of alarms, beeps and flashing warning lights as the controller and his assistant frantically moved between computer consoles, operating panels and monitors, trying to figure out what precisely was happening.

'This is crazy!' the senior controller shouted, his stress level rising perceptibly. 'I've got pressure differentials spiking all over the goddamned place.'

'There's no power from the surface barge!' the assistant called out.

'What in God's name is going on?'

The controller flicked through CCTV cameras all over the prison. Many did not function, some showed quiet, empty corridors while others revealed water rushing in through doors and along passageways.

'Where's the breach?' the controller demanded.

'There's more'n one, that's for sure.'

'Galley's showing four bars below normal. If it continues to drop the walls'll give.'

'Holy cow! We got a serious drop in pressure on level four. I can't stabilise it.'

'There's no compensation control. Do we have comms with the terminal?'

The assistant grabbed up a radio handset and pushed a pre-set frequency button. 'Mother one, this is Styx, copy!'

The speakers remained silent.

'Mother one, this is Styx!' the assistant repeated. 'We have an emergency situation, do you copy?'

'Styx,' a voice crackled over the speakers. 'This is mother one, come in.'

The senior controller grabbed the handset from his assistant. 'Be advised we have a serious emergency down here. I'm talking very serious. Remain on standby, OK?'

'Can you describe the nature of the emergency?'

'We're flooding on just about every level as far as we can tell! Stand by.'

The controller hit a speaker button on the phone and punched in a couple of numbers.

Mandrick looked around at the flashing red light on his desk phone, took another glance at the computer monitor to see how the virus was spreading, walked over and picked up the phone. 'Mandrick.'

'Warden. We have a crisis situation.'

'I'm listening.'

'The pressure's out of control. We're flooding. The perimeter's been breached in several places. We could be heading for total perimeter failure. We're not sure how or where it started. Maybe C cell. The equalisers aren't compensating. We've got a negative pressure migration to levels three and five which we are currently unable to control.'

'What about the access doors on those levels?' Mandrick asked casually, his voice booming over the speakers in the operations control room.

'When the pressure equalised most of the doors popped before I could set all the manual overrides. We need people to physically close them,' the controller said, looking at a monitor that showed a torrent of water gushing along a corridor. 'Right now I don't see how that's possible.'

'Your prognosis?' Mandrick asked as he reached for his waterproof bag.

'Well . . . the mains-power outage isn't good. It's like the barge has shut down.' The controller looked at a computer monitor that mirrored the one in Mandrick's office. 'The auto system has failed or is about to. It looks to me as if the program's erasing itself. I don't understand how we can have so many unrelated failures all happening at the same time.'

Mandrick was also curious since his virus program was only designed to affect the pressure compensators. 'Did you say that the surface power's been cut?' he asked, certain his virus was not supposed to cause anything like that to happen.

'Yes, sir. We're running on UPS auxiliary, emergency systems only.'

'Can we consolidate?' Mandrick wanted to know.

The controller looked around the room at the orchestra of complaining systems monitors and at his assistant who gave him a dour look before shaking his head. 'I'd have to say that's a negative, sir,' the controller finally said. Despite the seriousness of the emergency he was well aware of the implications of making such a firm decision. He could already see himself facing the judicial inquiry and being grilled for the reasons behind such a catastrophic assessment. 'If we move now we might be able to get everyone to the barges.'

'I understand,' Mandrick said, pouring himself a Scotch, taking a sip and then knocking it back, wincing as the fiery liquor coursed down his throat. 'Give the order to abandon the facility.'

The controller looked at his assistant just in case there was anything to suggest that the order was premature. Nothing was forthcoming.

'Did you hear me, controller?' Mandrick asked, his voice echoing in the OCR.

'Will do, sir . . . and sir?'

'Yes?'

'Good luck.'

'You too,' Mandrick said, replacing the receiver and picking up his bag. He paused to take a last look around, imagining the room flooded and wondering how long it would be, if ever, before anyone set a foot – or a fin – inside it again.

He headed across the room, operated the door which needed his help to open and stepped out into the corridor. Water several inches deep flowed past him from the steps above.

The alarms dimmed as a voice broke through them. 'ABANDON THE FACILITY!' it called out in a relatively calm voice. 'ALL PERSONNEL TO THE ESCAPE BARGES ON LEVEL TWO!'

Mandrick exhaled philosophically. He had done it. It was something he had, bizarrely perhaps, looked forward to for a long time. This was what he called power. He had single-handedly brought Styx to an end, the implications of which would spread around the globe. Some would rejoice, some would despair, while others would be horrified or even amused.

He looked down at the dirty, frothy water swirling around his feet, feeling the chill of it soaking into his socks. He smiled and headed up the stairs.

Several prison guards ran along a cell-block corridor that was ankle deep in water, flinging open cell doors and yelling for the inmates to get out. The Afghans needed no interpretation to understand the events taking place. Panic was the overriding emotion as prisoners and guards hurried together in the direction indicated by illuminated emergency arrows. A handful of prisoners following a guard turned a corner only to be struck by a torrent of water that washed them back. All save one, a man who was struck unconscious when his head hit the wall, managed to regain a footing and cling to the walls. They pulled themselves and their unconscious comrade along the corridor to a metal stairway that led out of the water and to the next level.

Stratton was running up the broad tunnel from the scrubber room when the klaxons first sounded. He paused at the entrance to the steeper, narrower tunnel that led to the upper level, noting the significant increase in the volume of water running down the guttering. As he headed up it he could only wonder what the hell Hamlin had done.

Stratton arrived at the access-level door that had a huge '5' painted on it to find it firmly shut. He pulled on the handle but it was like trying to move a mountain. Hamlin had got it wrong. The seals had collapsed, showing an equalising of pressure, but the door was firmly shut. Water was seeping in through a small gap in the seal at the bottom. He remembered the emergency manual overrides fitted to all access-level doors in the event of a pressure failure and found the small slot behind some fungus on the wall high and to the right of the door frame. He felt for the recessed hexagonal nut but without a key he would never be able to turn it.

Sounds came from behind him, penetrating the rhythmic toll of the alarms, and Stratton jerked around to see several figures approaching. It was the group of miners, led by the guard who had saved his life.

The guard went straight for the door and yanked on the handle. Unable to budge it he pulled his radio handset off the clip on his lapel and held it to his mouth. 'OCR! This is Zack on mine access to level five,' he shouted. 'I need the access door opened!'

There was no reply.

'Come on,' the guard said agitatedly. 'OCR. Open mine access level five. Come on, guys. Hear me!'

In the OCR the senior controller was preparing to abandon his post when he heard the call. His self-preservation urge was to get going but his conscience would not allow him to and he stepped back into the communications console, picked up the mike and hit a button on the control monitor. 'Zack. As far as I can tell all emergency manual overrides have been activated. Do you have your key?'

'Yes,' Zack shouted, feeling around the back of his waist belt and finding the heavy handle.

'When you get through head for the barges. I'll see you there.'

'Secure yourselves!' Zack shouted as he unhooked the handle from the back of his belt. 'Get away from the door! There could be a lotta water on the other side.'

Stratton noted the way the water was gushing fiercely from under the bottom of the door and pushed one hand behind several pipes up to his elbow, grabbing it tightly with the other. Prisoners scurried to find secure points.

Zack inserted the end of the key, which was like an old crank-starter, into the slot and positioned it over the hexagonal nut. He put all his weight against the handle, which took several jerks to get moving. When it eventually did it turned easily.

There was a grinding sound inside the door as the guard furiously wound the handle that operated a system of low-ratio gears. For every spin the lock moved barely a millimetre inside the door. It was taking an age. Every man strengthened his grip on his strongpoint in anticipation of the deluge to come. Just when it seemed as if the mechanism had failed and the guard's efforts were in vain the door burst open in front of a massive wall of water. The door slammed into the wall, almost coming off its hinges, and the sea crashed into the narrow corridor as if a dam had burst.

Two of the prisoners and the other guard, who'd been at the rear of the column, immediately lost their hold and were swept away down the corridor, their cries quickly muffled as the water slammed them into the walls before engulfing them.

Zack was struck on his side by the initial impact and although he managed to cling to a pipe for a few seconds he soon lost his handhold. Stratton automatically stretched a hand out to him and caught hold of his harness strap. Stratton's arm around the pipe felt like it was going to rip out of his shoulder as the guard thrashed around in a desperate effort to grab anything that was fixed to the wall. The most powerful initial thrust of the water was quickly spent and as Zack gripped a bracket Stratton released him. The panting guard looked Stratton in the eye and gave him a nod.

Without wasting another second Zack got to his feet. 'Get going!' he shouted to everyone in front of and behind him. 'Move! Move!'

The prisoners needed no encouragement as they scrambled through the door.

Stratton joined the group, hurrying up the inclined corridor where it met a main-line tunnel running across its path, water splashing along it. Cardboard cartons and various wrappings covered the surface as if the intruding ocean had emptied out a storeroom of some kind.

Zack stopped at the junction to guide his men in

the direction of the flashing emergency arrows. 'That way, that way. Go! Go!'

The men scurried around the corner, looking like half-drowned cats, exhausted but with plenty of energy left to save their own lives.

As Stratton reached the junction he saw a sign below one of the emergency lights that indicated the hospital was in the opposite direction to the escape barges. He took a moment to consider his options. They were basically to forget the mission and save himself without further ado. Or risk a couple more minutes to try and find his target. Gann had said that Durrani was in the hospital – where he might still be. Or the Afghan might already be on his way to the escape barges. Gann had implied that the tablet had been found. But no one had expected this level of mayhem. Anything could have happened. Stratton was suddenly feeling lucky. Perhaps Hamlin's diversion might work in his favour. He might still be able to complete his mission after all.

Stratton moved off in the direction of the hospital.

'Hey!' the guard shouted.

Stratton paused to look back, wondering if Zack was coming after him. But the guard had not moved and was simply looking at him curiously. 'The barges are this way,' he said.

'I know.'

Zack looked bemused as Stratton continued on his way. He shook his head and turned to follow his men.

'Hey, Zack,' Stratton shouted.

The guard looked back at him.

Stratton was standing in the near-darkness in knee-deep water with trash floating all around him. 'Thanks,' he said.

Zack remained confused by Stratton's choice of direction but acknowledged the prisoner's gratitude with a wave of his hand.

Stratton disappeared and Zack caught up with his men. They climbed several ladders and stairways, scurried along a corridor through an open pressure door, and met up with several more prisoners and guards coming from another direction. Together they surged through a doorway leading into what a sign above described as the escape room.

It was a large cavern containing two open airlock doors. A couple of guards stood outside each, ushering men through. The airlocks were short passageways into two escape barges. These were rudimentary vessels made of riveted plates of steel, their interiors lined with simple benches and dozens of large gas cylinders fixed into brackets against the walls. The floor was covered in rough wooden decking below which the bilges were visible. There were no portholes.

'Find a seat and strap yourselves in,' a guard ordered.

Anxious Afghan and Western prisoners, all dripping wet, some bruised and injured, sat side by side, fastening seat belts around their waists. A guard vomited up part of his fear. Several dripping-wet CIA men ran in and joined their enemies as the klaxons continued to wail, adding to the urgency of the collective desperation.

The operations controller emerged from one of the barges and walked towards Zack who was standing outside the entrance to the other vessel. 'Are you full?' he asked.

'Almost,' Zack said. 'How many do you think we're down?'

'Rough count I'd say we were down eighteen prisoners, five guards, two service staff. Anyone seen the doc?'

There was no reply.

Hank Palmerston squelched into the hall ahead of a handful of prisoners and a guard, all of whom looked exhausted and bedraggled. 'I got two people trapped in C cell,' Hank said angrily. 'Your fuckin' door won't open.'

'I didn't build the goddamn place,' the controller shouted back. He walked over to a wall between the two airlocks where a systems panel displayed various valves and gauges.

'We gotta get that door open,' Hank persisted, following him.

'You had the brief when you got here. When the power failed their door should've gone to manual override. They have a key in the room.'

'Well, something ain't working.'

The controller ignored Hank as he checked various gauges.

'You're just gonna leave 'em there?' Hank growled.

'They're probably already dead.'

'That ain't good enough.'

The controller left the panel and walked past him. 'Zack. Your barge leaves now. I'll wait as long as I can before I push off.'

Zack ushered his guards into his barge and prepared to close the airtight door.

'Are you gonna help my guys or not?' Hank asked angrily.

The controller walked over to a guard, pulled a crank key off his belt and held it out to Hank. 'I've got a job to do. *You* go save 'em.'

Hank took the handle and looked back at the entrance to the room. The water was flooding in.

'C cell's on level one but as you know you've got to pass through level three to get to it from here,' the controller said, trying to maintain his calm. 'Before you go you might want to consider the chances that you'll make it back here.'

'You ain't gonna wait?'

'I'll wait as long as I can!' the controller shouted at the top of his voice. 'That means when I think the remaining escape barge is at risk by staying here we're cutting loose! With or without you. Is that clear?' he shouted, his face red.

Hank looked at the other guards, realised that he was being unreasonable and lost some of his steam. 'Do you know where Mandrick is?' he asked in a more subdued voice.

'At his own presidential escape pod if he has any sense. It's easier to get to him from C cell than back here but if you do get your guys out you won't all fit in it. My guess is that Mandrick's already gone, anyway.'

Hank wasn't just frustrated because of his missing people. The flooding prison had also drowned his future.

Everything he had worked for was about to be washed up on the beach and he knew who was behind it. He gripped the crank handle firmly as if it had become a weapon and hurried out of the room.

The controller faced Zack who was waiting for any changes to his orders. 'Get going.'

Zack walked into the airlock and with the controller's help closed the outer watertight door. He marched down the short connecting corridor and into the barge. 'Let's go,' he said and the nearby guards closed the inner door and screwed the cleats home, making it watertight. 'Everyone make sure you're secure in your seats. It's gonna be a bumpy ride.' Zack went to the instrument panel and turned several dials as gas hissed from pipes along the ceiling. He concentrated on a series of gauges as their needles climbed.

'Listen up. This is how it's gonna work. When the barge releases it's gonna float straight to the surface. Like I said, it'll be a bumpy ride. The barge might go up at an angle which is why you stay strapped into your seats. There's a drag cable on the bottom to stop it inverting – if it works. If you start feeling a little weird don't worry about it. When we hit the surface we're gonna remain at Styx depth pressure inside here. The barge'll expand a little but the system's designed to compensate for the pressure. Anyone starts getting pains, live with it. We got no medical aid for the bends on board. On the surface we wait for the emergency crews who should already be waiting for us. We've got enough air to last twenty-four hours. That's more than enough for the crews to attach a decompression system

378

to that docking hatch,' Zack said, pointing to a hatch in the roof. 'We'll all stay in here, in our seats until the barge decompresses. We got a little water, no food, and a bucket latrine over there so sit tight and relax. Breathe easy. Any of you Talibutts speak English translate what I said for the others. You can also pass it on that if any of you guys wanna fuck around, try any of your suicide shit, I'll kill yer.'

'And you'll have a little help too,' said one of the burly white prisoners, eyeing the Afghans with a sour grimace.

'The emergency team'll be accompanied by armed guards,' Zack went on. 'So if any of you are thinking this could be a good time to make a break for it, forget it. They'll shoot to kill anyone trying to escape.'

Zack faced the panel and turned several wheels that allowed water to flood the short corridor between the outer and inner doors. One of the guards watched through a small glass porthole in the door. When the corridor was full Zack operated a gas-activated mechanism. There was a series of loud clunks and then the barge jolted heavily. This was followed by the sound of creaking as if the barge was stretching. Another massive jolt suddenly shook the vessel. Many of those inside feared that it signalled a disaster about to happen. A long silence followed, broken only by the gentle hissing of gas. One side of the barge started to rise and the water under the decking rushed to the opposite row of benches, drenching the legs of those sitting there. Zack secured himself into a seat as the barge levelled out before rising up on the other side. This time those sitting on the other row got a soaking. The entire barge creaked and groaned as the outside pressure reduced.

Zack stared at the main depth gauge on the panel. The needle dropped from the fifty-metre mark and speedily made its way to the forty-metre marker.

Stratton walked into the hospital to find Christine crouched over Doctor Mani who was lying on the floor on his back. Durrani was on his side not far away and Stratton went directly to him. He turned the Afghan over to make two immediate discoveries. First, the cut in his abdomen was open and the tablet had obviously been removed. Second: the man was dead.

Stratton looked at Mani who was barely conscious. Blood seeped from the dressing that both he and Christine were holding against his gut.

'We have to get out of here,' Stratton shouted above the sound of the klaxons.

Christine did not respond. Her hands were trembling and only then did Stratton notice in the poor light that her face was badly bruised. Her eyes were glazed and staring ahead as if she was looking at nothing.

'Hey,' he said in a softer voice as he touched her shoulder.

She snapped a look at him, her eyes filled with anger.

He held her gaze, trying to appear sympathetic. 'Let me take over,' he said, putting his hand on the dressing, hoping the offer might signal his friendship.

The gesture appeared to have the desired effect. Her expression softened as if she had returned from wherever she'd been and her eyes flickered as they moistened.

Stratton felt for a pulse in Mani's neck. The doctor's heart was beating rapidly, along with his breathing. The man was slipping away as his blood flowed from his body. He would not last long without a massive blood transfusion and surgery to close the internal injury. The journey to the escape barge would kill him even if Stratton could carry him all the way there. 'Can you hear me?' he asked him.

Mani's eyes flickered open and he looked at Stratton like a child waking up to find his father there, happy to see him. 'Is it bad?' he asked.

'You've lost a lot of blood,' Stratton said.

'I thought so.'

'Did you take anything from the Afghan's belly? Was it you who opened him up?' Stratton asked.

A frown grew on Mani's brow as he fought to collect his thoughts. He smiled. 'It was very small,' he said. Then he had a sudden thought: 'Was he a spy?'

Christine began to take an interest in the odd conversation.

'Where is it?' Stratton asked.

Mani started to slip away, his eyes glazing over.

'Doc . . . Is it here, in this room?' Stratton persisted.

Mani struggled to hold on to consciousness. 'Mandrick has it,' he gasped. 'I gave it to Mandrick . . .'

It was his last word. The air left his lungs and his muscles relaxed.

Stratton got to his feet, fighting to retrieve the map of the prison in his memory and see the warden's escape pod on it.

Christine withdrew her bloody hands, unsure where

to wipe them. As she got to her feet she realised that Stratton's clothes were soaked through. At the same time it became apparent to her that the cacophony of alarms was not inside her head but was real. 'What's happening?' she asked.

'We need to get out of here.'

She didn't move, wanting to know more. She was stubborn by nature and did not follow others easily, regardless of how obvious the reasons might be.

'The prison's flooding. Everyone's evacuating. If we hurry we might make it to the escape barges.'

Christine did not need any more information. Together she and Stratton hurried out of the hospital. When they reached the steps leading down to the main corridor, Christine paused in horror as if she had not quite believed what she'd been told. 'What happened?' she asked as she caught up with Stratton and entered the water, which was thick with debris and seaweed.

'This is what you get when you play with electricity,' he said as he waded ahead of her through thousands of assorted ration packs and plastic cutlery.

Hank Palmerston made his way up the final stairway to level one and along a poorly lit corridor. At the end of it, around a slight bend, he saw Mandrick pulling on a wetsuit. The scene was illuminated by a bright halogen light from inside the hatch of a sophisticated escape pod, its interior the size of a Smart car.

'Taking your time, Mandrick?' Hank called out as he approached.

Mandrick was surprised to see the CIA man but he

382

quickly composed himself and zipped up the front of the suit. 'I'm in no great hurry,' he said, picking up his waterproof bag.

'This all your doing?' Hank said, closing the gap between them.

'I have to take the credit.'

'How'd you do it, cutting the power and bypassing all the safety procedures?'

'I used a virus program. It was far more effective than I expected. Cost me five hundred dollars from a hacker in Moscow. Well worth the investment.'

'So how's it all work from here? I'm curious. I mean, soon as you pop to the surface you'll get picked up along with everyone else. My boys'll be waiting for you when you open the hatch.'

'Forgive me if I sound smug but I had thought of that. This is a very sophisticated pod. It doesn't have to be on the surface to decompress. I can do it right here without leaving the dock. Like every good captain I'll be the last to leave my sinking ship.'

'Then in your own sweet time you'll float up to the surface – during the night, I expect.'

'A calculable risk.'

'Sink the pod and swim ashore,' Hank said, stepping closer while deciding on the best way to take Mandrick down.

'I think I can make it by daylight – or be well out of the area, at least.'

'I suppose you have enough to buy a nice little house in some far-flung corner of the globe?'

'A nice *big* house, actually.' Mandrick held up his

waterproof bag. 'But you're right. I should get a nice little one at first – low profile and all that.'

'If we don't find a body, Mandrick, we won't stop looking for you.'

'That has been my biggest concern. But luck clearly favours the bold. At the very last moment – less than an hour ago, in fact – I believe I found myself a little insurance.'

'What kind of insurance?'

'To be honest I'm not entirely sure. Something we found stitched inside the gut of one of your Afghans – the one you interrogated about the helicopter he shot down . . . Durrani. Yes, I do listen to your interrogations.' Mandrick opened the waterproof bag, removed his minicomputer and lifted the flap to reveal the small card. 'I suspect it's what Gann believed Charon was after. It must be valuable . . . if not to the CIA then to someone else. It'll become clear once I find out what it is. It's going to be fun. Maybe it'll give me something to do during those long evenings in front of a cosy log fire. Or perhaps I'll go for the moonlit beach. I haven't made up my mind yet.'

'So do you wanna make a deal – right now?' Hank took a step closer, trying to figure his way through this. Mandrick was far too confident and since he'd told him the essence of his plan it suggested that he did not believe Hank would get out of the doomed prison alive. Hank only had one weapon to stack a fight in his favour.

'You're not in a position to make any deals. Besides, there's only room for one in this pod. Sorry.'

Hank let his hand fall by his side. He still had the heavy crank key. He held it like a club and moved forward to close the gap between himself and Mandrick even further. 'You ain't going anywhere, my friend.'

Mandrick took the pistol from the bag and aimed it at him.

Hank stopped in his tracks. This was the closest to checkmate that he had ever been. He'd had a gun pointed at him before, but not by someone like Mandrick. He knew Mandrick's background. He'd been one of the South African's selectors. Hank took a step back and dropped the crank key. 'OK. You win. Get on your way. I won't try and stop you . . . We'll finish this some other time − if I ever get out of here, which is probably a long shot by now.'

'Sorry about this, Hank. But we'll have to finish it now. You might get lucky.' Mandrick pulled the trigger.

The sound of the shot was deafening in the small rock corridor. Hank staggered back, dropped to his knees, felt his chest and looked at the blood on his hands in disbelief.

'Look at it this way,' Mandrick said. 'I'm doing you a favour. You'd probably end up suffocating to death in some black freezing-cold air pocket all alone. It's better this way.'

Hank looked into Mandrick's eyes as he struggled to breathe. Mandrick pulled the trigger again and this round went through Hank's head, killing him instantly.

Mandrick placed the bag into the pod, paused to check that he had everything and climbed through the narrow opening. Halfway in he turned onto his back and with barely enough room to manoeuvre he sat up, grabbed the edge of a door that had a small glass peep-hole in it and swung it shut. He pushed down a lever and twisted it, securing the door before shuffling further back into the pod. He heaved himself into a comfort-able bucket seat, a line of air bottles to one side and a small operations panel with various dials and gauges in front of him.

Leaning back, Mandrick pulled down the inner hatch, locked the seal and looked up at a waterproof instruc-tion pamphlet attached to the bulkhead above him. He read the first-stage instructions and compared an illus-tration with the various valves and levers surrounding him. To begin the decompression sequence he pressed a button, starting a small electrical pump that began to remove gas from the pod to reduce the inside pressure.

Chapter 16

Stratton and Christine hurried past the access tunnel that led down to level five and the mine beyond and found the stairs further on that connected to the upper levels. When they reached the top Stratton stopped on a long gantry that headed in two directions. He pointed to his left. 'Head down that way. Follow the arrows to the escape barges. Good luck.' He moved off in the opposite direction.

'Where're you going?' Christine called out. She started to follow him.

He stopped, frustrated by her obstinacy. 'You're the type that never does as she's told, aren't you?'

'I like to know what's going on, yes. Why aren't you heading for the escape barges?'

Stratton gritted his teeth in irritation. 'I need to get what I came down here for. Now you know. Go.'

Christine grabbed hold of his arm as he turned to move away. 'Maybe I don't trust you. There's no cause worth dying for. Maybe you know of another way out of here.'

'It just so happens that could be true. I also think your chances are better if you go for the barges – that way.' Stratton pulled away and continued along the gantry. When he looked back she was still following him. He stopped and raised his hands to the heavens. 'What is your *problem*, woman? What is it that you are so stupidly suspicious about that you're prepared to die to find out?'

'Tell me where you're going and I'll leave you be.'

He looked into the young woman's eyes. Her expression was still determined. Time was running out. 'I have to find Mandrick. OK? Goodbye.' He hurried along the gangway and around a corner to a narrow staircase that led up. As he reached for the rail he realised she was still behind him. 'You've got to be kidding me. You said you wouldn't follow if I told you where I was going.'

'I didn't know you were going after Mandrick.'

'Go away,' Stratton said with a harshness of tone that unnerved her.

'I can't,' Christine said, suddenly overwhelmed by everything. 'I want to escape. I'm scared. If it wasn't for you I'd be running like a jackrabbit to the barges. My mission now is about getting to Mandrick too. But you're not running away. You're not scared. Maybe you know something I don't, maybe I'm all wrong about you but I don't think so. You're charging headlong into the fight with the battlements falling down around you. I always dreamed I would be like that if it ever came down to it, but I'm not. Not without you.'

'You want to work together on this?'

'Yes,' she said, gritting her teeth.

'Then go hold one of the barges. I'll get Mandrick and drag his sorry arse back and we can both have him.'

Stratton ran up the steps, leaving Christine watching him, her glare turning downright acid.

When he disappeared at the top she looked around at the crumbling prison. Sea water was cascading down walls, the dim emergency lights were flickering, the klaxons were fading as the emergency power grew weaker. In stark contrast a jaunty computerised voice announced the time. Remaining there a single minute more was madness.

Stratton scurried along the narrow corridor and as he turned the corner he saw Hank lying on his back, his eyes open, blood trailing from a hole in his head. Stratton moved past him to the watertight door at the end of the tunnel and he peered through the small porthole.

'We're too late,' Christine said, standing over Hank.

Stratton continued looking through the porthole. He considered ignoring her but decided that was clearly a waste of time. 'Yes and no,' he said. 'The pod's still attached.'

'Can we open it?'

'If we could the pod would probably jettison and we'd drown a second later.' He looked at Christine thoughtfully. 'We need to get to the surface.'

Something behind him caught her attention. Her mouth slowly opened. 'Is that an escape barge?'

Stratton turned to follow her gaze through the window. The massive, black barge was moving gracefully away, a huge drag cable trailing beneath it. It slowly tipped up at one end, levelled out, tipped a little the other way and then began to rise.

'There's still one more left. Let's go.' Stratton started to head off, pausing to pick up the crank key beside Hank before continuing along the corridor and down the stairs, Christine hot on his heels.

They ran along the gantry, reaching the entrance to the tunnel they had come along minutes before, and came to an abrupt stop. Sea water was pouring from it like a waterfall and cascading into the chasm below.

'Can we get through that?' she asked, addressing the question to herself as much as to him.

'We have to,' Stratton said. He leaned across the torrent to plant an arm on the edge of the tunnel. He reached inside and took hold of one of a stack of conduits bolted to the stone. A firm tug proved that it was secure. 'Go for it,' he shouted above the din of the rushing water.

Christine didn't hesitate, jumping past him to grab hold of the conduit. She pulled herself into the tunnel, fighting against the flow. Stratton leapt in close behind her and they headed into near-darkness as the emergency lighting grew even dimmer.

The going was hard. Their feet constantly slipped out from beneath them due to the force of the water. 'Watch out!' Christine suddenly shouted as she pulled herself tight against the wall.

Stratton did the same as several tables, carried on the flood, came bumping down the corridor at speed. Both he and the girl managed to avoid being struck.

Christine moved a few metres further on to a large

bracket which she wrapped her arms around in order to snatch a breather. Stratton pulled ahead of her. 'Keep going.'

She grabbed a pipe as far ahead as she could reach and pulled herself along.

They rounded a bend where the light grew in intensity to discover that it was an emergency light illuminating a sign above a door across the tunnel from them: ESCAPE ROOM. Christine pulled herself opposite the door, wondering if they could cross the gap without being swept back the way they had come. Stratton made his way further up the tunnel. Without any hesitation he pressed his feet against the wall while holding on to a pipe and, as if he was starting a backstroke race, pushed off for the other side.

He turned onto his front as he reached the opposite wall and grabbed for a hold, moving with the water until he reached the door. Large metal brackets were fixed to the wall either side of it and he grabbed the first, pulling himself against the door, which was in a small recess. He reached a hand out to Christine. 'Go for it!' he shouted.

She did not hesitate and threw herself across the gap to grab his hand. As she secured herself he banged on the steel door. The noise of their efforts seemed to be swallowed up by the sound of the rushing water. Stratton took the crank key that he had hooked inside the waist of his trousers and repeatedly struck it against the door.

He repeated the noisy assault as he searched for a way to open the door but there did not appear to be one. They feared the worst.

'They've gone, haven't they?' Christine said, knowing the answer.

Stratton stopped banging. 'I think you're right,' he said, searching in vain further along the walls to either side of the door for a manual-override slot to fit the key into.

'What about the ferries?' she asked.

'They're further on up there,' he said, pointing in the direction they had been going. 'But the doors into the dock won't operate without the OCR even in an emergency.'

A body lying face down in the water drifted past. Judging by the uniform it was that of a prisoner. It was a chilling illustration of the fate that lay ahead for them.

Stratton thought about his diving set outside the dock by the facility umbilical. But even if there was a chance of getting to it, which he could not see, there was only one set and he would have to abandon Christine. It didn't look like an option either way.

'Do we have any choices left?' she asked.

'Only thing I can think of is to find somewhere we can breathe.'

'You think they'll send a search team in here within the next six months, if ever?'

'It's possible,' he said, not believing it.

'OK, so let's go find somewhere we can stay warm, get three squares a day and breathe for the next six months,' she said sardonically. 'That wasn't aimed at you, by the way. This is all my fault. I held you up.'

'I don't think so.'

'I did and you know it. I'm a pig-headed bitch.'

'Listen. If you're going to be my best friend for the rest of my life you'd better stop whingeing.'

Christine looked into Stratton's eyes, unable to suppress a slight smile. Then something caught her eye as it floated towards her and she plucked it out of the water. It was a ration pack. 'We have dinner at least.'

'What is it?'

She held it closer to the light to read the label. 'Chicken supreme.'

'That's very good, you know.'

She appreciated his humour in the face of such adversity.

'I know where there's an air-storage chamber,' Stratton said. 'Might even be some electricity.'

'What are we waiting for?'

'Hold on to me. Let's stay together.'

'For the rest of my life,' she said as she grabbed hold of his arm and he let go of the door bracket.

They shot down the tunnel, fending themselves off the sides. They soon reached the metal gantry, spilling out of the tunnel onto it as the water plummeted to the lower levels. Stratton got to his feet and they hurried to the stairs and down them. They crossed to another flight of steps, scurried down them to a broad tunnel that was waist-deep in water that was not flowing as fast as in the previous one and headed past a sign directing them towards the hospital. Stratton was encouraged by the shallower water that suggested, for the time being at least, that the prison was not necessarily filling from the bottom up.

They reached the narrower access tunnel that led

down to level five and the mine to find the water cascading down it more vigorously than before.

'We're heading down?' Christine asked.

Stratton nodded. 'Let's hope this one hasn't filled yet.'

He entered the tunnel and, holding firmly on to the side, made his way down the slope. Christine was close behind him in the near-darkness.

They reached the open pressure door with '5' stencilled on it and continued down the increasingly steep incline. The water became deeper as they descended and was chest high by the time they arrived at the larger corridor that led towards the scrubber room and the mine.

'This is good. I was worried this tunnel would be completely filled by now.'

'Yeah, this is really good news,' Christine said, feeling very cold and unable to hold back her cynicism.

They passed the battered bodies of the guard and prisoners who had been washed down the tunnel when the level five pressure door had burst open. The corpses were floating together in a recess.

Stratton arrived at the entrance to the scrubber and pump room where the engines were now silent, and climbed in through the doorway. The hissing had been replaced by a forced bubbling sound as the water only just lapped over the valve on the stack of huge air bottles that Hamlin had opened.

'This the place?' Christine asked as she moved inside.

'All the air you can breathe.'

'If there was a search team, you think they'd come this far down?'

'Sure. Might even be a priority. Probably more chance of surviving longer here than anywhere else.'

'I never tire of your optimism,' she said, looking behind the door and suddenly jumping back, startled. 'Jesus Christ!'

Gann was standing against the wall, his right arm gone at the shoulder, his face seriously charred. The flesh was practically burned away, exposing his teeth and cheekbone. One of his eyes was gone. He appeared to be dead at first but then he moved his head stiffly to face them, his one eye minus its eyelid moving in its socket. When he recognised Stratton he took a step forward, reaching out to him with his remaining hand. But he was so weak that he could barely stand.

Stratton stood his ground as Gann forced himself to take another painful step. He moved close enough to grab feebly at the front of Stratton's jacket with his charred fingers. He tried to say something, but his lips were gone and his throat was so horribly burned that he was unable to form a word. His knees suddenly gave way and he dropped face down into the water where he stayed.

'Was that Gann?' Christine asked.

'Yes,' Stratton said, turning away and wading over to the rack of gas cylinders. He reached into the water for the bubbling valve and turned it off.

'The lights are brighter in here,' she noted.

'I think there's a power line into here directly from the barge. What are your electrical skills like?'

'I can change a fuse, a spark plug.'

'Pity.'

395

'Why?'

'If we can find a power link to the barge we might be able to turn it on and off. Make a signal of some kind.'

'I like it.'

'The water will eventually stop rising – that's if there's nowhere for the air to escape in the roof. We put the air valve on trickle flow and . . . you know. Wait.'

Stratton climbed the rack to get out of the water.

Christine climbed up beside him. 'Hey, we're alive and breathing and in a while we'll be dry. That's way ahead of where I thought we'd be when we were outside the escape room.'

'I'm sorry it's not any better.' He was disappointed that he had been unable to get them out.

She put her hand on his and squeezed it. 'My name's Christine, by the way.'

'John,' he said.

'Where are you from? I guess we have no more need for secrets.'

'I'm a Brit.'

'I figured out *that* much.'

'I'm from a town in the south of England. Poole. Don't suppose you've even heard of it.'

She shook her head apologetically. 'England's on my list of must-see places . . . I'm curious as hell about you. Who do you work for? If you don't want to tell me I'll put it down to you being optimistic about us surviving and I'd probably be happier that way.'

'British military intelligence,' Stratton said.

She was surprised to find his timing and apparent lack of optimism amusing.

'We lost something in Afghanistan. The Taliban found it and it ended up in here.'

'Why didn't you just ask us? I thought we were the great alliance.'

'I understand it would've been embarrassing for our side if you guys found out what it was.'

'Oh.' Christine nodded. 'Bummer, you dying just to save someone an embarrassment.'

Stratton had to concede that one. 'What are you dying for?'

'Mine isn't much better . . . The White House wanted this place closed down and they needed evidence of the shenanigans going on down here. We decided to pool with the feds in the end but, well, you know better than anyone how that one ended . . . It was my stupid ego that killed me. I could've got out earlier but I had to go that one step beyond where I was asked to.'

'Yeah, that'll do it sometimes.'

'How'd you get in here without our help?'

'I didn't. My lot conned the White House into running a security exercise. We offered to test the prison – see if I could escape from it.'

'They bought that?'

Stratton put out his hands – he was the proof.

'So how's it going?'

'I'm still working on it.'

They both chuckled.

The lights suddenly went dimmer.

'The thought of Mandrick getting away with this really pisses me off,' she said.

'Maybe he won't.'

'I'd like to know it, though . . . I hope the lights don't go off completely,' Christine said, her fears momentarily getting the better of her.

'There's a box of candles in that room up there,' Stratton said, indicating the transformer room. 'We won't sit in the dark.'

She looked at him again. 'You're very comforting, aren't you? You been in this business long?'

'A few years . . . I always believed there was a solution, even to the most desperate situation. Somewhere, somehow there's one for this. Now, maybe it requires a much higher intelligence or strength than we possess to find it.'

'Or luck.'

'Or luck . . . But it's there.'

Christine noted that the water had risen several inches since they'd climbed the rack. 'I think we should head for a higher spot to sit or we'll soon have to swim—'

'Shh!' Stratton interrupted.

She obeyed, watching him, his brow furrowed, eyes searching the far wall for something.

Stratton had picked up on a sound that did not belong with the others. It came again. A single short ping, like metal striking metal, but muffled as if it was a long way away.

Christine heard it too. 'Others made it down here.'

That was a possible explanation but Stratton had another on his mind.

The noise came again. He jumped off the rack into the water that was now close to his shoulders, started to wade through it, then changed to the breaststroke and powered himself towards the door.

'What makes you think they're in any better situation than we are?' she shouted.

He ignored her and swam through the door. The lights flickered. Christine was suddenly alone.

'I'll check it out with you,' she called out. She jumped in and followed him.

She caught him up outside and he headed deeper into the main tunnel, the surface of the water now close to the ceiling. Stratton stuck to the side closest to the scrubber room, hoping to find an opening or a corridor that would lead to where the noise had come from. He considered the possibility of not being able to return to the scrubber room but he still felt compelled to find the source of the noise. He could never ignore his instincts when they were this strong.

Stratton came to the top of a door and glanced back to see that Christine was closing in on him. He ducked beneath the surface to feel if it was open.

It was slightly ajar and he heaved against it, wedging his body into the gap and pushing the door open wide enough to get through.

He broke the surface to find himself in a small room with a raised floor. A single emergency light provided some weak illumination. He pulled himself out of the water onto the raised ground.

Christine broke the surface and swam to the edge of the floor. After pulling herself out of the water she stood beside Stratton, rubbing her arms against the cold that was gripping her. Stratton put a finger to his lips. They were in a miners' storeroom. There were piles of picks, hammers and shovels, drill bits and chisels, mining helmets, harnesses and overalls. Stratton tested the light on one of the helmets. It worked and he left it on to provide more light.

The sound came again, still with the muffled effect that made it seem like it was coming from beyond the walls although now it was louder than before. Stratton put his hands on the wall as if trying to feel where the noise was coming from.

Christine looked back at the water rising above the top of the door they had just come through. She wondered if they would be able to make it back to the scrubber room.

The metallic tap came again. Stratton followed the wall to the edge of the floor where it disappeared under the water and he crouched to examine the spot. He climbed off the platform into the water and quietly sank below the surface.

Christine watched as the water was disturbed further along the wall.

A moment later Stratton surfaced. 'There's a way through.'

'Can you tell me why we're doing this?' she asked.

'Not exactly,' he replied.

She nodded. 'OK.'

'It's a hole, right below me, a metre or so down. I'll see you on the other side.' He ducked below the surface again and was gone. Christine did not lack courage and lowered herself into the water. The cold attacked her immediately. She was blindly following a man she didn't know into oblivion and was doing so without much of a second thought. It didn't feel like the wrong thing to do, either. She took a breath and ducked under the water.

Stratton surfaced inside a large natural cave that was brightly illuminated by a string of small halogen spot-lights hooked onto the walls. There was a large rudimentary triangular metal framework made up of dozens of pieces of iron lengths welded or fixed together with clamps, bolts and cables. An acetylene bottle and gun leant against a wall. A pulley hung from the apex of the framework near the ceiling with a cable running through it, one end disappearing into the water, the other over a rocky plateau above him.

Christine surfaced beside him, wiped the water from her face and eyes and looked surprised at the contents of the cave.

Stratton climbed out onto the plateau to see Hamlin propped against a winch that was secured to the rock floor. He had a hammer in one hand and a chisel in the other. He looked as if he was asleep. Christine climbed out of the water as Stratton went to Hamlin's side and put a hand on his chest.

Hamlin opened his eyes and took a moment to focus on the face above him. 'Ahh, the ferryman,' he said, a smile forming on his lips. 'Come to take me to Hades? I do believe I'm finally ready.'

The end of the cable that came from the pulley at the top of the derrick-like construction was secured onto the winch drum which Hamlin had evidently been trying to free.

'How you doing, Tusker?' Stratton asked in a soft, friendly voice.

'Not too good . . . Gann screwed me up,' Hamlin said, releasing the hammer and chisel. 'I warned you he was a son of a bitch.'

'If it makes you feel any better he isn't any more.'

Hamlin nodded approval and as he took in a breath it was accompanied by a gasp of agony. Several of his ribs were clearly cracked or broken. He took a moment to concentrate on his breathing, keeping it as shallow as possible to reduce the pain. 'Gettin' outta here is all I've ever wanted to do,' he said.

'You can still make it,' Stratton said, fishing for the 'how' of Hamlin's escape plan, wondering how lucid the older man was and if he would share whatever it was he had been coveting. Stratton had no doubt that Hamlin had hatched some kind of plan.

Hamlin shook his head in disagreement. 'Gettin' through that goddamned sump nearly killed me . . . You know how many times I've swum through there? Gotta be more'n a thousand.'

'How'd you find this place?'

'They let me alone for hours at a time to repair the mining stores next door. I found it when I was snoopin' around one day. I flooded it so they'd never find it. Last two years've been the most enjoyable I've had in any prison. Maybe even beats some years when I wasn't . . . Building it a little at a time, day by day, gave me something to wake up to.'

'Building what?' Stratton asked.

'Gettin' all the right pieces was tough . . . especially the plates. Then gettin' 'em through that damn sump. That was as much of a challenge as puttin' it together.'

'You built it in here?' Stratton asked, looking at the derrick again.

Christine did not have a clue what either man was going on about but she sat back, listening intently.

'Piece by damned piece.' A spasm suddenly shot through Hamlin's body and he went rigid as he fought the pain. A moment later it subsided and he took a breath. He looked over at Christine. 'Wish I'd gotten to know you better, ferryman. Takes a special kinda guy to find a chick in a disaster at the bottom of the ocean.'

There was a distant rumble, followed by a surge of water from the sump. The level increased dramatically. Christine looked with concern at Stratton, fearful that they would not make it back to the air supply.

Stratton got to his feet, frustrated with the old man's ramblings, and wondered if he could figure out for himself what Hamlin had built. He studied the framework, noting the cable leading from the pulley down into the water with another, thinner cable coming out beside it where it was wrapped several times around a large rock to secure it.

Christine stepped beside him and kept her voice low, though even a gentle whisper echoed in the cavern. 'Should we try and get him back to the air bottles?'

'He won't make it,' Stratton replied, looking at the water where the cables went into it. It was separated from the sump by a natural wall of rock but there was

403

something that looked different about it. He crouched and brushed the surface with his hand and the water that churned up was white as milk. 'This water comes directly from outside.'

'We're just above the sea bed here,' Hamlin said. 'The opening down there is big enough to drive a truck through. It's what started me on the idea.'

Stratton crouched beside Hamlin again. 'What is it you built, Tusker?'

Hamlin looked into his eyes. 'First one was made two and a half thousand years ago.'

Stratton looked back at the water, the cable going up to the ceiling, the spacious cave, the entrance apparently big enough to drive a truck through, the metal plates that Hamlin had described. He looked back at Hamlin who was wearing a smirk.

'A bell?' Stratton asked.

Hamlin's smirk broadened before a painful cough wiped it away. 'Finished it a couple weeks ago,' he said, recovering. 'Took me a week to get it outside. I got pretty damn good at holding my breath.'

Hamlin's expression turned serious as he held out a hand. Stratton took hold of it. 'Take it up for me . . . prove to those sons of bitches that I could do it.'

The water level rose again, creeping up the rock and reducing the surface area of the small plateau they were on.

'Release that cable,' Hamlin said, indicating the winch. 'I don't have the strength any more.'

Stratton took hold of the hammer, glanced at Christine who was struggling to make some sense of what was taking place, and took a heavy swing at the bracket holding the cable to the drum. It snapped off and the end of the cable shot up through the pulley and down into the milky water where it disappeared. 'That other one too?' Stratton asked, indicating the thinner cable tied around the rock.

'No.' Hamlin said, waving his hand. 'You'll need that . . . You said you knew diving.'

'Yes.'

'Inside the top . . . a tap . . . your air. Rest you'll have to figure out,' Hamlin said, growing weaker.

The water trickled over the rock wall and into the milky pool. It slowly covered Hamlin's feet, rising towards his backside. 'Help me up, will yer?' Hamlin asked.

Stratton put his hands under Hamlin's armpits and pulled the older man to his feet. Hamlin winced but fought the pain, indicating that he wanted to stand on his own. Stratton let him go and Hamlin shuffled to the edge of the milky pool.

'That leads to the bell,' Hamlin said, indicating the thin cable. 'Good luck, ferryman . . . Race you to the top.' Hamlin dived into the milky water and disappeared below the surface.

Christine stared after him. Stratton tore his gaze from the place where Hamlin had dived into the water and looked at her.

'You want to take another dive into what could turn out to be nowhere?' Stratton asked.

'You really believe that crazy old man's built a diving bell? One that'll actually work?'

'I wouldn't stake my life on it under normal conditions.'

'You're serious?'

'One thing I *do* know. We follow him out there, we're never coming back.'

Christine swallowed gently as she looked around the ever-shrinking cave and back into his eyes. 'I've been following you into oblivion most of the time I've known you. Why stop now?'

Stratton nodded, lowered himself into the water, grabbed the cable and pulled himself below the surface.

Christine watched him go. Without wasting another second to consider the wisdom of it she jumped into the milky water, grabbed hold of the cable, took a deep breath and pulled herself beneath the milky surface.

Hamlin emerged from the vast cloud of milky water that covered the sea bed like an impenetrable mist. He took a final stroke towards the surface, eyes wide and looking up. Bubbles escaped from his mouth as he ascended, travelling alongside him like pilot fish. He maintained his composure as best as he could until the spasms of asphyxiation took hold of him and he shuddered as he drowned. His body went limp and the bubbles alongside him grew larger.

Hamlin's body gradually expanded, his clothes tightening around his flesh before they ripped open. His skin stretched and gave way as it tore in places. His eyes popped from their sockets and fluid escaped from his ears seconds before his skull cracked open. More bubbles escaped from his flesh and blood, his bones splitting as the rapidly expanding gases freed themselves from the marrow. A trail of human detritus floated from the wrecked torso, lengths of intestinal tubing swelling like a string of balloons. The heavier parts of Hamlin's body sank back down while thousands of smaller bits of him, buoyed up by gases, headed towards the sunlight. Moments later a million of his bubbles broke the sunlit surface and mingled with the air.

In the distance the prison's security vessel was moored alongside one of the escape barges. Suddenly, a hundred metres away, the surface erupted as if a huge whale was trying to reach the skies. It was the second escape barge, on its side. It had ascended at speed from its undersea mooring. It came out of the water several metres before its weight dragged it back down. When it next came up it flopped over onto its underside and levelled out, the water cascading off the flat roof and down the sides.

Chapter 17

Stratton pulled himself along the thin cable, unable to make out anything by its shape or shade. The cable continued down for several metres where he hit the jagged sea bed with the side of his body, still unable to see anything through the white 'milk'. He pulled himself along the bottom, quickly reliving the nightmare of his recent near-drowning.

As his lungs started to complain of the lack of oxygen his head struck something metal. It was a piece of angle iron secured to one side of a large drum of some sort. The cable coiled around the drum, effectively coming to its end, and Stratton released it to feel his way beyond it. There were several more cables criss-crossing iron struts but the gaps between them were too small to crawl through. He was running out of air and suppressing uncontrollable thoughts of returning to the cave.

Stratton stretched out his hands in every direction to work out the shape of the construction and discovered that the struts formed a rough circle. He moved over the drum and through this circle to find himself inside a container, which he followed up into a narrow dead end. He was rapidly heading into oxygen deficit and Hamlin's words telling him to look for a tap echoed in his head. He found a small pipe that led to what was clearly a large metal gas bottle but without a valve at the connection. He quickly followed it in the other direction to find what could be described as a tap and tried to turn it but it wouldn't budge.

Something grabbed Stratton's leg and Christine climbed up beside him. Her hands felt up his arms and to his hands and together they fought to turn the valve. Their lungs were bursting, both of them with only seconds left before they would involuntarily gulp in water. The tap suddenly moved and they could hear the hiss of escaping gas.

Stratton spun the tap open as quickly as he could and pushed his face into the highest part of the bell, pressing his lips to the metal ceiling in search of the gas. A pocket of air quickly grew and he gulped in a breath, at the same time pulling Christine up alongside him. She took in a lungful of air while choking violently. Now their faces were pressed together in the ever-increasing air pocket.

The water level gradually dropped and the bell, which had initially been leaning at an angle, moved upright as it became buoyant. Stratton felt around in the darkness in order to find out more about Hamlin's rudimentary construction and its operating system. 'You OK?' he asked.

'Yes,' Christine said finally after clearing her throat. 'I didn't think we were going to make it that time.'

'You get used to that.'

'Do you have a sense of humour apart from at times like this?'

'I'm best when I'm scared shitless.'

The bell started to ascend but it did not travel far before coming to a creaky halt as the cable below went taut.

Stratton felt around the bell's interior from top to bottom. 'I've got to believe Hamlin put some kind of light in here. He had good attention to detail.'

Christine helped him search. 'I've found a wire . . . it splits and there are clips on the ends.'

'Now look for a battery.' Stratton felt around the base of the bell where Hamlin would have put anything heavy to help keep the vessel from inverting. 'I have it,' he said.

She grabbed his arm, found his hand and put the clips in it. He attached one to a terminal and as soon as he touched the other a small halogen light flickered on at the top of the bell. The tiny space was flooded with light.

Stratton secured the clip and looked at Christine who was staring at him. He smiled. 'Welcome aboard the *Nautilus*.' He pointed to an inscription scrawled on the bulkhead.

They proceeded to examine the bell and its contents. The outer shell was little more than metal plates fixed to struts of angle iron, some welded, other parts bolted together with rubber in between that acted as a seal. Struts also formed a bench that Stratton sat on to get a clearer perspective on his surroundings. Christine sat opposite him.

The cross-struts gave the framework its strength and all in all Stratton was impressed. 'You have to hand it to the old man,' he said.

Two large gas bottles were lashed either side of the small chamber. 'These are our breather mixes – argon and oxygen,' Stratton explained, feeling the cylinders' cold metal skins. There was a smaller bottle lashed beside one of them with a valve on the end which he turned on briefly to check that it had gas. 'This is pure oxygen. We'll need that to increase the oxygen percentage as we ascend.'

A metal container was secured under one of the brackets and Stratton untied it to see what it was. It contained liquid and he removed a cap on the side, smelled it and put it to his lips. 'Water,' he said, offering Christine some. 'Just a sip.'

She took it from him and relished a mouthful of the refreshing liquid. 'I don't know how much sea water I've drunk,' she said, taking another small sip.

Stratton removed a plastic bundle from one of the struts and tore it open. 'Blankets,' he said, handing them to her. She took them eagerly and immediately wrapped one around herself.

A white plastic board was fixed to the bulkhead. It had two columns of figures written on it in indelible ink. 'This looks like an ascent table,' he said. 'Just five stop numbers and a time beside each . . . Give me your watch.'

Christine screwed the cap back onto the water container and checked the timepiece on her wrist. 'It's broken,' she said, examining the broken glass.

'Hamlin wasn't wearing one. Check that box.'

She leaned down and opened a metal box tied to one of the braces between her feet. 'Pliers, screwdriver . . . and a watch,' she said, holding it out to him.

Stratton inspected it. It was a waterproof digital model and appeared to be working. 'You're not claustrophobic, I hope.'

'I've got too much else scaring the crap out of me . . . What's next?'

'We figure out how to head up.'

He looked down at the milky water surrounding their feet. 'This milk doesn't help any . . . I'm going to turn the gas off for a moment while we figure this out.' He reached up for the tap and closed it. The hissing ceased.

'Why's the water white?'

'A Gulf of Mexico phenomenon,' Stratton said, squatting down and reaching into the water to feel around the drum. 'Some kind of mineral washed down from the coast . . . The key to going up is obviously this cable drum . . . There's something clamped to the cable stopping it from unrolling . . . Hand me those pliers.'

Christine gave him the tool and he reached down to find the clamp and figure out how to release it. He felt a clip of some kind which he took a grip on before pausing. 'I can't feel how this clamp works.' He decided to pull on the clip, which felt as if it was moving out of a hole in the block secured around the cable. The clip came away and the block opened and fell off the cable. The drum immediately started to turn.

'We're going up,' Stratton said, looking perplexed.

'That's good, right?' Christine asked, wondering why he appeared to be so concerned.

The drum turned easily, paying out the cable as they rose. Stratton checked the ascent table. 'There's no depth here.'

'How do we know when to stop?'

'There has to be a depth gauge.'

Christine quickly inspected the contents of the box. 'Nothing.'

'There must be something,' Stratton said, checking around the nooks and crannies of the small space with increased desperation. 'It's one of the essential factors in decompression.'

'What else could you use if you didn't have a depth gauge?' she asked, unsure exactly what she was looking for.

'I don't know. There must be something. Hamlin had to know the decompression stop depths.'

The white water around their feet disappeared and was replaced by clear water. The drum was suddenly visible as they rose out of the milk, rotating quickly as it paid out the cable.

'We've got to stop it!' Stratton said, lowering himself to apply pressure to the drum with his foot in an effort to put the brakes on. It had no effect and he stood on it with both feet. Christine jumped down alongside him and together they tried to stop the drum from turning. But the cable continued to pay out.

'This is not good,' Stratton said, looking around. 'We're missing something. The answer is staring us in the face.' No sooner had the words left his mouth when there was a heavy clunk and the drum stopped turning, bringing the bell's ascent to a halt.

They climbed off the drum and Stratton crouched to inspect it. 'You sweet and brilliant man, Tusker Hamlin . . . It's another clamp. And there are others attached to the cable around the drum. We don't need a depth gauge. The cable's pre-set for every stop.'

Christine slumped back down onto her cross-brace and pulled her blanket back round her. She offered one to Stratton who took it and did the same.

He consulted the table, checked the watch and hit a button on the side of it. 'Four and a half hours. Then we move up to the next stop.'

She exhaled noisily. 'Is it going to be this easy?'

'I doubt the decompression will be perfect. There's always risks even with the most sophisticated set-ups. It'll be a resounding success if we're barely alive by the time we see daylight . . . We're going to have to watch each other for any symptoms. There'll also be a carbon dioxide build-up. We'll have to flush the air every so often.'

'What are the signs?'

'Discoloration – the lips, for instance. Light-headedness. Talking crap.'

'I think I've suffered from it before,' Christine said, trying to match his humour. But there were too many fears for her to keep it up for long. 'Is there enough air for the two of us? Hamlin planned this trip for one.'

Stratton shrugged. 'My maths doesn't extend to cubic litres and oxygen consumption at partial pressures. Sorry.'

He decided to set the tap to a gentle flow of air. 'If these bottles are full we should have enough.'

'How come you know so much about diving?'

'Ever heard of the SBS?'

'You were a courier?

'A what?'

'SBS is a courier company — isn't it?'

'No, I wasn't a courier . . . It's like your navy SEALs.'

'Oh. OK. Makes sense,' Christine said, wrapping her arms around herself, feeling the cold.

Stratton moved to the end of his strut and lifted his blanket to make some room. 'Sit over here. We need to keep warm.'

'Not the old Eskimo ploy,' she said, moving across the bell to sit beside him.

'The lengths I go to to use that line.'

They pulled their legs out of the water, propped them on the opposite strut and adjusted the blankets. Stratton put an arm around the girl and they got as comfortable as they could.

'What happened to Durrani?' he asked.

'He killed Mani and I think he intended to kill me. But he hesitated for some reason. I guess he was in a lot of pain. Then the lights went out. I punched him in the chest with everything I had. He must've been in bad shape. When the lights went back on he was lying on the floor, gasping for air . . . I've never seen anyone die up close before today.'

'How'd you get so beaten up?'

'That bastard Mandrick.'

'What's the deal with him?'

'Works for the crooked corporation that owns Styx. They were making money from the mine, cheating Uncle Sam. Small potatoes. But a good enough reason for us to shut down the interrogation cell before it became an embarrassment . . . Mandrick kept all the dirt on a small computer. He liked insurance. It was all the proof I needed. But I blew it . . . Doesn't matter now, though. We got what we wanted in the end. At the risk of sounding mercenary, this works out pretty good for us.'

'Glad someone's happy.'

Christine looked at Stratton. 'He has what you came for.'

Stratton had not forgotten.

'He'll get picked up when he surfaces,' she said. 'The feds still want him.'

'That's not good for me, though. The feds'll get what I came for . . . But he knows they'll be waiting for him. That's why he's still down there. That pod's designed to decompress at depth. He'll surface when it's done . . . You have any idea what time it is?'

'It was around four p.m. when I went to see Mandrick. Dinner's at six but I wanted to see him a couple of hours earlier. It couldn't have been more than an hour after that when the alarms went off.'

'That means it'll be dark when we surface. He needs it to be dark. We're ten miles off the coast. Not a problem if you're wearing the right gear. He'll be miles out of the area by dawn. On the road by late morning.'

Christine had nothing consolatory to offer.

'Unless we're there when he surfaces,' Stratton added.

'He must've started his decompression long before us.'

Stratton had already thought of that.

She wondered what was going through his mind. 'Why do I get the feeling you're planning on taking another risk before we're even done with this one?'

'I want to finish what I came for.'

'I've been around special ops for a few years now and I've never met anyone like you before. What drives you?'

'I don't know.'

'Fear of failing? No. I have that but I'm not in your league.'

'I get as scared as the next person. I suppose I just don't know when to quit until I'm in over my head. Then I have to figure how to get out. So far I've been lucky.'

'You've solved one puzzle for me.'

'What's that?'

'I've wanted to be like you all my life. But I never made it because deep down I didn't really believe you existed . . . Thanks.'

'You hitting on me?'

'Could be my last chance. This is the new me. It's your fault. I see what I want and now I'm going for it.'

They chuckled together.

'We should relax and save our air,' Stratton said. 'Try to sleep. I'll stay awake.'

Christine rested her head comfortably against him, enjoying the closeness despite the circumstances. He placed the palm of his hand against the side of her head.

She mused thoughtfully for some time but her eyelids soon grew heavy as the events of the day drained her. Seconds after closing her eyes she fell into a deep sleep. It seemed to her as though only a few minutes had passed before the digital clock chirped.

She sat up, wondering where she was for a second.

Stratton took the pliers and reached down into the water. He jiggled with the clamp and a few seconds later the drum began to roll and the bell ascended.

He adjusted the gas, adding some oxygen to the mix, breathing in and out deeply, hoping he might spot any dangerous symptoms before they incapacitated him. He had experienced decompression sickness before during a familiarisation exercise in an RAF decompression chamber before a week of HALO jumps with the SAS. The team had been inside a large chamber containing chairs and tables and had been invited to occupy themselves with a variety of games such as kit construction or drawing pictures. In Stratton's case he'd had to continually subtract seven from four hundred.

It was odd the way some had reacted differently to others. And at different periods of the decompression process. Some people had lasted barely a minute before they'd begun to act strangely, drawing wildly or becoming hysterical. One of the guys had started to do a little jig. Assistants wearing oxygen masks had been on hand to give oxygen immediately to anyone who showed signs of going under. Stratton had concentrated everything he had into subtracting his numbers and when the decompression had reached a dangerous level the pressure had been reversed and the exercise brought to a stop. When Stratton had reviewed his maths afterwards he'd found that he'd only made a couple of mistakes and had wondered if that was down to poor arithmetic or if he had started to succumb.

The bell came to a sudden stop and Christine tried to make herself comfortable against him once again but she was becoming fidgety. She chuckled to herself as she pulled the blanket down. Stratton was immediately aware of a change in her.

'Let's go for a swim,' Christine said, giggling.

Stratton reached for the oxygen bottle and turned it on, giving the bell a good burst to increase the partial pressure, hoping that was the right solution. Christine started to relax and although she was breathing heavily at first she calmed down to a normal level and lay quietly against him.

He offered her the water container, which was getting light. She took a small sip. He elected to pass on his drink for the moment and replaced the cap.

The hours passed by slowly but the stop times became shorter until they reached the final one. Stratton set the digital watch. 'How're you feeling?' he asked.

'I'm OK. I was in and out of dizziness a few times.'

'You have any muscle pains . . . headaches?'

'My head's fine. I think I'm OK everywhere else, too. This isn't the most comfortable eight hours I've ever spent . . . except for the company, which I've enjoyed more than I can remember enjoying anyone's company before.'

'Do I need to give you a little more oxygen?'

Christine smiled. 'I'm not talking crap,' she said,

looking into his eyes. 'You're a hell of a guy, whoever you are.'

Stratton looked a little embarrassed, unused as he was to compliments. It made him even more attractive to her and she kissed him gently on the side of his mouth. 'Whatever happens . . . thanks.'

'It was my pleasure.'

She rested her head on his shoulder again.

'We're ten metres from the surface, give or take whatever the tide's doing.'

Christine looked at Stratton in surprise. 'Only ten? You mean we've made it?'

'Only thing I remember about decompression stops is the last one is usually ten metres from the surface.'

'I don't believe it – I mean, I do. I just don't.'

'I can feel pins and needles in my fingers.'

'Me too. Is that bad?'

'We'll probably need a recompression. But I think we'll be fine,' he said, getting off the strut to sit opposite her.

Christine could see he had something on his mind. 'What is it?' she asked.

'Mandrick. I can't let him go.'

'What can you do about it?'

'I can be there when he surfaces.'

'You don't know when that'll be. He might wait down there for hours.'

'No. He has air limits too. He'll do around the same time as us. But if I'm down here when he surfaces I'll lose him.'

'Is it OK to skip this last stop?'

'It won't kill me. As long as I can get to a chamber soon after.'

'And if you can't?'

'There'll be one on board the rescue craft.'

'So your plan is to swim around up there, hoping he pops up right beside you?'

'You've got a better idea?'

'Yes. You've done your job as best you could. You nearly died, half a dozen times, trying to succeed. You said yourself it was only to save someone an embarrassment.'

'That's what it is to them. Not to me.'

Christine's expression softened. 'Why am I trying to argue with you?' She removed her blanket. 'OK – I'm coming with you.'

'No, you're not. There's the clock,' Stratton said, putting it in her hand. 'When it beeps get out and swim to the surface.'

She let the clock slip through her fingers. It plopped into the water and disappeared. 'Oops,' she said, looking at him.

'You're a stubborn bitch.'

A strange sound like a distant grating stopped them arguing.

'What's that?' Christine asked.

'No idea.'

The noise grew louder and the bell began to vibrate.

'A boat?' she asked, looking up.

'No,' Stratton said, looking down.

The cable was rattling where it joined the drum, the vibrations growing with each passing second. The bottom of the bell suddenly moved as if it was being yanked to one side. It started to lean over and they could make out something rising out of the gloom towards them.

It was Mandrick's pod, caught on the cable and coming up at them like a torpedo.

It slammed into the base of the bell with tremendous force, almost smashing the drum from its housing and tipping the bell onto its side. Water flooded in as the bell inverted.

Stratton and Christine were tossed around as if they were inside a washing machine. Then the bell stabilised and started to plummet.

Stratton grabbed Christine with one hand and the struts now above him with the other. The bars had twisted in the impact and the drum was threatening to block their escape. The bell sank rapidly as Stratton fought to pull himself through a small gap. He released Christine in an effort to free himself and when he'd got outside he reached back into what now felt like a cage for her. She was clutching him through a gap too small to pull herself through. Stratton reached in through the largest gap, grabbed her brutally and yanked her over. He pulled with all his might as his lungs cried out for air, suddenly fearful he might have to let her go.

Then, as if a door had opened, she popped through the struts and as the bell continued its journey back to the depths they headed up, swimming for their lives.

Stratton broke the surface, gasping for air. A second later Christine appeared beside him, fighting to stay on the surface as she too gulped for breath.

Stratton saw the pod only metres away as three large red bags inflated around it. There was a cluster of bright lights in the distance beyond, undoubtedly the rescue mission but probably too far away for them to see the pod unless someone was actually looking at it.

Stratton swam towards it as the hatch began to open. He tried to climb onto the pod but the large inflation bags made it difficult to do so.

Mandrick rose out of the hatch, looked towards the emergency crews in the distance and, satisfied that he was far enough away, began to make ready for his departure. He pulled out his waterproof bag and placed it on the side of the hatch. Then he removed a knife from his belt and stabbed the nearest inflation bag. As the gas escaped he slashed another and was about to slice the third when, to his utter amazement, he saw Christine on the other side of it.

'I don't believe it,' he said, stupefied. 'Christine. You have to be the most tenacious person I have ever known.'

'That's what my mother always told me,' Christine said, seeing the waterproof bag in Mandrick's hand.

Stratton surfaced behind Mandrick's back, took hold of the pod and eased himself out of the water.

'This is the end of the road, Mandrick,' Christine said.

'You must be referring to yourself,' Mandrick said as he reached down into the pod.

Stratton wrapped his arm around Mandrick's neck, the bone of his forearm across his throat. 'She was definitely referring to you,' he said, gripping Mandrick's hand that held the knife.

With his other hand Mandrick pulled a Very pistol out of the pod and aimed it at Christine. 'Release me or I'll put this flare through her head. Don't doubt it.'

Stratton froze.

'Take your arm away,' Mandrick shouted.

Stratton loosened his grip. 'You can't get away,' he said, his mind racing for a solution.

'For the last time, move away or she's dead,' Mandrick said.

As Stratton released him he noticed a strap hanging loosely from the back of Mandrick's life jacket. He hooked it over the hatch lever as he moved away. 'Whatever you say. Just don't shoot.'

'Only if I have to. I don't want to give away my position, now, do I?'

Mandrick buried the knife's blade in the remaining inflation bag. The pod quickly began to sink. Mandrick released the knife, grabbed his waterproof bag and went to climb out of the hatch when he discovered he was held fast from behind. He struggled to pull himself free as water flooded into the pod. His actions quickly became desperate as he thrashed from side to side in an effort to break his bonds.

Stratton and Christine floated in the water, watching as the pod filled and sank beneath the surface. In a final act of fury Mandrick wildly aimed the Very pistol at Stratton and fired. The flare shot across the water in a bright red light in the direction of the rescue craft and Mandrick disappeared below the surface.

At the same time, to Stratton's horror, Christine shot below the surface. He immediately thought that she had somehow become entwined with the pod, took a deep breath and was about to follow her when she surfaced, spluttering for air, beside him.

When she regained her composure she looked at him with a pleased expression on her face. 'Sometimes, when you want something bad enough the risks don't matter.'

Stratton was unsure what she meant.

She held up Mandrick's waterproof bag.

Stratton grinned. 'That's my girl.'

A boat powered towards them, silhouetted in the lights of the emergency crews behind it. It was a semi-rigid inflatable and a figure in the bows was shining a searchlight on the pair in the water. The engines clunked into neutral as the craft came alongside.

'I don't believe it. It's Stratton,' an Englishman called out.

Stratton recognised Todd's voice seconds before he saw his beaming face.

Paul came to stand beside his colleague. 'Christ! How the bloody hell . . . ?' he exclaimed. Then he hurried to help the pair into the boat.

They wrapped them in blankets and stood back looking at them in wonder.

'Before you do anything else,' Stratton said to Paul, 'our chip is inside that bag. The rest belongs to her.'

Paul took the waterproof bag while Stratton opened his blanket for Christine. She slid beside him and he wrapped them both up. 'Oh, and Paul? I think we might need a recompression chamber, and soon.'

Paul nodded to the coxswain who slipped the engines

into gear and powered the inflatable towards the main rescue party.

'Do you think they have one we can use together?' Christine asked. 'I've gotten to like sharing confined spaces with you.'

'That's what I call risky,' said Stratton.

'It's my new middle name,' she said.